BEAUTIES, BEASTS AND ENCHANTMENT
CLASSIC FRENCH FAIRY TALES

BEAUTIES, BEASTS AND ENCHANTMENT
CLASSIC FRENCH FAIRY TALES

TRANSLATED AND WITH AN
INTRODUCTION BY
Jack Zipes

NAL BOOKS

NEW AMERICAN LIBRARY

A DIVISION OF PENGUIN BOOKS USA INC., NEW YORK
PUBLISHED IN CANADA BY
PENGUIN BOOKS CANADA LIMITED, MARKHAM, ONTARIO

Published simultaneously in Canada by Penguin Books Canada Limited.

 NAL BOOKS TRADEMARK REG. U.S. PAT. OFF. AND FOREIGN COUNTRIES
REGISTERED TRADEMARK—MARCA REGISTRADA
HECHO EN DRESDEN, TN, U.S.A.

SIGNET, SIGNET CLASSIC, MENTOR, ONYX, PLUME, MERIDIAN
and NAL BOOKS are published in the United States by
New American Library, a division of Penguin Books USA Inc.,
1633 Broadway, New York, New York 10019,
and in Canada by Penguin Books Canada Limited,
2801 John Street, Markham, Ontario L3R 1B4

LIBRARY OF CONGRESS CATALOGING-IN-PUBLICATION DATA
Beauties, beasts, and enchantment.
    Summary: A collection of French fairy tales originally written
in the seventeenth and eighteenth centuries.
    1. Fairy tales—France—Translations into English. 2. French fiction—
17th century—Translations into English. 3. French fiction—
18th century—Translations into English. 4. Fairy tales—Translations
from French. [1. Fairy tales. 2. Folklore—France] I. Zipes, Jack David.
PQ1278.B39   1989   398.21'0944   89–8247
ISBN 0-453-00693-0

Designed by Julian Hamer

First Printing, October, 1989

1   2   3   4   5   6   7   8   9

PRINTED IN THE UNITED STATES OF AMERICA

For Jacques Barchilon
Who has worked wonders
for the conte de fées

CONTENTS

INTRODUCTION
The Rise of the French Fairy Tale
and the Decline of France

Your people, . . . whom you ought to love as your
children, and who up to now have been passionately
devoted to you, are dying of hunger. The culture
of the soil is almost abandoned; the towns and
the country are being depopulated; every trade is
languishing and no longer supports the workers. All
commerce is destroyed. . . . The whole of France is
nothing but a huge hospital, desolated and without
resources.
— Fénelon, *Letter to King Louis XIV*, 1694

UNTIL the 1690s the oral folk tale in France was not deemed worthy of
being transcribed and transformed into literature, that is, written down and
circulated among literate persons. In fact, with the exception of several
significant collections of tales in Italy, *The Entertaining Nights* (1550–53)
by Giovan Francesco Straparola and *The Pentameron* (1634–36) by
Giambattista Basile, most of the European aristocracy and intelligentsia
considered the folk tale part of the vulgar people's tradition, beneath the
dignity of cultivated people and associated with pagan beliefs and superstitions that were no longer relevant in Christian Europe. If the literate
members of the upper classes acknowledged the folk tale at all, it was as
crude entertainment, divertissement, anecdote, or homily in its oral form
transmitted through such intermediaries as wet nurses, governesses, servants, peasants, merchants, and village priests.

From the late Middle Ages up through the Renaissance, folk tales were
told by non-literate peasants among themselves at the hearth, in spinning
rooms, or in the fields. They were told by priests in the vernacular as part of
their sermons to reach out to the peasantry. Literate merchants and travelers transmitted them to people of all classes in inns and taverns. They were
told to children of the upper class by nurses and governesses. They were

1

remembered and passed on in different forms and versions by all members of society and told to suit particular occasions—*as talk*. Gradually, however, this talk became elevated, cultivated, made acceptable, and entered French salons by the middle of the seventeenth century. Only by 1690, in fact, was it regarded worthy of print, and by 1696 there had arisen a veritable vogue of printed fairy tales: the literary fairy tale had come into its own, and French aristocratic writers for the most part established the conventions and motifs for a genre that is perhaps the most popular in the western world—and not only among children.

How did all this come about? Why the change in attitude toward the lowly oral folk tale? What kinds of literary fairy tales were created?

Though it is impossible to fix a date for the rise of the literary fairy tale in France, its origins can be located in the conversation and games developed by highly educated aristocratic women in the salons that they formed in the 1630s in Paris and that continued to be popular up through the beginning of the eighteenth century. Deprived of access to schools and universities, French aristocratic women began organizing gatherings in their homes to which they invited other women and gradually men in order to discuss art, literature, and topics important to them such as love, marriage, and freedom. In particular, the women wanted to distinguish themselves as individuals who were above the rest of society and deserved special attention. Generally speaking, these women were called *précieuses* and tried to develop a *précieux* manner of thinking, speaking, and writing to reveal and celebrate their innate talents that distinguished them from the vulgar elements of society. Most important here was the emphasis placed on wit and invention in conversation. A *précieux* (and numerous men were included in this movement) was capable of transforming the most banal cliché into a brilliant and unique bon mot. Although they had a tendency to be effete and elitist, these women were by no means dilettantes. On the contrary, some of the most gifted writers of the time, such as Mlle. de Scudéry, Mlle. de Montpensier, Mme. de Sévigné, and Mme. de Lafayette, came out of this movement, and their goal was to gain more independence for women of their class and to be treated more seriously as intellectuals. In fact, one of the most important consequences of *préciosité* was its effect on women from the lower aristocracy and bourgeoisie, who were inspired to struggle for more rights and combat the arbitrary constraints placed on their lives in a patriarchal social system.

The women who frequented the salons were constantly seeking innovative ways to express their needs and to embellish the forms and style of speech and communication that they shared. Given the fact that they had all been exposed to folk tales as children and that they entertained themselves with conversational games that served as models for the occasional lyric and the serial novel, it is not by chance that they turned to the folk tale as a source of amusement. About the middle of the seventeenth century aristocratic women started to invent parlor games based on the plots of tales with the purpose of challenging one another in friendly fashion to see who could create the more compelling narrative. Such challenges led the women, in particular, to improve the quality of their dialogues, remarks, and ideas about morals, manners, and education, and at times to question male standards that governed their lives. The subject matter of the conversations consisted of literature, mores, taste, love, and etiquette, whereby the speakers all endeavored to portray ideal situations in the most effective oratory style, which would gradually be transmuted into literary forms and set the standards for the *conte de fée*, or what we now call the literary fairy tale.

By the 1670s we find various references in letters about the fairy tale as an acceptable *jeu d'esprit* in the salons. In this type of game, the women would refer to folk tales and use certain motifs spontaneously in their conversations. Eventually they began telling the tales as a literary divertimento, intermezzo, or as a kind of after-dinner dessert invented to amuse other listeners. This social function of amusement was complemented by another purpose, namely, that of self-portrayal and representation of proper aristocratic manners. The telling of fairy tales enabled women to picture themselves, social manners, and relations in a manner that represented their interests and those of the aristocracy. Thus, they placed great emphasis on certain rules of oration such as naturalness and spontaneity and themes such as freedom of choice in marriage, fidelity, and justice. The teller of the tale was to make it "seem" as though the tale were made up on the spot, as though it did not follow prescribed rules. Embellishment, improvisation, and experimentation with known folk or literary motifs were stressed. The procedure of telling a tale as bagatelle worked as follows: the narrator was requested to devise a tale based on a particular motif; the adroitness of the narrator was measured by the degree with which she was inventive and natural; the audience responded politely with a compliment; then another member of the audience was requested to tell a tale, not in direct competition with the other teller, but in order to continue the game and vary the possibilities for invention and symbolic expression that often used code words such as *galanterie, tendresse*, and *esprit* to signal the qualities that distinguished their protagonists.

By the 1690s the "salon" fairy tale became so acceptable that women and men began writing down their tales for publication. The "naturalness" of the tales was, of course, feigned, since everyone prepared their tales very carefully and rehearsed them before going to a salon. Most of the notable writers of the fairy tale learned to develop this literary genre by going to the salons or homes of women who wanted to foster intellectual conversation.

And some writers, such as Mme. d'Aulnoy, Mme. de Murat, and Mlle. L'Héritier, even had their own salons. Moreover, for festivities at Louis XIV's court and at aristocratic homes, especially during the Carnival period, people attended dressed as nymphs, satyrs, fawns, or other fairy-tale figures. There were spectacular ballets and plays that incorporated fairy-tale motifs, as in the production of Molière and Corneille's *Psyché* (1671), which played a role in the development of the beauty-and-the-beast motif in the works of Mme. d'Aulnoy. In this regard, the attraction to the fairy tale had a great deal to do with the Sun King's desire to make his court the most radiant in Europe, for the French aristocracy and bourgeoisie sought cultural means to translate and represent this splendor in form and style to themselves and the outside world. Thus, the peasant contents and the settings of the oral folk tales were transformed to appeal to aristocratic and bourgeois audiences.

The transformation of the oral folk tale into a literary fairy tale was not superficial or decorative. The aesthetics that the aristocratic women developed in their conversational games and in their written tales had a serious aspect to it: though they differed in style and content, these tales were all anticlassical and were written in implicit opposition to the leading critic of the literary establishment, Nicolas Boileau, who championed Greek and Roman literature in the famous "Quarrel of the Ancients and Moderns" (1687–96) as the models for contemporary French writers to follow. Instead, the early French fairy-tale writers used models from French folklore and the medieval courtly tradition. In addition, since the majority of the writers and tellers of fairy tales were women, these tales displayed a certain resistance toward male rational precepts and patriarchal realms by conceiving pagan worlds in which the final say was determined by female fairies, extraordinarily majestic and powerful fairies, if you will. To a certain extent, *all* the French writers of fairy tales, men and women, "modernized" an oral genre by institutionalizing it in literary form with utopian visions that stemmed from their desire for better social conditions.

Despite the fact that their remarkable fairy tales set the tone and standards for the development of most of the memorable literary fairy tales in the West up to the present, they and their utopian visions are all but forgotten, not only in English-speaking countries but also in France itself. The major representative of this genre known today is Charles Perrault, who published the verse fairy tales *Donkey-Skin* and *The Foolish Wishes* in 1694 and a slim volume of eight prose fairy tales, *Histoires ou contes du temps passé*, in 1697. Though finely wrought, these tales are not indicative of the great vogue that took place, nor are they representative of the utopian (and sometimes dystopian) verve of the tales. To appreciate the value of Perrault's tales and how different they are, they must be seen in their historical context.

There were approximately three waves of the French fairy-tale vogue: (1) the experimental salon fairy tale, 1690–1703; (2) the Oriental tale, 1704–20; and (3) the conventional and comical fairy tale, 1721–89. These waves overlap somewhat, but if we understand the reasons for their origins and changes, we will grasp some of the underlying meanings in the symbols of the tales that are not readily apparent.

THE SALON FAIRY TALE

When Marie-Catherine d'Aulnoy included the fairy tale *The Island of Happiness* in her novel *Histoire d'Hippolyte, Comte de Douglas* in 1690, she was not aware that she was about to set a trend in France. Within five years the literary fairy tale became the talk of the literary salons, or what had been the talk of these salons now came to print: her tales were followed by Mlle. L'Héritier's *Oeuvres Meslées* (1695); Mlle. Bernard's *Inès de Cordoue* (1695), a novel that includes a version of *Riquet à la houppe*; Mlle. de la Force's *Les Contes des Contes* (1697); Perrault's *Histoires ou contes du temps passé* (1697); Mme. d'Aulnoy's four-volume *Les Contes des fées* (1697–98); the Chevalier de Mailly's *Les Illustres Fées, contes galans* (1698); Mme. de Murat's *Contes de fées* (1698); Nodot's *Histoire de Mélusine* (1698); Prechac's *Contes moins contes que les autres* (1698); Mme. Durand's *Comtesse de Mortane* (1699); Mme. de Murat's *Histoires sublimes et allégoriques* (1699); Eustache Le Noble's *Gage touché* (1700); Mme. d'Auneuil's *Tiranie des fées détruite* (1702); and Mme. Durand's *Petits Soupers de l'année 1699* (1702).

The main reason for the publication of these tales—and perhaps the stress should be on making the tales *public*, or letting a greater public outside the salons know about the tales that were told in them—is that France had entered a major crisis about 1688, and conditions of living began to deteriorate at all levels of society. Indeed, even the aristocracy and haute bourgeoisie were not exempt. Due to the fact that Louis XIV continued to wage costly wars and sought to annex more land for France, the taxes for all classes became exorbitant, and at various times during the latter part of his reign there were years of bad crops due to terrible weather and devastation of human lives due to the wars. The steady increase of debt, taxation, and poor living conditions resulted in extreme misery for the peasantry and an austere life for the bourgeoisie and aristocracy. Moreover, this was the period when Louis XIV became more orthodox in his devotion to Catholicism under the influence of Madame de Maintenon, became more rigid in his cultural taste, and more arbitrary and willful as absolutist king. His reign, which had begun during an "Age of Reason," turned reason against itself to justify his desires, tastes, and ambition for glory, and this solipsism led to irrational policies that were destructive for the French people and soundly criticized by the highly respected Fénelon, the Archbishop of Cambrai, who in some way became the moral conscience of the ancien régime during its decline.

Given these dark times and the fact that writers were not allowed to directly criticize Louis XIV due to censorship, the fairy tale was regarded as a means to vent criticism and at the same time project hope for a better world. The very first fairy tale that Mme. d'Aulnoy wrote in 1690 is a good example of how writers saw the fairy tale as a narrative strategy to criticize Louis XIV and to elaborate a code of integrity, for many French writers were intent at that time to establish standards of manners, correct speech, justice, and love. In d'Aulnoy's *The Happy Island*, Prince Adolph fails to attain complete happiness because he sacrifices love for glory in war. It is because he does not esteem the tenderness of Princess Felicity enough to remain faithful to her that he destroys himself. *The Happy Island* is a utopian tale because it confronts male desire as a destructive force and suggests that there is an element missing in life that women can provide if utopia is to be attained and maintained. The paradise associated with the Princess Felicity will remain beyond our reach, and it is this longing for paradise, for a realm that is just and allows for natural feelings to flow, that was the basis for most of the literary fairy tales produced during the 1690s in France. In this sense, the utopian impulse was not much different from the utopian impulse that led peasants to tell their folk tales. But the wish fulfillment in the oral tales of the peasants rose from completely different circumstances of oppression and longing. The salon tales were marked by the struggles within the upper classes for recognition, sensible policies, and power.

Interestingly, almost all of the major fairy-tale writers of the 1690s were on the fringe of Louis XIV's court and were often in trouble with him or with the authorities. For instance, Mme. d'Aulnoy had been banished from the court in 1670, returned to Paris in 1690, and became involved in a major scandal when one of her friends killed her husband. Mme. de Murat was banished from the court in 1694 when she published a political satire about Madame de Maintenon, Scarron, and Louis XIV. Mlle. de La Force was sent to a convent in 1697 for publishing impious verses. Catherine Bernard was not accepted at court and remained single to maintain her independence. The Chevalier de Mailly was an illegitimate son of a member of the Mailly family, and though accepted at court, he caused difficulties by insisting that his bastard status be recognized as equal to that of the legitimate sons of the de Mailly family. Even Charles Perrault, who had been a loyal civil servant as long as his protector, Jean Baptiste Colbert, controller general of finances, was alive, fell into disfavor in 1683 and opposed the official cultural policy of Louis XIV until his death in 1701.

It would be an exaggeration to say that the first wave of salon fairy-tale writers were all malcontents opposed to Louis XIV's regime, for they all mixed in the best circles and were considered highly respectable and talented writers. Nevertheless, with the exception of Perrault, they were not part of the literary establishment and made names for themselves in a new genre that was looked upon with suspicion. Even the respectable Fénelon, who was a member of the court's inner circle and as the preceptor of the Duc de Bourgogne, Louis XIV's grandson, wrote fairy tales in the 1690s in an experiment to expand the Dauphin's mind through pleasurable reading, did not publish these tales until the 1730s. In other words, there was something inherently suspicious and perhaps subversive about the development of the literary fairy tale, and the French writers always felt compelled to apologize somewhat for choosing to write fairy tales. Though apologetic, they knew what they were doing.

Most of the early writers came to Paris from the provinces and were steeped in the folklore of their region. Before they published their tales, we must remember, they first practiced them orally and recited them in the salons. Whenever they wrote them down, they circulated them among their friends—they all knew one another and moved in the same circles—and made changes before the tales were printed. Some of them, like Perrault and Mlle. L'Héritier, were relatives and exchanged ideas. In addition, Perrault clearly had contact with Catherine Bernard, as their two versions of *Riquet with the Tuft* reveal. In particular, the women shared their ideas for their tales and discussed their dreams and hopes with one another in private and in their letters. When Madame Murat was banished to the provinces, she used to stay up into the early hours of the morning, telling tales to her friends, among whom was Mlle. de La Force, who used to distribute her tales among her friends and discuss them before being placed in a convent.

All the writers revised their tales to develop a *précieux tone*, a unique style, that was not only supposed to be gallant, natural, and witty, but inventive, astonishing, and modern. Their tales are highly provocative, extraordinary, bizarre, and implausible. They wrote in hyperbole to draw attention to themselves and their predicaments, and they were not afraid to include sadomasochistic elements and the macabre in their tales.

Many critics and educators have often complained that the Grimms' tales are too harsh and cruel to be read to children, and some have even gone so far as to maintain that German fairy-tale writers indulged themselves in violence. But in fact, the salon tales of the refined French ladies make the Grimms' tales look prudish. In particular, Mme. D'Aulnoy was a genius in conceiving ways to torture her heroines and heroes. She had them transformed into serpents, white cats, rams, monkeys, deer, and birds. Some of her heroines are whipped, incarcerated, and tantalized by grotesque fairies or sinister princes. Some of her heroes are treated brutally by ugly fairies who despise them because they want to marry an innocent, beautiful princess. A good many of her tales end tragically because the protagonists cannot protect themselves from those forces undermining their natural love.

The cruel events, torture, and grotesque transformations in d'Aulnoy's tales were not exceptional in the fairy tales written by women. In *The Discreet Princess* (1695) Mlle. L'Héritier has Finette brutalize the prince on three different occasions before she mercifully allows him to die. In *Riquet with the Tuft* (1696) Mlle. Bernard ends her tale by placing her heroine in a most cruel dilemma with two ugly gnomes. Mlle. de la Force depicts a brutal king as a murderer whose ferocity knows no bounds in *The Good Woman* (1697), while in *Fairer than a Fairy* (1697) she has a prince and princess demeaned and compelled to perform arduous tasks before they can marry and live in peace. Finally, Mme. de Murat has a sadistic sprite place two lovers in an unbearable situation at the end of *The Palace of Revenge* (1698), and she often has sets of lovers deceive and maltreat each other, as in *Anguillette* (1698) and *Perfect Love* (1698).

However, it was not only the women writers who wove violence and brutality into their tales. Perrault dealt with incest in *Donkey-Skin* (1694) and portrayed on ogre cutting the throats of his own daughters in *Little Thumbling* (1697). The Chevalier de Mailly had a penchant for transforming his protagonists into beasts, and in *The Queen of the Island of Flowers* (1698) he has a princess persecuted in a sadistic manner.

The brutality and sadomasochism in French fairy tales can be interpreted in two ways. On the one hand, it is apparent that the protagonist, whether male or female, has to suffer in order to demonstrate his or her nobility and *tendresse*. Therefore, a cruel trial or suffering became a conventional motif in the tales, part of the compositional technique to move the reader to have sympathy for the protagonist. On the other hand, much of the cruelty in the tales is connected to forced marriage or the separation of two lovers who come together out of tender feelings for each other and not because their relationship has been arranged. Since many of the female writers had been victims of forced marriages or refused to marry in order to guard their independence, there is an apparent comment on love, courtship, and marriage in these tales that, despite all the sentimentality, was taken seriously by the writers and their audiences.

In general, the fairy tales of the first phase of the vogue were very serious in tone and intent. Only here and there in the works of Mme. d'Aulnoy and Perrault do we find ironic and humorous touches. The fairy tales were meant to make readers realize how deceived they were if they compared their lives to the events in these tales. There was no splendid paradise in Louis XIV's court, no genuine love, no reconciliation, no tenderness of feeling. All this could be, however, found in fairy tales, and in this regard the symbolic portrayal of the impossible was a rational endeavor on the part of the writers to illuminate the irrational and destructive tendencies of their times.

THE ORIENTAL FAIRY TALE

The second phase of the fairy-tale vogue was only partially connected to the utopian critique of the first phase. The major change, the attraction to oriental fairy tales, stemmed from two factors: the salons had abandoned the fairy-tale games, and the major writers of fairy tales had either died or been banished from Paris by 1704. To fill the gap, so to speak, some writers began to turn toward oriental literature (it is interesting to note that the classical literature of Greece and Rome was ignored again). The most significant work of this period was Antoine Galland's translation *Les Mille et Une Nuits* (1704–17) of the Arabian collection of *The Thousand and One Nights*. Galland (1646–1715) had traveled and lived in the Middle East and had mastered Arabic, Hebrew, Persian, and Turkish. After he published the first four volumes of *The Thousand and One Nights*, they became extremely popular, and he continued translating the tales until his death. The final two volumes were published posthumously. Galland did more than translate. He actually adapted the tales to suit the tastes of his French readers, and he invented some of the plots and drew material together to form some of his own tales. His example was followed by Pétis de La Croix (1653–1713), who translated a Turish work by Sheikh Zadah, the tutor of Amriath II, entitled *L'Histoire de la Sultane de Perse et des Visirs. Contes turcs* (*The Story of the Sultan of the Persians and the Visirs. Turkish Tales*) in 1710. Moreover, he also translated a Persian imitation of *The Thousand and One Days*, which borrowed material from Indian comedies. Finally, the Abbé Jean-Paul Bignon's collection, *Les Aventures d'Abdalla, fils d'Anif* (1712–14), purported to be an authentic Arabic work in translation, but was actually Bignon's own creative adaptation of oriental tales mixed with French folklore.

Why all this interest in oriental fairy tales?

One explanation is that the diminishing grandeur of Louis XIV's court and the decline of France in general compelled writers to seek compensation in portrayals of exotic countries. Certainly for the readers of that time, the oriental tales had a unique appeal because so little was known about the Middle East, and whereas the French had developed extensive commercial relations with the Orient, this appeal became even greater. Of course, the men who stimulated the interest in the oriental fairy tales were scholars, and their reason for turning to Arabic, Persian, and Turkish folklore had more to do with their academic interests than with compensation for the decline of French glory. Whatever the reason for the second phase, it is important to point out that women stopped playing the dominant role and that the tales were no longer connected to the immediate interests of the aristocracy and haute bourgeoisie.

THE COMIC AND CONVENTIONAL FAIRY TALE

By 1720 the interest in the literary fairy tale had so diminished that writers began parodying the genre, developing it along conventional lines or utilizing it for children's literature. Claude Philippe de Caylus' tales in *Féerie novelles* (1741) and *Contes orientaux tirés des manuscrits de la bibliothèque du roi de France* (1743) are indicative of attempts to poke fun at the fairy-tale genre. De Caylus is not overly sarcastic, but he does reverse the traditional courtly types to reveal how ridiculous they and the court are. Most of his narratives are short, dry, and witty, and are connected to the style of caricature that he was developing at that time. Actually, his work had been preceded by Anthony Hamilton (1644–1719), who had earlier written much longer burlesques of the oriental trend in such tales as *Fleur d'Epine* and *Les Quatre Facardins* that were only published after his death in 1730.

In a more serious vein, Mlle. de Lubert and Mme. de Villeneuve carried on the salon tradition. For instance, Mlle. de Lubert, who rejected marriage in order to devote herself to writing, composed a series of long, intricate fairy tales from 1743 to 1755. Among them, *Princesse Camion* (1743) is a remarkable example of a sadomasochistic tale that is intriguing because of the different tortures and transformations that she kept inventing to dramatize the suffering of her protagonists. Mlle. de Villeneuve's major contribution to the fairy tale had more to do with her ability to transcribe a discourse on true love and class differences in marriage into a classic fairy tale, *Beauty and the Beast* (1740), than with writing a horror fairy tale like Mlle. de Lubert. Mme. de Villeneuve's tale employs almost all the traditional fairy-tale and folklore motifs in a conventional manner, but to her credit, she was the first writer to develop the plot of *Beauty and the Beast* as we generally know it today, and her addition of dream sequences was an innovative touch that later writers of fairy tales such as Novalis and E.T.A. Hoffman developed more fully.

The "conventionalization" of the salon tale meant that the genre had become part of the French cultural heritage and was open to parody, as we have seen, but also open to more serious cultivation as in the works of Mlle. de Lubert and Mme. de Villeneuve. More important, it meant that the literary fairy tale could convey standard notions of propriety and morality that reinforced the socialization process in France. What might have been somewhat subversive in the salon fairy tale was often "conventionalized" to suit the taste and values of the dominant classes and the regime by the middle of the eighteenth century. This was the period when there was a great debate about the meaning of *civilité*, and literature was regarded as a means of socialization through which norms, mores, and manners were to be diffused. Therefore, it is not by chance that the literary fairy tale for children was established during the eighteenth century by Mme. Leprince de Beaumont and not by Mme. d'Aulnoy or Perrault. Both the debate about civility and the acceptance of the fairy tale as a proper literary genre had to reach a certain stage before the tale could be conventionalized as children's literature.

It is extremely important to note that Mme. Leprince de Beaumont's shorter version of Mme. de Villeneuve's *Beauty and the Beast* was published in an educational book entitled *Le Magasin des Enfants* in 1757. In fact, she published several fairy tales in this volume, all with the didactic purpose of demonstrating to little girls how they should behave in different situations. Therefore, her *Beauty and the Beast* preaches domesticity and self-sacrifice for women, and her *Prince Désir and Princess Mignone*, based on an old Breton folk tale, teaches a lesson about flattery and narcissism. One of the dangers in Mme. Leprince de Beaumont's conventionalizing the fairy tale for pedagogic purposes led to the undermining of the subversive and utopian quality of the earlier tales. However, conventionalization did not necessarily bring about a total watering down and depletion of the unusual ideas and motifs of the literary fairy tale and folk tale. It actually led to a more general acceptance and institutionalization of the literary fairy tale as genre for all ages and classes of readers. Such institutionalization set the framework within which other writers would create, play with those motifs, characters, and *topoi* that had been developed, and revise them in innovative ways to generate new forms, ideas, and motifs.

For instance, many of the literary fairy tales of the 1690s and early part of the eighteenth century found their way into cheap popular books published in a series called the *Bibliotheque Bleue* (known in England as chapbooks) and distributed by traveling book pedlars called *colporteurs*. The tales were rewritten (often drastically) and reduced to a more simple language so that the tales, when read in villages, were taken over by the peasants again and incorporated into the folklore. These tales were told and retold thousands of times and reentered the literary fairy tale genre through fairy-tale writers exposed to this amalgamated "folklore." The interaction between the oral and literary retellings of tales became one of the most important features in the development of the literary genre as it was institutionalized in the eighteenth century. The most obvious sign that the literary fairy tale had become an institution in France was the publication by Charles Mayer of the *Cabinet des fées* (1785–89), a forty-one-volume set of the best-known salon fairy, comical, and conventional tales of the preceding century. From this point on, the French literary fairy tales were diffused and made their mark through translations in most of the western world.

In point of fact, then, though the original French fairy tales are no longer read, they have never been forgotten. They have come down to us today in various forms and have inspired writers like Wieland, Goethe, the Brothers Grimm, Andersen, George Sand, and numerous others. Thus, the literary fairy tale keeps thriving and makes itself felt not only through literature in remarkable works by such contemporary authors as Angela Carter, Margaret Atwood, Michael Ende, and others, but through stage adaptations and film productions. The best of the contemporary fairy tales also keep alive the utopian quest and questioning spirit of the earlier salon tales. Written because of dissatisfaction with their times, these fairy tales still have a certain captivating charm that is not confined to the particular historical period in which they were conceived and written. They embrace the future. They anticipate hopes and wishes that we ourselves have yet to fulfill. In that sense, they are still modern, and—who knows?—may even open up alternatives to our postmodern dilemmas.

A NOTE
ON THE TRANSLATION

I BEGAN this project with the intention of editing John Robinson Planché's translations of French fairy tales that were published in two nineteenth-century collections entitled *Four-and-twenty Fairy Tales selected from those of Perrault, etc.* (1858) and *Countess D'Aulnoy's Fairy Tales* (1885). Planché (1796–1880) was a distinguished British archaeologist and versatile writer who wrote over seventy works including numerous fairy-tale plays, a history of costumes, poems, songs, and essays. Initially I believed that his translations would enable me to accomplish two purposes at the same time: publish the major French fairy tales that led to a great vogue and brought about the establishment of the fairy tale as a serious literary genre in Europe; and reintroduce the gifted Planché to the English-speaking world. Historically, both the tales and Planché have suffered from neglect by critics and the general reading public.

The more I examined Planché's translations, however, the more I realized that they were somewhat too anachronistic and inaccurate. Once I had compared the original tales in the *Cabinet des Fées* (1786–89), a vast collection of forty-one volumes, with Planché's translations, I decided to create my own selection and to retranslate the tales using Planché's versions as the basis for my work since, to his credit, his renditions contained a certain style and idiomatic characteristics that I felt helped recapture the highly mannered style of the French authors. Moreover, as an expert in clothes, customs, and architecture, Planché provided accurate descriptions of the garments, buildings, and manners of French society during the ancien régime and even documented his translations with footnotes.

Since Planché did not include all the tales that I chose for my collection, I did completely new translations of Perrault's *Little Red Riding Hood, The Fairies, The Donkey Skin,* and *The Foolish Wishes,* d'Aulnoy's *The Island of Happiness,* Bignon's *Princess Zeineb and the King Leopard,* Leprince de Beaumont's *Beauty and the Beast,* L'Héritier's *The Discreet Princess,* Bernard's *Riquet with the Tuft,* and de Mailly's *The Queen of the Island of*

Flowers. In the case of Perrault's *The Donkey Skin* and *The Foolish Wishes*, which were written in rhymed verse, I decided to render them into prose because I found it extremely difficult to recapture the seventeenth-century puns, historical references, and courtly style in English verse. To my knowledge, the only other translations of these two tales are also in prose and are inaccurate in many instances. I have endeavored to be as faithful to the text as one can be when translating a poem into prose, and in certain instances where the meaning was unclear, I have tried to make the prose version more cogent.

One of the major difficulties in doing these translations involved the transcribing of the verse morals that appear at the end of Perrault's, d'Aulnoy's, and de Murat's tales, and are also embedded in d'Aulnoy's tales. In most cases I sacrificed meter and style to meaning; in some cases, particularly in d'Aulnoy's tales, I endeavored to temper the bombastic and lavish tone and style. There are, of course, major stylistic differences among the authors, and I have tried to respect them as much as possible so that the reader can see how these French authors experimented with language and set standards of courtly and civil discourse. For instance, it will become obvious that the women writers were more inventive and imaginative in their discourse and in conceiving intrigues and plots in their tales, which were highly elaborate, while the male writers tended to be more succinct and make one major point in language that was highly economical. It was through language that all these writers tried to represent themselves as unique and gifted individuals, whose words about values, norms, politics, and civility were to be taken seriously.

The French fairy tales written from 1690 to 1789 formed part of a serious debate about the manners, politics, and values of that time. They were *not* intended for children at first, though some of the tales were later adapted for young people. The only writer in this collection who wrote expressly for children was Marie-Jeanne Leprince de Beaumont, whose version of *Beauty and the Beast* supplanted Gabrielle-Suzanne de Villeneuve's more intricate version. In general, all the tales in the present collection have had a remarkable influence on western culture and bear the impact of oral tales and folklore. In this sense, the French literary fairy tales were among the first in history to bring together the interests of the upper and lower classes in tales that are often stunning because of their extravagant ideas, incredible violence, and utopian longing.

I would like to express my gratitude to LuAnn Walther, who has been most supportive of my work, and to Susan Rogers, who assumed control of the project at a crucial transitional period. Catherine Vellay-Vallantin and Jacques Barchilon, whose work in the field is exemplary, both gave me invaluable advice about the social and historical background of the tales, while Carol Dines helped me revise many of the tales and gave me excellent suggestions for changes. Last but not least, I owe a great debt to John Paine, whose skillful and sensitive editing of the tales has helped keep their magic alive.

—Jack Zipes
Minneapolis, 1989

Charles Perrault

Charles Perrault (1628–1703) was born in Paris into one of the more distinguished bourgeois families of the time. His father, Pierre Perrault, was a lawyer and member of the Paris Parlement, and his four brothers—he was the youngest—all went on to become renowned in such fields as architecture, theology, and law. In 1637 Perrault began studying at the Collège de Beauvais (near the Sorbonne), but at the age of fifteen he stopped attending school and largely taught himself all he needed to know so he could later take his law examinations.

It was about this time that Perrault took an interest in the popular movement against King Louis XIV, and his early poetry expressed a sympathy for bourgeois opposition to the crown because the king had deprived the bourgeoisie of certain privileges and offices. However, Perrault became somewhat fearful and gradually switched his position to support the king as the bourgeoisie made peace with Louis XIV in 1649. In 1651 he passed the law examinations at the University of Orléans, and after working for three years as a lawyer, he left the profession to become a secretary to his brother Pierre, who was the tax receiver of Paris.

Perrault, who had already written some minor poems, became more and more interested in literature. In 1659 he published two important poems, "Portrait d'Iris" and "Portrait de la voix d'Iris," and by 1660 his public career as a poet was in full swing when he composed several poems in honor of Louis XIV. In 1663 Perrault was appointed secretary to Jean Baptiste Colbert, controller general of finances, perhaps the most influential minister in Louis XIV's government. For the next twenty years, until Colbert's death, Perrault was able to accomplish a great deal in the arts and sciences due to Colbert's powerful support.

In 1671 he was elected to the French Academy and was also placed in charge of the royal buildings. He continued writing poetry and took an active interest in cultural affairs of the court. In

1672 he married Marie Guichon, with whom he had three sons. She died at childbirth in 1678, and he never remarried, supervising the education of his children by himself.

When Colbert died in 1683, Perrault was dismissed from government service, but he had a pension and was able to support his family until his death. Released from administrative duties, Perrault concentrated more on literary affairs, and in 1687 he helped inaugurate the "Quarrel of the Ancients and the Moderns" (la Querelle des Anciens et des Modernes) by reading a poem entitled "Le Siècle de Louis le Grand." Perrault took the side of modernism and believed that France and Christianity—here he sided with the Jansenists, who sought to purify Catholicism and make it more mystical—could progress only if they incorporated pagan beliefs and folklore and developed a culture of enlightenment. On the other hand, Nicolas Boileau, the literary critic, and Jean Racine, the dramatist, took the opposite viewpoint and argued that France had to imitate the great empires of Greece and Rome and maintain stringent classical rules in respect to the arts. This literary quarrel, which had great cultural implications, lasted until 1697, at which time Louis XIV decided to end it in favor of Boileau and Racine. This decision did not stop Perrault, however, from incorporating his ideas into his poetry and prose.

Perrault had always frequented the literary salons of his niece Mlle. L'Héritier, Mme. d'Aulnoy, and other women, and he had been annoyed by Boileau's satires written against women. Thus, he wrote three verse tales, *Griselidis* (1691), *Les Souhaits Ridicules* (The Foolish Wishes, 1693) and *Peau d'Ane* (Donkey Skin, 1694) along with a long poem, *Apologie des femmes* (1694), in defense of women, a defense, which is, however, questionable. His poems use a highly mannered style and folk motifs to stress the necessity of an enlightened attitude of fairness toward women, but fairness on male terms.

In 1696 Perrault embarked on a more ambitious project. He transformed several popular folk tales, including all their superstitious beliefs and magic, into moralistic tales that would appeal to children and adults and demonstrate a modern approach to literature. He had a prose version of *La Belle au Bois Dormant* (The Sleeping Beauty in the Woods) printed in the journal *Mercure Galant* in 1696, and in 1697 he published an entire collection of tales entitled *Histoires ou contes du temps passé*, which consisted of a new version of *Sleeping Beauty*, *Le Petit Chaperon Rouge* (Little Red Riding Hood), *Barbe Bleue* (Blue Beard), *Cendrillon* (Cinderella), *Le Petit Poucet* (Little Thumbling), *Riquet à la Houppe* (Riquet with the Tuft), *Le Chat botté* (Puss in Boots), and *Les Fées* (The Fairies).

Although *Histoires ou contes du temps passé* was published under the name of Pierre Perrault Darmancour, Perrault's son, and although some critics have asserted that the book was indeed written or at least cowritten by his son, recent evidence has shown clearly that this could not have been the case, especially since his son had not published anything up to that point. Perrault was simply using his son's name to mask his own identity so that he would not be blamed for reigniting the Quarrel of the Ancients and the Moderns.

Numerous critics have regarded Perrault's tales as written directly for children, but they overlook the fact that no children's literature per se existed at that time and that most writers of fairy tales were composing and reciting their tales for their peers in the literary salons. Certainly, if Perrault intended them to make a final point in the Quarrel of the Ancients and the Moderns, he obviously had an adult audience in mind that would understand his humor and the subtle manner in which he transformed folklore superstition to convey his position about the "modern" development of French civility.

There is no doubt but that, among the writers of fairy tales during the 1690s, Perrault was the greatest stylist, which accounts for the fact that his tales have withstood the test of time. Furthermore, Perrault claimed that literature must become modern, and his transformation of folk motifs and literary themes into refined and provocative fairy tales still speaks to the modern age, ironically in a way that may compel us to ponder whether the Age of Reason has led to the progress and happiness promised so charmingly in Perrault's tales.

THE MASTER CAT
OR
PUSS IN BOOTS

A MILLER bequeathed to his three sons all his worldly goods, which consisted just of his mill, his ass, and his cat. The division was made quickly, and neither notary nor attorney were called, for they would have soon consumed all of the meager patrimony. The eldest received the mill; the second son, the ass; the youngest got nothing but the cat.

Of course, the youngest was upset at inheriting such a poor portion. "My brothers may now earn an honest living as partners," he said, "but as for me, I'm bound to die of hunger once I have eaten my cat and made a muff of his skin."

The cat, who had heard this speech but pretended not to have been listening, said to him with a sober and serious air, "Don't trouble yourself, master. Just give me a pouch and a pair of boots to go into the bushes, and you'll see that you were not left with as bad a share as you think."

Although the cat's master did not place much stock in this assertion, he had seen the cat play such cunning tricks in catching rats and mice—hanging himself upside down by the heels or lying in the flour as if he were dead—that he did not abandon all hope.

As soon as the cat had what he had asked for, he boldly pulled on his boots. Then he hung the pouch around his neck, took the strings in his forepaws, and went to a warren where a great number of rabbits lived. He put some bran and lettuce into his pouch and, stretching himself out as if he were dead, he waited for a young rabbit little versed in the wiles of the world to look for something to eat in the pouch. He had hardly laid down when he saw his plan work. A young scatterbrain of a rabbit entered the pouch, and master cat instantly pulled the strings, bagged it, and killed it without mercy. Proud of his catch, he went to the king's palace and demanded an audience. He was ushered up to the royal apartment, and upon entering, he made a low bow to the king. "Sire," he said, "here's a rabbit from the warren of my lord, the Marquis de Carabas (such was the name he fancied to call his master). He has instructed me to present it to you on his behalf."

"Tell your master," replied the king, "that I thank him and that he's given me great pleasure."

After some time had passed, the cat hid in a wheatfield, keeping the mouth of the pouch open as he always did. When two partridges entered it, he pulled the strings and caught them both. Then he went straight to the king and presented them to him just as he had done with the rabbit. The king was equally pleased by the two partridges and gave the cat a small token for his efforts.

During the next two or three months the cat continued every now and then to carry presents of game from his master to the king.

One day, when he knew the king was going to take a drive on the banks of a river with his daughter, the most beautiful princess in the world, he said to his master, "If you follow my advice, your fortune will be made. Just go and bathe in the river where I tell you, and leave the rest to me."

The "Marquis de Carabas" did as his cat advised, little expecting that any good would come of it. While he was bathing, the king passed by, and the cat began to shout with all his might, "Help! Help! My lord, the Marquis de Carabas is drowning!"

At this cry the king stuck his head out of the coach window. Recognizing the cat who had often brought game to him, he ordered his guards to rush to the aid of the Marquis de Carabas. While they were pulling the poor marquis out of the river, the cat approached the royal coach and told the king that some robbers had come and carried off his master's clothes while he was bathing, even though he had shouted "Thieves!" as loud as he could. But in truth the rascal had hidden his master's clothes himself under a large rock. The king immediately ordered the officers of his wardrobe to fetch one of his finest suits for the Marquis de Carabas. The king embraced the marquis a thousand times, and since the fine clothes brought out his good looks (for he was handsome and well built), the king's daughter found him much to her liking. No sooner did the Marquis de Carabas cast two or three respectful and rather tender glances at her than she fell in love with him. The king invited him to get into the coach and to accompany them on their drive.

Delighted to see that his scheme was succeeding, the cat ran on ahead and soon came upon some peasants mowing a field.

"Listen, my good people," he said, "you who are mowing, if you don't tell the king that this field belongs to my lord, the Marquis de Carabas, you'll all be cut into tiny pieces like minced meat!"

Indeed, the king did not fail to ask the mowers whose field they were mowing.

"It belongs to our lord, the Marquis de Carabas," they said all together, for the cat's threat had frightened them.

"You can see, sire," rejoined the marquis, "it's a field that yields an abundant crop every year."

Master cat, who kept ahead of the party, came upon some reapers and said to them, "Listen, my good people, you who are reaping, if you don't say that all this wheat belongs to my lord, the Marquis de Carabas, you'll all be cut into tiny pieces like minced meat!"

A moment later the king passed by and wished to know who owned all the wheatfields that he saw there.

"Our lord, the Marquis de Carabas," responded the reapers, and the king again expressed his joy to the marquis.

Running ahead of the coach, the cat uttered the same threat to all whom he encountered, and the king was astonished at the great wealth of the Marquis de Carabas. At last master cat arrived at a beautiful castle owned by an ogre, the richest ever known, for all the lands through which the king had driven belonged to the lord of this castle. The cat took care to inquire who the ogre was and what his powers were. Then he requested to speak with him, saying that he could not pass so near his castle without paying his respects. The ogre received him as civilly as an ogre can and asked him to sit down.

"I've been told," said the cat, "that you possess the power of changing yourself into all sorts of animals. For instance, it has been said that you can transform yourself into a lion or an elephant."

"It's true," said the ogre brusquely. "And to prove it, watch me become a lion."

The cat was so frightened at seeing a lion standing before him that he immediately scampered up into the roof gutters, and not without difficulty, for his boots were not made to walk on tiles. Upon noticing that the ogre resumed his previous form a short time afterward, the cat descended and admitted that he had been terribly frightened.

"I've also been told," said the cat, "but I can't believe it, that you've got the power to assume the form of the smallest of animals. For instance, they say that you can change yourself into a rat or mouse. I confess that it seems utterly impossible to me."

"Impossible?" replied the ogre. "Just watch!"

Immediately he changed himself into a mouse, which began to run about the floor. No sooner did the cat catch sight of it than he pounced on it and devoured it.

In the meantime the king saw the ogre's beautiful castle from the road and desired to enter it. The cat heard the noise of the coach rolling over the drawbridge and ran to meet it.

"Your Majesty," he said to the king, "welcome to the castle of my lord, the Marquis de Carabas."

"What!" exclaimed the king. "Does this castle also belong to you, Marquis? Nothing could be finer than this courtyard and all these buildings surrounding it. If you please, let us look inside."

The marquis gave his hand to the young princess, and they followed the king, who led the way upstairs. When they entered a grand hall, they found a magnificent repast that the ogre had ordered to be prepared for some friends who were to have visited him that day. (But they did not presume to enter when they found the king was there.) The king was just as much delighted by the accomplishments of the Marquis de Carabas as his daughter, who doted on him, and now, realizing how wealthy he was, he said to him, after having drunk five or six cups of wine, "The choice is entirely yours, Marquis, whether or not you want to become my son-in-law."

After making several low bows, the marquis accepted the honor the king had offered him, and on that very same day, he married the princess. In turn, the cat became a great lord and never again ran after mice, except for his amusement.

MORAL

Although the advantage may be great
When one inherits a grand estate
From father handed down to son,
Young men will find that industry
Combined with ingenuity,
Will lead more to prosperity.

ANOTHER MORAL

If the miller's son had quick success
    In winning such a fair princess,
By turning on the charm,
Then regard his manners, looks, and dress
    That inspired her deepest tenderness,
For they can't do one any harm.

CINDERELLA
OR
THE GLASS SLIPPER

ONCE upon a time there was a gentleman who took the haughtiest and proudest woman in the world for his second wife. She had two daughters with the same temperament and the exact same appearance. On the other hand, the husband had a daughter whose gentleness and goodness were without parallel. She got this from her mother, who had been the best person in the world.

No sooner was the wedding over than the stepmother's ill-humor revealed itself. She could not abide the young girl, whose good qualities made her own daughters appear all the more detestable. So she ordered her to do all the most demeaning tasks in the house. It was she who cleaned the plates and the stairs, who scrubbed the rooms of the mistress and her daughters. She slept on a wretched straw mattress in a garret at the top of the house while her stepsisters occupied rooms with parquet floors and the most fashionable beds and mirrors in which they could regard themselves from head to toe. The poor girl endured everything with patience and did not dare complain to her father, who would have only scolded her since he was totally under the control of his wife. Whenever she finished her work, she would sit down near the chimney corner among the cinders. Consequently she was commonly called Cindertail. The second daughter, however, was not as malicious as her elder sister, and she dubbed her Cinderella. Nevertheless, Cinderella looked a thousand times more beautiful in her shabby clothes than her stepsisters, no matter how magnificent their clothes were.

Now, the king's son happened to give a ball and to invite all the people of quality. Our two young ladies were included in the invitation, for they cut a grand figure in this country. Of course, they were very pleased and began planning which would be the best gowns and headdresses to wear. This meant more misery for Cinderella because she was the one who ironed her sisters' linen and set their ruffles. Nothing was talked about but the style in which they were to be dressed.

"I'll wear my red velvet dress," said the elder sister, "and my English point-lace trimmings."

"I only have my usual petticoat to wear," said the younger, "but to make up for that I'll put on my gold-flowered mantua and my necklace of diamonds."

They sent for a good hairdresser to make up their double-frilled caps and brought their patches from the best shopkeeper. They summoned Cinderella and asked her opinion, for she had excellent taste. Cinderella gave them the best advice in the world and even offered to dress their hair for them, a favor they were eager to accept. While she went about it, they said to her, "Cinderella, wouldn't you like to go to the ball?"

"Alas! Ladies, you're playing with me. That would not befit me at all."

"You're right. People would have a great laugh to see a Cindertail at a ball!"

Any other person but Cinderella would have messed up their hairdos, but she was good-natured and dressed them to perfection. They could eat nothing for nearly two days because they were so excited. More than a dozen laces were broken in making their waists as small as possible, and they were constantly standing in front of their mirrors. At last the happy evening arrived. They set off, and Cinderella followed them with her eyes as long as she could. When they were out of sight, she began to cry. Her godmother, who came upon her all in tears, asked what was troubling her.

"I should so like—I should so like—" She sobbed so much that she could not finish the sentence.

"You'd like to go to the ball. Is that it?"

"Ah, yes!" said Cinderella, sighing.

"Well, if you'll be a good girl, I shall enable you to go." She led her from her chamber into the yard and said, "Go to the garden and bring me a pumpkin."

Cinderella left immediately, gathered the finest pumpkin she could find, and brought it to her godmother, unable to guess how a pumpkin would enable her to go to the ball. Her godmother scooped it out, leaving nothing but the rind. Then she struck it with her wand, and the pumpkin was immediately transformed into a beautiful coach gilded all over. Next she looked into the mousetrap, where she found six live mice. She told Cinderella to lift the door of the trap a little, and as each mouse ran out, she gave it a tap with her wand. Each mouse sprouted into a fine horse, producing a fine team of six handsome, dappled, mouse-gray horses. Since her godmother had some difficulty in choosing something for a coachman, Cinderella said, "I'll go and see if there's a rat in the rattrap. We could make a coachman out of him."

"You're right," said her godmother. "Go and see."

Cinderella brought her the rattrap, which contained three large rats. The fairy selected one with the most ample beard, and after touching it, the rat was changed into a fat coachman, who had the finest moustaches that had ever been seen. Then she said, "Go into the garden, where you'll find six lizards behind the watering pot. I want you to bring them to me."

Cinderella had no sooner brought them than her godmother transformed them into six footmen, who immediately climbed up behind the coach in their braided liveries and perched there as though they had done nothing else all their lives. Then the fairy said to Cinderella, "Well, now you have something to take you to the ball. Are you satisfied?"

"Yes, but am I to go in these dirty clothes?"

Her godmother merely touched her with her wand, and her garments were instantly changed into garments of gold and silver dotted with jewels. She then gave her a pair of glass slippers, the prettiest in the world. When she was thus attired, she got into the coach, but her godmother warned her, "Above all, do not stay past midnight. If you remain at the ball one moment too long, your coach will again become a pumpkin; your horses, mice; your footmen, lizards; and your clothes will become cinder-covered rags." She promised her godmother she would not fail to leave the ball before midnight, and so she departed, overcome with joy.

Upon being informed that a grand princess had arrived whom nobody knew, the king's son went forth to greet her. He gave her his hand to help her out of the coach and led her into the hall where the company was assembled. All at once there was dead silence. The guests stopped dancing and the fiddlers ceased playing, so engrossed was everybody in regarding the beauty of the unknown lady. All that was heard was a low murmuring, "Oh, how lovely she is!" The king himself, old as he was, could not take his eyes off her and whispered to the queen that it was a long time since he had seen anyone so beautiful and so pleasant. All the ladies were busy examining her headdress and her clothes because they wanted to obtain some similar garments the very next day, if they could find the appropriate materials and tailors.

The king's son conducted her to the place of honor and then led her out to dance. She danced with so much grace that everyone's admiration increased. A very fine supper was served, but the prince could not eat anything because he was so wrapped up in watching her.

She sat beside her sisters and showed them a thousand civilities. She shared with them oranges and citrons that the prince had given her, and her sisters were quite surprised because they did not recognize her at all. While they were conversing, Cinderella heard the clock strike a quarter to twelve. She immediately made a low curtsy to the company and departed as quickly as she could.

As soon as she arrived home, she looked for her godmother, and after having thanked her, she said she wished very much to go to the ball again the next day because the king's son had invited her. While she was busy in telling her godmother all that had happened at the ball, the two sisters knocked at the door, and Cinderella opened it.

"How late you are!" she said to them, yawning, rubbing her eyes, and stretching as if she had only just awoke. However, she had not had the slightest inclination to sleep since she had left them.

"If you had been at the ball," said one of her sisters, "you would not have been bored. The most beautiful princess attended it—the most beautiful in the world. She paid us a thousand attentions, and also gave us oranges and citrons."

Cinderella was beside herself with delight. She asked them the name of the princess, but they replied that nobody knew her. Moreover, the king's son was stumped and would give anything in the world to know who she was. Cinderella smiled and said, "She was very beautiful, then? Heavens! How fortunate you are!—Couldn't I have a chance to see her? Alas! Jayotte, would you lend me the yellow gown you wear every day?"

"Indeed," said Jayotte, "I like that! Lend my gown to a dirty Cindertail like you! I'd have to be quite mad to do something like that!"

Cinderella fully expected this refusal and was delighted by it, for she would have been greatly embarrassed if her sister had lent her the gown.

The next evening the two sisters went to the ball, and so did Cinderella, dressed even more splendidly than before. The king's son never left her side and kept saying sweet things to her. The young lady enjoyed herself so much that she forgot her godmother's advice and was dumbfounded when the clock began to strike twelve, for she did not even think it was eleven. She rose and fled as lightly as a fawn. The prince followed her, but could not catch her. However, she dropped one of the glass slippers, which the prince carefully picked up. Without coach or footmen, Cinderella reached home out of breath and in shabby clothes. Nothing remained of her finery, except one of her little slippers, the companion to the one that she had dropped. The guards at the palace gate were asked if they had seen a princess depart. They answered that they had only seen a poorly dressed girl pass by, and she had more the appearance of a peasant than a lady.

When the two sisters returned from the ball, Cinderella asked them if they had enjoyed themselves as much as the first time and if the beautiful lady had been present. They said yes, but that she had fled as soon as the clock had struck twelve, and she had been in such haste that she had dropped one of her glass slippers, the prettiest in the world. The king's son had picked it up and had done nothing but gaze at it during the remainder of the evening. Undoubtedly, he was very much in love with the beautiful person who had worn the slipper.

They spoke the truth, for a few days later there was a flourish of trumpets. The king's son proclaimed that he would marry her whose foot would exactly fit the slipper. His men began by trying it on the princesses, then on the duchesses, and so on throughout the entire court. However, it was all in vain. Soon it was taken to the two sisters, who did their utmost to force one of their feet into the slip-per, but they could not man-age to do so.

Cinderella, who witnessed their efforts and recognized the slipper, said with a smile, "Let me see if it will fit me."

Her sisters began to laugh and ridicule her. The gentle-man who had been entrusted to try the slipper looked at-tentively at Cinderella and found her to be very beautiful. So he said, "It is a proper request. I have been ordered to try the slipper on everyone without exception." He asked Cinderella to sit down, and upon placing the slipper under her little foot, he saw it go on easily and fit like wax.

The astonishment of the two sisters was great, but it was even greater when Cinderella took the other little slipper out of her pocket and put it on the other foot. At that moment the godmother arrived. With a tap of her wand Cinderella's clothes became even more magnificent than all the previous garments she had worn. The two sisters then recognized her as the beautiful person they had seen at the ball. They threw themselves at her feet, begging her pardon for the harsh treatment they had made her endure.

Cinderella raised and embraced them, saying that she forgave them with all her heart and begged them to love her well in the future. Adorned as she was, she was conducted to the young prince. He found her more beautiful than ever, and a few days later he married her. Cinderella, who was as kind as she was beautiful, gave her sisters apartments in the palace and had them married the very same day to two great noblemen of the court.

MORAL

A woman's beauty is quite a treasure
We never cease to admire.
Yet graciousness exceeds all measure.
There's nothing of virtue higher.
The fairy, according to our story,

Contributed it to Cinderella's glory
And taught her what becomes a queen,
(Left in a moral to be gleaned.)

Beautiful ladies, it's kindness more than dress
That wins a man's heart with greater success.
So, if you want a life filled with bliss,
The truest gift is graciousness.

ANOTHER MORAL

No doubt it is a benefit
To have strong courage and fine wit,
To be endowed with common sense
And other virtues to possess
That Heaven may dispense.
But these may prove quite useless—
As well as many others—
If you strive to gain success
And neglect godfathers or godmothers.

BLUE BEARD

ONCE upon a time there was a man who had fine town and country houses, gold and silver plates, embroidered furniture, and gilded coaches. Unfortunately, however, this man had a blue beard, which made him look so ugly and terrifying that there was not a woman or girl who did not run away from him.

Now, one of his neighbors was a lady of quality who had two exceedingly beautiful daughters. He proposed to marry one of them, leaving the choice up to the mother which of the two she would give him. Yet neither one would have him, and they kept sending him back and forth between them, not being able to make up their minds to marry a man who had a blue beard. What increased their distaste for him was that he had already had several wives, and nobody knew what had become of them.

In order to cultivate their acquaintance, Blue Beard took the sisters, their mother, three or four of their most intimate friends, and some young people who resided in the neighborhood, to one of his country estates, where they spent an entire week. Their days were filled with excursions, hunting and fishing, parties, balls, entertainments, and feasts. Nobody went to bed, for their nights were spent in merry games and gambols. In short, all went off so well that the younger daughter began to find that the beard of the master of the house was not as blue as it used to be and that he was a very worthy man.

The marriage took place immediately upon their return to town. At the end of a month Blue Beard told his wife that he was obliged to take a journey concerning a matter of great consequence, and it would occupy him at least six weeks. He asked her to amuse herself as best as she could during his absence and to take her closest friends into the country with her if she pleased, and to offer them fine meals.

"Here are the keys to my two great storerooms," he said to her. "These are the keys to the chests in which the gold and silver plates for special occasions are kept. These are the keys to the strongboxes in which I keep my money. These keys open the caskets that contain my jewels. And this is the passkey to all the apartments. As for this small key," he said, "it is for the little room at the end of the long corridor on the ground floor. Open everything and go everywhere except into that room, which I forbid you to enter. My orders are to be strictly obeyed, and if you dare open the door, my anger will exceed anything you have ever experienced."

She promised to carry out all his instructions exactly as he had ordered, and after he embraced her, he got into his coach and set out on his journey. The neighbors and friends of the young bride did not wait for her invitation, so eager were they to see all the treasures contained in the country mansion. They had not ventured to enter it while her husband was at home because they had been frightened of his blue beard. Now they began running through all the rooms, closets, and wardrobes. Each apartment outdid the other in beauty and richness. Then they ascended to the storerooms, where they could not admire enough the elegance of the many tapestries, beds, sofas, cabinets, stands, tables, and mirrors in which they could see themselves from head to foot. Some mirrors had frames of glass, and some of gold gilt, more beautiful and magnificent than they had ever seen. They could not stop extolling and envying the good fortune of the new bride.

In the meantime, she was not in the least entertained by all these treasures because she was so impatient to open the little room on the ground floor. Her curiosity increased to such a degree that, without reflecting how rude it was to leave her company, she ran down a back staircase so hastily that she nearly tripped and broke her neck on two or three occasions. Once at the door she paused for a moment, recalling her husband's prohibition. What misfortune might befall her if she disobeyed? But the temptation was so strong that she could not withstand it. She took the small key, and with a trembling hand she opened the door of the little room.

At first she could make out nothing, since the windows were shuttered. After a short time, though, she began to perceive that the floor was covered with clotted blood of the dead bodies of several women suspended from the walls. These were all the former wives of Blue Beard, who had cut their throats one after the other. She thought she would die from fright, and the key to the room fell from her hand. After recovering her senses a little, she picked up the key, locked the door again, and went up to her chamber to compose herself. Yet she could not relax because she was too upset. Then she noticed that the key to the room was stained with blood. She wiped it two or three times, but the blood would not come off. In vain she washed it, and even scrubbed it with sand and grit. But the blood remained, for the key was enchanted, and there was no way of cleaning it completely. When the blood was washed off one side, it came back on the other.

That very evening Blue Beard returned from his journey and announced that he had received letters on the road informing him that the business on which he had set forth had been settled to his advantage. His wife did all she could to persuade him that she was delighted by his speedy return. The next morning he asked her to return his keys. She gave them to him, but her hand trembled so much that he did not have any difficulty in guessing what had occurred.

"Why is it," he asked, "that the key to the little room is not with the others?"

"I must have left it upstairs on my table," she replied.

"Bring it to me right now," said Blue Beard.

After several excuses she was compelled to produce the key. Once Blue Beard examined it, he said to her, "Why is there blood on this key?"

"I don't know," answered the poor woman, paler than death.

"You don't know?" Blue Beard responded. "I know well enough. You wanted to enter the room! Well, madam, you will enter it and take your place among the ladies you saw there."

She flung herself at her husband's feet, weeping and begging his pardon. One glance at her showed that she truly repented of disobeying him. Her beauty and affliction might have melted a rock.

"You must die, madam," he said, "and immediately."

"If I must die," she replied, looking at him with eyes bathed in tears, "give me a little time to say my prayers."

"I shall give you a quarter of an hour," Blue Beard answered, "but not a minute more."

As soon as he had left her, she called for her sister and said, "Sister Anne"—for that was her name—"go up, I beg you, to the top of the tower and see if my brothers are coming. They promised me that they would come to see me today. If you see them, give them a signal to make haste."

Sister Anne mounted to the top of the tower, and the poor distressed creature called to her every now and then, "Anne! Sister Anne! Do you see anyone coming?"

And sister Anne answered her, "I see nothing but the sun making dust, and the grass growing green."

In the meantime Blue Beard held a cutlass in his hand and bellowed to his wife with all his might, "Come down quickly, or I'll come up there."

"Please, one minute more," replied his wife. Immediately she repeated in a low voice, "Anne! Sister Anne! Do you see anyone coming?"

And sister Anne replied, "I see nothing but the sun making dust, and the grass growing green."

"Come down quickly," roared Blue Beard, "or I shall come up there!"

"I'm coming," answered his wife, and then she called, "Anne! Sister Anne! Do you see anyone coming?"

"I see," said sister Anne, "a great cloud of dust moving this way."

"Is it my brothers?"

"Alas! No, sister, I see a flock of sheep."

"Do you refuse to come down?" shouted Blue Beard.

"One minute more," his wife replied, and then she cried, "Anne! Sister Anne! Do you see anything coming?"

"I see two horsemen coming this way," she responded, "but they're still at a great distance." A moment afterward she exclaimed, "Heaven be praised! They're my brothers! I'm signaling to them as best I can to hurry up."

Blue Beard began to roar so loudly that the whole house shook. So his poor wife descended to him and threw herself at his feet, all disheveled and in tears.

"It's no use," said Blue Beard. "You must die!"

He seized her by the hair with one hand and raised his cutlass with the other. He was about to cut off her head when the poor woman looked up at him. Fixing her dying gaze upon him, she implored him to allow her one short moment to collect herself.

"No, no," he said, lifting his arm, "commend yourself as best you can to Heaven."

At that moment there was such a loud knocking at the gate that Blue Beard stopped short. The gate was opened, and two horsemen burst through. With drawn swords they ran straight at Blue Beard, who recognized them as the brothers of his wife—one a dragoon, the other a musqueteer. Immediately he fled, hoping to escape, but they pursued so quickly that they overtook him before he could reach the step of his door and passed their swords through his body, leaving him dead on the spot. The poor woman, who was nearly as dead as her husband, did not have the strength even to rise and embrace her brothers.

Since Blue Beard had no heirs, his widow inherited all his wealth. She employed part of it to arrange a marriage between her sister Anne and a young gentleman who had loved her a long time. Another part paid for commissions for her two brothers so they could become captains. The rest she used for her marriage to a worthy man who made her forget the miserable time she had spent with Blue Beard.

MORAL

Curiosity, in spite of its charm,
Too often causes a great deal of harm.
A thousand new cases arise each day.
With due respect, ladies, the thrill is slight,
For as soon as you're satisfied, it goes away,
And the price one pays is never right.

ANOTHER MORAL

Provided one has common sense
And learns to study complex texts,
It's easy to trace the evidence
Of long ago in this tale's events.

No longer are husbands so terrible,
Or insist on having the impossible.
Though he may be jealous and dissatisfied,
He tries to do as he's obliged.
And whatever color his beard may be,
It's difficult to know who the master be.

LITTLE THUMBLING

ONCE upon a time there was a woodcutter and his wife who had seven children, all boys. The eldest was but ten years old and the youngest only seven. People were astonished that the woodcutter had had so many children in such a short time, but the fact is that his wife did not mince matters and seldom gave birth to less than two at a time. They were very poor, and having seven children was a great burden to them, since not one was able to earn his own living.

What distressed them even more was that the youngest son was very delicate and rarely spoke, which they considered a mark of stupidity instead of good sense. Moreover, he was very little. Indeed, at birth he was scarcely bigger than one's thumb, and this led everyone to call him Little Thumbling. This poor child became the family scapegoat and was blamed for everything that happened. Nevertheless, he was the shrewdest and most sensible of all the brothers, and if he spoke but little, he listened a great deal.

One year there was a disastrous harvest, and the famine was so severe that these poor people decided to get rid of their children. One evening, when they were all in bed and the woodcutter was sitting by the fire with his wife, he said with a heavy heart, "It's plain that we can no longer feed our children. I can't let them die of hunger before my eyes, and I've made up my mind to lose them tomorrow in the forest. We can do this without any trouble when they are making bundles of firewood. We only have to disappear without their seeing us."

"Ah!" the woodcutter's wife exclaimed. "Do you really have the heart to abandon your own children?"

Her husband tried in vain to convince her how their terrible poverty necessitated such a plan, but she would not consent to the deed. However poor, she was their mother. After reflecting on how miserable she would be to see them die of hunger, though, she finally agreed and went to bed weeping.

Little Thumbling had heard everything they said, for while he had been lying in his bed, he had realized that they were discussing their affairs. He had got up quietly, slipped under his father's stool, and listened without being seen. Going back to bed, he did not sleep a wink the rest of the night because he was thinking over what he should do. He rose early the next morning and went to the banks of a brook, where he filled his pockets with small white pebbles and then returned home. Little Thumbling revealed nothing of what he had heard to his brothers.

Later they set out all together. They entered a dense forest, where they were unable to see one another once they were ten paces apart. The woodcutter began to chop wood, and his children, to pick up sticks and make bundles. Seeing them occupied with their work, the father and mother gradually stole away and then fled in an instant by a small, winding path. When the children found themselves all alone, they began to cry with all their might. Little Thumbling let them scream since he was fully confident that he could get home again. He had dropped the white pebbles in his pockets all along the path.

"Don't be afraid, brothers," he said. "Our father and mother have abandoned us here, but I'll lead you safely home. Just follow me."

They followed him, and he led them back to the house by the same path that they had taken into the forest. At first they were afraid to enter the house. Instead, they placed themselves next to the door to listen to the conversation of their parents.

Now, after the woodcutter and his wife had arrived home, they found ten crowns that the lord of the manor had sent them. He had owed them this money for a long time, and they had given up all hope of ever receiving it. This put new life into these poor, starving people. The woodcutter sent his wife to the butcher's right away, for it had been many a day since they had eaten anything. She bought three times as much as was necessary for two persons, and when they sat down at the table again, she said, "Alas! Where are our poor children now? They would make a good meal out of our leftovers. But it was you, Guillaume, who wanted to lose them. I told you we'd repent it. What are they doing now in the forest? Alas! Heaven help me! The wolves have probably eaten them already! What a monster you must be to get rid of your children this way!"

When she repeated more than forty times that they would repent it and that she had told him so, the woodcutter lost his temper. He threatened to beat her if she did not hold her tongue. It was not that the woodcutter was not perhaps even more sorry than his wife, but that she browbeat him. He was like many other people who are disposed to women who can talk well but become irritated by women who are always right.

"Alas!" His wife was in tears. "Where are my children now, my poor children!"

She uttered these words so loudly that the children began to cry at the door, "Here we are! Here we are!"

She rushed to open the door, and embracing them, she exclaimed, "How happy I am to see you again, my dear children! You're very tired and hungry. And how dirty you are, Pierrot! Come here and let me wash you."

Pierrot was her eldest son, and she loved him most of all because he was somewhat redheaded, which was the color of her hair too. They sat down to supper and ate with an appetite that pleased their father and mother. They all talked at once and related how frightened they had been in the forest. The good souls were delighted to see their children around them once more, but their joy lasted just as long as the ten crowns. When the money was spent, they relapsed into their former misery and decided to lose the children again. And to do so they were determined to lead them much farther from home than they had the first time.

They discussed this in secret, but were overheard by Little Thumbling, who counted on getting out of the predicament the way he had before. Yet when he got up early to collect some pebbles, he found the house door double-locked. He could not think of what to do until the woodcutter's wife gave them each a piece of bread for their breakfast. Then it occurred to him that he might use the bread in place of the pebbles by throwing crumbs along the path as they went. So he stuck his piece in his pocket.

The father and mother led them into the thickest, darkest part of the forest, and as soon as they had done so, they took a sidepath and left them there. Little Thumbling was not at all worried, for he thought he would easily find his way back by following the crumbs he had scattered along the path. But he was greatly surprised when he could not find a single crumb: the birds had eaten them all up. Now the poor children were in great trouble. The farther they wandered, the deeper they plunged into the forest. Night arrived, and a great wind arose, filling them with fear. They imagined that they heard wolves howling on every side of them. "They're coming to devour us!" They scarcely dared to turn their heads. Then it began raining so heavily that they were soon drenched to the skin. With each step they took, they slipped and tumbled into the mud. They got up all covered with mud and did not know what to do with their hands. Little Thumbling climbed up a tree to try to see something from the top. After looking all around, he saw a little light, like that of a candle, faraway on the other side of the forest. When he climbed down from the tree and reached the ground, he could no longer see the light. This was a great disappointment to him, but after having walked on with his brothers for some time in the direction of the light, he saw it again as they emerged from the forest. Then again, when they descended into the ravines, they kept losing sight of the beaming light and became frightened. Eventually, however, they reached the house where the light was burning and knocked at the door. A good woman came to open it and asked them what they wanted. Little Thumbling told her that they were poor children who had lost their way in the forest and begged her for a night's lodging out of charity. Seeing how lovely the children were, she began to weep and said, "Alas! My poor boys, don't you know where you've landed? This is the dwelling of an ogre who eats little children!"

"Oh, madam!" replied Little Thumbling, who trembled from head to toe just as all his brothers did. "What shall we do? It's certain that the wolves of the forest will devour us tonight if you refuse to take us under your roof. That being the case, we'd rather be eaten by your husband. If you're kind enough to plead for us, perhaps he'll take pity on us."

The ogre's wife, who believed she could manage to hide them from her husband till the next morning, allowed them to come in and led them to a spot where they could warm themselves by a good fire, for there was a whole sheep on the spit roasting for the ogre's supper. Just as they were beginning to get warm, they heard two or three loud knocks at the door. The ogre had come home. His wife immediately made the children hide under the bed and went to open the door. The ogre first asked if his supper were ready and if she had drawn the wine. With that he sat down to his meal. The mutton was almost raw, but he liked it all the better for that. He sniffed right and left, saying that he smelt fresh meat.

"It must be the calf that you smell. I've just skinned it," said his wife.

"I smell fresh meat, I tell you," replied the ogre, looking suspiciously at his wife. "There's something here I don't understand." Upon saying these words, he rose from the table and went straight to the bed. "Ah!" he exclaimed. "This is the way you deceive me, cursed woman! I don't know what's holding me back from eating you as well! It's a lucky thing that you're an old beast!"

He dragged the boys from under the bed one after the other. "Here's some game that comes just in time for me to entertain three ogre friends of mine who are coming to see me tomorrow." The poor children fell on their knees, begging for mercy, but they were facing the most cruel of all the ogres. Far from feeling pity for them, he was already devouring them with his eyes. He said to his wife, "They will be perfect as dainty bits once you make a good sauce for them." He fetched a large knife, and as he approached the poor children, he whetted it on a long stone that he held in his left hand. He had already grabbed one of the boys when his wife said to him, "Why do you want to do it at this hour of the night? Won't you have time enough tomorrow?"

"Hold your tongue," the ogre replied. "They'll be all the more tender."

"But you already have so much meat," his wife responded. "Here's a calf, two sheep, and half a pig."

"You're right," the ogre said. "Give them a good supper to fatten them up, and then put them to bed."

Overjoyed, the good woman brought them plenty for supper, but they could not eat because they were so paralyzed with fright. As for the ogre, he seated himself to drink again, delighted to think he had such a treat in store for his friends. So he emptied a dozen goblets, which was more than usual and affected his head somewhat, and he was obliged to go to bed.

Now, the ogre had seven daughters who were still quite young. These little ogresses had the most beautiful complexions due to eating raw flesh like their father. But they had very small, round gray eyes, hooked noses, and large mouths with long teeth, extremely sharp and wide apart. They were not very vicious as yet, but they showed great promise, for they had already begun to bite little children to suck their blood. They had been sent to bed early, and all seven were in a large bed, each having a golden crown on her head. In the same room there was another bed of the same size. It was in this bed that the ogre's wife put the seven little boys to sleep, after which she went to sleep with her husband.

Little Thumbling noticed that the ogre's daughters had golden crowns on their heads. Fearing that the ogre might regret not having killed him and his brothers that evening, he got up in the middle of the night. He took off his nightcap and those of his brothers, crept over very softly, and swapped them for the crowns of the ogre's seven daughters. These he put on his brothers and himself so that the ogre might mistake them for his daughters, and his daughters for the boys whose throats he longed to cut.

Everything turned out exactly as he had anticipated. The ogre awoke at midnight and regretted that he had postponed what he might have done that evening until the next morning. Therefore, he jumped out of bed and seized his large knife. "Let's go and see how our little rascals are doing. We won't make the same mistake twice." So he stole up to his daughters' bedroom on tiptoe and approached the bed in which the little boys were lying. They were all asleep except Thumbling, who was dreadfully frightened when the ogre placed his hand on his head to feel as he had in turn felt those of his brothers.

After feeling the golden crowns, the ogre said, "Upon my word, I almost made a mess of a job! It's clear I must have drunk too much last night." He then went to the bed where his daughters slept, and after feeling the nightcaps that belonged to the boys, he cried, "Aha! Here are our sly little dogs. Let's get to work!" With these words he cut the throats of his seven daughters without hesitating. Well satisfied with his work, he returned and stretched himself out in bed beside his wife. As soon as Little Thumbling heard the ogre snoring, he woke his brothers and told them to dress themselves quickly and follow him. They went down quietly into the garden and jumped over the wall. As they ran throughout the night, they could not stop trembling, for they did not know where they were going.

When the ogre awoke the next morning, he said to his wife, "Go upstairs and dress the little rascals you took in last night."

The ogress was astonished by her husband's kindness, never suspecting the sort of dressing he meant her to give them. Thus she merely imagined that he was ordering her to go and put on their clothes. When she went upstairs, she was greatly surprised to find her daughters murdered and swimming in their blood. All at once she fainted (for this is the first thing that most women do in similar circumstances). Fearing that his wife was taking too long in carrying out her task, the ogre went upstairs to help. He was no less surprised than his wife when he came upon the frightful spectacle.

"Ah! What have I done?" he exclaimed. "The wretches shall pay for it, and right now!" He threw a jugful of water in his wife's face, and after reviving her, he said, "Quick! Fetch my seven-league boots so I can go and catch them."

After setting out, he ran far and wide and at last came upon the track of the poor children, who were not more than a hundred yards from their father's house. They saw the ogre striding from hill to hill and stepping over rivers as easily as if they were the smallest brooks. Little Thumbling noticed a hollow cave nearby and hid his brothers in it, and while watching the movements of the ogre, he crept in after them. Now the ogre, feeling tired because his long journey had been to no avail, needed to rest, especially since seven-league boots make the wearer quite exhausted. By chance he sat down on the very rock in which the little boys had concealed themselves. Since the ogre was worn out, he soon fell asleep and began to snore so terribly that the poor children were just as frightened as they had been when he had grabbed the large knife to cut their throats.

Little Thumbling was not so much alarmed and told his brothers to run straight into the house while the ogre was sound asleep and not to worry about him. They took his advice and quickly ran home. Little Thumbling now approached the ogre and carefully pulled off his boots, which he immediately put on himself. The boots were very large and very long, but since they were fairy boots, they possessed the quality of increasing or diminishing in size according to the leg of the person who wore them. Thus they fit him just as if they had been made for him. He went straight to the ogre's house, where he found the wife weeping over her murdered daughters.

"Your husband is in great danger. He's been captured by a band of robbers, who have sworn to kill him if he doesn't give them all his gold and silver," Thumbling said to her. "He saw me just at the moment they had their daggers at his throat, and he begged me to come and ask you to give me all his valuables without holding anything back. Otherwise, they'll kill him without mercy. Since time was of the essence, he insisted I take his seven-league boots so that I might go faster and also so that you'd be sure I wasn't an imposter."

The good woman was very much alarmed by this news and immediately gave Thumbling all the money she could find, for the ogre was not a bad husband to her, even though he ate little children. So, loaded down with the ogre's entire wealth, Little Thumbling rushed back to his father's house, where he was received with great joy.

Many people differ in their account of this part of the story. They assert that Little Thumbling never committed the theft, and that he only considered himself justified in taking the ogre's seven-league boots because the ogre had used them expressly to run after little children. These people argue that they got their story from good authority and had even eaten and drunk in the woodcutter's house.

They maintain that after Little Thumbling had put on the ogre's boots, he went to the court. There, he knew, they were anxious to learn about the army and the outcome of a battle that was being fought two hundred leagues away. He went to the king and told him, "If you so desire, I will bring back news of the army before dusk." The king promised him a large sum of money if he did so, and Little Thumbling brought news that very evening.

Since this first journey gave him a certain reputation, he earned whatever he chose to ask. Not only did the king pay liberally for taking his orders to the army, but numerous ladies gave him any price he named for news of their lovers, and this became the best source of his income. Occasionally he met some wives who entrusted him with letters for their husbands, but they paid him so poorly that he did not even bother to put down what he got among his receipts.

After he had been a courier for some time and saved a great deal of money, he returned to his father. You cannot imagine how joyful his family was at seeing him again. He made them all comfortable by buying newly created positions for his father and brothers. In this way he made sure they were all established, and at the same time he made certain that he did perfectly well at the court himself.

MORAL

No longer may children be such a hardship,
If possessed of charm, good looks, and wit.
But if one's weak and falters in the fray,
He'll soon be mocked until he runs away.
Yet there are times when the child, the least expected,
May return with a fortune, his honor resurrected.

THE SLEEPING BEAUTY
IN THE WOODS

ONCE upon a time there was a king and a queen who were quite
disturbed at not having any children. Indeed, they were so disturbed that
no words can express their feelings. They visited all the baths in the world.
They took vows, pilgrimages—everything was tried, and nothing succeeded. At last, however, the queen became pregnant and gave birth to a
daughter. At the christening all the fairies who could be found in the
realm (seven altogether) were asked to be godmothers so that each would
give the child a gift. According to the custom of the fairies in those
days, the gifts would endow the princess with all the perfections that could
be imagined.

After the baptismal ceremonies the entire company returned to the king's
palace, where a great banquet was held for the fairies. Places were laid for
each, consisting of a magnificent plate with a massive gold case containing
a spoon, fork, and knife of fine gold, studded with diamonds and rubies.
But as they were all about to sit down at the table, an old fairy entered the
palace. She had not been invited because she had not left the tower in
which she resided for more than fifty years, and it was supposed that she
had either died or had become enchanted.

The king ordered a place to be set for her, but he could not give her a
massive gold case as as he had with the others because the seven had been
made expressly for the seven fairies. The old fairy thought that she was
being slighted and muttered some threats between her teeth. One of the
young fairies who chanced to be nearby overheard her, and thinking that
she might wish the little princess bad luck, hid herself behind the tapestry
as soon as they rose from the table. "That way I'll have the last word and
repair any evil the old woman might do."

Meanwhile, the fairies began to bestow their gifts upon the princess. The
youngest fairy decreed, "She will be the most beautiful person in the
world." The next fairy declared, "She will have the temperament of an
angel." The third, "She will evince the most admirable grace in all she

does." The fourth: "She will dance to perfection." The sixth: "She will play every instrument in the most exquisite manner possible."

Finally the turn of the old fairy arrived. Her head shook more with malice than with age as she declared, "The princess will pierce her hand with a spindle and die of the wound."

This terrible gift made the entire company tremble, and no one present could refrain from tears. At this moment the young fairy stepped from behind the tapestry and uttered in a loud voice, "Comfort yourselves, King and Queen, your daughter will not die. It's true that I don't have sufficient power to undo entirely what my elder has done. The princess will pierce her hand with a spindle. But instead of dying, she'll only fall into a deep sleep that will last one hundred years. At the end of that time, a king's son will come to wake her."

In the hope of avoiding the misfortune predicted by the old fairy, the king immediately issued a public edict forbidding all his subjects to spin with a spindle or to have spindles in their house under pain of death.

After fifteen or sixteen years had passed, the royal couple and their court traveled to one of their country residences, and one day the princess happened to be exploring it. She went from one chamber to another, and after arriving at the top of a tower, she entered a little garret, where an honest old woman was sitting by herself with her distaff and spindle. This good woman had never heard of the king's prohibition of spinning with a spindle.

"What are you doing there, my fair lady?" asked the princess.

"I'm spinning, my lovely child," answered the old woman, who did not know her.

"Oh, how pretty it is!" the princess responded. "How do you do it? Let me try and see if I can do it as well."

No sooner had she grasped the spindle than she pricked her hand with the point and fainted, for she had been hasty, a little thoughtless, and moreover, the sentence of the fairies had ordained it to be that way. Greatly embarrassed, the good old woman called for help. People came from all quarters. They threw water on the princess's face. They unlaced her stays. They slapped her hands. They rubbed her temples with Queen of Hungary's water. Nothing could revive her. Then the king, who had run upstairs at the noise, remembered the prediction of the fairies and wisely concluded that this must have happened as the fairies said it would. Therefore, he had the princess carried to the finest apartment in the palace and placed on a bed of gold and silver embroidery. One would have said she was an angel, so lovely did she appear, for her swoon had not deprived her of her rich complexion: her cheeks preserved their crimson color, and her lips were like coral. Her eyes were closed, but her gentle breathing could be heard, and that indicated she was not dead. The king commanded that she be left to sleep in peace until the hour arrived for her waking.

The good fairy who had saved her life by decreeing that she should sleep for one hundred years was in the Kingdom of Mataquin, twelve thousand leagues away. When the princess met with her accident, she was informed of it instantly by a little dwarf who had a pair of seven-league boots (that is, boots that enable the wearer to cover seven leagues at a single stride). The fairy set out immediately, and an hour afterward she was seen arriving in a chariot of fire drawn by dragons. The king advanced and offered his hand to help her out of the chariot. She approved of all that he had done. Yet since she had great foresight, she thought to herself that when the princess awoke, she would feel considerably embarrassed at finding herself all alone in that old castle. So this is what the fairy did:

With the exception of the king and queen, she touched everyone in the castle with her wand—governesses, maids of honor, ladies-in-waiting, gentlemen, officers, stewards, cooks, scullions, boys, guards, porters, pages, footmen. She also touched all the horses in the stables, their grooms, the great mastiffs in the courtyard, and little Pootsie, the princess's tiny dog lying on the bed beside her. As soon as she touched them, they all fell asleep, and they were not to wake again until the time arrived for their mistress to do so. Thus they would all be ready to wait upon her if she should want them. Even the spits that had been put down to the fire, laden with partridges and pheasants, went to sleep, and the fire as well.

All this was done in a moment, for the fairies never lose much time when they work. Then the king and queen kissed their dear daughter without waking her and left the castle. They issued a proclamation forbidding anyone to approach it. These orders were unnecessary, for within a quarter of an hour the park was surrounded by such a great quantity of trees, large and small, interlaced by brambles and thorns, that neither man nor beast could penetrate them. Nothing more could be seen than the tops of the castle turrets, and these only at a considerable distance. Nobody doubted but that was also some of the fairy's handiwork so that the princess might have nothing to fear from the curiosity of strangers during her slumber.

At the end of the hundred years, a different family from that of the sleeping princess had succeeded to the throne. One day the son of the king went hunting in that neighborhood and inquired about the towers that he saw above the trees of a large and dense wood. Every person responded to the prince according to the story he had heard. Some said that it was an old castle haunted by ghosts. Others, that all the witches of the region held their Sabbath there. The most prevalent opinion was that it was the abode of an ogre who carried away all the children he could catch and ate them there at his leisure, since he alone had the power of making a passage through the wood. While the prince tried to make up his mind what to believe, an old peasant spoke in his turn and said to him, "Prince, it is more than fifty years since I heard my father say that the most beautiful princess ever seen is in that castle. He told me that she was to sleep for a hundred years and was destined to be awakened by a chosen king's son."

Upon hearing these words, the young prince felt all on fire. There was no doubt in his mind that he was destined to accomplish this wonderful adventure, and impelled by love and glory, he decided on the spot to see what would come of it. No sooner had he approached the wood than all those great trees and all those brambles and thorns opened on their own accord and allowed him to pass through. Then he began walking toward the castle, which he saw at the end of the long avenue that he had entered. To his surprise, the trees closed up as soon as he passed, and none of his attendants could follow him. Nevertheless, he continued to advance, for a young and amorous prince is always courageous. When he entered a large forecourt, everything he saw froze his blood with terror. A frightful silence reigned. Death seemed to be everywhere. Nothing could be seen but the bodies of men and animals stretched out and apparently lifeless. He soon discovered, however, by the shining noses and red faces of the porters that they were only asleep; their goblets, which still contained a few drops of wine, sufficently proved that they had dosed off while drinking. Passing through a large courtyard paved with marble, he ascended a staircase. As he entered the guardroom, he saw the guards drawn up in a line, their carbines shouldered, and snoring their loudest. He traversed several apartments filled with ladies and gentlemen all asleep; some standing, others seated. Finally he entered a

chamber completely covered with gold and saw the most lovely sight he had ever looked upon—on a bed with curtains open on each side was a princess who seemed to be about fifteen or sixteen. Her radiant charms gave her such a luminous, supernatural appearance that he approached, trembling and admiring, and knelt down beside her. At that moment the enchantment ended. The princess awoke and bestowed on him a look more tender than a first glance might seem to warrant.

"Is it you, my prince?" she said. "You have been long awaited."

Charmed by these words, and still more by the tone in which they were uttered, the prince hardly knew how to express his joy and gratitude to her. He assured her he loved her better than he loved himself. His words were not very coherent, but they pleased her all the more because of that. The less eloquence, the more love, so they say. He was much more embarrassed than she was, and one ought not to be astonished at that, for the princess had had time enough to consider what she should say to him. There is reason to believe (though history makes no mention of it) that the good fairy had procured her the pleasure of very charming dreams during her long slumber. In short, they talked for four hours without expressing half of what they had to say to each other.

In the meantime the entire palace had been roused at the same time as the princess. They all remembered what their tasks were, and since they were not all in love, they were dying with hunger. The lady-in-waiting, as hungry as any of them, became impatient and announced loudly to the princess that dinner was ready. The prince assisted the princess to rise. She was fully dressed, and her gown was magnificent, but he took care not to tell her that she was attired like his grandmother, who also wore stand-up collars. Still, she looked no less lovely in it.

They passed into a salon of mirrors, in which stewards of the princess served them supper. The violins and oboes played antiquated but excellent pieces of music. And after supper, to lose no time, the chaplain married them in the castle chapel, and the maid of honor pulled the curtains of their bed closed.

They did not sleep a great deal, however. The princess did not have much need of sleep, and the prince left her at sunrise to return to the city, where his father had been greatly worried about him. The prince told him that he had lost his way in the forest while hunting, and that he had slept in the hut of a charcoal-burner, who had given him some black bread and cheese for his supper. His father, who was a trusting soul, believed him, but his mother was not so easily persuaded. Observing that he went hunting nearly every day and always had some story ready as an excuse when he had slept two or three nights away from home, she was convinced that he had some mistress. Indeed, he lived with the princess for more than two years and had two children by her. The first was a girl named Aurora, and the second, a son, called Day because he seemed even more beautiful than his sister.

In order to draw a confession from him, the queen often said to her son that he ought to settle down. However, he never dared to trust her with his secret. Although he loved her, he also feared her, for she was of the race of ogres, and the king had married her only because of her great wealth. It was even whispered about the court that she had the inclinations of an ogress: whenever she saw little children passing, she had the greatest difficulty restraining herself from pouncing on them. Hence, the prince refused to say anything about his adventure.

Two years later, however, the king died, and the prince became his successor. Thereupon, he made a public declaration of his marriage and went in great state to fetch his queen to the palace. With her two children on either side of her, she made a magnificent entry into the capital.

Some time afterward the king went to war with his neighbor, the Emperor Cantalabutte. He left the regency of the kingdom to his mother, the queen, and placed his wife and children in her care. Since he was likely to spend the entire summer in battle, the queen mother sent her daughter-in-law and the children to a country house in the forest, as soon as he was gone, so that she might gratify her horrible longing more easily. A few days later, she followed them there, and one evening she said to her steward, "I want to eat little Aurora for dinner tomorrow."

"Ah, madam!" exclaimed the steward.

"That is my will," said the queen (and she said it in the tone of an ogress longing to eat fresh meat), "and I want her served up with *sauce Robert.*"

The poor man plainly saw that it was useless to trifle with an ogress. So he took his knife and went up to little Aurora's room. She was then about four years old, and when she skipped over to him, threw her arms around his neck with a laugh, and asked him for some sweets, he burst into tears. The knife fell from his hands. Soon he went down into the kitchen court, killed a little lamb, and served it with such a delicious sauce that his mistress assured him she had never eaten anything so good. In the meantime he carried off little Aurora and gave her to his wife to conceal in the lodging she occupied at the far end of the kitchen court.

A week later, the wicked queen said to her steward, "I want to eat little Day for supper."

Determined to deceive her as before, he did not reply. He went in search of little Day and found him with a tiny foil in his hand, fencing with a large monkey, though he was only three years old. He carried him to his wife, who hid him where she had concealed his sister. Then he cooked a tender little goat in place of little Day, and the ogress thought it most delicious.

Thus far all was going well, but one evening this wicked queen said to the steward, "I want to eat the queen with the same sauce that I had with the children."

This time the poor steward despaired of being able to deceive her again. The young queen was now twenty years old, not counting the hundred years she had slept. Her skin was a little tough, though it was white and beautiful. Thus, where in the menagerie was he to find an animal that was just as tough as she was?

To save his own life he resolved he would cut the queen's throat and went up to her apartment intending to carry out this plan. He worked himself up into a fit and entered the young queen's chamber, dagger in hand. However, he did not want to take her by surprise and thus repeated respectfully the order he had received from the queen mother.

"Do your duty!" said she, stretching out her neck to him. "Carry out the order given to you. Then I shall behold my children, my poor children, that I loved so much."

She had thought they were dead ever since they had been carried off without explanation.

"No, no, madam!" replied the poor steward, touched to the quick. "You shall not die, and you shall see your children again, but it will be in my house, where I have hidden them. And I shall again deceive the queen mother by serving her a young hind in your stead."

He led her straight to his own quarters, and after leaving her to embrace her children and weep with them, he cooked a hind that the queen ate at supper with as much appetite as if it had been the young queen. She felt content with her cruelty and intended to tell the king on his return that some ferocious wolves had devoured his wife and two children.

One evening when she was prowling as usual around the courts and poultry yards of the castle to inhale the smell of fresh meat, she overheard little Day crying in a lower room because his mother wanted to slap him for having been naughty. She also heard little Aurora begging forgiveness for her brother. The ogress recognized the voices of the queen and her children and, furious at having been duped, she gave orders in a tone that made everyone tremble, "Bring a large copper vat into the middle of the court early tomorrow morning."

When it was done the next day, she had the vat filled with toads, vipers, adders, and serpents, intending to fling the queen, her children, the steward, his wife, and his maidservant into it.

"Bring them forth with their hands tied behind them," she commanded.

When they stood before her, the executioners began preparing to fling them into the copper vat when the king, who was not expected back so soon, entered the courtyard on horseback. He had ridden posthaste, and greatly astonished, he demanded to know the meaning of the horrible spectacle, but nobody dared to tell him. Then the ogress, enraged at the sight of the king's return, flung herself headfirst into the vat and was devoured by the horrible reptiles that she had commanded to be placed there. The king could not help but feel sorry, for she was his mother, but he speedily consoled himself in the company of his beautiful wife and children.

MORAL

To wait so long,
To want a man refined and strong,
Is not at all uncommon.
But: rare it is a hundred years to wait.
Indeed there is no woman
Today so patient for a mate.

Our tale was meant to show
That when marriage is deferred,
It is no less blissful than those of which you've heard.
Nothing's lost after a century or so.
And yet, for lovers whose ardor
Cannot be controlled and marry out of passion,
I don't have the heart their act to deplore
Or to preach a moral lesson.

RIQUET WITH
THE TUFT

ONCE upon a time there was a queen who gave birth to a son so ugly and misshapen that for a long time everyone doubted if he was in fact human. A fairy who was present at his birth assured everyone, however, that he could not fail to be pleasant because he would have a great deal of intelligence. She added that he would also have the ability to impart the same amount of intelligence to that person he came to love by virtue of this gift she was giving him. All this somewhat consoled the poor queen, who was very much distressed at having brought such a hideous little monkey into the world. Sure enough, as soon as the child was able to talk, he said a thousand pretty things. Futhermore, there was an indescribable air of thoughtfulness in all his actions that charmed everyone. I have forgotten to say that he was born with a little tuft of hair on his head, and this was the reason why he was called Riquet with the Tuft (Riquet being the family name).

At the end of seven or eight years, the queen of a neighboring kingdom gave birth to two daughters. The first of them was more beautiful than daylight, and the queen was so delighted that people feared her great joy might cause her some harm. The same fairy who had attended the birth of little Riquet with the Tuft was also present on this occasion, and to moderate the queen's joy, she declared that this little princess would be as stupid as she was beautiful. The queen was deeply mortified by this, but a few minutes later her chagrin became even greater still, for she gave birth to a second child who turned out to be extremely ugly.

"Don't be too upset, madam," the fairy said to her. "Your daughter will be compensated in another way. She'll have so much intelligence that her lack of beauty will hardly be noticed."

"May heaven grant it," replied the queen. "But isn't there some way to give a little intelligence to my older daughter who is so beautiful?"

"I can't do anything for her, madam, in the way of wit," said the fairy, "but I can do a great deal in matters of beauty. Since there's nothing I would not do to please you, I shall endow her with the ability to render any person who pleases her with a beautiful or handsome appearance."

As these two princesses grew up, their qualities increased in the same proportion. Throughout the realm everyone talked about the beauty of the older daughter and the intelligence of the younger. It is also true that their defects greatly increased as they grew older. The young daughter became uglier, and the older more stupid every day. She either gave no answer when addressed, or she said something foolish. At the same time she was so awkward that she could not place four pieces of china on a mantel without breaking one of them, nor drink a glass of water without spilling half of it on her clothes. Despite the great advantage of beauty in a young person, the younger sister always outshone the elder whenever they were in society. At first everyone gathered around the more beautiful girl to admire her, but soon left her for the more intelligent sister to listen to the thousand pleasant things she said. In less than a quarter of an hour, not a soul would be standing near the elder sister while everyone would be surrounding the younger. Though very stupid, the elder sister noticed this and would have willingly given up all her beauty for half the intelligence of her sister.

The queen, discreet though she was, could not help reproaching the elder daughter whenever she did stupid things, and that made the poor princess ready to die of grief. One day, when she had withdrawn into the woods to bemoan her misfortune, she saw a little man coming toward her. He was extremely ugly and unpleasant, but was dressed in magnificent attire. It was young Riquet with the Tuft. He had fallen in love with her from seeing her portraits, which had been sent all around the world, and he had left his father's kingdom to have the pleasure of seeing and speaking to her. Delighted to meet her thus alone, he approached her with all the respect and politeness imaginable. After paying the usual compliments, he remarked that she was very melancholy.

"I cannot comprehend, madam," he said, "how a person so beautiful as you are can be so sad as you appear. Though I may boast of having seen an infinite number of lovely women, I can assure you that I've never beheld one whose beauty could begin to compare with yours."

"It's very kind of you to say so, sir," replied the princess, and there she stopped.

"Beauty is such a great advantage," continued Riquet, "that it ought to surpass all other things. If one possesses it, I don't see anything that could cause one much distress."

"I'd rather be as ugly as you and have intelligence," said the princess, "than be as beautiful and stupid as I am."

"There's no greater proof of intelligence, madam, than the belief that we do not have any. It's the nature of the gift that the more we have, the more we believe we are deficient in it."

"I don't know whether that's the case," the princess said, "but I know full well that I am very stupid, and that's the cause of the grief which is killing me."

"If that's all that's troubling you, madam, I can easily put an end to your distress."

"And how do you intend to manage that?" the princess asked.

"I have the power, madam, to give as much intelligence as anyone can possess to the person I love," Riquet with the Tuft replied. "And as you are that person, madam, it will depend entirely on whether or not you want to have so much intelligence, for you may have it, provided that you consent to marry me."

The princess was thunderstruck and did not say a word.

"I see that this proposal torments you, and I'm not surprised," said Riquet with the Tuft. "But I'll give you a full year to make up your mind."

The princess had so little intelligence, and at the same time had such a strong desire to possess a great deal, that she imagined the year would never come to an end. So she immediately accepted his offer. No sooner did she promise that she would marry Riquet with the Tuft twelve months from that day than she felt a complete change come over her. She found she possessed an incredible facility to say anything she wished and to say it in a polished yet easy and natural manner. She commenced right away, maintaining an elegant conversation with the prince. Indeed, she was so brilliant that he believed that he had given her more wit than he had kept for himself.

When she returned to the palace, the whole court was at a loss to account for such a sudden and extraordinary change. Whereas she had formerly said any number of foolish things, she now made sensible and exceedingly clever observations. The entire court rejoiced beyond belief. Only the younger sister was not quite pleased, for she no longer held the advantage of intelligence over her elder sister. Now she merely appeared as an ugly woman by her side, and the king let himself be guided by the elder daughter's advice. Sometimes he even held the meetings of his council in her apartment.

The news of this change spread abroad, and all the young princes of the neighboring kingdoms exerted themselves to the utmost to gain her affection. Nearly all of them asked her hand in marriage, but since she found none of them sufficiently intelligent, she listened to all of them without promising herself to anyone in particular. At last a prince arrived who was so witty and handsome that she could not help feeling attracted to him. Her father noticed this and told her that she was at perfect liberty to choose a husband for herself and that she only had to make her decision known. Now, the more intelligence one possesses, the greater the difficulty one has in making up one's mind about such a weighty matter. So she thanked her father and requested some time to think it over.

By chance she took a walk in the same woods where she had met Riquet with the Tuft to ponder with greater freedom what she should do. While she was walking, deep in thought, she heard a dull rumble beneath her feet, as though many people were running busily back and forth. Listening more attentively, she heard voices say, "Bring me that cooking pot." "Give me that kettle." "Put some wood on the fire." At that same moment the ground opened, and she saw below what appeared to be a large kitchen full of cooks, scullions, and all sorts of servants necessary for the preparation of a magnificent banquet. A group of approximately twenty to thirty cooks came forth, and they took places at a very long table set in a path of the woods. Each had a larding pin in hand and a cap on his head, and they set to work, keeping time to a melodious song. Astonished at this sight, the princess inquired who had hired them.

"Riquet with the Tuft, madam," the leader of the group replied. "His marriage is to take place tomorrow."

The princess was even more surprised than she was before, and suddenly she recalled that it was exactly a year ago that she had promised to marry Prince Riquet with the Tuft. How she was taken aback! The reason why she had not remembered her promise was that when she had made it, she had still been a fool, and after receiving her new mind, she had forgotten all her follies. Now, no sooner had she advanced another thirty steps on her walk than she encountered Riquet with the Tuft, who appeared gallant and magnificent, like a prince about to be married.

"As you can see, madam," he said, "I've kept my word to the minute, and I have no doubt but that you've come here to keep yours. By giving me your hand, you'll make me the happiest of men."

"I'll be frank with you," the princess replied. "I've yet to make up my mind on that matter, and I don't believe I'll ever be able to do so to your satisfaction."

"You astonish me, madam."

"I can believe it," the princess responded, "and assuredly, if I had to deal with a stupid person—a man without intelligence—I'd feel greatly embarrassed. 'A princess is bound by her word,' he'd say to me, 'and you must marry me as you promised to do so.' But since the man with whom I'm speaking is the most intelligent man in the world, I'm certain he'll listen to reason. As you know, when I was no better than a fool, I could not decide whether I should marry you. Now that I have the intelligence that you've given me and that renders me much more difficult to please than before, how can you expect me to make a decision today that I couldn't make then? If you seriously thought of marrying me, you made a big mistake in taking away my stupidity and enabling me to see clearer."

"If a man without intelligence would be justified in reproaching you for your breach of promise," Riquet with the Tuft replied, "why do you expect, madam, that I should not be allowed to do the same? This matter affects the entire happiness of my life. Is it reasonable that intelligent people should be placed at a greater disadvantage than those who have none? Can you presume this, you who have so much intelligence and have so earnestly desired to possess it? But let us come to the point, if you please. With the exception of my ugliness, is there anything about me that displeases you? Are you dissatisfied with my birth, my intelligence, my temperament, or my manners?"

"Not in the least," replied the princess. "I admire you for everything you've just mentioned."

"If so," Riquet with the Tuft responded, "I'll gain my happiness, for you have the power to make me the most pleasing of men."

"How can that be done?"

"It can if you love me sufficiently to wish that it should be. And to remove your doubts, you should know that the same fairy who endowed me

at birth with the power to give intelligence to the person I chose also gave you the power to render handsome any man who pleases you."

"If that's so," the princess said, "I wish with all my heart that you may become the most charming and handsome prince in the world."

No sooner had the princess pronounced these words than Riquet with the Tuft appeared to her eyes as the most handsome, strapping, and charming man she had ever seen. There are some who assert that it was not the fairy's spell but love alone that caused this transformation. They say that the princess, having reflected on her lover's perseverance, prudence, and all the good qualities of his heart and mind, no longer saw the deformity of his body nor the ugliness of his features. His hunch appeared to her as nothing more than the effect of a man shrugging his shoulders. Likewise, his horrible limp appeared to be nothing more than a slight sway that charmed her. They also say that his eyes, which squinted, seemed to her only more brilliant for the proof they gave of the intensity of his love. Finally, his great red nose had something martial and heroic about it. However this may be, the princess promised to marry him on the spot, provided that he obtained the consent of the king, her father.

On learning of his daughter's high regard for Riquet with the Tuft, whom he also knew to be a very intelligent and wise prince, the king accepted him with pleasure as a son-in-law. The wedding took place the next morning, just as Riquet with the Tuft had planned it.

MORAL

That which you see written down here
Is not so fantastic because it's quite true:
We find what we love is wondrously fair,
In what we love we find intelligence, too.

ANOTHER MORAL

Nature very often places
Beauty in an object that amazes,
Such that art can ne'er achieve.
Yet even beauty can't move the heart
As much as that charm hard to chart,
A charm which only love can perceive.

LITTLE RED RIDING HOOD

ONCE upon a time there was a little village girl, the prettiest in the world. Her mother doted on her, and her grandmother even more. This good woman made her a little red hood which suited her so well that wherever she went, she was called Little Red Riding Hood.

One day, after her mother had baked some biscuits, she said to Little Red Riding Hood, "Go see how your grandmother's feeling. I've heard that she's ill. You can take her some biscuits and this small pot of butter."

Little Red Riding Hood departed at once to visit her grandmother, who lived in another village. In passing through the forest she met old neighbor

wolf, who had a great desire to eat her. But he did not dare because of some woodcutters who were in the forest. Instead he asked her where she was going. The poor child, who did not know that it is dangerous to stop and listen to a wolf, said to him, "I'm going to see my grandmother, and I'm bringing her some biscuits with a small pot of butter that my mother's sending her."

"Does she live far from here?" the wolf asked.

"Oh, yes!" Little Red Riding Hood said. "You've got to go by the mill, which you can see right over there, and hers is the first house in the village."

"Well, then," said the wolf, "I'll go and see her, too. You take that path there, and I'll take this path here, and we'll see who'll get there first."

The wolf began to run as fast as he could on the shorter path, and the little girl took the longer path. What's more, she enjoyed herself by gathering nuts, running after butterflies, and making bouquets of small flowers that she found along the way. It did not take the wolf long to arrive at the grandmother's house, and he knocked:

"Tick, tock."

"Who's there?"

"It's your granddaughter, Little Red Riding Hood," the wolf said, disguising his voice. "I've brought you some biscuits and a little pot of butter that my mother's sent for you."

The good grandmother, who was in her bed because she was not feeling well, cried out to him, "Pull the bobbin, and the latch will fall."

The wolf pulled the bobbin, and the door opened. He pounced on the good woman and devoured her quicker than a wink, for it had been more than three days since he had eaten last. After that he closed the door and lay down in the grandmother's bed to wait for Little Red Riding Hood, who after a while came knocking at the door.

"Tick, tock."

"Who's there?"

When she heard the gruff voice of the wolf, Little Red Riding Hood was scared at first, but she thought her grandmother had a cold and responded, "It's your granddaughter, Little Red Riding Hood. I've brought you some biscuits and a little pot of butter that my mother's sent for you."

The wolf softened his voice and cried out to her, "Pull the bobbin, and the latch will fall."

Little Red Riding Hood pulled the bobbin, and the door opened.

Upon seeing her enter, the wolf hid himself under the bedcovers and said to her, "'Put the biscuits and the pot of butter on the bin and come lie down beside me."

Little Red Riding Hood undressed and got into the bed, where she was quite astonished to see how her grandmother appeared in her nightgown.

"What big arms you have, grandmother!" she said to her.

"The better to hug you with, my child."

"What big legs you have, grandmother!"

"The better to run with, my child."

"What big ears you have, grandmother!"

"The better to hear you with, my child."

"What big eyes you have, grandmother!"

"The better to see you with, my child."

"What big teeth you have, grandmother!"

"The better eat you with!"

And upon saying these words, the wicked wolf pounced on Little Red Riding Hood and ate her up.

MORAL

One sees here that young children,
Especially pretty girls,
Who're bred as pure as pearls,
Should question words addressed by men.
Or they may serve one day as feast
For a wolf or other beast.
I say a wolf since not all are wild
Or are indeed the same in kind.
For some are winning and have sharp minds.
Some are loud, smooth, or mild.
Others appear plain kind or unriled.
They follow young ladies wherever they go,
Right into the halls of their very own homes.
Alas for those girls who've refused the truth:
The sweetest tongue has the sharpest tooth.

THE FAIRIES

ONCE upon a time there was a widow who had two daughters. The older one was often mistaken for her mother because she was so much like her in looks and character. Indeed, both mother and daughter were so disagreeable and haughty that it was impossible to live with them. The younger daughter, who looked exactly like her father and took after him in her kindness and politeness, was one of the most beautiful girls ever seen.

Since we naturally tend to be fond of those who resemble us, the mother doted on her elder daughter while she hated the younger. She made her eat in the kitchen and work from morning till night. Among the many things that this poor child was forced to do, she had to walk a mile twice a day to fetch water from a spring and tote it back in a large jug. One day, when she was at the spring, a poor woman came up to her and asked her for a drink.

"Why, of course, my good woman," she said, and the pretty maiden at once stooped and rinsed out the jug. Then she filled it with water from the clearest part of the spring and offered it to the woman, helping to keep the jug raised so that she might drink more easily.

After the woman had finished drinking, she said, "You are so beautiful, so good and kind, that I can't resist bestowing a gift on you"—for she was a fairy who had assumed the form of a poor peasant in order to discover just how kind this young girl was. "I shall give you a gift," continued the fairy, "that will cause every word you utter to become either a flower or precious stone."

When this beautiful girl arrived home, her mother scolded her for returning so late.

"I'm sorry for having taken so long," the poor girl said, and on saying these words, two roses, two pearls, and two large diamonds fell from her mouth.

"What do I see here!" said her mother, completely astonished. "I believe I saw pearls and diamonds dropping from your mouth. Where do they come from, my daughter?" (This was the first time she had ever called her "my daughter.")

61

As countless diamonds fell from her mouth, the poor child naively told her all that had happened.

"Upon my word," said the mother, "I must send my daughter. Come here, Fanchon! Do you see what's falling from your sister's mouth when she speaks? Wouldn't you like to have the same gift? You only have to fetch some water from the spring, and if a poor woman asks you for a drink, you're to give it to her nicely and politely."

"You'll never get me to walk to the spring!" the rude girl responded.

"I'm insisting," her mother replied, "and you'd better go this instant!"

She left, sulking as she went. With her she took the most beautiful silver bottle in the house. No sooner did she arrive at the spring than a magnificently dressed lady emerged from the forest and asked her for a drink. This was the same fairy who had appeared to her sister, but she now put on the airs and the garments of a princess to see just how rude this girl could be.

"Do you think I came here just to fetch you a drink?" the rude and arrogant girl said. "Do you think that I carried this silver bottle just to offer a drink to a fine lady? Get your own drink if you want one!"

"You're not at all polite," the fairy replied without anger. "Well, then, since you're not very obliging, I'll bestow a gift on you. Every word uttered from your mouth will become either a snake or a toad."

As soon as her mother caught sight of her, she cried out, "Well then, daughter!"

"Well then, my mother," her rude daughter responded, spitting two vipers and two toads from her mouth.

"Oh heavens!" her mother exclaimed. "What do I see? Your sister's to blame, and she'll pay for it!"

She dashed off to beat her, but the poor child fled and took refuge in a nearby forest. The king's son, who was returning from a hunt, encountered her there, and observing how beautiful she was, he asked her what she was doing there weeping all alone.

"Alas, sir! My mother has driven me from home."

Seeing five or six pearls and as many diamonds fall from her mouth, the king's son asked her to tell him where they came from. She told him the entire story, and the king's son fell in love with her. When he considered that such a gift was worth more than a dowry anyone else could bring, he took her to the palace of the king, his father, where he married her.

As for the sister, she made herself so hated that her own mother drove her out of the house. This wretched girl searched about in vain for someone who would offer her shelter, and finally she went off to a corner of the forest, where she died.

MORAL

Diamonds and gold
Can do wonders for one's soul.
Yet kind words, I am told,
Are worth more on the whole.

ANOTHER MORAL

Virtue demands a great deal of effort,
For one must indeed be very good-natured.
Sooner or later it reaps its reward,
Which comes indeed when it's least sought.

THE FOOLISH WISHES

ONCE upon a time there was a poor woodcutter whose life was so hard that he longed to rest in the infernal regions of the world beyond. This tormented soul maintained that in all his days on earth, heaven had never granted him a single wish.

One day he was grumbling to himself in the forest when Jupiter appeared with thunderbolt in hand. It is impossible to describe the fear of the good man, who threw himself on the ground and cried, "I don't want a thing. No wishes. No thunder. My lord, let me live in peace!"

"Have no fear," said Jupiter. "I've come because I've been moved by your complaints, and I want to show you how unfair you've been to me. So listen: I, who reign supreme over the entire world, promise to grant you the first three wishes you make, no matter what they are. Just see that they make you happy. And since your happiness depends on your wishes, think carefully before you make them." With these words Jupiter returned to the heavens.

The woodcutter, now cheerful, picked up his bundle of sticks and carried them home on his back. Never had his burden seemed so light. As he was running along, he said to himself, "I mustn't be hasty in this matter. It's important, and I must ask my wife's advice."

Upon entering his cottage, he called, "Hey, Fanchon! Let's make a large fire, my dear. We're going to be rich for the rest of our lives. All we have to do is to make some wishes."

He told her what had happened, and on hearing the story his wife promptly began forming a thousand vast schemes in her mind. Nevertheless, she realized the importance of doing everything prudently.

"Blaise, my dear," she said to her husband, "let's not spoil anything by our impatience. Let's both mull over in our minds what's best for us. I suggest that we sleep on it and put off our first wish until tomorrow."

"I agree with you," said the good man Blaise. "But now, get some of the good wine behind the stack of sticks."

On her return, he leisurely drank the wine by a large fire and enjoyed the sweetness of relaxation. Leaning back in his chair, he said, "Since we have such a good blaze, I wish we had some sausage. That would go well with it."

He had hardly finished speaking when his wife was astonished to see a very long sausage approaching her from the chimney corner like a serpent. First she screamed, but then realized that this incident had been caused by her husband's foolish wish. Overcome by vexation, she began to scold and berate the poor man.

"You can have an empire of gold, pearls, rubies, diamonds, or fine clothes," she said, "but all you seem to want is a sausage!"

"Ah well, I was wrong," he replied. "I made a bad choice. In fact, I made an enormously bad choice. I'll do better next time."

"Sure, you will," she snapped. "I'll be long gone before that happens. You've got to be an ass to make a wish like that!"

Her husband became enraged and thought how nice it would be to be a widower, and—between you and me—this was not a bad idea.

"Men," he said, "are born to suffer! A curse on this sausage and all other sausages. I wish to God that the sausage was hanging from your nose, you vile creature!"

The wish was heard in heaven, and moments after he had uttered those words, the sausage attached itself to the nose of the agitated woman. This unforseen miracle made her immensely angry. Fanchon was pretty and had a great deal of grace. And, to tell the truth, this ornament did not improve her looks. Even though it merely hung down over her face, it prevented her from speaking easily. Her husband now had such a wonderful advantage that he thought his wish was not all that bad.

"Despite this terrible disaster, I could still make myself king," he said to himself. "In truth, there's nothing that can compare to the grandeur of sovereignty. But I must take the queen's feelings into account, for she'd suffer immensely if she had to take her place on the throne with a nose more than a yard long. I must see whether she wants to be a grand princess with that horrible nose or whether she wants to keep living as a woodcutter's wife with a nose like everyone else's."

Fanchon knew that she who wielded a scepter had a lot of power and that people must swear you have a well-formed nose if you wear a crown. Yet after thinking about the matter carefully, she realized that nothing could surpass the desire to be pleasant-looking. Thus she decided to keep her own nose rather than to become an ugly queen.

So the woodcutter did not change his lot. He did not become a potentate, nor did his purse become filled with gold coins. Happily he employed his last wish to have his wife restored to her former state.

MORAL

No doubt, men who are quite miserable,
Or blind, dumb, worried, and fickle
Aren't fit to make those wishes they should.
In fact, there are few among them who're able
To use such heaven's gifts for their own good.

DONKEY-SKIN

ONCE upon a time lived the most powerful king in the world. Gentle in peace, terrifying in war, he was incomparable in all ways. His neighbors feared him while his subjects were content. Throughout his realm the fine arts and civility flourished under his protection. His better half, his constant companion, was charming and beautiful. Such was her sweet and good nature that he was less happy as king and more happy as her husband. Out of their tender, pure wedlock a daughter was born, and she had so many virtues that she consoled them for their inability to have more children.

Everything was magnificent in their huge palace. They had an ample group of courtiers and servants all around them. In his stables the king had large and small horses of every kind, which were adorned with beautiful trappings, gold braids, and embroidery. But what surprised everyone on entering the stables was a master donkey in the place of honor. This discrepancy may be surprising, but if you knew the superb virtues of this donkey, you would probably agree that there was no honor too great for him. Nature had formed him in such a way that he never emitted an odor. Instead he generated heaps of beautiful gold coins that were gathered from the stable litter every morning at sunrise.

Now, heaven, which always mixes the good with the bad, just like rain may come in good weather, permitted a nasty illness to suddenly attack the queen. Help was sought everywhere, but neither the learned physicians nor the charlatans who appeared were able to arrest the fever, which increased day by day. When her last hour arrived, the queen said to her husband, "Before I die, you must promise me one thing, and that is, if you should desire to remarry when I am gone—"

"Ah!" said the king, "your concern is superfluous. I'd never think of doing such a thing. You can rest assured about that."

"I believe you," replied the queen, "if your ardent love is any proof. But to make me more certain, I want you to swear that you'll give your pledge to another woman only if she is more beautiful, more accomplished, and wiser than I."

Her confidence in her qualities and her cleverness were such that she knew he would regard his promise as an oath never to remarry. With his eyes bathed in tears, he swore to do everything the queen desired. Then she died in his arms.

Never did a king make such a commotion. Day and night he could be heard sobbing, and many believed that he could not keep mourning so bitterly for long. Indeed, some said he wept about his deceased wife like a man who wanted to end the matter in haste.

In truth, this was the case. At the end of several months he wanted to move on with his life and choose a new queen. But this was not easy to do. He had to keep his word, and his new wife had to have more charms and grace than his dead one, who had become immortalized. Neither the court, with its great quantity of beautiful women, nor the city, the country, or foreign kingdoms, where the rounds were made, could provide the king with such a woman.

The only one more beautiful was his daughter. In truth, she even possessed certain attractive qualities that her deceased mother had not had. The king himself noticed this, and he fell so ardently in love with her that he became mad. He convinced himself that this love was reason enough for him to marry her. He even found a casuist who argued logically that a case could be made for such a marriage. But the young princess was greatly troubled to hear him talk of such love and grieved night and day.

Thus the princess sought out her godmother, who lived at some distance from the castle in a grotto of coral and pearls. She was a remarkable fairy, far superior to any of her kind. There is no need to tell you what a fairy was like in those most happy of times, for I am certain that your mother has told you about them when you were very young.

Upon seeing the princess, the fairy said, "I know why you've come. I know your heart is filled with sadness. But there's no need to worry, for I am with you. If you follow my advice, there's nothing that can harm you. It's true that your father wants to marry you, and if you were to listen to his insane request, it would be a grave mistake. However, there's a way to refuse him without contradicting him. Tell him that before you'd be willing to abandon your heart to him, he must grant your wishes and give you a dress the color of the sky. In spite of all his power and wealth and the favorable signs of the stars, he'll never be able to fulfill your request."

So the princess departed right away, and trembling, went to her amorous father. He immediately summoned his tailors and ordered them to make a dress the color of the sky without delay. "Or else, be assured I will hang you all."

The sun was just dawning the next day when they brought the desired dress, the most beautiful blue of the firmament. There was not a color more like the sky, and it was encircled by large clouds of gold. Though the princess desired it, she was caught between joy and pain. She did not know how to respond or get out of her promise. Then her godmother said to her in a low voice, "Princess, ask for a more radiant dress. Ask for one the color of the moon. He'll never be able to give that to you."

No sooner did the princess make the request than the king said to his embroiderer, "I want a dress that will glisten greater than the star of night, and I want it without fail in four days."

The splendid dress was ready by the deadline set by the king. Up in the night sky the luster of the moon's illumination makes the stars appear pale, mere scullions in her court. Despite this, the glistening moon was less radiant than this dress of silver.

Admiring this marvelous dress, the princess was almost ready to give her consent to her father, but urged on by her godmother, she said to the amorous king, "I can't be content until I have an even more radiant dress. I want one the color of the sun."

Since the king loved her with an ardor that could not be matched anywhere, he immediately summoned a rich jeweler and ordered him to make a superb garment of gold and diamonds. "And if you fail to satisfy us, you will be tortured to death."

Yet it was not necessary for the king to punish the jeweler, for the industrious man brought him the precious dress by the end of the week. It was so beautiful and radiant that the blond lover of Clytemnestra, when he drove his chariot of gold on the arch of heaven, would have been dazzled by its brilliant rays.

The princess was so confused by these gifts that she did not know what to say. At that moment her godmother took her by the hand and whispered in her ear, "There's no need to pursue this path anymore. There's a greater marvel than all the gifts you have received. I mean that donkey who constantly fills your father's purse with gold coins. Ask him for the donkey skin. Since this rare donkey is the major source of his money, he won't give it to you, unless I'm badly mistaken."

Now this fairy was very clever, and yet she did not realize that passionate love counts more than money or gold, provided that the prospects for its fulfillment are good. So the forfeit was gallantly granted the moment the princess requested it.

When the skin was brought to her, she was terribly frightened. As she began to complain bitterly about her fate, her godmother arrived. She explained, "If you do your best, there's no need to fear." The princess had to let the king think that she was ready to place herself at his disposal and marry him while preparing at the same time to disguise herself and flee alone to some distant country in order to avoid the impending, evil marriage.

"Here's a large chest," the fairy continued. "You can put your clothes, mirror, toilet articles, diamonds, and rubies in it. I'm going to give you my magic wand. Whenever you hold it in your hand, the chest will always

follow your path beneath the ground. And whenever you want to open it, you merely have to touch the ground with my wand, and the chest will appear before you. We'll use the donkey's skin to make you unrecognizable. It's such a perfect disguise and so horrible that once you conceal yourself inside, nobody will ever believe that it adorns anyone so beautiful as you."

Thus disguised, the princess departed from the abode of the wise fairy the next morning as the dew began to drop. When the king started preparations for the marriage celebration, he learned to his horror that his bride-to-be had taken flight. All the houses, roads, and avenues were promptly searched, but in vain. No one could conceive of what had happened to her. Sadness and sorrow spread throughout the realm. There would be no marriage, no feast, no tarts, no sugar-almonds. The ladies at the court were quite disappointed not to be able to dine, but the priest was most saddened, for he had been expecting a heavy donation at the end of the ceremony as well as a hearty meal.

Meanwhile the princess continued her flight, dirtying her face with mud. When she extended her hands to people she met, begging for a place to work, they noticed how much she smelled and how disagreeable she looked, and did not want to have anything to do with such a dirty creature, even though they themselves were hardly less vulgar and mean. Farther and farther she traveled and farther still until she finally arrived at a farm where they needed a scullion to wash the dishclothes and clean out the pig troughs. She was put in a corner of the kitchen, where the servants, insolent and nasty creatures all, ridiculed, contradicted, and mocked her. They kept playing mean tricks on her and harassed her at every chance they had. Indeed, she was the butt of all their jokes.

On Sundays she had a little time to rest. After finishing her morning chores, she went into her room, closed the door, and washed herself. Then she opened the chest and carefully arranged her toilet articles in their little jars in front of her large mirror. Satisfied and happy, she tried on her moon dress, then the one that shone like the sun, and finally the beautiful blue dress that even the sky could not match in brilliance. Her only regret was that she did not have enough room to spread out the trains of the dresses on the floor. Still, she loved to see herself young, fresh as a rose, and a thousand times more elegant than she had ever been. Such sweet pleasure kept her going from one Sunday to the next.

I forgot to mention that there was a large aviary on this farm that belonged to a powerful and magnificent king. All sorts of strange fowls were kept there: chickens from Barbary, rails, guinea fowls, cormorants, musical birds, quacking ducks, and a thousand other kinds, which were the match of ten other courts put together. The king's son often stopped at this charming spot on his return from the hunt to rest and enjoy a cool drink. He was more handsome than Cephalus and had a regal and martial appearance that made the proudest batallions tremble. From a distance Donkey-Skin admired him with a tender look. Thanks to her courage, she realized that she still had the heart of a princess beneath her dirt and rags.

"What a grand manner he has!" she said, even though he paid no attention to her. "How gracious he is, and how happy must be the woman who has captured his heart! If he were to honor me with the plainest dress imaginable, I'd feel more decorated than in any of those I have."

One Sunday the young prince was wandering adventurously from courtyard to courtyard, and he passed through an obscure hallway, where Donkey-Skin had her humble room. He chanced to peek through the keyhole, and since it was a holiday, she had dressed herself up as richly as possible in her dress of gold and diamonds that shone like the sun. Succumbing to fascination, the prince kept peeking at her, scarcely breathing because he was filled with such pleasure. Her magnificent dress, her beautiful face, her lovely manner, her fine traits, and her young freshness moved him a thousand times over. But most of all, he was captivated by the air of grandeur mingled with modest reserve that bore witness to the beauty of her soul.

Three times he was on the verge of entering her room because of the ardor that overwhelmed him, but three times he refrained out of respect for the seemingly divine creature he was beholding.

Returning to the palace, he became pensive. Day and night he sighed, refusing to attend any of the balls even though it was Carnival. He began to hate hunting and attending the theater. He lost his appetite, and everything saddened his heart. At the root of his malady was a deadly melancholy.

He inquired about the remarkable nymph who lived in one of the lower courtyards at the end of the dingy alley where it remained dark even in broad daylight.

"You mean Donkey-Skin," he was told. "But there's nothing nymphlike or beautiful about her. She's called Donkey-Skin because of the skin that she wears on her back. She's the ideal remedy for anyone in love. That beast is almost uglier than a wolf."

All this was said in vain, for he did not believe it. Love had left its mark and could not be effaced. However, his mother, whose only child he was, pleaded with him to tell her what was wrong, yet she pressured him in vain. He moaned, wept, and sighed. He said nothing, except that he wanted Donkey-Skin to make him a cake with her own hands. And so, his mother could only repeat what her son desired.

"Oh, heavens, madam!" the servants said to her. "This Donkey-Skin is a black drab, uglier and dirtier than the most wretched scullion."

"It doesn't matter," the queen said. "Fulfilling his request is the only thing that concerns us." His mother loved him so much that she would have served him anything on a golden platter.

Meanwhile, Donkey-Skin took some ground flour, salt, butter, and fresh eggs in order to make the dough especially fine. Then she locked herself alone in her room to make the cake. She washed her hands, arms, and face and put on a silver smock in honor of the task that she was about to undertake. It is said that in working a bit too hastily, a precious ring happened to fall from Donkey-Skin's finger into the batter. But some claim that she dropped the ring on purpose. As for me, quite frankly, I can believe it because when the prince had stopped at the door and looked through the keyhole, she must have seen him. Women are so alert that nothing escapes their notice. Indeed, I pledge my word on it that she was convinced her young lover would gratefully receive her ring.

There was never a cake kneaded so daintily as this one, and the prince found it so good that he immediately began ravishing it and almost swallowed the ring. However, when he saw the remarkable emerald and the narrow band of gold, his heart was ignited by an inexpressible joy. At once he put the ring under his pillow. Yet that did not cure his malady. Upon seeing him grow worse day by day, the doctors, wise with experience, used their great science to come to the conclusion that he was sick with love.

Whatever else one may say about marriage, it is a perfect remedy for love sickness. So it was decided that the prince should marry. After he deliberated for some time, he finally said, "I'll be glad to get married provided that I marry only the person whose finger fits this ring."

This strange demand surprised the king and queen very much, but he was so sick that they did not dare to say anything that might upset him. Now a search began for the person whose finger might fit the ring, no matter what class or lineage. The only requirement was that the woman be ready to come and show her finger to claim her due.

A rumor was spread throughout the realm that to claim the prince, one had to have a very slender finger. Consequently, every charlatan, eager to make a name for himself, pretended that he possessed the secret of making a finger slender. Following such capricious advice, one woman scraped her finger like a turnip. Another cut a little piece off. Still another used some liquid to remove the skin from her finger and reduce its size. All sorts of plans imaginable were concocted by women to make their fingers fit the ring.

The selection was begun with the young princesses, marquesses, and duchesses, but no matter how delicate their fingers were, they were too large for the ring. Then the countesses, baronesses, and all the rest of the nobility took their turns and presented their hands in vain. Next came well-proportioned working girls who had pretty and slender fingers. Finally, it was necessary to turn to the servants, kitchen help, minor servants, and poultry keepers, in short, to all the trash who with their reddened or blackened hands hoped for a happy fate just as much as those with delicate hands. Many girls presented themselves with large and thick fingers, but trying the prince's ring on their fingers was like trying to thread the eye of a needle with a rope.

Everyone thought that they had reached the end because the only one remaining was Donkey-Skin in the corner of the kitchen. And who could ever believe that the heavens had ordained that she might become queen?

"Why not?" said the prince. "Let her try."

Everyone began laughing and exclaimed aloud, "Do you mean to say that you want that dirty wretch to enter here?"

But when she drew a little hand as white as ivory and of royal blood from under the dirty skin, the destined ring fit perfectly around her finger. The members of the court were astonished. So delirious were they that they wanted to march her to the king right away, but she requested that she be given some time to change her clothes before she appeared before her lord and master. In truth, the people could hardly keep from laughing because of the clothes she was wearing.

Finally, she arrived at the palace and passed through all the halls in her blue dress whose radiance could not be matched. Her blonde hair glistened with diamonds. Her blue eyes, so large and sweet, whose gaze always pleased and never hurt, were filled with a proud majesty. Her waist was so

slender that two hands could have encircled it. All the charms and ornaments of the ladies of the court dwindled in comparison. Despite the
rejoicing and commotion of the gathering, the good king did not fail to
notice the many charms of his future daughter-in-law, and the queen was
also terribly delighted. The prince, her dear lover, could hardly bear the
excitement of his rapture.

Preparations for the wedding were begun at once. The monarch invited
all the kings of the surrounding countries, who left their lands to attend the
grand event, all radiant in their different attire. Those from the East were
mounted on huge elephants. The Moors arriving from distant shores were
so black and ugly that they frightened the little children. People embarked
from all the corners of the world and descended on the court in great
numbers. But neither prince nor king seemed as splendid as the bride's
father, who had purified the criminal and odious fires that had ignited his
spirit in the past. The flame that was left in his soul had been transformed
into devoted paternal love. When he saw her, he said, "May heaven be
blessed for allowing me to see you again, my dear child."

Weeping with joy, he embraced her tenderly. Everyone wanted to share
in his happiness, and the future husband was delighted to learn that he was
to become the son-in-law of such a powerful king. At that moment the
godmother arrived and told the entire story of how everything had happened and culminated in Donkey-Skin's glory.

Evidently, the moral of this tale implies it is better for a child to expose
oneself to hardships than to neglect one's duty.

Indeed, virtue may sometimes seem ill-fated, but it is always crowned
with success. Of course, strongest reason is a weak dike against mad love
and ardent ecstacy, especially if a lover is not afraid to squander rich
treasures.

Finally, we must take into account that clear water and brown bread are
sufficient nourishment for all young women provided that they have good
habits, and that there is not a damsel under the skies who does not imagine
herself beautiful and somehow carrying off the honors in the famous beauty
contest between Hera, Aphrodite, and Athena.

> The tale of Donkey-Skin is hard to believe,
> But as long as there are children on this earth,
> With mothers and grandmothers who continue to give birth,
> This tale will always be told and surely well received.

Marie-Jeanne L'Héritier

Marie-Jeanne L'Héritier de Villandon (1664–1734) was a niece of Charles Perrault and the daughter of Nicolas L'Héritier, seigneur de Nouvelon et de Villandon, a noted historian and writer. Her mother was reported to be quite erudite; her brother led a distinguished career as mathematician and man of letters; her sister, Mlle. de Nouvelon, was a poet. Given such a literary and scholarly family, it was not by chance that Mlle. L'Héritier decided to dedicate herself to writing. Unlike many other women writers of her time, however, she did not become involved in any scandals nor suffered banishment to a convent. She never married or had any lovers. She was known for being studious, clever, honorable, and on close terms with the most influential women of her time. She was invited to attend the gatherings at the more illustrious of the salons in Paris and eventually maintained her own literary salon, in which she often recited her tales, poetry, and other works before she published them.

Mlle. L'Héritier's first major work was *Oeuvres meslées* (1695–98), which contained *L'Innocente tromperie*, *L'Avare puni*, *Les Enchantements de l'éloquence ou Les Effets de la Douceur*, and *L'Adroite Princesse ou Les Aventures de Finette*, which was dedicated to Henriette Julie de Murat. It was followed immediately by *Bigarrures ingénieuses* (1696), which reprinted *Les Enchantements* and *L'Adroite Princesse* and included a new fairy tale entitled *Ricdin-Ricdon*. These early collections were influenced by Perrault, Mme. d'Aulnoy, and Mme. de Murat, who were all close friends of hers, and contained her major contributions to the fairy-tale mode.

As her reputation grew, she won various literary prizes and was elected member of the Académie des Ricovrati de Padova in 1697. Mlle. L'Héritier was supported in her work by her patron, the Duchess of Nemours, Marie d'Orléans de Longueville, whose memoirs she edited in 1709. After her patron's death, she received a modest pension from Chauvelin that enabled her to live in a proper way until her death. In addition, she inherited Mlle. de Scudéry's salon, for whom she wrote the eulogy *L'Apothéose de Mlle Scudéry* (1702).

All Mlle. L'Héritier's works tended to be moralistic and conformed to the general literary taste of the day. For example, two of her works, *La Pompe Dauphine* (1711) and *Le Tombeau du Dauphin* (1711), were dedicated to the king and the royal family and are filled with short, didactic pieces that celebrated virtuous courtly manners. Mlle. L'Héritier also liked to display her extensive knowledge in works such as *L'Erudition Enjouée* (1703) and *Les Caprices du Destin* (1718), which included short literary essays, histories, poems, and tales.

Even though Mlle. L'Héritier published few fairy tales after her three major works in 1695, she is historically important because her first three prose tales signaled the beginning of the mode of fairy-tale writing that was to become so popular in France for the next hundred years. *L'Adroite Princesse* (The Discreet Princess) is undoubtedly her most significant tale and reveals Mlle. L'Héritier's attitudes about the standards of proper comportment for young ladies. As in most of her tales, magical elements and imagination are not celebrated so much as reason and sobriety. In fact, *The Discreet Princess* was written in such a dry, succinct manner that it was considered to be one of Perrault's tales for over one hundred fifty years. However, Perrault would never have allowed a young woman to triumph over a man, no matter how villainous he was. To Mlle. L'Héritier's credit, she demonstrated the qualities women needed to survive in courtly society, and her skillful transformation of folk motifs and themes rendered *The Discreet Princess* one of the more amusing narratives of that period.

THE DISCREET PRINCESS
OR
THE ADVENTURES OF FINETTE

DURING the time of the First Crusade, a king of a country in Europe decided to go to war against the infidels of Palestine. Before undertaking such a long journey, he put the affairs of his kingdom into such good order and placed the regency in the hands of such an able minister that he was entirely at ease. What worried this king most, though, was the care of his family. He had recently lost his wife, who had failed to give birth to a son before her death. On the other hand, he was the father of three princesses, all of marriageable age. My chronicle has not indicated what their true names were. I only know that people were quite simple during these happy times, and customarily gave eminent people surnames according to their good or bad characteristics. Thus they called the eldest princess "Nonchalante," the second "Babbler," and the third "Finette." All of these names suited the characters of the three sisters.

Never was anyone more indolent than Nonchalante. The earliest she ever woke up was one in the afternoon, and she was dragged to church in the same condition as when she got out of bed. Her clothes were all in disarray, her dress loose, sans belt, and often she wore mismatched slippers. They used to correct this mistake during the day, but could never prevail upon this princess to wear anything but slippers, for she found it extremely exhausting to put on shoes. Whenever Nonchalante finished eating, she would camp at her dressing table until evening. She employed the rest of her time until midnight by playing and snacking. Since undressing her took almost as long as getting her dressed, she never succeeded in going to bed until dawn.

Babbler led a different kind of life. Extremely active, this princess spent little time caring about her looks, but she had such a strong propensity for talking that from the moment she woke to the time she fell asleep again, her mouth was never shut. She knew everything about the bad households, the love liaisons, and the intrigues not only at the court, but also among the most petty of the bourgeoisie. She kept a record of all those wives who

77

stole from their families at home in order to make a more dazzling impression when they went out into society. She was informed precisely about what a particular countess's lady-in-waiting and a particular marquis's steward earned. In order to be on top of all these insignificant affairs, she listened to her nurse and seamstress with greater pleasure than she would to an ambassador. Finally, she shocked everyone, from the king down to his footmen, with her pretty stories. She did not care whom she had for a listener provided she could prattle. Such a longing to talk had another bad effect on this princess. Despite her high rank, her familiarity emboldened young men around the court to talk sweetly to her. She listened to their flowery speeches merely so that she could have the pleasure of responding to them. No matter what the consequences of her actions might be, she had to hear others talk or gossip herself from morning till night.

Neither Babbler nor Nonchalante ever bothered to occupy herself by thinking, reflecting, or reading. They never troubled themselves about household chores or entertained themselves by sewing or weaving. In short, these two sisters lived in eternal idleness and ignorance.

The youngest of the three sisters had a very different character. Her mind and hands were continually active, and she had a surprising vivacity that was put to good use. She knew how to sing and dance and play musical instruments to perfection. She was remarkably nimble and successful in all those little manual chores with which her sex generally amused themselves. Moreover, she put the king's household into perfect order and prevented the pilferings of the petty officers through her care and vigilance, for even in those days princes were cheated by those who surrounded them.

Finette's talents did not stop there. She had great judgment and such a wonderful presence of mind that she could immediately find ways to get out of any kind of predicament. By using her insights, this young princess had discovered a dangerous trap that a perfidious ambassador of the neighboring kingdom had set for her father in a treaty that he was about to sign. To punish the treachery of this ambassador and his master, the king changed the articles of the treaty, and by wording it in the terms that his daughter dictated to him, he in turn deceived the deceiver. Another time the princess discovered some cheating by a minister against the king, and through the advice she gave her father, he managed to foil this disloyal man. In fact, she gave so many signs of her intelligence that this is why the people called her Finette.

The king loved her far more than his other daughters and depended so much on her good sense that if he had not had any other child but her, he would have departed for the Crusade without feeling uneasy. However, his faith in Finette's good behavior was offset by his distrust of his other daughters. Therefore, to make sure that his family would be safeguarded in the way he believed he had done for his subjects, he adopted the following measures that I am now going to relate.

The king was on intimate terms with a fairy, and went to see her in order to express the uneasiness he felt concerning his daughters.

"It's not that the two eldest have ever done the least thing contrary to their duty," he said. "But they have so little sense, are so imprudent, and live so indolently that I fear that they will get caught up in some foolish intrigue during my absence or do something foolish merely to amuse themselves. As for Finette, I'm sure of her virtue. However, I'll treat her as I do her sisters to make everything equal. This is why, wise fairy, I'd like you to make my daughters three distaffs out of glass. And I'd like you to make each one so artfully that it will break as soon as its owner does anything against her honor."

Since this fairy was extremely skillful, she presented the king with three enchanted distaffs within seconds, taking great care to make them according to his conditions. But he was not content with this precaution. He put the princesses into a high tower in a secluded spot. The king told his daughters that he was ordering them to live in that tower during his absence and prohibited them from admitting any people whatsoever. He took all their officers and servants of both sexes from them, and after giving them the enchanted distaffs, whose qualities he explained to them, he kissed the princesses, locked the doors of the tower, took away the keys, and departed.

You may perhaps believe that these princesses were now in danger of dying from hunger. Not at all. A pulley had been attached to one of the windows of the tower, and a rope ran through it, to which the princesses tied a basket that they let down to the ground. Provisions were placed into this basket on a daily basis, and after they pulled up the basket, they carefully coiled the rope in the room.

Nonchalante and Babbler led a life of despair in this desolate place. They became bored beyond expression, but they were forced to have patience because they had been given such a terrible picture of their distaffs that they feared that their least slip might cause them to break.

As for Finette, she was not bored in the least. Her needlework, spinning, and music furnished her with abundant amusement. Besides this, the minister who was governing the state had the king's permission to place letters into the basket, which kept the princesses informed about what was happening in the kingdom or outside it. Finette read all the news with great attention and pleasure, but her two sisters did not deign to participate in the least. They said they were too sorrowful to have the strength to amuse themselves with such weighty matters. They needed cards to entertain themselves during their father's absence.

Thus they spent their time by grumbling continually about their destiny, and I believe they even said, "It is much better to be born happy than to be

born the daughter of a king." They often went to the windows of the tower
to see at least what was happening in the countryside, and one day, when
Finette was absorbed in some pretty work in her room, her sisters saw a
poor woman clothed in rags and tatters at the foot of the tower. She
pathetically cried out to them about her misery and begged them with clasped
hands to let her come into the castle. "I'm an unfortunate stranger who knows
how to do a thousand things, and I shall serve you with the utmost fidelity."

At first the princesses recalled their father's orders not to permit anyone
to enter the tower, but Nonchalante was so weary of attending herself, and
Babbler was so bored at having nobody to talk to but her sisters, that the
desire of the one to be groomed and the other to gossip made them decide
to admit this poor stranger.

"Do you think," Babbler said to her sister, "that the king's order was
meant to include this un-
fortunate wretch? I believe
we can admit her without
anything happening."

"Sister, you may do what-
ever you please," Noncha-
lante responded.

Babbler had only waited
for her sister to consent, and
she immediately let down
the basket. The poor woman
got into it, and the princesses pulled her up with
the help of the pulley.

When this woman drew
nigh, her horrid dirty clothes
almost turned their stom-
achs. They would have given
her others, but she told them
she would change her clothes
the next day. At present, she
could think of nothing but
her work. As she said these
words, Finette entered the
room. She was stunned to
see this unknown person
with her sisters. They told
her the reasons that had induced them to pull her up, and Finette, who
saw that she could do nothing about it, concealed her disappointment at
their imprudence.

In the meantime the princesses' new servant explored the tower a hundred times under the pretext of doing her work, but in reality to see what was located where in it. In truth, this ragged creature was none other than the elder son of a powerful king, a neighbor of the princesses' father. One of the most cunning men of his time, this young prince completely controlled his father. Actually, this did not require much ability, because the king had such a sweet and easy disposition that he had been named "The Gentle." As for this young prince, who always acted with artifice and guile, the people called him Rich-in-Craft, a name commonly shortened to Rich-Craft.

His younger brother had as many good qualities as Rich-Craft had bad ones. Despite their different characters, however, such a tight bond existed between these two princes that everyone was surprised by it. Besides the younger prince's good qualities, his handsome face and graceful figure were so remarkable that he was generally called Bel-a-voir.

It was Rich-Craft who had instigated the deceitful act of his father's ambassador who had tried to change the treaty, an act that had been foiled by Finette's quick mind. Ever since she had turned the tables on them, Rich-Craft, who had not shown a particularly great love for the princess's father before this, now developed an even stronger aversion for him. Thus, after he had learned about the precautions that the king had taken in regard to his daughters, he decided to have some pernicious fun by undermining the prudence of such a distrustful father. Accordingly, Rich-Craft obtained permission from his father to take a journey, and he found a way to enter the tower, as you have already seen.

In examining the castle, Rich-Craft observed that the princesses could easily make themselves heard by people passing by, and he concluded that he'd best stay in his ragged disguise for the rest of the day because if they realized who he was, they could easily call out and have him punished for his rash undertaking. That night, however, after the princesses had dined, he pulled off his rags and revealed himself as a cavalier in rich attire dotted with gold and jewels. The poor princesses were so frightened by this disclosure that they all ran from him as fast as they could. Finette and Babbler, who were very nimble, quickly reached their rooms, but Nonchalante, who was not accustomed to moving fast, was soon overtaken.

Rich-Craft threw himself at her feet. He declared who he was and told her that the reputation of her beauty and the sight of her portraits had induced him to leave his delightful court in order to pledge his eternal devotion and propose to her. Nonchalante was at such a loss for words that she could not answer the prince, who remained kneeling. Meanwhile he kept saying a thousand sweet things and made a thousand protestations, and he ardently implored her, "Take me this very moment for your husband." Due to her weak backbone, she did not have the strength to gainsay him and told him without thinking that she believed him to be sincere and accepted his proposal. No greater formalities than these concluded the marriage.

At that moment, however, her distaff broke into a thousand pieces.

Babbler and Finette were extraordinarily anxious. They had made it back to their separate rooms and locked themselves in. These rooms were at some distance from each other, and since neither princess knew anything about the other's fate, they did not sleep a wink all night long.

The next morning the wicked prince led Nonchalante into a ground apartment at the end of the garden, where she told him how greatly she was disturbed about her sisters. She dared not show herself to them, for fear they would find fault with her marriage. The prince told her he would make sure that they would approve and, after talking some more, he locked Nonchalante in her room. Then he searched carefully all over the castle to locate the other princesses. It took some time before he could discover in what rooms they had locked themselves, but eventually Babbler's longing to talk all the time caused her to grumble to herself.

Rich-Craft went to the door, looked through the keyhole, and spoke to her. He told her everything that he had previously told her sister. "I swear I entered the tower only to offer my hand and heart to you." This seducer was the consummate actor and played his role perfectly, for he had had a lot of practice. He praised her wit and beauty in exaggerated terms, and Babbler, who was convinced that she had great qualities, was foolish enough to believe everything he told her. She answered with a flood of words that showed how receptive she was. Certainly this princess had an extraordinary capacity for chatter to have acquitted herself as she did, for she was extremely faint after not having eaten a morsel all day. In fact, she had nothing fit to eat in her room because she was extremely lazy and had not thought of anything but endless talking. Whenever she needed anything, she usually depended on Finette, who was always prudent and kept an abundance of fine biscuits, pies, macaroons, and jams of her own making in her room. Weakened by her severe hunger pangs, Babbler was moved by the protestations that the prince made through the door. At last she opened it and was at the mercy of the artful seducer.

Given her hunger, they decided to adjourn to the pantry, where he found all sorts of refreshments, since the daily basket furnished the princesses with more than enough. Babbler was still at a loss to know what had happened to her sisters, but she got it into her head—and I am not sure what her reasons were—that they were both locked up in Finette's room and had all they needed. Rich-Craft used all the arguments he could to substantiate this belief and told her that they would go and find the princesses toward evening. Not entirely in agreement with him on this matter, she said they would go and find them as soon as they had finished eating.

In short, the prince and princess began eating with big appetites. When they were finished, Rich-Craft asked to see the most beautiful apartment in the castle. He gave his hand to the princess as she led him there, and when they entered, he began to exaggerate his love and the advantages she would have in marrying him. He told her, just as he had done with her sister Nonchalante, that she should accept his proposal immediately because if she were to see her sisters beforehand, they would certainly oppose it. "Since I'm one of the most powerful of the neighboring princes, they'll probably think I'm better suited for your elder sister, and she'll never consent to a match she might desire herself." After many words that signified nothing, Babbler acted just as extravagantly as her sister had done; she agreed to become Rich-Craft's wife.

She never thought about her glass distaff until it shattered into a hundred pieces.

Toward evening Babbler returned to her room with the prince, and the first thing she saw was the shards of her glass distaff littering the floor. She was very troubled by this sight, and the prince asked why she was so concerned. Since her passion for talking made her incapable of holding her tongue about any subject, she foolishly told Rich-Craft the secret of the distaff. The prince laughed evilly to himself because the princesses' father would now be wholly convinced of his daughters' bad conduct.

Meanwhile, Babbler no longer wished to search for her sisters, for she had reason to fear that they would not approve of her conduct. The prince himself proposed that he undertake this task and told her, "I know how to win their approval, never fear." After this assurance the princess, who had not slept at all that night, grew very drowsy, and when she fell asleep, Rich-Craft locked her in her room as he had previously done with Nonchalante.

Once this devious prince had locked up Babbler, he went into all the rooms of the castle, one after another. When he found them all open except one that was locked from the inside, he concluded that was where Finette had gone. Since he had created a routine of compliments, he used the same ones at Finette's door that he had used with her sisters. But this princess was not so easy to dupe, and listened to him for a good while without responding. At last realizing that he knew she was in that room, she told him if it were true that he had such a strong and sincere affection for her, he should go down into the garden and shut the door after him. Then she would talk to him as much as he wanted from the window of her room that overlooked the garden.

Rich-Craft would not agree to this, and since the princess persisted in refusing to open the door, this wicked prince lost his patience. Fetching a large wooden log, he broke the door in. However, he found Finette armed with a large hammer, which had been accidentally left in a wardrobe in her room. Her face was red with emotion, and her eyes sparkled with rage, making her appear even more enchanting and beautiful to Rich-Craft. He would have cast himself at her feet, but as she retreated, she said boldly, "Prince, if you approach me, I'll split your skull with this hammer."

"What's this I hear, beautiful princess!" Rich-Craft exclaimed in his hypocritical tone. "Does the love I have for you inspire you with such hatred?"

He then began to speak to her across the room, describing the passionate ardor that the reputation of her beauty and wonderful wit had aroused in him. "The only reason I put on such a disguise was to offer my hand and heart." He told her she ought to pardon the violent love that caused him to break open her door. Finally he tried to persuade her, as he had with her sisters, that it was in her interest to take him for a husband as soon as possible, and he assured her he did not know where her sisters had gone. This was because his thoughts had been wholly fixed on her, and he had not gone to the trouble of looking for them.

The discreet princess pretended to be appeased and told him, "I simply must find my sisters, and after that we will do what has to be done together." But Rich-Craft answered that he could not agree to search for her sisters until she had consented to marry him, for her sisters would certainly oppose their match due to their seniority. Finette, who had good reason to distrust this treacherous prince, became even more suspicious at this answer. She trembled to think of what disaster had befallen her sisters and was determined to revenge them. So this young princess told Rich-Craft that she would gladly consent to marry him, but since she was of the opinion that marriages made at night always turned out to be unhappy, she requested that he postpone the ceremony until the next morning. She added that she would certainly not mention a word of this to her sisters and asked him to give her only a little time to say her prayers. Afterward she would take him to a room where there was a very good bed, and then she would return to her own room until the morning.

Rich-Craft was not very courageous, and as he watched the large hammer, which she played with like a fan, he consented and retired to give her some time to pray. No sooner was he gone than Finette rushed to one of the rooms of the tower, and made a bed over the hole of a sink. This room was as clean as any other, but all the garbage and dirty water were thrown down the hole which was very large. Finette put two weak sticks across it and then made a clean bed on top of them. After that she quickly returned to her room. A few minutes later Rich-Craft made his appearance, and the princess led him into the room where she had made his bed and then retired.

Without undressing, the prince hastily threw himself onto the bed. His weight immediately broke the small sticks, and he began falling to the bottom of the drain, unable to stop himself. Along the way he received twenty blows on his head and was bruised all over. The prince's fall made a great noise in the pipe, and since it was not far from Finette's room, she knew that her trick had worked. It is impossible to describe the pleasant feeling and joy she had as she heard him muttering in the drain. He certainly deserved his punishment, and the princess had every reason to feel satisfied.

But her joy was not so consuming that she forgot her sisters, and her first concern was to go and look for them. It was quite easy to find Babbler. Rich-Craft had double-locked that princess in her room and had left the key in the door. So Finette entered eagerly, and the noise she made startled her sister, throwing her into a great state of confusion. Finette told how she had defeated the wicked prince who had come to insult them, and on hearing that news, Babbler was thunderstruck, for despite all her talk about how smart she was, she had been foolish enough to have ridiculously believed every word Rich-Craft had told her. The world is still full of such dopes like her. However, she managed to cover up the extent of her sorrow and left the room with Finette to look for Nonchalante.

They searched all the rooms of the castle, but in vain. At last Finette thought to herself that they should look in the garden apartment, where, indeed, they found Nonchalante half dead with despair and fatigue, for she had not had anything to eat all day. Her sisters gave her all the assistance she needed. Then they recounted their adventures to one another, and Nonchalante and Babbler were overcome with remorse. Afterward, all three went to bed.

In the meantime Rich-Craft spent a very uncomfortable night, and when day came, he was not much better. The prince found himself in an underground sewer, though he could not see how horrible it was because no light could penetrate there. Nevertheless, after he had struggled painfully for some time, he found the end of the drain, which ran into a river at a considerable distance from the tower. Once there, he was able to make himself heard by some fishermen, who dragged him out in such a state that he aroused their compassion.

Rich-Craft ordered the men to carry him to his father's kingdom to recover from his wounds in seclusion. The disgrace that he had experienced caused him to develop such an inveterate hatred for Finette that he thought less about getting well than he did about getting revenge.

Meanwhile, Finette was very sad. Honor was a thousand times dearer to her than life, and the shameful weakness of her sisters had thrown her into such despair that she had great difficulty overcoming it. At the same time, the constitution of her sisters took a turn for the worse as a result of their worthless marriages, and Finette's patience was put to the test.

Rich-Craft, long a cunning villain, had continued to hatch ideas since this incident so that he could perpetrate even greater villainy. Neither the drain nor the bruises disturbed him as much as the fact that he had encountered someone more clever than he was. He knew the effects that his two marriages had had, and to tempt the princesses, he had great boxes filled with the finest fruit placed beneath the windows of the castle. Nonchalante and Babbler, who often sat at the windows, could not help but see the fruit, and they immediately felt a passionate desire to eat some. They insisted that Finette go down in the basket to get some of the fruit for them. So great was the kindness of that princess and so willing was she to oblige her sisters that she did as they requested and brought back some fruit, which they devoured with great avidity.

The next day fruits of another kind appeared, and again the princesses wanted to have some. And again Finette complied with kindness. But Rich-Craft's officers, who were hiding and who had missed their target the first time, did not fail the second. They seized Finette and carried her off in plain view of her sisters, who tore out their hair in despair. Rich-Craft's guards were efficient and took Finette to a house in the country, where the prince was residing in order to regain his health. Since he was so infuriated with the princess, he said a hundred brutal things to her, which she answered with courage and greatness of soul worthy of the heroine she was. At last, after having kept her prisoner for some days, Rich-Craft had her brought to the top of an extremely high mountain, where he immediately followed. There he announced to her they were going to put her to death in such a manner that would sufficiently avenge all the injuries she had caused him. Then the wicked prince demonstrated his barbaric nature by showing her a barrel lined with knives, razors, and hooked nails all around the inside. "In order to punish you the way you deserve," he said, "we're going to put you into that barrel and roll you from the top of this mountain down into the valley."

Though Finette was no Roman, she was no more afraid of this punishment than Regulus was at the sight of a similar destiny. Instead of admiring her heroic character, however, Rich-Craft became more enraged than ever. Determined to put a quick end to her life, he stooped to look into the barrel, the instrument of his vengeance, to see whether it was properly furnished with all its murderous weapons.

Finette, who saw her persecutor absorbed in examining the barrel, swiftly pushed him into it and kicked the barrel down the mountain. As she ran away, the prince's officers, who had been appalled at how cruelly their master had planned to treat this charming princess, did not make the slightest attempt to stop her. Besides, they were so frightened by what had

happened to Rich-Craft that they could think of nothing but how to stop
the barrel, which was rolling pell-mell down the mountain. However, their
efforts were for naught. He rolled down to the bottom, where they drew
him out wounded in a thou-
sand places.

Rich-Craft's accident made
the gentle king and Prince
Bel-a-voir extremely sad. As
for the people of their country,
they were not at all moved,
since Rich-Craft was universally
hated. They were astonished that
the young prince, who had such
noble and generous sentiments,
could love his unworthy elder
brother. But that was due to
the loyalty and good nature of
this prince, and Rich-Craft was
always astute enough to exploit
his compassionate feelings and
make his brother beholden to
him. Therefore, Bel-a-voir did

not leave a thing undone to cure him as soon as possible. Yet despite
all the care everyone took of Rich-Craft, nothing did him any good. On
the contrary, his wounds grew worse every day, and it appeared that he
would be suffering from them for a long time.

After escaping from this terrible danger, Finette returned safely to the
castle, where she had left her sisters, but it was not long before she was
faced with new troubles. Both of her sisters gave birth to sons, and Finette
was mortified by such a predicament. However, her courage did not abate,
and her desire to conceal her sisters' shame made her determined to expose
herself to danger once more.

To accomplish her plan, she first took the precaution to disguise
herself as a man. The children of her sisters she put into boxes in
which she made little holes so they could breathe. Then she took these
boxes and several others and rode on horseback to the capital of the
gentle king.

When Finette entered the city, she learned of the generous manner in
which Bel-a-voir was paying for any medicine that might help his brother.
Indeed, such generosity had attracted all the charlatans in Europe. At that
time there were a great many adventurers without jobs or talent who
pretended to be remarkable men that had been endowed by heaven to cure

all sorts of maladies. These men, whose entire science consisted of bold deceit, found great credence among the people because of the impression they created by their outward appearance and by the bizarre names they assumed. Such quacks never remain in the place where they were born, and the exoticism of coming from a distant place is often considered a proof of quality by the common people.

The ingenious princess, who knew all this, gave herself a very strange name for that kingdom. Then she let it be known that the Cavalier Sanatio had arrived with marvelous secrets that cured all sorts of wounds, no matter how dangerous and infected. Bel-a-voir immediately sent for this supposed cavalier, and Finette swept in with all the airs of one of the best physicians in the world and said five or six words in a cavalier way. That is, she was the perfect doctor.

The princess was surprised by the good looks and pleasant manner of Bel-a-voir, and after conversing with him some time with regard to Rich-Craft's wounds, she told him she would fetch a bottle with an extraordinary elixir. "In the meantime I'll leave two boxes I've brought that contain some excellent ointments appropriate for the wounded prince." After the supposed physician left and did not return, everyone began to feel anxious. When at last they were going to send for him, they heard the bawling of young infants in Rich-Craft's room. This surprised everybody, for no one had seen any infants there. After listening attentively, however, they found that the cries came from the doctor's boxes. The noise was caused by Finette's little nephews. The princess had given them a great deal to eat before she came to the palace, but since they had now been there a long time, they were hungry and expressed their needs by singing a most doleful tune. Someone opened the boxes, and the people were greatly surprised to find two pretty babes in them. Rich-Craft realized immediately that Finette had played a new trick on him and threw himself into a rage. His wounds grew worse and worse because of this, and everyone realized that his death could not be prevented.

Seeing Bel-a-voir overcome with sorrow, Rich-Craft, treacherous to his last breath, thought to exploit his brother's affection. "You've always loved me, Prince," he said, "and you're now lamenting my imminent loss. I can have no greater proof of your love for me. It's true I'm dying, but if you've really ever cared for me, I hope you'll grant me what I'm going to ask of you."

Bel-a-voir, who was incapable of refusing anything to a brother in such a condition, gave him his most solemn oath to grant him whatever he desired.

As soon as he heard this, Rich-Craft embraced his brother and said to him, "Now I shall die contented because I'll be revenged. The favor I want you to do is to ask Finette to marry you after I die. You'll undoubtedly obtain this wicked princess for your wife, and the moment she's in your power, I want you to plunge your dagger into her heart."

Bel-a-voir trembled with horror at these words and repented the imprudence of his oath. But now was not the time to retract it. He did not want his despair to be noticed by his brother, who died soon after. The gentle king was tremendously affected by his death. His subjects, however, far from mourning Rich-Craft, were extremely glad that his death guaranteed the succession for Bel-a-voir, whom everyone considered worthy of the crown.

Once again Finette had returned safely to her sisters, and soon thereafter she heard of Rich-Craft's death. Some time later, news reached the three princesses that the king, their father, had returned home. He rushed to the tower, and his first wish was to see the distaffs. Nonchalante went and brought the distaff that belonged to Finette and showed it to the king. After making a very low curtsy, she returned it to the place whence she had taken it. Babbler did the same. In her turn, Finette brought out the same distaff, but the king now grew suspicious and demanded to see them all together. No one could show hers except Finette. The king was so enraged by his two elder daughters that he immediately sent them away to the fairy who had given him the distaffs, asking her to keep his daughters with her as long as they lived and to punish them the way they deserved.

To begin the punishment of these princesses, the fairy led them into a gallery of her enchanted castle where she had ordered the history of a vast number of illustrious women who had made themselves famous by leading busy, virtuous lives to be depicted in paintings. Due to the wonderful effects of fairy art, all these figures were in motion from morning until night. Trophies and emblems honoring these virtuous ladies were everywhere, and it was tremendously mortifying for the two sisters to compare the triumphs of these heroines with the despicable situation to which their imprudence had reduced them. To complete their grief, the fairy told them gravely that if they had occupied themselves like those they saw in the pictures, they would not have gone astray. She told them, "Idleness is the mother of all vice and the source of all your misery." Finally the fairy added that to prevent them from ever falling into the same bad habits again and to make up for the time they had lost, she was going to employ them in the most coarse and mean work. Without any regard for their lily-white complexions, she sent them to gather peas in the garden and to pull out the weeds. Nonchalante could not help but despair of leading such a disciplined life, and she soon died from sorrow and exhaustion. Babbler, who some time afterward found a way to escape from the fairy's castle by night, broke her skull against a tree and died in the arms of some peasants.

Finette's good nature caused her to grieve a great deal over the fate of her sisters, but in the midst of her sorrow, she was informed that Prince Bel-a-voir had requested her hand in marriage. What's more, her father had already consented without notifying her, for in those days the inclination of the partners was the last thing one considered in arranging marriages. Finette trembled at the news. She had good reason to fear that Rich-Craft's hatred might have infected the heart of a dear brother, and she was worried that this young prince only sought to victimize her for her brother's sake. So concerned was she about this that she went to consult the wise fairy, who appreciated her fine qualities in the same way she had despised Nonchalante's and Babbler's bad ones.

The fairy would reveal nothing to Finette and only remarked, "Princess, you're wise and prudent. Up to now you've taken the proper precautions with regard to your conduct, and that has enabled you to bear in mind that *distrust is the mother of security.* Remember the importance of this maxim, and you'll eventually be happy without needing the help of my art."

Since she was not able to learn anything more from the fairy, Finette returned to the palace extremely upset. Some days later she was married by an ambassador in the name of Prince Bel-a-voir and conducted to her spouse in a splendid equipage. After she crossed the border, she was escorted in the same magnificent manner upon entering the first two cities of King Gentle's realm, and in the third city she met Bel-a-voir, who had been ordered by his father to go and welcome her. Everybody had been surprised by the prince's sadness at the approach of a marriage that he had so zealously pursued. Indeed, the king had to reprimand him and send him to meet the princess against his inclinations.

When Bel-a-voir saw how charming she was, he complimented her in such a confused manner that the courtiers, who knew how witty and gallant he was, believed him so strongly moved by love that he had lost his presence of mind. The entire city shouted for joy, and there were concerts and fireworks everywhere. After a magnificent supper, preparations were made for conducting the royal couple to their apartment.

Finette, who kept thinking about the fairy's maxim, had a plan. She won over one of the women, who had the key of the closet of the apartment designated for her. She gave orders to the woman to carry into that closet some straw, a bladder, some sheep's blood, and the entrails of some of the animals that had been prepared for supper. Then the princess used a pretext to go in. Making a figure from the straw, she put into it the entrails and bladder full of blood. Then she dressed it up in a woman's night-clothes. After she had finished making this pretty dummy, she rejoined her company, and some time later, she and her husband were conducted to their apartment. When they had allowed as much time at the dressing table as was necessary, the ladies of honor took away the torches and retired. Finette immediately placed the straw dummy in the bed and hid herself in a corner of the room.

After heaving two or three deep sighs, the prince drew his sword and ran it through the body of the supposed Finette. All at once he saw the blood trickle out, and the straw body did not move.

"What have I done?" Bel-a-voir exclaimed. "What! After so many cruel struggles with myself—after having weighed everything carefully whether I should keep my word at the expense of a dreadful crime, I've taken the life of a charming princess, whom I was born to love! Her charms captivated me the moment I saw her, and yet I didn't have the strength to free myself from an oath that a brother possessed by fury had exacted from me. Ah, heavens! How could anyone think of punishing a woman for having too much virtue? Well, Rich-Craft, I've satisfied your unjust vengeance, but now I'll revenge Finette by my own death. Yes, beautiful princess, this same sword will—"

As he was saying these words, Finette heard the prince looking for his sword, which he had dropped in his great agitation. Since she did not want him to commit such a foolish act, she cried, "My prince, I'm not dead! Your good heart made me anticipate your repentance, and I saved you from committing a crime by playing a trick that was not meant to harm you."

She then told Bel-a-voir about the foresight she had had in regard to the straw figure. The prince was ecstatic to find Finette alive, and expressed his gratitude to her for her prudence and preventing him from committing a crime which he could not think about without horror. He could not understand how he could have been so weak and why he had not discovered the futility of that wicked oath sooner that had been exacted from him by his deceitful brother.

However, if Finette had not always been convinced that distrust is the mother of security, she would have been killed, and her death would have caused that of Bel-a-voir. Then afterward, people would have discussed the prince's strange emotions at their leisure.

Long live prudence and presence of mind! They saved this couple from the most dreadful of misfortunes and provided them with the most lovely destiny in the world. The prince and princess retained the greatest tenderness for each other and spent a long succession of beautiful days in such honor and happiness that would be difficult to describe.

Catherine Bernard

Catherine Bernard (1662–1712) was born in Rouen and moved to Paris during her youth. Since she was related to Corneille and Fontenelle, she was soon introduced to the literary circles of Paris and established herself in 1687 as a talented author with a series of novels under the general title *Les Malheurs de L'amour* (The Misfortunes of Love): *Eléonor d'Yvrée* (1688), *Le Comte d'Amboise* (1689), and *Inès de Cordoue* (1696). It was as a writer of tragedies, however, that she became famous. In 1689 her first play, *Léodamie*, was performed twenty times, and was followed by *Brutus* (1690), which had even greater success than the play by Voltaire, who had been influenced by her work.

Like many women writers of her time, who were not independently wealthy and remained single, Mlle. Bernard led an austere and modest life. In addition to her novels and tragedies, she wrote a number of poems that were published in different anthologies of the seventeenth century. Since she could not support herself from her writing alone, she accepted the patronage of the Chancelière de Pontchartrain, one of the more influential ladies at King Louis XIV's court.

Mlle. Bernard's *Riquet à la Houppe* (Riquet with the Tuft) appeared in her novel *Inès de Cordoue* in 1696 along with one other tale, *Le Prince Roiser*. There is some question as to whether she wrote her tale before Charles Perrault wrote his or vice versa. It is more than likely, since they moved in the same literary circles, that there was a mutual influence, and that both may have been acquainted with an oral folk tale that served as the basis of *Riquet*. The differences between the two versions are very interesting. Perrault's tale is more imaginative and optimistic from a male viewpoint. To bring about the happy end, he has his princess comply with a male code of reasoning. Bernard's version is more realistic and corresponds to the general theme of her novel, *The Misfortunes of Love*. Unlike Perrault, she took a more critical view of forced marriages and depicted the quandary many women felt when they were obliged to enter into contractual marriages. To this extent, Bernard's tale, which helped inaugurate the fairy-tale mode in France, is a significant social document that can be considered part of the debate about the role of women and women's education that was prevalent during the ancien régime.

RIQUET
WITH THE TUFT

A GRAND nobleman of Grenada, whose wealth was equal to his high birth, experienced a domestic calamity that poisoned all the treasures of his fortune. His only daughter was so stupid that her naturally beautiful features only served to make her appearance distasteful. Her movements were anything but graceful. Her figure, though slender, made an awkward impression since it lacked sprightliness.

Mama—that was the name of this girl—did not possess enough intelligence to know that she was not intelligent, but she did have enough to realize she was looked upon with disdain, even though she could not figure out why. One day, when she was out walking by herself, as was her habit, she saw a man hideous enough to be a monster emerge from the ground. As soon as she caught sight of him, she wanted to flee, but he called her back.

"Stop," he said to her. "I have something unpleasant to tell you, but I also have something nice to promise you. Even with your beauty you have something—and I don't know what's caused it—that makes people regard

you with disfavor. It has to do with your incapacity to think, and without my making a value judgment, this fault makes you as inferior as I am, for my body is like your mind. That's the cruel thing I have to say to you. But from the stunned manner in which you're looking at me, I think I've given your mind too little credit, for I fear I've insulted you. This is what makes me despair as I broach the subject of my proposition. However, I'm going to risk making it to you. Do you want intelligence?"

"Yes." Mama responded in a manner that might have indicated no.

"Very good," he said. "Here's the way. You must love Riquet with the Tuft. That's my name, and you must marry me at the end of the year. That's the condition I'll impose on you. Think it over. If you can't, repeat the words that I'm going to say to you as often as possible. They'll eventually teach you how to think. Farewell for a year. Here are the words that will dissipate your indolence and at the same time cure your imbecility:

> Love can surely inspire me
> To help me shed stupidity.
> And teach me to care with sincerity
> If I have the right quality."

As Mama began to utter these words properly, her poise improved immensely—she became more vivacious, and her movements more free. She kept repeating the verse and soon departed for her father's house, where she told him something coherent, then a little later, something intelligent, and finally, something witty. Such a great and rapid transformation did not go unnoticed. Lovers came in droves. Mama was no longer alone at the balls or during promenades. Soon she made men unfaithful and jealous. People talked only about her and for her.

Among the men who found her charming, it was easy for her to find someone more handsome than Riquet with the Tuft. The mind that her benefactor had given her started to work against him. The words that she conscientiously repeated filled her with love, but the effect was contrary to Riquet's intentions: the love was not for him.

She favored the most handsome of those men who sighed for her, although he was not the best match with regard to his wealth. Thus her father and mother, who saw that they had wished this misfortune on their daughter by desiring she should have a mind, and who realized that they could not deprive her of it, thought at least they should give her lessons against love. But prohibiting a young and pretty person from loving is like preventing a tree from bearing leaves in May. She only loved Arada more—that was the name of her lover.

She made sure not to tell anyone about how she happened to obtain her mind. Her vanity caused her to keep this a secret. She had enough intelligence to understand the importance of hiding the mystery of how she had managed to become so.

The year that Riquet with the Tuft had given her to make a decision drew to an end. With great anguish she awaited the deadline. Her mind, now her bane, did not let one single torturous consequence escape her. To lose her lover forever, to be under the power of someone about whom the only thing she knew was his deformity, which was perhaps his least fault, and finally to marry someone and to accept his gifts that she did not want to return—these thoughts kept passing through her mind.

One day, when she was contemplating her cruel destiny and wandering off alone, she heard a loud hubbub and subterranean voices singing the words Riquet with the Tuft had taught her. She shuddered when she heard them, for it was the signal of disaster. Soon the ground opened. She descended gradually and saw Riquet with the Tuft surrounded by creatures who were just as deformed as he was. What a spectacle for a person who had been pursued by the most charming men in her country! Her torment was even greater than her surprise. Unable to speak, she let loose a flood of tears. This was the only human quality she possessed that was beyond the control of the mind that Riquet with the Tuft had given her. In turn, he regarded her sadly.

"Madam," he said, "it's not difficult to see that I'm more distasteful to you than when I first appeared before you. I myself am bewildered by what has happened in giving you a mind. But in the last analysis, you're free to make a choice: marry me or return to your former condition. I'll send you back to your father's house the way I found you, or I'll make you mistress of this kingdom. I am king of the gnomes, and you would be queen. If you can excuse my shape and overlook my repulsive deformities, you could enjoy a great many pleasures here. I am master of all the treasures locked up in the earth, and you would be mistress of them. With gold and intelligence, who could want more from life?" Seeing she was unconvinced, he continued, "I'm afraid that you've developed some kind of false squeamishness. I must seem inadequate in the midst of all my riches. But if I and my treasures don't please you, just speak up. I'll take you away from here and bring you home because I don't want anything to trouble my happiness here. You have two days to become acquainted with this place and to decide my fate and yours."

After leading her into a magnificent apartment, Riquet with the Tuft left her. She was attended by gnomes of her sex, whose ugliness did not repel her as much as that of the men. They entertained her with a meal and good company. After dinner she saw a play in which the deformities of the actors prevented her from developing any interest in the subject of the drama. That evening a ball was held in her honor, but she attended it without desiring to please anyone. Indeed, she felt an innate disgust that made it impossible for her to show Riquet her appreciation for all the pleasures he provided.

In order to save herself from this odious husband, she would have returned to her stupidity without feeling grief if she had not had a lover, but it would have meant losing a lover in a most cruel manner. It is also true that she would lose her lover by marrying the gnome—she would never be able to see Arada, speak with him, or send him news about herself, for Riquet would suspect her of infidelity. In sum, by getting rid of the man she loved, she was going to marry a husband who would always be odious even when he was pleasant. Moreover, he was a monster.

The decision was a wrenching one to make. When the two days had passed, her mind was not any more made up than before. She told the gnome that it had not been possible for her to reach a decision.

"That's a decision against me," he told her. "So now I'll return you to your former condition that you didn't dare to choose."

She trembled. The idea of losing her lover through the disdain he would show her provided such a powerful spur that she felt compelled to renounce him.

"Well, then!" the gnome said to her. "You've decided. It must be up to you."

Riquet with the Tuft did not make it difficult. He married her, and Mama's intelligence increased even more through this marriage. Her unhappiness, though, increased in proportion to the growth of her mind. She was horrified to have given herself to a monster, and she couldn't comprehend how she spent one moment with him.

The gnome realized very well how much his wife hated him, and he was hurt by it, even though he prided himself on the force of his intelligence. This aversion was a constant reproach to his deformity and made him detest women, marriage, and curiosity so much so that he became distraught. He often left Mama alone, and since she was reduced to just thinking, she became convinced that she had to make Arada see with his own eyes that she was not unfaithful. She knew he could get to this place because she had so easily managed to get there herself. At the least she had to send him news about herself and explain her absence because of the gnome who had abducted her. Once Arada saw him, he would know she was faithful.

There is nothing that an intelligent woman in love cannot do. She won over a gnome attendant, who carried news about her to Arada. Fortunately, this was still during the time that lovers were faithful to each other. He had become despondent over Mama's absence without becoming bitter about it. He was not even plagued by suspicion. He maintained that if he died, he would not have the least negative thought about his mistress and did not want to seek a cure for his love. It is not difficult to believe that with such feelings, he was willing to risk his life to find Mama as soon as he knew where she was. Nor did she forbid him from coming there.

Mama's cheerfulness returned gradually, and her beauty made her even more perfect, but the amorous gnome caused her to worry. He had too much intelligence and knew Mama's repugnance for him too well to believe that she had become accustomed to being there and had become sweeter so suddenly. Mama was imprudent enough to get dressed up, and he was smart enough to realize that he was not worthy of this. Long did he search until he discovered a handsome man hiding in his palace. As a result, he thought up an extremely fine way both to revenge himself and take care of the lover. First, Riquet ordered Mama to appear before him.

"It doesn't amuse me to make complaints and reproaches," he said. "I let human beings have their share of them. When I gave you a mind, I presumed I would enjoy it. However, you've used it against me. Still, I won't deprive you of it completely. You've submitted to the law that was imposed on you. But even if you did not break our agreement, you didn't observe it to the letter. Let us compromise. You shall have a mind during the night. I don't want a stupid wife, but you shall be stupid during the day for whomever you please."

All at once Mama felt a dullness of mind that she did not understand anymore. During the night her ideas were aroused again, and she wept over her misfortune. She was not able to console herself or find the ways through her wisdom to help herself.

The following night she noticed that her husband was sleeping soundly. She placed an herb on his nose that increased his oblivion and made it last as long as she wished. She got up and crept away from the object of her wrath. Led by her dreams, she went to the place where Arada was dwelling. She thought that he might be looking for her and found him in a lane where they had often met. He asked her all kinds of questions. Mama told him about her misfortunes, which abated because of the pleasure she derived in relating them to him.

The next night they met at the same place without being followed, and their meetings continued for such a long time that their misfortune now enabled them to taste a new kind of happiness. Mama's mind and love provided her with a thousand ways to be charming and to make Arada forget that she lacked intelligence half the time.

Whenever the lovers felt the dawn of day approaching, Mama went to wake the gnome. She took care to remove the herb that made him drowsy as soon as she was beside him. Although she now became an imbecile again, she used the time to sleep.

Such bittersweet happiness could not last forever. The leaf that made Riquet sleep also made him snore, and, thinking his master was grumbling, a half-asleep servant ran to him, saw the herb that had been placed on his nose, and removed it because he thought that was disturbing him—a cure that made three people unhappy all at the same time. Riquet saw that he was alone and searched for his wife in a rage. Either chance or his bad luck led him to the place where the two lovers had abandoned themselves to each other. As he approached, he heard them swear eternal love to each other. He did not say a word. He touched the lover with a wand that transformed his shape into one exactly like his own. And after looking back and forth and back and forth, Mama could no longer distinguish who her husband was. Thus she lived with two husbands instead of one, never knowing whom she should address her lamentations for fear of mistaking the object of her hatred for the object of her love.

But perhaps she hardly lost anything there. In the long run lovers become husbands anyway.

Charlotte-Rose Caumont de La Force

Charlotte-Rose Caumont de La Force (1650–1724) was born into one of the oldest and most esteemed families of France. Due to the family lineage, she was accepted at King Louis XIV's court under the tutelage of Madame de Maintenon and was named maiden of honor to the queen and the dauphine. During her adolescence she developed into one of the most scheming young ladies at the court. She became involved in various intrigues and had numerous love affairs despite the fact that she was notoriously ugly. She had a penchant for younger men, and at one point she fell in love with Charles Briou, the son of the president of the Paris Parlement, who was much younger than her and very naive. His family did not sanction his seeing her, so they carried on a clandestine love affair. Eventually, through her connections, she managed to obtain the king's permission to marry Briou in 1687. However, his father and her family interfered and had the marriage annulled. Some years later, in 1697, there was another great scandal, caused this time by some impious verses she wrote, and this act led to Mlle. de La Force's expulsion from the court: Louis XIV gave her the option of having her pension taken away from her, which would have left her penniless, or allowing her to keep it and live in a convent. She chose the convent.

Before her exile Mlle. de La Force had begun publishing historical romances, *Histoire secrète du duc de Bourgogne* (1694), *Histoire secrète de Marie de Bourgogne* (1696), and *Histoire de Marguerite de Valois* (1696), which were extremely well received because they depicted fascinating abductions, scandals, love affairs, disguises, and duels that had little to do with history and a great deal to do with the court society of that time. Mlle. de La Force had a great flair for writing exciting romances and continued publishing works in this vein such as *Gustave Vasa* (1698) and *Histoire secrète de Catherine Bourbon* (1703) after her banishment from the court.

With regard to her fairy tales, Mlle. de La Force was considered an entertaining storyteller, and she often attended salons and soirees in Paris, where she recited her tales. Among her acquaintances were such well-known fairy-tale writers as Antoine Hamilton, Mme. D'Aulnoy, and Mme. de Murat. She circulated her tales in manuscript form and revised them before she eventually published them anonymously under the title *Les Contes des Contes* (1697). They contained *Plus Belle que Fée, Persinette, L'Enchanteur, Tourbillon, Verd et Bleu, Le Pays des Délices, La Puissance d'Amour,* and *La Bonne Femme.* There is a great similarity between these tales and her romances. Mlle. de La Force wrote for an aristocratic audience long if not verbose fairy tales that were filled with motifs taken largely from the courtly romance tradition. Her favorite plots involved crossed lovers, infidelity, and the power of love. Her most serious fairy tale, and most interesting from an autobiographical viewpoint, is *La Bonne Femme* (The Good Woman). It was probably written just after Mlle. de la Force had moved to the convent, and it reflects her attitude toward the decadent courtly life of her time and the constraints placed on true love. She clearly identified with the good woman, who in turn supported the idyllic love affairs of the four young protagonists of her tale. Though she herself had been the perpetrator of many intrigues at Louis XIV's court, she stated in a memoir that she had never been malicious or vengeful and had always opposed the constraints that had been imposed on her and members of her sex. Indeed, she had always sought to pursue an independent life, and her fairy tales and romances provided her with an important outlet, especially after she was obliged to spend the latter part of her life in a convent.

THE GOOD WOMAN

ONCE upon a time there was a Good Woman who was kind, candid, and courageous. She had experienced all the vicissitudes that cause turbulence in one's life, for she had resided at the court and had endured all the storms that are commonplace there: treason, perfidy, infidelity, loss of wealth, loss of friends. Consequently, she became so disgusted with living where pretension and hypocrisy had established their empire and so tired of lovers who never were what they appeared to be that she decided to leave her own country and settle where she could forget the world and where the world would no longer hear about her.

When she believed herself far enough away, she built a cottage in an extremely pleasant spot. All she had to do then was to buy a flock of sheep, which furnished her with food and clothing. Not long thereafter she found herself perfectly happy. "So there does exist a way of life in which one can be content," she said, "and the choice I've made leaves nothing to be desired." She spent each day plying her distaff and tending her flock. Sometimes she would have liked a little company, but she was afraid of the trouble friends had always brought upon her.

She was gradually getting accustomed to the life she led when, one day, as she was gathering her little flock, the sheep began to flee from her, scattering all over the countryside. In fact, they fled so fast that there were soon hardly any sheep to be seen. "Am I a rapacious wolf?" she cried. "What's the meaning of this strange incident?" She called a favorite ewe, but it did not seem to know her voice. She raced after it, yelling, "I don't mind losing all the rest of the flock if only you would stay with me!" But the ungrateful creature continued its flight and disappeared with the rest.

The Good Woman was deeply distressed at the loss she had sustained. "Now I've got nothing left," she cried. "Maybe I won't even find my garden, or my little cottage will no longer be in its place." She returned slowly, for she was very tired from running after the sheep. After she exhausted a small stock of cheese, she lived off fruit and vegetables for some

She had nothing more to spin. She had nothing more to eat. Leaning on her distaff, she went into a little wood. In looking around for a place to die, she was astonished to see three little children come running toward her. They were all more beautiful than the brightest day imaginable. She was delighted to see such charming company, and they gave her a hundred caresses. As she sat on the ground in order to hug them more easily, one threw its arms around her neck, the other hugged her waist from behind, and the third called her "Mother." Long did she wait for someone to fetch them, believing that whoever had led them there would not neglect to come back for them. But the day passed without anyone appearing.

She decided to take them to her own home. "Heaven has sent me this little flock to replace the one I lost." There were two girls, who were only two or three years old, and a little boy of five. Each had a ribbon around its neck, to which was attached a small jewel. One was a golden cherry enameled with crimson and engraved with the word "LIRETTE." She thought, "This must be the little girl's name." The other had a medlar with "MIRTIS" written on it. And the little boy had an almond of green enamel around which was written "FINFIN." The Good Woman felt sure that these were their names.

The little girls had some jewels in their headdresses that were more than enough to put the Good Woman in comfortable circumstances. Soon thereafter she bought another flock of sheep and surrounded herself with everything necessary for maintaining her interesting family. She made their winter clothing from the bark of trees, and in the summer they had white cotton dresses that were bleached in a fine way. Even though they were quite young, they tended the flock, and this time the sheep were more docile and obedient to them than toward the large dogs that guarded them. These dogs were also gentle and attached to the children, who as they grew larger spent their days in most innocent ways. They loved the Good Woman, and all three were extremely fond of one another. They occupied themselves by tending their sheep, fishing with a line, spreading nets to catch birds, working in a little garden of their own, and using their delicate hands to cultivate flowers.

There was one rose tree that the young Lirette especially liked. She watered it often and took great care of it. She thought nothing so beautiful as a rose. One day she felt a desire to open a bud and find its heart. In doing so, she pricked her finger with a thorn. The pain was sharp, and she began to cry. The handsome Finfin, who seldom left her side, approached her, and when he saw how she was suffering, he also began to cry. He took her little finger, pressed it, and gently squeezed the blood from it.

The Good Woman, who saw their alarm at this accident, approached, and after learning what had happened, she asked, "Why were you so inquisitive? Why did you destroy the flower you loved so much?"

"I wanted its heart," Lirette replied.

"Such desires are always fatal," the Good Woman replied.

"But, Mother," Lirette pursued, "why does this beautiful flower that pleases me so much have so many thorns?"

"To show you that we must distrust the greater part of those things that please our eyes, and that the most pleasant objects hide snares that may be most deadly to us."

"What?" Lirette replied. "Shouldn't one love everything that's pleasant?"

"No, certainly not," the Good Woman said, "and you must take care not to do so."

"But I love my brother with all my heart," she replied. "He's so handsome and charming."

"You may love your brother," her mother replied, "but if he weren't your brother, you shouldn't love him."

Lirette shook her head, and thought that this rule was very hard. Meanwhile Finfin was still occupied with her finger; he squeezed the juice of the rose leaves on the wound and wrapped it up in them. The Good Woman asked him why he did that.

"Because I think that the remedy may be found in the same thing that has caused the evil."

The Good Woman smiled at this reason. "My dear child, not in this case."

"I thought it was in all cases," he said. "You see, sometimes when Lirette looks at me, she troubles me a great deal. I feel quite upset, and a moment later those same looks give me a pleasure I can't describe. When she scolds me sometimes, I'm very wretched, but if later she says one gentle word to me, I'm joyous again."

The Good Woman wondered what these children would think of next. Since she did not know their relation to one another, she dreaded that they would become too loving. "I'd give anything to learn if they are brother and sister." Her lack of knowledge about this point caused her much anxiety, but their extreme youth put her at ease.

Finfin already paid a great deal of attention to little Lirette, whom he loved much better than Mirtis. At one time he had given her some young partridges, the prettiest in the world, that he had caught. One that she reared became a fine bird with beautiful feathers. Lirette loved it inordinately and gave it to Finfin. It followed him everywhere, and he taught it a thousand amusing tricks. One day he took it with him when going to tend his flock. On returning home he could not find it and looked for it everywhere. He was greatly distressed by his loss, and Mirtis tried to console him without success. "Sister," he replied. "I'm despondent. Lirette will be angry, and nothing you can say will rid me of my grief."

"Well, brother," she said, "we'll get up very early tomorrow and go in search of another one. I can't bear to see you so miserable."

While she was saying this, Lirette arrived, and once she learned the cause of Finfin's grief, she said to him, "We'll find another partridge. It's just the condition in which I see you that gives me pain."

These words sufficed to restore serenity to Finfin's heart and countenance. "Why couldn't Mirtis restore my spirits with all her kindness," he asked himself, "while Lirette did it with a single word? Two is one too many—Lirette is enough for me."

On the other hand, Mirtis saw plainly that her brother made a distinction between her and Lirette. "There aren't enough of us here, being three," she said. "I ought to have another brother who would love me as much as Finfin does my sister."

Lirette had just turned twelve, Mirtis, thirteen, and Finfin, fifteen, when one evening after supper they were all seated in front of the cottage with the Good Woman, who would give them lessons in a hundred pleasant things. Young Finfin watched Lirette playing with the jewel on her neck and asked his dear mama what it was for. She replied that she had found one on each of them when they had fallen into her hands. Then Lirette said, "If mine would only do what I tell it to do, I'd be glad."

"And what would you like to have it do?" asked Finfin.

"You'll see," she said as she took the end of the ribbon. "Little cherry, I'd like to have a beautiful house of roses."

All at once they heard a slight noise behind them. Mirtis turned around first and uttered a loud cry. She had good reason to do so: one of the most charming cottages imaginable had replaced the Good Woman's cottage. It was not very high, but the roof was formed from roses that bloomed in winter as well as in summer. They entered it and found the most pleasant apartments magnificently furnished. In the middle of each room was a rose bush in full bloom and in a precious vase. As they entered the first room, they found the partridge that Finfin had lost. Onto his shoulder it flew and gave him a hundred caresses.

"Do I only have to wish?" Mirtis asked as she took the ribbon of her jewel in her hand. "Little medlar, give us a garden more beautiful than our own." No sooner had she finished speaking than a garden of extraordinary beauty appeared with everything that could be imagined in the most perfect condition.

The young children began immediately to run down the beautiful lanes among the flower beds and around the fountains.

"Wish for something, brother," Lirette said.

"But I don't have anything to wish for," he said, "except to be loved by you as much as you are loved by me."

"Oh," she replied, "my heart can satisfy you on this account. That doesn't depend on your almond."

"Well, then," Finfin said, "little almond, little almond, I wish that a great forest would rise near here in which the king's son would go hunting and then fall in love with Mirtis."

"What have I done to you?" the beautiful girl replied. "I don't want to leave the innocent life we lead."

"You're right, my child," said the Good Woman, "and I admire the wisdom of your sentiments. Besides, they say that this king is a cruel usurper who's put the rightful sovereign and his entire family to death. Perhaps the son is no better than his father."

The Good Woman, however, was quite unsettled by the unusual wishes of these wonderful children. That night she retired into the House of Roses, and in the morning she found a large forest close to the house. It formed a fine hunting ground for our young shepherds, and Finfin often hunted deer, harts, and roebucks there. He gave the lovely Lirette a fawn whiter than snow, and it followed her just as the partridge followed him. When they were separated for a short period of time, they wrote to each other and sent their notes by these messengers. It was the prettiest sight in the world.

The little family went on living peacefully like this, occupying themselves in different ways according to the seasons. They tended their flocks, year round but in the summer their work was most pleasant. They hunted a good deal in the winter with bows and arrows, and sometimes they went such a long distance that they returned to the House of Roses almost frozen and dragging their feet behind them.

The Good Woman would receive them by a large fire and would not know which one to begin warming first. "Lirette, my daughter Lirette," she would say, "place your feet here." And taking Mirtis in her arms, "Mirtis, my child," she would continue, "give me your beautiful hands to warm. And you, my son, Finfin, come nearer." Then placing all three of them on a sofa, she would take care of them in the most charming and gentle manner.

Thus did they spend their days in peace and happiness. The Good Woman was struck by the affection between Finfin and Lirette, for Mirtis was just as beautiful and charming as Lirette, yet Finfin certainly did not love her as fervently as the other. "If they are brother and sister, as I believe their beauty indicates," the Good Woman said, "what shall I do? They're so similar in everything that they must assuredly be of the same blood. If this is the case, then their affection for each other is dangerous. If not, I could make it legitimate by letting them marry. And since they both love me so much, their union would give me joy and peace in my old age."

In her uncertainty she ordered Lirette, who was rapidly approaching womanhood, never to be alone with Finfin. For better security she instructed Mirtis to always go with them. Lirette obeyed her without any objections, and Mirtis also did what she had commanded. Meanwhile the Good Woman had heard about a clever fairy in the vicinity and decided to look for her and find out something about the past of these children.

One day, when Lirette wasn't feeling well and Mirtis and Finfin were out hunting, the Good Woman thought it a convenient opportunity to go in search of Madame Tu-tu, for such was the name of the fairy. Leaving Lirette at the House of Roses, she had not gone far before she came upon Lirette's fawn, which was heading toward the forest. At the same time she saw Finfin's partridge coming from it. They came together right near her, and she was astonished to see a little ribbon around each one of their necks with a paper attached to it. She called the partridge, which flew to her, and took the paper. It contained these lines:

> Soar to Lirette, dear bird, take to the air.
> Cut off from her presence, I languish.
> Give her my love and make her hear
> My ardor and silent anguish,
> For her heart is much too cold, I fear.
> Oh I'd be content one day to see
> That Lirette might change and come to care
> The way I do with great sincerity.

"What words!" The Good Woman cried. "What phrases! A simple friendship doesn't express itself with so much warmth." Then she stopped the fawn, which came to lick her hand, and she unfastened the paper from its neck, opened it, and read these words:

> The sun is setting—you're hunting yet.
> You left while it was turning light.
> Come back, dear Finfin, I think you forget,
> Without you my day is like eternal night.

"They're acting just as people did when I was in society," the Good Woman remarked. "Who could have taught Lirette so much in this desolate spot? What can I do to cut the root of such a pernicious evil before it has a chance to grow?"

"Eh, madame, why are you so anxious?" the partridge asked. "Let them alone. Those who are guiding them know better than you."

The Good Woman was speechless, for she realized that the partridge must possess some kind of supernatural power. In her fright the notes fell from her hands, and the fawn and the partridge picked them up. The one ran and the other flew, and the partridge cried out so often "Tu-tu" that the Good Woman thought it must be that powerful fairy who had caused it to speak. She regained her senses a little after thinking about this incident, but she no longer felt equal to her undertaking and retraced her steps to the House of Roses.

Meanwhile, Finfin and Mirtis had hunted the entire day, and since they had become tired, they placed their game on the ground and sat down to rest under a tree, where they fell asleep. The king's son had also gone hunting in the forest that day. He became separated from his entourage and came to the spot where our young shepherd and shepherdess were resting. He looked at them some time with wonder: Finfin had made a pillow out of his game bag, and Mirtis's head reclined on Finfin's chest. The prince thought Mirtis so beautiful that he quickly dismounted from his horse to examine her features more closely. He judged by the bags they were carrying and their simple apparel that they were only some shepherd's children. He sighed from grief, having already sighed from love, and this love was followed instantly by jealousy. The position in which they lay made him believe that such familiarity could result only from lovers' affection.

Uneasy, he could not stand their prolonged repose, so he touched the handsome Finfin with his spear. Finfin jumped up, and upon seeing a man before him, he passed his hand over Mirtis's face and woke her. In calling her "sister," he immediately gave the young prince the reassurance that he needed. Mirtis stood up quite astonished, for she had never seen any other man but Finfin. The young prince was the same age as she, and he was superbly attired. His face had a charming expression, and he began saying many sweet things to her. She listened to him with a pleasure that she had never before experienced, and she responded to him in a simple manner, full of grace. Finfin saw that it was getting late, and the fawn had not arrived with Lirette's letter. Therefore, he told his sister it was time to go.

"Come, brother," she said to the young prince, giving him her hand, "come with us to the House of Roses." Since she believed Finfin to be her brother, she thought any man who was as handsome as he must be her brother, too. The young prince did not need much urging to follow her. Finfin threw the game he had shot on the back of his fawn, and the handsome prince carried Mirtis's bow and game bag.

This was the way they arrived at the House of Roses. Lirette came out to greet them and gave the prince a warm welcome before turning toward Mirtis. "I'm delighted that you've had such a good catch."

They all went together to find the Good Woman, and the prince enlightened her about his high birth. She paid him the respect due such an illustrious guest and gave him a fine room in their home. He remained two or three days, long enough to complete his conquest of Mirtis, which was in keeping with the wish that Finfin had made with his little almond.

Meanwhile, the prince's entourage had been astonished to have lost track of him. They found his horse, and they looked for him everywhere. His father, the wicked king, was furious when they reported they could not find him. His mother, a charming woman who was the sister of the king whom her husband had cruelly murdered, was in a state of extreme grief at the loss of her son. In her distress she secretly sent a messenger in search of Madame Tu-tu, an old friend of hers whom she had not seen for some time because the king hated her and had insulted her outrageously by harming a person she had dearly loved.

Madame Tu-tu arrived in the queen's chamber without anyone noticing her. After they embraced each other affectionately—there is not much difference between a queen and a fairy, since they have almost the same power—the fairy Tu-tu told her that she would see her son very soon. She begged her not to become upset by anything that might happen, for if she was not very mistaken, she could promise her something delightful and quite unexpected. "One day you will be the happiest of mortals."

After making many inquiries about the prince and searching for him carefully, the king's men finally found him at the House of Roses. Then they escorted him back to the king, who scolded him brutally, as though he were not the most handsome young man in the world. The prince remained very sad at his father's court and kept thinking about his beautiful Mirtis. Finally he could no longer contain his grief and took his mother into his confidence, who offered him a good deal of consolation.

"If you'll mount your beautiful palfrey, and go to the House of Roses," he said, "you'll be charmed by what you see."

The queen gladly agreed to do this and took her son with her, who was enchanted by the prospect of seeing his dear mistress again. The queen was astonished by Mirtis's great beauty and also by that of Lirette and Finfin. She embraced them with as much tenderness as she would her own children. Moreover, she immediately developed an immense liking for the Good Woman. In fact, she admired the house, the garden, and all the rare things she saw there.

When she returned, the king asked her to give an account of her journey. Naturally, she did this, and he felt a desire to go as well and see the wonders that she had described. His son asked permission to accompany him, and he consented with a sullen air: he never did anything graciously.

As soon as he saw the House of Roses, he coveted it. Paying not the least attention to the charming inhabitants of this beautiful place, he exercised his royal prerogative and began taking possession of their property by announcing that he would sleep there that evening. The Good Woman was very annoyed by his decision, for she sensed uproar and disarray, and this frightened her. "What's happened to the happy tranquillity I once enjoyed here!" she exclaimed. "The slightest change in fortune's ways always appears to destroy the calm in my life!"

She gave the king an excellent bed and withdrew to her little family. The wicked king went to bed, but found it impossible to fall asleep. Opening his eyes, he saw a little old woman at the foot of his bed. She was perhaps a yard high and about as wide, and she made frightful grimaces at him. Since cowards are generally fearful, he was in a terrible fright. A thousand needles he felt pricking him all over. In this tormented state of mind and body was he kept awake the whole night. Furious about it, he stormed and swore in language that was not at all in keeping with his dignity.

"Sleep, sleep, sire," the partridge said, who was roosting in a porcelain vase, "or at least let us sleep. If being king means that one must always be so anxious, I prefer being a partridge than being a king."

The king was even more alarmed at these words. He commanded his men to seize the partridge, but she flew up when she heard this order and beat his face with her wings. Since he still saw the same vision and felt the same prickings, he was dreadfully frightened and became more furious. "Ah!" he said. "It's a spell that this sorceress whom they call the Good Woman has cast. I'll get rid of her and all her kin by putting them to death!"

Since he was unable to sleep, he got up, and as soon as it was dawn, he commanded his guards to seize the innocent little family and fling them into dungeons. What's more, he had them dragged before him so that he might witness their despair. Though those charming faces were wet with tears, he was not at all moved. On the contrary, he felt a malignant joy at the sight. His son, whose tender heart was torn apart by such a sad spectacle, could not look at Mirtis without agony. On such occasions a true lover suffers more than the person loved.

Just as they grabbed hold of those poor innocents and began leading them away, the young Finfin, who was unarmed and thus could not fight these barbarians, suddenly touched the ribbon on his neck and cried, "Little almond, I wish that we were freed from the king's power!"

"And with his greatest enemies, my dear cherry!" Lirette continued.

"And let's take the handsome prince with us, my dear medlar!" added Mirtis.

No sooner had they uttered these words than they found themselves with the prince, partridge, and fawn, all in a chariot that rose into the air, and they soon lost sight of the king and the House of Roses.

However, Mirtis soon repented her wish. She was aware that she had been inconsiderate in allowing herself to be carried away by an impulse that she could not control. Therefore, she kept her eyes lowered during the entire journey and felt very much abashed. The Good Woman gave her a severe glance and said, "My daughter, you've not done a good thing to separate the prince from his father. No matter how unjust he may be, the prince shouldn't leave him."

"Ah, madam," the prince replied, "please don't think it ill that I've been given the pleasure of traveling with you. I respect my father, but I would have left him a hundred times before this if not for the virtue, kindness, and tenderness of my mother that always detained me."

As he finished speaking, they found themselves descending in front of a beautiful palace. They stepped from the chariot and were welcomed by Madame Tu-tu. She was the most lovely person in the world—young, lively, and gay. She paid them a hundred compliments and confessed that it was she who had given them all the pleasures that they had enjoyed in their lives and had also given them the cherry, almond, and medlar, whose powers were at an end since they had now arrived in her realm. Then, addressing the prince in private, she told him that she had heard more than a thousand times that his father had made his life miserable. "I'm telling you all this in advance so that you will not accuse me of doing evil things to the king." Indeed, she had played some tricks on him, but that was the full extent of her vengeance.

After that she assured them that they would all be very happy with her: "You will have flocks to keep, crooks, bows, arrows, and fishing rods so that you can amuse yourselves in a hundred different ways." She gave all of them, including the prince, the most elegant kind of shepherds' clothes. Their names and emblems were on their crooks, and that very evening the young prince exchanged crooks with the charming Mirtis. The next day Madame Tu-tu led them to the most delightful promenade in the world and showed them the best pastures for their sheep and a fine countryside for hunting.

"You can go as far as that beautiful river," she said, "but never go to the opposite shore. You may hunt in this wood, but beware of passing a great oak tree in the middle of the forest. It's very remarkable, for it has a trunk and roots of iron. If you go beyond it, you may experience a catastrophe, and I won't be able to protect you. Besides, I wouldn't be in a position to assist you right away because a fairy has plenty of things to keep her busy."

The young shepherds assured her that they would do exactly as she said, and all four led their flocks into the meadows. That left Madame Tu-tu alone with the Good Woman, who appeared to be somewhat anxious.

"What's the matter, madam?" the fairy asked. "What cloud has come over your mind?"

"I won't deny it," the Good Woman said. "I'm uneasy at leaving them together like that. For some time now I've noticed with sorrow that Finfin and Lirette love each other more than is decent, and to add to my trouble, another attachment has developed—the prince and Mirtis are fond of each other. Their youth, I'm afraid, makes them susceptible to their feelings."

"You've brought up these two young girls so well," Madame Tu-tu replied, "that you needn't fear anything. I'll answer for their discretion, and I'll clear up the matter about their destiny."

Then she informed her that Finfin was the son of the wicked king and brother of the young prince. In turn, Mirtis and Lirette were sisters and daughters of the king whom the cruel usurper had murdered. The wicked king had ascended the throne after having committed a hundred atrocities, which he wished to crown by the murder of the two infant princesses. The queen had done all she could to dissuade him, but since she had not succeeded, she had called upon the fairy to help her. She then told the queen that she would save them, but she could only do so by taking her eldest son with them. But she promised the queen she would see them again someday under happier circumstances. "Given those conditions, the queen consented to a separation, which of course appeared at first very hard. And I carried all three off and confided them to your care as the person most worthy of such a task."

After telling her this, the fairy begged the Good Woman to be at ease and assured her that the union of these young princes would restore peace to the kingdom and Finfin would reign with Lirette. The Good Woman listened to this talk with great interest, but not without letting some tears fall. Surprised, Madame Tu-tu asked why she was crying.

"Alas!" she said. "I fear they'll lose their innocence due to the grandeur to which they'll be elevated. Such a splendid future is certain to corrupt their virtue."

"No," replied the fairy. "You needn't fear such a great misfortune. The principles you've instilled in them are too excellent. It's possible to be a king and yet an honest man. You know that there's already one in this world who's the model of a perfect monarch. Therefore, set your mind at rest. I'll be with you as much as possible, and I hope you won't be melancholy here."

The Good Woman believed her, and after a short time she felt completely satisfied. The young shepherds were also very happy and did not ask for anything but to continue living as they were. Everything was tranquil; they found pleasure in one another's company each day; and the time passed only too quickly.

The wicked king learned that they were with Madame Tu-tu, but despite all his power he could not get them away from her. He knew that she used magic to protect them and could not deceive her with his tactics. Indeed, he had not been able to take possession of the House of Roses due to the continual tricks played on him by Madame Tu-tu, and he hated her as well as the Good Woman more than ever. And now his hatred extended to his own son as well.

The king used all sorts of stratagems in order to get one of the four young shepherds into his power, but his power did not extend to the realm of Madame Tu-tu. Then one unlucky day (there are some which we cannot avoid), these charming shepherds were nearing the fatal oak when the beautiful Lirette noticed a bird with unusual feathers on a tree about twenty yards away. She impulsively shot an arrow, and when she saw the bird fall dead, she ran to pick it up. All this was done within a moment and without reflection. Consequently, poor Lirette found herself transfixed to the spot. It was impossible for her to return. She wanted to but could not manage it. She discovered her mistake, and all she could do was to reach out with her arms for pity to her brothers and sisters. Mirtis began to cry, and Finfin ran to her without a moment's hesitation.

"I'll perish with you," he cried as he joined her.

Mirtis wanted to follow them, but the young prince held her back. "Let's go and tell Madame Tu-tu what has happened," he said. " That's the best way to help them."

Suddenly they saw the wicked king's men seize them, and all they could do was to cry adieu to one another. The king had arranged to have this beautiful bird placed there by his hunters as a snare for the shepherds. Indeed, he had fully expected everything to happen as it did. They led Lirette and Finfin before the cruel monarch, who abused them terribly and had them confined in a dark, strong prison. It was then they began to lament the fact that their little cherry and almond had lost their powers. The fawn and the partridge looked for them, but when the fawn was not able to espy them, she shed some tears of grief and heard orders shouted to have her seized and burned alive. So she saved herself by running quickly to Mirtis. The partridge was luckier since she saw Lirette and Finfin every day through the grating of their prison. Fortunately for them, the king had not thought of separating them. When one is in love with someone, suffering together is a pleasure.

The partridge flew back every day and brought news to Madame Tu-tu, the Good Woman, and Mirtis. Mirtis was very unhappy, and if she had not had the handsome prince, she would have been inconsolable. She decided to write to the poor captives via the faithful partridge and hung a little bottle of ink around her neck with some paper and put a pen in her beak. The good partridge carried all this to the bars of the prison, and our young shepherds were delighted to see her again. Finfin extended his hand and took from her everything she brought. Afterward they began to read as follows:

Mirtis and the Prince to Lirette and Finfin

We want you to know that we're languishing during this cruel separation. We keep sighing, and this separation may perhaps kill us. We would already have died if we had not been sustained by hope. That hope has supported us ever since Madame Tu-tu assured us that you were still alive. Believe us, dear Lirette and Finfin, we shall meet again and be happy despite the malice we have encountered.

Lirette and Finfin to Mirtis and the Prince

We've received your letter with great pleasure. It made us happier than we had anticipated. In these regions of horror our torments would be insufferable but for the sweet consolation we derive from each other's presence. Since we are close to each other, we don't feel pain, and love renders everything delightful. Adieu, dear prince, adieu, dear Mirtis. Encourage your mutual feelings. Keep alive your tender fidelity. You hold out a hope to us that we can share. The greatest blessing which can happen to us is being once again in your company.

After Finfin attached this note to the partridge's neck, she swiftly flew away with it. The young shepherds received great consolation from it, but the Good Woman had not been comforted from the moment she had been separated from her dear ones, whom she knew to be in so much danger. "How quickly my happiness has changed!" she said to Madame Tu-tu. "I seem to have been born only to be continually disturbed. I thought I had taken the proper steps to guarantee my peace of mind. How short-sighted I was!"

"Don't you know," the fairy replied, "that there's no place in this world in which one can live happily?"

"I do," the Good Woman replied mournfully. "If one can't find happiness in one's self, it's seldom found anywhere else. But, madam, please have consideration for the fate of my children!"

"They didn't remember the orders I gave them," Madame Tu-tu remarked. "But let's think of a way to help them."

Madame Tu-tu entered her library with the Good Woman. She read nearly the entire night, and after opening a large gold-trimmed book that she had frequently passed over despite its beauty, she was suddenly plunged into a state of extreme sadness. After some time passed and day was breaking, the Good Woman observed a few tears fall on the book and took the liberty of asking why the fairy was so sad.

"I'm saddened by the irrevocable decree of fate that these pages have revealed," she said, "and I shudder to tell you what I've learned."

"Are they dead?" the Good Woman cried.

"No," Madame Tu-tu responded, "but nothing can save them unless you or I appear before the king and satisfy his vengeance. I must confess to you, madam, that I don't have enough affection for them, nor enough courage to expose myself to his fury. Indeed, it is too much to ask anyone to make such a sacrifice."

"Pardon me, madam," the Good Woman said with great firmness. "I'll go to this king. No sacrifice is too great for me if it will save my children. I'll gladly pour out every drop of blood that I have in my veins for them."

Madame Tu-tu was struck with admiration by such a grand gesture. "I promise to help you in any way I can, but I find myself limited in this instance due to the mistakes the young people have made." The Good Woman then took leave of her, refusing to tell Mirtis or the prince about her plans, for fear she would distress them and weaken her own determination.

She set out, the partridge flying by her side, and as they passed the iron oak, the bird snatched a little moss from its trunk with her beak and placed it into the Good Woman's hands. "When you are in the greatest danger," she said to her, "throw this moss at the feet of the king."

The Good Woman had barely time to treasure these words when she was seized by some of the wicked king's soldiers, who were always stationed on the borders of Madame Tu-tu's domain. When they led her before the king, he said, "I've got you at last, you wicked creature, and I'm going to put you to death by the most cruel torture!"

"I came expressly for that purpose," she replied. "You may exercise your cruelty on me anyway you want. Only spare my children, who are so young and incapable of having offended you. I offer my life for theirs."

All who heard these words were filled with pity at her magnanimity. The king alone was unmoved. Seeing his queen shedding a flood of tears, he became so angry with her that he would have killed her if her attendants had not interposed themselves between them. With piercing shrieks she fled the room.

The barbarous king had the Good Woman locked up and ordered his men to feed her well to make her approaching death more frightful to her. He commanded them to fill a pit with snakes, vipers, and adders, looking forward keenly to having the pleasure of pushing the Good Woman into it. What a horrible kind of execution! It makes me shudder to think of it!

Regretfully the unjust king's officers obeyed him, and after they had carried out this frightful order, the king advanced to the spot. They were about to bind the Good Woman when she begged them not to, assuring them that she had sufficient courage to meet death with her hands free. Feeling that she had no time to lose, she approached the king and threw the moss at his feet. At that very moment he was stepping forward to inspect the dreadful pit. His feet slipped on the moss, and he fell in. No sooner did he reach the bottom than the bloodthirsty reptiles pounced on him and stung him to death. Meanwhile, the Good Woman found herself transported instantly in the company of her dear partridge to the House of Roses.

While these things were taking place, Finfin and Lirette were almost dead with misery in their frightful prison. Their innocent affection alone kept them alive. They were saying sad, touching things to each other when they noticed the doors of the dungeon open all of a sudden and admit Mirtis, the handsome prince, and Madame Tu-tu. Embracing, they all spoke at the same time, but the fairy did not neglect in the midst of this joyful confusion to announce the death of the king.

"He was your father as well as the prince's," she said. "but he was unnatural and tyrannical and would have put the queen, your dear mother, to death a hundred times. Let us now go and find her."

They did this, and on hearing about the king's death her good nature made her feel some regret because he had been her husband. Finfin and the prince also paid their honorable respects to his memory. Thereafter, Finfin was acknowledged king, and Mirtis and Lirette princesses. Then they all went to the House of the Roses to see the generous Good Woman, who thought she would die from joy as she embraced them. They all stated that they owed their lives to her, and more than their lives, since they were also obliged to her for their happiness.

From that moment on, they considered themselves perfectly happy. The marriages were celebrated with great pomp. King Finfin wed Princess Lirette, and Mirtis, the prince. When these splendid marriages were over, the Good Woman asked permission to retire to the House of Roses. They were very unwilling to consent to this, but yielded since she wished it so sincerely. The widowed queen also desired to spend the rest of her life with the Good Woman, along with the partridge and the fawn. They were quite disgusted with the world and found peace and quiet in that charming retreat. Madame Tu-tu often went to visit them, as did the king and queen and the prince and princess.

> Happy are those who can imitate
> The deeds the Good Woman accomplished.
> Such magnanimity is truly great
> And deserves its rewards at the finish.
>
> Perilous rocks can be avoided
> If only one learns how to navigate
> And steer wisely with great courage.
> Moreover, virtue and common sense necessitate
> That they too receive their due homage.

Jean de Mailly

The Chevalier Jean de Mailly (?–1724) was a godson of Louis XIV and the illegitimate son of one of the members of the de Mailly family. He spent his youth in the army, and at one point he caused a scandal by taking his family to court to make them admit that he was illegitimate. In the process he insisted that all the most honorable men were bastards and died in obscurity. He did not want this to be his fate but he never managed to achieve much fame, for very little is known about the chevalier's life except that he was a prolific writer, publishing over twenty books from the early 1690s until his death. These works dealt with such diverse subjects as history, nature, hunting, literature, and culture, and among the more important are: *Rome galante* (1685), *Les Disgrâces des amants* (1695), *Aventures et Lettres glantes, avec la Promenade des Tuilleries* (1697), *Les Entretiens des Cafés de Paris* (1702), *Diverses Aventures de France et d'Espagne* (1707), *L'Eloge de la Chasse* (1723), and *Principales Merveilles de la Nature* (1723).

Since there were few literary genres that the Chevalier de Mailly did not attempt and few topics that he did not treat, it is not surprising that he also tried his hand at writing and translating fairy tales. His major works were *Les Illustres Fées* (1698), *Recueil de Contes Galans* (1699), and the translation of Persian tales, *Le Voyage et les Aventures des trois Princes de Sarendip* (1719). Mailly's fairy tales were often based on oral folk tales and were filled with action and scant description. He was obviously fascinated by the marvels of nature and how things were transformed in mysterious ways. Animals in particular played an important role in his fairy tales and were often depicted as helpers. De Mailly was not a great stylist, nor did he develop extraordinary plots as did most of the women writers of fairy tales. His best tale was clearly *La Reine de l'Isle des Fleurs* (The Queen of the Island of Flowers), which appeared in *Les Illustres Fées*. This narrative is characteristic of many of his tales, which conveyed an implicit critique of the court society: his emphasis on transformation and change reflected his discontent with the petty jealousies at court as well as his yearning for idyllic social relations that he envisioned as possible only in a fairy tale.

THE QUEEN OF THE
ISLAND OF FLOWERS

T HERE was once a queen in the realm of the Island of Flowers who lost her husband when she was very young. They had loved each other tenderly, and that mutual affection had produced two perfectly beautiful princesses, whom the queen raised with great care. She had the pleasure of watching them develop more charming qualities every day. In particular, the elder sister became incomparably beautiful by the age of fourteen, and this made her mother somewhat uneasy because she knew that the Queen of the Islands would be jealous.

The Queen of the Islands believed herself to be the most beautiful queen in the world, and demanded that all other marvelous people acknowledge her superiority. Obsessed by this vanity, she had compelled her husband to conquer all the neighboring islands. Although he was just and would not have undertaken such a task, he was so captivated by her that he did not think about anything after the conquests but how to please her. Thus he imposed a law on all the princes he had defeated, obliging them to send all princesses of rank to pay homage to his wife's beauty as soon as they reached the age of fifteen.

The Queen of the Island of Flowers knew of this obligation and intended to have her elder daughter walk before the throne of this superb queen when she turned fifteen. The beauty of the young princess had already caused such a sensation that reports about her extraordinary features had been spread all over, and the Queen of the Islands, who had heard a good deal of talk about it, awaited her arrival with some concern. Indeed, her concern was the foreshadowing of the envy that soon possessed her. She paled in comparison with the princess's stunning beauty and could not help agreeing with everyone that she had never seen anyone as beautiful. That is, it was understood that she meant only after her, for the self-love that consumed the queen prevented her from believing that any princess could be more beautiful. Therefore she treated the princess with civility, thinking that the princess would not dare challenge her superiority. However, all the men and women of the court so acclaimed the princess's beauty that the queen grew spiteful and lost her composure. She withdrew to her room, pretending to be sick, in order not to witness the triumphs of such a charming rival. Then she sent a message to the Queen of the Island of Flowers that she could no longer see her because she had become indisposed. As a result she advised her to return to her realm and to take her daughter with her.

The Queen of Flowers had spent a long time at that court on a previous occasion and had made friends with the queen's lady of honor. This lady now advised her confidentially to take her leave of the Queen of the Islands and to flee her dominions as soon as possible. The lady of honor, a good woman who promised to remain friends with the Queen of the Island of Flowers, was caught between the obligations of friendship and loyalty to the queen whom she served. She believed that she had found the right balance by warning the queen, her friend, only that the queen, her mistress, was somewhat displeased and could not tell her why. "Return to your realm without wasting any time, and once there, keep the princess from leaving the palace for six months, no matter what the cause or occasion may warrant." Moreover, she promised the Queen of the Island of Flowers to use all her influence to soften the attitude of her mistress.

The Queen of the Island of Flowers realized from her friend's mysterious warning that her daughter had a great deal to fear from the vengeful queen, which could only be due to the fact that the queen had felt greatly offended by the commotion that the charming princess's beauty had caused at the court. So she conducted her daughter back to her realm and diligently led her into the palace.

Since she knew that the irritable queen had been given quite extensive secret powers by the fairies, she warned her daughter that she would be in great danger if she left the palace. With all her authority as queen and with all her tenderness as mother, she said, "Do not leave the palace without requesting my permission, no matter what the reason be." The queen did everything possible to entertain the princess, and she herself rarely left the palace in order to keep her daughter company and to make her confinement more tolerable.

On precisely the last day that the six months were to end, a large and joyous festival was held in a charming meadow at the far end of the avenue leading to the palace. Thus, the princess was able to watch the preparations from the window of her apartment, and since she was very bored and had been deprived of the pleasure of a promenade for so long, she begged the queen to permit her to take a walk in the meadow. The queen, who believed that the danger had passed, gave her consent, and she herself decided to go with her. They were followed by the entire court, which was charmed to see the princess enjoy her liberty after having been detained in the palace for six months without the queen ever explaining why.

Overjoyed to walk down a path lined with flowers after such a long time, the princess was traipsing a few steps ahead of her mother when the ground yawned open at her feet; after swallowing her, it closed up again. What a cruel spectacle! The queen fainted from pain, while her other daughter, the younger princess, shed tears, refusing to leave the spot where she had seen her sister disappear.

This accident shocked the entire court. Nothing like this had ever been seen before. Doctors were called to save the queen, and after she was revived by their remedies, she ordered a deep pit to be dug, but they were very surprised when they were unable to find a trace of the princess.

She had gone right through the earth and found herself in a desert where she saw rocks and woods but not the slightest sign of human beings. The only living thing she encountered was a marvelously comely little dog. No sooner did she appear than he ran right to her, and she petted him a thousand times. Since she was utterly bewildered to be in the middle of such a terrible adventure, she took the pretty and affectionate dog into her arms. After holding him a few moments, she put him down, uncertain where to go. Then she noticed the dog trot forward and turn his head every now and then as though he wanted her to follow him. So she let him lead her, not knowing where he was headed. She did not walk very far before she found herself on the brink of a valley lined with fruit trees that bore flowers and fruit at the same time. Even as she noticed that the ground was also covered with fruit and flowers, she saw a fountain outlined with turf in the middle of a beautiful flower bed. She approached it and found that the water was as clear as spring water. When she sat down on the grass, she was suddenly so overcome and horrified by her woes that she broke into tears. Everything frightened her, and she did not see any way of obtaining help. "At least I've found some means to protect myself against hunger and thirst," she told herself, taking some fruit and helping herself to the water with her bare hands. All the same, she still did not see any way she could protect herself against wild animals. Therefore, she kept thinking that she was in danger of being devoured.

Once she realized that she had to be resolute no matter what might happen, she tried to forget her suffering by petting her little dog. She spent the day on the edge of the fountain, but as night approached, her fears increased, and she did not know what to do. However, her little dog began to tug her dress. At first she did not pay much attention to this, but he persisted. Taking a firm grip of her dress, he ran three steps in front of her. In a moment he returned and tugged her again. Clearly he wanted her to follow him along that path, and finally she allowed him to lead her to the foot of a large rock, where she saw a large opening. It appeared that the little dog, who again kept tugging her dress as he had done before, wanted her to enter.

The princess was surprised to discover a pleasant cave illuminated by the glistening stones that formed it, as though the sun itself were shining within. She noticed a bed covered with moss in the farthest corner of the cave. She went over there to lie down and relax, and the little dog, who was constantly at her heels, followed her. Since she was exhausted from her worry and the travails of the day, she fell asleep.

At daybreak she was wakened by the singing of birds perched in the trees around the rock. If her predicament had been different, she would have been charmed by this, for she had never before heard a warbling so diverse and melodious. Awake like her, the little dog approached her feet in a touching fashion, as if he wanted to kiss them. She stood up and went outside to breathe the sweetest air imaginable, for the temperature was most pleasant. The little dog began to walk ahead of her and returned as he had done before to tug her dress. She let herself be guided again, and he led her back to that pleasant flower bed and the edge of the fountain where she had spent part of the previous day. She partook of some fruit and water and found herself satisfied by this kind of meal. Such was the way she spent several months, and since she did not encounter anyone hostile, her fear and suffering gradually diminished, and her solitude became more tolerable. Her little dog, who was always so cheerful and affectionate, contributed a great deal to her change in mood.

One day she noticed that he had become melancholy and did not allow himself to be petted anymore. Afraid he had become sick, she led him to a spot where she had once watched him eat some herbs that she now hoped would cure him, but she was unable to get him to take any. His sadness lasted the entire day and night, and he groaned a great deal. Finally the princess went to sleep, and when she awoke, her first concern was to look for her little dog. Since she did not find him at her feet where he usually slept, she rose urgently to find out what had become of him. Upon leaving the cave, she heard the voice of a man groaning, and she noticed an old man. He disappeared from sight the instant he became aware that she had seen him.

Once again she was overcome by surprise—a man in a place where there had been no one for several months! The disappearance of her little dog, though, stunned her more than anything else. Since he had been so loyal from the very first day of her disgrace, she thought that perhaps the old man had abducted him. She began exploring behind the rock, immersed in her thoughts, when all of a sudden she found herself being enveloped by a thick cloud and transported through the air. Since resistance was futile, she let herself be carried, and at the end of the day the cloud dissipated and she found herself, without knowing how everything had happened, in one of the avenues of the palace where she had been born.

As she approached the palace, she saw a sad spectacle. Everyone she encountered was dressed in mourning. Consequently, she feared that she had lost either the queen, her mother, or the princess, her sister. When she drew closer to the palace, she was recognized, and the air was filled with cries of joy. Alerted by these voices, her sister, who was now queen, ran to the princess, embraced her tenderly, and told her that she was going to give her back her crown. "Our subjects obliged me to take it after Mother's death. She died several days after that tragic accident that led to your disappearance."

The two princesses were both very noble; each sought to cede the crown to the other until finally the elder accepted it, but only on the condition that the authority would be shared. However, the younger princess declared that she would not accept this as a condition since she was quite content to have the honor of obeying a queen who possessed the charm of her sister.

The princess took the crown, as was her right, and occupied herself with carrying out the tasks in the memory of her mother. At the same time she gave her sister a thousand signs indicating how much she appreciated her generosity in ceding her crown. Then, since she had been greatly moved by the loss of the little dog that had been so loyal to her for so long in her solitude, she ordered her attendants to search for him over all the regions of the known world. Yet none of her attendants were able to obtain news of the dog, and she was so upset that her suffering led her to announce: "The queen will give half of her dominions to whoever can recover the dog for her." Her sister was astonished by such a lavish proposal and used a thousand different arguments in vain to try to dissuade her.

Of course, such a great reward motivated the courtiers, and everyone departed to try his luck. Yet, like those before them, they returned without any good news. Now her torment became so excessive that she was moved to proclaim: "The queen will marry whoever brings her the little dog." Without him, she felt—she said this in order to excuse herself—she could not live. Since everyone hoped to attain such an extraordinary prize, the court became deserted.

One day, while most of them were abroad searching for the dog, the queen was informed that there was a sinister-looking man in her chamber with her sister, and he wanted to talk to her. She ordered her attendants to admit him, and he told the queen that he had come to offer the return of her little dog about whom she had talked so much. Her sister spoke first: "The queen cannot make a decision to marry without the consent of her subjects. On an occasion as important as this, it is necessary to assemble her council." The man consented to submit his case to the deliberations of the council, which was to meet the next day. Saying nothing to oppose the princess, the queen ordered an apartment in the palace to be prepared for this man who had such high aspirations. When the princess was alone with the queen, she tried to convince her how wrong she had been to have offered such a great reward for a little dog and compelled her to renounce her bizarre plans. The queen was so upset that her condition provided them with a pretext as to why she had not said a word to the sinister-looking man. The council assembled the next day, and the princess went there to resolve everything. She intended to offer this sinister man a good deal of money as the reward for finding the little dog, and if he refused, he was to be thrown out of the kingdom without allowing him to speak again to the queen.

The man rejected the money and withdrew. The princess told her sister about the council's resolution and that the man had withdrawn after rejecting the offer of money. The queen agreed that everything had been done properly but that since she was her own mistress, she was going to depart the next day and roam the world until she found her little dog. "I intend to return the crown to you." Her sister was horrified by the queen's resolution, for she truly loved her. Therefore, she did everything she could to get the queen to change her mind, assuring her with remarkable unselfishness that she would never accept the crown.

As they were having this sad conversation, one of the queen's chief officers came to the door of her chamber and informed her that the sea was filled with ships. The two princesses went to a balcony and saw a grand navy approaching at full sail. After looking at it for a while, they judged by its splendor that it had not come to wage war: all the ships were trimmed gallantly with thousands of flags, streamers, and pennants. Their impression was confirmed when they saw one of the smaller ships advance, bearing a white streamer as a sign of peace. The queen ordered some servants to run to the port and go to the admiral of this navy to learn where it had come from. Shortly thereafter, she was informed that the prince of the Island of Emeralds requested the liberty of landing in her realm, offering her his humble respects. The queen sent her chief officers to the prince's ship to give him her compliments and to assure him that he was welcome indeed. Then she took a seat on her throne and waited for him. When he appeared, she left her throne and even took a few steps toward him. This meeting took place with great civility and wit on both sides.

The queen had the prince conducted to a magnificent apartment, and after he requested a special audience, she granted him one for the next day. When the hour for his audience arrived, the prince was led into the queen's chamber. Only her sister was allowed to remain near her. When he approached, he told the queen that what he had to relate would amaze everyone but herself, because she would quickly realize that his story was true. Indeed, she was the only one who knew the real circumstances.

"My kingdom borders on the dominions of the Queen of the Islands," he continued. "My realm is a peninsula that has a small passage to her kingdom. One day, as I was out hunting, which is a passion of mine, I saw a stag right in the middle of one of her forests. But, I had the misfortune of encountering the queen. Even worse, I didn't realize it was her because she did not have a retinue. So I didn't stop to offer my respects as I should have. You know better than anyone, madam, that she's very vindictive and has remarkable fairy powers. This I discovered right then and there. The ground opened under my feet, and I found myself in a faraway region transformed into a little dog. That was where I had the honor of meeting you, madam. After six months had passed, the queen's vengeance was still not complete, and so she changed me into a hideous old man. Since I was so afraid of disgusting you in this condition, I went to live in a dense forest, where I spent another three months. However, I was lucky enough to encounter a beneficent fairy, who saved me from the power of the imperious Queen of the Islands. This fairy told me everything that had happened to you, madam, and where I could find you. Now I've come to offer you the devotion of a heart that has known no other power over it than your own ever since that first day I met you in the desert."

After this narrative, the prince informed the queen that the fairies had deprived the Queen of the Islands of their fairy gifts because of the way she had abused them. Then the prince had many other conversations with the queen, and they agreed to tie the eternal knot together. Once their decision was made public, it was universally applauded, and for good reason: never in the world have subjects lived under such gentle rule, one they enjoyed for almost a century because the king and queen reigned and lived happily together until they reached an extremely ripe old age.

Henriette Julie de Murat

Henriette Julie de Castelnau, Comtess de Murat (1670–1716) was born in Brest, Brittany, and was strongly influenced by the traditions and folklore of that region. Both her parents came from old noble families, and at the time she was born, her father was governor of Brest. When Henriette Julie turned sixteen she was sent to Louis XIV's court in Paris to marry Comte de Murat. Soon after her arrival and marriage, she caused a sensation and impressed Queen Marie-Thérese by wearing the traditional peasant costumes of Brittany.

Madame de Murat was known for her great beauty, wit, and independence. However, since she was courted by numerous famous people, she let this flattery go to her head. In addition, her nonconformism and flair for attention made important members of the court extremely envious. Given the enemies she made and her zest for adventure, she was often in trouble with the king. Finally, in 1694 when she published a pamphlet entitled *Histoire de la courtisane Rhodope*, a political satire about Scarron, Louis XIV, and Madame de Maintenon, she was banished. It appears that her husband, who had played a minor role in her life, had died before this banishment. At any rate, Madame de Murat was sent alone to Loches, a small city in the provinces of France, where she remained until 1715.

It was in Loches from 1694 to 1715 that Madame de Murat wrote and published her most significant works: *Histoire galante des habitants de Loches* (1696), *Les Mémoires de la Comtesse de Murat ou la defense des dames* (1697), *Contes de fées* (1698), *Les nouveaux contes de féés* (1698), and *Histoires sublimes et allégoriques* (1699). As in Paris, Madame de Murat, who missed the cultural life of the court, caused somewhat of a commotion in the provincial city of Loches. Given her vivacious temperament, she organized all kinds of gatherings at her house, which were reported to be scandalous. In fact, however, Mme. de Murat simply endeavored to recreate an atmosphere similar to Paris, and she loved to converse, dance, and stay up until late in the morning telling fairy tales with some of her best friends like Charlotte-Rose de la Force, who also published tales during this period. In addition to these soirees and numerous mysterious journeys, Madame de Murat astonished the people of Loches by wearing a red cloak to church every Sunday.

Though Madame de Murat constantly sought to obtain a pardon from Louis XIV, she was never successful. She returned to Paris briefly in 1715, after Louis XIV's death. But even then the duration of her residence there was very short because she was already suffering from chronic nephritis and kidney stones that caused her extreme pain. Therefore, she retired to her chateau, La Buzadière, where she died in 1716.

Madame de Murat composed her fairy tales during her exile in Loches to relieve herself of boredom. A born storyteller, she recalled the tales and legends that she had heard during her childhood in Brittany, and she amused herself by retelling them in her own versions to her friends. Then she would either record these oral versions in a journal that she kept or prepare them for publication. Most of her tales concern the issue of *tendresse*, marriage, and power struggles among the aristocracy. Madame de Murat's basic philosophy—live for the moment, and live according to your feelings—is the dominant theme in her tales. But she does not preach or predict a happy end when one subscribes to such a philosophy. In fact, nothing is predictable in her tales because even the power of fairies was never sufficient in her mind to guarantee a happy end. This becomes evident in one of her best tales, *Le Palais de la vengeance* (The Palace of Revenge), which was first published in *Les nouveaux contes de fées* in 1698. Moreover, *The Palace of Revenge* is interesting because it conveys her sentiments about banishment and boredom. What appears to be an idyllic dream for a couple living at a bustling court turns out to be a nightmare in disguise.

THE PALACE
OF REVENGE

THERE was once a king and queen of Iceland, who had a daughter after twenty years of married life. Her birth gave them the greatest pleasure, since they had given up hope of having a successor to the throne. The young princess was named Imis, and from the very beginning her budding charms promised that she would be marvelously beautiful and radiant when she grew older.

No one in the universe would have ever been worthy of her if Cupid had not thought it a point of honor to bring such a wonderful person under his sway. Therefore, he arranged to have a prince born in the same court who was just as charming as the lovely princess. He was called Philax and was the son of a brother of the King of Iceland. He was two years older than the princess, and they were brought up together with all the freedom natural to childhood and close relatives. The first sensations of their hearts were mutual admiration and affection, and both found nothing more beautiful in their eyes as the other. Consequently, they could not find a single attraction in the world that interfered with the feeling each had for the other, even though they had yet to discover its name.

The king and queen were pleased to see the children's mutual affection grow. They loved young Philax, for he was a prince of their blood, and no child had ever wakened fairer hopes. Everything seemed to favor Cupid's plans to make Prince Philax the happiest of men.

The princess was about twelve years old when the queen, who was extremely fond of her, wanted to have her daughter's fortune told by a fairy whose extraordinary powers had created a sensation at that time. The queen set out in search of this fairy and took along Imis, who was despondent because she had to separate from Philax. Moreover, she wondered time and again why people troubled themselves about the future when the present was so pleasant. Philax remained with the king, and there was nothing at the court that could compensate for the absence of the princess.

Arriving at the fairy's castle, the queen was magnificently received, but the fairy was not at home. Her usual residence was on the summit of a mountain some distance away, where she absorbed herself in the profound study that had made her famous throughout the world. As soon as she heard about the queen's arrival, she returned to the castle. The queen presented the princess to her, told her her name and the hour of her birth, which the fairy already knew quite well even though she had not been there. The fairy of the mountain knew everything. She promised the queen an answer in two days and then returned to the summit of the mountain. On the morning of the third day she came back to the castle, requested that the queen descend into the garden, and gave her some tablets of palm leaves closely shut, which she was ordered not to open except in the presence of the king. To satisfy her curiosity to some degree, the queen asked her several questions in regard to the fate of her daughter.

"Great queen," the fairy of the mountain replied, "I can't tell you precisely what sort of catastrophe threatens the princess. I see only that love will have a large share in the events of her life, and that no beauty will ever arouse such passionate emotions as that of Imis will do."

One didn't have to be a fairy to foresee that the princess would have admirers. Her eyes already seemed to demand love from everyone's heart that the fairy assured the queen most people would feel for her. In the meantime, Imis, much less uneasy about her destiny than about her separation from Philax, amused herself by gathering flowers. Because she was only thinking about his love and was impatient to depart, however, she forgot the bouquet she had begun to make and unthinkingly threw them away. Then she hastened to rejoin the queen, who was taking her leave of the fairy of the mountain. The fairy also embraced Imis and gazed at her with the admiration she deserved.

"Since it's impossible for me, beautiful princess, to change the decree of destiny in your favor, I'll at least try to let you escape the disasters that it's preparing for you." Upon saying this, she gathered a bunch of lilies of the valley and addressed the youthful Imis again. "Always wear these flowers that I'm giving you," she said. "They'll never fade, and as long as you wear them, they'll protect you from all the evils with which fate threatens you."

Then she fastened the bouquet on the headdress of Imis. The flowers, obedient to the fairy's wishes, were no sooner placed in the princess's hair than they adjusted themselves and formed a sort of aigrette, whose whiteness seemed to prove only that nothing could eclipse Imis's fair complexion.

After thanking the fairy a thousand times, the queen bade her farewell and went back to Iceland, where the entire court impatiently awaited the princess's return. The eyes of Imis and her lover sparkled radiantly and beautifully with a joy that has never been seen before. The mystery of the lilies of the valley was revealed to the king alone. It had such a pleasing effect in the princess's beautiful brown hair that everyone assumed that it was simply an ornament that she herself had culled in the fairy's gardens.

The princess told Philax much more about the grief she felt at her separation from him than about the misfortunes that the fates had in store for her. Although Philax was worried by them, he was happy just to be with her in the present; the evils of the future were as yet uncertain. In fact, they forgot them and abandoned themselves to the delight of seeing each other again.

In the meantime, the queen recounted the events of the journey to the king and gave him the fairy's tablets. The king opened them and found the following words written in letters of gold:

Fate for Imis hides despair
Under hopes that seem most fair.
She'll be miserable as can be
Because of too much felicity.

The king and queen were very disturbed by this oracle and vainly tried to interpret it. They said nothing about it to the princess in order to spare her unnecessary sorrow.

One day, while Philax was hunting, a pleasure he indulged in frequently, Imis went walking by herself in a labyrinth of myrtles. She was melancholy because Philax had been gone so long, and she reproached herself for succumbing to an impatience that he evidently did not share. She was absorbed in her thoughts when she heard a voice:

"Why do you torment yourself, beautiful princess? If Philax does not appreciate the happiness of being loved by you, I've come to offer you a heart a thousand times more grateful—a heart deeply smitten by your charms—and a fortune remarkable enough to be the object of desire of everyone in the world except yourself."

The princess was astonished when she heard this voice. She had imagined herself alone in the labyrinth, and since she had not uttered a word, she was even more surprised that this voice had responded to her thoughts. She looked around and saw a little man appear in the air, seated upon a cockchafer.

"Fear not, fair Imis," he said to her. "You have no lover more submissive than I, and although this is the first time I've appeared to you, I've loved you for a long time and have gazed upon you every day."

"You astonish me!" the princess replied. "What's that you said? You've watched me and know my thoughts? If so, you must be aware that it's useless to love me. Philax, to whom I've given my heart, will continue to rule over it because of his charm, and although I'm unhappy with him, I've never loved him so much as I do at this moment. But tell me who you are, and where you first saw me."

"I'm Pagan the Enchanter," he replied, "and I have power over everyone but you. I saw you first in the gardens of the fairy of the mountain. I was hidden in one of the tulips you had gathered, and I took it as a good sign that you were induced to choose the flower I was concealed in. I had hoped you would carry me away with you, but you were too pleasantly occupied by thinking about Philax. You threw away the flowers as soon as you had gathered them and left me in the garden the most enamored of creatures. From that moment on, I've felt that nothing could make me happy except the hope of being loved by you. Think favorably of me, fair Imis, if this be possible, and permit me occasionally to remind you of my affection."

With these words he disappeared. The princess returned to the palace, where the sight of Philax dissipated the alarm she felt. She was so eager to hear him apologize for the length of time he had spent hunting that she nearly forgot to tell him what had occurred. But at last, she told him what she had seen in the labyrinth of myrtles. Despite his courage the young prince was alarmed at the idea of a winged rival because he could not fight for the hand of the princess with him on equal terms. Still, the plume of the lilies of the valley protected her against enchantments, and the affection Imis had for him gave him no cause to fear any change in her heart.

The day after this incident in the labyrinth, the princess woke and saw twelve tiny nymphs seated on honey bees fly into her room. They carried minuscule golden baskets in their hands and approached Imis's bed, where they greeted her, and then placed their baskets on a table of white marble that was standing in the center of the room. As soon as the baskets were placed on it, they grew to an ordinary size. The nymphs left them there and greeted Imis again. One approached the bed nearer than the rest, let something fall on it, and then flew away.

Although she was astonished by such a strange sight, she picked up the object that the nymph had dropped beside her. It was a marvelously beautiful emerald, and the moment the princess touched it, the emerald opened and revealed a rose leaf on which she read these verses:

> Let the world learn to its surprise
> The wondrous power of your eyes.
> Such is the love I bear, you'll see,
> It makes even torture dear to me.

The princess had difficulty recovering from her surprise, and at last she called her attendants, who were just as surprised at the sight of the baskets. The king, queen, and Philax rushed to her chamber on hearing the news of this extraordinary event. When the princess revealed to them what had happened, she told them about everything except the letter of her lover. She thought she was not bound to say anything about it except to Philax. The baskets were carefully examined and found to be filled with extraordinarily beautiful jewels of such great value that everyone's astonishment increased.

The princess would not touch anything, and when she found a moment when nobody was listening, she drew close to Philax and gave him the emerald and the rose leaf. He read his rival's letter with much disquietude, and Imis consoled him by tearing the rose leaf to pieces before his eyes. Alas, how dearly were they to pay for that act!

Some days elapsed without the princess hearing anything from Pagan. She thought that her contempt for him would put an end to his passion, and Philax expected the same thing. So he returned to his hunting as usual. When he stopped beside a fountain to refresh himself, he had the emerald with him that the princess had given him. Recalling with pleasure how little value she had placed on it, he drew it from his pocket to look at it. But no sooner was it in his hand than it slipped through his fingers, and no sooner did it touch the ground than it changed into a chariot. Two winged monsters emerged from the fountain and harnessed themselves to it. Philax gazed at them without alarm, for he was incapable of fear. Nevertheless, he could not avoid feeling some distress when he found himself being transported into the chariot by an irresistible power, and at the same moment raised into the air by the winged monsters, who pulled the chariot along with alarming speed.

Night fell, and the huntsmen, after searching for Philax in vain throughout the wood, went back to the palace, where they imagined he had returned alone. But he was not to be found there, nor had anyone seen him since he had set out with them for the chase.

The king commanded them to renew their search. The entire court shared his majesty's anxiety. They returned to the wood and ran all over looking for him. It was daybreak before they retraced their steps to the palace; however, they had been unable to obtain any news about the prince's whereabouts. Imis had spent the night despairing of her lover's absence, which she could not comprehend. She had ascended to the battlements of the palace to watch for the return of the search party, hoping she would see him arrive in their company. No words can express her grief when Philax did not appear, and when she was informed that it had been impossible to discover what had happened to him, she fainted. Carrying her into the palace, one of her women undressed her and put her to bed. In her haste, however, she took the plume of the lilies of the valley out of the princess's hair that guarded her against the power of enchantment. The instant it was removed, a dark cloud filled the apartment, into which Imis vanished. The king and queen fell into deep despair when they learned about her disappearance, and there was nothing that could console them.

On recovering from her swoon, the princess found herself in a chamber of multicolored coral with a floor made of pearls. She was surrounded by nymphs, who waited on her with the most profound respect. They were very beautiful and dressed in a magnificent and tasteful manner. Imis first asked them where she was.

"You're in a place where you're adored," one of the nymphs said to her. "Fear nothing, fair princess, you'll find everything you can desire here."

"Then Philax is here!" the princess exclaimed, her eyes sparkling with joy. "My only desire is to be fortunate enough to see him again."

"You cherish the memory of an ungrateful lover too long," Pagan said, making himself visible to the princess. "Since that prince has deserted you, he's no longer worthy of your affection. Let resentment and respect for your own pride combine with the feelings I have for you. Reign forever in these regions, lovely princess. You'll find immense treasures in them, and every kind of conceivable delight will accompany your steps."

Imis replied to Pagan's words with tears alone, and since he was afraid to embitter these tears, he left her. The nymphs remained with her and used everything within their power to console her. They served her a magnificent meal, but she refused to eat. By the following morning, though, her desire to see Philax once more made her determined to live. She took some food, and the nymphs conducted her through various parts of the palace to take her mind off her sorrow. It was built entirely of shiny shells mixed with precious stones of different colors that produced the finest effect in the world. All the furniture was made of gold, and it was clear from such wonderful craftsmanship that only fairies could have made it.

After they had shown Imis the palace, the nymphs led her into the gardens, which were indescribably beautiful. She found a splendid chariot drawn by six stags and led by a dwarf, who requested that she get in. Imis complied, and the nymphs seated themselves at her feet. They were driven to the seaside, where a nymph informed the princess that Pagan, who reigned on this island, had used the power of his art to make it the most reigned on this island, had used the power of his art to make it the most

After they had shown Imis the palace, the nymphs led her into the gardens, which were indescribably beautiful. She found a splendid chariot drawn by six stags and led by a dwarf, who requested that she get in. Imis complied, and the nymphs seated themselves at her feet. They were driven to the seaside, where a nymph informed the princess that Pagan, who reigned on this island, had used the power of his art to make it the most beautiful in the universe. The sound of instruments interrupted the nymph's talk. The sea appeared to be entirely covered with little boats built of scarlet coral and filled with everything necessary to create a splendid aquatic entertainment. In the middle of the small craft was a much larger barque on which Imis's initials, formed by pearls, could be seen everywhere. Drawn by two dolphins, the barque approached the shore. The princess got in, accompanied by her nymphs. As soon as she was on board, a superb meal appeared before her, and her ears were entertained at the same time by exquisite music that emanated from the boats around her. Songs lauding her were sung, but Imis did not pay any attention. She remounted her chariot and returned to the palace overcome with sadness.

In the evening Pagan appeared again, and he found her more inappreciative of his love than ever before, but he was not discouraged and was confident that his constancy would have an effect. He had yet to learn that the most faithful are not always the most happy when it comes to love.

Every day he offered the princess entertainments worthy of arousing the admiration of the entire world, but they were lost upon the person for whom they were invented. Imis thought of nothing but her missing lover.

In the meantime, that unfortunate prince had been transported by the winged monsters to a forest belonging to Pagan, called the Dismal Forest. As soon as Philax arrived there, the emerald chariot and monsters disappeared. Surprised by this miracle, the prince summoned all his courage to help himself. It was the only aid on which he could count in that place. He first explored several of the roads through the forest. They were dreadful, and the sun could not illuminate a way out of the gloomy forest. There was not a soul to be found, not even an animal of any kind. It seemed as though the beasts themselves were horrified of this dreary abode.

Philax lived on wild fruit and spent his days in the deepest sorrow. His separation from the princess caused him great despair, and sometimes he occupied himself by using his sword to carve the name of Imis on the tree trunks. Although these rank growths were hardly befitting for such a tender purpose, when we are truly in love, we frequently make the least suitable things express our feelings.

Continuing to advance through the forest every day, the prince had been journeying nearly a year when one night he heard some plaintive voices. Try as he might, he could not distinguish any words. Alarming as these wailing sounds were at such a dark hour—in a place where the prince had not encountered a soul—he desperately sought some kind of company. "If I could at least find someone as wretched as I," he said to himself, "he could console me for the misfortunes I have experienced." Thus he waited impatiently for morning, when he could search for the people whose voices he had heard. He walked toward that part of the forest where he thought the sounds had come from, but he searched all day in vain. At last, however, toward evening he discovered a spot barren of trees. There sprawled the ruins of a castle that appeared to have been enormous at one time. He entered a courtyard that had walls made of green marble and still seemed somewhat splendid. Yet he found nothing but huge trees standing irregularly in various spots of the enclosure. Noticing something elevated on a pedestal of black marble, he found on closer inspection a jumbled pile of armor and weapons, heaped one on top of the other. Ancient helmets, shields, and swords formed a sort of motley trophy. He had been looking for some inscription that might tell him who had been the former owners, and he found one engraved on the pedestal. Time had nearly effaced the characters, and he had great difficulty in deciphering these words:

TO THE IMMORTAL MEMORY OF THE GLORY OF THE FAIRY CÉORÉ
IT WAS HERE
THAT ON THE SAME DAY
SHE TRIUMPHED OVER CUPID
AND PUNISHED HER UNFAITHFUL LOVERS

This inscription did not provide Philax with nearly enough information to solve the mystery. Therefore, he was about to continue his search through the forest when night overtook him. He sat down at the foot of a cypress, and no sooner did he begin to relax than he heard the same voices that had attracted his attention the previous evening. He was not so much surprised by this as when he noticed that it was the trees themselves that uttered these complaints just as if they had been human beings. The prince rose, drew his sword, and struck the cypress nearest him. He was about to repeat the blow when the tree exclaimed, "Stop! Stop! Don't insult an unfortunate prince who's no longer in a position to defend himself!"

Philax stopped, and as he adjusted to the extraordinary nature of this happenstance, he asked the cypress what miracle had transformed it into a man and a tree at the same time.

"I'll gladly tell you," the cypress replied, "especially since this is the first opportunity in two thousand years that fate has afforded me the chance of relating my misfortunes and I don't want to lose it. All the trees you see in this courtyard were princes, renowned in their time for their rank and valor. The fairy Céoré reigned in this country. Beautiful though she was, her powers made her more famous than her beauty. These other charms she used to bring us under her spell. She had become enamored of the young Orizée, a prince whose remarkable qualities made him worthy of a better fate—I should tell you," the cypress added, "he's the oak you see beside me."

Philax looked at the oak and heard it breathe a heavy sigh as it recalled its misfortune.

"To attract this prince to her court," the cypress continued, "the fairy had a tournament proclaimed. We were all quick to seize this opportunity to acquire glory, and Orizée was one of the princes who contended. The prize consisted of a fairy armor that made the wearer invulnerable. Unfortunately, I was the winner. Céoré was annoyed that fate had not favored her inclinations and, deciding to avenge herself on us, she enchanted all the mirrors that lined a gallery in her castle. Those who saw her reflection in these fatal mirrors just once could not resist having the most passionate feelings for her. It was in this gallery that she received us the day after the tournament. We all saw her in these mirrors, and she appeared so beautiful that those among us who had been indifferent to love up until then stopped being so from that point on, and those who were in love with others became unfaithful all at once. We no longer thought of leaving the fairy's palace. Our only concern was to please her. The affairs of our realms no longer mattered to us. Nothing seemed of consequence except the hope of being loved by Céoré. Orizée was the only one she favored, and the passion of the other princes merely gave the fairy opportunities of sacrificing them to this lover who was so dear to her, and causing the fame of her beauty to spread throughout the world. Love appeared for some time to soften Céoré's cruel nature, but at the end of four or five years she displayed her former ferocity. Abusing the power of her enchantment over us, she used us to avenge herself on neighboring kings for the slightest offence by the most horrible murders. Orizée tried in vain to prevent her cruel acts. She loved him but would not obey him. Having returned one day from subduing a giant whom I had challenged on her orders, I had the vanquished giant's arms brought before her. She was alone in the gallery of mirrors. I laid the giant's spoils at her feet and declared my feelings for her with indescribable ardor, augmented no doubt by the power of the enchantment that surrounded me. But far from showing the least gratitude for my triumph or for the love I felt for her, Céoré treated me with utmost contempt. Into a boudoir she withdrew and left me alone in the gallery in a state of utter despair and rage. I remained there for some time, not knowing what to do because the fairy's enchantments did not permit us to fight with Orizée. Since she was concerned about the life of her lover, the cruel Céoré had deprived us of the natural desire to avenge ourselves on a fortunate rival when she aroused our jealousy. Finally, after pacing the gallery for some time, I remembered that it was in this place that I had first fallen in love with the fairy and exclaimed, 'It's here that I first felt that fatal passion which now fills me with despair. You wretched mirrors that have pictured the unjust Céoré to me so often with a beauty that enslaved my heart and reason, I'm going to punish you for the crime of making her too appealing to me.' Upon saying this, I snatched the giant's club that I had brought to give the fairy as a present, and I dashed the mirrors to pieces. No sooner were they broken than I felt an even greater hatred for Céoré than my former love. At the same time, the other princes who had been my rivals felt their spells broken, and Orizée himself became ashamed of the love the fairy had for him. Céoré vainly tried to retain her lover by her tears, but he did not respond to her grief. Despite her cries, we set out all together, determined to flee from the terrible place. Yet as we passed through the courtyard, the sky appeared to be on fire. A frightful clap of thunder was heard, and we found we could not move. The fairy appeared in the air, riding on a large serpent, and she addressed us in a tone that revealed her rage. 'Faithless princes,' she said, 'I'm about to punish you by a torture that will never end because of the crime you've committed in breaking my chains, which were too great an honor for you to bear. As for you, ungrateful Orizée, I'll triumph after all in the love you've felt for me. I'm going to plague you with the same misfortune that your rivals will experience. Now, I command in memory of this incident that when mirrors become commonly used throughout the world, it will always be a definite sign of infidelity whenever a lover breaks one.' The fairy vanished after having uttered these words. We were changed into trees, but cruel Céoré left us our reason, undoubtedly with the intention to increase our suffering. Time has destroyed the superb castle that was the avenue of our misfortune, and you're the only man we've seen during the two thousand years that we've been in this frightful forest."

Philax was about to reply to the cypress tree's story when he was suddenly transported into a beautiful garden. There he found a lovely nymph who approached him with a gracious air and said. "If you wish, Philax, I'll allow you to see Princess Imis in three days."

The prince was ecstatic when heard such an unexpected offer and threw himself at her feet to express his gratitude. At that same moment Pagan was aloft, concealed in a cloud with the Princess Imis. He had told her a thousand times that Philax was unfaithful, but she had always refused to believe a word of this jealous lover. He now conducted her to this spot, he said, to convince her of the fickleness of the prince. The princess saw Philax throw himself at the nymph's feet with an air of extreme delight, and she became despondent. No longer did she deceive herself of something that she was afraid to believe more than anything in the world. Pagan had placed her at a distance from the earth that prevented her from hearing what Philax and the nymph had said—it was by his orders that the nymph had appeared before Philax.

Pagan led Imis back to his island, where, after having convinced her of Philax's infidelity, he found that he had only increased the beautiful princess's grief without making her any more positive toward him. To his despair he found that his plan of alleged infidelity had failed despite the fact that it had seemed so promising. Therefore, he was now determined to avenge himself for the constancy of these lovers. He was not cruel like the fairy Céoré, his ancestress, so he conceived a different kind of punishment from the one she had used to torment her unfortunate lovers. He did not wish to destroy either the princess, whom he had loved so tenderly, or even Philax, whom he had already made suffer so much. Consequently he limited his revenge to the destruction of a feeling that had opposed his own.

Erecting a crystal palace on his island, he took great care to put everything in it that would make life pleasant. However, there would be no way to leave this castle. He enclosed nymphs and dwarfs to wait on Imis and her lover, and when everything was ready for their reception, he transported the two of them there. At first they thought themselves at the height of happiness and blessed Pagan a thousand times for softening his anger. As for Pagan, although he at first could not bear to see them together, he hoped that this spectacle would one day prove less painful. In the meantime, he left the crystal palace after engraving this inscription on it with a stroke of his wand:

> Absence, danger, pleasure, pain,
> Were all employed, and all in vain.
> Imis and Philax could not be severed.
> Pagan, whose power they dared defy,
> Condemned them for their constant tie
> To dwell in this place together forever.

They say that at the end of some years, Pagan was as much avenged as he had hoped and that the beautiful Imis and Philax fulfilled the prediction of the fairy of the mountain. Indeed, they fervently kept seeking to recover the aigrette of the lilies to destroy their enchanted palace in the exact same way that they had previously used the lilies to protect themselves against the evil that had been predicted for them.

> Until that moment a fond pair had been blessed
> And cherished in their hearts love's constant fire.
> But Pagan taught them by that fatal test
> That even of bliss human hearts could tire.

Jean-Paul Bignon

Jean-Paul Bignon (1662–1743), the son of Jérome II and Suzanne Phélypeaux de Pontchartrain, chose to enter the ecclesiastical orders at an early age in order to pursue his scholarly interests. In 1684 he was accepted into the Novitiate de l'Oratoire, and in 1685 he went to a retreat at St.-Paul-aux-Bois, the diocese of Soissons, for five years in order to devote himself to a systematic study of the classics. At the beginning of 1691 he was ordained a priest and became director of all the academies in the kingdom, one of the most important educational positions in the ancien régime. In 1693 he was made abbot of St.-Quentin-en-Isle, but continued to function as the director of academies. Bignon endeavored to keep out of the quarrels between the Jansenists and Jesuits, and he gradually became one of the most influential figures in the domain of the arts and sciences during his lifetime. As a member of the Académie Française and president of the Academy of Sciences for forty years, he constantly supported the work of the most promising intellectuals in France.

In 1700 he was appointed director of the libraries and the bureau of censorship. In 1702 Bignon took over the directorship of the *Journal des scavans* (Journal of Scholars and Scientists) and reorganized it so that more intellectuals could contribute to the publication and enhance the quality of the articles. Bignon constantly sought ways to improve the conditions of scholarship in France, and after he became royal librarian in 1718 he brought about major changes in the library system, increasing the holdings and providing wide public access to the libraries. Toward the end of his life he had an expensive chateau built for himself near Melun, and he gave his retreat the name *Isle-Belle*, or Beautiful Island.

Bignon was more than a strong administrator. He was a noted public speaker, poet, and scholar. He published numerous essays and wrote an important biography entitled *Vie de François Lévesque, prêtre de l'Oratoire* (1684). Since he was most active in intellectual circles during the height of the fairy-tale vogue, he evidently decided to make a contribution to it by writing a collection of tales entitled *Les Aventures d'Abdalla, fils d'Anif* (1712–14). Bignon combined oriental motifs with French folklore to depict the exotic adventures of Abdalla, who encounters Zeineb during his travels. Each episode of the book is a tale unto itself, and Zeineb's first-person narrative is extremely important because of the role it plays in the Beauty and the Beast tradition. It is more than likely that Madame de Villeneuve knew this version, and it may have served as the basis for her tale that later influenced Madame Leprince de Beaumont.

PRINCESS ZEINEB
AND KING LEOPARD

I AM the daughter of King Batoche, who rules over the easternmost part
of the Island of Gilolo. My name is Zeineb, and I have five older sisters.
One day my father went hunting in the mountains, and after he had gone a
long way, he eventually reached a desolate spot and was extremely surprised
to find a beautiful palace that he had never seen before. Anxious to find out
more about this unknown mansion, he started to approach it. Yet he froze
as a terrifying voice called him by name and threatened him with immediate death unless he sent one of his daughters within three days. King
Batoche raised his eyes and saw a leopard at a window. The fire emanating
from the eyes of this beast terrified him. In fact, so great was my father's
fright that he fled the spot with his men without daring to reply.

My sisters and I were all upset by the sadness that overcame our father,
especially since it was quite visible on his face. We hugged him and urged
him to tell us what was troubling his heart. After we had persisted for a long
time, he finally told us.

"It's a matter of my life or yours," he said. "Ah, I'd much rather die than
lose the children I so dearly love."

Tears were in his eyes as he began telling us what he had seen and how
he had been threatened in such a terrible way.

"If that's the only dreadful thing that's been disturbing you, my dear
father," our eldest sister said, "console yourself. I'll depart tomorrow. Perhaps this leopard won't be as merciless as you think."

The king vainly tried to oppose her plan, for she let herself be guided to the
secluded palace. But when the doors opened and the leopard showed himself,
my sister found him so horrible that she forgot all her good resolutions,
turned around, and fled. When my four other sisters saw her return, they
scolded her harshly for having so little courage, and the next day they all
tried their luck together. But their courage failed them in the same way that
it had failed our eldest sister. As a result, the king's life depended solely on
me.

145

When I took my turn, I was more fearless than they. Not only did I withstand the dreadful gaze of the leopard at the window when I arrived, but I also had the courage to enter the marvelous palace with my mind firmly made up not to leave until I had completely brought everything to light. As soon as I was in the courtyard, the doors closed. A group of nymphs who were quite comely but, due to some miracle, could not talk, appeared before me and began serving me. I was led into a magnificent apartment and spent the entire day regarding the beautiful features of the palace and its gardens. My evening repast was delicious, and I went to sleep in a bed that was better than any in King Batoche's palace. But a thousand troubling things were soon to follow.

Shortly after I was in bed, I heard his steps, and it would not have taken much to have frightened me to death. He rushed into my room and made a terrible noise, brandishing teeth, claws, and tail. Then he stretched his whole body alongside me. I had left him plenty of space because, believe me, I did not occupy much myself. The beast behaved himself in an astonishingly discreet way: he did not touch me at all and left before daybreak. I would have liked to have taken advantage of this time to have slept, but my fear was much too overwhelming. The same nymphs who had served me the day before came to wake me and get me dressed. They did not neglect a thing to make me comfortable. I had a royal lunch and heard a musical concert during the afternoon. My pleasure was made complete when I observed that the leopard did not appear during the entire day. Indeed, this day set the tone for all the days that followed, but, to tell the truth, I spent many nights without daring to sleep. Finally, the discretion demonstrated by the leopard enabled me to regain my tranquillity.

Ten months went by like this, and at the end of this time, I succumbed to a curious desire that had possessed me from the start and one I had continually resisted: I wanted to know whether the leopard by day was also a leopard by night.

I rose from the bed while he slept, avoiding any contact with him. Then I tiptoed all around the room, searching for something to light it. I suspected that the beast's skin was lying on the ground. In fact, I found it and was then overcome by a mad whim—for what else could I call my behavior? I boldly tore the skin to pieces without considering what might happen. After this rash act I lay down again on my edge of the bed as if nothing had happened.

My companion got up at his usual time, and when he discovered that his skin was gone, he began to wail. I responded by coughing to make him aware that I was awake.

"It's superfluous now to continue taking precautions," the groaning man said to me sadly. "I'm a powerful king who was placed under a magic spell by a magician serving my enemies. My enchantment would have been over now, and I had decided to share my throne and my bed with you. But alas, your curiosity has set me back, and it is now as if I had never suffered anything! Why did you act against your better judgment? Common sense should have told you that you can't act recklessly in a place where you don't know the laws."

I frankly confessed my mistake and begged him to consider that girls are naturally curious. I told him he should be grateful to me for not having looked sooner for the answer to his mysterious appearance. This excuse spoiled everything, and he heaped upon me a new flood of reproaches. Finally, the enchanted king calmed down and momentarily revealed his splendid face, which radiated a sudden light. But as he felt dark forces about to act on him again, he bade farewell and taught me some words that I was to pronounce against anyone I wanted to restrain from doing something until I pronounced some other words that would free that person to continue his actions. No sooner did I learn them than the palace disappeared along with all its pleasant things, and I found myself alone and completely naked lying on a rock.

Tears poured from my eyes as I cursed my curiosity and imprudence. Daylight came, and I was obliged out of shame to look around for something to cover me. I noticed some clothes near the spot where I was lying and went over to pick them up. They were my own clothes, which had been almost worn out over those ten months by all the abuses of exposure. I put on those sad rags as best I could and, fearing that my mistake had caused my father's death, I thought it wiser to leave my country and to go begging rather than to appear before my sisters in my sorry condition. Smearing my face with dirt, I summoned up my courage to begin my wandering.

After a long and fatiguing journey I arrived at a seaport where an old Moslem who was heading to Borneo to do some trading took pity on me and took me on board his ship. We had a safe voyage and let down the anchor in a bay of that large island, even though I was not sure why. After descending with many other people weary of the sea, I left their company without anyone noticing, since I had no desire to go with their leader, who was on his way to the coastal cities where business called him. Instead, I went into the interior of the island, which was very populous, and in three months I reached the pretty city of Soucad, which got its name from the large river that crosses it.

I noticed from the very first that the embroidery decorating the clothes of the women was extremely coarse, and I was convinced that I was more skillful in doing this simple work than the women of Borneo, and that I had found a source that would provide me with work. Once my skill became known, I soon had success beyond my greatest expectations. I rented a small cottage and in a short time established an honest business for myself. I did not have any difficulty learning the language because people use approximately the same language in Soucad as they do in Gilolo. For six or seven months I was able to work in peace and gradually regained the beauty that people had flattered me with having—good looks that had almost entirely disappeared due to the exhaustion and misery I had suffered. I drew the attention of many people. Among them were three of the most distinguished young men of the city, who conspired together to discover whether I was a cruel beauty. They agreed among themselves that one of them, who was considered an artful seducer, would make the first attempt. He came to my house that very evening and began the conversation by asking me to make an embroidered belt for him. Then he talked about his feelings for me: no beauty intended for easy conquest has ever heard so many professions of friendship and favors all at once. When dinnertime arrived, he wanted to entertain me, and though he saw I was repulsed by the idea, he insisted, and I consented. The meal was exquisite, and he did not forget little sweet songs to accompany it. In fact, my lover made it quite clear from several brazen looks that he expected me to be most obliging to him.

Since an open window in my room made him feel uncomfortable, he went over to shut it. While he was closing it, however, I pronounced those powerful words King Leopard had taught me. I put him into a trance so that he had to keep closing and reclosing the window. As for me, I went to bed as I ordinarily did without any difficulties. The poor spellbound man spent the entire night closing that window. The next morning I released him and let him go with a good warning to behave better in the future.

His comrades, who had been waiting impatiently for him in a street since daybreak, ran toward him as soon as he appeared. He cleverly led them to believe that he had been perfectly well received and described his good fortune to them in glowing colors that set them afire. They drew lots to see which one would enjoy the expected happiness next, and the day seemed long to the one who won. However, the night was much more tedious for him because he was obliged to wind a reel of silk for the exact same time that the other had spent closing the window. The third young man was tricked just like his friends, and he had to comb my hair the entire night because of my orders.

These young men did not have the strength to conceal their misadventures for long. All three were outraged, and their tenderness changed into obsessive hate. Therefore, they agreed to denounce me to the judges as the most despicable sorceress in the world. As a result, I was taken from my house and imprisoned. My powerful and motivated adversaries worked feverishly at getting ready for my trial. Since I did not deny a single fact they accused me of, the affair would not have lasted four days if I had not distributed some money among several of the judges through the help of a good friend who was kind enough to do this. The decision was postponed for three whole months due in part to the money and in part to the fact that two of the other judges were appreciative of my charms. They did everything they could to save me, convinced that I would not be ungrateful after such a great service. Nevertheless, in the end my persecutors won, and I was condemned to be burned alive.

After this cruel sentence had been pronounced, I was led to the stake set up in the most beautiful square in Soucad. When I arrived there, they told me what to expect when one is to be executed in a public ceremony, and they bound me to the stake with a large chain. The people hurled insults at me: "She's a sorceress!" "She's an enemy of the human race!" They accused me of all the bad things that had happened naturally or accidentally to all those people who had bought my work. They were delighted to see the executioner advance toward the stake with a flaming torch in his hand, but this unsuspecting crowd was greatly surprised a moment later to see this same executioner become immobile and entranced. The only thing he could do was to hold his burning torch. This effect had been induced by the words that I had secretly pronounced against him. Everyone was in suspense due to this strange incident. Then their mood changed all at once, and they could not stop themselves from laughing as they watched how ridiculous a figure the executioner cut.

The three young men were present and had a large number of partisans in the crowd. They became extraordinarily furious at seeing an event that reminded them of what had happened to them. They cried out that this was public proof of my guilt and that they should quickly reduce to ashes a woman who even at the point of death had abominable ties with evil spirits. The mob was moved by these words and ran to the nearby houses to fetch firebrands. I prepared again to stop this riot when an uproar mixed with acclamations caught their attention in the main street that emptied into the square.

The King of Soucad himself had caused this pleasant commotion. After a long absence he had wanted to surprise his people by making a sudden appearance. Since he was greatly beloved, everyone's attention was drawn to him and away from the stake, executioner, victim, and judges.

The king had gotten out of his carriage and was riding slowly on horseback in order to be better seen. He advanced right into the middle of the square and saw a spectacle that he found rather strange, since it did not fit the public joy that had been aroused by his happy return. When he turned toward the stake, he granted me the reprieve that only he could give and had me untied. Immediately I ran to embrace the knees of my liberator, who looked at me very attentively. He dismounted and embraced me with a joy that equaled the amazement of all the spectators. I did not dare to raise my eyes, but finally, once I glimpsed the person from whom I had received such a surprising reprieve, I recognized King Leopard, whose image had remained deeply engraved in my mind.

It is impossible to express the feelings of my heart, my thoughts, and what I wanted to say. I could not form a single coherent sentence. My gratitude and joy took away all the words that came to my mind. The king had me climb into his carriage without getting in himself and conducted me to his palace in triumph. Some days later, he married me in a solemn ceremony and empowered me to reign in his dominions. The first merciful act I asked him to perform was to pardon my accusers. Then I gave the judges who had let themselves be bribed by my money the punishment they deserved. On the other hand, those judges who had been moved by my beauty were punished in a more lenient way.

Gabrielle-Suzanne de Villeneuve

Gabrielle-Suzanne Barbot Gallon de Villeneuve (1695–1755) was the daughter of a nobleman of La Rochelle. Not much is known about her life except that she married Jean-Baptiste de Gallon, seigneur de Villeneuve, who was a lieutenant colonel in the army. Soon thereafter he died, and she moved to Paris and remained a widow for the rest of her life. She lived with the famous French dramatist Prosper Jolyot de Crébillon and began a career as writer to support herself. Encouraged by Crébillon's son, Claude, himself an accomplished writer, Mme. de Villeneuve achieved a modest success as a novelist and also published poetry in the magazine *Mercure*. Among her best works are: *Les Contes marins ou la jeune Américaine* (1740), *Les Belles solitaires* (1745), *La Jardinière de Vincennes* (1750–53), *Le Beau-frère supposé* (1752), *Le Juge prévenu* (1754), *Anecdotes de la cour d'Alphonese XI, roi de Castille* (1755).

Mme. de Villeneuve worked within the tradition of the sentimental novel; she liked to write about vicissitudes of young lovers and add moral reflections about their destinies. Her major accomplishment was the story *La Belle et la Bête* (Beauty and the Beast), which was included in *Les contes marins ou la jeune Américaine* (1740).

Since Mme. de Villeneuve's version is exceedingly long and intricate, her version is not as well-known as that of Mme. Leprince de Beaumont, whom she influenced. However, it is a fascinating narrative about the manners and social class attitudes that reveals how closely the fairy tale was bound to the development of civility in France and reflected questions of socialization.

THE STORY
OF
BEAUTY AND THE BEAST

IN a country far from here, there was a large city where business had been flourishing. Among its citizens was a merchant who succeeded in everything he tried. Fortune responded kindly to his wishes and always showered him with her fairest favors. But if he had immense wealth, he also had a great many children: six boys and six girls. None of them were settled in life. The boys were too young to think about it; the girls were too proud because of their wealth and found it difficult to decide among their suitors. That is, their vanity was inflamed by the attentions of the handsomest young gentlemen.

Then an unexpected reverse of fortune struck home and disturbed their happiness. Their house caught fire, and the splendid furniture, account books, notes, gold, silver, and all the valuable goods that formed the merchant's principal wealth, were besieged by this tempestuous fire, which was so violent that few of the things could be saved.

This first disaster was but the forerunner of others. The father, who had prospered in everything until that moment, lost all the ships he had at sea at the time, either due to shipwreck or pirates. His representatives caused him to become bankrupt, and his foreign agents were treacherous. In short, after enjoying the most opulent way of life, he suddenly fell into the most abject poverty. He had nothing left but a small country house situated in a desolate spot more than a hundred miles from the city. Impelled to seek a place of refuge after his house had burned to the ground, he took his family to this isolated spot. All were in despair at such a drastic change. His daughters were especially horrified by the prospect of the life they would have to lead in such dull and solitary place. For a time after their father made his intention known, they hoped that their lovers who had proposed to them in vain would now be only too happy to find they were inclined to listen to them. They imagined that their many admirers would all strive to be the first to propose marriage. But they did not stay deluded very long, for they had lost their greatest asset when their father's splendid fortune had

153

disappeared like a flash of lightning, and their time for choosing had gone with it. Their crowd of admirers vanished at the moment of their downfall; their beauty was not sufficiently commanding to retain one of them. Their friends were no more generous than their lovers. From the hour they became poor, everyone, without exception, did not want to know them anymore. Some were even cruel enough to impute their misfortunes to their own acts. Those whom the father had most obliged were his most vehement slanderers: they reported that all the catastrophes had resulted from his bad conduct, lavishness, foolish extravagance, and that of his children.

Thus, the best thing this wretched family could do was to leave this city, where everybody took pleasure in insulting them as a result of their misfortune. Having no resources whatsoever, they secluded themselves in their country house, situated in the middle of an almost impenetrable forest. Indeed, it could well be considered the saddest abode in the world. What misery they had to endure in this frightful solitude! They were forced to do the meanest work. No longer in the position to have anyone to wait upon them, the unfortunate merchant's sons were compelled to divide the servants' duties among themselves and also had to make a country living. As for the daughters, they had plenty of things to do. Like poor peasant girls, they were obliged to use their delicate hands to do all the farm chores. Forced to wear only woolen dresses; they had nothing to gratify their vanity; they lived off what the land produced. Although they were limited to basic necessities, they still retained a refined and dainty taste and they constantly missed the city and its attractions. Yet just the memory of the mirthful and pleasurable days of their youth caused them great anguish.

The youngest girl, however, displayed greater perseverance and resolution in their common misfortune than her sisters. She bore her lot cheerfully and with a strength of mind much beyond her sixteen years. This is not to say that she was not at first melancholy. Alas, who would not have been affected by such misfortunes? But after mourning her father's bad luck, she decided it would be better to cheerfully accept the position she was placed in and to forget a world that she and her family had found so ungrateful in their time of adversity.

Eager to console her father and her brothers by her pleasant disposition and sprightliness, she did everything during this sad period she could to amuse them. The merchant had spared no cost in her education, nor in that of her sisters. Since she sang in a charming way and accompanied this by playing various instruments exceedingly well, she asked her sisters to join her, but her cheerfulness and patience only made them more miserable. These girls, who were inconsolable because of their bad luck, thought their youngest sister displayed poor spirit and even weakness to be so merry in the state to which Providence had reduced them.

"How happy she is," the eldest said. "She was made for such coarse occupations. With such low notions, what else would she have done in the world?"

Such remarks were unjust. This adorable and good-natured person was much more suited to shine in society than any of her sisters. A generous and tender heart showed in her every word and deed. She was just as sensitive about the reverse of fortune that had recently overwhelmed her family as any of her sisters, but through a strength of mind uncommon in her sex, she concealed her sorrow and rose above her misfortunes. So much steadiness they considered insensitivity. But one tends to judge things hastily when one is envious.

Every person who knew her true character was impelled to prefer her over her sisters. Although she distinguished herself through her good nature, she was also so beautiful that she was called "Beauty." Known by this name only, what more was needed to increase the envy and hatred of her sisters? Her charms and the general esteem in which she was held might well have induced her to hope for a much more advantageous marriage than her sisters, but she was moved solely by her father's misfortunes. Far from delaying his departure from a city in which she had enjoyed so much pleasure, she had done all she could to help him. This young girl found the same tranquillity in solitude that she had had at the center of the world. To amuse herself in her hours of relaxation, she would dress her hair with flowers, and, like the shepherdesses of former times, this rustic life made her forget all those opulent things that had most gratified her. Every day brought her some new innocent pleasure.

Two years passed, and the family was just beginning to become accustomed to country life when the merchant received a sign of hope that their prosperity might be restored. The father was informed that one of the vessels he had thought was lost had arrived safely in port with a rich cargo. His informants added that they feared his agents would take advantage of his absence and sell the cargo at a low price, fraudulently allowing them to make a great profit at his expense. He conveyed these tidings to his children, who were immediately convinced that they would soon be able to return from exile. The girls, much more impatient than the boys, were eager to set out instantly and to leave everything behind them. But the father, who was more prudent, asked them to control their excitement. Although he was needed by his family because it was harvest time, he decided to leave his sons in charge of the work in the fields and set out on the long journey.

His daughters, with the exception of the youngest, were certain that they would soon be restored to their former splendor. They imagined that even if their father's cargo might not be considerable enough to allow them to live in the great metropolis, he would at least have enough for them to live in a less expensive city. They hoped they would be able to find good society there, attract admirers, and profit by the first proposal made to them. They hardly recalled the drudgery they had undergone for the past two years and believed that they had already climbed out of the pit of poverty and miraculously fallen into the lap of plenty. As a result, they overwhelmed their father with foolish requests, for solitude had not cured them of the taste for luxury and show. They asked him to purchase jewelry, clothes, and headdresses. Each one outdid the other in her demands so that the total far exceeded their father's supposed fortune.

Beauty, who was no slave of luxury, prudently realized that if he fulfilled her sisters' requests, it would be useless for her to ask for anything. All the same, her father was astonished by her silence and interrupted his insatiable daughters. "Well, Beauty, don't you desire anything? What shall I bring you? Speak freely."

"My dear papa," the charming girl replied, embracing him affectionately, "I only want one thing, and it's more precious than all the ornaments my sisters have asked for. I shall be extremely happy merely to see you return in perfect health."

This unselfish response filled her sisters with shame and confusion. They were so angry that one of them, who spoke for the rest, said with bitterness, "This little girl wants to make herself seem important and fancies that she distinguishes herself by these affected heroics. Surely nothing can be more ridiculous."

But the father, touched by her remark, could not help showing his joy and appreciation that she had asked nothing for herself. He begged her to choose something, if for no other reason than to soften the ill-will that his other daughters had toward her. He remarked that her indifference to dress was not natural at her age.

"Very well, my dear father," she said, "since you want me to make a request, I'm going to ask you to bring me a rose. I've a great love for that flower, and ever since I've lived in this desolate spot, I've not had the pleasure of seeing one." By this request she obeyed her father and at the same time avoided making him go to any expense for her.

At last the day arrived for this good old man to leave his family. He traveled as fast as he could to the great city, for the prospect of a new fortune had reinvigorated him. But he did not obtain the reward he had hoped for. His vessel had indeed arrived, but his partners, believing him to be dead, had taken possession of the entire cargo and had disposed of it. Thus, instead of gaining possession of what belonged to him, he had to endure all sorts of legal chicanery to get it. He did indeed manage to win over them, but after more than six months of trouble and expense, he was not any richer than before. His debtors had become insolvent, and he could hardly defray his own costs. Thus did his riches elude him.

To add to all these unpleasant things, he was obliged to to start home in the most dreadful weather. Exposed on the road to piercing blasts of snow, he thought he was going to die from exhaustion, but when he found himself within a few miles of his house (which he had not reckoned leaving for such false hopes, and indeed Beauty had shown sense in mistrusting these hopes) his strength returned to him. It was late and he would need some hours to cross the forest, but he wanted to continue on. Soon he was overtaken by nightfall and, buried in the snow with his horse, he suffered from the intense cold. Not knowing which way to turn, he thought his last hour had come. There was no hut to be seen, although the forest was filled with them. A tree hollowed by age was the best shelter he could find, and he was only too happy to hide himself in it. This tree protected him from the cold and saved his life. His horse saw another hollow tree a short distance away and was led by instinct to take shelter there.

The night seemed to never end. He was not only famished but frightened by the roaring of the wild beasts that were constantly passing him. It was impossible to relax even for an instant. Nor did his troubles and anxiety end with the night. No sooner did he have the pleasure of seeing daylight than his distress heightened. The ground was so deeply covered with snow, he could not find the path. Only after a great effort and frequent falls did he succeed in discovering something like a path on which his horse could keep its footing.

Proceeding without knowing the direction, he chanced upon an avenue leading to a beautiful castle, where the snow had, oddly, not fallen. The avenue consisted of four rows of orange trees bearing flowers and fruit. Statues were scattered here and there regardless of order or symmetry—some were in the middle of the road, others among the trees—and all made in the strangest fashion. They were life-size and had the color of human flesh. Though in different poses and in various dresses, the greatest number represented warriors.

Arriving at a courtyard, he saw a great many more statues, but he was suffering so much from cold that he did not stop to examine them. An agate staircase with balusters of chased gold led him inside to several magnificently furnished rooms. Now that he was bathed in a gentle warmth, he felt refreshed. Still, he needed to eat and did not know whom he should address. This magnificent edifice appeared to be inhabited only by statues. A profound silence reigned throughout. Nevertheless, it did not have the air of an old palace that had been deserted. The halls, rooms, and galleries were all open. It just seemed that there was no living thing in this charming place.

Weary of wandering through this vast dwelling, he stopped in a salon that had a roaring fire. Assuming that it had been prepared for someone who would soon appear, he drew near the fireplace to warm himself and wait, but no one came. Seated on a sofa near the fire, a sweet sleep closed his eyelids, and he was no longer in a condition to observe anyone enter. Fatigue induced him to sleep; hunger woke him. He had been suffering from it for the past twenty-four hours, and exploring this palace had increased his appetite. When he opened his eyes, he was astonished to see an elegantly set table. A light meal would not have satisfied him, and the sumptuous food invited him to devour everything.

His first concern was to utter his thanks loudly to those from whom he had received so much kindness, and he then decided to wait quietly until his host decided to make himself known. However, just as fatigue had caused him to sleep before, now a full belly produced the same effect. In fact, this second time he slept for at least four hours. Upon waking, he saw another table in place of the first table. It was made of porphyry, and some kind hand had set out a meal consisting of cakes, preserved fruits, and liqueurs. This likewise seemed laid out for him, and he benefited from this kindness by eating everything.

However, after realizing there was nobody who could inform him whether this palace was inhabited by men or gods, he became afraid, for he was naturally timid. Therefore, he decided to go back through all the apartments and express his great thanks to the genius to whom he was indebted for so much kindness. Moreover, he sought in the most respectful manner to induce him to appear. Yet all his efforts were in vain: there were neither servants nor signs that could enable him to ascertain whether the palace was inhabited. As he began to reflect more on what he should do, he began to think—he could not imagine why—that some good spirit had given him this mansion and all the riches it contained as a present. This idea seemed like an inspiration, and without further delay, he reinspected everything and took possession of all the treasures he could find. He began pondering what he would give to each of his children, selecting the apartments that would particularly suit them and enjoying the delight beforehand that his journey would afford them. Then he entered the garden, where in spite of the severity of the winter, the rarest flowers were producing the most delicious scents in the mildest and purest air. Birds of all kinds blended their songs with the rushing noise of water and brought about a pleasant harmony.

The old man was ecstatic amid such wonders and said to himself, "I don't think my daughters will find it difficult to accustom themselves to this delightful abode. I can't believe that they'll miss or prefer the city to this mansion. I'm going to set out right away!" he cried, carried away by a joy rather uncommon for him. "I'm already happy at the thought of their happiness."

Upon entering the charming castle, he had taken care to unbridle his horse and let him make his way to a stable he had observed in the forecourt, located at the end of a lane ornamented by palisades and formed by rose bushes in full bloom. He had never seen such lovely roses, and their perfume reminded him that he had promised to bring Beauty a rose. So he picked one and was about to gather enough to make a half-dozen bouquets when a most frightful noise made him turn around. He was tremendously alarmed at seeing a horrible beast beside him. It had a trunk resembling an elephant's which it placed on the merchant's neck. "Who gave you permission to gather my roses?" the beast asked with a terrifying voice. "Wasn't it enough that I kindly allowed you to remain in my palace? Instead of feeling grateful, rash man, I find you stealing my flowers! Your insolence shall not go unpunished."

The good man, who was already overwhelmed by the unexpected appearance of this monster, thought he would die of fright at these words and quickly threw away the fatal rose. "Ah, my lord," he said, prostrating himself before him, "have mercy on me! I'm not ungrateful! I was saturated by all kindness, and I did not imagine that such a slight liberty would offend you in any way."

The monster replied angrily, "Hold your tongue, you prating fool. I don't care for your flattery, nor for the titles you bestow on me. I'm not 'my lord.' I am the Beast, and you won't escape the death you deserve."

The merchant was dismayed by such a cruel sentence. Thinking that submission was the only means of saving his life, he responded in a truly touching manner, "The rose I dared to take is for one of my daughters, called Beauty." Then, whether he hoped to escape death, or to induce his enemy to feel sorry for him, he told him all about his misfortunes. He related to him the object of his journey and dwelled on the little present he was bound to give Beauty, adding that it was the only thing she had asked for, while the riches of a king would hardly have sufficed to satisfy the wishes of his other daughters. So, he explained, when the opportunity arose to satisfy Beauty's modest wish, he believed that it was possible to do this without any unpleasant consequences, and now he asked pardon for his involuntary mistake. The Beast reflected for a moment, and then spoke in a milder tone, "I'll pardon you, but only on the condition that you'll give me one of your daughters. Someone must make up for the mistake."

"Just Heaven!" replied the merchant. "How can I keep my word? Could I be so inhuman as to save my own life at the expense of one of my children's? Under what pretext could I bring her here?"

"It's not necessary to have a pretext," interrupted the Beast. "No matter which daughter you bring here, I expect her to come willingly, or I won't have her. Go and see if there's one among them who has enough courage and love for you to sacrifice herself to save your life. You appear to be an honest man. Give me your word of honor to return in a month. If you convince one of them to come back with you, she'll remain here and you'll return home. If you can't do this, swear you'll return here alone, after bidding them farewell forever, for you'll belong to me. Don't imagine," the monster continued, grinding his teeth, "that by merely agreeing to my proposition you'll be saved. I warn you, if you think you can escape me, I'll come searching for you and will destroy you and all your kin, even if you have a hundred thousand men to defend you."

Even though the good man felt certain it would be useless to test the affection of his daughters, he accepted the monster's proposition. He promised to return to him at the designated time and surrender himself. "Beast, you won't have to search for me." After this assurance he thought to take leave of the Beast, whose presence was most distressing to him. The reprieve that he had obtained was not very long, yet he feared the creature might revoke even that. He expressed his desire to depart, but the Beast told him he could not do so till the following day.

"You'll find a horse ready at break of day. He'll carry you home quickly. Adieu. Go and have your supper, and wait for my orders."

More dead than alive, the poor man returned to the salon in which he had feasted so heartily. His supper had been laid before a large fire, and he was induced to sit and enjoy it. However, the delicacy and richness of the dishes no longer had any appeal for him. Overwhelmed by grief, he would not have sat down at all, but he feared that the Beast was hiding somewhere, observing him, and he did not want to arouse his anger by slighting his generosity. In turn he tasted the various dishes as best his troubled heart would permit. At the end of the meal a great noise was heard in the adjoining apartment, and he was sure it was his formidable host. Since he could not manage to avoid his presence, he tried to recover from the alarm this sudden noise had caused him. At that moment the Beast appeared and asked him abruptly if he had eaten a good supper. The good man replied in a modest and timid tone that, thanks to his attention, he had eaten heartily.

"Promise me," the monster replied, "to keep your word as a man of honor by bringing me one of your daughters."

The old man, who was distressed by this conversation, swore he would fulfill what he had promised. He would return in a month alone or with one of his daughters, if he found one who loved him enough.

"I warn you again," the Beast said, "to take care not to deceive her about the sacrifice you must exact from her, or the danger she will incur. Depict my face to her as it is. Let her know what she is about to do. Above all, her decision must be a firm one. There'll be no time for reflection after you've brought her here. There can be no turning back. You'll be lost as well and won't be able to obtain her liberty to return."

Overcome by this speech, the merchant reiterated his promise to comply with all that was prescribed to him. The monster was satisfied with his answer. Thereupon, he ordered him to retire and not rise until he saw the sun and heard a golden bell.

"You'll have breakfast before setting out," he said. "And you may take a rose with you for Beauty. The horse that will carry you will be ready in the courtyard. I reckon on seeing you again in a month if you're an honest man. If you fail to keep your word, I'll pay you a visit."

Not desiring to prolong a conversation already too painful for him, the good man made a low bow to the Beast, who told him again not to worry about the road which he was to take when it came time to return to the Beast's palace. The same horse he would mount the next morning would be found at his gate and would suffice for him and his daughter.

Despite the fact that the old man was not inclined to go to sleep, he did not dare disobey the orders he had received. Obliged to lie down, he did not rise until the sun began to brighten the chamber. After he had his breakfast, he descended into the garden to pluck the rose that the Beast had ordered him to take to Beauty. How many tears this flower caused him to shed! But the fear of bringing new disasters upon himself made him restrain his tears, and without further delay he went in search of the horse that had been promised him. He found a light but warm cloak on the saddle. As soon as the horse felt him on his back, he set off at an incredible speed, and the merchant lost sight of the fatal palace. He now experienced as much joy as he had felt when he had first seen the palace, but with one difference: the delight of leaving the palace was made bitter by the cruel necessity compelling him to return.

"What have I pledged?" he asked while his courser carried him with a swiftness and lightness known only in fairyland. "Shouldn't I give myself up right away and become the victim of this monster who thirsts for the blood of my family? I've managed to prolong my life by a promise that's just as unnatural as it is indecent. How could I think of extending my days at the expense of my daughters? Could I be so barbaric as to take one to him and watch him, no doubt, devour her before my eyes?" But all at once, he interrupted himself and cried, "Miserable wretch that I am, what have I to fear? If I could somehow overcome my fear, I would not have to commit such a cowardly act. She's got to know her fate and consent to it. I see no chance that she'll be inclined to sacrifice herself for an inhuman father, and it would be better if I didn't propose such a thing at all. It's unjust. But even if the affection that they all entertain for me should induce one to commit herself, just the sight of the Beast will destroy her constancy, and I won't be able to complain.

"Ah, you imperious Beast! You've done this on purpose! By setting an impossible condition for escaping your fury for this trite mistake, you've added insult to injury! I can't bear to think about it. I'd rather expose myself to your rage than attempt a useless mode of escape, which my paternal love trembles at employing. Let me retrace the road to this frightful palace, without deigning to purchase the remnant of a life at such a miserably high price. I'll return and terminate my miserable existence this very day!"

At these words he endeavored to retrace his steps, but he found it impossible to turn the bridle of his horse. Therefore, he allowed himself to be carried forward against his will, but he was determined at least not to propose anything to his daughters. Already he saw his house in the distance, and his resolve increased more and more as he approached. "I won't speak to them about the danger that threatens me," he said. "I'll have the pleasure of embracing them once more. I'll give them my last words of advice and beg them to live on good terms with their brothers, whom I shall also implore not to abandon them."

In the midst of this reverie he reached the door of his house. The appearance of his own horse, which had found its way home the previous evening, had alarmed his family. His sons had scattered in the forest and looked for him everywhere. His daughters had been anxious to hear some tidings of him and were at the door in order to obtain the first news. Since he was mounted on a magnificent steed and wrapped in a rich cloak, they did not recognize him. At first they mistook him for a messenger that he had sent, and the rose, which they saw attached to the pommel of the saddle, made them relieved about his welfare.

When their troubled father approached nearer, however, they recognized him and showed their pleasure at seeing him return in good health. But the sadness depicted in his face—his eyes were filled with tears that he vainly tried to restrain—changed their joy to anxiety. All of them rushed forward to inquire about the cause of his troubles. He made no reply, but as he gave Beauty the rose, he remarked, "Here's what you requested, but you and the others will pay dearly for it."

"I was saying this very moment," the eldest daughter exclaimed, "that she'd be the only one whose errand you'd carry out. At this time of the year, a rose must have cost more than what you would have had to pay for us five together, and judging from the looks of it, the rose will be faded before the day is ended. Oh well, it doesn't matter. You were determined to please the fortunate Beauty at any price."

"It's true," the father replied mournfully, "that this rose has cost me a lot, and a lot more than all the ornaments that you wished for. It's not in money, however, and I only wish to Heaven that I could have purchased it with all I am yet worth in the world."

These words aroused the children's curiosity and weakened the resolution he had made not to reveal anything about his adventure. He informed them about his troubles in the city that made his journey unsuccessful and all that had taken place in the palace of the monster. After this revelation, despair took the place of hope and joy.

The daughters, seeing all their plans annihilated by this thunderbolt, uttered dreadful cries. More courageous, the brothers maintained resolutely that they would not allow their father to return to this frightful castle; they would indeed save the world from this horrible Beast, if he had the temerity to search for him. Although moved by their affection, the good man forbade them to resort to violence and told them, "Since I have given my word, I would rather kill myself than fail to keep it."

Nevertheless, they tried to find some means to save his life. Filled with courage and filial affection, the young men offered to replace their father by sending one of them to become the victim of the Beast's wrath. But the monster had said explicitly that he wanted one of the daughters. The brave brothers did all they could to inspire their sisters with the same heroism. However, their jealousy of Beauty was sufficient to create an invincible obstacle.

"It's not just," they said, "that we should perish in such a frightful manner for a mistake that we didn't commit. It would be like making us Beauty's victims. Now, any one of us would be glad to sacrifice herself for her, but duty doesn't demand such a sacrifice in this case. This is all the result of this unfortunate girl's moderation and perpetual preaching! Why couldn't she be like us and ask for a good stock of clothes and jewels? Even if we didn't get them, it didn't cost anything for the asking. We have no reason to reproach ourselves for having indiscreetly exposed the life of our father. If she hadn't sought to show off with a feigned indifference—she's always more favored than we are anyhow—he would have undoubtedly found enough money to content her. Oh no, she had to have her peculiar whim satisfied, and that's what has brought about this disaster for all of us. She's the one who's at fault, and they want us to pay the penalty. We'll not be her dupe. She's brought it on herself, and she must find the solution."

Beauty, whose grief had almost made her faint, suppressed her sobs and said to her sisters, "I'm the cause of this misfortune. It's I alone who must rectify everything. I admit that it would be unjust to allow you to suffer for my mistake. Alas! It was an innocent wish. How could I have foreseen the desire to have a rose in the middle of summer would be punished so cruelly? However, the mistake's been made. It doesn't matter whether I'm innocent or guilty. It's only fair that I should be the one to expiate it, for it can't be imputed to anyone else. I'll risk my life to release my father from his fatal commitment," she continued in a firm tone. "I'll go find the Beast, and I'll be only too happy to die to save the life of the person from whom I received mine. So, you can be quiet now. Don't worry about my changing my mind. I only ask one favor of you during this month, and that's to spare me your reproaches."

So much firmness in a girl of her age surprised them all, and the brothers, who loved her tenderly, were moved by her determination. They paid her a tremendous amount of attention and felt their imminent loss keenly. Far from opposing such a pious and generous purpose—saving their father's life—they shed tears and gave their sister all the praise her noble resolution merited. After all, she was only sixteen and had a long life ahead of her that she was willing to sacrifice to a cruel monster.

The father was the only one who would not consent to his youngest daughter's plan, but the other daughters insolently reproached him, accusing him of caring only for Beauty in spite of the misfortune that she had caused. "You're just sorry it's not one of us who is going to pay for Beauty's imprudence."

This unjust charge forced him to desist. Besides, Beauty made it clear to him that if he would not accept her as his replacement, she would do it in spite of his protests and go to find the Beast alone. Thus she would perish without saving him. "How do we know," she asked, forcing herself to appear calmer than she really felt, "perhaps the dreadful fate that seems to await me conceals another as fortunate as this seems terrible?"

When her sisters heard her speak this way, they smiled maliciously at such a wild idea and such self-delusion. But the old man, finally persuaded by all her reasons, remembered an ancient prediction that this daughter would save his life and be a source of happiness to her entire family. So he stopped opposing Beauty's will, and gradually they began to speak about their departure as something almost insignificant. It was she who set the tone of the conversation, and in the presence of the family she appeared to consider it as a happy event. She did this only to console her father and brothers, however, and not upset them more than necessary. Although her sisters appeared impatient to see her depart and Beauty was dissatisfied with their conduct toward her, she divided among them what little property and jewels she had at her disposal.

They were delighted to have this new proof of her generosity, but this did not soften their hatred toward her. In fact, their hearts jumped for joy when they heard the horse neigh that was sent to carry away their amiable sister. The father and the sons were so upset that they could not restrain their feelings as the fatal moment arrived. They proposed to strangle the horse, but Beauty remained composed and showed them again on this occasion the absurdity of such a plan and the impossibility of carrying it out. After taking leave of her brothers, she embraced her hard-hearted sisters, and it was such a tender farewell that she drew some tears from them, and they believed for the space of a few minutes that they were almost as upset as their brothers.

During these brief yet lingering leave-takings, the good man, pressed by his daughter, had mounted his horse. She placed herself behind him with as much alacrity as one embarking on a pleasant journey. The animal flew instead of galloping, yet its extreme swiftness did not inconvenience her in the least. The strides of this unique horse were so gentle that Beauty felt no more shaken by him than by the breath of a zephyr.

During the journey her father offered her the opportunity a hundred times to dismount, saying he would go on alone to find the Beast, but it was all in vain. "Think about it, my dear child," he said, "there's still time. This monster is more terrible than you can imagine. No matter how firm your resolution may be, I fear it will fail once you see him. Then it will be too late. You'll be lost, and we'll both perish."

"If I were going to seek this terrible beast with the hope of being happy," Beauty replied, "that hope would most likely fail me upon seeing him. But since I'm anticipating a speedy death that I believe is unavoidable, what does it matter whether my destroyer is charming or hideous?"

As they conversed, they were enveloped by night, but the horse galloped just as swiftly in the dark. Suddenly the darkness was exploded by a most unexpected spectacle of all kinds of beautiful fireworks—flowerpots, catherine wheels, suns, bouquets—which dazzled the eyes of our travelers. This remarkable display illuminated the entire forest and caused a gentle heat to be diffused through the air. Such heat was certainly welcome, for the cold in this country was keenly felt at night.

By this charming light the father and daughter saw that they were approaching an avenue of orange trees. As soon as they entered it, the fireworks stopped, but illumination was maintained by the statues, which held burning torches in their hands. In addition, innumerable lamps fronted the palace, symmetrically arranged in forms of true-lover's knots and crowned ciphers consisting of double *LL*'s and double *BB*'s. On entering the court they were received by an artillery salute that, added to the sound of a thousand instruments—some soft, some martial—had a fine effect.

"The Beast must be very hungry indeed," Beauty said half jestingly, "to create such a grand, joyful welcome at the arrival of his prey." Despite her trepidation of an event that, according to all appearances, was about to end her life, she could not help noting the magnificent objects that succeeded each other and afforded her the most beautiful spectacle she had ever seen. Nor could she refrain from saying to her father, "The preparations for my death are more splendid than the bridal pomp of the greatest king of the world."

The horse stopped at the foot of the flight of steps. She dismounted quickly, and as soon as her father had done likewise, he led her through a vestibule to the salon in which he had been so well entertained. There they found a large fire, lighted candles emitting an exquisite aroma, and a table splendidly laid out. The good man, accustomed to the manner in which the Beast regaled his guests, told his daughter, "This meal is intended for us, so help yourself." Beauty did not create any difficulty, convinced as she was that nothing would prevent her death. On the contrary, she imagined that her behavior would make the Beast aware of the repugnance she felt in coming to him. She hoped that her frankness might soften him, and even that her adventure might be less sad than she had at first apprehended. The formidable monster had not shown himself, and the whole palace exuded joy and magnificence. "My arrival has given rise to all this, and it does not seem likely that it has been designed for a funeral ceremony," she thought.

Her hope did not last long, however. The monster made himself heard. A frightful noise caused by his enormous bulk, the terrible clank of his scales, and an awful roaring, announced his arrival. Beauty was seized with terror. Embracing his daughter tightly, the old man began to shriek. As Beauty watched the Beast approach, she started shuddering. Nevertheless, she soon regained control of herself and advanced with a firm step and modest air, greeting him respectfully. This behavior pleased the monster. After examining her, he said to the old man—in a tone that might have

filled the boldest heart with terror, even though it was actually without anger—"Good evening, my good friend." Turning to Beauty, he also said to her, "Good evening, Beauty."

The old man, terrified that at any second something awful was going to happen to his daughter, did not have the strength to reply. But Beauty was not upset and said in a sweet, firm voice, "Good evening, Beast."

"Have you come here voluntarily?" the Beast inquired. "And will you consent to let your father depart without following him?"

Beauty replied that she had no other intention.

"So! And what do you think will become of you after his departure?"

"Whatever you like," she said. "My life is in your hands, and I shall submit myself blindly to the fate that you've determined for me."

"I'm satisfied with your submission," the Beast replied, "and since it appears that they have not brought you here by force, you'll remain here with me. As for you, good man," he said to the merchant, "you'll depart tomorrow at daybreak. The bell will warn you and don't delay after your breakfast. The same horse will carry you back, but when you're with your family again, don't ever dream of revisiting my palace. Remember, you're forbidden to come here. As for you, Beauty," the monster turned and addressed her, "lead your father into the adjoining wardrobe and choose anything that both of you think will give pleasure to your brothers and sisters. You'll find two trunks. Fill them. It's only right that you should send them something sufficiently valuable for them to remember you by."

In spite of the monster's generosity, the approaching departure of her father caused Beauty extreme grief. However, she was determined to obey the Beast, who left them after having said, as he had on entering, "Good night, Beauty. Good night, good man."

When they were alone, the good man embraced his daughter and wept incessantly. The idea of leaving her with the monster was a most cruel trial for him. He regretted ever having brought her to this place. The gates were open, and he wanted to take her away again, but Beauty convinced him of the dangerous consequences of doing such a thing.

Thereupon they entered the wardrobe that had been pointed out to them, only to be surprised at the treasures it contained. It was filled with apparel so superb that a queen could not wish for anything more beautiful or in better taste. The world has never seen a wardrobe as full.

When Beauty had chosen the dresses she thought the most suitable— they were above the present situation of the family, since they corresponded to the riches and generosity of the Beast—she opened a closet whose door was rock crystal and mounted in gold. Although such a magnificent exterior made her think she would find some rare and precious treasures, she discovered such an extraordinary mass of jewels that her eyes could hardly stand their splendor. Acting from a feeling of obedience, Beauty took a huge amount without hesitation. Then she divided it as best she could into the lots she had already made. On opening the last cabinet, one filled with gold coins, though, she changed her mind. "I think," she said to her father, "that it would be better to empty these trunks and to fill them with coins that you can give to your children at your pleasure. This way you won't be obliged to tell your secret to anyone, and you'll be able to keep your wealth without any danger. The advantage that you'd derive from the possession of these jewels, although their value might be more considerable, would be fraught with complications. For one, in order to obtain money, you'd be forced to sell them to people who would only regard you with envy. Your confidence in them might even prove fatal to you. Gold coins, on the other hand, will place you beyond the reach of any such misfortune by giving you the means to acquire land and houses and to purchase rich furniture, ornaments, and precious stones."

The father agreed with her, but since he wanted to bring his daughters some dresses and ornaments, he took those things that he had selected for his own use out of the trunks in order to make room for the gold and presents for his daughters. However, the huge amount of coins that they put into the trunks did not fill them, for they had compartments that stretched at will. So he found room for the jewels he had put aside. In fact, these trunks contained more than he could ever wish for. "All this money will put me in a position to sell my jewels at my own convenience," he said to Beauty. "Following your advice, I'll hide my wealth from the world, and even from my children. If they knew how rich I was, they'd pester me to abandon the country, the only place that has allowed me to find happiness and to live without the perfidy of false friends, with whom the world is filled." Alas, the trunks were so immensely heavy that an elephant would have sunk under their weight, and the hope he had begun to cherish appeared to him a cheat and nothing more. "The Beast is mocking us," he said. "He's pretending to give me wealth and then makes it impossible for me to carry it away."

"Don't be so hasty with your judgment," Beauty replied. "You haven't requested his generosity in any indiscreet way, nor have you appeared to be greedy or opportunistic. Railing at him would be without point. Since the monster has granted you this wealth, I believe he'll certainly find the means of allowing you to enjoy it. We just have to close the trunks and leave them here. I'm sure he knows the best way to send them."

Nothing could have been more prudent than this advice. The good man did as she said and went back into the salon with her. Seated together on the sofa, they found breakfast instantly served. The father ate with more appetite than he had done the preceding night. All that had occurred had alleviated his despair and revived his faith. He would have departed without concern if the Beast had not been so cruel to tell him that he was forbidden to see this palace ever again. The good man was not completely stunned by this order, though, for there is no evil without remedy but death. He thought, "The order may not be irrevocable," and this reflection prepared him to leave his host in a more optimistic mood. On the other hand, Beauty was not so hopeful. She was not at all convinced that her future would be a happy one, and she feared that the rich presents with which the monster bestowed on her family was but the price of her life. He would devour her immediately once he was alone with her. At the least she envisioned a perpetual prison as her fate, and her only companion this frightful Beast.

This reflection plunged her into a profound reverie, but a second stroke of the bell warned them that it was time to separate. They descended into the court, where her father found two horses, one loaded with the two trunks, and the other intended for him. His horse, the same horse that he had ridden before, was covered with a good cloak, and the saddle had two bags attached to it full of provisions. The Beast's care and attention furnished them again with something to talk about, but the horses, neighing and stamping with their hoofs, made them realize that it was time to part. Since the merchant was afraid of irritating the Beast by his delay, he bade his daughter an eternal farewell. Then the two horses set off faster than the wind, and Beauty instantly lost sight of them. She wept as she climbed the stairs to the room designated for her, and for some time she lost herself in sad reflections.

At last she felt overcome with sleep, something that she had been unable to enjoy during the past month. Having nothing better to do, she was about to go to bed when she noticed a serving of chocolate on the table. She took it, half asleep, and her eyes closed immediately. Into a quiet slumber she fell.

During her slumber she dreamed that she was on the bank of a canal a long way off. Both its sides were adorned by two rows of orange trees and flowering myrtles of immense size. Engrossed by her sad situation, she lamented the misfortune that condemned her to spend the rest of her days in this place.

A young man, as handsome as any portrait of Cupid ever made, spoke to her in a voice that touched her heart: "Don't believe, Beauty, that you'll remain as unhappy as you are now. In this place will you receive the reward they've unjustly denied you elsewhere. Let your keen mind help you extricate me from the appearance that disguises me. Once you've seen me, judge whether my company is contemptible and whether I am preferable to a family unworthy of you. Wish, and all your desires will be fulfilled. I love you tenderly. You alone can bestow happiness on me by being happy yourself. Never deny me this. Since you surpass all other women by the qualities of your mind as well as by your beauty, we shall be perfectly happy together."

This charming apparition then knelt at her feet and made her the most flattering promises in the most tender language. He urged her in the warmest terms to listen to his wishes and assured her that she would be entirely her own mistress.

"What can I do?" she said to him eagerly.

"Be gracious," he said. "Don't judge with your eyes and above all, don't abandon me. Release me from the terrible torment that I must endure."

After this first dream, she imagined she was in a magnificent room with a lady whose majestic mien and surprising beauty created a feeling of profound respect in her heart. This lady said to her affectionately, "Charming Beauty, don't regret that you've left your home. A more illustrious fate awaits you. But if you want to attain it, beware of allowing yourself to be swayed by appearances."

Her sleep lasted more than five hours, during which she saw the young man in a hundred different places and under a hundred different circumstances. Sometimes he offered her fine entertainment; sometimes he made her the most tender protestations. How pleasant her sleep was! She would have liked to have prolonged it, but her eyes were opened by the light of day and could not be induced to close again. Beauty believed she had had only a pleasant dream.

A clock struck noon, repeating her own name twelve times, and it obliged her to rise. She then saw a dressing table covered with everything necessary for a lady. After having dressed herself with a feeling of inexplicable pleasure, she went into the salon, where her dinner was served.

When one eats alone, a meal is very soon over. On returning to her room, she threw herself onto the sofa, and the young man about whom she had dreamed arose in her mind again. "I can make you happy" were his words. Probably this horrible Beast, who seems to command everything here, keeps him in prison, she thought. How can I get him out? I was told not to be deceived by appearances, but I understand nothing. How foolish I am! I amuse myself by looking for reasons to explain an illusion formed by sleep and which my waking has destroyed. I really shouldn't pay any attention to it. I should just concern myself with my present fate and seek only those amusements that will prevent me from being overcome by melancholy.

Shortly afterward she began to wander through the numerous apartments of the palace. She was enchanted with them, for she had never seen any place so beautiful. The first room she entered was a large cabinet of mirrors in which she saw herself reflected on all sides. Eventually a bracelet suspended from a girandole caught her eye. She found that it held a miniature portrait of the handsome cavalier she had seen in her sleep. How had she recognized him so quickly? His features were already deeply impressed on her mind and perhaps in her heart. She hastily, joyfully placed the bracelet on her arm without thinking about whether this was the correct thing to do. Then she left this cabinet and went into a gallery full of pictures, where she found the same portrait. Life-size this time, it appeared to regard her with such tender attention that she blushed, as if this picture had been the person himself, or as if he were reading her mind.

Continuing her ramble, she found herself in a salon filled with different kinds of instruments. Since she knew how to play almost all of them, she tried several, preferring the harpsichord to the others because it allowed her to both play and sing. From this salon she entered another gallery similar to the one with the paintings, only it contained an immense library. She liked reading, and ever since her sojourn in the country she had been deprived of this pleasure, for her father had been forced to sell his books. Her great desire for learning could easily be satisfied in this place and would help her ward off the boredom of always being alone. The day passed before she could see everything. As night approached, all the apartments were illuminated by scented candles placed in candelabras either of crystal or of diamonds and rubies.

At the usual hour Beauty found her supper arranged with the same delicacy and neatness as before. No human figure presented itself to her view; her father had told her she would be alone. She was just beginning to get accustomed to this solitude when the Beast made himself heard. Since she had never been alone with him before, she did not know

what would happen during this encounter and even feared that he was coming to devour her. Is it any wonder that she trembled? However, once the Beast arrived—and his approach was by no means furious—her fears dissipated.

"Good evening, Beauty," the monstrous giant said in a rough voice.

She returned his greeting with a calm but somewhat tremulous voice. Among the different questions the monster put to her, he asked how she had amused herself.

"I've spent the day by inspecting your palace," Beauty replied, "but it's so vast that I haven't had time to see all the apartments and splendors it contains."

"Do you think you can get accustomed to living here?"

The girl replied politely that she could easily live in such a beautiful abode. After an hour's conversation, Beauty discovered that the terrible timbre of his voice was due only to the nature of the organ, and that the Beast tended to be more stupid than ferocious. After a while he asked her bluntly if she would marry him. This unexpected request renewed her fears, and she could not prevent herself from uttering a terrible shriek, "Oh! heavens, I'm lost!"

"Not at all," the Beast replied quietly. "But without frightening yourself, reply properly. Tell me succinctly yes or no."

Beauty replied, trembling, "No, Beast."

"Well, since you don't want to, I'll leave you," the docile monster replied. "Good evening, Beauty."

"Good evening, Beast," said the frightened girl, gratified to see him depart.

Extremely relieved by discovering that she did not have to fear any violence, she lay quietly down and went to sleep. Immediately her dear Unknown returned to her dreams and said in a tender tone, "How overjoyed I am to see you once more, dear Beauty! But what pain has your severity caused me! I know that I must expect to be unhappy for a long time." Her vision changed again: the young man appeared to offer her a crown, and sleep depicted him in a hundred different ways. Sometimes he seemed to be at her feet, sometimes abandoning himself to the most excessive delight. Other times he shed a flood of tears, which touched the depths of her soul. This mixture of joy and sadness lasted throughout the night. When she awoke, her imagination was full of this dear object, and she sought out his portrait to compare it once more with her recollections and to see if she hadn't been deceived. She ran to the picture gallery, where she recognized him even more clearly than before. She stood there a long time admiring him! Eventually feeling ashamed of her weakness, she contented herself by looking at the miniature on her arm.

Finally she put an end to these tender reflections and descended into the garden, where the fine weather seemed to invite her to take a stroll. She was enchanted; never had she seen anything in nature so beautiful. The groves were adorned with remarkable statues and innumerable fountains that cooled the air and shot up so high that the eye could scarcely follow them. What surprised her most was that she recognized places she had dreamed about when she had seen the Unknown. Especially when she saw the grand canal lined with orange and myrtle trees, she could think only of her vision, which no longer appeared to be a fiction. She believed she understood the mystery: the Beast kept someone shut up in his palace. She decided to clear up the matter that very evening by questioning the monster, from whom she expected a visit at the usual hour.

She continued to walk the rest of the day as long as her strength permitted without being able to see everything. The apartments she had not been able to inspect the evening before were no less worthy of her admiration. Besides the instruments and rare objects with which she was surrounded, she found plenty to occupy herself in another small sitting room filled with purses, shuttles for knotting, and scissors for cutting. It was equipped for all kinds of ladies' work. Moreover, care had been taken to place a cage filled with rare birds in this boudoir, and when Beauty arrived, they performed a remarkable concert. They also came and perched on her shoulders, each of these loving little creatures vying with one another to see which could nestle closest to her. "What pleasant prisoners," she said. "I'm only annoyed that you're so far from my apartment. I'd like the pleasure of hearing you sing more often."

No sooner had she said this than, to her surprise, she opened a door and found herself in her own room, which she had thought was far from this boudoir, especially since she arrived there only after winding through a labyrinth of apartments. A wall panel opening into the gallery had concealed the nearness of the birds from her, one that was very convenient since it completely shut out all noise when she desired peace and quiet.

Continuing her wandering, Beauty spied another feathered group: parrots of all kinds and colors. As soon as she approached, they all began to chatter. One said, "Good day"; another asked her for some breakfast; one more gallant begged a kiss; several sang opera tunes, others declaimed verses composed by the best authors; all exerted themselves to entertain her. Not only were they as gentle and as affectionate as the inhabitants of the boudoir aviary, but she delighted in finding creatures with which she could talk, for she did not like silence. She put several questions to some of them, who answered her like intelligent creatures, and she selected one among them as the most amusing. The others were envious of this favoritism and complained sadly. So she consoled them by some caresses and gave them permission to pay her a visit whenever they pleased.

Not far from this spot she saw a numerous troop of monkeys, capuchins great and small, some with human faces, others with beards blue, green, black, and crimson. Advancing to meet her at the door of their apartment, they made her low bows, accompanied by countless capers that testified to how highly honored they felt by her visit. To celebrate this occasion, they danced on the tightrope and jumped about with a skill and an agility beyond example.

Beauty was delighted by the monkeys, but disappointed at not finding anything that could enlighten her about the whereabouts of the handsome unknown. Since there seemed to be no hope she could get to the bottom of it, she began to regard her dream simply as an illusion and did her best to drive it from her mind. Her efforts were in vain.

After praising and caressing the monkeys, she said she would like some of them to follow her to keep her company. Instantly two tall young apes in court dress, who appeared to have been waiting only for her orders, advanced and placed themselves ceremoniously beside her. Two sprightly monkeys acted as her pages and picked up her train. A facetious baboon, dressed as a Spanish gentleman of the chamber, presented his neatly gloved paw to her. Accompanied by this singular cortege, Beauty proceeded to the supper table. During her meal the smaller birds whistled an accompaniment to the voices of the parrots in perfect harmony and sang the finest and most fashionable tunes. While the concert was being performed, the monkeys took it upon themselves to wait on Beauty. They decided on their various ranks and duties in an instant, and began waiting on her with all the attention and respect that royal officers pay to queens.

As she rose from the table, another troupe proceeded to entertain her with an extraordinary spectacle. They were an acting company of sorts, who enacted a tragedy in the most extraordinary fashion. These signor monkeys and signora apes, in stage dresses covered with embroidery, pearls, and diamonds, mimed all the actions corresponding to the words of their parts, spoken with great distinctness and proper emphasis by the parrots. They did all this so cleverly, indeed, that if she had not realized that the birds were concealed in the wig of one actor or under the mantle of another she would have believed that these new-fashioned tragedians were speaking themselves. The drama appeared to have been written expressly for the actors, and Beauty was enchanted. At the end of the tragedy one of the performers advanced to pay Beauty a polished compliment, thanking her for the indulgence with which she had listened to them. Then everyone departed, except the monkeys of her household and those selected to keep her company.

After supper the Beast paid her his usual visit, and after the same questions and the same answers, the conversation ended with "Good night, Beauty." The lady apes of the bedchamber undressed their mistress, put her to bed, and made sure to open the window of the aviary so that the birds, who began warbling much more softly than they did during the day, might induce slumber and afford her the pleasure of seeing her charming lover once more.

Several days passed without her feeling bored. Every moment brought new pleasures. In three or four lessons each of the monkeys succeeded in training a parrot to act as an interpreter, and they replied to Beauty's questions with as much promptitude and accuracy as the monkeys themselves had done by gestures. In short, Beauty found nothing to complain about except the obligation of enduring the presence of the Beast every evening. However, she thought, "His visits are short, and it is undoubtedly due to him that I have all the most entertaining amusements imaginable."

Sometimes the monster's gentleness led Beauty to believe that she could ask for an explanation of the person she saw in her dreams. Yet she was quite aware that the Beast was in love with her and feared that such questioning might arouse his jealousy. So she had the prudence to remain silent and did not venture to satisfy her curiosity.

After several tours of the palace she managed to visit every apartment in this enchanted place, but one likes to return to look at things that are rare, unique, and lavish. So Beauty turned her steps toward a large salon that she had seen only once before. This room had four windows in it on each side. Only two were open, letting in a glimmering light. Beauty wanted to have more light, but when she opened another window, she found it looked only into some enclosed space that although large, was obscure. She could distinguish nothing but a distant gleam that appeared to come through a thick crepe curtain. While pondering why this place had been designed thus, she was suddenly dazzled by bright lights. A curtain rose, and Beauty discovered a well-lighted theater. People of both sexes, exceedingly beautiful and handsome, were sitting on the benches and in the boxes. A sweet symphony began immediately, and when it ended, human actors came onstage to perform a fine tragedy. This was followed by a short piece equal in elegance to its predecessor. Beauty was fond of plays, the only pleasure she had missed when she left the city.

She wanted to know what sort of material the drapes of the box next to her were made of, but she found herself prevented from doing so by a glass that separated them. Thus she discovered that she had not seen actual objects but their reflections through a crystal mirror, which conveyed everything that happened on the stage on the finest city in the world. What a master stroke in optics to be able to reflect from such a distance! She remained in her box some time after the play ended in order to watch the fine company leave. Darkness gradually ensued. Delighted by this discovery, which she promised to take advantage of on a frequent basis, she descended into the gardens. "Marvelous events are starting to seem normal to me," she thought. "I'm overjoyed to find they are all performed for my benefit and amusement."

After supper the Beast came as usual to ask her what she had been doing during the day. Beauty gave him an exact account of all her amusements and told him she had been to the theater.

"Do you like it?" the clumsy creature inquired. "Wish for whatever you want, and you shall have it. You're very pretty."

Beauty smiled to herself at the coarse manner in which he paid her compliments, but she did not smile at his usual question, "Will you marry me?" This put an end to her good mood, and she abruptly answered, "No."

His docility during this last encounter, though, did not reassure but alarmed her. "What's to come of all this?" she said to herself. "The fact that he continues to ask me to marry him proves that he persists in loving me, and his generosity confirms it. Even though he does not insist on my compliance, or show any signs of resentment at my refusal, how am I to know that he won't eventually lose patience, and that I won't die as a consequence?" These reflections rendered her so thoughtful that it was almost daylight before she went to bed. The Unknown, who but awaited that moment to appear, reproached her tenderly for her delay. He found her melancholy, lost in thought, and inquired what could have upset her in such a place. She answered that nothing displeased her except the monster whom she saw every evening. She should have become accustomed to him, but he was in love with her, and this love made her fear that some violence might occur. "It's clear from the foolish compliments he pays me that he wants to marry me," Beauty said to her lover. "Would you advise me to consent? Alas! Even if he were as charming as he is frightful, you have made my heart inaccessible to him and to all others. Nor do I blush when I confess that I can love no one but you."

Such a sweet confession could only flatter the Unknown, yet, he replied to her only by saying, "Love him who loves you. Do not be misled by appearances, and release me from prison."

These words, continually repeated without any explanation, caused Beauty tremendous distress. "What do you want me to do?" she said to him. "I'd risk anything to set you free, but my wish is useless so long as you refrain from providing me with the means to act upon it."

The Unknown gave her an answer, but it was so confused that she could not comprehend it. Instead she envisioned a thousand amazing things. She saw the monster on a throne blazing with jewels; he called to her and invited her to sit beside him. A moment afterward the Unknown compelled him suddenly to descend, taking his place. Then the Beast regained the advantage, and the Unknown disappeared in his turn. He spoke to her from behind a black veil, which made his voice a horrifying groan.

Her entire night was spent in this manner. Yet despite the distress it caused her, she felt it ended all too soon, since her awakening deprived her from seeing the object of her affection. After she had finished dressing, various sorts of handiwork, books, and animals occupied her attention until the hour when the play was to begin. She arrived just in time, but she was not in the same theater, but at the opera. As soon as she was seated, the performance commenced. The spectacle was magnificent and the spectators just as grand. The mirrors reflected distinctly the most minute details of the dresses of even the people in the pit. Delighted to see human forms and faces, many of which she recognized as former acquaintances, she would have been even more pleased if when she spoke to them, they could have heard her.

Beauty was more charmed by this day's entertainment than with the previous one, and the rest of the day she spent as she had done since her arrival. The Beast came in the evening, and after his visit she retired as usual. The night resembled former nights, that is, spent in pleasant dreams. When she awoke, she found the same number of domestics ready to wait on her. But after dinner she was occupied in different ways. The day before, on opening another of the windows, she had found herself at the opera. To diversify her amusements, she now opened a third window and discovered all the pleasures of the Fair of St. Germain, which was far more splendid than it is at present. But since it was not time yet for the best company to attend the fair, she could observe and examine everything at her leisure. She saw the rarest items and the most extraordinary products of nature and works of art. The most trivial entertainments were open to her. She found time to watch a puppet show while waiting for more refined performances and was delighted by a splendid comic opera. At the end of the events she saw well-dressed people visiting the tradesmen's shops, and she recognized in the crowd several professional gamblers who flocked to the fair as their workplace. She observed people who lost their money to more clever folks and left the fair with less joy than when they had entered. The smart gamblers, who did not stake their whole fortunes on the turn of a card and who used their skill to profit, could not conceal from Beauty their sleight of hand. She longed to warn the victims of the tricks that led them to be plundered, but being more than a thousand miles away, she could not possibly come to their aid. Everything she heard and saw distinctly without being able to make herself heard or seen by others. The reflections and echoes that conveyed all these sights and sounds to her did not work in reverse. Placed above the air and wind, everything came to her like a thought. Realizing her predicament, Beauty gave up at her vain attempts at contact.

It was past midnight before she thought it time to retire. Her desire for some refreshment might have indicated to her the lateness of the hour, but she had found liqueurs and baskets filled with everything necessary for a meal in her box. Her supper was light and quick because she was in a hurry to go to bed. The Beast observed her impatience and came merely to say good night so that she would have more time to sleep and visit with the Unknown.

The following days passed in a similar fashion. She found an inexhaustible source of fresh entertainment in her windows: the first of the other three windows showed an Italian comedy; the second, the Tuileries, the resort of all the most distinguished and beautiful of both sexes; and the last was far from the least pleasant, for it allowed her to see all the important events taking place in the world. Sometimes it depicted the reception of a grand ambassador, or the marriage of famous people, or an exciting revolution. At this window did she witness the last revolt of the Janizaries to the very end.

No matter what time it was, she was certain to find something at the palace to entertain her. Even the boredom she had initially felt as she listened to the Beast had vanished. Her eyes had become accustomed to his ugliness. She was prepared for his foolish questions, and wanted their conversations to last longer, even though the same four or five sentences, always coarsely uttered and resulting only in yes or no, were not much to her taste.

Since Beauty's slightest wishes were anticipated, she took more care in dressing and grooming herself, even though she was certain that no one could see her. But she owed this attention to herself, and she took pleasure in dressing herself according to the customs of all the various nations on the globe. She could do this quite easily, since her wardrobe furnished her with everything she needed, and every day its contents changed. As she regarded herself in the different dresses, her mirror revealed that she suited the mode of the different countries, and her animals affirmed this fact according to their talents—the monkeys by their actions, the parrots by their language, and the other birds by their songs.

Beauty should have been perfectly happy with such a delightful life, but everything has a way of growing stale. The greatest happiness fades when it is always the same and continually comes from the same source, and when we find ourselves excluded from fear and hope. Beauty felt all of this, and in the midst of her prosperity she began to have thoughts about her family that troubled her. Her happiness could not be perfect as long as she was denied the pleasure of telling her relatives how happy she was. Since she had become more familiar with the Beast, either due to the habit of seeing him or the gentleness she had discovered in his nature, she ventured to ask him a question. She did not take this liberty, however, until she had obtained his promise that he would not be angry with her. The question she put to him was: "Are we the only two persons in this castle?"

"Yes, I swear to you," the Beast replied rather excitedly, "and I guarantee that you and I, the monkeys, and the other animals are the only living creatures in this place." Offering no more than this, the Beast departed more abruptly than usual.

Beauty had asked this question only to ascertain whether her lover might not be confined somewhere in the palace, for she would have liked to see and speak with him. This happiness she would have purchased at the price of her own freedom and all the pleasures that surrounded her. Once convinced that the charming youth existed only in her imagination, though, she began to regard this palace as a prison that one day would be her tomb.

These melancholy thoughts overcame her that night. She dreamed she was weeping on the banks of a great canal when her dear Unknown, alarmed at her sadness, came forth and pressed her hand tenderly between his own. "What's the matter, my beloved Beauty?" he asked. "Who could have offended you, and what can possibly have disturbed your tranquillity? By my love for you, I implore you to explain to me why you're so upset. You won't be refused a thing. You're sole sovereign here, and everything is yours to command. Why are you overwhelmed by sorrow? Is it the sight of the Beast that upsets you? Then you must be rescued from him."

At these words Beauty imagined she saw the Unknown draw a dagger and prepare to plunge it into the throat of the monster, who made no attempt to defend himself. On the contrary, he offered his neck to the blow with calm submission that caused Beauty, even though she had quickly risen to protect the Beast, to fear the Unknown would carry out his purpose before she could prevent him. The instant she realized his intention, she shouted with all her might, "Stop, you barbarian! Don't harm my benefactor. Kill me instead!"

The Unknown, who continued striking at the Beast despite Beauty's shrieks, said to her angrily, "So, you don't love me any longer! How can you take the side of this monster who bars my way to happiness?"

"You're ungrateful," she replied, still struggling with him. "I love you more than my own life and I'd rather lose it than stop loving you. I'd abandon everything that the world can offer without a sigh to follow you into the wildest desert. But these tender feelings cannot dispel my gratitude. I owe everything to the Beast. He anticipates all my wishes. I'm indebted to him for the joy of knowing you, and I'd sooner die than see you harm him in any way."

After several similar struggles the dream visions vanished, and Beauty saw the lady who had appeared to her some nights before. "Courage, Beauty," she said. "Be a model of female generosity. Show yourself to be as

wise as you are charming. Don't hesitate to sacrifice your passion to your duty. Take the true path to happiness, and you'll be blessed, provided you're not misled by deceiving appearances."

When Beauty awoke she pondered this mysterious vision, but it still remained an enigma. During the day her desire to see her father replaced the anxiety caused by these dreams of the monster and the Unknown. Thus, even though she was surrounded by the greatest luxuries, she no longer had her peace at night or contentment by day. The only distraction she could find was in the theater. She attended an Italian comedy, but after the first scene she departed for the opera, which she left almost as quickly. Her melancholy followed her everywhere. She opened each of the six windows many times without finding a minute's respite from her cares. Such days and nights of continual agitation weighed on her and began to have an effect on her appearance and her health.

She took great pains to conceal from the Beast the depths of her sorrow, and even though the monster frequently surprised her with tears in her eyes, he did not press his inquiries when she told him that she was suffering only from a headache. One evening, however, her sobs betrayed her, and she felt unable to pretend any longer. After she admitted everything, the Beast wanted to know what had caused her to become so unhappy that she yearned to see her family. So upset did the Beast become that he sat down and heaved a deep sigh (it was more like a howl that would have frightened anyone to death). "What now, Beauty?" he replied. "Do you want to abandon an unfortunate beast? I can't believe that you have so little gratitude! When have I failed to make you happy? Hasn't the care I've given you allayed your hatred? Unjust, that's what you are. You prefer your father's house and your sisters' envy. You'd rather tend the flocks with them than enjoy the sweet benefits of life here. It's not love for your family but antipathy to me that makes you long to depart."

"No, Beast," Beauty replied timidly, soothingly. "I don't hate you, and I'd regret never being able to see you again. But I can't overcome the desire I have to be with my family. Permit me to go away for two months. I promise you that I'll return with pleasure to spend the rest of my days with you, and I'll never ask another favor."

While she spoke, the Beast stretched himself on the ground with his head thrown back, and only his sorrowful sighs revealed that he was still alive. Finally he answered her: "I can't refuse you anything, even though it may cost me my life. But what does that matter? In the cabinet adjoining your apartment you'll find four chests. Fill them with anything you like for yourself or for your family. If you break your word, you'll repent it, and regret the death of your poor Beast only after it's too late. Return at the end of two months, and you'll still find me alive. You won't need an equipage for your journey back to me. Merely take leave of your family the night before you go to sleep and when you're in bed, turn your ring so that the stone faces inside and say with a firm voice, 'I wish to return to my palace, and behold my Beast again.' Good night. Fear nothing. Sleep in peace. You'll see your father early tomorrow morning. Adieu, Beauty."

As soon as she was alone, she quickly filled the chests with the most beautiful treasures imaginable, and only when she tired of putting things into the chests did they appear to be full. After these preparations she went to bed. The thought of seeing her family so soon kept her awake through most of the night, and sleep stole upon her only toward the hour when she was wont to stir. In her dreams she saw her charming Unknown, but not as he had formerly appeared. Stretched out on a bed of turf, he appeared prey to the keenest sorrow. Touched by seeing him in such a state, Beauty imagined she could alleviate his profound distress by asking him what had caused it. Her lover looked at her full of despair and said, "How can you ask me such a question? You're inhuman. Aren't you aware that your departure means my death?"

"Don't succumb to sorrow, dear Unknown," she replied, "my absence will be brief. I want only to reassure my family concerning the cruel fate they imagine has befallen me. I'll return immediately afterward to this palace, and I won't leave you anymore. How could I abandon a residence that so delights me? Besides, I've given my word to the Beast that I'll return. Then again," she said, prompted by a new thought, "why must this journey separate us at all? Be my escort. I'll postpone my departure another day in order to obtain the Beast's permission. I'm sure he won't refuse me. If you agree to my proposal, we won't have to part. We'll return together. My family will be delighted to see you, and I'll make sure they treat you the way you deserve to be treated."

"I can't accede to your wishes," the Unknown replied, "unless you decide never to return here. It's the only way that I can leave this spot. You must decide what you want. The inhabitants of this palace have no power to compel you to return. Nothing can happen to you except that the Beast will be grieved."

"You're not taking into account," Beauty replied quickly, "that he told me he'd die if I broke my word to him."

"What does that mean to you?" the lover remarked. "Is it really a misfortune if your happiness costs the life of a mere monster? What use has the world for him? Will anything be lost by the destruction of a creature who's the horror of all nature?"

"Ha!" Beauty exclaimed almost angrily, "I want you to know that I'd give my life to save his, and that this monster is only one in form. His heart is humane, and I won't have him punished for a deformity made less hideous by his actions. I refuse to repay his kindness with such loathsome ingratitude."

The Unknown interrupted her, inquiring what she would do if the monster tried to kill him. Whom would she help if it were decreed that one of them must slay the other?

"I love only you," she replied. "But no matter how great my affection, I won't let it weaken my gratitude to the Beast. If I were to find myself placed in such a dire predicament, I'd escape the remorse resulting from such a combat by taking my own life. But why indulge in such dreadful specula-tions? No matter how impossible, the idea freezes my blood. Let's change the subject."

Thereupon, she set an example by professing the most flattering things that a tender woman in love could ever say to her lover. Unrestrained by the rigid customs of society, for slumber left her free to act naturally, she admitted her love to him with a frankness from which she would have shrunk when in full possession of her reason.

Her sleep was long, and when she awoke, she was uncertain the Beast had kept his promise until she heard the sound of a familiar human voice. Quickly pulling back her curtains, she was bewildered to find herself in a strange apartment with furniture not nearly as superb as that in the Beast's palace. This marvel induced her to rise hastily and open the door of her chamber. The next room was just as unfamiliar, but what astonished her even more was finding in it the four chests that she had filled the previous evening. The fact that she and her treasures had been conveyed to this strange place was proof of the power and generosity of the Beast. But where in fact was she?

Finally she heard her father's voice. Rushing out, she flung her arms around his neck. Her appearance astounded her brothers and sisters. They stared at her as if she had come from some other world. Her entire family embraced her with the greatest of delight, but in their hearts her sisters were annoyed at seeing her, for their envy had not disappeared. After many caresses on all sides the good man asked to speak with her privately, not only to learn from her own lips of all the circumstances of such an extraordinary journey, but also to inform her of the state of his own fortune, part of which he had set aside for her. He told her that on the same evening that he had left the Beast's palace, he had reached his own house without feeling the least exhausted. While on the road he had debated how he could best conceal his trunks from his children, hoping they could be carried into a small, secret cabinet adjoining his bedroom, to which he alone had the key. Finally dismissing this notion as impossible as he dismounted at his door, he turned around to find the horse that had been carrying the trunks had run away, and thus he was suddenly spared of the trouble of hiding his treasures. "I assure you," the old man told his daughter, "I wasn't bothered by the loss of the riches, for I hadn't owned them long enough to regret much losing them. The incident did seem to me, though, to be a gloomy omen. I was convinced that the perfidious Beast would act similarly toward you. I feared that the favors he had bestowed on you would not be any more lasting, and this thought upset me greatly. To conceal it, I pretended to be in need of rest, but it was only to abandon myself to my grief without holding anything back, for I regarded your destruction as certain. However, my sorrow was soon lifted by the sight of the trunks that I thought I had lost, and my hopes for your happiness were revived. I found the trunks placed in my cabinet precisely as I had wished them. The keys, which I had forgotten and left behind me on the table in the salon where we had spent the night, were in the locks. This incident provided me with new proof of the Beast's kindness, and his painstaking care overwhelmed me with gladness. No longer did I doubt that your adventure would be to your benefit, and I reproached myself for unjustly suspecting that generous monster and his honor. Therefore, I begged his pardon a hundred times for the abuse that in my distress I had heaped on him in my mind.

"Without informing the children of the extent of my wealth, I contented myself with distributing the presents you had sent them and showing them some moderately costly jewels. Afterward I pretended to have sold them and used the money in sundry ways to improve our income. I've bought this house and have servants to relieve us from the work that we were formerly forced to do of necessity. The children lead a life of leisure, and that's all I desire. Before all of this, ostentation and luxury caused envious people to hate me, and I'd incur their hatred again if I were to live in the style of a very wealthy man. Beauty, many proposals have been made to your sisters, and I'll soon be marrying them off. Your arrival is fortuitous because now I can give them the portion of the wealth you've brought me as you think fit. Then, once they're settled, we'll live, my daughter, with your brothers, for whom your presents were inadequate consolation for your loss. Or if you prefer, we two will live together apart from them."

Touched by her father's kindness and his assurance regarding her brothers' love, Beauty thanked him tenderly for his offer, but thought it wrong to conceal from him that she had not returned to stay. The good man was distressed to learn that he would not have the support of his child in his declining years. "However, I shall not attempt to dissuade you from carrying out any duty that you think necessary."

In turn, Beauty related to him all that had happened to her since they had parted and described to him the pleasant life she led. The good man was captivated by the charming account of his daughter's adventures and blessed the Beast for his kindness. His delight was even greater still when Beauty opened the chests and displayed the immense treasures they contained. She persuaded him that he could freely dispose of the wealth he himself had brought to benefit his daughters, since these last testimonies of the Beast's generosity would provide him with ample means to live agreeably with his sons.

The good man, realizing that this monster's mind was too noble to be lodged in such a hideous body, deemed it his duty to advise his daughter to marry him despite his ugliness, and used the strongest arguments to induce her to do so: "You shouldn't be directed by your eyes alone. You've been continually exhorted to let yourself be guided by gratitude. By following such encouragement you've been guaranteed happiness. It's true that this advice was given to you only in dreams, but these dreams are too significant and too frequent to be attributed to chance. They promise you benefits sufficient to conquer your repugnance. Therefore, the next time the Beast asks you to marry him, I advise you not to refuse. You've admitted that he loves you tenderly. Take the proper steps to make your union with him indissoluble. A pleasant husband is far preferable to one whose only merit is that he's handsome. How many girls are compelled to marry rich brutes—much more brutish than the Beast, who's only one in form and not in his feelings or his actions?"

Beauty admitted that all these arguments were sound, but she found it impossible to consent to marry a horrid monster who appeared to be as stupid as he was gigantic. "How can I accept him for a husband?" she asked her father. "I don't have any feelings for him, and his conversation doesn't have the charm to compensate for his ugliness. What else would hold my attention and relieve such wearisome companionship? I can't simply dismiss his company. I hear nothing beyond five or six questions concerning my health or appetite, followed by a 'Good night, Beauty,' a chorus my parrots know by heart and repeat a hundred times a day. I don't have the strength to endure such a union, and I'd rather perish immediately than to die every day from fright, sorrow, disgust, and weariness. The only thing in his favor is the consideration he demonstrates in confining himself to very short visits that occur only once a day. Is that enough to inspire one with affection?"

The father admitted that his daughter was quite right, but since he had perceived so much civility in the Beast, he could not believe him as stupid as she said. In his opinion, all the order, opulence, and good taste that he had noticed throughout the Beast's palace were not the mark of a fool. In sum, he found him highly worthy of his daughter's consideration.

Beauty might have felt more inclined to listen to the monster, had not her nocturnal lover's appearance thrown an obstacle in the way. The comparison she drew between these two admirers could not help but be unfavorable to the Beast. The old man himself was fully aware of the vast distinction to be made between them, but despite this he used every argument he could to overcome her repugnance. "Remember the advice of the lady who warned you not to be swayed by appearances. Her speeches seem to imply that the young Unknown will only make you miserable."

Talking reasonably about love is easier than conquering it. Beauty did not have the strength to listen to the repeated requests of her father, and he left her without persuading her. It was already well into the night, and although Beauty was delighted to see her father once more, she was glad to be left alone so that she could rest. Her heavy eyelids held out the hope that her slumber would soon allow her to behold her beloved Unknown again. She was eager to enjoy this innocent pleasure, and her quickly beating pulse testified to the joy of her gentle heart. But even though her excited imagination projected scenes in which she had usually held sweet conversations with that dear Unknown, it did not have sufficient power to conjure up his form as she so ardently desired. She awoke several times, but on falling asleep again there were no cupids fluttering around her couch. In a word, instead of a night filled with the sweet dreams she had expected in the arms of sleep, she had an interminably long one filled with endless anxiety. She had never known anything like it in the Beast's palace, and she had a mingled feeling of relief and impatience when daybreak came at last.

Her father, who had become a wealthy man thanks to the Beast's generosity, had left his country house in order to more easily arrange the marriages of his daughters, and now resided in a very large city. Here he had gained new friends, or rather, new acquaintances, because of his wealth, and the news of his youngest daughter's return soon spread to this circle of acquaintances. Everybody was eager to meet her, and when they did, they were all as much charmed by her intellect as by her beauty. The peaceful days she had spent in her isolated palace, the innocent pleasures with which gentle slumber had invariably provided her, the thousand amusements that prevented boredom from penetrating her heart—in short, all the care and attention of the monster had combined to make her even more beautiful and charming than she had been when her father had parted from her.

She was admired by all who saw her. Her sisters' suitors did not deign to excuse their infidelity by even the slightest pretext, but simply fell in love with her and neglected their lady companions. Beauty, far from responding to the mounting attention she received from this crowd of admirers, did all she could to discourage them and induce them to return to their former mistresses. Despite all her caution, however, she did not escape the jealousy of her sisters.

Far from concealing their feelings, the inconstant lovers invented new entertainments every day with the purpose of courting her, and even beseeched her to bestow the prize in the games that took place in her honor. Though Beauty was not blind to the mortification she was causing her sisters, she was unwilling to reject their ardent and flattering requests outright, and she satisfied them all by declaring that she would alternate with her sisters in presenting the prize to the winner. Whereas she selected a flower or some such trifle, she left it up to her elder sisters, when their turn came, to bestow jewels, diamond crowns, costly weapons, or superb bracelets (presents that her generous hand had provided them, but she took not the slightest credit for this). In need of nothing thanks to the treasures lavished on her by the monster, she divided all the most rare and elegant articles she had brought among her sisters. Since she bestowed nothing but trifles on the young men and left her sisters the pleasure of giving more generous prizes, she reckoned that she would secure for her sisters the love as well as the gratitude of the youthful combatants. But these lovers sought only to gain her heart, and the simplest gift from her hand was more precious to them than all the marvelous treasures heaped upon them by her siblings.

Though the entertainment at her family's house was vastly inferior to that which she had enjoyed in the Beast's palace, she was sufficiently amused so that time did not hang heavily on her hands. Yet despite the gratification of seeing her beloved father, despite the pleasure of being with her brothers, who in a hundred ways proved the extent of their affection, and despite the amusing conversations with her sisters, whom she loved though they did not love her in return, she missed her pleasant dreams. To her great sorrow her Unknown did not come to speak to her tenderly while she slept under her father's roof. Not did the attention shown to her by the former admirers of her sisters compensate for the loss of that pleasurable illusion. Even if she had been the kind of young woman who feels flattered by such conquests, she still would have been able to perceive a vast difference between their attentions and those of the Beast and her charming Unknown.

Though their advances were received by her with the greatest indifference, Beauty realized that her coolness had no effect on them. They were obstinately bent on competing with one another to prove the intensity of their passion. Consequently, she thought it her duty to make them clearly understand they were wasting their time. The first she tried to edify was one who had courted her eldest sister. She told him that she had returned only to attend the marriage of her sisters, particularly that of her eldest sister, and that she was about to urge her father to settle everything immediately. Instead Beauty found that she faced a man who no longer saw any charms in her sister. He sighed only for Beauty, and her coldness and disdain, her threat to depart before the expiration of the two months—in short, nothing discouraged him. Extremely disturbed at having failed at attaining her goal, Beauty held a similar conversation with the others and was mortified to find them equally infatuated. To complete her distress, her unjust sisters, who regarded her as a rival, developed an unconcealed hatred toward her. While Beauty was deploring the great effect of her charms, she suffered another setback when she learned that her new admirers believed each to be the cause of the other's rejection and were bent on fighting among themselves to settle the issues.

All these annoying incidents made her decide to return sooner than she had planned. Her father and brothers did all they could to detain her, but she remained firm in her resolution. Neither the tears of her father nor the pleas of her brothers could prevail on her to change her mind. The most they could obtain from her was a promise to defer her departure for as long as she could.

The two-month deadline had come and gone. Each morning she was determined to bid adieu to her family, but did not have the heart to say farewell when night arrived. Torn between affection and gratitude, she could not lean to the one without doing injustice to the other. In the midst of her predicament she needed nothing less than a dream to help her decide. She imagined herself at the Beast's palace, where she was walking down a secluded path that ended in a thicket full of brambles. This thicket concealed the entrance to a cave, and soon she heard terrible groans issuing from it. She recognized the voice of the Beast and ran to his assistance. The monster appeared in her dream stretched along the ground in the throes of death, and he reproached her for causing his demise. "You've repaid my affection with the basest ingratitude!" She then saw the lady who had appeared to her before in her sleep. In a severe tone she said that it would be her destruction if she hesitated any longer to fulfill her commitment. "You have given your word to the Beast you would return in two months, and that time has expired. The delay of another day will be fatal to the Beast. The trouble you are creating in your father's house and the hatred of your sisters ought to increase your desire to return to the Beast's palace, where everything is arranged to delight you."

Terrified by this dream that warned of causing the Beast's death, Beauty awoke with a start and immediately went to tell her family that she could no longer delay her departure. This news produced diverse responses. Her father's tears bespoke his feelings quite clearly. Her brothers protested and claimed that they would not allow her to leave. Her lovers swore in despair that they would not allow the house to be robbed of its brightest jewel. Her sisters, however, far from being distressed by her departure, were loud in their praise of her sense of honor. They pretended to possess the same virtue themselves and had the audacity to assure her that if they had pledged their word to the Beast as she had done, they would not have allowed his ugliness to have interfered with their duty. They would have long since been on their road back to the marvelous palace. In this way did they conceal the cruel jealousy that rankled in their hearts. Since Beauty was charmed by their apparent generosity, she thought only of convincing her brothers and her lovers about her obligation to leave them. However, her brothers loved her too much to consent to her going, and her lovers were too infatuated to listen to reason. All of them were unaware of the way in which Beauty had arrived at her father's house, and they were certain that the horse that had first conveyed her to the Beast's palace would be sent to take her back again. So they decided among themselves to prevent it.

Her sisters concealed their joy by pretending sorrow as the hour approached for Beauty's departure, but they were really frightened to death lest anything delay her. Yet Beauty was firm in her resolution and knew when duty called. Having no more time to lose if she was to help the Beast, her benefactor, stay alive, she took leave of her family at nightfall and said farewell to all those interested in her destiny. She assured them, "Whatever steps you take to try to prevent my departure, I shall nevertheless be in the Beast's palace the next morning before you are stirring. All your schemes are fruitless, for I have decided to return to the enchanted palace."

When she went to bed, she did not forget to turn her ring. Sleeping soundly, she did not wake until the clock in her chamber struck noon and chimed her name to music. On hearing that sound, she knew that her wishes had been fulfilled. The moment she stirred, her couch was surrounded by all her animals, who had been eagerly waiting to serve her, and all expressed their happiness at her return and their sorrow due to her long absence.

This day seemed longer to her than any she had previously spent in that palace, not so much because she missed those she had left but because she was eager to see the Beast again and apologize for her conduct. She was also motivated by another desire: she longed to hold another one of those sweet conversations with her dear Unknown in her sleep. Alternately the Beast and the Unknown were the subjects of her reflections. One moment she reproached herself for not returning the affection of a lover who in the form of a monster displayed a noble mind; the next she deplored having set her heart on a vision who had no existence except in her dreams. As she went back and forth, she began to doubt whether she really should prefer the imaginary devotion of a phantom to the real affection of the Beast. The very dreams in which the Unknown appeared to her had been invariably accompanied by warnings not to trust her eyes, and now she feared it was but an idle illusion conceived from the vapors of the brain and destroyed by the light of day.

So she remained undecided: she loved the Unknown, but did not want to displease the Beast. Seeking relief from her thoughts, she decided to distract herself by going to a French comedy, which she found exceedingly poor. Shutting the window abruptly, she hoped she would be better amused at the opera, but she thought the music miserable. The Italians were equally unable to entertain her, for their commedia del l'arte seemed to her to lack cleverness, wit, and action. Wherever she went, she encountered only that which seemed distasteful and wearisome. The gardens had no appeal for her. Though her retinue tried to entertain her, the monkeys failed to amuse her by their frisking, and the parrots and other birds had no success with their chattering and singing.

Impatient for the Beast's visit, she expected to hear the noise of his approach at any second, but he did not appear at the appointed hour. Alarmed, almost angry at his delay, she tried in vain to account for his absence. Torn between hope and fear, her mind was awhirl and her heart was plagued by melancholy.

She descended into the gardens, determined not to reenter the palace until she had found the Beast, but she could not find a trace of him anywhere. She called him, and the only response was her echo. After more than three hours of this fruitless searching, she was overcome by fatigue and sank onto a garden bench. She thought, "The Beast is either dead or has abandoned this place." She imagined herself alone in that palace without the hope of ever leaving it. "I miss my conversations with the Beast, even though they were not entertaining," she realized, amazed to discover she had so much feeling for him. She blamed herself for not having married him, and thinking she had caused his death (for she feared her long absence had brought it about), she heaped the keenest, most bitter reproaches on herself.

In the midst of her sad reflections she realized that she was seated on the very path of which she had dreamed during the last night she had spent under her father's roof. She had seen the Beast expiring in some strange cave. Convinced that she had not been conducted to this spot by chance, she stood and hurried toward the thicket, which, she found, was not impenetrable, and she discovered an opening that seemed the one she had seen in her dream. Since the moon gave off but a feeble light, her monkeys immediately appeared with a sufficient number of torches to cast light into the cave and reveal the Beast stretched on the earth asleep, or so she thought. Far from being alarmed at the sight of him, Beauty was delighted. Approaching him boldly, she placed her hand upon his head and called to him several times. She found him cold and motionless. Certain he was dead, she uttered the most mournful shrieks and exclaimed the most touching endearments in the world.

Despite her certainty he was dead, she still made every effort to revive him. Placing her hand on his heart, she felt to her great joy that it still beat. Without hesitating, Beauty ran out of the cave to the basin of a fountain, where she cupped her hands to carry water. With it she rushed back and sprinkled him. But since she could bring only a little at a time and spilt some of it on the way, her help would have been meager had not the monkey courtiers flown to the palace and returned speedily with a vase for water as well as the proper restoratives. She made him smell and swallow them, and they produced such an excellent effect that he soon began to stir. She encouraged him with her voice and caressed him as he recovered.

"You've caused me a good deal of worry," she told him kindly. "I didn't know how much I loved you, but the fear of losing you has proved to me that I've been attached to you by stronger ties than gratitude. I swear to you that I had resolved in my mind to kill myself if I had failed in reviving you."

At these tender words the Beast felt perfectly recovered and replied in a still feeble voice, "It's very kind of you, Beauty, to love such an ugly monster, but you've done well. I love you better than my life. I thought you'd never return; and the grief has nearly killed me. Your love has now restored my desire to live. You had better retire, and rest assured that you'll soon be happy, since your good heart makes you worthy of such happiness."

Never before had Beauty heard such a lengthy speech from the Beast. Though it was not overly eloquent, its gentleness and sincerity pleased her. She had expected to be scolded, or at least to have been reproached, and from this moment on she had a better opinion of his character. She no longer thought he was so stupid and even considered his short answers proof of his prudence. More kindly disposed toward him than ever, she retired to her apartment, her mind occupied with the most gratifying thoughts.

Beauty was extremely exhausted, and her heavy eyelids promised her the refreshment of sweet sleep. As soon as she lay her head on her pillow, she fell fast asleep and her dear Unknown appeared to her instantly. What tender words he uttered to express his pleasure at seeing her again! He assured her that she would be happy and that she needed only follow the impulse of her good heart. Beauty asked him if her happiness would derive from her marriage with the Beast. The Unknown replied that this was the only means of obtaining it. She was somewhat annoyed by this, thinking it even extraordinary that her lover would advise her to make his rival happy.

After this first dream she thought she saw the Beast dead at her feet. An instant afterward the Unknown reappeared and disappeared again just as quickly, giving way to the Beast. But what she observed most distinctly was the lady, who said to her, "I'm pleased with you. Continue to follow the dictates of reason, and don't worry about a thing. I'll assume the task of making you happy."

Beauty professed a partiality for the Unknown and a repugnance for the monster, whom she could not consider lovable. The Lady smiled at her objections and advised her not to worry about her affection for the Unknown because the emotions she felt were not incompatible with the decision she had made to do her duty. "Follow your inclinations without resisting them, for your happiness will be attained by your marriage to the Beast."

This dream, which ended only with her sleep, provided her with an inexhaustible source of reflections. As in those that had preceded it, this vision had had more coherence than is usually found in dreams, and therefore she decided to consent to this strange union. Still, the image of the Unknown rose constantly to trouble her. It was the sole obstacle, but not a slight one. Uncertain of the course she ought to take, she attended the opera, but without solving her dilemma. At the end of the performance she sat down to supper, and only when the Beast arrived was she able to make up her mind.

Far from reproaching her for her overlong absence, the monster acted as if the pleasure of seeing her had made him forget his past misery. On entering Beauty's apartment, he seemed to have no other concern but of ascertaining if she had amused herself, if she had been well received, and if her health had been good. Answering these questions, she added politely, "I have paid dearly for all the pleasures your care enabled me to enjoy by the cruel pain I suffered on my return on finding you in such a sad state."

The Beast thanked her brusquely, and then as he was about to take his leave, he asked her as usual if she would marry him.

Beauty was silent for several moments, but at last she said to him, trembling, "Yes, Beast, I'd like to very much. If you'll pledge me your faith, I'll give you mine."

"I do," the Beast replied, "and I promise never to have any wife but you."

"Then I accept you for my husband," Beauty responded, "and swear to be a tender and faithful wife to you."

No sooner had she uttered these words than she heard an immense explosion. It was clearly a signal of rejoicing, for when she looked out her windows, the sky was all ablaze with the light of twenty thousand fireworks, which continued rising for three hours. They formed true-lovers' knots and beneath them Beauty's initials appeared on elegant shields in well-defined letters, "Long live Beauty and her husband."

After this display had ended, the Beast took his leave, and Beauty retired to rest. No sooner was she asleep than her dear Unknown paid her his customary visit. "How deeply I'm obliged to you, charming Beauty," he said. "You've released me from the frightful prison in which I've suffered for so long. Your marriage with the Beast will restore a king to his subjects, a son to his mother, and life to a whole kingdom. We shall all be happy."

Upon hearing these words, Beauty was bitterly annoyed, and she was further disturbed when she noticed that the Unknown, far from showing the despair her engagement should have caused him, gazed at her with sparkling eyes of joy. She was about to express her discontent to him when the lady, in her turn, appeared in her dream.

"There you are, victorious!" she said. "We owe everything to you, Beauty. You've allowed gratitude to triumph over every other feeling. No one but you would have had the courage to keep her word at the expense of her desires, or would have risked her life to have saved that of her father. Thanks to your virtue, you'll enjoy more happiness than anyone has ever known. You know very little at present, but the rising sun will reveal more."

When the lady had disappeared, Beauty saw the unknown youth again, but this time he was stretched along the ground as in death. She spent the entire night having such dreams, but they had become familiar to her and did not prevent her from sleeping long and soundly. It was broad daylight when she awoke. Sunlight streamed into her apartment with more radiance than usual, for her monkeys had not closed the shutters. Since she thought the sight that met her eyes was only a continuation of her dreams, her joy and surprise were unparalleled when she discovered that her beloved Unknown lay beside her. Fast asleep, he looked a thousand times handsomer than he had looked in her dreams. To assure herself that it was truly he, she sprang from the bed and snatched up the miniature she usually wore on her arm from her dressing table. She was not mistaken. She spoke to him in the hope of waking him from the trance into which he seemed to have been thrown by some wonderful power. Since her voice did not arouse him, she shook him by the arm. This effort was just as ineffectual and served only to convince her that he was under an enchanted spell, and that she must wait until the end of the charm. "For it is reasonable to suppose," she told herself, "that it has a limited duration."

How delighted she was to find herself engaged to him, for it was he alone who had made her hesitate. How delighted she was to find that she had done out of duty that which she wanted to do out of inclination. She no longer doubted the promise of happiness that had been made to her in her dreams. She now knew that the lady had told her the truth: her love for the Unknown was not incompatible with the affection she entertained for the Beast. They were one and the same person.

In the meantime, however, her husband did not awake. After a light repast she endeavored to spend the time in her usual occupations, but they seemed to her insipid. Undecided as to whether she should leave her apartments or just to sit idly by, she picked up some music and began to sing. When her birds heard her, they joined her in a concert. It was more charming to her than she expected, since it might be interrupted any moment by the awakening of her husband. Moreover, she hoped she could dissolve the spell by the harmony of her voice.

The spell was indeed soon broken, but not by the means she imagined. She heard first the sound of a chariot rolling beneath her windows and then several voices approaching. At that moment the monkey who served as captain of the guard announced the arrival of two ladies, interpreted via the beak of his parrot. From her windows Beauty eyed the chariot that brought them. It was a wholly strange kind of a chariot, unsurpassed in its beauty. Four white stags with horns and hoofs of gold and wearing superb harnesses drew this equipage, and its unique appearance increased Beauty's desire to become acquainted with the owners.

As the voices drew closer, she realized that the ladies had nearly reached the antechamber, and she considered it proper to advance and receive them. One of the ladies she recognized as the lady she had seen in her dreams. The other was just as beautiful, and her noble, distinguished bearing indicated clearly that she was an illustrious personage. She was no longer in the bloom of youth, but her air was so majestic that Beauty was uncertain which of the two strangers she ought to address first. She was still pondering this dilemma when the lady of her dreams, who appeared to have precedence over the other, turned to her companion and said, "Well, Queen, what do you think of this beautiful girl? To her you're indebted for your son's coming back to life, for you must admit that the deplorable circumstances under which he existed could not be called living. Without her you would never have seen the prince again. He would have had to remain in the horrible shape in which he had been transformed if he hadn't found the one and only in the world whose virtue and courage matched her beauty. I think you will be pleased to learn that the son she has restored to you is her husband. They love each other, and they only need your consent to make their happiness complete. Will you refuse to bestow it on them?"

On hearing this, the queen embraced Beauty affectionately and exclaimed, "Far from refusing my consent, their union will provide me with the greatest felicity! Charming and virtuous child, to whom I owe so much, tell me who you are. Name the sovereigns so blessed as to have given birth to such a perfect princess?"

"Madam," Beauty replied modestly, "it's long since I've had a mother, and my father is a merchant more distinguished in the world for his honesty and misfortunes than for his birth."

The astonished queen recoiled a pace or two on hearing this frank declaration and exclaimed, "What? You're only a merchant's daughter? Ah, great fairy!" She cast a mortified look at her companion. She said nothing further, but her manner sufficiently expressed her thoughts, and her disappointment was visible in her eyes.

"You appear to be dissatisfied with my choice," the fairy said haughtily. "You regard the status of this young person with contempt, and yet she was the only creature in the world capable of carrying out my project of making your son happy."

"I'm deeply grateful to her for what she's done," the queen replied, "but, my powerful spirit, I cannot refrain from pointing out to you the incongruity of mixing the noble blood that runs in my son's veins with that of this person whose ancestry is obscure. I confess I'm quite discouraged by the prospects of the prince's future happiness if it must be purchased by an alliance so degrading to us and so unworthy of him. Can you not find a maiden somewhere in the world whose birth is equal to her virtue? I know many excellent princesses by name. Why can't I be permitted to hope that he'll be allowed to marry one of those?"

Just then the handsome Unknown appeared. The arrival of his mother and the fairy had aroused him, and the sound of their voices was more effective than all of Beauty's efforts because this was the nature of the spell. The queen took him in her arms for a long time without saying a word. She had found her son again, and his fine qualities made him worthy of all her affection. What joy for the prince to see himself released not only from his horrible form but his stupidity as well. This had caused him especial pain because it had been imposed artificially and had in no way obscured his reason.

After expressing his filial love to his mother, the prince paused to pay his thanks to the fairy, prompted by duty and gratitude. Though he did so most respectfully, he was as brief as possible in order to turn his attention toward Beauty. That he had regained his natural form thanks to the object of his affection made her even more precious to him. Having already expressed his feelings by tender glances, he was about to confirm in the most touching speech what his eyes had spoken when the fairy stopped him, requesting that he be the judge between her and his mother. "Your mother," she said, "condemns the engagement you have entered into with Beauty. She believes that Beauty's birth is too much beneath yours. For my part, I think that her virtues make up for that inequality. It's up to you, Prince, to declare your feelings. And so you won't feel any restraint in telling us your true sentiments, you should know that you have full freedom of choice. Although you've pledged your word to this charming person, I vow that Beauty will release you from your promise without the least hesitation, although it is through her kindness that you've regained your natural form. And I also assure you that her generosity will make her so impartial that she'll give you the freedom to offer your hand to any person the queen would like to propose. —What do you say, Beauty?" the fairy asked, turning toward her. "Have I been mistaken in interpreting your feelings thus? Would you take a husband who'd marry you with regrets?"

"Certainly not, madam," replied Beauty. "I'd freely renounce the honor of being his wife. When I accepted him, I believed I was taking pity on a creature below humanity. I became engaged to him only because of my affection for him, and ambition played no role in my thoughts. Therefore, great fairy, I implore you not to demand a sacrifice from the queen, whom I cannot blame, for it is in truth a delicate matter."

"Well, Queen, what do you say to that?" the fairy inquired with disdainful displeasure. "Do you consider that princesses, who are so due to the caprice of fortune, deserve the high rank they've been given more than this young maiden? For my part, I think she should not be discriminated against because of her birth, from which she has elevated herself through her behavior."

The queen replied with no little embarrassment, "Beauty is incomparable! Her merit is infinite. Nothing can surpass it. But, madam, can't we find some other way of rewarding her? Do I have to sacrifice the hand of my son?" Turning to Beauty, she continued, "Yes, I owe you more than I can pay. Therefore, I shall set no limits on whatever you desire. Ask boldly and I'll grant you anything with that sole exception. The difference won't seem so great to you. Choose a husband from among the nobles of my court. No matter how high in rank, he'll have good reason to bless his good fortune, and for your sake, I'll place him so near the throne that your position will be scarcely less enviable."

"I thank you, madam," Beauty replied, "but I require no reward. I'm more than repaid by the pleasure of having broken a spell that had deprived a great prince of his mother and of his kingdom. My happiness would have been perfect if I had done this service for my own sovereign. All I desire is that the fairy restore my father to me."

The prince, whom the fairy had commanded to be silent during this conversation, could no longer restrain himself. Flinging himself at the feet of the fairy and his mother, he implored them in the strongest terms not to plunge him anew into misery by sending Beauty away and depriving him of the happiness of being her husband.

Upon hearing this plea, Beauty gazed at him with an air both of tenderness and noble pride. "Prince," she said, "I can't conceal my affection for you. Your disenchantment is a proof of it, and it would be useless to try to disguise my feelings. Why should I pretend? We must disavow evil impulses, but mine are perfectly innocent and are authorized by the generous fairy, to whom we are both so much indebted. But if I could decide to sacrifice my feelings to my duty to save the Beast, you must realize that I won't falter now that it's no longer the interest of the monster that's at stake, but your own. I'm well satisfied just to know your true identity. I'm willing to renounce the glory of being your wife. I'll go so far as to say that even if your mother yields to your pleas and grants you what you ask, it would not alter the case in my own mind. I repeat, I ask no favor but that of being allowed to return to the bosom of my family, where I'll cherish the memory of your goodness and affection forever."

"Generous fairy!" the prince exclaimed, clasping his hands in supplication, "for mercy's sake, don't allow Beauty to depart! I'd rather you make me into the monster again because then I'll be her husband. She pledged her word to the Beast, and I prefer that happiness to my restored self if I must purchase it so dearly!"

The fairy gave no answer, but gazed steadily at the queen, who was moved by such true affection, but whose pride remained unshaken. Her son's despair affected her, yet how could she not forget that Beauty was a merchant's daughter and nothing more? Nevertheless, she feared the fairy's silence, which sufficiently demonstrated her indignation. In her extreme confusion she was speechless, fearing to end this fateful conversation with a decision that would offend the protective spirit. When no one spoke for some minutes, the fairy broke the silence. Casting an affectionate eye at the lovers, she said, "I find you worthy of each other. It would be a crime to separate two such excellent people, and I promise you, you won't be separated. Believe me, I have sufficient power to keep my promise."

The queen shuddered at these words and would have protested, but the fairy anticipated her by stating, "As for you, Queen, the little value you set upon virtue unadorned by the vain titles that you alone respect would be cause enough for me to heap the bitterest reproaches on you. But I'm going to pardon your fault that comes from pride of birth, and I'll take no other vengeance than undermining your prejudices. Later on you'll thank me for doing this."

Hearing this, Beauty embraced the fairy's knees and exclaimed, "Oh, please don't expose me to the misery of being told all my life that I'm unworthy of the rank to which your generous heart would elevate me. Pray consider that this prince, who now believes that his happiness would be made complete if he were to marry me, may shortly share the opinion of his mother."

"No, no, Beauty, you have nothing to fear," the fairy replied. "The evils you anticipate cannot happen. I know a sure way of protecting you from them, and if the prince should become capable of despising you after marriage, he must find some other reason than the inequality of your rank. Your birth is not inferior to his own. In fact, the advantage is considerably on your side, for the truth is," she said sternly to the queen, "that you're looking at your niece, and what should make her even more worthy of your respect is that she's mine as well! She's the daughter of my sister, who, unlike you, wasn't a slave to rank, which has no luster without virtue. Since she knew how to estimate true worth, she did your brother, the King of the Fortunate Island, the honor of marrying him. I preserved this fair fruit of their union from the fury of a fairy who wanted to be her stepmother. From the moment of her birth I destined her to become the wife of your son. I wished to keep from you the results of my good service to give you an opportunity of showing your confidence in me, for I had reason to believe that it seemed greater than it was. You might have trusted me to watch over the destiny of the prince. I have given you proof enough of my interest in him, and you needn't have worried that I'd expose him or you to disgrace. I feel convinced, madam," she continued with a smile that still held a trace of bitterness, "that you won't object to honoring us with your consent."

Both astonished and mortified, the queen did not know what to answer. The only way to atone for her fault was to confess it frankly and show sincere repentance. "I'm guilty, generous fairy," she said. "Your good deeds should have made me realize that you would not allow my son to form an alliance unworthy of him. But please pardon the prejudices of my rank, which urged that royal blood could not marry one of humbler birth without degradation. I admit that I deserve to be punished by your giving Beauty to a mother-in-law more worthy of her, but I know you look too kindly on my son to make him the victim of my error. As to you, dear Beauty," she continued, embracing her tenderly, "you musn't resent my opposition. It was prompted by my desire to have my son marry my niece, whom the fairy has often assured me was living despite all appearances to the contrary. She had drawn such a charming portrait of her that, without knowing you were she, I loved you enough to risk offending the fairy in order to preserve the throne and my son's heart for you."

Once more she caressed Beauty, and the maiden received these signs of affection with respect. The prince, for his part, was enraptured by this pleasant news, though he expressed his delight in looks alone.

"See how we're all satisfied!" the fairy said. "And now, to terminate this happy adventure we only need the consent of the prince's royal father. But we'll soon see him here."

Beauty requested her permission to allow the person who had brought her up, and whom she had regarded as her father until now, to witness her happiness.

"I admire such consideration," the fairy said. "It's worthy of a beautiful soul, and since you desire it, I'll make it my business to inform him."

She then took the queen by the hand and led her away under the pretext of showing her the enchanted palace. In fact, though, she wished to leave the newly engaged couple alone to talk for the first time without the restraint of illusion. And when they would have followed, she forbade them.

The happiness in store for them filled both lovers with equal delight, for they had not the slightest doubt of the other's affection. Their conversation was confused and unconnected, and they mutually pledged their troth a hundred times. These were more convincing proofs of love than the most eloquent speeches. After having exhausted all that love prompts to those whose hearts have truly been touched, Beauty asked her lover to tell her not only about the misfortune that caused him to be so cruelly transformed into a beast, but also about all the events of his life before that shocking metamorphosis. Although the prince had regained his natural form, his eagerness to obey her had not abated, and without further ado, he began his story:

The king, my father, died before I was born, and the queen would never have been consoled for his loss if her concern for her child had not triumphed over her sorrow. My birth brought her extreme delight. The sweet task of rearing the fruit of the affection of such a dearly beloved husband was destined to dissipate her mourning. Wholly focused on looking after my education and well-being, she was aided by a fairy of her acquaintance, who showed the greatest desire to keep me safe from all kinds of accidents. As greatly as the queen was obliged to her, she was not, however, pleased when the fairy requested that she place me entirely in her hands. This fairy did not have the best of reputations: she was said to be capricious in her favors, and she was feared more than loved. Even if my mother had been wholly convinced of the goodness of her nature, she would never have agreed to part with me.

Fearing the fatal consequences of this vindictive fairy's resentment, however, she took the advice of several wise men and did not flatly refuse. She thought if she voluntarily trusted in the fairy's care, there would be no reason to suppose she would do me any harm, for experience had shown that she took pleasure in hurting those only who she thought had offended her. The queen realized this full well, but was reluctant to forgo the pleasure of looking upon me with a mother's eyes, which continually discovered charms I owed solely to her.

She was still undecided when a powerful neighbor invaded my kingdom with a formidable army, imagining it an easy matter to seize the dominions of an infant whose mother governed the realm. The queen quickly raised an army to oppose him, and with a courage exceeding that of her sex, she placed herself at the head of her troops and marched to defend our frontiers. It was only after being compelled to leave me that she could not avoid entrusting my education to the fairy. I was placed in her hands after my mother had sworn by all she held most sacred that she would promptly bring me back to the court as soon as the war was over, which she calculated would not last more than a year at the most. However, despite all the victories she gained over the enemy, she found it impossible to return to the capital as soon as she had expected. After driving the foe out of our dominions, she sought to take advantage of her victory by pursuing him on his own territory. She conquered entire provinces, won battle after battle, and finally forced the vanquished enemy to sue for a degrading peace, which he obtained only under the hardest conditions. After this glorious success the queen returned triumphantly, looking forward to the pleasure of seeing me once more. However, during her return march she learned that her vile foe had surprised and massacred our garrisons in violation of the treaty, and retaken nearly all the places he had been compelled to cede. So she was obliged to retrace her steps. Honor prevailed over the affection that drew her toward me, and she resolved never to sheathe her sword till she had totally incapacitated her enemy. A considerable time she spent on this second expedition. She had imagined that two or three campaigns would suffice, but she had to contend with an adversary who was as cunning as he was false. He managed to cause rebellions in some of our own provinces and to corrupt entire battalions, and that treachery forced the queen to remain in arms for fifteen years. She never sent for me because she always hoped that each month of her absence would be her last and that she was on the point of seeing me again.

Meanwhile, the fairy had lavished her care and attention on my education, in keeping with her promise. From the day she took me out of my kingdom, she never left me, nor stopped proving her interest in all that pertained to my health and amusement. My respect for her showed my awareness of her kindness, since I demonstrated the same deference and attention that I would have shown my mother, and gratitude inspired me with just as much affection for her as for my mother.

For a long time she appeared satisfied with my behavior, but one day, without telling me why, she set out on a journey. She did not return from this trip for several years, and when she did, she found herself admiring the results of her nurture to the point of developing tender feelings for me quite different from those of a mother. Whereas she had previously permitted me to call her "mama," she now forbade me. I obeyed her without inquiring why, or suspecting the demands she was about to place on me.

When she began harping continually on my ingratitude, I saw clearly that she was dissatisfied, but I couldn't imagine why, nor did I feel I deserved such reproaches. I was particularly bewildered because they were always preceded or followed by the most tender caresses. Since I was not old enough to comprehend all this, she was compelled to explain herself.

One day, when I had voiced my impatience and regret for the continued absence of my mother, the fairy reproached me. I assured her that my affection for my mother in no way minimized my feelings for her. She replied that she wasn't jealous, although she had done a great deal for me and was determined to do even more. However, I had to marry her in order to enable her to carry out her plans with greater freedom. She wanted me to love her not as a mother, but as a mistress. What's more, she was certain that I'd be grateful for her proposal and joyfully accept it. For her, it was simply a question of informing me of the pleasant certitude that I'd become the husband of a powerful fairy who would protect me from all dangers and procure for me a life full of charms and glory.

This proposal put me in a very awkward position. I knew enough about the ways of my own world to be aware that the happiest wedded couples were those whose ages and characters matched. Those who had married under different circumstances were pitied because they usually found that the strong differences between them became a source of constant misery. Since the fairy was old and haughty, I could not believe that my future would be as pleasant as she predicted. In no way did I have the kind of feelings for her as one should for a woman with whom we intend to spend the rest of our days. Besides, I was not inclined to become engaged at such an early age. My only desire was to see the queen again and to distinguish myself at the head of her forces. I sighed for liberty from the fairy. That was the only thing that could give me hope, and the only thing the fairy refused to grant.

I had often implored her to allow me to share the dangers the queen faced in order to protect my kingdom, but my pleas had been fruitless up till then. Pressured to reply to the fairy's astounding declaration, I at first was quite perplexed, but then I reminded her, "You've often told me that I have no right to dispose of my hand without my mother's consent and certainly not during her absence."

"That's precisely my opinion," she replied. "I don't want you to do otherwise. I'll be quite content to refer the matter to the queen."

Her desire to obtain my mother's sanction, of which she was certain, obliged her to grant me what she had always denied me—to seek out my mother—even without my asking. But it was on the condition, by no means pleasant to me, that she accompany me. I did what I could to dissuade her, but found it impossible, and we set out together with a large escort.

We arrived on the evening before a crucial battle. The queen had maneuvered with such skill that the next day was certain to decide the fate of the enemy, who would no longer have any resources if he lost the battle. My arrival provoked much cheering in the camp and gave additional courage to our troops, who interpreted my coming as a good omen. The queen thought she would die from joy, but her initial delight was succeeded by the greatest alarm. Whereas I imagined I would achieve a measure of glory, the queen trembled at the danger to which I was about to expose myself. Since she was too kindhearted to prevent me, she begged me in the name of all her affection to take as much care of myself as honor would permit and implored the fairy not to abandon me. Her pleas were unnecessary, for the danger alarmed the fairy just as much as the queen. She did not, in fact, have a spell to protect me from the accidents of war, but she did accomplish a great deal by quickly inspiring me with the art and the wisdom of commanding an army.

The most experienced captains were surprised as I assumed total control of the battlefield and led our men to complete victory. In the process I also had the good fortune of rescuing the queen from being taken prisoner and thus saving her life. The enemy was pursued with such vigor that he abandoned his camp, lost his supplies, and more than three-fourths of his army, while the losses on our side were paltry. The only advantage of which the foe could boast was a scratch I received. However, the queen feared that if the war continued, a more dire fate would befall me. So, in opposition to the whole army, which had been invigorated by my presence, she sued for peace and gave the enemy more advantageous terms than he could have ever hoped for.

Shortly thereafter we returned in triumph to our capital. My involvement during the battle and the continual presence of the old fairy had prevented me from telling the queen what had occurred during her absence. Therefore, she was completely taken aback when the fairy told her, in so many words, that she had decided to marry me immediately. This declaration was made in this very palace, but at that time it was not as superb as it is at present. It had been a country residence of the late king, and he had been prevented from improving it by a thousand other tasks. My mother, who cherished everything he had loved, had selected it above all others as a place of retirement after the stress and strain of the war. When the fairy declared her intention, she was unable to control her feelings and exclaimed, "Madam, have you considered the absurdity of the match you've proposed?"

In truth, it was impossible to conceive of one more ridiculous. In addition to the the fairy's age, she was almost decrepit and horribly ugly. Nor was this due to the passage of time. Had she been pretty in her youth, she might have preserved some portion of her beauty through the aid of her art. But since she was naturally hideous, her power could only endow her with the appearance of beauty for one day each year, and once that day ended, she returned to her former state.

The fairy was astounded at the queen's exclamation. Her self-love prevented her from truly seeing how horrible she looked, and she reckoned that her power sufficiently compensated for the loss of a few charms of her youth. "What do you mean by an absurd match?" she said to the queen. "Have you thought how imprudent you are to make me remember what I've chosen to forget? You should be congratulating yourself on having a son so charming that his qualities have induced me to choose him over the most powerful genii of all the elements. And since I've deigned to lower myself to marry him, respectfully accept the honor I'm good enough to confer and don't allow me any time to change my mind."

The queen was as proud as the fairy and had never realized that there was a rank on earth higher than a throne. Therefore, she belittled the so-called honor that the fairy offered her. Since she had always ruled over all who approached her, she did not at all want a daughter-in-law to whom she herself had to pay homage. So she refused to reply but just stood stock still, looking at me for assistance. Just as astounded as she, I returned her gaze in the same manner. The fairy could not fail to see that our silence expressed sentiments diametrically the opposite of the joy that she had meant to arouse.

"What's the meaning of this?" she asked sharply. "How come mother and son are saying nothing? Has this pleasant surprise deprived you of the power of speech? Or are you so blind and rash as to reject my offer? Tell me, Prince," she said to me, "are you so ungrateful and imprudent as to despise my kindness? Are you now refusing to give me your hand?"

"Yes, madam, I refuse," I replied instantly. "Although I'm sincerely grateful to you for past favors, I cannot agree to pay my debt in this fashion, and with the queen's permission, I refuse to give up my freedom so soon. Let me have another way of acknowledging your good deeds that I won't find impossible. As for what you have proposed, please excuse me, for—"

"What? You insignificant creature!" the fairy interrupted furiously. "You dare to resist me? And you, foolish queen? How can you regard his pride and not become angry! What am I saying? Not get angry! It's you who's started it! Your own insolence has inspired him with the audacity to refuse me!"

Already stung by the fairy's contemptuous words, the queen could control herself no longer. By chance she happened to glance at a nearby mirror at the moment the wicked fairy provoked her: "What answer can I give you that you shouldn't give to yourself?" the queen remarked. "Look at the people reflected by this mirror without any bias, if you will, and it will speak for me."

The fairy easily grasped the queen's meaning. "So it's your precious son's beauty that makes you so vain," she said. "This is what's exposed me to such a humiliating refusal! I appear unworthy of him. Very well," she continued, raising her voice in a rage, "since I've taken such great pains to make him charming, it's only fitting that I should complete my work and give you both a remarkably unique reason to make you remember what you owe me. Go, wretch!" she said to me. "Boast that you've refused to give me your heart and your hand. Give them to that woman you find more worthy than I."

Upon saying this, my terrible lover gave me a severe blow on the head. To the ground I was dashed face first, feeling as though I had been crushed by a mountain. Angered by this insult, I struggled to rise, but found the weight of my body had become so great that I could not lift myself. All that I could do was to support myself on my hands, which suddenly had become two horrible paws, and the sight of them made me realize the change I had undergone. I glanced into that fatal mirror, and in an instant saw the same form that you encountered. No longer had I any doubts of my cruel, swift transformation.

My despair paralyzed me. The queen almost went out of her mind at the dreadful sight. Then the wrathful fairy put the finishing touch on her barbarity by ironically informing me, "Go! Make illustrious conquests more worthy of you than a majestic fairy. And since intelligence isn't necessary when one is so handsome, I command you to seem as stupid as you are hideous. You will remain in this condition until a beautiful girl comes to seek you of her own free will even though she's fully convinced you'll devour her. And after discovering that her life is not in danger, she must develop such tender love for you that she'll agree to marry you. Until you encounter this rare maiden, it's my pleasure that you remain an object of horror to yourself and to all who behold you. As for you, too happy mother of so lovely a child," she said to the queen, "I warn you that if you tell anyone that this monster is your son, he'll never recover his natural shape. He's not to be able to use concern, ambition, or his charming mind to regain his shape. Adieu! Don't be impatient. You won't have long to wait, for such a darling will undoubtedly soon find a way to remedy his misfortune."

"Ah, you cruel fiend!" exclaimed the queen. "If my refusal has offended you, wreak your vengeance on me. Take my life, but don't, I implore you, destroy your own work."

"You're forgetting yourself, great princess," the fairy replied, still ironical. "You demean yourself too much. I'm not beautiful enough for you to condescend to entreat me. I am, however, firm in my resolutions. Adieu, powerful queen. Adieu, handsome prince. It wouldn't be fair of me to stay any longer and annoy you with my hateful presence. Before I leave, though, I still have the charity to warn you," she said, addressing herself to me, "that you must forget who you are. If you allow yourself to be flattered by vain respects or by pompous titles, you'll be lost irretrievably! And you'll also be lost if you dare make use of the intelligence I've allowed you to keep to shine in conversation."

With these words she vanished, leaving the queen and me in a state that can neither be described nor imagined. Lamentations are the consolation of the unhappy, but our misery was too deep to seek such relief. My mother was determined to stab herself, and I wanted to fling myself into the adjacent moat. Without revealing our intentions to each other, we were on the verge of carrying out these fatal projects when out of nowhere appeared a female whose majestic mien inspired us with profound respect. She reminded us that it was cowardice to succumb even to the greatest misfortunes. "There is no evil that cannot be overcome with time and courage." The queen, however, was inconsolable. Tears streamed from her eyes, and not knowing how to inform her subjects that their sovereign was transformed into a horrible monster, she abandoned herself to the most fearful despair. The fairy (for that was what she was, and the same whom you have seen here) understood both her misery and embarrassment, and reminded her of her vital obligation to conceal this dreadful adventure from her people. "Instead of yielding to despair, you would do better to seek some way to combat the harm already done."

"Can one be found that's powerful enough to prevent the fulfillment of a fairy's spell?" the queen asked.

"Yes, madam," replied the fairy, "there's a remedy for every ill. I'm a fairy just like the one whose fury you have just felt, and my power is equal to hers. It's true that I can't immediately make up for the harm she's done you, for we're not permitted to act in direct opposition to each other. What's more, she is older than I, and age has a particular claim to respect among us. But since she could not avoid adding a condition indicating how the spell might be broken, I'll help you break it. I must confess that it will be a difficult task to end this enchantment, but it doesn't appear to be impossible. Let me exert all the means of my power and see what can be done."

From inside her robe she drew a book, and after taking a few mysterious steps, she seated herself at a table and read for a considerable time with such intense concentration that drops of perspiration beaded on her forehead. Then she closed the book and meditated profoundly. The expression on her face was so grave that for some time we were led to believe that she considered my misfortune irreparable. After she recovered from her trance and her features resumed their natural beauty, though, she informed us that she had discovered a remedy for our disasters. "It will be slow," she said, "but it will be sure. Keep your secret. Don't let anyone suspect you're concealed beneath this horrible disguise, for in that case you'll deprive me of the power that I need to rescue you. Your enemy hopes you'll divulge it. That's the reason why she didn't rob you of your power of speech."

The queen soon found that total silence would be impossible to impose, for two of her women had been present at the fatal transformation and had rushed from the apartment in terror. This in turn must have excited the curiosity of the guards and courtiers. She imagined that by this time the whole court was buzzing, and that the entire kingdom, and even the entire world, would quickly receive the news. However, the fairy knew a way to prevent the disclosure of the secret. She made several circles, at first solemnly, then rapidly, uttering words we did not understand, and she finished by raising her hand with the air of someone who issues commands with absolute authority. The spell she cast was so powerful that every living creature in the palace was changed into a statue. Look all around you. They're all still standing in the same poses as when the fairy's potent spell surprised them. The queen, who happened to glance at that moment out onto the main courtyard, observed this transformation overtaking a baffling number of people. The silence that suddenly replaced the bustling hubbub made the queen sorry for the many innocents deprived of life for my sake. The fairy comforted her by saying that she would keep her subjects thus only as long as was necessary to make sure they would be discreet. "Though I am compelled to take such a precaution, I promise that the period they spend in this state will not be added to the years allotted them. They'll be much younger because of it," the fairy said, "so you can stop feeling badly and leave them here with your son. He'll be quite safe, for I've raised such thick fogs around the castle that no one can possibly enter it unless we think it fitting. Now, let me take you where your presence is necessary. Your enemies are plotting against you, and you must be careful to proclaim to your people that the fairy who educated your son is keeping him near her for an important purpose and is also keeping all the people who were part of your entourage."

Not without shedding a flood of tears did my mother leave me. The fairy reassured her that she would always watch over me and swore that I had only to ask and all my wishes would be fulfilled. She added that my misfortunes would soon end, provided that neither the queen nor I created an obstacle through some act of unwisdom. All these promises did not console my mother. She wanted to remain with me and to have the fairy, or some other capable soul, govern the kingdom. But when fairies give orders, they expect to be obeyed, and my mother, fearing that her refusal would add to my misery and deprive me of this beneficent spirit's aid, consented to the fairy's demand. She saw a beautiful chariot approach that was drawn by the same white stags that brought her here today. The fairy made the queen mount beside her, and she had scarcely time to embrace me, for not only her affairs demanded her presence elsewhere, but she was warned that to tarry any longer would work to my detriment as well. She was transported with extraordinary speed to the spot where her army was encamped. They were not surprised to see her arrive with this equipage because everybody thought the old fairy was accompanying her. So the younger one kept herself invisible and departed again to return immediately to this place, which she quickly decorated with everything that her imagination could conceive and her art could provide.

This good-natured fairy also permitted me to add whatever I desired, and after doing all she could for me, she left me with words of encouragement and promised to come occasionally and inform me of any turn in events that would be in my favor.

I thought myself alone in the palace, but everything was not as it seemed. I was served as if I were living in the midst of my courtiers, and my occupations were nearly the same as those that were afterward yours: I read, I went to the theater. I also cultivated a garden to amuse myself and found that whatever I planted grew to perfection the very same day. In no time at all I produced the bower of roses to which I am indebted for the happiness of beholding you here.

My benefactress came to see me often, and her presence and promises alleviated my distress. It was through her that the queen received news of me, and I news of her. Then one day I saw the fairy arrive with joy sparkling in her eyes. "Dear prince," she announced, "the moment of good fortune is approaching!"

Then she informed me that the man whom you believed to be your father had spent a very uncomfortable night in the forest. She related to me in a few words the reason why he had undertaken the journey, without revealing to me your real parentage, and she told me that the worthy man was compelled to seek refuge from the misery he had endured during the past twenty-four hours.

"I'm going to give orders for his reception," she said. "It must be a pleasant one, for he has a charming daughter. I plan to have her release you from the spell. I've examined the conditions that my cruel companion laid down for your disenchantment, and fortunately she did not ordain that your rescuer must come here out of love for you. On the contrary, she insisted that the maiden expect no less than death and yet expose herself to it voluntarily. I've thought of a scheme to compel her to take that step: It's to make her believe that her father's life is at stake, and that she has no other means of saving him. I know that she asked him to bring her a single rose in order to spare him any undue expense on her account, while her sisters have overwhelmed him with extravagant requests. He'll naturally take the first available opportunity to fulfill her wish. Hide yourself in this arbor, and grab him the moment he tries to pick your roses. Threaten him with death as punishment for his audacity unless he gives you one of his daughters; or, rather, unless she's willing to sacrifice herself according to the condition set by our enemy. This man has five daughters besides the one I've destined for you, but not one of them is sufficiently magnanimous to purchase the life of their father at the price of their own. Only Beauty is capable of such a grand gesture."

I did exactly what the fairy commanded, and you know, lovely princess, what success I had. To save his life, the merchant promised what I demanded, even though I saw him depart still uncertain that he would return with you, for I couldn't imagine that my desire would be fulfilled. What torment I suffered during the month he requested with his family. I longed for its end even as I was certain of my disappointment. I couldn't imagine that a lovely and charming girl would have the courage to seek out a monster who she believed would devour her. Even if I supposed that she had sufficient fortitude, she would have to live with me without repenting the step she had taken, and that appeared to me to be an invincible obstacle. Besides, how could she look upon me without dying from fright? I spent a miserable existence absorbed by these melancholy reflections, and never was I more to be pitied.

The month, however, elapsed, and my protectress announced your arrival. You remember, no doubt, the pomp and splendor with which you were received. Not daring to express my delight in words, I endeavored to show it to you by the most magnificent displays. Greatly concerned about me, the fairy prohibited me from making myself known to you. No matter how terrified you became, no matter what kindness you showed me, I was not permitted to please you, to express any fondness, or to reveal to you in any way who I was. I could have recourse, however, to showing an excessive good nature, since the malignant fairy had thankfully forgotten to forbid this.

These prohibitions seemed hard to me, but I was compelled to obey them, and I decided to appear before you for only a few moments every day and avoid long conversations in which my heart might betray its tenderness. When you arrived, charming princess, the first sight of you produced exactly the opposite effect on me that my monstrous appearance must have had on you. For me, to see you was to love you. I trembled when I entered your apartment, and I was filled with rapture on finding that you could look at me with greater intrepidity than I looked at myself. You made me overjoyed when you declared that you would remain with me. An impulse of self-love that I retained even under that most horrible of forms led me to believe that you had not found me so hideous as you had anticipated.

Your father departed in contentment, but my sorrow was to increase when I began to reflect that I was not allowed to win your favor in any way except by indulging your whims and taste. Your demeanor and conversation were as refined as they were unpretentious. Everything about you convinced me that you acted solely on the principles dictated to you by reason and virtue, and consequently it would not be luck that would determine my fate. I was despondent at being forbidden to address you in any other language than that which the fairy had dictated, which she had expressly chosen as crude and stupid. I vainly tried to convince her it was unnatural to expect you to accept my proposal to marry you. Her answer was always, "Patience, perseverance, or all is lost." To make up for my silly conversation, she assured me she would surround you with all sorts of pleasures and give me the advantage of seeing you constantly without alarming you, or being compelled to say rude and impertinent things to you. She made me invisible, and I had the gratification of seeing you attended by spirits who were also invisible or appeared to you in the shapes of various animals.

In addition to all this, the fairy arranged for you to see my natural form in your nightly slumbers and in portraits by day, and she made it speak to you in your dreams as I would have spoken to you myself. You gained a confused notion of my secret and my hopes, which she urged you to realize. Through the use of a studded mirror I witnessed all your encounters and was able to know all you uttered or imagined. However, this state of affairs was not enough to make me happy. I was only this way in a dream, and my sufferings were real. The intense love you had aroused in me led me to complain about the restraints under which I lived, and I became even more wretched when I realized that this beautiful setting no longer had any charms for you. Your tears pierced my heart. When you asked me whether I was alone here, I was on the verge of discarding my feigned stupidity and giving you assurances by pledging my troth. These vows would have been uttered in language that would have surprised you and caused you to suspect that I was not such a coarse brute as I pretended. Thankfully, the fairy, who remained invisible to you, appeared in a threatening manner before me. Oh, heavens! What an extreme she went to silence me! She approached you with a dagger in hand and indicated that the first word I uttered would cost you your life. I was so frightened that I instantly relapsed into my affected imbecility.

My sufferings were not yet at an end. You expressed a desire to visit your father, and I gave you permission without hesitation, for I could not have refused you anything. Still, I regarded your departure as my death blow, and without the fairy's help I would have expired. The kind creature never left my side during your absence. She saved me from destroying myself, which I would have done in my despair, not daring to hope that you would return. The time you had spent in this palace had made my condition more intolerable than it had been previously because I felt I was the most miserable of all men without the hope of making it known to you.

My most pleasant occupation was wandering through the places that you had frequented, but my grief was increased by no longer seeing you there. The evenings when I had had the pleasure of conversing with you for a moment were even more painful to me. Those two months, the longest I had ever known, ended at last, and you did not return. It was then my misery reached its climax. The fairy's power was too weak to prevent my sinking into utter despair, and the precautions she took to prevent my attempting suicide were useless. I had a sure way to elude her power—it was to refrain from eating. She managed to sustain me for some time by using her magic skills, but once she exhausted all her secrets, I grew weaker and weaker until I had just a few moments to live. It was then that you arrived to snatch me from the grave.

Your precious tears were more effective than all the cordials of the disguised genii who cared for me and prevented my soul from departing. Once I realized from your lamentations that I was dear to you, I knew what perfect happiness was, and that happiness reached its height when you agreed to let me become your husband. Still, I was not permitted to divulge my secret to you, and the Beast was compelled to leave you without daring to reveal the prince. You know the coma into which I fell, and which ended only with the arrival of the fairy and the queen. When I awoke, I found myself as you see me now without knowing how the transformation had taken place.

You have witnessed what followed, but you could gain only a vague idea of the woe that my mother's obstinacy caused me when she opposed a marriage so suitable and glorious. I had resolved, Princess, to become a monster again rather than abandon the hope of being the husband of such a virtuous and charming maiden. Even if the secret of your birth had remained a mystery forever, my love and gratitude for you would have more than guaranteed me that I would be the most fortunate of men in having you as my wife.

The prince finished his story, and Beauty was about to respond when she was interrupted by a burst of loud voices and martial instruments. They did not seem to signal anything sinister, and the prince and princess looked out of the window, as did the fairy and queen, who had returned from their tour. The fanfare had announced the arrival of a man who, from all appearances, was no less than a king. His escort was obviously a royal one, and his demeanor had a majestic air that corresponded to his magnificent entourage. Even though this monarch was not in the prime of his life, he cut such a fine figure that it was clear that few could have equaled him in the flower of his youth. He was followed by twelve of his bodyguard and some courtiers in hunting garments who seemed as astonished as their master to find themselves in a castle that had been unknown to them until then. He was received by invisible creatures with the same honors that would have been paid to him in his own dominions. Shouts of joy and flourishes of trumpets were heard, but no one was to be seen.

Once the fairy caught sight of him, she immediately said to the queen, "Here's the king, your brother, and the father of Beauty. He hardly expects the pleasure of seeing you both here. This will make him all the more happy since, as you know, he believes his daughter long since dead. He's still mourning her, just as he also mourns his wife, whom he remembers with a great deal of affection."

This news made the queen and young princess even more eager to embrace this monarch, and they reached the courtyard just as he dismounted. He saw them without recognizing them; however, they clearly were coming to greet him. He was making up his mind how and in what terms he should pay his compliments to them when Beauty flung herself at his feet, embraced his knees, and called him "Father!"

The king raised her and hugged her tenderly without understanding why she addressed him in this fashion. He imagined she must be some orphan princess who sought his protection from some oppressor, and who made use of this most touching expression in order to have her request granted. He was about to assure her that he would do all in his power to assist her when he recognized his sister, who embraced him in her turn and presented her son. She then told him how indebted they were to Beauty and how the frightful enchantment had just been ended. The king praised the young princess and wanted to know her name. But the fairy interrupted him and asked if it was necessary to name her parents. "Have you ever met anyone whom she sufficiently resembles that will enable you to guess her parentage?"

"If I were to judge only from her features," he said, gazing at her earnestly, unable to restrain a few tears, "the name she gave me is legitimately mine. Despite that evidence, though, and the emotion her presence arouses in me, I daren't hope she's the daughter whom I have long mourned. I had the most positive proof that she had been devoured by wild beasts. Yet," he continued, still examining her features, "she perfectly resembles my tender, incomparable wife whom death snatched from me. Oh, how wonderful it would be if I could have the pleasure of hoping she is the fruit of that charming marriage sundered much too soon!"

"You may, my lord," the fairy replied. "Beauty is your daughter. Her birth is no longer a secret here. The queen and prince know who she is. I had you direct your steps this way on purpose to inform you, but this is not the proper place for me to recount the details of this adventure. Let us enter the palace. After you've had a short rest, I'll tell you all you wish to know. Then, after you've fully experienced the joy at finding a daughter so beautiful and virtuous, I'll give you additional news that will please you just as much."

The king, accompanied by his daughter and the prince, was ushered by the monkey officers into the apartment designated for him by the fairy, who in turn took this opportunity to restore freedom to the statues so that they could relate what they had witnessed. Because their fate had aroused the compassion of the queen, the fairy wanted her to be the agent of their resurrection. Placing her wand in the queen's hand, she had her make several circles in the air. Then she pronounced: "Be revived! To you has your king been restored!" All of a sudden the statues began to move, walk, and act as they had done in the past, retaining only a confused idea of what had happened to them.

After this ceremony the fairy and queen returned to the king, whom they found conversing with Beauty and the prince, caressing each in turn and most fondly his daughter. A hundred times he inquired how she had been saved from the wild beasts who had carried her off, not recalling she had told him from the first that she knew nothing about what had happened and had even been unaware about the true circumstances of her birth. A hundred times the prince kept repeating, without anyone listening, how indebted he was to the Princess Beauty. He wanted the king to know of the promises that the fairy had made him about marrying the princess, and he implored him not to refuse giving his kind consent to the alliance. In the midst of all this entered the queen and the fairy. Now that the king had regained his daughter, he fully appreciated his happiness, but he was still unaware as to whom he was indebted for this precious gift.

"It is to me," the fairy said. "I alone can explain all the adventures to you, and I won't limit my good news to this alone. I have other tidings in store for you that are just as pleasant. Therefore, great king, you'll be able to mark this day as one of the happiest of your life."

Since the company saw that the fairy was about to begin a tale, they fell silent and gave her their rapt attention. She rewarded this attention by delivering the following discourse directed at the king:

"Beauty, my lord, and perhaps the prince, are the only people present who are not acquainted with the laws of the Fortunate Island. Therefore, I must explain those laws to them. The inhabitants of that island, even the king himself, are allowed perfect freedom to marry according to their inclinations so that they will have no obstacle whatsoever to their happiness. It was due to this privilege that the monarch in our presence selected a young shepherdess for his wife, whom he came upon one day while hunting. Considering her charms and wisdom worthy of his throne, he raised her to a rank from which her low birth normally would have excluded her, for she deserved it because of her noble character and pure mind. He continually had reason to rejoice in the selection he had made. Her gentleness, her obliging disposition, and her affection for him matched her personal charms. But he did not long enjoy the happiness of having her by his side. After she had made him the father of Beauty, he was compelled to travel to the frontiers of his kingdom to suppress some revolts about which he had been given word. During this period he lost his dear wife, and this loss distressed him profoundly because, in addition to the love with which her beauty had aroused in him, he had had the greatest respect for her many rare qualities. Despite her youth and the slight education she had received, he had found her naturally endowed with consummate judgment, and his wisest ministers had been astonished not only by the excellent advice she had given, but the policy by which she had enabled him to succeed in all his undertakings."

The king, who still brooded over his loss, and whose imagination still pictured the death of his dear wife, could not listen to this account without being strongly moved. Noticing this, the fairy said, "Your feelings prove that you deserved that happiness. I won't dwell any longer on a subject that's so painful to you, but I must reveal to you that the so-called shepherdess was a fairy. If I may, let me continue this story for the sake of the others."

Moreover, she was my sister. Having heard that the Fortunate Island was a charming country and having also heard a wealth of praise for its laws and the gentle nature of its king's government, she had been particularly eager to visit it. The dress of a shepherdess was the only disguise she assumed, since she intended to enjoy that country for a short time. The king encountered her during her stay, and her youth and beauty touched his heart. For his part, she yielded to a desire to discover if the qualities of his mind equaled those she found in his person. Confident in her powers as a fairy, she felt she could place herself beyond the reach of his advances anytime she wished if he became too insistent, or if he were to presume to take advantage of the humble position in which he had found her. Unworried about any feelings he might arouse in her, convinced that her virtue was enough to protect her against the snares of love, she attributed her desire to a simple curiosity to discover if there were still men on earth capable of loving virtue unembellished by those wondrous ornaments more radiant and respectable to vulgar souls. These ornaments have fatal attractions that often make virtue out of the most abominable vices.

With this idea in mind, she was not inclined to retire to the common asylum of us fairies, as she had at first proposed. Instead she chose to inhabit a small cottage she had built for herself in the isolated spot accompanied by a phantom representing her mother. When the king met these two persons there, they appeared to sustain themselves by tending a so-called flock, which in fact had no fear of the wolves because they were actually genii. It was in that cottage that she was receptive to his attention, and he gained the conquest he desired. She could not resist the offer of his crown, and he now knows the extent of his obligations to her at a time when he imagined she owed everything to him.

This is proof positive that ambition played no part in the consent she gave to his wishes. You all are aware that fairies look upon the greatest kingdoms as naught but baubles that we bestow on anyone as we please. Still, she appreciated his generous behavior, and since she considered herself fortunate to be uniting herself to such an excellent man, she rashly became engaged without thinking about the danger she would incur. You see, our laws expressly forbid our

forming unions with those who possess less power, especially when we have not arrived at that age when we are privileged to exercise our authority over other fairies. Until our turn comes to preside over others, we are subordinate to our elders, and to keep us from abusing our power, we are allowed only to place our hearts at the disposal of a spirit or sage whose knowledge is at least equal to our own. It is true that after that period we are free to form whatever alliance we please, but we seldom avail ourselves of that right and never without causing scandal to our order. Those who do are generally old fairies who almost always pay dearly for their folly, for they marry young men who despise them, and although they are not punished as criminals, they are sufficiently punished by the bad conduct of their husbands, since the only penalty we impose upon them is that they are not permitted to avenge themselves on their spouses. The trouble that almost invariably follows an indiscretion relieves the offenders of the desire to reveal the great secrets of our art to those profane persons from whom they expected respect and attention.

My sister, however, held neither of these positions. Endowed with every charm that could inspire affection, she was not of age and paid heed only to her heart. She hoped she could keep her marriage a secret, and she even succeeded for a brief time, for we rarely make inquiries about those who are absent from our midst. Each fairy is occupied with her own affairs as she flies throughout the world, doing good or evil, according to her inclination, and she is not obliged upon her return to account for her actions, unless she has been guilty of an act that causes talk, or unless some beneficent fairy moved by the unjust persecution of some unfortunate mortal raises a complaint against the offender. In short, some unforeseen event must arise to cause us to consult the general book that spiritually records all we do at the very second we do it. With these exceptions, we only have to appear in a general assembly three times a year, and since we travel swiftly, the entire affair does not take up more than a couple of hours.

My sister too was obliged to "enlighten" the throne (such is our phrase for the performance of that triannual duty). Whenever she had to attend, she arranged a hunting party or journey of pleasure for the king some distance away, and after his departure she feigned some indisposition in order to remain alone in her room. Sometimes she said that she had letters to write or that she wished to rest. Nobody had any suspicion in the palace or among us that she had anything of importance to conceal. I, however, knew about her secret and warned her of the catastrophic consequences. Still, she loved the king too well to repent the step she had taken. She even wanted to justify it in my eyes and insisted that I pay him a visit. Without flattering you, sire, I confess that even though you did not sway me entirely to excuse her weakness, I was at least considerably less surprised by her actions, and I tried harder to keep everything secret.

For two years her pretense was successful, but she eventually betrayed herself. You see, we are generally obliged to do a certain number of good deeds in the world and to give an account of them. When my sister gave hers, it was apparent that she had limited her beneficial excursions to the confines of the Fortunate Island. Several of our bad-tempered fairies found fault with her conduct, and consequently our fairy queen demanded to know why she had restricted her good deeds to this small corner of the earth. "You know," she said, "that a young fairy is obligated to travel far and wide, and demonstrate our good will and power to the universe at large."

Since this was not a new regulation, my sister could neither complain about it nor find a pretext for refusing to obey it. She promised therefore to do so, but her eagerness to be at the king's side, her fear that her absence would be discovered at the palace, and the impossibility of acting secretly on a throne did not permit her to absent herself long or often enough to fulfill her promise. In fact, at the next assembly she had difficulty proving that she had left the Fortunate Island even for a quarter of an hour.

Very much displeased with her, our queen threatened to destroy that island to prevent her from continuing to violate our laws. This threat made her so distraught that even the most dim-witted fairy could see that her interest in that fatal island was extreme. Her confusion convinced the wicked fairy who turned the prince here into a frightful monster that if she opened the great book, she would find an important entry that would allow her to exercise her propensity for mischief. "It's there," she exclaimed, "that the truth will appear. We shall learn what has really kept her busy!" With these words she opened the volume before the whole assembly and read the details of all that had taken place during the last two years in a loud and distinct voice.

Upon learning about the degrading alliance, all the fairies were in an uproar, and they overwhelmed my wretched sister with the cruelest reproaches. Our order stripped her of her powers, and she was condemned to remain a prisoner among us. If her punishment had consisted of just the first penalty, she would have consoled herself, but the second sentence was far more terrible and made her feel the rigor of both. The loss of her dignity affected her but slightly, but since she loved the king so tenderly, she begged with tears in her eyes to let them be satisfied with degrading her. "Do not deprive me of the pleasure of living like a simple mortal with my husband and dear daughter."

Her tears and supplications touched the hearts of the younger judges, and I sensed from the murmur that arose that if the votes had been counted at that instant, she would certainly have escaped with a reprimand. But one of the eldest, who had obtained the name among us of the "Mother of the Seasons" due to her extreme decrepitude, did not give the fairy queen time to admit that pity had touched her heart as well as the others.

"There's no excuse for this crime!" cried the detestable old creature in her cracked voice. "If it's permitted to go unpunished, we'll be forever exposed to similar insults. The honor of our order is wholly at stake. This miserable being who's attached to earth does not regret losing her rank, which elevates her a hundred degrees higher above monarchs than they are above their subjects. She tells us that her affections, her fears, and her wishes, are all directed toward her unworthy family. It's through them we must punish her. Let her husband mourn her! Let her daughter, the shameful fruit of her illegal marriage, become the bride of a monster in order to make up for the folly of a mother who allowed herself to be captivated by the frail, contemptible beauty of a mortal!"

This cruel speech revived the severity of many who had been previously inclined to mercy. Those who continued to pity her were too few to offer any opposition, and the sentence was to be carried out strictly. Even our queen, who seemed to feel compassion, became severe again and supported the majority vote in favor of the ill-tempered fairy's motion. What's worse, in pleading for a revocation of this cruel decree, my sister tried to move her judges to pity and pardon her marriage by drawing such a charming portrait of the king that it inflamed the heart of the fairy who had opened the book. However, this budding passion served only to increase the hatred the wicked fairy already bore for my unfortunate sister.

Unable to resist her desire to see this mortal, the fairy concealed her passion under the pretext of being curious to learn if he deserved such a sacrifice by a fairy. Since she had obtained the sanction of the assembly regarding the guardianship of the prince, she would not have ventured to leave him for any length of time if the ingenuity of love had not given her the idea of placing a protecting genius and two inferior and invisible fairies to watch over him during her absence. After taking this precaution, nothing prevented her from following her desire that speedily carried her to the Fortunate Island.

In the meantime, the women and officers of the imprisoned queen, surprised that she did not emerge from her private chamber, became worried. Since she had given express orders not to disturb her, they spent the night without knocking at the door. At last, though, their impatience prevailed over all other considerations. They knocked loudly, and when no one answered, they forced the doors, believing some accident had befallen her. Although they had prepared themselves for the worst, they were nevertheless astonished to find no trace of her. They called her and hunted for her in vain. They imagined a thousand reasons for her disappearance, each more absurd than the other, never suspecting that she had left on her own free will. Since she was omnipotent in the kingdom, and the sovereign jurisdiction the king had given her was not disputed by anyone, everybody had obeyed her cheerfully. The affection she had for her monarch and her daughter and her adoring subjects prevented them from supposing she had fled. Where could she go to be happier? Similarly, what man would dare carry off a queen in the midst of her guards in the heart of her palace? Such a scoundrel must have left traces indicating the road he had taken.

There was no doubt about the disaster, even though the causes were unknown. Moreover, there was another evil to dread, namely, the feelings with which the king would receive this fatal news. Although those responsible for the queen's safety were innocent, they were by no means convinced that they would not feel his wrath. They believed they must either flee the kingdom and thus appear guilty of a crime they had not committed, or must find some means of concealing this misfortune.

After a long discussion they could devise no other plan than that of persuading him the queen was dead. This scheme they put into action immediately. They sent a courier to inform him that she had been suddenly taken ill, and a second followed a few hours afterward, bearing the news of her death in order to prevent his love from inducing him to return post haste to court, for his appearance would have upset all the measures they had taken for their safety. They paid all the funeral honors due to the rank of his supposedly deceased wife, and they honored his affection and the sorrow of a people who wept at her loss as sincerely as the king did himself.

This cruel incident was always kept a profound secret from him, although it was known to every inhabitant of the Fortunate Island, for the surprise at her disappearance had spread rapidly among the people. His distress because of her loss was proportionate to his love, and he found no consolation except in the innocent caresses of his infant daughter, whom he sent for. He was now determined never again to be separated from her. She was charming, and as a living image of her mother, she constantly reminded him of the queen.

When the hostile fairy who had caused all this trouble arrived, she did not escape paying the price for her curiosity. His dashing looks produced the same effect on her heart as it had previously done on that of his wife, but this experience did not lead her to pardon my sister. Instead, she ardently sought to commit the same mistake. Hovering about him invisibly, she could not tear herself away. Because she saw that he was inconsolable, that she had no hope of success, she was afraid to add the shame of his refusal to the pain of disappointment, and thus she did not dare make herself known. On the other hand, when she imagined what might happen if she revealed herself, she thought she might make him accustomed to her by skillful manipulation and perhaps in time induce him to love her. But in order to bring this about, she had to be introduced.

After she thought a great deal about finding a suitable pretext of showing herself, she hit on one. There was a queen in the vicinity who had been driven out of her dominions by a usurper who had murdered her husband. This unhappy princess was roving the world to find asylum and an avenger. The fairy carried her off, and after placing her in a secure spot, she put her to sleep and assumed her form. Soon the king beheld the disguised fairy flinging herself at his feet and imploring his protection and assistance to punish the assassin of a husband she professed to miss as much as he did his queen. She declared that her love for her husband alone compelled her to take this course, and that she would gladly give a crown to whoever avenged her dear husband.

The unhappy tend to commiserate with each other, and so he took an interest in her misfortunes, particularly because she was mourning the loss of a beloved spouse. By mixing her tears with his, she talked to him constantly about the queen. He gave her his protection and lost no time in reestablishing her authority in the kingdom she pretended to rule by punishing the rebels and the usurper. But she would neither return to her realm nor leave his side. She implored him in the name of her own security to govern the kingdom, since he was too modest to accept it as a gift from her. Moreover, she requested permission to reside at his court. He could not refuse this new request, and he thought he needed her to help raise his daughter, for the cunning fairy knew quite well that the child was the sole object of his affection. Feigning an immense fondness for her, she continually held her in her arms. Anticipating the request he was going to make to her, she earnestly asked to be permitted to take charge of his daughter's education, saying that she would have no heir but that dear child. "I already regard her as my own. She's the only being I love in this world because she so reminds me of a daughter I had by my husband, who perished along with him."

This proposal appeared to him so beneficial that he did not hesitate to place the fairy in complete charge of the princess. She performed her duties to perfection, and through her talent and affection she gained his implicit trust and a love akin to that for a tender sister. However, this hardly satisfied her: her sole desire was to become his wife, and she did everything she could to achieve this goal. However, even if he had never been the husband of the most beautiful of fairies, she was not formed to inspire him with love. The shape she had assumed could not compare to the queen whose place she wanted to steal. In fact, this figure was extremely ugly, and since she was naturally ugly herself, she only had the power of appearing beautiful one day in the year.

Aware of this discouraging fact, she became convinced that if she wanted to succeed, she had to have recourse to other charms than beauty. She plotted secretly to compel the people and nobility to petition him to take another wife and to select her as the one desired. After she had held some suspicious conversations with him to sound out his inclinations, though, he was easily able to discover the source of the urgent demands that kept pestering him. He declared absolutely that he would not hear of giving a stepmother to his daughter, nor lower her position by making her subordinate to a queen. She was to maintain her rank as the highest person in the kingdom next to himself and the acknowledged heir to his throne. He also told the false queen, "I shall be obliged to you if you return to your own dominions immediately and without fuss. I promise you that when you are settled there, I shall provide you with all the services you can expect from a faithful friend and a generous neighbor." Moreover, he made it clear to her that if she did not do this willingly, she ran the risk of being compelled to do so.

Such an invincible obstacle had he created to her love that she was thrown into a terrific rage. This, however, she took pains to hide. She feigned so much indifference about the matter that she succeeded in convincing him that her attempt had been caused by ambition and the fear that he would have eventually taken over her realm. "Despite the earnestness with which I seemed to offer my realm to you, I preferred to let you believe I had been insincere in making the offer rather than let you suspect my real sentiments."

Her fury became even more violent because she had to suppress it. She was certain that it was Beauty who took precedence over policy in his heart and caused him to reject such a glorious opportunity of increasing his empire. Developing a hatred for her as passionate as that for his wife, she was determined to get rid of her. She was fully convinced that if she were dead, his subjects would renew their remonstrances and would compel him to change his mind to get him to leave a successor to the throne. The good woman was no longer of an age to give him one, but she did not care a fig about that. The queen whose resemblance she had assumed was still young enough to have many children, and her ugliness was no obstacle to a royal and political alliance.

Despite the official declaration he had made, people thought that if his daughter died, he would yield to the continual pressure of his council. People also believed that his choice would fall upon this so-called queen, and thus she was surrounded by innumerable parasites. With the aid of one of these flatterers, whose wife was as base as her husband and as wicked as she was herself, she conceived a plan to kidnap his daughter. She had appointed this woman governess to the little princess, and these wretches settled on a plan to smother her and report that she had suddenly died. To ensure that nobody surprised them, they decided to commit this barbarous murder in a nearby forest. Out there they could not possibly be blamed for not having called for help before she died, since their excuse that they were too far away to get any would seem legitimate. The husband of the governess proposed to go in search of aid as soon as the tender victim of their fury was dead, and to forestall arousing any suspicion, he was to appear shocked at finding he was too late when he returned. He even rehearsed his sorrow and consternation.

When my wretched sister had found herself deprived of her power and condemned to a cruel imprisonment, she asked me to console her husband and to watch over the safety of her child. This precaution was wholly unnecessary. The tie that binds us, and the pity I felt for her, was ample assurance that I would protect him, and her pleas were not needed to increase the zeal with which I hastened to fulfill her request.

I saw you, sire, as often as prudence permitted without incurring the risk of arousing the suspicions of our enemy, who would have denounced me as a fairy who placed sisterly affection over the honor of her order and protected guilty human beings. I did my best to convince the fairies that I had abandoned my sister to her unhappy fate. By doing this, I thought I could be more free to serve her. Since I watched every move of the treacherous admirer, not only with my own eyes, but with those of my genii servants, I was aware of her horrible intentions. I could not oppose her by open force, and though I could have easily destroyed the couple into whose hands she had placed the innocent child, prudence restrained me. In fact, had I carried off my niece, the malignant fairy would have taken her back from me without my being able to defend her.

One of our laws states that we must be a thousand years old before we can dispute the power of the elder fairies. Either this or we must become a serpent. We call this condition the "terrible act" because it is fraught with danger, and the bravest among us shudder at the thought of undertaking it. Long will we hesitate before taking such a risk because of its consequences. Without an urgent reason such as hatred, love, or vengeance, there are few who do not prefer waiting for time to pass rather than acquiring their privilege by that dangerous transformation, in which the greater number are destroyed. I was in this position. I needed ten years before I was to become a thousand, and thus I had to resort to artifice. Taking the form of a monstrous she-bear, I hid myself in the forest chosen for the detestable deed. When the wretches arrived to carry out the barbarous order they had received, I flung myself on the woman as she placed her hand on the mouth of the child in her arms. Her fright made her drop the precious burden, but she was not allowed to escape so easily. The horror I felt at her unnatural conduct inspired me with the ferocity of the brute whose form I had assumed. I strangled her as well as the traitor who accompanied her, and I carried off Beauty. Rapidly stripping off her clothes and dyeing them with the blood of her enemies, I tore them in several places and scattered them about the forest so that the fairy would not suspect the princess had escaped. After doing this, I withdrew, delighted at having succeeded so completely.

The fairy believed her object had been attained, and the death of her two accomplices was to her advantage, for she alone knew the secret, and their fate was only what she herself had had in mind to reward their criminal services. Another circumstance was also in her favor: some shepherds who had seen this affair from a distance ran for help, and a mass of people arrived just in time to see the infamous wretches die. This precluded all possibility of suspecting that she had anything to do with it.

The same circumstances benefited my undertaking as well. The wicked fairy was just as convinced by this incident as the eyewitnesses. The event happened so naturally that she did not have the slightest doubt about it, and she did not even bother to exert her skills to make certain the child had died. I was delighted that she thought herself so safe. I could not have offered strong resistance if she had attempted to recover little Beauty, because in addition to the already cited reasons making her my superior, she had the advantage of having received that child from the king. He had given her his authorization, which only he could have retracted. Thus, short of his wresting his daughter himself out of her hands, nothing could have interfered with her right to exercise control over the princess until she was married.

Although I now had one worry less, I found myself facing another when I recalled that the Mother of the Seasons had condemned my niece to marry a monster. At that time she was only three years old, and I hoped to study the situation and devise some way to prevent this curse from being fulfilled to the letter. I had plenty of time to ponder, and therefore my first need was to find some spot where I could keep my precious charge safe.

Complete secrecy was necessary. I dared not place her in a castle or exercise any of the magnificent wonders of our art for her benefit, for our enemy would have noticed it, and the anxiety it would have aroused would have been fatal to us. I thought it better to assume a humble garb and place the infant under the care of the first person with an honest face under whose roof she would live comfortably.

Chance soon favored my intentions. I found what suited me exactly: a small house in a village. Since the door was open, I entered. The cottage seemed to belong to a peasant in comfortable circumstances. I saw by the light of a lamp three peasant women asleep beside a cradle. The cradle, however, did not at all match the overall simplicity of the room. Everything about it was sumptuous. I concluded that its little occupant was ill, and that the deep sleep into which its nurses had fallen resulted from the long hours they had spent watching over it. I approached silently with the intention of curing the infant, pleasantly anticipating the surprise of these women on awaking to find their invalid miraculously restored to health. I was about to take the child out of the cradle in order to cure it, but my good intentions were in vain: it died the instant I touched it.

Immediately it occurred to me that I should make good use of this sad event and substitute my niece for the dead child, who fortunately happened to be a girl. I lost no time in making the exchange, and after carrying the lifeless infant away, I buried it carefully. Then I returned to the house and knocked long and loudly at the door to waken the sleepers.

Feigning a provincial dialect, I told them that I was a stranger to those parts in need of a night's lodging. They kindly offered me one and then went to look at their nursling, whom they found quietly asleep in seemingly perfect health. They were astonished and delighted, not realizing that I had deluded them. They told me that the child was the daughter of a rich merchant. One of their party had been her wet nurse, and after having weaned her, she had returned her to her parents. All too soon, however, the child had fallen ill in her father's house and had been sent back to the country in hope that the change of air would do her good. They added, with satisfied looks, that the experiment had produced better results than all the remedies tried before the child had been brought to them. They decided to carry her back to her father as soon as it was daylight, and give him the pleasure of knowing as soon as possible that his daughter had recovered. Moreover, they also expected to receive a liberal reward since the child was his particular favorite, although the youngest of twelve.

They set out at sunrise, and I pretended to continue my journey, congratulating myself on having provided for my niece's safety so well. To guarantee that my plan would succeed and to induce the so-called father to form an even stronger attachment to the little girl, I assumed the form of a fortune-teller. Arriving at the merchant's door just as the nurses reached it with the child, I followed them into the house. He received them with joy, and after taking the little girl in his arms, he abandoned himself to his paternal feelings that came more from his natural kindness than true blood ties.

I took advantage of this opportunity to increase the interest he had in his supposed daughter. "Look well at this little one, my good gentleman," I said in the language customary of the class indicated by my dress. "She'll bring great honor to your family. She'll bring you immense wealth and save your life as well as the lives of all your children. She'll be so beautiful that she'll be called Beauty by all who behold her." As a reward for my prediction, he gave me a gold coin, and I withdrew perfectly satisfied. I no longer had any reason to stay with the race of Adam, and I leisurely returned to Fairyland, intending to remain there for some time. I spent my days quietly consoling my sister, giving her news of her dear daughter, and assuring her that the king had not forgotten her, but cherished her memory as fondly as he had in the past.

Such was our situation while the great king was suffering from this newest calamity. Being deprived of his child revived all the pain he had felt at the loss of her mother. Although he could not positively name the fairy as the spiteful perpetrator of the accident, he found it impossible to regard her in a civil fashion. Though she did not seem guilty of intentional harm, the event had turned out to be fatal because she had neglected to ensure that the young princess was properly attended and protected.

After the delirium of his grief had subsided, she imagined that there was no obstacle preventing him from marrying her. She had her emissaries renew her proposal, but she was rebuffed. Indeed, she was mortified as he declared, "Not only are my intentions unchanged with regard to remarriage, but even if something were to make me change my mind, it would never be in your favor." In addition to this declaration, he ordered her to leave his kingdom immediately, for her presence continually reminded him of his child and added to his grief. Such was the pretext he used for taking this measure, but his principal object was to end the intrigues she was constantly plotting.

She was furious, but she was obliged to obey without avenging herself, for I had persuaded one of our older fairies to protect him. Her power was considerable because, aside from her age, she had the advantage of having been a serpent four times. There are honors and powers attached to the terrible act in relation to the extreme dangers involved. Out of consideration for me, this fairy took him under her protection and made it impossible for the indignant lover to do him any harm.

This development profited the queen whose form this wicked fairy had assumed. She awoke her from her magic sleep, and the fairy concealed the criminal use she had made of her features and put her conduct in the best light. She did not forget to emphasize how well she interceded with the king in her behalf and the trouble she had saved her. Moreover, she gave her the best advice she could on how to maintain herself in the future. It was at that time that this wicked fairy returned to the young prince to console herself for the king's indifference, and she resumed taking care of him. Then she became too fond of him, but since she was not able to get him to love her, she made him feel that terrible effect of her fury.

In the meantime, I had eventually reached the privileged age, and my power was augmented, but my desire to serve my sister and her husband convinced me that I still did not have enough. So, out of my sincere friendship that blinded me to the danger involved, I decided to commit the terrible act. I became a serpent, fortunately survived the ordeal, and thereby gained the power to act openly in favor of those persecuted by my malicious companions. If I cannot always undo their fatal spells completely, I can at least counteract them by my skill and by my advice.

My niece was among those whom I could benefit only partially. Not daring to reveal my deep interest in her destiny, I believed that my best option was to allow her to continue to pass as the merchant's daughter. I visited her in various guises and always returned satisfied, for her virtue and beauty equaled her good sense. At the age of fourteen she had already demonstrated great fortitude during the trials that her so-called father had to endure, and I was delighted to find that the cruelest reverses had not affected her steadfastness. On the contrary, through her cheerfulness and charming conversation, she had succeeded in calming the hearts of her father and brothers. How I rejoiced in observing that her sentiments were worthy of her birth.

These pleasant reflections were, however, mixed with a great deal of bitterness when I remembered that despite her numerous perfections, she was destined to be the wife of a monster. I toiled and studied night and day to find some means of saving her from such a great misfortune, and became desperate when I was unable to find one.

This worry did not prevent me from paying the king occasional visits. His wife, deprived of that liberty, constantly implored me to go and see him, and despite the protection of our friend, her affectionate heart caused her continual concern about him. "The instant you lose sight of him, sister, will be the last of his life. Then he will be sacrificed to the fury of our enemy." She was so obsessed by this fear that she gave me hardly a moment's rest. No sooner did I bring her news of him than she implored me so earnestly to return that I couldn't possibly refuse her.

Touched by her distress, I wanted to put an end to it. Therefore, I used the same weapon that my cruel fellow fairy had used against her—I proceeded to open the great book. Fortunately, this occurred at the very moment the wicked fairy was holding that conversation with the queen and prince that ended in his transformation. Not a word did I miss, and I was overjoyed to find that, without knowing it, she had neutralized the harm the Mother of the Seasons had wreaked in dooming Beauty to be the bride of a monster.

To crown our good fortune, the fairy added conditions so advantageous that they almost seemed made on purpose to oblige me, for she provided my sister's daughter with an opportunity of proving that she was worthy of being the product of the purest fairy blood.

Our slightest gesture indicates to us that which would take an ordinary mortal three days to explain. By uttering but one contemptuous word, I informed the assembly that our enemy had condemned herself according to the same law she had used to punish my sister ten years before. My sister's weakness in love was far more natural than that of an elder fairy of the highest order, and I detailed the base, wicked actions that had accompanied that wild passion. I maintained that if so many infamous deeds were allowed to go unpunished, mortals would be justified in saying that fairies existed only to dishonor nature and torment the human race. Presenting the book to them, I closed my brusque speech with the single word: "Behold!"

It had a most powerful effect. Friends of mine, both young and old, were present, and they treated the amorous old fairy as she deserved. She had not succeeded in becoming the king's wife, and in addition to that disgrace,she was degraded from our order and imprisoned as in the case of the queen of the Fortunate Island.

"This meeting was held while she was with you, madam, and your son," she said, bringing the tale to a close. "As soon as she appeared among us, she was told of her sentence. I had the pleasure to be present, and after I closed the book, I descended rapidly from the middle region of the sky in which our empire is situated to combat the despair to which you were ready to abandon yourselves. I performed my journey as quickly as I had my laconical address. I arrived in time to promise you my assistance, for I had all sorts of reasons to come.

"Your virtues and misfortunes," said the fairy, turning to the prince, "offered such advantages to Beauty that I realized you were the monster who suited my purpose. I deemed you worthy of each other, and I felt convinced that when you became acquainted, your hearts would do each other justice.

"You know," she continued, addressing the queen, "what I have since done to achieve my goal, and how I compelled Beauty to come to this palace, where her encounters with the prince in the dreams I conjured for her had the effect I desired. They kindled love in her heart without diminishing her virtue or weakening the sense of duty and gratitude that drew her to the monster. In short, I have fortunately carried out my scheme to perfection. Yes, Prince, you no longer have anything to fear from your enemy. She is stripped of her power and will never again harm you by other spells. You have fulfilled the conditions she imposed on you exactly as you were supposed to. If you had not done so, you would still be bound by them, despite her eternal degradation. You have made yourself beloved without the aid of your rank or intelligence, and you, Beauty, are also released from the curse pronounced upon you by the Mother of the Seasons. You voluntarily accepted a monster for your husband. She can demand nothing more from you, and everything points now to your happiness."

The fairy fell silent at last, and the king threw himself at her feet. "Great fairy," he exclaimed, "how can I thank you for all the favors you have bestowed on my family? My gratitude far exceeds my power of speech. All the same, my majestic sister," he added, "that title of kinship emboldens me to ask one further favor. Despite the obligation I already owe you, I must confess that I'll never be truly happy as long as I'm deprived of my beloved fairy queen. Your account of what she has done and suffered has increased both my love and my distress, as if they had not already reached their peak. Ah, madam, can't you crown all your deeds by letting me see her?"

His plea was in vain. If the fairy had had the power to perform this deed, she would not have waited for the request, but she could not alter what the council of fairies had decreed. The young queen was a prisoner in the middle regions, and there was not the shadow of a chance that he would be allowed to see her. The fairy was about to explain this to him and kindly encourage him to wait patiently for some unforeseen event until she could take advantage of when an enchanting melody reached their ears and interrupted her. The king, his daughter, the queen, and the prince were transported with delight, but the fairy experienced another sort of emotion. This music indicated the triumph of some fairy, and she could not imagine what fairy had achieved a victory. Her fears suggested that it was either the wicked fairy or the Mother of the Seasons, who in her absence had either obtained liberty or the permission to persecute the lovers anew.

She was still puzzled when her fairy sister, the queen of the Fortunate Island, suddenly appeared in the midst of the charming group. She was just as lovely as she had been when the king had lost her. The monarch recognized her instantly and his ardor overwhelmed the respect he owed her. He embraced her with such delirious joy that the queen herself was taken aback.

Her sister could not imagine what fortunate miracle had brought about her liberty until the royal fairy informed her that she owed her happiness solely to her own courage, which had induced her to risk her own life to save another's. "You're aware," she said to the fairy, "that the daughter of our queen was received into the order at her birth, and that her father was not a sublunary being but the sage Amadabak, whose alliance is an honor to the fairy race, and whose sublime knowledge invests him with much higher powers. Despite this, however, his daughter was required to become a serpent at the end of her first hundred years. When the fatal day arrived, our queen, who was as tenderly anxious as any mother regarding the fate of her dear infant, could not bear to expose her to the abundant chances of destruction in such a form, since the misfortunes of those who had perished were only too well-known to her.

My wretched plight had deprived me of all hope of ever seeing my affectionate husband and my lovely daughter again. Having developed a total antipathy for a life in which I was doomed to spend separated from them, I offered without the slightest hesitation to become a crawling reptile in place of the young fairy. Here, I was delighted to see, lay a quick and honorable way of ending my devastating misery, either by death or by a glorious emancipation that would make me mistress of my own actions and thereby enable me to rejoin my husband.

"Our queen did not hesitate a second to accept this offer, so appealing did I make it to her maternal love. Embracing me a hundred times, she promised to restore my freedom unconditionally and reestablish all my privileges if I was fortunate enough to survive the perilous task unharmed. I managed to do so, and the fruit of my labors was enjoyed by the young fairy for whom I had substituted. The success of my first trial encouraged me to undergo a second for my own benefit. So I tried a second transformation and was equally fortunate. This last act made me an elder, and consequently independent. I didn't waste any time in taking advantage of my liberty and flew here to rejoin my family that I cherish with all my heart."

As the fairy finished her account, her listeners began embracing each other again in charming confusion. Each caressed another almost without knowing what they were doing. Beauty was particularly enchanted by the fact that she belonged to such an illustrious family and no longer feared degrading the prince, her cousin, by compelling him to form an alliance beneath him.

Although she was delirious with happiness, she did not forget the worthy man whom she had formerly believed to be her father. She reminded her fairy aunt about her promise to allow him and his children to have the honor of attending her marriage. Even as she broached the matter, though, they spied the approach of sixteen people on horseback from the window. Most of them had hunting horns and appeared to be considerably confused, since their horses had evidently run away with them. Beauty instantly recognized them as the six sons of the worthy merchant, the five daughters, and their five lovers.

Everyone but the fairy was surprised at their abrupt appearance, and those who appeared were just as astonished at finding themselves carried by the speed of their unmanageable horses to a palace utterly unknown to them. It had happened in this way: they were out hunting when their horses suddenly formed a squadron that galloped off with them at such a great speed that all their efforts to rein them in were completely useless. Paying little heed to her present dignity, Beauty rushed out to embrace them.

The good man himself was the next to appear, but he was not in the same state of confusion. When a horse had neighed and scratched at his door, he was positive that it sought him on orders from his dear daughter. He mounted it without fear and was perfectly at ease to let the steed go where it would. Thus he was not at all surprised to find himself in the courtyard of a palace that he now saw for the third time. Why else would he have been conducted to it but to witness the marriage of Beauty and the Beast?

The moment he saw her, he ran to her with open arms, blessing the happy occasion of seeing her again, and he heaped praise on the generous Beast who had permitted him to return. Looking all around for the Beast in order to offer him his humblest thanks for all the favors he had conferred on his family and particularly his youngest daughter, he was distressed at not finding him and even began to worry that he had drawn the wrong conclusions. Still, the presence of all his children seemed to support his assumption since they would scarcely have been all gathered if some solemn ceremony, such as a marriage, was not to be celebrated.

These thoughts racing through the good man's mind did not prevent him from hugging Beauty fondly and bathing her cheeks with tears of joy. After allowing him this initial expression of his feelings, the fairy said, "Enough, good man. You've caressed this princess enough. It's time that you stop regarding her as a father and learn that the title is not yours to claim. You must now do homage to her as your sovereign. She's the Princess of the Fortunate Island, daughter of the king and queen you see before you. She's about to become the wife of this prince. Here is the prince's mother, sister of the king. I'm a fairy, her friend, and Beauty's aunt. As to the prince," the fairy added, noting the expression of the good man's face, "he's better known to you than you imagine, but he's changed a great deal since you last saw him. In a word, he was the Beast."

The father and his sons were delighted by this wonderful news, while the sisters felt a painful envy. Though their attempt at feigning satisfaction deceived no one, the others pretended to believe they were sincere. As to the lovers, who had abandoned their hope of ever possessing Beauty and returned to their first attachments only in their despair, they did not know what to think.

The merchant could not help weeping, uncertain whether his tears were caused by the pleasure of seeing Beauty's happiness or by the sorrow of losing such a perfect daughter, and his sons were aroused by similarly mixed feelings. Beauty, greatly moved by this evidence of their love, implored those on whom she now depended, as well as her future husband, to permit her to reward such tender attachment. Her request, testifying to the goodness of her heart, was too sincere to be rejected. So they were overwhelmed with gifts, and by permission of the king, the prince, and the queen, Beauty continued to call them by the tender names of father, brothers, and even sisters, though she knew quite well that her "sisters" were so neither in their hearts nor blood. In return, she requested that they call her by the name they were accustomed to when they believed her to be a member of their family. The old man and his children were appointed to respected positions at Beauty's court. The lovers of her sisters, whose feelings for Beauty might easily have been revived had they not known it to be useless, thought themselves quite fortunate to be allied to young women for whom Beauty retained so much goodwill.

After all those she had invited to her wedding had arrived, the celebration went forth without delay. The festivities lasted many days and eventually ended only because the fairy aunt of the young bride pointed out to the newlyweds the propriety of leaving that beautiful retreat and returning to their dominions to show themselves to their subjects. "You must remember to look after your kingdom, for many necessary tasks demand your attention."

They had entirely forgotten about their realm and royal duties, so enchanted had they been by the palace and by the pleasure of expressing their love to each other. Indeed, the newly married couple told the fairy that they wanted to abdicate and give their power to anyone she might select, but the wise fairy made it clear to them that they were under just as great an obligation to fulfill their destiny as rulers of a nation as that nation was to remain loyal to them.

They yielded to these just remonstrances, but the prince and Beauty stipulated that they be allowed to visit that spot occasionally to cast aside the cares of their rank and office for a while. "Furthermore, we want to be waited on by the invisible genii and animals who attended us before." Indeed, they made use of this permission as often as possible, and their presence seemed to enrich the spot. Everyone was eager to please them. The genii awaited their visits with impatience and testified in a hundred ways the delight their return provided them.

The fairy, whose foresight neglected nothing, gave them a chariot drawn by twelve white stags with golden horns and hoofs, like those she drove herself. The speed of these animals was almost greater than that of thought, and if one was drawn by them, one would easily make the tour of the world in two hours. Because of this conveyance they lost no time in traveling. Frequently they used this elegant equipage to visit their father, the King of the Fortunate Island, who had grown so young again thanks to the return of his fairy queen that he resembled his son-in-law. He also felt as happy since he was just as enamored of his wife and eager to demonstrate his unceasing affection to her, while she, on her part, responded to his love with all the tenderness that had previously caused her so much misfortune.

Her subjects had rejoiced as joyously when she returned as they had wept with grief at her loss. She had always loved them dearly, and since she now had no restraints on her will, she showered them with all the benefits they desired for many centuries. Her power, aided by the friendship of the queen of the fairies, preserved the life, health, and youth of her husband for ages. He passed away only because no mortal can live forever.

The queen and her sister took the same good care of Beauty, her husband, the queen, his mother, the old man, and his entire family. Never has the world known mortals who lived so long. The prince's mother had this marvelous story recorded in the archives of her kingdom and in those of the Fortunate Island so that it might be handed down to posterity. They also distributed copies throughout the universe so that the world at large would never cease talking about the wonderful adventures of Beauty and the Beast.

Jeanne-Marie Leprince
de Beaumont

Jeanne-Marie Leprince de Beaumont (1711–80) was born in Rouen and was given an excellent education. She married M. de Beaumont, a dissolute libertine, in 1743, but the marriage was annulled after only two years. In 1746 she departed for England, where she earned her living as a governess, and she often returned to France for visits. She also remarried, this time to a certain M. Pichon, and raised several children in England. At the same time she began publishing novels and stories with a strong didactic bent. Her first work was a novel entitled *Le Triomphe de la Vérité* (1748), which was published in France. It was in London, however, that she made a name for herself by publishing short stories in magazines and producing collections of anecdotes, stories, fairy tales, commentaries, and essays directed at specific social and age groups. For instance, she published a series of pedagogical works with the following titles: *Le Magasin des Enfants* (1757), *Le Magasin des Adolescents* (1760), *Le Magasin des Pauvres* (1768), *Le Mentor moderne* (1770), *Manuel de la jeunesse* (1773), and *Magasin des dévotes* (1779).

In 1762 she returned to France, where she continued her voluminous production, and retired to a country estate in Haute-Savoie in 1768. Among her major works of this period were: *Mémoires de la Baronne de Batteville* (1776), *Contes moraux* (1774), *Oeuvres mêlées* (1775). By the time of her death, she had written over seventy books.

Mme. Leprince de Beaumont's major fairy tales were all published in *Le Magasin des Enfants*, and they include: *La Belle et la Bête*, *Le Prince Chéri*, *Le Prince Désir*, *Fatal et Fortuné*, *Le Prince Charmant*, *La Veuve et les deux filles*, *Aurore et Aimée*, *Le Pêcheur et le Voyageur*, *Joliette*, and *Bellotte et Laidronette*. Her version of *Beauty and the Beast*, which was based on Mme. de

Villeneuve's longer narrative, is perhaps the most famous in the world. Her emphasis was on the proper upbringing of young girls like Beauty, and she continually stressed industriousness, self-sacrifice, modesty, and diligence in all her tales as the qualities young ladies must possess to attain happiness. She was one of the first French writers to write fairy tales explicitly for children, and one can see from the two tales presented here that she keeps her language and plot simple to convey her moral messages. Though her style is limited by the lesson she wants to teach, she is careful not to destroy the magic in her tales, which triumphs despite her preaching.

BEAUTY
AND
THE BEAST

ONCE upon a time there was an extremely rich merchant who had six children, three boys and three girls. Since he was a sensible man, the merchant spared no expense in educating them, hiring all kinds of tutors for their benefit.

His daughters were very pretty, but everyone admired the youngest one in particular. When she was a small child, they called her simply "Little Beauty." The name stuck and as a result it led to a great deal of envy on the part of her sisters. Not only was the youngest girl prettier, she was also better natured. The two elder girls were very arrogant because their family was rich. They pretended to be ladies and refused to receive visits of daughters who belonged to merchant families. They chose only people of quality for their companions. Every day they went to the balls, the theater, and the park, and they made fun of their younger sister, who spent most of her time reading books.

Since these girls were known to be rich, many important merchants sought their hand in marriage. But the two elder sisters maintained that they would never marry unless they found a duke, or at the very least, a count. But Beauty—as I have mentioned, this was the name of the youngest daughter—thanked all those who proposed marriage to her and said that she was too young and that she wanted to keep her father company for some years to come.

Suddenly the merchant lost his fortune, and the only property he had left was a small country house quite far from the city. With tears in his eyes he told his children that they would have to go and live in this house and work like farmers to support themselves. His two elder daughters replied that they did not want to leave the city and that they had many admirers who would be only too happy to marry them even though they no longer had a fortune. But these fine young ladies were mistaken. Their admirers no longer paid them any attention now that they were poor. Moreover, since they were so arrogant, everyone disliked them and said, "They don't deserve to be pitied.

It's quite nice to see pride take a fall. Now let's see them pretend to be ladies while minding sheep in the country."

Yet at the same time people said, "As for Beauty, we're distressed by her misfortune. She's such a good girl. She has always been kind to poor people. She's so sweet and forthright!"

Several gentlemen still wanted to marry her, despite the fact that she told them that she could not abandon her poor father in his distress. She was going to follow him to the country to console him and help him in his work. Poor Beauty had been greatly upset by the loss of her fortune, but she said to herself, "My tears will not bring back my fortune. So I must try to be happy without it."

When they arrived at the country house, the merchant and his three sons began farming the land. Beauty rose at four o'clock every morning and occupied herself by cleaning the house and preparing breakfast for the family. At first she had a great deal of difficulty because she was not accustomed to working like a servant. But after two months she became stronger, and the hard work improved her health. After finishing her chores, she generally read, played the harpsichord, or sung while spinning. On the other hand, her two sisters were bored to death. They rose at ten, took walks the entire day, and entertained themselves by bemoaning the loss of their beautiful clothes and the fine company they used to have.

"Look at our little sister," they would say to each other. "She's so thick and stupid that she's quite content in this miserable situation."

The good merchant did not agree with them. He knew that Beauty was more suited to stand out in company than they were. He admired the virtues of this young girl—especially her patience, for her sisters were not content merely to let her do all the work in the house, but also insulted her every chance they had.

After living a year in this secluded spot, the merchant received a letter informing him that a ship containing his merchandise had just arrived safely. This news turned the heads of the two elder girls, for they thought that they might put an end to their boredom and would finally be able to leave the countryside. When they saw their father getting ready to depart for the city, they begged him to bring them back dresses, furs, caps, and all sorts of finery. Beauty asked for nothing because she thought that all the profit from the merchandise would not be sufficient to buy what her sisters had requested.

"Don't you want me to buy you something?" her father asked her.

"Since you are so kind to think of me," she replied, "please bring me a rose, for there are none here."

Beauty was not really anxious to have a rose, but she did not want to set an example that would disparage her sisters, who would have said that she had requested nothing to show how much better she was.

The good man set out for the city, but when he arrived, he found there was a lawsuit concerning his merchandise, and after a great deal of trouble, he began his return journey poorer than before.

He had only thirty miles to go before he would reach his house and was already looking forward to seeing his children again, but in passing through a large forest to get to his house, he got lost in a raging snowstorm. The wind was so strong that he was twice knocked from his horse. When night fell, he was convinced that he would die of hunger and cold, or else be eaten by the wolves that were howling all around him. Suddenly he saw a light at the end of a long avenue of trees. It appeared to be quite some distance away, and he began walking in that direction. Soon he realized that the light was coming from a huge palace that was totally illuminated. Thanking God for sending this help, the merchant hurried toward the castle. Imagine his surprise, though, when he found nobody in the courtyards! His horse, which had followed him, saw a large, open stable and walked inside. Upon finding hay and oats, the poor animal, who was dying of hunger, began eating with a rapacious appetite. The merchant tied the horse up in the stable and walked toward the palace without encountering a soul. When he entered a large hall, however, he discovered a good fire and a table set with food for one. Since the sleet and snow had soaked him from head to foot, he approached the fire to dry himself. "The master of this house will forgive the liberty I'm taking," he said to himself, "and I'm sure that he'll be here soon."

He waited a considerable time, but when the clock struck eleven and he still did not see anyone, he could not resist his pangs of hunger anymore. Trembling all over, he took a chicken and devoured it in two mouthfuls. As he became more hardy, he left the hall and wandered through several large, magnificently furnished apartments. Finally he found a room with a good bed, and since it was past midnight and he was tired, he decided to shut the door and go to bed. It was ten o'clock when he woke the next day, and he was greatly surprised to find clean clothes in place of his own, which had been completely muddied.

"Surely," he said to himself, "this palace belongs to some good fairy who has taken pity on my predicament."

He looked out the window and no longer saw snow but an enchanting vista of arbors of flowers. He returned to the large hall where he had dined the night before and saw a small table with a cup of chocolate on it.

"I want to thank you, madam fairy," he said aloud, "for being so kind to think of breakfast for me."

After drinking his chocolate, the good man went to look for his horse. As he passed under an arbor of roses, he remembered Beauty's request, and he plucked a rose from a branch heavy with those flowers. All of a sudden

he heard a loud noise and saw a beast coming toward him. It looked so horrible that he almost fainted.

"You're very ungrateful," the beast said in a ferocious voice. "I saved your life by receiving you in my castle, and then you steal my roses, which I love more than anything else in the world. You will have to die for this mistake. I'll give you a quarter of an hour to ask for God's forgiveness."

The merchant threw himself on his knees and pleaded with clasped hands: "Pardon me, my lord. I didn't think that I'd offend you by plucking a rose. One of my daughters had asked me to bring her one."

"I'm not called 'lord' but Beast. I prefer that people speak their minds, so don't think that you can move me by flattery," replied the monster. "But are you telling me that you have daughters . . .? I'll pardon you on one condition, that one of your daughters comes here voluntarily to die in your place. Don't try to reason with me. Just go. And if your daughters refuse to die for you, swear to me that you'll return within three months."

The good man did not intend to sacrifice one of his daughters to this hideous monster, but he thought, "At least I'll have the pleasure of embracing them one more time."

So he swore he would return, and the Beast told him he could leave whenever he liked. "But," he added, "I don't want you to part empty-handed. Go back to the room where you slept. There you'll find a large, empty chest. You may fill it with whatever you like, and I shall have it carried home for you."

The Beast withdrew, and the good man said to himself, "If I must die, I shall still have the consolation of leaving my children with something to sustain themselves."

He returned to the room where he had slept, and upon finding a large quantity of gold pieces, he filled the chest that the Beast had mentioned. After closing it, he went to his horse in the stable, and left the palace with a sadness that matched the joy that he had experienced upon entering it. His horse took one of the forest roads on its own, and within a few hours the good man arrived at his small house, where his children gathered around him. But instead of returning their caresses, the merchant burst into tears at the sight of them. He held the branch of roses that he had brought for Beauty, and he gave it to her, saying, "Beauty, take these roses. They will cost your poor father dearly."

Immediately thereafter he told his family about the tempestuous adventure that he had experienced. On hearing the tale, the two elder daughters uttered loud cries and berated Beauty, since she did not weep.

"See what this measly creature's arrogance has caused!" they said. "Why didn't she settle for the same gifts as ours? But no, our lady had to be different. Now she's going to be the cause of our father's death, and she doesn't even cry."

"That would be quite senseless," replied Beauty. "Why should I lament my father's death when he is not going to perish? Since the monster is willing to accept one of his daughters, I intend to offer myself to placate his fury, and I feel very fortunate to be in a position to save my father and prove my affection for him."

"No, sister," said her three brothers, "you won't die. We shall go and find this monster, and we'll die under his blows if we can't kill him."

"Don't harbor any such hopes, my children," said the merchant. "The Beast's power is so great that I don't have the slightest hope of killing him. And I'm delighted by the goodness of Beauty's heart, but I won't expose her to death. I'm old, and I don't have much longer to live. Therefore, I'll lose only a few years of my life that I won't regret losing on account of you, my dear children."

"Rest assured, Father," said Beauty, "you won't go to this palace without me. You can't prevent me from following you. Even though I'm young, I'm not so strongly tied to life, and I'd rather be devoured by this monster than to die of the grief that your loss would cause me."

Arguments were in vain: Beauty was determined to depart for this beautiful palace. And her sisters were delighted because the virtues of their younger sister had filled them with a good deal of envy. The merchant was so concerned by the torment of losing his daughter that he forgot all about the chest that he had filled with gold. But as soon as he retired to his room to sleep, he was quite astonished to find it by the side of his bed. He decided not to tell his children that he had become rich, for his daughters would want to return to the city and he was resolved to die in the country. But he confided his secret to Beauty, who informed him that several gentlemen had come during his absence and that two of them loved her sisters. She pleaded with her father to let her sisters get married, for she was of such a kind nature that she loved them and forgave with all her heart the evil they had done her.

When Beauty departed with her father, the two nasty sisters rubbed their eyes with onions to weep. But her brothers wept in truth, as did the merchant. The only one who did not cry was Beauty, because she did not want to increase their distress.

The horse took the road to the palace, and by nightfall they spotted it all alight as before. The horse was installed in the stable, and the good man entered the large hall with his daughter. There they found a table magnificently set for two people. However, the merchant did not have the heart to eat. On the other hand, Beauty forced herself to appear calm, and she sat down at the table and served him. Then she said to herself, "It's clear that the Beast is providing such a lovely feast to fatten me up before eating me."

After they had finished supper, they heard a loud roar, and the merchant tearfully said good-bye to his daughter, for he knew it was the Beast. Beauty could not help trembling at the sight of this horrible figure, but she summoned her courage. The monster asked if she had come of her own accord and, continuing to shake, she responded yes.

"You are, indeed, quite good," said the Beast, "and I am very much obliged to you. As for you, my good man, you are to depart tomorrow, and never think of returning here. Good-bye, Beauty."

"Good-bye, Beast," she responded.

Suddenly the Beast disappeared.

"Oh, my daughter!" said the merchant, embracing Beauty. "I'm half dead with fear. Believe me, it's best if I stay."

"No, my father," Beauty said firmly. "You're to depart tomorrow morning, and you'll leave me to the mercy of Heaven. Perhaps Heaven will take pity on me."

When they went to bed, they thought they would not be able to sleep the entire night. But they were hardly in their beds before their eyes closed shut. During her sleep Beauty envisioned a lady who said to her, "Your kind heart pleases me, Beauty. The good deed you're performing to save your father's life will not go unrewarded."

When Beauty woke the next morning, she told her father about the dream, and though this consoled him somewhat, it did not prevent him from sobbing loudly when he had to tear himself away from his dear child. After he departed, Beauty sat down in the great hall and began to weep as well. Yet since she had a great deal of courage, she asked God to protect her and resolved not to grieve anymore during the short time she had to live. Convinced that the Beast was going to eat her that night, she decided to take a walk in the meantime and explore the splendid castle. She could not help but admire its beauty, and was quite surprised when she found a door on which was written: "BEAUTY'S ROOM." She opened the door quickly and was dazzled by the magnificence that radiated throughout the room. But what struck her most of all was a glass-walled bookcase, a harpsichord, and numerous books of music. "He doesn't want me to get bored," she whispered to herself. "If I'm only supposed to spend one day here, he wouldn't have made all these preparations."

This thought renewed her courage. She opened the library, chose a book, and read these words on it: "Your wish is our command. You are queen and mistress here."

"Alas!" she said with a sigh. "My only wish is to see my poor father again and to know what he's doing at this very moment."

She had said this to herself, so you can imagine her surprise when she glanced at a large mirror and saw her house, where her father was arriving with an extremely sorrowful face. Her sisters went out to meet him, and despite the grimaces they made in pretending to be distressed, the joy on their faces at the absence of their sister was visible. A moment later, everything in the mirror disappeared, and Beauty could not but think that the Beast had been most compliant and that she had nothing to fear from him.

At noon she found the table set, and during her meal she heard an excellent concert, even though she did not see a soul. That evening as she was about to sit down at the table, she heard the noise made by the Beast. She could not keep herself from trembling.

"Beauty," the monster said to her, "would you mind if I watch you dine?"

"You're the master," replied Beauty, trembling.

"No," responded the Beast. "You are the mistress here, and you only have to tell me to go if I bother you. Then I'll leave immediately. Tell me, do you find me very ugly?"

"Yes, I do," said Beauty. "I don't know how to lie. But I believe that you're very good."

"You're right," said the monster. "But besides being ugly, I'm not intelligent at all. I know quite well that I'm just a beast."

"A stupid person doesn't realize that he lacks intelligence," Beauty replied. "Fools never know what they're lacking."

"Enjoy your meal, Beauty," the monster said to her, "and try to amuse yourself in your house, for everything here is yours. I'd feel upset if you were not happy."

"You're quite kind," Beauty said. "I assure you that I am most pleased with your kind heart. When I think of that, you no longer seem ugly to me."

"Oh, yes," the Beast answered, "I have a kind heart, but I'm still a monster."

"There are many men who are more monstrous than you," Beauty said, "and I prefer you with your looks rather than those who have pleasing faces but conceal false, ungrateful, and corrupt hearts."

"If I had the intelligence," the Beast responded, "I'd make a fine compliment to thank you. But I'm so stupid that I can only say that I'm greatly obliged to you."

Beauty ate with a good appetite, for she was no longer afraid of the Beast. She nearly died of fright, though, when he asked, "Beauty, will you be my wife?"

She did not answer right away, for she feared enraging the monster by refusing him. At last, however, she said with a quaver, "No, Beast."

The poor monster meant merely to sigh, but he made such a frightful whistle that it echoed through the entire palace. Beauty soon regained her composure, for the Beast said to her in a sad voice, "Farewell, then, Beauty."

He left the room, turning from time to time to look at her as he went. When Beauty was alone, she felt a great deal of compassion for the Beast. "It's quite a shame," she said, "that he's so ugly, for he's so good."

Three months Beauty spent in great tranquillity. Every evening at supper the Beast paid her a visit and entertained her in conversation with plain good sense, but not what the world calls wit. Every day Beauty discovered new qualities in the monster. She became so accustomed to seeing him that she adjusted to his ugliness, and far from dreading the moment of his visit, she often looked at her watch to see if it was nine o'clock yet, for the Beast never failed to appear at that hour.

Only one thing troubled Beauty. Before she went to bed every night, the Beast would ask her if she would be his wife, and he seemed deeply wounded when she refused.

"You're making me uncomfortable, Beast," she said one day. "I'd like to say I'll marry you, but I'm too frank to allow you to believe that this could ever happen. I'll always be your friend. Try to be content with that."

"I'll have to," responded the Beast. "I am honest with myself, and I know I'm quite horrid-looking. But I love you very much. However, I'm happy enough with the knowledge that you want to stay here. Promise me that you'll never leave me."

Beauty blushed at these words, for she had seen in her mirror that her father was sick with remorse for having lost her, and she wished to see him again.

"I could easily promise never to leave you," she said. "But I have such a desire to see my father again that I would die of grief if you were to refuse me this request."

"I'd rather die myself than to distress you," the monster said. "I'll send you to your father's home. You will stay with him, and your poor beast will die of grief."

"No," Beauty said. "I love you too much to want to cause your death. I promise to return in a week's time. You've shown me that my sisters are married and my brothers have left home to join the army. Just let me stay a week with my father since he's all alone."

"You will be there tomorrow morning," the Beast said. "But remember your promise. You only have to place your ring on the table before going to bed if you want to return. Farewell, Beauty."

As was his custom, the Beast sighed when he said these words, and Beauty went to bed very sad at having troubled him. When she awoke the next morning, she found herself in her father's house, and when she rang a bell at her bedside, it was answered by a servant who uttered a great cry upon seeing her. Her good father came running when he heard the noise and almost died of joy at seeing his dear daughter again. They kept hugging each other for more than a quarter of an hour. After their excitement subsided, Beauty recalled that she did not have any clothes to wear. But the servant told her that he had just found a chest in the next room, and it was full of dresses trimmed with gold and diamonds. Beauty thanked the good Beast for looking after her. She took the least sumptuous of the dresses and told the servant to lock up the others, for she wanted to send them as gifts to her sisters. But no sooner had she spoken those words than the chest disappeared. Her father remarked, "The Beast probably wants you to keep them for yourself." Within seconds the dresses and the chests came back again.

As Beauty proceeded to get dressed, a message was sent to inform her sisters of her arrival, and they came running with their husbands. Both sisters were exceedingly unhappy. The oldest had married a young gentleman who was remarkably handsome, but was so enamored of his own looks that he occupied himself with nothing but his appearance from morning until night and despised his wife's beauty. The second sister had married a man who was very intelligent, but he used his wit only to enrage everyone, first and foremost his wife. The sisters almost died of grief when they saw Beauty dressed like a princess and more beautiful than daylight. It was in vain that she hugged them, for nothing could stifle their envy, which increased when she told them how happy she was.

The two envious sisters descended into the garden to vent their feelings in tears. "Why is this little prig happier than we are?" they asked each other. "Aren't we just as pleasing as she?"

"Sister," said the oldest, "I've just had an idea. Let's try to keep her here more than a week. That stupid beast will become enraged when he finds out that she's broken her word, and perhaps he'll devour her."

"Right you are, sister," responded the other. "But we must show her a great deal of affection to succeed."

Having made this decision, they returned to the house and showed Beauty so much attention that she wept with joy. Once the week had passed, the two sisters tore their hair and seemed so distressed by her departure that she promised to remain another week. Even so, Beauty reproached herself for the grief she was causing her poor Beast, whom she loved with all her heart. In addition, she missed not being able to see him any longer. On the tenth night she spent in her father's house, she dreamt that she was in the palace garden and saw the Beast lying on the grass nearly dead and reprimanding her for her ingratitude. Beauty woke with a start and burst into tears.

"Aren't I very wicked for causing grief to a beast who's gone out of his way to please me?" she said. "Is it his fault that he's so ugly and has so little intelligence? He's so kind, and that's worth more than anything else. Why haven't I wanted to marry him? I'm more happy with him than my sisters are with their husbands. It is neither handsome looks nor intelligence that makes a woman happy. It is good character, virtue, and kindness, and the Beast has all these good qualities. It's clear that I don't love him, but I have respect, friendship, and gratitude for him. So there's no reason to make him miserable, and if I'm ungrateful, I'll reproach myself for the rest of my life."

With these words Beauty placed her ring on the table and lay down again. No sooner did her head hit the pillow than she fell asleep, and when she woke the next morning, she saw with joy that she was in the Beast's palace. She put on her most magnificent dress to please him and spent a boring day waiting for the evening to arrive. But the clock struck nine, and Beast did not appear.

Now Beauty feared that she had caused his death. She ran throughout the palace, sobbing loudly. After searching everywhere, she recalled her dream and ran into the garden toward the canal, where she had seen him in her sleep. There she found the poor Beast stretched out unconscious. She thought he was dead. Without concern for his horrifying looks, she threw herself on his body and felt his heart still beating. So she fetched some water from the canal and threw it on his face.

Beast opened his eyes and said, "You forgot your promise, Beauty.

The grief I felt upon having lost you made me decide to fast to death. But I shall die content since I have the pleasure of seeing you one more time."

"No, my dear Beast, you shall not die," said Beauty. "You will live to become my husband. I give you my hand and swear that I belong only to you from this moment on. Alas! I thought that I only felt friendship for you, but the torment I am feeling makes me realize that I cannot live without you."

Beauty had scarcely uttered these words when the castle radiated with light. Fireworks and music announced a feast. These attractions did not hold her attention, though. She returned her gaze to her dear Beast, whose dangerous condition made her tremble. How great was her surprise when she discovered that the Beast had disappeared, and at her feet was a prince more handsome than Eros himself, who thanked her for having put an end to his enchantment. Although she should have been only concerned about the prince, she could not refrain from asking what had happened to the Beast.

"You're looking at him right at your feet," the prince said. "A wicked fairy condemned me to remain in this form until a beautiful girl consented to marry me, and she prohibited me from revealing my intelligence. You were the only person in the world kind enough to allow the goodness of my character to touch you. In offering you my crown, I'm only discharging the debt I owe you."

Beauty was most pleasantly surprised and assisted the handsome prince in rising by offering her hand. Together they went to the castle, where Beauty was overwhelmed by joy in finding her father and entire family in the hall, for the beautiful lady who had appeared to her in her dream had transported them to the castle.

"Beauty," said this lady, who was a grand fairy, "come and receive the reward for your good choice. You've preferred virtue over beauty and wit, and you deserve to find these qualities combined in one and the same person. You're going to become a great queen, and I hope that a throne will not destroy your virtuous qualities. As for you, my young ladies," the fairy said to Beauty's two sisters, "I know your hearts and all the malice they contain. You shall become statues while retaining your ability to think beneath the stone that encompasses you. You will stand at the portal of your sister's palace, and I can think of no better punishment to impose on you than to witness her happiness. I'll allow you to return to your original shape only when you recognize your faults, but I fear that you'll remain statues forever. Pride, anger, gluttony, and laziness can all be corrected, but some sort of miracle is needed to convert a wicked and envious heart."

The fairy waved her wand and all at once transported everyone in the hall to the prince's realm, where his subjects rejoiced upon seeing him again. Then he married Beauty, who lived with him a long time in perfect happiness because their relationship was founded on virtue.

PRINCE DÉSIR
AND
PRINCESS MIGNONE

ONCE upon a time there was a king who was passionately in love with a princess, but she could not marry because she was under a magic spell. When he went in search of a fairy to learn what he could do to win this princess's hand, the fairy said to him, "This princess has a large cat that she's very fond of, and she's destined to marry the man who's nimble enough to tread on her cat's tail."

Saying to himself, "That won't be difficult," the king left the fairy determined to crush the cat's tail without fail. So he ran to the princess's palace, and Minon came toward him, raising its back as it was accustomed to do. The king responded by lifting his foot, and just as he was sure he would step on the cat's tail, Minon turned around so quickly that his majesty trod on nothing but the floor. For a week he tried to step on this fatal tail, but it seemed to be full of quicksilver, so continually was it in motion. At last the king had the good fortune of surprising Minon while he was sleeping, and he stamped on its tail with all his might. Minon awoke with a horrible squeal. Suddenly it took the form of a huge man and looked at the king with eyes full of rage.

"You will wed the princess," he said, "because you've destroyed the enchantment that prevented you from doing so. But I'll be avenged. You will have a son who'll turn unhappy once he discovers that he has a nose that's too long. And if you dare reveal this curse, you will die immediately."

Although the king was very frightened by the sight of this giant, who was a sorcerer, he could not help but laugh at this threat. "If my son has a nose that's too long," he said to himself, "he'll always be able to see or feel it, unless he's either blind or has no hands."

Since the sorcerer had disappeared, the king went looking for the princess. She consented to marry him, but his happiness was brief, for he died at the end of eight months. A month later, the queen gave birth to a little prince, who was named Désir. He had the most beautiful blue eyes, and a pretty little mouth, but his nose was so big that it covered half his face.

When she saw this great nose, the queen was inconsolable, but her ladies in attendance told her that the nose was not as large as it appeared to be. "It's a Roman nose, and if you study history, you'll learn all heroes have large noses." The queen, who doted on her newborn, was charmed by these words, and after continually looking at Désir, his nose did not appear so large after all.

The prince was carefully reared, and as soon as he could talk, they told all sorts of shocking stories in front of him about people with short noses. They allowed no one to come near him, but those whose noses in some degree resembled his own. Indeed, all the courtiers pulled the noses of their children several times a day to make them long enough to pay their respects to the queen and her son. (It was no use pulling, though, because they appeared snub-nosed beside Prince Désir.) As soon as he could read, they taught him history, and when they spoke of any great prince or beautiful princess, they always spoke of their long noses. Désir became so accustomed to regarding the length of a nose as a mark of beauty that he would not have wished his smaller even for a crown.

When he reached the age of twenty, they thought of marrying him and showed him portraits of several princesses. He became captivated by that of Mignone's. She was the daughter of a great king and heiress to several kingdoms, but this did not matter a whit to Désir because he was so enchanted by her beauty.

This princess whom he found so charming had a little turned-up nose, which made her face the prettiest in the world, but which created a predicament for Désir's courtiers. They had acquired the habit of ridiculing little noses, and they could not keep from smiling when they saw the princess's nose. However, Désir would allow no raillery on the subject and banished two men from his court who dared to disparage Mignone's nose. The other courtiers learned from this example and corrected themselves, and there was one who said to the prince that, in truth, a man could not be handsome without a large nose, but that female beauty was altogether different. "A scholar who speaks Greek told me he read in an old Greek manuscript that the beautiful Cleopatra had the tip of her nose turned up."

The prince gave a magnificent present to the person who told him this good news, and he sent ambassadors to demand Mignone's hand in marriage. They granted his request, and he rode more than three miles to meet her along the way because he was so eager to see her. But when he advanced to kiss her hand, the sorcerer descended, carried off the princess right in front of him, and left him inconsolable. Désir made up his mind not to return to his kingdom until he had rescued Mignone. He would not allow any of his courtiers to follow him, and since he was mounted on his good horse, he put the bridle on his neck and let him lead the way.

The horse entered a large plain, and Désir traveled all day without seeing a single house. The master and his horse were both dying of hunger when toward evening the prince at last saw a cave that appeared to emit light. Entering, he saw a little woman who seemed to be more than a hundred years old. She put on her spectacles to look at the prince, but she took a long time in adjusting them because her nose was too short. The prince and the fairy (for that was what she was) both burst out laughing at seeing each other, and both cried at once, "Ah, what a droll nose!"

"Not so droll as yours," Désir said to the fairy. "But, madam, let's leave our noses as they are, and be so kind as to give me something to eat, for I'm dying of hunger, and so is my poor horse."

"With all my heart," the fairy said. "Although your nose is ridiculous, you're no less the son of my best friend. I loved the king, your father, like my own brother. He had a very handsome nose, that prince!"

"And what's wrong with mine?"

"Oh, there's nothing wrong," the fairy replied. "On the contrary, there's just too much of it. But never mind, one may be a very good man, even with a long nose. I've told you that I was your father's friend. He came to see me often back then, and apropos of those days, let me tell you I was then very pretty, and he used to say so. I must tell you a conversation we had together the first time he saw me—"

"Madam," Désir said, "it will be my pleasure to listen to you once I've had something to eat. Please, remember that I've not eaten all day."

"Poor boy," the fairy said. "You're right. I forgot all about that. I'll give you your supper right away, and while you're eating, I'll tell you my story in as few words as possible. I'm not fond of long stories, you know. Too long a tongue is even more insufferable than a long nose, and I remember when I was young, I was admired because I wasn't a great prattler. They told this to the queen, my mother. In spite of the way you see me now, I'm the daughter of a great king. My father—"

"Your father ate when he was hungry," the prince interrupted.

"Yes, without a doubt," the fairy replied, "and you'll eat also in a moment. I only wanted to tell you that my father—"

"And I'll listen to nothing until I've eaten!" said the prince, beginning to get angry. He calmed down, however, because he needed the fairy, and said to her, "I know the pleasure I'd have in listening to you would make me forget my hunger, but my horse can't listen to you, and he needs food."

The fairy was pleased by this compliment. "You won't wait much longer," she said, calling her servants. "You're very polite, and despite the enormous size of your nose, you're very good-looking."

"May the plague take the old woman for going on so about my nose," the prince said to himself. "You'd think that my mother had stolen that part of her nose that makes hers so deficient. If I didn't want something to eat so badly, I'd leave this chatterbox. Where did she ever get the idea that she's not an incessant talker? You've got to be a great fool not to know your own defects. This must come from being born a princess. No doubt, flatterers have spoiled her and have convinced her that she talks very little."

While the prince mulled over these thoughts, the servants set the table, and he could not but stare in amazement at the fairy, who asked them a thousand questions merely for the pleasure of talking. Above all he admired the tact of a lady-in-waiting who, no matter what the fairy said, praised her mistress for her discretion.

"Well," he thought while eating, "I'm charmed at having come here. This example makes me see how wisely I've acted in not listening to flatterers. Such people's praise is shameless. They hide our defects from us and change them into perfections. As for me, I'll never be their dupe. Thank God, I know my faults!"

Poor Désir was thoroughly convinced of this and did not feel that those who had praised his nose mocked him just as the lady-in-waiting mocked the fairy (for the prince saw that she turned aside from time to time to giggle). As for him, he did not say a word.

"Prince," the fairy said when she saw he was satisfying his hunger, "please turn yourself a little. Your nose is casting a shadow that prevents me from seeing what's on my plate. Now, come, let's talk about your father. I went to his court when he was a little boy, but it's forty years since I withdrew to this solitary place. Tell me a little about the way they live at court these days. Do the ladies still love rushing from place to place? In my time they could be seen on the same day at the assembly, the theater, the promenades, and the ball—how long your nose is! I can't get accustomed to the sight of it!"

"Indeed," Désir replied, "I wish you'd stop talking about my nose. It is what it is. What does it matter to you? I'm content with it and don't want it any shorter. Everyone's nose is just as it pleases Providence."

"Oh! I see plainly that you're angry, my poor Désir," the fairy said. "However, it wasn't my intention to annoy you. Quite the contrary. I'm one of your friends, and I'd like to do you a favor. It's just that I can't help but being shocked by your nose. I'll try not to talk about it, however. I'll even force myself to think you're snub-nosed, although to tell the truth, there's enough material in that nose of yours to make three reasonable noses."

Désir, who had finished eating, became so impatient with the endless talk the fairy kept up on the subject of his nose that he threw himself on his horse and rode off. He continued his journey and wherever he passed, he thought everybody mad because they talked about his nose. So accustomed had he been to hearing that his nose was handsome that he could never admit to himself that it was too long. The old fairy, who wanted to do him a favor in spite of himself, got it into her head to get Mignone from the sorcerer and lock her up in a crystal palace. Then she placed this palace on Prince Désir's way. Ecstatic, he tried to break the crystal, but he found it impossible to do. In despair he approached so that he could at least speak to the princess. For her part, she pressed her hand close to the glass. He wanted to kiss it, but no matter how he turned, he could not get his lips near it. His nose prevented him. For the first time he realized how extraordinarily long it was, and he grabbed it with his hand to bend it to one side. "I must confess," he said, "that my nose *is* too long."

All at once the crystal palace collapsed, and the old woman, holding Mignone by the hand, said to the prince, "Admit that you're greatly indebted to me. I could have talked myself blue, and you still wouldn't have believed that you had a defect until it became an obstacle that hindered the fulfillment of your wishes."

Thus does self-love conceal the deformities of our soul and body from us. Reason seeks in vain to reveal them to us. We do not admit that we have them until the moment when this same self-love discovers that they oppose its interests. Désir, whose nose now became an ordinary one, had learned his lesson. He married Mignone and lived happily with her for a great number of years.

Philippe de Caylus

Anne-Claude-Philippe de Tubières Grimoard de Pestels de Le-
vis, Comte de Caylus (1692–1765) was born into one of the most
respected aristocratic families in France. Caylus was given a remarkably well-rounded education and then entered military service
in 1709 as a musketeer. After fighting in the War of the Spanish
Succession and distinguishing himself in Fribourg, he took time
off from the army and traveled to Italy, where he studied the
classical arts. By 1715 he had resigned from the army and began
dedicating his life to the study of the arts and sciences. Undertaking a long voyage to the Middle East and China to collect cultural
artifacts and to study foreign customs, he did not return to Paris
until 1717. From then on, Caylus devoted himself to painting,
sculpture, music, and engraving, and built up a vast collection of
Greek, Roman, Egyptian, and French art works. His major contribution to the arts was in the field of engraving and painting. One
of the best engravers of his times, he became known for engravings
in the manner of Rubens, Van Dyck, and Leonardo da Vinci and
also created numerous caricatures. In addition, he worked with
chemists to develop processes that would make paint more indel-
ible and also to tint marble. Throughout his life he was a generous
patron of the arts and artists and also assisted scientists in their
research.

Caylus was unusually prolific and versatile as a writer. He wrote
novels, anecdotal stories, studies of the theater, painting, artifacts,
and engraving, and personal memoirs. Among his more important
scholarly works are: *Recueil d'antiquités égyptiennes, étrusques,
grecques, romaines et gauloises* (1752–67), *Nouveaux Sujets de
peinture et de Sculpture* (1755), and *Recueil de peintures antiques*
(1757).

His prose fiction in such works as *Histoire de Guillaume, cocher*
(1735) and *Mémoires de l'académie des Colporteurs* (1745) was witty
and charming, and he wrote several books of lively fairy tales:

Féeries nouvelles (1741), *Contes orientaux tirés des manuscrits de la bibliothéque du roi de France* (1743), *Cinq Contes des Fées* (1745), *Le Pot-Pourri* (1748), and *Le Loup galeux et la Jeune Vieille* (1744), which is sometimes attributed to Madame de Villeneuve. Caylus's attitude toward the fairy-tale tradition was an ironic one. He had been a child when the fairy tale had been in vogue and had been part of the salon life of Paris. However, the fairy tale had lost its ties to the salons and courtly life by the time he began composing his tales, and it was more a subject to be parodied than a means of compensation that enabled women writers to express social criticism and utopian longings. *La Princesse Minutie et le Roi Floridor* (Princess Minute and King Floridor), which appeared in *Féeries nouvelles* (1741), is a good example of his tongue-in-cheek attitude toward the fairy-tale tradition and the pretentiousness of court society. Nothing is to be taken seriously in this tale, and one is left wondering whether the happy end is but a mockery of the traditional fairy-tale ending.

PRINCESS MINUTE
AND
KING FLORIDOR

ONCE upon a time there was a king and queen who died young and left a very fine empire to their only daughter, who was then only thirteen years of age. She thought she knew how to reign, and all her good subjects, without knowing quite why, convinced themselves she was right. However, being a queen is a profession that is not without its difficulties.

At least the king and queen had the consolation of knowing when they died that they were leaving their daughter under the protection of a friendly fairy. Her name was Mirdandenne. She was a very good soul, but had a major fault: she never gave in when she thought she was right, even though she might be biased. As for the little princess, she was so tiny that they called her Minute.

This fine kingdom was governed by obstinacy and frivolity, for the princess's passion for trifles had never been corrected, and it was because of her that all those little knickknacks were invented that have since spread all over the world. The princess was deluded by the grandeur of her ideas and showed it in a thousand different ways. Let me point out just one: she would not retain a general who had distinguished himself by deeds rendered to the state as head of her army. Indeed, she even exiled him from the court. And why? Because he had appeared in her presence with a hat bound with silver when his coat was laced with gold. She thought that any man who was guilty of such negligence at court would also allow himself to be surprised by the enemy for the same reason. The discernment that she thought she had shown in this instance, and the wisdom that the fairy found in some of her other frivolous ideas, were enough to make the most sound person unstable.

Now, near this great country was a kingdom so tiny that I hardly know what to compare it to. The queen mother who had reigned over it for a long time in the name of one Prince Floridor had recently died. Floridor, who was the most affectionate son possible, felt this loss acutely and always retained a feeling of gratitude for the things she had given him. One of the greatest was a perfect education—the most perfect and, as far as his physical prowess was concerned, the most rigid. Thus he was both robust and active, and possessed a refined and sound mind. Handsome and well formed, this young prince governed wisely without abusing his sovereign power, for he restrained his desires carefully. In short, he was a charming person: his subjects adored him, and the strangers who visited the court agreed that he would have brought happiness to the greatest empire. But one thing they did not know was that he owed a great number of his qualities to a charming ant, who had been attached to him from his early childhood.

At the death of the queen the good ant was his sole consolation. He did not take a single step without previously consulting this ant, who had chosen as her residence a wooded area in the palace gardens. He often abandoned the court and its pleasures to go and converse with her, no matter what the weather. And no matter how severe the winter, she always came out of her anthill, which was the best supervised for a hundred miles around, and gave him prudent and wise advice.

You may have guessed that the pretty ant in question was a fairy. Her history, which dates back seven thousand years, has been chronicled down to the twenty-two-thousandth year of the world at the four-hundred-and-sixtieth page of the volume for that year. This ant could have easily given the king, whom she loved very much, several kingdoms—for fairies dispose of them as they please—but the ant was prudent, and prudence is always guided by justice. It was not that she did not heartily desire to see Floridor advance in the world. Rather, she wanted him to increase his glory only by employing those qualities that she had instilled in his heart.

Naturally patient, the ant waited for an opportunity to bring the virtues of her pupil to light. And sure enough, Minute's conduct and Mirdandenne's bias soon furnished her with one. The flame of revolt was kindled in Minute's mighty kingdom. When this news was confirmed by all the newspapers, the good fairy ant told King Floridor to set out, attended simply by a groom, in order to help the queen, his neighbor. Before he departed, she gave him a common sparrow, a little carving knife, and a walnut shell. "My gifts," she said, "seem very ordinary, but put your mind at ease. They'll be of service to you when you're in need."

He immediately assured her that he had complete confidence in her, since she had done many favors for him in the past. After bidding her a tender farewell, he set out on his journey, and every inhabitant of his little kingdom felt as sad about his departure as they would a brother, son, or bosom friend.

Arriving in the capital of Queen Minute's realm, he found it in a frenzy. The people had heard that a neighboring king leading one of the most dreadful armies imaginable was advancing rapidly with the intention of taking over the kingdom. Floridor learned that the queen had withdrawn to a pleasant residence that she owned near the capital, in which she had collected all sorts of glittering trinkets. However, she had a motive for this retreat: she wanted to have time to reflect seriously and without any interruption whether her troops should wear blue or white cockades. Incidentally, the queen was twenty years old by this time.

King Floridor discovered the road that led to this country villa and proceeded there as quickly as possible. His handsome face made Mirdandenne partial to him, and the compliments he paid her and the queen only increased her good opinion of him. Naturally, when he offered his services, he was extremely well received because the state was in a very embarrassing predicament.

Floridor found Minute charming, and from the moment he saw her, he fell desperately in love with her. The zeal and alacrity that always accompany love showed in his every word and gesture and glistened in his eyes. As he began to investigate the existing state of affairs, he wanted to use the fairy's powers, but Mirdandenne's lack of forethought had led her long ago to give her wand to Minute to keep her amused. The princess had used it so often that as a result, it was worn out and no longer had any power or virtue, particularly for important things. When Floridor returned to the capital, moreover, he found neither fortifications nor ammunition for waging a war.

Meanwhile, the invader, whom Floridor considered a rival for Minute's hand, advanced nearer and nearer. Finding no other recourse, he proposed that the queen take flight and proudly offered her asylum in his kingdom. Prudence suggested a course that his courage condemned, but he had to save the unfortunate queen, and only made this proposition on the condition that once she was safe, he be allowed to return and risk his life in battle to save her legitimate title. Mirdandenne was convinced that the king's proposal was a good one, but the queen consented to depart only when they promised her that her horse would have a rose-colored harness. Floridor also agreed to give her the sparrow that the fairy ant had given him. The bird was quickly obtained, and though they needed urgently to depart, they had to wait till the harness that the queen had requested could be procured from the city. At last it came, and Floridor and Minute, with no other accompaniment but Mirdandenne, took the road to his realm.

Floridor was enchanted at being allowed to conduct Minute to his kingdom and at having the opportunity to make himself useful to the woman he adored. Being in love and traveling are two things that make people exceedingly talkative. Floridor blushed in telling of the limited extent of his realm, and he could not refrain from mentioning the debts he owed to the good ant. When he came to recount the details of their parting, the queen found the sparrow, little knife, and walnut to be very strange presents. She was eager to see the walnut, and the king gave it to her without hesitation. As soon as it was in her hand, she cried, "Heavens, what do I hear!" She put her ear to it with the utmost attention and then said with a mixture of surprise and curiosity, "I can hear little voices of men, neighing of horses, and trumpets very distinctly. In short, I hear a very strange murmur, and it's the prettiest thing in the world!"

While the king watched his beloved Minute amuse herself, he noticed that the scouts of the rebels were closing in on them and about to take them prisoners. Faced with the impending danger, he reached mechanically for the walnut and accidentally broke it. Out jumped thirty thousand armed men—infantry, cavalry, and dragoons—with artillery and all the necessary ammunition. He placed himself at their head, and after showing a bold front to the enemy, he did not even have to strike a blow, but beat the most dignified retreat in the world. In this way he was able to command the mountains along the way and save the queen from the hands of her rebellious subjects. After such a fine military maneuver, which was not accomplished without much exhaustion and concern for the queen's safety, they stopped for several days in the mountains. Since the entire country was up in arms, however, they saw another army as they began their march again. This one was much larger than the one they had escaped, and Floridor would have been extremely rash to fight it. In this dire predicament, what did the queen do? She requested the little knife for some trivial purpose. On discovering that it did not cut to her fancy, she threw it away, saying, "What a dull knife!"

However, the moment it pierced the ground, it made a considerable hole. Struck by its power, the king immediately used it to cut deep entrenchments all around the mountain, making their position impregnable. When this operation was finished—and it took him only minutes to make the circle—the sparrow he had given to Minute flew to the summit of the mountain. Flapping its wings as it hovered, it cried in a terrible voice, "Let me deal with them! You're about to see a wonderful game. Descend the mountain and march upon the enemy. You have nothing to fear."

They immediately followed the sparrow's orders while the bird lifted the mountain as easily as a straw. Into the air he flew with it and let it fall on the army of the enemy, covering the majority of their forces. The rest took flight and left the passage free. The king, who was primarily concerned with getting the queen to safety, urged the horses to go faster, but since the pace of an army is necessarily slow, he would have liked the army to reenter the walnut shell. No sooner did he utter this wish than it occurred. He put the shell in his pocket, and they arrived in his little kingdom, where the good ant greeted them with every sign of friendship.

When Floridor was convinced that Minute had everything she needed in the palace, he began making his preparations to depart in a cheerful mood.

Not only had the good ant assured him she would look after the queen, but during their recent journey he had taken the opportunity to declare his love to Minute, which she had been kind enough to approve. Thus, when he was finally obliged to leave her, they bid tender adieus. Off Floridor went with no other aid but a letter from Minute addressed to her good and faithful subjects, in which she requested them to obey King Floridor's commands.

The good ant did not give him back the walnut or the little knife. On the other hand, the queen wanted him to have the sparrow, and requested that he carry it with him at all times along with an embroidered silk scarf that she herself had made for him. The king followed the exact same route that he had taken to his country with the queen, not only because lovers like to revisit places associated in their memories with their loves, but because it was also the shortest route. When he approached the transplanted mountain, the sparrow flew into the air, picked it up with the same facility as before, and carried it back to its previous spot. Then, in that terrible voice he knew how to assume, the sparrow said to the people whom he found shut up under the mountain, "Be faithful to Minute, and do what King Floridor orders in her name."

After saying this, the strange sparrow disappeared. The mountain, it seems, was hollow, and these people had been enclosed in it as under a bell. They did not suffer from want during the time of their imprisonment, and once the soldiers and officers saw the light of day again, they ran pell-mell to Floridor. So impressed were they by his handsome features that they regarded him as a demigod and were ready to worship him. The king was touched by their obedience and, after being shown the letter with which he was charged, they swore new vows of fidelity to the lawful queen in his presence.

He made the army pass in review and chose fifty thousand of the finest men, whose devotion a general needs if he is to have success. Then he established strict rules of discipline for this new army and used himself to set their example. With these troops he became invincible and defied the countless forces of the usurper, whom he slew with his own hand in one of the last battles. This death enabled Minute to regain a kingdom that had been utterly lost to her. Floridor marched through all the provinces of this great state and reestablished her authority. Thereafter, he rushed back to his kingdom to rejoin her.

What a change he found in the character and mind of this lovely queen! The counsels of the good ant and, above all, love and the wish to be worthy of Floridor had completely corrected her only fault. She was ashamed of having always done little things with great help, while her lover had done such great things with so little.

They married and lived happily ever after.

Mlle. de Lubert

Mademoiselle de Lubert (c.1710–c.1779) was the daughter of the president of Parlement in Paris. Not much is known about her life except that she rejected marriage in order to dedicate herself to her writing. She was able to do this because she was independently wealthy. As her career advanced, she developed good relations with Fontenelle, Voltaire, and La Condamine, who praised her works.

Mlle. de Lubert wrote poetry and prose and had a special talent for combining motifs from ancient romances with traditional folk tales to produce long fairy tales that are extraordinarily imaginative and complex. Her major works include: *Les Princes des Autruches* (1743), *Le Prince Glacé et la Princesse Etincelante* (1743), *La Princesse Camion* (1743), *La Princesse Couleur de Rose et le Prince Céladon* (1743), *La Veillée galante* (1747), *Histoire de la princesse Foirette, et d'autres contes* (1750), *Blancherose* (1751), *Mourat et Turquia* (1752), and *Léonille* (1755).

Writing in the tradition of Mme. d'Aulnoy, Mlle. de Lubert had a penchant for the grotesque and bizarre mixed with sadism. Monsters and tortures abound in her works, and there is an obvious influence of the theater, ballet, and opera on them. Mlle. de Lubert sought to transform the scenes in her works into theatrical spectacles. In turn, these unusual scenes created an atmosphere that allowed her to treat such serious themes as forced marriages, fidelity, and authority with a great deal of freedom. In *Princess Camion* are characters and incidents that prefigure the grotesque in Kafka, and although they are also somewhat ludicrous, Mlle. Lubert's fairy tales may be interpreted as ironical commentaries about courtly manners that seemed absurd to her. In this respect, we must consider her perspective as that of a single woman opposed to marriage and traditional social norms, who saw her tales as a subversive means to make her critical private views extraordinarily public.

THE PRINCESS
CAMION

ONCE upon a time there was a king and queen who placed all their hopes for a successor in their only son, for the queen did not bear any other children. By the time Prince Zirphil was fourteen, he was marvelously handsome and learned everything taught him with ease. The king and queen were tremendously fond of him, and their subjects adored him, for whereas he was friendly to everyone, he knew how to make distinctions among those who approached him. Since he was an only son, the king and queen decided he should marry as soon as possible in order to secure the succession to the crown.

Therefore, they had their men travel by foot and on horseback to look for a princess worthy of the heir apparent, but they failed to find anyone suitable. At last, after the long, careful search, the queen was informed that a veiled lady requested a private audience regarding an important affair. The queen immediately ascended her throne in the audience chamber and ordered the lady to be admitted. The lady approached without removing her white crepe veil, which hung all the way to the ground. Arriving at the foot of the throne, she said, "Queen, I'm astonished that you thought of marrying your son without consulting me. I'm the fairy Marmotte, and my name is sufficiently well-known to have reached your ears."

"Ah, madam," the queen said, quickly descending her throne and embracing the fairy, "I'm sure you'll pardon my fault when I tell you that people related stories to me about your wonders as though they were nursery tales. But now that you've graced this palace by coming here, I no longer doubt your power. I beg you, do me the honor of giving me your advice."

"That's not a sufficient answer for a fairy," Marmotte replied. "Such an excuse might perhaps satisfy a common person, but I'm mortally offended, and to begin your punishment, I command you to have Zirphil marry the person I've brought with me."

Upon saying these words, she felt around in her pocket and took out a toothpick case. When she opened it, out came a little ivory doll, so pretty and well made that the queen could not help admiring it despite her unease.

"This is my goddaughter," the fairy said, "and I had always destined her for Zirphil."

The queen soaked herself in her tears. She implored Marmotte in the most touching terms not to expose her to the ridicule of her people, who would laugh at her if she announced such a marriage.

"Laugh, will they, madam?" the fairy exclaimed. "Indeed, we shall see if they have reason to laugh! We shall see if they laugh at my goddaughter, and if your son doesn't adore her. I can tell you that she deserves to be adored. It's true that she's tiny, but she has more sense than your entire kingdom put together. When you hear her speak, you'll be surprised yourself—for she can talk, I promise you. Now, then, little Princess Camion," she said to the doll, "speak a little to your mother-in-law, and show her what you can do."

Then the pretty Camion jumped on the queen's fur tippet and paid her a little compliment so tender and sensitive that her majesty stopped crying and gave the Princess Camion a hearty kiss.

"Here, Queen, is my toothpick case," the fairy said. "Put your daughter-in-law in it. I want your son to become acquainted with her before marrying her. I don't think it will take long. Your obedience may soften my anger, but if you act contrary to my orders, you, your husband, your son, and your kingdom will all feel the effect of my wrath. Above all, take care to put her back into her case early in the evening because it's important that she doesn't stay out late."

As she finished saying this, the fairy raised her veil, and the queen fainted from fright when she saw an actual marmot—black, sleek, and as large as a human being. Her attendants rushed to her assistance, and when she recovered, she saw nothing but the case that Marmotte had left behind her.

Putting her to bed, they went to inform the king about the accident. He arrived very anxious, and the queen sent everyone away. In a flood of tears she told the king about what had just happened. At first the king did not believe it, not until he saw the doll that the queen drew from the case.

"Heavens!" he cried, and after reflecting a moment, he asked, "Why is it that kings are exposed to such great misfortunes? Ah, we're placed above other men only to feel the cares and sorrows that are part of our existence more acutely."

"And in order to set greater examples of fortitude, sire," added the doll in a small, sweet, distinct voice.

"My dear Camion," the queen said, "you speak like an oracle."

After the three of them had conversed for an hour, they decided not to reveal the impending marriage until Zirphil, who had gone hunting for three days, returned and agreed to obey the fairy's command. In the interim the queen and the king withdrew to the privacy of their rooms in order to talk to little Camion. Since she had a highly cultivated intellect, she spoke well and with an unusual turn of thought that was very pleasing. Although she was vivacious, her eyes had a fixed expression that was not very pleasant. Moreover, it disturbed the queen because she had begun to love Camion and feared the prince might take a dislike toward her.

More than a month passed since Marmotte had appeared, but the queen still had not dared to show Zirphil his intended. One day he entered the room while she was in bed. "Madam," he said, "the most unusual thing happened to me some days ago while I was hunting. I had wanted to keep it from you, but it's come to seem so extraordinary that I must tell you about it no matter what.

"I had followed a wild boar and chased it into the middle of the forest without observing that I was alone. When I saw him jump into a great hole that opened up in the ground, my horse plunged in after it, and I continued falling for half an hour. At last I found myself at the bottom of this hole without having hurt myself. Instead of encountering the boar, which, I confess, I was afraid of facing, I saw a very ugly woman who asked me to dismount and follow her. I didn't hesitate giving her my hand, and she opened a small door that had previously been hidden from view. I entered with her into a salon of green marble, where there was a golden bathtub covered with a curtain of very rich material. The curtain rose, and I saw a person of such marvelous beauty in the tub that I thought I would faint. 'Prince Zirphil,' said the bathing lady, 'the fairy Marmotte has enchanted me, and it's only through your aid that I can be released.'

" 'Speak, madam,' I said to her. 'What must I do to help you?'

" 'You must either marry me this instant or skin me alive.'

"I was just as surprised by the first alternative as I was alarmed by the second. She read the embarrassment in my eyes and said, 'Don't think I'm jesting, or that I'm proposing something you may regret. No, Zirphil, dismiss your fears. I'm an unfortunate princess who's detested by a fairy. She's made me half woman, half whale because I wouldn't marry her nephew, the King of the Whiting—he's frightful and even more wicked than he is hideous. She's condemned me to remain in my present state until a prince named Zirphil fulfills one of the two conditions that I've just proposed. To expedite this matter, I had my maid of honor take the form of a wild boar, and it was she who led you to this spot, where you'll remain until you fulfill my desire in one way or the other. I'm not mistress here, and Citronette, who you see with me, will tell you that this is the only way it can be.'

"Imagine, madam," the prince said to the queen, who was listening attentively, "what a state I was in when I heard these words! Although the whale-princess's face was exceedingly pleasing and her charms and misfortunes made her extremely intriguing, the fact that she was half fish horrified me, and the idea of skinning her alive threw me into utter despair. 'But, madam,' I said to her at length (for my silence was as stupid as it was insulting), 'isn't there a third way?' No sooner had I uttered those unfortunate words than the whale-princess and her attendant uttered shrieks and lamentations that were enough to pierce the vaulted roof of the salon. 'Ungrateful wretch! Cruel tiger, and everything that is most ferocious and inhuman!' the whale-princess exclaimed. 'Do you want to condemn me to the torture of seeing you perish as well? If you don't grant my request, the fairy has assured me you'll die, and I'll remain a whale my entire life.'

"Her reproaches pierced my heart. She raised her beautiful arms out of the water and joined her charming hands together to implore me to decide quickly. Citronette fell at my feet and embraced my knees, screaming loud enough to deafen me. 'But how can I marry you?' I asked. 'What sort of ceremony could be performed?' 'Skin me,' she said tenderly, 'and don't marry me. I prefer that.'

" 'Skin her!' screamed the other. 'You have nothing to fear.'

"I was in an indescribable state of confusion, and while I was trying to make up my mind, their shrieks and tears increased until I had no idea what would become of me. After a thousand and one struggles, I cast my eyes once more on the beautiful whale. I confess, I found an inexpressible charm in her features. Throwing myself on my knees close to the tub, I took her hand. 'No, divine princess,' I said to her. 'I won't skin you. I'd prefer to marry you!'

"As I said these words, joy lit the princess's countenance, but a modest joy, for she blushed and lowered her beautiful eyes. 'I'll never forget the favor you're doing for me,' she said. 'I'm so overwhelmed with gratitude that you can demand anything from me after this generous act.'

" 'Don't waste time,' the insufferable Citronette said. 'Tell him quickly what he must do.'

" 'It's sufficient,' said the whale princess blushing again, 'that you give me your ring, and that you take mine. Here's my hand. Receive it as a pledge of my faith.'

"No sooner did I perform this tender exchange and kiss the beautiful hand she held out to me than I found myself on my horse again in the middle of the forest. After calling my attendants, they came to me, and I returned home unable to say a word because I was so completely astounded. Since then I've been transported every night, without knowing how, into the beautiful green salon, where I spend the night near an invisible person. She speaks to me and tells me that the time hasn't come yet for me to know who she is."

"Ah, my son," the queen interrupted, "is it really true that you're married to her?"

"I am, madam," the prince replied. "Yet even though I love my wife enormously, I would have given her up if I could have escaped the salon without resorting to the marriage."

Upon saying these words, a little voice that came from the queen's purse said, "Prince Zirphil, you should have flayed her. Your pity may perhaps be fatal to you."

Surprised by this voice, the prince was speechless. The queen vainly tried to conceal the cause of his astonishment from him, but he quickly searched the purse hanging on the armchair near the bed and drew out the toothpick case, which the queen took from his hand and opened. Princess Camion immediately emerged, and the dumbfounded prince threw himself onto his knees by the queen's bedside to inspect her more closely.

"I swear, madam," he cried, "this is my dear whale in miniature! Is this some jest? Did you only want to frighten me by allowing me to believe so long that you wouldn't approve of my marriage?"

"No, my son," the queen replied. "My grief is real, and you've exposed us to the most cruel misfortunes by marrying that whale. In fact, you were promised to the Princess Camion, whom you see in my hands."

Then she related to him what had happened between her and the fairy Marmotte. The prince did not interrupt because he was so astonished that she and his father had agreed to a proposal that was so patently ridiculous.

"Heaven forbid, madam," he said when the queen had finished, "that I should ever oppose your majesty's plans, or that I should act contrary to the wishes of my father, even when he commands me to do something impossible as this appears to be. But if I had consented, could I really have fallen in love with this pretty princess? Would your subjects ever have—"

"Time is a great teacher, Prince Zirphil," Camion interrupted. "But what is done is done. You can't marry me now, and my godmother is a person who won't easily tolerate anyone breaking his word to her. Tiny as I am, I feel the unpleasantness of this predicament as acutely as the largest woman would. But since you're not so much to blame, except for having been a mite too hasty, I may be able to persuade the fairy to mitigate the punishment."

After saying these words, Camion fell silent, exhausted from having said so much.

"My darling," the queen said, "I implore you to get some rest. I fear you might become ill, and then you'll be in no condition to speak to the fairy when she comes to torment us. You're our only hope, and no matter how she may punish us, I won't feel it so deeply if Marmotte doesn't take you from us."

Princess Camion felt her little heart beat at these words. Since she was quite exhausted, however, she could only kiss her hand and let some tiny tears drop on it. Moved by this incident, Zirphil begged Camion to permit him to kiss her hand in turn. She gave it to him with much grace and dignity and then reentered her case. After this tender scene the queen rose in order to tell the king what had happened and to take every sensible precaution against the fairy's anger.

In spite of a double guard in front of Zirphil's apartment, he was carried off at midnight and found himself as usual in the company of his invisible wife. But instead of hearing the sweet, touching things she usually said to him, she wept and refused to speak at all.

"What have I done?" he asked after he tired of asking her to confide in him. "You weep, dear princess, when you ought to console me for all the danger I've incurred due to my tender feelings for you."

"I know everything," the princess said, her voice racked by sobs. "I know all the misery that may happen to me. But you, ungrateful man, you're the one I have most to complain about!"

"Oh, heavens!" Zirphil cried. "With what do you reproach me?"

"The love Camion has for you and the tenderness with which you kissed her hand."

"The tenderness!" the prince replied quickly. "You know too little about it if you can accuse me so lightly. Besides, even if Camion could love me—which is impossible, since she only saw me for a moment—how can you worry when you've had proofs of my commitment to you? I should accuse you of injustice. If I looked at her with any attention, it was because her features reminded me of yours, and being deprived of the pleasure of beholding you, anyone who resembles you gives me the greatest satisfaction. Show yourself to me again, my dear princess, and I'll never look at another woman."

The invisible lady appeared to be consoled by these words, and she approached the prince. "Pardon my spate of jealousy," she said. "I have too much reason to fear they'll take me from you not to feel troubled by an incident that seemed to announce the beginning of that separation."

"But," the prince said, "can't I know why you're no longer permitted to show yourself? If I've rescued you from Marmotte's tyranny, how can it be that you can be subjected to it again?"

"Alas!" the invisible princess said. "If you had decided to flay me, we would have been very happy. But you were so horrified by that proposal that I didn't dare push you further."

"Pray, how did Camion chance to learn about this adventure?" the prince interrupted. "She told me nearly the exact same thing."

No sooner did he finish saying these words than the princess uttered a frightful shriek. Surprised, the prince rose hastily. His alarm was enormous when he saw the hideous Marmotte in the middle of the room. She held the beautiful princess, who was now neither half whale nor invisible, by the hair. He was about to grab his sword when the princess tearfully begged him to temper his anger because it would be to no avail against the fairy's power. The horrible Marmotte was grinding her teeth and spewed a blue flame that scorched his beard.

"Prince Zirphil," she said to him, "a fairy protects you and prevents me from exterminating you, your father, your mother, and your kin. But since you've married without consulting me, you'll at least suffer in regard to everything that's dear to you. Neither your torment nor that of your princess will ever end until you've obeyed my commands."

When she finished speaking, the fairy, princess, salon, and palace all disappeared together, and he found himself in his own apartment in his nightdress and with his sword in his hand. So astonished and infuriated was he that he did not feel the severity of the cold, though it was the middle of winter. The cries he made caused his guards to enter the room, and they begged him to go to bed or to allow them to dress him. Deciding to get dressed, he went to the queen's chamber, who, for her part, had spent the night in the cruelest state of anxiety. She had been unable to sleep, and in order to induce slumber she had wanted to talk over her despair with tiny Camion. When she had looked for her toothpick case, though, Camion had disappeared. Afraid she might have lost her in the garden, the queen got up, and after ordering torches to be lit, she searched for her without success. Camion had vanished. Therefore, the queen retired to bed again in an alarming state of sorrow. She was giving fresh vent to her grief as her son entered, but he was so distressed himself that he did not notice her tears. Yet she saw how disturbed he was and exclaimed, "Ah! No doubt you've come to bring some dreadful tidings to me!"

"Yes, madam," the prince replied. "I've come to tell you that I'll die if I don't find my princess."

"What?" the queen cried out. "Do you already love that unfortunate princess, my dear son?"

"Do you mean your Camion?" the prince asked. "Madam, how can you suspect me of such a thing? I'm speaking of my dear whale-princess. She's been torn away from me. It's for her alone that I live, and the cruel Marmotte has carried her away!"

"Ah, my son," the queen said. "I'm far more unhappy than you. They may have taken away your princess, but they've also robbed me of my Camion! She's been missing from her case since last night!"

Then they told each other their respective adventures and wept together over their common misfortunes. The king was informed about the sorrow of the queen and the grief of his son. He entered the apartment in which this tragic scene was taking place, and since he was an extremely clever man, it occurred to him immediately to post a large reward for finding Camion. Everybody agreed that this was a capital idea, and even the queen, in spite of her great grief, confessed that only an extraordinary mind could have thought of such a novel expedient. The handbills were printed and distributed, and the queen became rather calm in the hope of soon hearing some tidings of her little princess. As for Zirphil, Camion's disappearance interested him no more than her presence had. He decided to seek out a fairy about whom he had heard, and after receiving the permission of the king and queen, he departed with a single equerry to accompany him.

A great distance separated his country and that inhabited by the fairy, but neither time nor obstacles checked the ardor of young Zirphil. Through countless countries and kingdoms he passed. Nothing in particular happened to him because he was not looking for any adventures. Since he was as handsome as Cupid and brave as his sword, he could have had plenty of adventures if he had sought them.

After traveling for a year, he arrived at the beginning of the desert in which the fairy had her abode. He dismounted from his horse and left his equerry in a cottage with orders to wait for him there. Into the desert, which was frightful due to its desolation, he entered. Only screech owls inhabited it, but their cries did not alarm the valiant spirit of our prince.

One evening he saw a light at a distance, and this made him think, I must be approaching the famous grotto. Indeed, who but a fairy could live in such a horrible desert? He walked all night long, and finally at daybreak he discovered the grotto, but a lake of fire separated him from it, and all his valor could not protect him from the flames that spread left and right. He searched around for a long time to see what he could do, and his courage nearly failed him when he found not even a bridge.

Despair proved his best friend, for in a frenzy of love and anguish he decided, "I'll end my days in the lake if I cannot cross it." No sooner did he make this strange resolution than he threw himself bodily into the flames. From the first he felt a gentle warmth that hardly inconvenienced him, and he swam to the other side without the least trouble. As soon as he got there, a young and beautiful salamander emerged from the lake and said, "Prince Zirphil, if your love is as great as your courage, you may hope for everything from the fairy Lumineuse. She favors you, but she wants to test you."

Zirphil made a profound bow to the salamander in acknowledgment, for she plunged again into the flames before he had time to speak. He continued on his way, and after a while he arrived at the foot of an enormous rock that glowed so radiantly that it appeared to be on fire. It was such a large carbuncle that the fairy was lodged inside in a very comfortable manner. As soon as the prince approached, Lumineuse emerged from the rock, and he prostrated himself before her. Then she raised him and asked him to enter.

"Prince Zirphil," she said, "a power equal to mine has neutralized the benefits I bestowed on you at birth, but since I am very concerned for your future, I'll do the best I can for you. Indeed, you'll need as much patience as courage to foil the wickedness of Marmotte. I can tell you nothing more."

"At least, madam," the prince replied, "do me the favor of informing me if my beautiful princess is unhappy, and if I may hope to see her again soon."

"She's not unhappy," the fairy responded. "But you won't be able to see her until you've pounded her in the mortar of the King of Whiting."

"Oh, heavens!" the prince cried. "Is she in his power? Now I'll not only have to dread the consequences of his fury, but also the even greater horror of pounding her with my own hands!"

"Summon your courage," the fairy replied. "Don't hesitate to obey. Your entire happiness, and your wife's as well, depend on it."

"But she'll die if I pound her," the prince said, "and I'd rather die myself."

"Be off," the fairy said, "and don't argue! Each moment you lose adds to Marmotte's fury. Go and look for the King of the Whiting. Tell him you're the page I promised to send him, and rely on my protection."

Then she took a map and pointed out the road that he had to take to reach the dominions of the King of Whiting. Before she took leave of him, she informed him that the ring that the princess had given him would show him what he should do whenever the king commanded him to perform a difficult task. He departed, and after traveling some days, he arrived in a meadow that stretched down to the seashore, where a small sailing vessel made of mother-of-pearl and gold was moored. Looking at his ruby, he saw himself in it going on board the vessel. Therefore, he embarked and cast off, whereupon the wind took the boat out to sea. He had been sailing for several hours when the vessel finally docked at the foot of a crystal castle built upon wooden piles. He jumped ashore and entered a courtyard that led to a magnificent vestibule and countless apartments whose walls were remarkably cut from rock crystal, producing the most beautiful effect in the world. The castle appeared to be inhabited only by people with heads of all sorts of fish. Convinced this was the dwelling of the King of Whiting, he shuddered with rage. However, he restrained himself so he could ask a turbot, who had the manner of a captain of the guard, how he could manage to see the King of Whiting. The man-turbot made a grave signal for him to advance, and he entered the guard chamber, where he saw a thousand armed men with pike heads formed in rows through which he was to pass.

Making his way through this infinite crowd of fish-men, he came to the throne room. There was not much noise, for the courtiers could not speak since the greater number of them had whiting's heads. He saw several who appeared to be of a higher rank than the rest due to the air they assumed with the crowd surrounding them. Once he arrived at the king's room, he saw the council, composed of twelve men who had shark heads, emerge. After a while the king himself appeared. He had a whiting's head like many of the others, but he could speak. He had fins on his shoulders, and from his waist down he was a veritable whiting. He wore only an extremely radiant scarf made of the skin of goldfish and a helmet in the form of a crown, from which rose a codfish's tail as a plume. Four whiting carried him in a bowl of Japanese porcelain as large as a bathful of sea water. His greatest pride consisted in having it filled twice a day by the dukes and peers of his kingdom, and this position was extremely sought after.

Very large, the King of Whiting had more the air of a monster than of anything else. After he had spoken to several petitioners, he noticed the prince. "Who are you, my friend?" he asked. "By what chance do I see a man here?"

"My lord," Zirphil said, "I'm the page the fairy Lumineuse promised you."

"I know what she's up to," the king laughed, showing teeth like those of a saw. "Lead him into my seraglio, and let him teach my crayfish to talk."

Immediately a squad of whiting surrounded him and led him away. As he passed through the apartments again, all the fish, even those in highest favor, professed a great deal of friendship for him by various signs. The whiting led him through a delightful garden at the end of which was a charming pavilion built entirely of mother-of-pearl and ornamented with great branches of coral. The favorite whiting brought him into a similarly decorated apartment that had windows overlooking a magnificent stretch of water. They indicated that this was to be his residence, and after showing him a little room at one corner of the salon, which he understood was to be his bedroom, they retired, and he remained alone, astonished to find himself something like a prisoner in the palace of his rival.

He was contemplating his situation when the doors of his room opened. Ten or twelve thousand crayfish, who were conducted by one larger than the rest, entered and placed themselves in straight lines that nearly filled the apartment. The one marching at their head mounted a table near him and said, "Prince, I know you, and you owe much to my care, but since it is rare to find gratitude in men, I won't tell you what I've done for you, for fear you'd destroy the sentiments you've aroused in me. Therefore, let me merely inform you that these are the crayfish of the King of Whiting. They alone speak in this empire, and you've been chosen to teach them the language of refinement, the customs of the world, and the means of pleasing their sovereign. You'll find them intelligent, but you must choose ten every morning to pound in the king's mortar to make his broth."

Once this crayfish stopped speaking, the prince replied, "I had no idea, madam, that you had taken an interest in my affairs. The gratitude I already feel toward you should induce you to abandon the bad opinion you've developed toward men in general, for on the bare assurance you've given me of your friendship, I feel deeply obligated to you. But what I am anxious to learn is how I should go about reasoning with the beings whose education I am in charge of. If I could be sure that they had as much intelligence as you, I'd be honored to do this work. But if I find them difficult to teach, I'll have less courage to punish them for faults for which they are not responsible. And if I live with them, how can I have the heart to have them tortured?"

"You are obstinate and a great talker," the crayfish interrupted. "But we know exactly how to take care of you." Upon saying this, she rose from the table, and after jumping to the ground, she took her real form of Marmotte (for she was that wicked fairy).

"Oh heavens!" the prince cried. "So this is the person who boasts that she's interested in my affairs—she who's done nothing but make me miserable! Ah, Lumineuse, you've abandoned me!"

No sooner had he finished uttering those words than the marmot jumped through the window into the reservoir and disappeared, leaving him alone with twelve thousand crayfish. After reflecting somewhat on how he should proceed to educate them, during which time they waited in complete silence, it occurred to him that he might find his beautiful and unfortunate princess among them. "Hideous Marmotte has ordered me to pound ten of them every morning. And why should I be chosen to pound ten of them every morning if not to drive me mad? Never mind, let's look for her. Let's at least try to recognize her even if I die of grief before her eyes." Then he asked the crayfish if they would kindly permit him to search for one of his acquaintances among them.

"We know nothing about it, my lord," offered one of them. "But you can make whatever inquiry you please up to the time we must return to the reservoir, for we spend every night there."

Zirphil began his inspection, and the more he looked, the less he discovered, but he surmised from the few words that he drew from those he interrogated that they were all princesses transformed by Marmotte's wickedness. This caused him inconsolable grief because he had to choose ten for the king's broth.

When evening came, the crayfish repeated that they had to retire to the reservoir. Not without pain did he relinquish his search for the sweet princess. He had been able to interrogate only a hundred and fifty crayfish during the entire day, but since he was certain that at least she was not among them, he decided to take ten from that number. No sooner did he choose them than he proceeded to carry them to the king's offices. Suddenly he heard peals of laughter from the victims he was about to crush and stopped dead, so surprised that he could not speak. As he continued walking, he interrupted them to inquire what they found so amusing under their present circumstances. They renewed their loud laughter so heartily that he could not help participating in their mirth in spite of himself. They wanted to speak, but could not do so because they were laughing so hard. They could only utter, "Oh, I can't say any more!" "Oh, I'll die from it!" "No, there's nothing in the world so amusing!" And then they roared again.

At last he reached the palace with them all laughing together, and after he showed them to a pike-headed man who seemed to be the head cook, a mortar of green porphyry ornamented with gold was placed before him. Into this he put his ten crayfish, and prepared to pound them. Just then the bottom of the mortar opened and emitted a radiant flame that dazzled the prince. Then it closed again and appeared perfectly empty: the crayfish had vanished. This simultaneously astonished and gratified him because he had been loath to pound such merry creatures. On the other hand, the man-pike seemed sadly distressed by this incident and wept bitterly. The prince was just as much surprised by this as he was by the laughter of the crayfish. However, he could not determine the reason for this, since the pike-head could not talk.

He returned to his pretty rooms and was disturbed to find the crayfish had already gone back to the reservoir. The next morning they reentered without Marmotte, and he looked for his princess. Since he was still not able to discover her, he again chose ten of the youngest crayfish for pounding. Then the same thing occurred—they laughed, and the man-pike wept when they disappeared in the flame. For three months this extraordinary scene was repeated every day. He heard nothing from the King of Whiting, and he was uneasy only because he had not discovered his beautiful princess.

One evening, after returning from the kitchen to his apartment, he crossed the king's gardens and passed near a palisade surrounding a charming grove. In the middle of it was a little sparkling fountain, where he heard someone chatting. Since he believed that all the inhabitants of that kingdom were incapable of speaking, this surprised him. He advanced quietly and heard a voice that said, "But, Princess, if you don't reveal yourself, your husband will never find you."

"What can I do?" said the other voice, which he recognized as the one he had so often heard. "Marmotte's cruelty compels me to remain silent, and I can't reveal myself without risking his life as well as my own. The wise Lumineuse, who's helping him, is hiding my features from him in order to protect both of us. It's absolutely necessary that he pound me. It's an irrevocable sentence."

"But why must he pound you?" the other inquired. "You've never told me your history. Your confidante, Citronette, would have told me if she hadn't been chosen for the king's broth last week."

"Alas!" the princess replied. "That unfortunate lady has already undergone the torture that still awaits me. If only I were in her place! I'm sure she's in her grotto by this time."

"But," the other voice replied, "since it's such a beautiful night, tell me now why you've been subjected to Marmotte's vengeance. I've already told you who I am, and I'm burning with impatience to know more about you."

"Although it will revive my grief," the princess remarked, "I can't refuse to satisfy you, especially since I must talk about Zirphil. I take pleasure in everything that pertains to him."

You can easily judge how delighted the prince felt at this fortunate moment. He glided quietly into the grove, but since it was very dark, he did not see anything. However, he listened with all his might, and this is what he heard word for word:

My father was king of a country near Mount Caucasus. He reigned to the best of his ability over a people of incredible wickedness. They were perpetually revolting, and often the windows of his palace were broken by stones they hurled. The queen, my mother, who was a very accomplished woman, composed speeches for him to make to the disaffected, but if he succeeded in appeasing them one day, the next produced new troubles. The judges became tired of condemning people to death, and the executioners of hanging them. At last things reached such a state that my father saw that all our provinces were united against us, and he decided to withdraw from the capital so that he would no longer have to witness so many unpleasant scenes. He took the queen with him and left the government of the kingdom to one of his ministers, who was very wise and less timid than my father. My mother was expecting to give birth to me and traveled with some difficulty to the foot of Mount Caucasus, which my father had chosen for his abode. Our wicked subjects joyfully fired guns at their departure and strangled our minister the next day, saying that he had wanted to carry matters with too high a hand and that they preferred their former sovereign. My father was not at all flattered by their preference and remained hiding in his little retreat, where I soon saw the light of day.

They named me Camion because I was so tiny. Moreover, since the king and queen were tired of the honors that had cost them so dearly, they concealed my high birth from me. I was brought up as a shepherdess. At the end of ten years (which appeared to them like ten minutes because they were so happy in their retreat), the fairies of the Caucasus, who had become infuriated by the wickedness of the people of our kingdom, decided to restore order there. One day, as I was tending my sheep in the meadow next to our garden, two old shepherdesses approached and begged me to give them shelter for the night. They had such a dejected air that my soul was moved with compassion. "Follow me," I said. "My father, who's a farmer, will gladly welcome you." I ran to the cottage to announce their arrival to him. He came to greet them and received them with a good deal of kindness, as did my mother. Then I brought in my sheep and set milk before our guests. Meanwhile, my father prepared them a nice little supper, and the queen—who, as I told you before, was a clever woman—entertained them in a wonderful manner.

I had a little lamb of which I was extremely fond, and my father called me to bring it to him so he might kill and roast it. I was not accustomed to oppose his will and therefore took it to him. But I was so distressed that I sat down to weep beside my mother, who was so occupied in talking to these good women that she did not pay any attention to me. "What's the matter with the little Camion?" one of them said, who saw me in tears.

"Alas, madam!" I said to her. "My father's roasting my pet lamb for your supper."

"What!" said the one who had not yet spoken. "Is it on our account that pretty Camion is thus distressed?" Standing up, she struck the ground with her stick, and a magnificently set table rose from it. The two old women became two beautiful ladies dressed in dazzling precious stones. I was so transfixed that I did not even pay attention when my little lamb bounded into the room and made a thousand capers that amused the entire company. After kissing the hands of the beautiful ladies, I ran to pet him. Imagine my shock when I found his wool made all of silver purl and covered with knots of rose-colored ribbon.

My father and mother fell at the feet of the fairies, for, I need not tell you, this is what they were. The more majestic of them raised them, saying, "King and queen, we've known you for a long time, and your misfortunes have aroused our pity. Don't imagine that greatness exempts anyone from the evils of humankind. You must know through experience that the more elevated the rank, the more keenly these evils are felt. Your patience and virtue have raised you above your misfortunes, and it's time to give you your reward. I'm the fairy Lumineuse, and I've come to inquire what your majesties would find most pleasant. Come, speak! Don't worry about putting our power to the test. Consult each other, and your wishes will be fulfilled. But say nothing with regard to Camion: her destiny is separate from yours. The fairy Marmotte has been envious of the splendid fate promised her and has obscured it for a time. But we do know Camion will learn the value of her happiness only by experiencing the evils of life. We can protect her only by softening them. That's all we're permitted to tell you. Now, speak. We can do anything you want with that one exception."

After this speech the fairies fell silent. The queen turned to the king so that he might reply, for she was crying because I was doomed to be unhappy. But my father was in no better condition to speak than she was. He uttered pitiful cries, and on seeing them in tears, I left my lamb to come weep with them. The fairies waited patiently and in perfect silence until our tears dried. At last my mother nudged the king gently: they were waiting for his reply. He took his handkerchief from his eyes and said that since it was fated that I should be miserable, they could offer him nothing that would please him. "I refuse the happiness you promise me because I'll always feel embittered by thinking about what dear Camion has to dread." Seeing that the poor man could say no more, the queen begged the fairies to take their lives on the day my sad destiny was to be fulfilled because her only wish was not to be compelled to witness my misery. The good fairies were touched by the extreme grief that reigned in the royal family and talked together in a whisper. At last Lumineuse said to the queen, "Be consoled, madam. The misfortunes threatening Camion are not so great and they'll end happily. Indeed, from the moment that the husband destined for her obeys the commands of fate, our sister's malevolence will have no more power over her. Believe me, she'll be happy with him, for the prince we've chosen is worthy of her.

"All we can tell you is that you must never forget to lower your daughter every morning into your well. She must bathe in it for half an hour, every morning. If you observe this rule strictly, she may escape the evil with which she is threatened. At the age of twelve, the critical period of her fate will commence. If she reaches the age of thirteen safely, there'll be nothing more to fear. This is all that concerns her. Now, make a wish for yourselves, and we'll satisfy your desires."

The king and queen looked at each other, and after a short silence the king asked to become a statue until I had completed my thirteenth year. The queen made a modest request, that the temperature of the well in which I was to be dipped always correspond to the season. The fairies were charmed by this excess of parental tenderness and added that the water would be orange-flowered water, and that the king could resume his natural form whenever the queen threw this water on him. "You can, of course, become a statue again whenever you please." After lauding the king and queen for their moderation, they eventually took their leave of us with the promise: "We'll aid you whenever you need help if you just burn a bit of the silver purl with which Camion's lamb is covered."

When they vanished, I felt anguish for the first time in my life as I watched my father become a great black marble statue. The queen burst into tears, and I did, too, but since everything must have an end, I stopped crying and occupied myself by consoling my mother because I felt a sudden increase of both sense and sensitivity.

The queen spent her days at the feet of the statue, and I milked my ewes after bathing each day as they had ordered. We lived off the food produced by the milk because the queen would not take anything else, and only out of love for me could she be prevailed upon to go on with a life so filled with bitterness. "Alas, my daughter!" she sometimes said. "Our grandeur and high birth have been of no use to us! (By this time she had revealed my rank to me.) It would have been better to have been born into the lower classes. A crown has brought such disaster to us! Only virtue and my affection for you, my dear Camion, enable me to withstand these catastrophes. There are moments when my soul seems eager to leave me, and I confess, I feel pleasure in thinking that I shall soon die. It's not for me you should weep, but for your father, whose grief is even greater than mine. It has brought him to the extremity of desiring a fate worse than death. Never forget, my dear, the gratitude you owe him."

"Alas, madam!" I said. "I'm incapable of ever forgetting it, and still less can I forget that you're keeping yourself alive only in order to help me."

I was bathed regularly every day, and every day my mother sadly viewed the king as an inanimate statue. However, she did not dare recall him to life for fear of inflicting him with the pain of witnessing my threatened misfortune. Since the fairies had not specified what we were to fear, we lived in mortal dread. My mother in particular imagined no end of frightful things because her imagination had an unlimited scope to cover. As for me, I did not trouble myself much about it, for youth is the only time that we enjoy the present.

My mother told me repeatedly that she felt a great desire to bring my father back to life again, an inclination I shared as well. At last, after six months had passed and she found that the fairies' bath had greatly enriched both my body and mind, she decided to satisfy this longing, if only to give the king the pleasure of seeing my progress. Therefore, she asked me to bring her some water from the well. Accordingly, after my bath I drew up a vase of this marvelous water, and no sooner did we sprinkle the statue than my father became a man again. The queen threw herself at his feet to ask pardon for having troubled his repose. He raised her and after embracing her tenderly, he readily forgave her, and she introduced me to him.

"I'm ashamed to tell you that he was both delighted and surprised. For how can you believe me, beautiful princess, when I am the most hideous of crayfish?" the voice said hesitatingly.

"Alas! I don't have any trouble believing you," replied the one to whom she spoke. "I too might boast of having been beautiful, but how is it possible to appear so in these frightful shells? Please continue, for I'm eager to hear the rest of your story."

"Very well, then," said the other voice:

The king was enchanted with me and gave me numerous caresses. Then he asked the queen if she had any news to tell him. "Alas!" she said. "Who in this desolate spot could come and tell me any? Besides, since I've been solely occupied in lamenting your transformation, I've taken little interest in the world, which means nothing to me without you."

"Well," the king said, "I'll tell you some news then, for don't think that I've always been asleep. The fairies who are protecting us have disclosed to me the punishment of my subjects. They've made an immense lake out of my kingdom, and all the inhabitants are men-fish. A nephew of the fairy Marmotte whom they have set up as their king persecutes them with unparalleled cruelty: he devours them for the least fault. At the end of a certain time a prince will arrive who'll dethrone him and reign in his stead. It's in this kingdom that Camion will attain perfect happiness. This is all I know, and it wasn't a bad way of spending my time, given the fact that I was able to discover these things," he said laughing. "The fairies came every night to inform me of what was going on, and I would have perhaps learned much more if you had let me remain a statue a little longer. However, I'm so delighted to see you once more that I don't think I'll want to become a statue again very soon."

We spent some time in the happiest manner possible. Nevertheless the king and queen were rather anxious as I approached the age of thirteen. Whenever the queen bathed me, she took great care to ensure the prediction would not be fulfilled. But who can boast of escaping her destiny? One morning, when my mother had risen early and was gathering some flowers to decorate our cottage—my father was fond of them—she saw an ugly animal, a marmot, come out from beneath a tuberose. This beast threw itself on her and bit her nose. She fainted from the pain of the bite, and when my father did not see her return at the end of an hour, he went looking for her. You can imagine how upset he was at finding her covered with blood and nearly dead! He uttered fearful cries and I ran to his aid. Together we carried the queen into the house and put her to bed, where it took more than two hours for her to revive. At last she began to give some signs of life, and we had the pleasure of seeing her recover from all but the pain of the bite, which caused her a good deal of suffering.

Right away she asked, "Did Camion go bathing?" We had quite forgotten it, though, in our anxiety about her. She was very alarmed at hearing this. However, on seeing that nothing had happened to me as yet, she became reassured.

The day passed without any other trouble. The king had taken out his gun and went searching all over for the horrid beast without being able to find it. The next day at sunrise the queen awoke and came to fetch me to make up for the fault of the preceding morning. She lowered me into the well as usual, but alas, it was our unlucky day! Although the heavens were quite serene, all at once a dreadful clap of thunder pierced the air. Suddenly the sky was on fire, and a flaming dart soared from a burning cloud and flew into the well. In her fright my mother let go of the cord holding me, and I sank to the bottom. Although I was not hurt, you can imagine how horrified I was at discovering that I had been partially transformed into an enormous whale. I bobbed to the surface again and called the queen with all my might. She did not reply, and I wept bitterly as much for her loss as for my transformation. Then I felt an invisible power forcing me to descend to the bottom of the well. Upon reaching it I entered a crystal grotto where I found a kind of nymph. She was quite ugly, resembling an immensely fat frog. However, she smiled at my approach and said to me, "Camion, I'm the Nymph of the Bottomless Well. I have orders to welcome you and to make you undergo the penance to which you've been sentenced for having failed to bathe. Follow me, and don't try to object."

"Alas, what could I do? I was so distressed and so faint at finding myself on dry ground that I didn't have the strength to speak. She dragged me, not painlessly, into a salon of green marble adjoining the grotto. There she put me into an immense golden tub filled with water, and I began to recover my senses. The good nymph appeared delighted at this. "I'm called Citronette," she said. "I've been appointed to wait on you, so you can order me to do anything you want. I know the past and the present perfectly, but I cannot determine the future. Command me, and at least I can make the time of your penance less annoying to you."

I embraced the good Citronette after she said these words and told her about my past. Then I inquired about the fate of the king and queen. She was about to reply when a hideous marmot as large as a human being entered the salon. I was petrified with horror. She walked on her hind legs and leaned on a gold wand, giving her a dignified air. She approached the tub—in which I would gladly have drowned myself because I was so frightened—and she raised her wand to touch me. "Camion," she said, "you're in my power, and nothing can release you except your obedience and that of the husband whom my sisters have destined for you. Listen to me, and set aside your fear. It doesn't befit a person of your rank.

"Ever since your childhood I have wanted to care for you and marry you to my nephew, the King of Whiting. Lumineuse and two or three of my other sisters combined to deprive me of this right. I was provoked, and not being able to revenge myself on them, I decided to punish you for their audacity. Therefore, I condemned you to become a whale for at least half the term of your existence. My sisters protested so strongly against what they called my injustice that I reduced my term by over three-quarters, but I reserved the right of marrying you to my nephew in return for my compliance. Lumineuse, who's imperious and unfortunately my superior, would not listen to this arrangement. She had predestined you to a prince whom she protected. I was then compelled to consent to her plan in spite of my resentment. All that I could obtain was that the first person to rescue you from my claws would become your husband. Here are their portraits," she continued, showing me two gold miniature cases, "which will enable you to recognize them. But if one of them comes to rescue you, he must become your fiancé when you're in the tub, and he must tear off the whale skin before you can leave it. If he doesn't, you'll remain a fish forever. My nephew wouldn't hesitate a moment to carry out this order, but Lumineuse's favorite will consider it a horrible task because he has the air of a delicate gentleman. So you'd better put your mind to work and think up a way to make him skin you. After that you'll no longer be unhappy, if you can call it unhappiness to be a beautiful, fat, and well-fed whale up to your neck in water."

I did not reply, dejected as much by my present state as the thought of the flaying to which I had to submit myself. Marmotte disappeared and left me with the two miniature cases. I was weeping over my misfortunes without dreaming of looking at the portraits when sympathetic Citronette said, "Come, we musn't lament over catastrophes that can't be remedied. Let's see if I can't help console you. But first, try not to weep so much, for I have a tender heart and can't see your tears without feeling inclined to mix mine with them. Let's chase them away by looking at these portraits."

Upon saying this, she opened the first case and showed it to me. We both shrieked like Melusine at seeing a hideous whiting's head. True, it was painted to give all the advantages that could be given, yet in spite of that, nothing so ugly has ever been seen in the memory of humankind. "Take it away," I cried. "I can't bear the sight of it any longer. I'd rather be a whale all my life than marry that horrible whiting!"

She didn't give me time to finish heaping abuse on this monster, but exclaimed, "Look at this darling young man! Oh, as far as he's concerned, if he were to skin you, I'd be delighted."

I looked quickly to see if what she said was true, and I was soon quite convinced. A noble, charming expression, with fine eyes full of tenderness, adorned a face both mild and majestic. An air of intelligence permeated this fascinating and delightful portrait. A profusion of black hair with natural curls gave him a look that Citronette mistook for indifference, but which I interpreted, and I think rightly so, as conveying precisely the opposite sentiment.

I gazed at this handsome face without being aware of how much pleasure I was having. Citronette noticed it first. "'Without a doubt," she cried, "that's the one we'll choose."

This banter roused me from my reverie, and blushing at my ecstasy, I said, "Why should I trouble myself? Ah, my dear Citronette, this appears to me very much like another one of cruel Marmotte's tricks. She's made full use of her art to compel me to long for some similar living being who's impossible to find."

"What?" Citronette commented. "You're already having such tender thoughts about this portrait? Ah, truly, I didn't expect that so soon." I blushed again at this jest and became quite embarrassed at finding that I had too innocently betrayed the effect this beautiful painting had produced on my heart. Citronette again read my thoughts. "No, no," she said, embracing me. "Don't repent of your feelings. Your frankness charms me, and to console you, I'll tell you that Marmotte is not deceiving you. There really is a prince who's the original of the portrait."

This assurance filled me with joy momentarily, but the next instant that feeling departed when I remembered that this prince would never see me. I was in the depths of the earth, and Marmotte would prefer to allow her monster of a nephew to penetrate my abode than give the least assistance to a prince she hated. Hadn't her sisters destined him for me without her consent? I no longer concealed what I thought from Citronette. Indeed, the attempt would have been useless because she read my deepest secrets with surprising ease. Therefore, I decided it would be better to be candid. Moreover, she deserved my trust since she was so attached to me. Naturally, I found it a great consolation because I've felt from that time on, one can have a lot of happiness in being able to talk to someone when one's heart is consumed by one object. In fact, this is when I began to fall in love, and Citronette helped clear up the confusion that the beginning of passion produces in the mind. Clever and clear-sighted, she soothed my grief by allowing me to talk about it, and when I had exhausted words, she gently changed the subject to something that almost always, however, touched on my troubles or my affection.

She informed me that the king, my father, had been transported to the abode of the King of Whiting and that the queen had become a crayfish the very moment she lost me. I could not understand this and maintained, "One cannot just become a crayfish."

"Well," she responded, "can you explain how you've become a whale any better?"

She was right, of course. We are often surprised by things that happen to others, even though we don't notice when we go through even more astonishing things ourselves. I simply lacked experience to grasp this. Citronette laughed frequently at my innocence and was surprised to find me so eloquent in my affection, for truly I was spellbinding on that subject. And I found that love makes the mind more active. I could not sleep and woke the good-natured Citronette a hundred times during the night to talk to her about my prince. She had told me his name, that he hunted almost every day in the forest, and it was beneath this forest that I was interred. She proposed that we try to attract him to our dwelling, but I would not consent, although I was dying to do so. I was afraid he would die for want of air. It was different for us since we were accustomed to it. I was also afraid that I would be taking too great a liberty. Besides, I was upset that I would have to appear to him in the form of a whale, and I judged that his aversion for me would equal that which the King of Whiting's portrait had aroused within me. Citronette reassured me, saying that despite the whale's body, my face was charming. I believed it sometimes, but more often I was uneasy, and after having looked at myself, I could not imagine I was sufficiently beautiful to inspire love in a man who had made me so well acquainted with it. My self-love came to the aid of my prudence. Alas, how rarely are our virtues traced to purer inspirations!

I spent my time by devising ways that I could catch sight of him and make him see me. Each one that occurred to me I rejected, one after the other. Citronette was a great help to me at this time, for she had plenty of sense and even more gentleness and amiability. One day, when I was even sadder than usual—for love has the peculiar property of infecting gentle souls with melancholy—I saw the frightful Marmotte enter with two persons whom I did not recognize at first. I imagined she had brought her wretched nephew with her, and I uttered frightful shrieks as they approached. "Why, she couldn't cry louder if they were skinning her!" the horrid Marmotte exclaimed. "Look what terrible harm's been done to her!"

"Good gracious, sister," said one of the persons accompanying her and whom I then remembered with joy as having seen previously in our village. "Let's set a truce to your stories of skinning, and let's tell Camion what we've come to tell her."

"Gladly," Marmotte said, "but on the conditions agreed upon."

"Camion," the good fairy said, without replying to Marmotte, "we've become too upset by your plight not to think of a remedy, particularly since you've not deserved your fate. My sisters and I have decided to ameliorate it as much as we can. Therefore, this is what we've decided to do. You're about to be presented at the court of the prince to whom I've destined you from birth. But, my dear child, you won't appear there as you are. You're to return three nights a week and to plunge back into your tub. Until you're married—"

"And skinned!" interrupted the odious Marmotte, laughing violently.

The good fairy merely turned toward her, shrugged her shoulders, and continued, "Until you're married, you'll be a whale in this place. We can tell you no more. You'll be informed of the rest by degrees, but above all keep your secret. If a word of this is revealed, neither I nor my sisters can do anything for you, and you'll be at the mercy of my sister Marmotte."

"That's what I hope," the wicked fairy said, "and I daresay I already see her in my power. A secret kept by a girl would be a miracle."

"That's her own affair," Lumineuse said, for it was she who had already spoken. "To proceed, my daughter," she said, "you'll become a little doll made of ivory, but you'll be capable of thinking and speaking, and we'll preserve all your features. I'll give you a week to consider whether my proposal suits you. Then we'll return, and you can tell me if you agree to it, or if you'd prefer one of the two husbands chosen for you."

I had no time to reply. The fairies departed after these words, leaving me astounded by what I had just seen and heard. I remained with Citronette, who believed that it was a great treat for me to become an ivory doll. I sighed when I thought that my prince would never take a fancy to such a bauble, but at last the desire to become acquainted with him overcame my anxiety to please him, and I decided to accept. In fact, I was quite eager because Zirphil (they had mentioned his name) might possibly be forestalled by the King of Whiting, and this idea made me nearly die of grief.

Citronette told me that Prince Zirphil hunted daily in the forest above, and I made her take the form of a stag, hound, or wild boar every day so that she might bring me some news of him who occupied my heart. She described him to me as a hundred times more handsome than his picture, and my imagination embellished him to such a degree that I decided to see him or die.

One day before the expected arrival of the fairies, Citronette was roaming the forest in the form of a wild boar to find food for my curiosity when suddenly I saw her return, followed by the too charming Zirphil. I can't describe my joy and astonishment. What enchanted me most, though, was that this charming prince appeared equally delighted with me. Perhaps I desired this too much not to help deceiving myself. However, I thought I saw a look in his eyes that he knew the impression he had made. Citronette was more worried about my happiness than about our ecstasy. She aroused us by begging him either to skin or to marry me. Then I came to my senses and felt the danger of my situation. I joined in her entreaties and, thanks to our tears and pleas, we induced him to pledge himself to me. No sooner did I accept him than he vanished. I don't know how, but I found myself in my ordinary form, lying on a good bed. I was no longer a whale, but I was still in the depths of the earth in the green salon, and Citronette had lost the power of leaving it and of transforming herself.

I expected the fairies to be infuriated. My love had increased since I had become personally acquainted with the object of my desire, and I feared that my charming husband might be included in the vengeance of the fairies for not having waited until they could witness my marriage. Citronette had all she could do to reassure me, for I could not overcome my apprehension. At dawn Marmotte appeared, but I saw neither Lumineuse nor her companion. Not seeming more irritable than usual, Marmotte touched me with her wand without a word, and I became a charming little doll, which she put in her toothpick case. Then she went to the queen-mother of my husband and gave me to her with orders to wed me to her son or to expect all the evil she could inflict. Moreover, she told her that I was her goddaughter and was called Princess Camion. In truth, I took a great fancy to my mother-in-law. I considered her charming since she was the mother of my adorable Zirphil, and my caresses were returned. Every night I was transported into the green salon and enjoyed the pleasure of meeting my husband, for the same power controlled him and transported him likewise into the subterraneous dwelling. I did not know why they forbade me to tell him my secret since I was married, but I kept it in spite of my great desire to tell him.

"You'll see," the speaker continued with a sigh, "how impossible it is to avoid one's fate. But it's beginning to get light, and I'm quite weary from being out of the water so long. Let's return to the reservoir, and tomorrow, if we're not selected for the soup of that worthless king, we'll resume the thread of our conversation at the same hour. —Come, let's go.'

Zirphil did not hear any more and returned to his apartment, quite concerned at not having given some indication to his princess that he was so near. Yet the fear of increasing her misfortunes by such an indiscretion consoled him. The misery of knowing she was likely to perish by his hand made him determined to continue his diligent search among the crayfish.

He went to bed but not to sleep, for he did not close his eyes all night. To have found his princess in the form of a crayfish, ready to be made into soup for the King of Whiting, seemed a torture more frightful than even death itself. He believed that this had been her fate and was becoming terribly upset when he heard a great noise in the garden. At first he heard a jumbled sound, but after listening attentively, he distinguished flutes and conch shells. He rose and went to the window, from which he saw the King of Whiting, accompanied by the dozen sharks who composed his council, advancing toward the pavilion. He rushed to open the door, and after the retinue entered, the king had his tub filled with sea water by the peers of the realm who had been carrying it. After a short repose he made the council take their places and addressed the young prince. "Whoever you may be," he said, "you've apparently decided to make me die of hunger because you've been sending me a broth everyday that I can't swallow. However, I must tell you, young man, that if you are in league with evil powers to poison me, you're on the wrong side. As nephew of the fairy Marmotte, nothing can harm me."

The prince was astonished at being suspected of such a base act and was about to make a proud reply. As he raised his hand, however, he happened to gaze at his ring and saw Lumineuse, who placed her finger to her lips to warn him to be silent. (He had not thought of consulting his ring before this because he had been so overwhelmed by his grief.) Accordingly, he held his tongue, but he betrayed his indignation by his expression, which the sharks noticed because they made signs that appeared to say that they agreed with him.

"Ho, ho!" the king said. "Since this myrmidon appears so angry, we must make him work in front of us. Let them go to my kitchen. Let them bring the mortar for the crayfish. I'll give my council a treat."

A pike-head began carrying out the king's commands at once. At the same time the twelve sharks took a large net, threw it from the window into the reservoir, and drew in three or four thousand crayfish. While the council fished and the pike-head fetched the king's mortar, Zirphil contemplated the situation. "The most crucial moment of my life is approaching. My happiness or misery will depend on what I do right now." He armed himself with resolve for whatever might happen, placing all his hopes in the fairy Lumineuse. He implored her, "Take my side," and at the same time he looked at his ring and saw the beautiful fairy, who made a sign to him to pound courageously. This signal revitalized him and relieved him of some of the pain he felt in consenting to such a cruel act.

At last the horrid mortar was produced. Zirphil approached it boldly, prepared to obey the king. The council ceremoniously put in the crayfish, and the prince tried to pound them. Yet the same thing that had happened to the ones in the kitchen happened to them as well—the bottom of the mortar opened and flames devoured them. The king and his odious sharks amused themselves for a long time with this spectacle, never tiring of refilling the mortar. Finally, a single crayfish was left of the four thousand, one surprisingly large and fine. The king commanded it to be shelled so he could see if he would like to eat it raw. They gave it to Zirphil to shell, and he trembled all over at having to inflict this new torture. His trembling became even worse when this poor fish joined her two claws and said with eyes filled with tears, "Alas, Zirphil, what have I done to you to make you want to harm me so much?"

The prince was moved by these words, and his heart, pierced with grief. He looked at her sadly and at length took it upon himself to beg the king to allow her to be pounded. Ever covetous of his authority, the king was firm in his resolution. Indeed, he was enraged by this humble request and threatened to pound Zirphil himself if he did not shell it. The poor prince quivered as he touched the crayfish with a knife they supplied him. Again he looked at his ring and saw Lumineuse laughing and talking to a veiled person she held by the hand. He was baffled by this, and the king gave him no time to reflect. He cried out to him loudly to finish. The prince stuck the knife with such force under the shell of the crayfish that it cried piteously. He turned his eyes away from hers, unable to help shedding tears. Finally he resumed his task, but to his great astonishment, as he was about to finish the shelling, he found the wicked Marmotte in his hands. She jumped to the ground and uttered shrieks of mocking laughter. They were so loud and unpleasant that they prevented him from fainting; otherwise he would have slumped to the floor.

The king cried in surprise, "Why, it's my aunt!"

"Yes, it's no one but me," this annoying beast said. "But, my dear Whiting, I've come to tell you a terrible piece of news." Whiting grew pale at these words, and the council assumed an air of satisfaction that increased the bad mood of the king and his terrible aunt. "The fact is, my darling,"

Marmotte continued, "you must return to your watery dominions because this rash young man before you has chosen to display a constancy that nothing can shake. He's triumphed despite all the traps I set to prevent him from carrying off the princess I had destined for you."

Upon hearing these words, the King of Whiting fell into such a rage that he could not contain himself. He flailed about and showed his violent temper. Despite Marmotte's attempts to calm him, he broke his bowl into a thousand pieces, and since he was on dry ground, he fainted. Mad with rage, Marmotte turned to Zirphil, who had remained a silent spectator during this tragic scene. "You've triumphed, Zirphil," she said, "thanks to the power of a fairy whom I must obey. But your troubles haven't ended yet. You won't be happy until you give me the case that contained the cursed Camion. Even Lumineuse has agreed to this, and I've obtained her consent to make you suffer until that time." After saying this she took the King of Whiting on her shoulders and threw him into the reservoir along with the sharks, the palace, and all its inhabitants.

Zirphil found himself alone at the foot of a great mountain, in a country as arid as a desert. There was nothing to be seen—not a single house or even the large reservoir. Everything had vanished all at once. The prince was more upset than astonished by such an extraordinary event: he was accustomed to wonders but the continued persecution of the fairy Marmotte caused him to grieve.

"I'm sure that I've pounded my princess," he said. "Yes, I must have pounded her. Yet I'm none the happier for it. Ah, barbarous Marmotte! And you, Lumineuse, you've left me helpless even after I obeyed you at the expense of all that a heart as sensitive as mine could suffer!"

Grief and his scant rest of the night before threw him into such a state of weakness that he would have collapsed altogether if he had not summoned the courage to survive. "If I could only find some nourishment," he said. "However, I'm sure I can't find a single fruit in this horrible desert that can refresh me." No sooner had he uttered these words than his ring opened, and a tiny table covered with excellent viands emerged from it. Within seconds it grew large enough to accommodate him, and on it he found everything that could tempt his eyes and his appetite, for the repast was so beautifully arranged and the wine so delicious that nothing was lacking. He gave thanks to Lumineuse, for who else could have helped him so opportunely? He ate, drank, and felt his strength return.

After he had finished, the table shrank back into the ring. Since it was late, he did not make much progress in climbing the mountain, but stretched himself out under a wretched tree that had hardly enough leaves to protect him from the dew. "Alas!" he said as he lay down. "Such is the nature of man. He forgets the good that is past and concerns himself only with the evil in the present. Right now I'd gladly exchange that table for a couch a little less hard than this."

A moment later he felt himself lying in a comfortable bed, though he could see nothing because the darkness had seemingly increased. He ascertained that this was caused by large curtains surrounding his bed and protecting him from the cold and dew. After thanking the attentive Lumineuse again, he dropped off to sleep. At daybreak he awoke and found himself in a bed walled by curtains of yellow taffeta and silver. This bed had been placed in the middle of a satin tent of the same color, embroidered all over with bright silver letters forming Zirphil's name, and all of these supported by whales outlined by rubies. Everything that one could possibly need was to be found in this beautiful tent. If the prince had been in a more tranquil state of mind, he would have admired this elegant habitation, but he only glanced at the whales, dressed himself, and went out of the tent, which folded itself up and returned to the ring from which it had emerged.

He began to climb the mountain, no longer going to the trouble of looking for food or lodging because he was certain to have both as soon as he wished for them. His only worry was how to find Lumineuse, for his ring was mute on that subject, and he found himself in a country so unfamiliar and deserted that he was compelled to trust to chance.

After having spent several days in climbing without discovering anything, he arrived at the brink of a well that was cut into the rock. Seating himself beside it to rest, he began to exclaim as usual: "Lumineuse, why can't I find you?"

When he finished uttering these words, he heard a voice coming from the well: "Is it Zirphil who's speaking to me?"

His joy at hearing the voice was increased when he recognized whose it was. He rushed to the brink of the well and said, "Yes, it's Zirphil. And aren't you Citronette?"

"Yes," Citronette replied, emerging from the well and embracing the prince.

It is impossible to relate what pleasure Zirphil felt in seeing Citronette again. He overwhelmed the nymph with questions about the princess and herself. Finally, after the excitement of their initial encounter had subsided, they spoke more soberly with each other.

"I'm going to tell you everything you don't know," she said. "Ever since you pounded us, we've been enjoying a happiness lessened only by your absence. I've been awaiting your arrival here in behalf of the fairy Lumineuse to tell you what you still have to do in order to possess a princess who loves you as much as you love her. But since some time must elapse before you can attain this happiness, I'll tell you the rest of the marvelous story about your charming bride."

Zirphil kissed Citronette's hand a thousand times and followed her into her grotto, where he thought he would die of intermixed pleasure and woe, for in this spot had he seen his divine princess for the first time. After sharing a meal that sprang from the ring, he begged the good Citronette kindly to resume the narrative from the point that the princess had left off in the palace garden.

Since this is the spot where Lumineuse is to meet you, you'll learn all you want while waiting for her—you realize it's useless for you to run after her. She's entrusted you to my care, and a lover is less impatient when one talks to him about the lady he loves.

The fairy Marmotte knew about your marriage, and she had transformed our friend into an ivory doll, believing that you would be disgusted by her. Lumineuse conducted this affair herself, knowing that nothing could deprive you of the princess if you destroyed her enchantment by either marrying or skinning her. You chose the former alternative, and you know what followed. By night she resumed her natural form and lamented spending all her days in your royal mother's pocket, for Marmotte had been permitted by Lumineuse to torment the princess until you had fulfilled your destiny, which was to skin her. Marmotte was enraged at finding that you had married her before the King of Whiting, her nephew.

Since the princess was no longer a whale, there was no fish to skin, but Marmotte, who kept creating new obstacles, was to make you pound her and had forbidden the princess to tell you anything about it at the cost of your life. Moreover, Marmotte promised her she would later enjoy the greatest happiness. "How will he ever make up his mind to pound me?" she asked while waiting for you. "Ah, my dear Citronette, if it were only my life that Marmotte threatened, I'd give it cheerfully to protect my husband from the tortures they've prepared for him. But they're also after his life—that life which is so dear to me. Ah, Marmotte! Babarous Marmotte! How can you find pleasure in making me so miserable when I've never given you any reason to harm me?" She knew the period prescribed for your separation from her, but she did not dare tell you. You know the last time that you saw her that you found her in tears, and you asked her why. She pretended to accuse you of inconstancy because of your attentions to little Camion. You appeased her supposed jealousy, and the fatal hour for Marmotte to fetch her arrived. You were transported to the palace of your father while the princess and I were changed into crayfish and placed into a little cane basket, which the fairy put under her arm. After getting into a chariot drawn by two adders, we arrived at the palace of the King of Whiting. This palace had belonged to the princess's father, but the city had been changed into a lake and formed the reservoir that we inhabited. By the way, all the men-fish that you've seen had once been the wicked subjects of that good king.

I must tell you, my lord, that the unfortunate monarch and his wife were in despair the moment the princess sank to the bottom of the well. The fairies who had formerly come to their aid appeared and consoled them for their loss, but the unhappy couple knew that Camion was to be exiled to their kingdom and chose to be with her rather than far away in spite of what they had to fear from the cruelty and ferociousness of the King of Whiting. The fairies did not conceal the princess's future fate from them, and her father asked to be cook of the kitchen and keeper of the King of Whiting's mortar. The fairy immediately tapped her wand, and he became the pike-headed man you saw in that position. So you need no longer be surprised at his having wept bitterly whenever you brought the crayfish to pound. Since he knew that his daughter had to undergo this torture, he always thought she might be among them. The wretched monarch did not have a moment's rest because his daughter had no means of making herself known to him. What's more, the queen had requested to be changed into a crayfish in order to be with the princess.

As soon as we arrived at the palace, the fairy presented us to him and ordered him to have crayfish soup made for his dinner every day. We were then thrown into the reservoir. My first concern was to search for the queen in order to soothe the grief of the princess a little. But either by decree of fate or stupidity on my part, I found it impossible to discover her. We spent our days in this mournful search, and our most pleasant moments were those in which we recalled our past. Finally you arrived and they presented us to you, but the fairy had forbidden us to make ourselves known until you interrogated us, and we didn't dare to break this rule because we were severely punished for the most trivial offences.

The princess told me she thought she was going to die of fright when she observed you talking with the cruel Marmotte. We saw you impatiently searching among our companions, and it was obvious you had little chance of reaching us by the direction you took. We knew we had to be pounded, but we also learned that we would be restored to our former condition immediately after and that the wicked Marmotte would have no further power over us. On the same day you were to begin inflicting this torture on us, we were all gathered in the reservoir weeping over our destiny when Lumineuse appeared. "Don't weep, my children," that remarkable fairy said. "I've come to inform you that you'll escape the punishment with which they've threatened you, provided you go cheerfully to the mortar and don't answer any questions addressed to you. I can say no more at present—I'm in a hurry, but do as I've told you and you won't regret it. The young princess whose fate appears to be the cruelest is not to lose hope—she'll soon find relief."

We all thanked the fairy and appeared before you fully determined to keep our secret. You spoke to some, who gave you only vague replies, and after you had chosen ten, we returned to the reservoir, where the assurance of our imminent rescue invigorated us with a natural gaiety.

Lumineuse's last words relieved the beautiful Camion's heart, and that made her charming in her mother's eyes and mine, and we three were inseparable. Eventually your choice fell on me and the queen, and we had no time to say adieu to the princess. An unknown power acted on us at the moment and caused us to become so cheerful that we thought we'd die of laughter at the absurd things we said to each other. You carried us to the kitchen, and no sooner did we touch the bottom of the fatal mortar than Lumineuse herself came to our aid and restored me to my natural form and transported me to my usual abode. I also had the consolation of seeing the queen and our companions resume their forms, but I don't know what happened to them. The fairy embraced me and told me to wait for you and reveal everything when you came searching for the princess.

"I've awaited this moment with impatience, as you can well believe, my lord," Citronette said to the prince, who had been listening most eagerly to her. "Yesterday I was just about to sit at the mouth of the well when Lumineuse appeared and said, 'Our children are about to be made happy, my dear Citronette. Zirphil has only to retrieve Marmotte's toothpick case to fulfill his tasks since he's finally skinned the princess.' 'Ah, great queen!' I cried. 'Are you sure of this? Have we really been so fortunate?' 'Yes,' she replied. 'It's quite true. He thought he had only skinned Marmotte, but in reality it was the princess. Marmotte was concealed in the handle of the knife that he used, and the instant he had finished his task, she caused the princess to vanish and appeared in her place in order to intimidate him again!' "

"What!" cried the prince. "I actually harmed my charming bride? Was I so cruel? Did I torture her? Ah, heavens! She'll never pardon me. I don't deserve her pardon!" The unhappy Zirphil spoke so impetuously and upset himself so much that poor Citronette was sorry she had told him this news.

"What's that?" she said, seeing that he was quite overcome. "You didn't know it?"

"No, I didn't know that," he said. "What made me take the shell off that unfortunate and charming crayfish was the sight of Lumineuse in my ring speaking to a veiled person. She even laughed with her, and I imagined it was my princess. I thought that she had passed through the mortar like the rest. Ah, I'll never forgive myself for this mistake!"

"But, my lord," Citronette said, "the charm depended on your skinning or pounding her, and you hadn't done either. The person to whom

Lumineuse spoke was the princess's mother. They were waiting for the end of your adventure in order to seize your bride and protect her for you. It was quite necessary for it to happen that way."

"Nevertheless," the prince said, "if I had known it, I'd rather have pierced my own heart with that horrid knife!"

"But consider," Citronette said, "that in piercing your heart, you'd have left the princess eternally in the power of your frightful rival. It is far better to have shelled her than to have died and left her in misery."

This argument obviously placated the prince, and he consented to some nourishment to maintain his strength. They had just finished when the roof of the salon opened and Lumineuse appeared, seated on a carbuncle drawn by a hundred butterflies. She descended from the carbuncle, assisted by the prince, who drenched the hem of her garment with a flood of tears. The fairy raised him, saying, "Prince Zirphil, today you're to reap the fruit of your heroic endeavors. Console yourself, for you shall finally enjoy happiness. I've vanquished Marmotte's fury by my pleas, and your courage has disarmed her. Come with me to receive your princess from her hands and mine."

"Ah, madam," the prince cried, throwing himself at her feet, "am I dreaming? Can it be that happiness is at last mine?"

"You can rest assured," the fairy said. "Come to your kingdom and console the queen, your mother, for your absence and the death of the king, your father. Your subjects are waiting to crown you."

In the midst of his joy the prince felt a bitter pang on hearing about his father's death, but the fairy distracted him from his distress by seating himself beside her. Citronette she permitted to seat herself at their feet. Then the butterflies spread their radiant wings and set out for King Zirphil's empire.

On the way the fairy told him to open his ring, and he found the toothpick case he had to return to Marmotte. The king thanked the generous fairy a thousand times over, and they arrived at the capital of his dominions, where they were awaited with the utmost impatience. Zirphil's mother advanced to greet the fairy as she got out of her chariot, and all the people, who knew about Zirphil's return, shouted and acclaimed him. Such a reception relieved him somewhat of his grief, and he tenderly embraced his mother. Then they all went up to a magnificent apartment that the queen had prepared for the fairy.

No sooner did they enter than Marmotte arrived in a chariot lined with Spanish leather and drawn by eight winged rats. She brought with her the beautiful Camion as well as her father and mother. Lumineuse and the queen hastened to embrace Marmotte while Zirphil respectfully kissed her paw, which she laughingly extended to him. Thereupon he returned the toothpick case to her, and she permitted him to claim his bride and present her to the queen, who embraced her with a thousand expressions of joy.

The large, illustrious group of people began speaking all at once, and joy reigned supreme. Camion and her charming husband were the only ones unable to say a word, for they had too much on their minds. There was, however, an eloquence in their silence that affected everyone present. The good Citronette wept with happiness while kissing the hands of the divine princess.

At last Lumineuse took them both by the hand and advanced with them toward Zirphil's mother. "Behold, madam," she said. "Two young lovers who only await your consent to become happy. Do complete their happiness. My sister Marmotte, the king and queen here present, and I myself, all request that you do so."

The queen tenderly embraced the happy couple. "Yes, my children," she replied courteously, "live happily together, and permit me to participate in that happiness as I relinquish my crown to you."

Zirphil and the princess threw themselves at her feet, and she raised them and embraced them again. They implored her not to abandon them, but to help them by giving them her advice.

Then Marmotte touched the beautiful Camion with her wand: her clothes, already magnificent, became silver brocade embroidered with carat diamonds, and her beautiful locks fell down and rearranged themselves so exquisitely that the kings and queens declared that her appearance was perfectly dazzling. The toothpick case the fairy held was changed into a crown formed entirely from beautiful diamonds so well set that the whole palace became illuminated by it. Marmotte placed it on the head of the princess, and Zirphil in turn appeared in a suit similar to that of Camion's. Lastly, the ring that she had given him produced a crown exactly like hers.

They were married on the spot and proclaimed king and queen of that fine country. The fairies gave the royal wedding breakfast, and nothing was lacking. After spending a week overwhelming them with good things, they departed and conducted the king and queen, Camion's father and mother, back to their kingdom, where they had punished the old inhabitants and repopulated it with new people faithful to their master. As for Citronette, the fairies permitted her to come and spend some time with her beautiful queen, and they allowed Camion to see her whenever she pleased just by wishing for her.

At last the fairies departed, and never has the world seen two people so happy as King Zirphil and Queen Camion. Their greatest happiness they found in each other, and days seemed to them like moments. Having children completed their bliss, and they lived to an extreme old age loving and continually striving to please each other with the same ardor. When they died, their kingdom was divided, and after various changes it has come under the rule of one of their descendants and become the flourishing empire of the Great Mogul.

Marie-Catherine d'Aulnoy

Marie-Catherine Le Jumel de Barneville, Comtesse d'Aulnoy (c.1650–1705) was born in Barneville, Normandy, and came from a wealthy aristocratic family. During her youth she had two important formative influences: her aunt told her numerous folk tales, and her mother encouraged her to live as independently as possible. At fifteen she was married to François de la Motte, Baron d'Aulnoy, who was thirty years her senior and a notorious gambler and libertine. She had some children by him, but due to his poor character, she soon became disenchanted with her marriage and had several lovers. In 1669, with the help of her mother, Madame Guadagne (who had remarried after Baron de Barneville's death), and two men, Jacques-Antoine de Courboyer and Charles de la Moizière, who were their respective lovers, Mme. d'Aulnoy tried to implicate her husband in a crime of high treason against the king, which carried a capital punishment. However, the Baron d'Aulnoy managed to extricate himself from the affair and turned the tables on his wife: De Courboyer and de la Moizière were executed; Madame Guadagne escaped and made her way to England; Mme. d'Aulnoy was arrested briefly and then also managed to flee Paris. After taking refuge in a convent, Mme. d'Aulnoy apparently traveled extensively in Holland, England, and Spain, and may have acted along with her adventurous mother as a secret agent for France in those countries. She also had some more children and different lovers. However, it is not clear when she traveled, where she lived at any given time, or who her lovers were. What is known is that in 1685 she received permission to return to Paris and bought a house in the rue Saint-Benoit, which became one of the most interesting literary salons of the period.

By 1690 Mme. d'Aulnoy, an exceedingly bright and beautiful woman, began her public literary career with the publication of the novel *L'Histoire d'Hippolyte, comte de Douglas*, which contained the prose fairy tale, *L'île de la Félicité*, which anticipated the great fairy-tale vogue that commenced five years later. Her novel was a huge success, and that same year she published *Mémoires de la cour d'Espagne*, which appears to have been largely taken from an English book, since there is no evidence that Mme. d'Aulnoy had ever been at the Spanish court. The same holds true for her next book, *Relation du voyage d'Espagne* (1691), which contained the tale *Histoire de Mira*, based on the theme of Melusine. Her last book about journeys to foreign countries was *Mémoires de la cour d'Angleterre* (1695), which may also have been a fictive account and based on Mme. d'Aulnoy's own readings about the English court.

It became customary at Mme. d'Aulnoy's salon to recite fairy tales and on festive occasions to dress up like characters from fairy tales. She herself became one of the most gifted storytellers at her salon, and eventually she began publishing several volumes of fairy tales: *Les Contes des Fées*, vols. I–III (1696–97), *Les Contes des Fées*, vol. IV (1698), and *Contes Nouveaux ou Les Fées à la Mode*, vols. I–IV (1698). More than Charles Perrault, it was Mme. d'Aulnoy who was responsible for the extraordinary vogue of French fairy tales that swept the Parisian literary circles during the next ten years and continued less intensely until the publication of the *Cabinet des Fées* (1786–89).

On the basis of her so-called memoirs and fairy tales, Mme. d'Aulnoy was elected a member of the Académie des Ricovrati in Padova, and she continued to be active in the literary field by publishing other works such as *Sentiments d'une Ame pénitente* (1698) and *Le Comte de Warwick* (1703). In addition, Mme. d'Aulnoy managed to make time for intrigues. In 1699 she supposedly assisted her friend Mme. Ticquet, who assassinated her husband, a member of Parlement, because he had allegedly abused her. Mme. Ticquet was beheaded, and Mme. d'Aulnoy was fortunate to be exculpated from any wrongdoing.

In 1700 her husband died. Since they had been on terrible terms, his last act was to disinherit her. Nevertheless, she continued to maintain her salon and participate in the cultural life in Paris until her death in 1705.

Although Mme. d'Aulnoy was a mediocre stylist and her poetry is maudlin at times, she had such a powerful imagination and remarkable command of folktale motifs and characters that her fairy tales never ceased to captivate her readers. Moreover,

Mme. d'Aulnoy paid close attention to the details of dress, architecture, speech, and manners of her day, and she described these details in her fairy tales so accurately that they always had a ring of authenticity. Of course, her descriptions always tended to be hyperbolic: her heroines were the most beautiful; her heroes were the most charming and handsome; the castles were the most splendid. One refrain continues throughout her tales: "never has anyone seen anything so magnificent as this." This "never" that becomes "forever" in her tales revealed her longing for a world different from the one to which she had been exposed.

Mme. d'Aulnoy did not like constraints. In particular, she did not like the manner in which women were treated and compelled to follow patriarchal codes, and as we know, she did not even stop short of abetting execution or murder of men she considered unworthy or tyrannical. All her tales are filled with violence and violation of some kind or another that must be resolved, and in some cases, like *The Ram*, the resolution is not entirely satisfying. D'Aulnoy's tales are nightmarish because the fairies themselves are not always in agreement with one another, and thus humans must live under laws that they do not always understand and under fairy powers who are arbitrary, not unlike Louis XIV and his ministers. The only saving grace in the tales is love, or *tendresse*, that is, true natural feelings between a man and woman, and these feelings are constantly tested in extreme if not macabre ways. D'Aulnoy's repertoire of tortures and bestial transformations was immense. She stopped at nothing to make her lovers suffer, making their rescue all the sweeter.

Literary critics have often commented that the constant action in d'Aulnoy's tales emanated from the boredom that the aristocracy felt during the ancien régime and that the tales were a form of compensation for the frustration that she and others felt. However, d'Aulnoy was anything but bored, and her tales that originated from her active social life in the salons of that time were a means of confronting the frustrating conditions under which she lived and of projecting possibilities for change. Like her heroine Belle-Belle or the Chevalier Fortune, d'Aulnoy disguised her dreams in her symbolical tales and was not afraid to imagine or try anything if it meant the fulfillment of these dreams.

THE ISLAND
OF HAPPINESS

RUSSIA is a frigid country where one rarely sees the beautiful days of a mild climate. Its mountains are almost always covered with snow, and the trees are so loaded with icicles that when the sun casts its rays on them, they appear to be garnished with crystals. There are forests of enormous grandeur where white bears wreak terrible havoc, and the people are continually warring with them. Although they manage to kill the bears, it is not without difficulty and danger. Thus, in Russia hunting bears is considered both the most noble and most ordinary occupation.

Once upon a time the Russians were governed by a young prince named Adolph. Born under a lucky star, he was so handsome, polite, and intelligent that it would have been difficult to convince anyone that a person so accomplished lived in a country so coarse and savage. He had not yet turned twenty when he undertook a great war against the Muscovites and showed dauntless courage and remarkable leadership. When he allowed his army to rest, he himself did not rest. Instead he went on that dangerous quest for bears.

One day when he was carried away once again by his noble passion for hunting, he led a large retinue into a vast forest. All over he roved until he finally got lost. Just as he realized that he was alone, that it was late, and that he no longer knew where he was, a storm took him by surprise. He guided his horse down a wide track and vainly blew his hunting horn in order to alert some of his hunters. All at once the scant daylight that was left was transformed into the most obscure night, punctuated only by lightning. The thunder made a terrible noise as the rain storm increased. The prince at first took shelter under some trees, but he was soon compelled to leave that spot. All around the rain fell in torrents, and the paths were flooded. Deciding to get free of the forest and to seek some shelter from the tempest, he struggled with difficulty to reach open fields, where he found himself even more exposed to the inclement weather. He looked all around him and noticed a light in a spot that was very high up.

So he headed in that direction, arduously climbing by foot and leading his horse to the top of an almost inaccessible mountain. His way was obstructed by a multitude of boulders and sheer cliffs. For several hours he pressed on, sometimes on foot, sometimes on horseback, until he found himself nearing a cave. Through the opening he saw the light that he had already observed. He hesitated before entering, for he thought it might be the hideout of some robbers who frequently ravaged the countryside and who could rob and kill him. However, since the souls of princes possess a nobility and pride that sets them apart from other men, he reproached himself for his fear. Into the cave he advanced, hand on sword, ready to defend himself in case someone was bold enough to attack him.

Because of the noise he made when he entered, an old woman, whose white hair and mass of wrinkles revealed how ancient she was, emerged from the rear of the cave. As she approached him, she was visibly astonished.

"You're the first mortal I've ever seen here," she said. "Do you know, sir, who dwells here?"

"No, my good woman," Adolph responded. "I have no idea where I am."

"This is the abode of Eole, god of the winds," she stated. "This is where he retires with all his children. I'm their mother, and you've found me alone because they are all busy, each one doing good or evil in the world as his wont. But you seem drenched from the rain that has just fallen. Let me make a fire so you can dry yourself. I'm afraid, though, that I cannot offer you much here. The meals that the winds have are very light, and men need to eat something much more solid."

The prince thanked her for the kind welcome he had received and approached the fire, which leapt into flames almost immediately because the West Wind had just entered and blown on it. No sooner had he arrived than the Northeast Wind and many northerly gales returned to the cave. Eole was not tardy, and Boreas, the East, Southwest, and North Winds followed. They were all damp and had puffed cheeks and unkempt heads of hair. Their manners were not very civil or polite, and when they ventured to speak to the prince, they all but froze him with their breath. One recounted that he had dispersed an entire navy. Another recalled that he had caused many ships to perish. A third had kindly saved certain vessels from pirates who had wanted to seize them. Many of the gales reported how they had uprooted trees, knocked down houses, and overturned walls. In short, each one boasted of his exploits. After listening to all of them, the old woman suddenly showed signs of great uneasiness.

"Did any of you encounter your brother Zephir during your adventures?" she asked. "He's already late, and I confess I'm troubled that he's not going to return."

While all echoed that they had not seen him, Adolph noticed a young boy at the entrance of the cave. He was just as handsome as Cupid: he had wings made of white feathers mixed with the color of flesh that appeared to be fine and delicate and in perpetual motion. His blond hair fell carelessly in a thousand curls to his shoulders. His head was crowned by roses and jasmine, and he had a pleasant, jovial air about him.

"Where have you come from, you little rake?" the old woman cried huskily. "All your brothers are here. You're the only one who takes his time and who doesn't care at all about how much I might worry."

"Mother, I had no intention of returning so late," he said, "for I know that you don't like it. But I was in the gardens of Princess Felicity. She was taking a walk there with her nymphs. One made a garland of flowers for her. Another nymph, who was lying on the grass, opened her throat a little, and this gave me the freedom to approach her and give her a kiss. Several were dancing to songs. The beautiful princess was in an orange orchard, and my breath swept up to her mouth. I dallied around her and played gently with her veil. 'Zephir,' she said, 'I like that! You make everything so pleasant! I'm going to keep walking as long as you tarry. . . .' I must confess that such sweet words uttered by such a charming person captivated me, and I was no longer my own master. I would not have been able to leave her at all if I had not known how this would displease you."

Adolph listened with such great satisfaction that he felt sorry when Zephir fell silent. "Permit me, charming Zephir, to ask you where the country is that the princess reigns," he said.

"It is the Island of Happiness," responded Zephir. "Nobody, sir, can enter it. People have exhausted themselves in trying to find it, but their fate is such that they do not know how to find it. They have traveled all over in vain. Sometimes they even imagine that they have found it because they often arrive at other small ports possessing calm and tranquillity. Many people remain there happily, but these floating islands are quite mediocre compared with the Island of Happiness. People soon lose sight of them, and only desire, which allows mortals to hope for just a shadow of repose, keeps them searching. Every day I see distinguished men perish near there."

The prince continued to ply him with questions, which Zephir answered with great precision and intelligence. It was extremely late, and the good mother ordered all her children to go to their corners of the cave. Zephir offered the prince a bed in a spotless place less cold than the other caverns of this grotto. A small spot of fine grass grew there, covered with flowers, and Adolph threw himself down on it. The rest of the night he spent with Zephir, talking about the Princess Felicity.

"How I'd love to see her," he said. "Is it so absolutely impossible? Couldn't I succeed with your help?"

Zephir told him that such a venture would be very dangerous, but that if he had the courage to abandon himself to Zephir's guidance, he imagined there might be a way: he would put him on his wings and carry him through the vast ethereal regions. "I have a cloak I'll give you," he continued, "and when you put it on with the green side showing, you'll be invisible. No one will be able to perceive you, and this is absolutely vital for your protection, because if the guards of the island, who are terrible monsters, see you, they'll capture you, no matter how brave you may be."

Adolph had such an urgent desire to begin this great adventure that he accepted everything Zephir proposed with all his heart, no matter what danger he faced. No sooner did the sun begin to shine in its chariot of mother-of-pearls than the impatient Adolph woke a still dozing Zephir.

"I've given you hardly any time to rest," the prince said as he embraced him, "but it seems to me, my kind host, that it's already time to depart."

"Let's go, then," Zephir responded. "Far be it from me to complain. Let me thank you instead, for I must confess that I'm in love with a proud and pert rose, and I'd be in a good deal of trouble with her if I weren't there to see her as soon as it turns daylight. She is in one of Princess Felicity's flower beds."

So saying, he gave the prince the cloak that he had promised him. He wanted to carry him on his wings, but he did not find this way comfortable.

"Sir, I'm going to lift you," he said, "just as I lifted Psyche on Cupid's orders when I carried her to the beautiful palace that he had built for her."

So he took him in his arms, and after placing himself at the edge of a cliff, he rocked for some time in a steady motion until he spread his wings, took off, and began soaring through the air.

Although the prince was courageous, he could not help being afraid when he found himself aloft in the arms of a young adolescent. To reassure himself, he recalled that Zephir was a god and that Cupid himself, who seemed the smallest and weakest of all the gods, was the strongest and most awesome. Thus, abandoning himself to his destiny, he collected his wits and gazed attentively at all the places they flew over. But how was it possible to count the places! There were so many cities, kingdoms, seas, rivers, fields, deserts, woods, unknown territories, and diverse peoples! All these sights transported him into such a state of wonderment that he was unable to speak. Zephir told him about the names and customs of all those inhabitants of the earth. He flew gently, and they even took a rest on top of the formidable Caucasian Mountains, on Mount Athos, and on many others that they found along their way.

"Even though the beautiful rose whom I adore," Zephir said, "will sting me with her thorns, I can't cross such vastness without giving you the pleasure of admiring these wonders for the first time."

Adolph expressed his gratitude for Zephir's kindness and at the same time his concern that Princess Felicity would be unable to understand his language and he unable to speak hers.

"Don't fret over that," the god said. "The princess's knowledge is universal, and I'm convinced that you'll speak the same language soon enough."

He flew until that desired island was in sight, and the prince was so struck by all its beauties that he readily believed that it was indeed enchanted. The air was thoroughly perfumed with dew from the excellent waters of Nafre and Cordoue. The rain carried the scent of oranges. The water gushed up to the clouds. The forests were filled with rare trees, and the ground was covered with extraordinary flowers. Streams as clear as crystal flowed all over with a sweet murmur. The birds sang concerts that were superior to the music of the great masters. Exotic fruit grew there naturally, and throughout the island one could find tables covered with all the delicacies that one could desire. But the palace surpassed even all the rest: the walls were made of diamonds, and the ceilings and floors were made of precious gems that formed compartments. Gold glittered everywhere. The furniture was made by the hands of the most gallant fairies. Everything seemed so natural that one could not help but admire the magnificence and assortment all the more. After Zephir set the prince down in a pleasant green lawn, he said, "Sir, I've kept my word, and now it's up to you to do the rest."

They embraced each other, and Adolph gave him thanks befitting such a favor. Since the god was eager to see his mistress, he left him in those delightful gardens. Venturing down several alleys, Adolph saw grottos made expressly for pleasure. In one he noticed a white marble statue of Cupid so well made that it must have been the work of some divine sculptor. Instead of flames, a jet of water spurted from its torch, and the god was supported by grotto-work and seemed to be reading verses engraved on lapis lazuli. These proclaimed: "Love is the greatest of all blessings. Love alone is able to fulfill our desires. All other sweet things of life become dull if they are not mixed with love's attractive charms."

Adolph entered a honeysuckle arbor, where the sun could not penetrate the charming shade. Here he lay on a carpet of grass surrounding a fountain, and he yielded to the sweetness of slumber, for his heavy eyelids and exhausted limbs begged for a few hours of rest.

It was close to noon when he awoke. He was disappointed to have lost so much time, and to make up for it, he rushed toward the palace. As soon as he got near enough to it, he began to admire its beautiful features at a more leisurely pace than when he had been further away. It seemed that all the arts had competed with equal success to contribute to the magnificence and perfection of the building. Because the prince continued to wear the cloak on the green side, he could view everything without being seen. For a long time he searched for a way to enter the palace, but either the vestibule was closed or the doors of the palace were on the other side of the palace, for he saw no way to enter until he noticed a pretty young nymph opening a window made entirely of crystal. At the very same moment a dwarfish gardener ran to the spot, and the nymph let down a large gold filigree basket that had many ribbons and bows attached. Then she ordered the gardener to gather flowers for the princess, and the gardener promptly did as she was told. Consequently, Adolph threw himself on the flowers in the basket before the nymph had pulled it up to the window. (It should be noted that the green cloak that made him invisible also made him as light as the wind.)

As soon as he was inside, he entered a large salon, where he saw wonders that are difficult to recount. The nymphs were there in large numbers. The oldest among them seemed no more than eighteen, and a great many seemed to be younger. Some were blondes, others brunettes, and all had remarkable white, fresh complexions with beautiful features and regular teeth. In short, the nymphs could pass for the most perfect people imaginable. Adolph could have stayed in the salon all day admiring them if his curiosity had not been aroused by numerous voices marvelously harmonizing with some exceedingly well-played instruments. He advanced toward the chamber from which this pleasant harmony came, and as he entered, he heard the most touching words sung in a manner equally tender.

When first the prince had entered the salon, he had thought that nothing could equal the charms he saw there. However, he was wrong, for the musicians surpassed their beauty by far. Due to some miracle, he understood everything they said even though he did not know the language they used in this palace. He was standing behind one of the prettiest nymphs when her veil slipped to the ground. Without realizing that he would undoubtedly frighten her, he picked up the veil and gave it to her. Since the nymph did not see a soul, she uttered a great cry, and perhaps for the first time someone had become afraid in that beautiful place. All her companions gathered around her, asking her urgently what the matter was.

"You're going to think that I've been seeing things," she said, "but I assure you that my veil that just fell to the ground was returned to my hand by some invisible force."

Everyone burst into laughter, and several nymphs pranced toward the princess's chamber to amuse her with this story. Adolph followed. Thanks to the green cloak, he crossed anonymously through the rooms, galleries, and chambers until he finally reached that of the princess. She sat on a throne made of a single carbuncle more radiant than the sun, but the eyes of Princess Felicity far outshone the carbuncle. Her beauty was so perfect that she seemed a daughter of the heavens. Moreover, she cast a youthful aura of majestic confidence that aroused love and respect. She was dressed more in a gallant than a magnificent fashion: her blond hair was decorated with flowers and a scarf, and her robe was made of gauze mixed with gold. Around her frolicked many small cupids playing a thousand different games. Some took her hands and kissed them; others climbed her throne with the help of their companions and placed a crown on her head. The pleasures were also playing about her. In brief, everywhere the prince turned his eyes, he was struck by the most charming things imaginable, and he stood there like a man entranced. He could hardly stand the princess's explosive beauty, and he could not think of anything but this person whom he already adored. Because he was so agitated and excited, his green cloak fell to the ground, and he became visible.

The princess had never seen a human being, and so she was extremely surprised. In turn, when Adolph saw that he had exposed himself, he threw himself respectfully at her feet.

"Great princess," he said, "I've crossed the universe to admire your divine beauty. I want to offer you my heart and devotion. I hope you will not refuse me."

The princess, who was normally vivacious, remained silent and confused. Until then she had never seen anyone as remarkable as this creature, whom she believed to be unique in the world. This thought convinced her that he was the Phoenix, that bird so rare and vaunted, and feeling she was right in her mistake, she said, "Handsome Phoenix—for I can't believe that you are anyone else but Phoenix since you are so perfect and don't resemble anything that is on my island—I'm extremely grateful to have the pleasure of seeing you. It's a great shame that you are the only kind of your species. If there were many more birds like you, they would fill beautiful bird cages."

Adolph smiled at her gracious naiveté. He did not want the object of his already great passion to remain mistaken for long, for it might lead to misconceptions. Therefore, he took care to tell her everything about himself, and never has a pupil learned her lessons so quickly. In fact, she was ready to give them after just learning them.

Her natural intuition went further than what the prince could tell her. She loved him more than she loved herself, and he loved her more than he loved himself. The two lovers felt everything that love has to offer in sweetness, everything that the mind has to offer in vivacity, and everything that the heart has to offer in delights. Nothing disturbed their repose; everything contributed to their pleasures. They were never sick. They were never troubled by the slightest inconvenience.

Their youthfulness was not changed by the passing of the years, for in this delightful asylum everyone drank long draughts from the Fountain of Youth. Neither the anguishes of love, nor jealous suspicions, not even the petty quarrels that sometimes disturb the happy tranquillity of lovers until they make sweet amends—nothing of this kind happened to them. They were intoxicated with pleasure, and up to that time there had never been a mortal who had enjoyed such good luck as constant as that of the prince. But the condition of mortality bears with it sad consequences. Their good fortune could not last forever.

One day when Adolph was with the princess, it occurred to him to ask her how long he had been enjoying the pleasure of being with her. "The moments pass so quickly where you are," he continued, "that I haven't paid any attention to time since my arrival."

"I'll tell you," she said, "after you reveal to me how long you think you've been here."

He pondered this and said, "If I consult my heart and the gratification I've experienced, I'd believe that I've only spent a week here. But, my dear princess, according to certain things that I can recall to mind, it's been approximately three months."

"Adolph," she said more seriously, "it's been three hundred years."

Ah, if she had only known what those words would cost her, she would have never uttered them.

"Three hundred years!" cried the prince. "What's going on in the world? Who's governing it right now? What are the people doing there? When I return, who will recognize me, and whom will I be able to recognize? My dominions have undoubtedly fallen into somebody else's hands rather than those close to me. I cannot dare hope that there's anything left for me. I'm going to be a prince stripped of his robe. People will regard me like a ghost. I'll no longer know the manners and customs that I'll need to live."

Becoming impatient, the princess interrupted him. "What do you regret, Adolph? Isn't this price worth all the love and kindness I've shown you? I received you in my palace where you are the master. I've preserved your life for three centuries. You haven't aged at all and apparently, until now, you haven't been bored. You wouldn't have had any of this if it weren't for me."

"I'm not ungrateful, beautiful princess," he replied, somewhat confused. "I know all that I owe you. But ultimately, if I were dead at this moment, I would have perhaps performed such great deeds that my name would be eternally engraved in stone. As it is, I see with shame that there has been nothing virtuous about my actions, and my name is not famous. The brave Reginald may have ended in the arms of his Armida, but it was honor that tore him away from her."

"You barbarian!" the princess screamed as a flood of tears streamed from her eyes. "It will be honor that tears you away from me. You want to leave me, and you minimize the pain that it will cause me."

Upon saying this, she collapsed in a dead faint. The prince was greatly moved. He dearly loved her, but he reapproached himself for having spent so much time with a mistress without having done anything that would place his name among the ranks of heroes. He tried in vain to restrain himself and conceal his misgivings. However, he fell into an apathy that soon rendered him unrecognizable.

Now the prince, who had mistaken centuries for months, mistook months for centuries. The princess saw this and suffered greatly because of it. Not wanting him to remain out of a sense of obligation, she declared, "You are master of your destiny and can depart whenever you wish. All the same, I fear something terrible will happen to you."

Her last words caused him less pain than her first, which were not very pleasing themselves. Although he grew tender and melancholy when he thought about separating, his sense of his destiny was stronger, and at last he said farewell to the woman whom he had adored, and whom he still loved with a great deal of tenderness. He assured her that as soon as he had achieved a measure of glory and made himself more worthy of her magnanimity, he would return and acknowledge her as his sole sovereign and the only treasure of his life. But the princess was too intelligent to be misled, and she had sad forebodings that told her she was going to lose the person she cherished forever.

Despite the fact that she was terribly upset, she did not express her pain. She gave the indifferent Adolph magnificent weapons and the most magnificent horse in the world. "Bichar (that was the name of the horse) will conduct you," she said, "and he will take you wherever you must go to do battle and triumph. But don't place your foot on the ground no matter what happens in your country, for the fairy spirit that the gods have given me enable me to prophesy that if you neglect my advice, Bichar will not be able to extricate you from your trouble."

Promising her that he would obey her wishes, the prince kissed her beautiful hands a thousand times, and he was so eager to leave that delightful place that he even forgot to take his green cloak with him.

Once they reached the border of the island, the vigorous horse threw himself into the river with his master on top of him. After swimming across it, he galloped over hill and dale. He passed through fields and forests with such great speed that it seemed he had wings. But one evening, in a narrow, rutted path, filled with rocks and pebbles and bordered by thorn bushes, they encountered a wagon blocking the path. Loaded with different kinds of old wings, it had turned over on an old man who had been driving the wagon. His head was gray, his voice trembled, and the prince felt pity for the old man's distress since he was bearing the weight of the wagon. Bichar wanted to jump over the wagon blocking the way, and was about ready to soar over it when the good man cried, "Sir, have some compassion for my predicament. If you don't deign to help me, I'll soon be dead."

Adolph could not resist helping the old man. He put his feet on the ground, approached the man, and gave him his hand. But alas! He was tremendously surprised to see the man get up quickly and seize him before he could get ready to defend himself.

"Finally, the Prince of Russia!" the old man said in a terrible, menacing voice, "I've found you. I'm called Father Time, and I've been looking for you for three centuries. I've used all the wings this wagon is carrying to go around the universe in order to find you. But no matter where you may have hidden yourself, nothing that lives can escape me."

Thereupon, he clapped his hand on Adolph's mouth with such force that he prevented the prince from drawing breath until he was smothered. At this sad moment Zephir, who had witnessed everything, passed by, greatly disturbed by the misfortune of his dear friend. When the old barbarian left Adolph, Zephir approached and tried to bring him back to life with his sweet breath. His efforts were in vain, though. He took him in his arms just as he had done the first time, and weeping bitter tears, he brought him back to the gardens of Princess Felicity. He set him down in a grotto on a rock that was flat across the top. Then he covered him and surrounded him with flowers. After taking off his weapons, he formed a trophy with them and engraved an epitaph on a column of jasper that he placed near the unfortunate prince.

The sorrowful princess had been going every day to this grotto since the departure of her lover, adding a flood of tears to the flow of the stream. But then, what unexpected joy to find him again at the very moment when she believed him to be so far away! She imagined that he had just arrived and that, exhausted from the trip, he had fallen asleep. She contemplated whether she should wake him, and finally giving way to her tender feelings, she opened her loving arms to embrace him. As she approached, however, she began to realize her extreme misfortune, and she uttered such bitter cries that they could have moved the most insensitive heart.

She ordered the doors of her palace to be closed forever, and ever since that fatal day nobody has seen her. Her suffering is the reason why she rarely shows herself, and one never finds this princess without her being preceded by some anguish accompanied by sorrow or followed by disturbances. This is the company that is usually with her most of the time. Human beings can certainly bear witness to this, and ever since that deplorable adventure, everyone keeps saying that there is no avoiding Father Time. Nor is there perfect happiness.

BEAUTY WITH
THE GOLDEN HAIR

ONCE upon a time there was a princess who was more beautiful than anyone in the world, and she was called Beauty with the Golden Hair because her locks were radiant like the finest gold and fell in ringlets to her feet. She always appeared with her hair flowing in curls and crowned with flowers, and her dresses were embroidered with diamonds and pearls. It was impossible to look upon her without adoring her.

Now, among her neighbors was a young king who was rich, handsome, and unmarried. When he heard about Beauty with the Golden Hair—though he had never seen her—he fell so deeply in love with her that he could neither eat nor drink. Therefore, he decided to send an ambassador to ask her hand in marriage. He had a magnificent coach made for this envoy, gave him upward of a hundred horses and as many servants, and charged him specifically not to return without the princess. From the moment the ambassador took his leave, the entire court talked of nothing else, and the king, who never doubted that Beauty with the Golden Hair would consent to his proposal, immediately ordered fine dresses and splendid furniture to be prepared for her.

While the craftsmen were hard at work, the ambassador arrived at Beauty's court and delivered his brief message. However, she was either out of temper that day or found the proposal displeasing, for she told the ambassador that she was grateful to the king, but she had no inclination to marry. The ambassador left the princess's court, despondent at not being able to bring her with him. He carried back all the king's presents he had brought, for the prudent beauty was perfectly aware that young ladies should never accept gifts from bachelors. So she had refused beautiful diamonds and other valuable articles, retaining only a quarter pound of English pins so as not to affront the king.

When the ambassador reached the king's capital, where he was so impatiently awaited, everybody was disturbed that he had not brought back

Beauty with the Golden Hair. The king began to cry like a babe. They endeavored to console him, but without the least success.

At the king's court resided a young man who cut the finest figure in the kingdom. Indeed, he was as radiant as the sun. Due to his graceful manners and intelligence, he was called Avenant. Everybody loved him except envious colleagues, who were irritated that the king conferred favors upon him and confided to him daily about his affairs. Happening to be in the company of some people who were talking about the return of the ambassador, he told them the man had not done his best. "Why, if the king had sent me to Beauty with the Golden Hair," he said to them carelessly, "I'm certain she would have returned with me."

These mischief makers went directly to the king and said, "Sire, do you know what Avenant's been saying? He claims that if you had sent him to Beauty with the Golden Hair, he would have brought her back with him. See how malicious he is! He asserts he's handsomer than you, and that she would have become so fond of him that she would have followed him anywhere."

Upon hearing this, the king flew into a rage so terrible that he was quite beside himself. "Ha, ha!" he cried, "this petty minion laughs at my misfortune. He thinks he's superior to me. Go! Fling him into the great tower, and let him starve to death!"

The royal guards quickly searched out Avenant, who had quite forgotten what he had said. They dragged him to prison and beat him terribly. The poor youth had only a pittance of straw to lie upon and would have soon perished but for a tiny spring that trickled through the foundations of the tower. Since his mouth was continually parched with thirst, he kept refreshing himself by drinking drops of water from the spring.

One day when he was quite exhausted, he exclaimed with a heavy sigh, "Why is the king complaining? There's not a subject more loyal than I am. I've never done anything to offend him."

Just then the king happened to pass near the tower, and upon hearing the voice of one he had loved so dearly, he stopped to listen, even though the people who were with him hated Avenant and said, "That doesn't concern you, sire. Don't you know he's a rogue?"

The king replied, "Leave me alone. I want to hear what he has to say."

After listening to Avenant's complaints, tears welled in his eyes. He opened the door of the tower and called to the prisoner. Avenant came, knelt before him with deep humility, and kissed his feet. "What have I done, sire, to have earned such severe treatment?"

"You've boasted that if I had sent you to Beauty with the Golden Hair, you would certainly have brought her back with you."

"It's true, sire," Avenant remarked. "I believe I would have impressed her with your majesty's high qualities in such a persuasive manner she could not have refused you. By saying that, sire, I uttered nothing that was intended to offend you."

The king saw clearly that Avenant was innocent. He cast an angry look at the maligners of his favorite and took him away, sincerely repenting the wrong he had done to him.

After giving Avenant an excellent supper, he called him into his cabinet and said to him, "Avenant, I still love Beauty with the Golden Hair. Her refusal has not discouraged me, but I don't know what step to make to induce her to marry me. I'm tempted to send you to her to see if you might succeed."

Avenant replied that he was ready to obey him completely, and that he could set out the next day.

"Wait," said the king, "I want to give you a splendid equipage."

"It's unnecessary," Avenant answered, "I only need a good horse and letters of recommendation from your majesty."

The king embraced him, for he was delighted to find Avenant prepared to start so quickly.

On that Monday morning Avenant took his leave of the king and his friends, and proceeded on his mission, quite alone and without pomp or fanfare. His mind was occupied solely with schemes to induce the Beauty with the Golden Hair to marry the king. He had a writing case in his pocket, and when a good idea occurred to him for his introductory speech, he dismounted from his steed and seated himself under a tree to write it down so that he would not forget anything.

One morning he set out at the first peep of day, and while passing through a large meadow, a charming idea came into his head. He dismounted and seated himself beside some willows and poplars planted along the bank of a little river that bordered the meadow. After he had noted down his thought, he looked about him, delighted to find himself in such a beautiful spot. It was then that he spotted not far from him on the grass a large, gilded carp gasping and nearly exhausted: in trying to catch some flies, it had leapt right out of the water. Although it was a fish-day and Avenant might have carried it off for his dinner, he took pity on it. Picking it up, he put it gently back into the river. As soon as this lovely carp felt the freshness of the water, she began to recover. Down to the very bottom she glided and then rose again joyously to the bank of the stream. "Avenant," she said, "I thank you for your kindness. If it weren't for you, I would have died. You've saved me, and I shall do the same for you."

After this brief salute, she darted down again into the water, leaving Avenant astonished by her clarity of mind and civility.

As he continued his journey, the next day he saw a crow in great distress. The poor bird was being pursued by a large eagle, a great predator of crows. The eagle had nearly caught it and would have swallowed it like a lentil if Avenant had not felt compassion for its misfortune. "Just look," he cried, "how the strong oppress the weak. What right does the eagle have to eat the crow?" He seized his bow and arrow, which he always carried with him, and, taking good aim at the eagle, whizz! sent the shaft right through its body, and it fell dead.

The crow was delighted. Fluttering over to a tree and landing on a branch, it cried to him, "Avenant, you were very kind to rescue me, I who am only a poor crow. Believe me, I shall not be ungrateful and shall do as much for you."

Astonished by the crow's intelligence, Avenant resumed his journey. After entering a great wood early in the next morning, when there was scarcely light enough for him to see his way, he heard an owl screeching as though in desperate straits. "Eh, now," he said, "there's an owl in great trouble. It must be caught in some net." He searched all about and at last discovered some large nets that had been spread by fowlers during the night to catch small birds. "What a pity, " he said, "that men are only made to torment each other, or to persecute poor animals that do them no mischief." He drew his knife and cut the cords. The owl took flight, but swiftly returned on the wing and cried, "Avenant, it's needless for me to make a long speech. You realize now that I'm beholden to you. Everything's quite clear. The hunters would soon have been here. They would have captured me, and I would now be dead but for your assistance. I have a grateful heart, and I shall do as much for you."

These were the three most important adventures that Avenant experienced during his journey. So eager was he to reach its end that he lost no time in proceeding to the palace of Beauty with the Golden Hair. Everything about it was remarkable. As he looked about, he saw heaps of diamonds, strewn about like pebbles. In addition, there were elegant clothes, candied preserves, and coins—it was the most wonderful sight in the world. Avenant thought in his heart, if he could persuade the princess to leave all this for the king his master, he would be lucky indeed. Dressing in a suit of brocade with a plume of carnations and white feathers, he combed and powdered himself, washed his face, and wrapped a richly embroidered scarf around his neck. Finally he took a little basket containing a beautiful little dog that he had bought as he had passed through Bologna. Avenant was so handsome, so charming, and did everything with so much grace that when he presented himself at the palace gate the guards saluted him most respectfully and ran to inform Beauty with the Golden Hair that Avenant, ambassador from the king, her nearest neighbor, requested an audience with her.

Upon hearing the name of Avenant, the princess said, "That's a good omen. I'll wager he's a handsome fellow and pleases everybody."

"Yes, indeed, madam!" all her maids of honor exclaimed. "We saw him from the loft in which we were trimming your flax, and as long as he remained beneath our windows, we couldn't work."

"Very nice," Beauty with the Golden Hair replied, "amusing yourselves by looking at young men! Here, give me my grand gown of blue embroidered satin and arrange my blonde hair with the utmost of taste. Get me some garlands of fresh flowers, my high-heeled shoes, and my fan. Have the servants sweep my chamber and dust my throne, for I want him to declare everywhere he goes that I'm truly Beauty with the Golden Hair."

All her women rushed about to dress her regally. Such was their hurry that they bumped into one another and scarcely made any progress. At length, however, the princess strolled through her great gallery of mirrors to see if anything was missing. Then she ascended her throne of gold, ivory, and ebony, which emitted a perfume-like balsam, and she commanded her maids of honor to take their instruments and sing very softly so as not to disturb the audience.

Ushered into the hall where all the audiences were held, Avenant was so carried away with astonishment that ever since that time he has frequently commented on how he was scarcely able to speak. Nevertheless, he took courage and delivered his speech to perfection. He begged the princess not to humiliate him by refusing to return with him.

"Gentle Avenant," she replied, "the arguments you have produced are all extremely good, and I assure you I would be very happy to favor you more than anyone, but you must know that about a month ago I was walking by the riverside with my ladies-in-waiting, and when I pulled off my glove to take some refreshment, my ring slipped from my finger and unfortunately fell into the stream. I valued it more than my kingdom, so you can imagine my grief over its loss. I have made a vow never to listen to any offers of marriage if the ambassador representing the prospective husband does not restore to me my ring. Now you see what you have to do in this matter, for even if you were to talk to me for two weeks, night and day, you could never persuade me to change my mind."

Avenant was very much surprised by this answer. He made the princess a low bow and begged her to accept the little dog, the basket, and the scarf. But she replied that she would not accept any presents, and asked him to go and reflect on what she had said. When he returned to his lodgings, he went to bed without eating any supper, and his little dog, whose name was Cabriolle, would take none himself and lay down beside his master. All night long Avenant kept sighing. "How can I hope to find a ring that fell into a great river a month ago?" he said. "It would be folly to attempt looking for it. The princess set this condition only because she knew I could not possibly fulfill it." And then the despondent fellow sighed again.

Cabriolle, who had heard him, said, "My dear master, I beseech you not to despair of your misfortune. You're too likable not to be happy. Let's go to the riverside as soon as it is daylight."

Avenant gave him two little pats without saying a word, and since he was worn out with fretting, he fell asleep. As soon as Cabriolle saw the day break, he frisked about so that he woke Avenant. "Dress yourself, master, and let's go out."

Avenant was quite willing. He arose, dressed, and descended into the garden. From there he strayed automatically toward the river, where he strolled along the banks with his hat pulled over his eyes and his arms folded. He was thinking only of taking his departure when suddenly he heard his name being called: "Avenant! Avenant!" He looked all around

and saw no one. He thought he was dreaming and had resumed his walk when again the voice called: "Avenant! Avenant!"

"Who's calling me?" he cried.

Tiny Cabriolle, who was gazing down into the water, replied, "I can't believe my eyes, but I see a golden carp there."

Immediately the carp appeared on the surface and said to Avenant, "You saved my life in the meadow of nettle trees, where I would have perished if it hadn't been for your aid. I promised to do as much for you. Here, dear Avenant, is the ring that belongs to Beauty with the Golden Hair."

Avenant stooped, took the ring out of the carp's mouth, and thanked his friend a thousand times. Instead of returning to his lodgings, he went directly to the palace, followed by little Cabriolle, who was very glad he had induced his master to take a walk by the riverside. The princess was informed that Avenant requested to see her.

"Alas," she said, "the poor boy is coming to take his leave of me. He's convinced that it's impossible to provide me with what I want and is about to return with these tidings to his master."

After Avenant was introduced, he presented her with the ring. "Madam, I've obeyed your commands. Are you willing now to accept the king my master for your husband?"

When she saw her ring in perfect condition, she was so astonished that she thought she was dreaming. "My gracious Avenant, you must be truly favored by some good fairy. Naturally, there's no other way you could have done it."

"Madam" he answered, "I'm not acquainted with any fairy, but I was most desirous of obeying you."

"Since you are so obliging," she continued, "you must do me another service, if I am to marry. Not far from here lives a prince named Galifron, who has gotten it into his head he will make me his wife. He declared his intention to me accompanied by the most terrible threats. For instance, if I refuse him, he will ravage my kingdom. But you be the judge if I should accept him. He's a giant who's taller than a tower, and he eats men like a monkey eats chestnuts. When he ambles about his country, he carries in his pockets small cannons, which he uses for pistols, and when he shouts, those near him become deaf. I sent word to him that I didn't want to marry and that he must excuse me, but he's not stopped persecuting me. He kills all my subjects, and before anything can be done, you must fight him and bring me his head."

Avenant was astounded at this proposition. He pondered it for a few minutes and answered, "Well, madam, I'll fight Galifron. Even though I believe I'll lose, I'll die like a brave man."

The princess was in turn surprised by his determination. She said a thousand things to prevent his undertaking such an adventure, but they were all for naught. He withdrew to seek out weapons and anything else he might require. After he had made his preparations, he placed little Cabriolle in his basket again, mounted a fine horse, and rode toward Galifron's country. Along the way he asked people where Galifron was to be found, and everyone told him he was a demon whom nobody dared approach. The more he heard about him, the more his alarm increased. Cabriolle encouraged him by saying, "My dear master, when you fight him I'll bite his legs. Then as he stoops to get rid of me, you can kill him easily."

Avenant admired the wit of the little dog, but he knew well enough that his help would be of little avail. Finally he arrived in the vicinity of Galifron's castle. All the roads to it were strewn with the bones and bodies of men whom he had eaten or torn to pieces. Avenant did not wait long before he saw the monster coming through a wood. His head was visible above the highest trees, and he sang in a terrible voice:

"Ho! bring me some babies, fat or lean,
So I can crush them between my teeth!
I could eat oh so many, many, many,
That the world would not be left with any, any!"

Avenant immediately began to sing in the same spirit:

"Ho! Here comes Avenant on the spot
To take out your teeth and make them rot.
I'm not the greatest man you'll ever view,
But I'm big enough to conquer you!"

The rhymes were not quite adapted to the music, but he made them up in a great hurry, and it is really a miracle they were not much worse because he was terribly frightened. When Galifron heard these words, he looked all around him and caught sight of Avenant, who, sword in hand, uttered several taunts to provoke him. However, they were not necessary, for Galifron was in a dreadful rage. He snatched an iron club and would have crushed the gentle Avenant with one blow if a crow had not landed on his head at that instant and adroitly pecked out both his eyes with its beak. As blood poured down his face, he swung the club all about him like a madman. Avenant avoided his blows and kept thrusting with his sword until the giant fell down bleeding from a thousand wounds. Then Avenant ran his sword up to the hilt into Galifron's heart. Rejoicing in his good fortune, Avenant quickly cut off his head, and the crow, who had perched itself on the nearest tree, said to him, "I didn't forget the service you rendered me in killing the eagle that pursued me. I promised you I would return the favor. I trust I have done so today."

"I owe everything to you, Monsieur Crow," Avenant replied, "and I shall remain your servant."

Immediately Avenant mounted his horse, laden with the horrible head of Galifron. When he reached the city, the people followed him, crying, "Behold the brave Avenant, who has slain the monster!"

When the princess heard the uproar, she so trembled for fear they were coming to announce Avenant's death that she did not dare inquire what had happened. But within minutes she saw Avenant enter carrying the giant's head. The very sight of this filled her with terror, though there was no longer any reason to be alarmed.

"Madam," Avenant said to the princess, "your enemy is dead. I trust you'll no longer refuse the king my master."

"Ah, pardon me," Beauty with the Golden Hair said, "but I still must refuse him, unless you bring me some water from the Gloomy Grotto before my departure. Nearby is a deep cavern that is six miles long. At its mouth are two dragons who prevent anyone from entering: flames spew from their jaws and eyes. Inside the cavern is a deep pit into which you must descend: it is full of toads, adders, and serpents. At the bottom of this pit is a small hole, and the fountain of health and beauty flows through it. It is absolutely crucial that I obtain some of this water. Whatever it washes becomes something marvelous. If people are handsome, they remain so forever; if ugly, they become beautiful; if young, they remain young; if old, they become young again. You may well imagine, Avenant, that I would not leave my kingdom without some of this wonderful water."

"Madam," he replied, "you are so beautiful already that this water will be quite useless to you. But I'm an unfortunate ambassador, whose death you desire. So I shall go now to search for what you desire with the certainty that I'll never return."

Beauty with the Golden Hair remained immovable, and Avenant set out with little Cabriolle to seek the water of beauty in the Gloomy Grotto. Everyone he met on the road exclaimed, "It's a pity to see such a charming young man wantonly court destruction. He's going alone to the grotto, but even if he had a hundred men to back him, he'd not be able to accomplish his mission. Why does the princess demand the impossible?" Avenant kept going without saying a word, but he was in very low spirits.

When he was almost at the top of a mountain, he sat down to rest a little, allowing his horse to graze and Cabriolle to run after flies. He knew that the Gloomy Grotto was not far away and looked around to see if he could spot it. He caught sight of a tremendous chasm, as black as ink, from which thick smoke was rising. The next moment he saw one of the dragons, spitting out fire from his mouth and eyes. It had a green and yellow body, great claws, and a long tail wrapped in more than a hundred coils. Cabriolle saw all this as well and was so frightened he did not know where to hide himself.

Perfectly convinced he was going to his death, Avenant drew his sword and descended toward the cavern with a phial that Beauty with the Golden Hair had given him to fill with the water of beauty. He said to his little dog, Cabriolle, "It's all over for me. I'll never be able to obtain the water guarded by those dragons. When I'm dead, fill the phial with my blood and carry it to the princess so that she may see what her whim has cost. Then go to the king my master and tell him my sad story." As he uttered these words, he heard a voice calling: "Avenant! Avenant!"

"Who's calling me?" he cried. In the hollow of an old tree he spied an owl who said to him, "You let me out of the fowler's net, in which I was ensnared, and saved my life. I promised I would do the same for you, and now's the time. Give me your phial. I'm familiar with all the windings in the Gloomy Grotto. I'll fetch you some of the water of beauty."

You can imagine how delighted Avenant was to hear this. He quickly handed the phial to the owl, who entered the grotto without the least difficulty. In less than a quarter of a hour the bird returned with the phial full of water and tightly capped. Avenant was in ecstasy. He thanked the owl heartily, and after climbing back up the mountain, he returned to the city filled with joy. Once there he went straight to the palace and presented the phial to Beauty with the Golden Hair, who no longer had any excuses to make. Thanking him, she gave orders for everything to be prepared for her departure, and at last set out with him on their journey. She found him an exceedingly pleasant companion and said to him more than once, "If you had wished it, I would have made you king, and there would have been no occasion for us to leave my realm."

But his answer was always: "I'd never betray my master, not for all the kingdoms on the face of the earth, even though I find you more beautiful than the sun."

Finally they arrived at the king's capital city. Upon hearing that Beauty with the Golden Hair was approaching, his majesty went to meet her and gave her the most superb presents in the world. The marriage was celebrated with such great rejoicing that people could talk of nothing else. But Beauty with the Golden Hair, who secretly loved Avenant, was never happy when he was out of her sight. "I'd never have come here, except that he did impossible things for my sake. You should feel deeply indebted to him. He obtained the water of beauty for me so that I'll never grow old and always remain beautiful."

The envious courtiers, who heard the queen express herself in this way, said to the king, "You're not jealous and yet you have good cause to be so. The queen is so deeply in love with Avenant that she can neither eat nor drink. She can talk about nothing but him and about your obligation to him. Yet anyone you had sent to her would have done as much."

"Now that I think upon it, that's quite true," said the king. Let him be put in the tower with irons on his hands and feet."

Avenant was seized, and in return for his faithful service was fettered hand and foot in a dungeon. He was allowed to see no one but the jail keeper, who threw him a morsel of black bread through a hole and gave him some water in a clay pan. His little dog, Cabriolle, however, did not desert him. He came daily to console him and tell him all the news. When Beauty with the Golden Hair heard of Avenant's disgrace, she flung herself at the king's feet. With tears running down her cheeks, she implored him to release Avenant from prison. But the more she pleaded, the more angry the king became, for he thought to himself, "It's because she loves him." So he refused to budge in the matter, and the queen gave up urging him and fell into a deep melancholy.

Because of this, the king took it into his head that perhaps she did not think him handsome enough. He longed to wash his face with the water of beauty in the hope that the queen would then feel more affection for him. The phial full of this water stood on the chimneypiece in the queen's chamber, where she had placed it for the pleasure of looking at it more frequently. Unfortunately, one of her chambermaids, trying to kill a spider with a broom, knocked the phial off, and it broke in the fall. All the water was lost. Quickly, she swept the fragments of glass away, and not knowing what to do, it suddenly occurred to her that she had seen a phial full of water in the king's cabinet. It was as clear as the water of beauty and looked exactly the same. So, without saying a word to anyone, she adroitly managed to get it and placed it on the queen's chimneypiece.

The water in the king's cabinet, however, was used to execute princes and great noblemen who committed criminal offenses. Instead of beheading or hanging them, their faces were rubbed with this water, which had the fatal property of throwing them into a deep sleep from which they never awakened. So one evening the king happened to take the phial that he thought contained the water of beauty and, rubbing the contents well over his face, he fell into a profound slumber and died.

Little Cabriolle was the first to hear the news of the king's death and ran to tell Avenant, who begged him to find Beauty with the Golden Hair and remind her of the poor prisoner. Cabriolle slipped quietly through the crowd, for there was great confusion at court  due to the king's death, and he said to the queen, "Madam, do not forget poor Avenant."

She immediately recalled all that he had endured for her and his utter fidelity. Leaving the palace without speaking to a soul, she went directly to the tower, where she took the irons off his hands and feet with her own hands. Putting a crown of gold upon his head and a royal mantle over his shoulders, she said, "Come, charming Avenant, I want to make you king and take you for my husband."

He threw himself at her feet in joy and gratitude. Everybody was delighted to have him for their master. Their wedding was the most splendid the world has ever seen, and Beauty with the Golden Hair reigned long and happily with the handsome Avenant.

A kindly action never fail to do.
The smallest returns a blessing to you.
When Avenant saved the carp and crow,
And even showed compassion for the woes
Of a poor and unfortunate owl,
Who would have dreamed a mere fish or fowl
Would place him on the pinnacle of fame?
Yet his bravery ignited the princess's flame,
And he induced her to give her accord.
Unshaken in his loyalty he stood on the ford.
Innocent victim of a rival's hate.
When all seemed lost—when faced by his dark fate—
Just Providence reversed the ruthless doom
And gave virtue the throne, tyranny a tomb.

THE BLUE BIRD

ONCE upon a time there was a king who was extremely rich. For all his property and money, though, he was inconsolable when his wife suddenly fell ill and died. He shut himself up for a week in a small room and beat his head against the walls in his distress. Since his servants were afraid that he would kill himself, they put some mattresses between the tapestries and the walls so that he would not harm himself no matter how much he knocked himself about. Moreover, his subjects all agreed that they had better speak to him to alleviate his grief as best they could. Some prepared grave and serious speeches; others, charming and even lively addresses. But none made the least impression on him, for he barely heard a word they said.

At last a lady covered by black crape, veils, mantles, and other long mourning garments came before him. She wept so much and sobbed so loudly that he was quite astonished. She told him she would not attempt, as others had done, to mitigate his sorrow. Rather, she came to augment it, since nothing could be more just than to lament the loss of a good wife. "As for myself, I have lost the best of husbands and have made up my mind to weep as long as I have eyes in my head." Thereupon, she redoubled her groans, and the king, following her example, began to howl as well.

He paid more attention to this visitor than all the others and talked to her about the excellent qualities of his dear departed wife. In turn, she recapitulated all those of her beloved dead husband. They talked so much about their sorrow that they were eventually at a loss for words. When the cunning widow saw the subject was nearly exhausted, she raised her veil a little so that the grieving king could get a peek. Indeed, this poor mourner knew how to roll her large blue eyes and flutter long black lashes in a most effective manner. Her complexion was still blooming, and the king examined her with a great deal of attention. Gradually he spoke less and less about his wife, until he stopped discussing her altogether. The widow declared, however, that she would never stop mourning for her husband.

In response, the king implored her not to make her sorrow eternal, and soon, to everyone's astonishment, he declared that he would marry her. His mourning garments were exchanged for those with green and rose. Apparently, one needs only to determine a person's weakness in order

to gain his trust and do just what one wishes with him.

The king had had only a daughter by his first wife. Considered an eighth wonder of the world, she was named Florine because she was so sweet, young, and beautiful. Seldom was this artless maid seen in splendid attire; she preferred light morning dresses of taffeta fastened with a few jewels and qualities of the finest flowers, which produced an admirable effect when twined with her beautiful hair. She was only fifteen when the king was re-married.

The new queen sent for her own daughter, who had been brought up by her godmother, the fairy Soussio, but she was not particularly more graceful or beautiful because of this upbringing. Because Soussio loved her dearly, she had worked hard to make something out of her goddaughter, but her efforts were in vain. The girl's name was Truitonne, and her face was covered with reddish spots like those on the back of a trout. Her black hair was so greasy and dirty that no one would venture to touch it, and oil oozed out of her yellow skin. Her mother doted on her and talked about nothing but her charming Truitonne.

Since Florine possessed so many advantages over her daughter, however, the queen was stirred to use every possible means to belittle the unfortunate princess in the eyes of her father. Not a day passed that the queen and Truitonne did not play some mischievous trick on Florine. The princess, who was as mild as she was sensible, merely endeavored to keep herself beyond the reach of their malice.

One day the king remarked to the queen that Florine and Truitonne were of an age to be married, and that they should bestow the hand of one of them on the first prince who visited their court.

"I want my daughter married first," said the queen. "She's older than yours, and since she's a thousand times more charming, there should be no hesitation about the matter."

The king, who disliked arguments, replied that he was quite willing to do it this way and she was to arrange everything as she desired.

A short time afterward, it was learned that King Charmant was to arrive soon. No prince was more celebrated for gallantry and magnificence than he. In mind and appearance he was just as charming as his name implied. When the queen heard this news, she employed all the embroiderers, all the tailors, and all the artisans to make dresses for Truitonne. On the other hand, she not only requested that the king give nothing new to Florine, she also bribed the princess's ladies-in-waiting to steal all her clothes, headdresses, and jewels on the very day King Charmant arrived so that when she went to dress she could not find even a ribbon. Florine knew full well who had done her this turn, and she sent her servants to purchase materials for a new dress. However, all the tradesmen responded that the queen had forbidden them to furnish her with a single thing. Therefore, she was left only with the gown she had on her back, and this was very soiled. So ashamed was she of her appearance that when King Charmant arrived, she hid herself in a corner of the hall.

The queen received the royal visitor with great pomp and presented her daughter in a blaze of such magnificence that she looked even more ugly than usual. When King Charmant averted his eyes, the queen tried to convince herself that he was so stunned by her that he had to keep turning away to control his emotions. Thus, she continually pushed Truitonne before him, but he responded by inquiring, "Isn't there another princess, named Florine?"

"Yes," said Truitonne, pointing with her finger, "there she is, hiding herself because she's not dressed properly."

Upon being discovered, Florine blushed. So exceedingly beautiful did she look in her confusion that King Charmant was dazzled. He rose immediately and bowed profoundly to the princess. "Madam," he said, "your incomparable beauty makes the artificial aid of ornaments quite unnecessary."

"Sir," she replied, "I confess I'm not accustomed to wearing such a disgraceful dress as this, and I would have preferred to have escaped your notice."

"It would be impossible for such a marvelous princess like yourself to go anywhere and not have all eyes focused on her," he exclaimed.

"Ah," said the queen, greatly irritated, "it's nice listening to you pay these compliments. But believe me, sir, Florine is already enough of a flirt. She doesn't need such excessive flattery."

King Charmant quickly perceived the queen's motives for speaking this way, but since he was not accustomed to suppressing his inclinations, he continued to manifest his admiration for Florine. Indeed, he conversed with her for three whole hours.

The queen was in despair, and Truitonne inconsolable, because the princess had received such preference. Complaining bitterly to the king, they compelled him to consent to locking up Florine in a tower during King Charmant's stay so that they could not see each other.

No sooner did she return to her room than four masked men seized and carried her to a room at the top of the tower, where they left her greatly distressed, for she saw clearly that she was being treated this way to prevent her from pleasing King Charmant. He had already gained her affections, and she would willingly have accepted him for her husband.

Since he was not aware of Florine's violent abduction, he looked forward with the greatest impatience to the hour when he would meet her again. He talked about her to the gentlemen the king had placed in his company to do him honor, but they had been ordered by the queen to say the worst possible things about Florine they could imagine:

"She is coquettish, inconstant, and ill-tempered."

"She torments her friends and her servants."

"It is impossible to imagine anyone more slovenly."

"She is so niggardly that she prefers to dress like a poor shepherdess than spend the money allowed her by her father to purchase rich garments befitting her rank."

As each detail was mentioned, Charmant smarted, scarcely able to restrain his anger. "No," he said to himself, "it's impossible that Heaven would permit so worthless a soul to inhabit this masterpiece of nature. I admit she was badly dressed when I first saw her, but the shame she expressed proves that she was not accustomed to dressing so. How can she be ill-tempered and coquettish with such an enchanting air of mildness and modesty? It makes no sense! I can much more easily imagine that it's the queen who's slandering her. She's not her stepmother for nothing, and the Princess Truitonne, her own daughter, is such an ugly beast that it wouldn't be unusual for her to envy the most perfect of beings."

While he was pondering all of this in his mind, the courtiers suspected from his manner that he was displeased by their abuse of Florine. One courtier more astute than the rest changed his tune and began extolling the princess's virtues in order to discover the prince's true sentiments. Upon hearing this praise, Charmant woke as from a deep sleep. He participated eagerly in the conversation, and his features lit up with joy. Oh love, how hard you are to hide! You are visible everywhere—on a lover's lips, in his eyes, in the tone of his voice. When we truly love, both silence and speech, happiness and misery, equally express the passion we feel.

Impatient to learn if King Charmant was in love, the queen sent for the courtiers who had won the king's trust and spent the rest of the night interrogating them. Everything they reported served only to confirm the opinion she had already formed—the king was in love with Florine.

But how can I describe the melancholy state of that poor princess? She lay stretched on the floor in the keep of that terrible tower. "I wouldn't have to be pitied so much," she said, "if I had been locked up here before I had seen that charming monarch. My recollection of him only serves to increase my distress. I'm positive that the queen treated me this cruelly only to prevent my seeing him again. Alas, the little beauty that Heaven has bestowed on me has cost me a great deal of tranquillity." She then began to weep so bitterly that her worst enemies would have pitied her if they had witnessed her torment. And so the night passed.

The queen was anxious to win over King Charmant by showing him all the attention she could. She sent him the most costly and magnificent garments made in the newest fashion of that country, and also the Order of the Knights of Cupid, which she had compelled the king to institute the day they themselves had married in honor of their wedding. This badge was a golden heart enameled and colored like fire. It was surrounded by several arrows and pierced with one that bore the words, "One alone wounds me." For Charmant, however, the queen had a heart cut from a ruby as large as an ostrich's egg; each arrow was made of a single diamond the length of a finger, and the chain of the badge was composed of pearls, the smallest of which weighed a whole pound. In short, nothing like it had ever been seen in the world. Charmant was so astonished when he saw it that it was some time before he could speak. At the same time they gave him a beautifully illustrated book with pages of the finest vellum and a binding encrusted with gold and jewels. In it were written the statutes of the Order of the Knights of Cupid in a gallant, refined style. They told him that the princess he had seen requested that he be her knight and had sent him this present. Upon hearing this he imagined that they had come from his beloved. "My goodness," he cried, "does the beautiful Princess Florine think of me in this splendid and flattering way?"

"Sire," they replied, "you've confused the names. We come from the charming Truitonne."

"Truitonne! Is she the one who wants me to be her champion?" the king asked coldly. "I regret that I cannot accept this honor. A sovereign is not wholly his own master and cannot accept just any engagement that pleases him. I know the duties of a knight and would like to be able to fulfill them all. But I'd prefer not receiving the honor she has offered me rather than proving myself unworthy of it."

So saying, he put the heart, chain, and book back into the basket and sent them all back to the queen, who, along with her daughter, almost choked with rage at the contemptuous manner in which the illustrious foreigner had declined such a signal honor.

King Charmant visited the king and queen as often as he was permitted in the hope of meeting Florine in the royal apartments. His eyes searched everywhere for her. The moment he heard anyone enter the room, he turned sharply toward the door and seemed always restless and unhappy when it was not she. The malicious queen easily guessed what was on his mind, but she appeared to take no notice of it. She talked to him only about pleasure parties, and he replied with the most incongruous answers. At last he asked her plainly, "Where is the Princess Florine?"

"Sir," the queen replied haughtily, "her father has forbidden her to leave her apartment until my daughter is married."

"And what motive," inquired King Charmant, "can there be for making that beautiful princess a prisoner?"

"I don't know," the queen said, "and even if I did, I don't feel obligated to inform you."

Enraged, Charmant cast an angry glance at Truitonne. He thought to himself, "This little monster is the cause of my being deprived of the pleasure of seeing Florine." So he abruptly left the queen's presence, which gave him too much pain.

On returning to his room, he told a young prince, a cherished companion of his, to do his utmost to win the confidence of one of the princess's attendants so that he could speak to Florine for even one moment. This prince easily found some ladies of the palace whom he could trust, and one of them guaranteed him that Florine would be at a small lower window that very evening. This window overlooked the garden, and she could converse with Charmant from it, provided he was extremely careful and made sure that no one knew. "The king and queen are so severe," she added, "that they'll put me to death if they discover I've sided with Charmant's feelings."

Delighted that he had succeeded in his mission, the prince promised her anything she desired. Then he returned to his royal master and told him the appointed time of meeting. Meanwhile the confidante, who had deceived him, went and told the queen what had happened and waited for further instructions. The queen immediately decided to place her daughter at the little window and gave Truitonne special instructions. Despite the fact that she was naturally stupid, Truitonne was to carry them out without a mistake.

The night was so dark that King Charmant could not have possibly noticed the trickery, even if he had been suspicious. When he drew near the window, he was overflowing with joy and expressed a wealth of tender thoughts to the supposed Florine to convince her of his affection. Taking advantage of the situation, Truitonne told him that she felt like the most unfortunate person in the world in having such a cruel stepmother, and that she would continue to suffer until the queen's daughter was married. Charmant assured her that if she would accept him for her husband, he would be delighted to share his heart and crown with her. Thereupon, he drew his ring from his finger and, placing it on one of Truitonne's, begged her to receive it as a token of eternal fidelity and added, "You need only fix the hour for our flight."

Truitonne made the best possible answers she could to his ardent appeals. He noticed they were not very sensible, and they normally would have made him uneasy, but he thought they arose from the terror she felt at possibly being surprised by the queen. He left her only on condition that she would meet him again the next night at the same hour, which she promised faithfully to do.

Upon hearing of the good success of this meeting, the queen felt sure of everything. When the day was fixed for the elopement, King Charmant prepared to carry off his beloved in a flying chariot drawn by winged frogs, a present to him by a friend who was an enchanter. The night was pitch black, and Truitonne snuck out mysteriously through a little door. The king, who was waiting for her, received her in his arms with a hundred vows of everlasting affection. But since he was not eager to be flying about in his chariot for a long time before marrying his beloved princess, he asked her to tell him where she wanted their wedding to be held. She answered that she had a godmother named Soussio who was a celebrated fairy, and she felt they should go at once to Soussio's castle. Although the king did not know the way, he only had to mention to his great frogs where he wished to go. They were perfectly acquainted with the whole map of the world, and in no time they brought Charmant and Truitonne to Soussio's abode.

The castle was so brilliantly illuminated that Charmant would have discovered his mistake the moment he entered if the princess had not carefully covered herself with her veil. She asked for her godmother and contrived to see her alone. Telling her how she had ensnared Charmant, she entreated her to pacify him.

"Ah, my child," the fairy said, "the task won't be an easy one, for he is too fond of Florine. I feel certain he'll give us a great deal of trouble."

Meanwhile the king was awaiting them in a salon that had walls made of diamonds so pure and transparent that he saw Soussio and Truitonne conversing together through them. He thought he must be dreaming. "What?" he said. "Have I been betrayed? Have some demons brought this enemy of our peace to this place? Has she come to disturb our wedding? Where's my dear Florine? Perhaps her father has pursued her!"

A thousand thoughts ran through his mind, all of them disconcerting. But matters looked even worse when he entered the salon and Soussio addressed him in an authoritative tone, "King Charmant, here is the Princess Truitonne, whom you have pledged to marry. She is my goddaughter, and it's my desire that you marry her immediately."

"Me?" he exclaimed. "You want me to marry that little monster? You must think me a docile babe to propose such a thing. I've made no promise to her whatsoever, and if she's told you otherwise, then she has—"

"Hold your tongue," interrupted Soussio. "Don't you dare forget to show me the proper respect."

"I agree to respect you as much as a fairy can be respected," the king replied, "provided that you restore my princess to me."

"Aren't I your princess, faithless one?" Truitonne said, showing him his ring. "To whom did you give this ring as a pledge of your troth? With whom did you converse at the little window if not with me?"

"How's this possible?" he cried. "Have I been deceived? No! No, I'll not be your dupe! Come, my frogs, come! I want to leave here immediately!"

"Oho, it's not in your power to leave without my consent," exclaimed Soussio. At her touch his feet were fastened to the floor as if they had been nailed to it.

"You may stone me to death, you may flay me alive," cried the king. "I'll marry no one but Florine. My mind is made up. So you can do with me as you please."

Soussio tried sweet talk, threats, promises, prayers. Truitonne wept, shrieked, groaned, stomped, and became sullen again. The king merely surveyed them both with an air of the greatest indignation, not giving the slightest response to anything they said.

Twenty days and twenty nights passed without their ceasing to talk and without eating, sleeping, or sitting down. Finally Soussio became exhausted and lost her patience. "Well, since you so obstinately refuse to listen to reason," she said to the king, "choose right now whether you'll marry my goddaughter, or do penance for seven years as a punishment for breaking your word."

All of a sudden the king, who up to this time had been perfectly silent, exclaimed, "Do what you want with me, just so that I'm freed from this wretch."

"You're a wretch yourself!" Truitonne said angrily. "A petty king like you, with your marsh-bred postures. You come to my country, break your word to me, and insult me. Had you a groat's worth of honor in you, you'd behave differently!"

"How touching," said the king in an ironical tone. "I must be making a mistake not to take such a lovely person for my wife."

"No, no, she won't be your wife!" screamed Soussio in a rage. "You may now fly out of that window if you like, for you're to be a blue bird for the next seven years!"

At that very moment the king underwent a complete transformation: his arms grew feathers and formed wings; his legs and feet became black and scrawny and furnished with crooked talons; his body shrank. He was entirely covered with long, fine, thin feathers of celestial blue; his eyes became round and as bright as two stars; his nose was but an ivory beak; a white crest rose on his head in the form of a crown. He was able to sing and talk in a remarkable fashion, but all he uttered was a cry of anguish at seeing himself transformed into this condition. Then he flew from Soussio's fatal palace as fast as his wings could carry him.

Overwhelmed with grief, he flitted from branch to branch, selecting only those trees consecrated to love or sorrow. Sometimes he landed on myrtles, other times on cypresses, and sang the most lamentable tunes, deploring his sad fate and that of Florine. "Where have her enemies hidden her?" he asked. "What has become of that beautiful victim? Has the queen's barbarity permitted her to remain alive? Where should I search? Am I condemned to spend seven years without her? Perhaps during that period they'll compel her to marry, and I'll never regain the hope that sustains me." This whirl of thoughts tormented the blue bird to such a degree that he would have welcomed death.

Meanwhile the fairy Soussio sent Truitonne back to the queen, who was anxiously waiting learn all about the nuptials. When she heard from her daughter's lips all that had transpired, she became terribly enraged, and poor Florine was to feel her backlash. "She shall repent more than once for having captivated Charmant," the queen said.

To the tower she went with Truitonne, whom she had dressed in her richest clothes with a crown of diamonds on her head and a royal mantle whose train was carried by three daughters of the richest barons in the realm. On her thumb was King Charmant's ring, which Florine had noticed the day she had conversed with him. Florine was greatly surprised to see Truitonne in such splendid apparel.

"My daughter's come to bring you a wedding present," she said. "King Charmant was so madly in love with her that he's married her. Oh, you've never seen such a happy couple." Thereupon, they showed the princess heaps of gold and silver tissues, jewels, lace and ribbons, all contained in large baskets worked in gold filigree. While presenting these objects, Truitonne made sure that Florine noticed King Charmant's sparkling ring, and the latter became convinced of her misfortune. With an air of desperation she told them to remove the base gifts from her sight. "I wish to wear nothing but black, and, indeed, I shall soon be dead." Upon saying this, she fainted.

The cruel queen was delighted to have succeeded so well. She did not permit anyone to assist her, but left her alone in the most wretched state imaginable. Then she maliciously reported to the king that his daughter was so carried away by her emotions that she had lost control of her wits, and great care should be taken to prevent her leaving the tower. The king told her to manage the matter as she thought best, and that he would be satisfied as always.

When the princess recovered from her swoon and began to consider how they had behaved toward her, how her wicked stepmother had mistreated her, and how her hope of becoming King Charmant's wife had been destroyed, her anguish became so keen that she wept the entire night. In this wretched condition she went to an open window, where she uttered the most tender and touching lamentations. When day began to break, she shut the window, but continued to weep. The following night she again opened the window, sobbing and sighing and shedding a torrent of tears. Morning dawned, and she hid herself in the recesses of her chamber.

In the meantime King Charmant—or, to speak more correctly, the beautiful blue bird—kept flying around the palace, for he believed his dear princess was confined somewhere in it. If her lamentations were distressing, his were no less so. He approached the windows as near as he could in order to look into the rooms, but the fear of being noticed and recognized by Truitonne prevented his examining the rooms as closely as he wished. "It would cost me my life," he said to himself. "If these wicked princesses were to discover where I am, they'd take their revenge on me. I must keep my distance, or else I'll be exposed to extreme danger." For these reasons he took the greatest precautions and rarely sang except at night.

Now, there happened to be a towering cypress right in front of the window at which Florine usually sat. The blue bird came to perch on it, and no sooner had he done so than he heard someone lamenting. "How much longer shall I suffer?" she said. "Won't death kindly come to my aid? Those who fear death see him too soon. Yet I long for his coming, and he cruelly avoids me. Oh, barbarous queen! What have I done to you that you keep me in this horrible captivity? Don't you have ways enough to torment me? You need only make me witness the happiness your unworthy daughter enjoying the company of King Charmant!"

The blue bird heard every syllable of this lament in astonishment. He could hardly wait for daylight to arrive in order to catch a glimpse of the distressed lady, but just before morning dawned, she closed her window and retired. The bird, whose curiosity was awakened, did not fail to return the following night, and in the moonlight he saw a girl begin to sigh at the tower window.

"Oh, fortune," she exclaimed, "you who flattered me with the prospect of reigning, you who had kept my father's love alive, what have I done to deserve being plunged so suddenly into such bitter grief? Is it at such a tender young age as mine that one must begin to experience your inconstancy? Return, you cruel thing! Return, if you can. The only favor I ask of you is to end my unhappy fate."

The blue bird listened attentively, and the more he did, the more convinced he became that it was his charming princess who was doing the lamenting.

"Adorable Florine," he cried, "wonder of our days, why do you desire to terminate your life so hastily? Your misfortunes can still be remedied."

"Ah! Who's that speaking in such a consoling way?" she asked.

"An unfortunate king," replied the bird, "who loves you and will never love any other than you."

"A king who loves me!" replied Florine. "Is this a trap set for me by my enemy? Yet what would she gain by it? If she seeks to discover my sentiments, I'm ready to frankly own up to them."

"No, my princess," replied the bird. "The lover who's speaking to you is incapable of betraying you"—and as he uttered these words he flew to the window.

At first Florine was alarmed at the appearance of such an extraordinary bird, who spoke with as much sense as a man and yet had the small, sweet voice of a nightingale. The beauty of his plumage, however, and the words he uttered soon reassured her.

"May I be permitted once more to behold you, my princess?" he exclaimed. "Can I taste such perfect happiness and not die with joy? But, alas, how this happiness is troubled by your captivity, and the condition that the wicked Soussio has reduced me to for seven years."

"And who are you, charming bird?" the princess inquired, caressing him.

"You've pronounced my name," said the king, "and you pretend you do not know me?"

"What? The greatest monarch in the world, King Charmant?" cried the princess. "Can the little bird I hold in my hand be you?"

"Alas, beautiful Florine, it is but too true," the bird replied. "And if anything can console me, it's the feeling that I chose this pain instead of renouncing my love for you."

"For me?" said Florine. "Ah, don't attempt to deceive me. I know that you've married Truitonne. I recognized your ring on her hand. I saw her glistening with the diamonds you had given her. She came to insult me in my sad prison, wearing the rich crown and royal mantle she had received from your hands, while I was bound in chains and fetters."

"You've seen Truitonne dressed that way?" interrupted the king. "Did she and her mother dare tell you those jewels came from me? Oh, Heaven! Is it possible that I hear such awful lies, and that I cannot gain immediate revenge on the liars? I want you to know that they tried to deceive me: by basely using your name, they succeeded in getting me to elope with the ugly Truitonne. But the instant I discovered my error, I tried to flee from her, and eventually I chose to become a blue bird for seven years rather than betray the pledge of fidelity I made to you."

Florine was so pleased by her charming lover's explanation that she forgot the misery of her prison. She told him many things to console him in his sad circumstances, and assured him that she would have done as much for him. Day had dawned and the majority of the officers of the royal household risen before the blue bird and the princess had finished conversing. It cost them a thousand pangs to part, but they agreed they would meet every night in the same manner.

Their delight at having found each other was so great that it cannot be described. Both offered thanks to love and fortune, but Florine's happiness was tempered by her anxiety about the blue bird. "Who will protect him from the hunters?" she asked. "Or from the sharp talons of some eagle or hungry vulture? They'll eat him with relish not knowing that he's a great king. Oh, Heaven! What would become of me if some of his delicate feathers were blown to my window and announced to me the dreaded disaster?" This thought prevented the poor princess from closing her eyes, for when one loves, thoughts appear like facts, and what one would at another time think impossible seems certain to occur. So she spent the day in tears until the hour arrived for her to return to the window.

Hiding in a hollow tree, the charming bird occupied himself all day by thinking of his beautiful princess. "How happy I am to have found her," he said. "How fascinating she is! How deeply I appreciate the kindness she's extended to me." The tender lover counted every second he was condemned to spend in the shape that prevented his marrying her, and never was the termination of a sentence more ardently desired. Since he was eager to be as gallant to Florine as possible, he flew to the capital city of his own kingdom. Landing at his palace, he entered his cabinet through a broken pane of glass in one of the windows, took a pair of diamond earrings more perfect than any other in the world, and brought them that evening to Florine's cell, where he requested that she wear them.

"I'll consent," she said, "if you visit me by daylight, but since I only see you at night, I won't put them on."

The bird promised he would find a way to come to the tower whenever she wished. In response, she put on the earrings, and the night passed in tender discourse just like the night before.

The next day the blue bird returned to his palace, entered his cabinet by the broken window, and carried away the richest bracelets ever seen. Each was made of a single emerald cut in facets with a hole through the center to enable the wearer to pass her hands and arms through them. "Do you think," the princess said to him, "that my affection for you can be measured by presents? Ah, how you misjudge me."

"No, madam," he replied, "I don't believe that the trifles I offer you are required to keep your love, but mine will not permit me to neglect the least opportunity of showing you my respect, and when I am absent, these little trinkets will bring me to mind."

Florine said a thousand kind things to him on this subject, and he replied with as many no less tender. The following night the enamoured bird brought his beautiful lady a watch. It was encased in a single pearl, and the workmanship was superior to its luster.

"It's useless to present me with a watch," said the princess sweetly. "When you are absent, the hours seem endless, and when you are with me they pass so like a dream that I cannot time them with any precision."

"Alas, my princess," exclaimed the blue bird, "I agree with you and am certain that I feel the pain of absence and the pleasure of returning even more deeply than you do."

"After what you have suffered to remain true to me," replied the princess, "I truly believe that your affection and respect cannot be carried further."

As soon as morning appeared, the bird flew back to his hollow tree, where he lived on wild fruits. Sometimes he sang the finest tunes, to the great delight of all who passed that way. Since they could not see anything, they believed it must be the voice of a spirit. This belief became so widespread that eventually nobody dared enter the wood. A thousand fabulous adventures were told about those who had done so, and the general alarm insured the blue bird's safety. Not a day passed without his making Florine some present, either a pearl necklace, or the most brilliant and uniquely wrought rings, diamond loops, bodkins, and bouquets of

jewels in imitation of natural flowers, entertaining books, and interesting medals, until she possessed a stack of marvelous valuables. She wore her jewels only by night to please the king, and in the daytime, since she had no other place to put them in, she hid them carefully in the straw of her mattress.

Two years passed this way without Florine once complaining about her captivity. Indeed, how could she? She had the pleasure of conversing all night with the man she loved. Never were so many pretty speeches made. Though the bird spent

the whole day in a hollow tree and never saw anyone, they had a thousand new things to tell each other. Their love and wit alone furnished them with an inexhaustible abundance of subject matter for their conversation.

In the meantime the malicious queen vainly endeavored to marry off

Truitonne. She sent ambassadors with proposals to every prince she had ever heard of, but these envoys were sent packing almost as soon as they arrived. "If your mission concerned Princess Florine, you would be joyously received," was the answer. "But as for Truitonne, let her remain a virgin, for nobody will object."

These tidings infuriated both mother and daughter, and they vented their anger against the innocent princess. "What? This arrogant creature continues to thwart us despite her captivity?" they cried. "We shall never be able to forgive the injuries she has caused us! She must have some secret correspondence with foreign countries and thus must be guilty of high treason at the very least. Let's act on this suspicion and use every possible means to convict her."

So late did they finish their talk about this matter that it was past midnight when they decided to climb the tower to interrogate Florine. At the window with the blue bird, she was arrayed in all her jewels. Her beautiful hair was dressed with a nicety unusual for tormented souls. Her room and bed were strewn with flowers, and some Spanish pastilles that she was burning emitted an exquisite perfume. Listening at the door, the queen thought she heard a melody sung in a duet (Florine's voice was nearly divine), and these are the tender words she heard:

> "Oh, how wretched is our lot,
> Nor can we forget our torment,
>   Loving thus—while forced to part.
> But even though our woes are deep,
> And our cruel foes force us to weep,
>   Nothing will destroy our hearts."

A few deep sighs finished this little concert.

"Ah, my Truitonne, we've been betrayed," exclaimed the queen. All at once she opened the door and rushed into the room. Imagine the alarm of Florine at this sight! She promptly pushed open the window to give the royal bird an opportunity to fly off unperceived. She was much more anxious about protecting his life than her own, but he felt unable to fly away. His sharp eyes had discovered the danger—the queen and Truitonne—to which the princess was exposed. As they approached like Furies bent on devouring her, how troubled he was not to be able to defend her!

"Your intrigues against the state are detected," cried the queen. "Do not imagine your rank can save you from the punishment you deserve."

"Intrigues with whom, madam?" inquired the princess. "Haven't you been my jailer these two years? Have I seen any other people than those you have sent me?" While she spoke, the queen and her daughter examined her with great surprise. Her remarkable beauty and her extraordinary attire dazzled them.

"And where, madam, have you obtained these jewels that outshine the sun?" the queen asked. "Are we to believe there are mines in this tower?"

"I found them," answered Florine. "That's all I know about it."

The queen gazed at Florine with a penetrating look, trying to ascertain what was happening in the core of her heart. "We are not your dupes," she cried. "You think you can deceive us, but, Princess, we are aware of all you do from morning till night. These jewels have been given to you with the sole object of inducing you to sell your father's kingdom."

"I'm in a good position to deliver, aren't I?" replied Florine with a disdainful smile. "An unfortunate princess who has languished in captivity so long can be of great service, certainly, in a conspiracy of such a nature."

"And for whom, then,' added the queen, "are you so coquettishly dressed up? Your room is so full of perfume, and your attire so magnificent that it is as if you were at court."

"I have plenty of time on my hands," said the princess. "It's not unusual I should strive to wile away a few moments by taking care of the way I look. I spend so many hours in weeping over my misfortunes that my innocent occupation surely cannot be a subject of reproach."

"Indeed, indeed!" said the queen. "Let us just see if this innocent miss is not in league with our enemies." She began to hunt everywhere and, emptying the mattress, she found such an immense quantity of diamonds, pearls, rubies, emeralds, and topazes that she could not imagine where they all had come from. All the while she was intending to hide incriminating documents in some place so that their discovery would inculpate the princess. When she thought nobody was looking, she began thrusting them into the chimney, but by good luck the blue bird was perched there. He had eyes as sharp as a lynx and saw everything.

"Beware, Florine!" he cried. "Your enemy is trying to betray you."

This voice was so unexpected that it frightened the queen, and she became afraid to conceal the papers.

"Madam," said the princess, "you see that the spirits of the air are my friends."

"I believe," exclaimed the queen in a fit of rage, "that you are in league with demons. In spite of them, though, your father will have justice done."

"Would to heaven," cried Florine, "I only had to fear the fury of my father. But yours, madam, is much more terrible."

The queen left her, greatly disturbed by all she had seen and heard. She consulted her friends as to what should be done to the princess. They remarked that if Florine was being protected by some fairy or enchanter, any further persecution would only irritate her powerful friend. "It would be better first to discover the mystery." The queen approved this idea. She sent a young girl to sleep in Florine's apartment under the pretext that she was there to wait on her. The girl pretended to be naive, but Florine did not fall for such an obvious ruse. The princess regarded her as a spy, and she could only feel her torment more violently. "What now? Won't I ever be able to converse again with my dear bird?" she asked. "He has helped me endure my misfortunes, and I have soothed his troubles. Our affection was everything to us! What will become of him? What will become of me?" While thinking all these things, she shed rivers of tears. She no longer dared go to the little window, though she heard the bird fluttering around it. She was dying to open it, but she feared exposing the life of her dear lover.

A whole month passed without her appearing at the window. The blue bird was in despair. Complaint after complaint did he utter. How could he live without seeing his princess? He had never felt the pangs of solitude and the misery of his transformation so sharply. He sought in vain a remedy for both. Nothing brought him consolation.

After watching day and night for a whole month, the spy was eventually overwhelmed by drowsiness, and at last she sunk into a sound slumber. When Florine saw this, she opened her little window and said:

> "Bird as blue as cloudless sky,
> Come to my window, quickly fly!"

Those were her exact words without the slightest alteration. The bird heard them so distinctly that he was at the window in an instant. What delight once more to behold each other! How much they had to say to each other! They renewed their vows of love and fidelity a thousand times over. Seeing the princess unable to restrain her tears, her lover was tormented and did his utmost to console her. At last the hour of parting arrived, without the spy awakening, and they said good-bye to each other in the most touching manner.

The next night the spy fell asleep again. The princess lost no time in going to the window and calling as before:

> "Bird as blue as cloudless sky,
> Come to my window, quickly fly!"

The bird immediately arrived, and the night passed without discovery like the preceding one. The lovers were delighted. They hoped that the spy would find so much pleasure in sleeping that she would do so every night, and, in fact, the third did pass as happily.

On the one following, though, the sleeper was disturbed by a noise. Listening without appearing to be awake, and peeping as best she could, she saw the most beautiful bird in the world by the light of the moon. He talked to the princess, caressed her with his claw, and pecked her gently with his bill. She overheard part of their conversation and was extremely surprised, for the bird spoke like a lover, and the beautiful Florine answered him most tenderly. When day broke and they said their farewells, they parted with extreme sorrow, as though they had a presentiment of their coming misfortune. Bathed in tears, the princess threw herself on her bed, and the king returned to his hollow tree.

The spy ran to the queen and told her all she had seen and heard. The queen in turn sent for Truitonne and her confidantes. They talked the matter over for a long time and concluded that the blue bird was King Charmant. "What an affront!" cried the queen. "What an affront, my Truitonne! This insolent princess, whom I thought was so wretched, was quietly enjoying the most charming conversations with that ungrateful prince. Oh, I'll take such a bloody revenge that it will be the talk of the whole world!"

Truitonne begged her not to lose a moment, and since she considered herself more interested in the matter than the queen, she was bursting with joy at the thought of all that would be done to destroy the happiness of the lover and his mistress. The queen sent the spy back to the tower, ordering her not to show any suspicion or curiosity, but to appear more sleepy than ever. She went to bed early and snored as loudly as she could. The poor, deceived princess opened the little window and called:

> "Bird as blue as cloudless sky,
> Come to my window, quickly fly!"

but she called in vain the whole night long. He did not come, for the wicked queen had ordered swords, knives, razors, and daggers to be attached to the cypress tree so that when he darted toward the window these murderous weapons cut off his feet. In addition, some others lacerated his wings and stabbed his chest. Only with great difficulty, leaving behind him a long trail of blood, did he reach his own tree. Why weren't you there, lovely princess, to comfort that royal bird? And yet it would have been the death of her to have seen him in such a dismal condition.

Since he was convinced that it was Florine who had been guilty of this cruel treachery, he did not care a fig about his life. "Oh, barbarous princess," he exclaimed mournfully, "is this the way you repay the most pure and tender passion that ever was or will ever be? If you had wanted me to die, why didn't you perform the deed yourself? Death would have been sweet from your hand! I looked for you with so much love and trust. I suffered for you and suffered without complaining. And now you have sacrificed me to the cruelest of women, our common enemy! You've made your peace with her at the price of my life. It is you, Florine—you who has stabbed me! You have borrowed Truitonne's hand and guided it to my bosom!" These furious thoughts so overwhelmed him that he looked forward to his death.

However, his friend the enchanter, who had seen the flying frogs return without the king in the chariot, became so concerned about him that he went around the world eight times in search of him. On his ninth journey he passed through the forest in which the poor king was lying. As was his custom, he blew a long blast on his horn and then cried five times in a loud voice, "King Charmant! King Charmant! Where are you?"

The king recognized his best friend's voice and cried, "Come over to this tree, and behold the wretched king you cherish drowning in his own blood."

Quite surprised, the enchanter looked all around without seeing anyone. "I'm a blue bird," the king exclaimed in a feeble, plaintive voice.

After hearing this, the enchanter had no trouble locating him in his nest. Another person might have been dumbfounded, but he was well versed in every aspect of necromancy. He needed but a few words to stop the blood from flowing, and along with some herbs he found in the wood, he murmured a short spell and cured the king so well that it seemed he had never been wounded. Then he asked the king to tell him how he had become transformed into a bird, and who had wounded him so cruelly. The king satisfied his curiosity and informed him that it must have been Florine who had revealed the amorous mystery of the secret visits he paid her. To make her peace with the queen, she had consented to have the cypress tree filled with the daggers and razors that had almost hacked him to pieces. He denounced the treachery of the princess a thousand times and said he would have been happier if he had died without knowing the wickedness of her heart. The magician inveighed against her and against all her sex, and he advised the king to forget her. "What a misfortune it would be," he said, "if you were to continue loving that ungrateful lady. After what she's done to you, you have everything to fear."

The blue bird, however, could not share this view, for he still loved Florine too dearly, and the enchanter, who knew his real sentiments despite the care the king took to conceal them, said to him in a friendly manner:

"Crushed by Fortune's cruel blow,
Vainly Reason's voice is heard;
We but listen to our woe,
Neglecting wise and soothing words.
Leave old Time his work to do.
All things have their sunny side.
But until he brings it within view,
Naught but darkness will be spied."

The royal bird admitted the truth of these remarks and asked his friend to take him home and put him in a cage, where he would be safe from a cat's paw or murderous weapon.

"But," said the enchanter, "do you really want to remain in such a deplorable condition for five years? It is ill-suited to your duties and you dignity. Remember, you have enemies who claim that you're dead. They want to seize your kingdom. I fear very much that you'll lose it before you regain your proper form."

"Can't I enter my palace and govern as I used to do?" asked the king.

"Oh," exclaimed his friend, "the situation has changed. Those who would obey a man will not bow to a parrot. Those who feared you when you were a king surrounded by grandeur and pomp would be the first to pluck out all your feathers now that you're a little bird."

"Alas, for human weakness," cried the king. "Although a glittering exterior is nothing compared to virtue, it still wields a power over the minds of men that is difficult to combat. Well, then, let us be philosophers, and despise that which we cannot obtain. Our lot will be none the worse for it."

"I don't give up so easily," said the magician. "I still hope to hit upon some means of restoring you to your proper form."

Florine, sad Florine, was in despair at no longer seeing the king. She spent her days and nights at the window and constantly repeated:

> "Bird as blue as cloudless sky,
> Come to my window, quickly fly!"

The presence of her watchful attendant did not stop her, for her despair was so great that she did not care about the consequences. "What has happened to you, King Charmant?" she cried. "Have our mutual enemies made you feel the cruel effects of their rage? Have you fallen victim to their fury? Alas, alas! Have you perished? Shall I never see you again? Shall I never weary of my woes? Have you abandoned me to my hard fate?"

What tears, what sobs followed these tender complaints. How did the absence of such a dear and charming lover lengthen the dreary hours of her captivity. The princess was dejected, ill, thin, and changed. So convinced that something fatal had happened to the king, she could scarcely sustain herself.

The queen and Truitonne had triumphed. Their revenge gave them more pleasure than the offence that had annoyed them. And just what was this offence after all? King Charmant had refused to marry a little monster he had a thousand reasons to hate. In the meantime, Florine's father, who had reached a considerable age, fell ill and died. Now the fortunes of the wicked queen and her daughter assumed a new aspect. They were looked upon as favorites who had abused their influence. The people rose up and ran to the palace, demanding Princess Florine and claiming they would recognize her alone as their sovereign. The queen was affronted by this and tried to handle the affair in a haughty manner. She appeared on a balcony and threatened the insurgents. But the revolt became widespread, and the people broke into the apartments, pillaged them, and stoned her to death. Truitonne fled for protection to her godmother, the fairy Soussio, or she would have shared the fate of her mother. The nobles of the kingdom met immediately and climbed the tower, where the princess was lying gravely ill. She knew neither of her father's death nor of her enemy's punishment. When she heard the noise of people approaching, she was convinced they were coming to put her to death. She was not in the least alarmed, for life had become hateful since she had lost the blue bird. So when her subjects flung themselves at her feet and informed her of the happy change in her fortunes, she was quite indifferent. Still, they carried her to the palace and crowned her. Then her frail body was given great care, and her desire to search for the blue bird combined to restore her health. Soon she was able to appoint a council to govern the kingdom during her absence. Providing herself with jewels to the value of a thousand million francs, she set out on her journey one night quite alone, without anyone knowing where she was going.

The enchanter who managed the affairs of King Charmant, not having sufficient power to undo what Soussio had done, decided to seek her out and propose some arrangement whereby she would restore the king to his natural form. He called for his frogs and flew to the fairy, who was at that moment conversing with Truitonne. Enchanters and fairies are on an equal footing. These two had known each other for five or six hundred years, and during that time they had quarreled and made up again at least a thousand times.

She received him very politely. "What does my compeer want?" she said (this is the way they all address one another). "Is there anything I can do for you?"

"Yes, compeer," answered the magician, "you can. It concerns one of my best friends, a king whom you have made very unhappy."

"Aha! I understand you, compeer," cried Soussio. "I'm very sorry, but there's no hope for him unless he consents to marry my goddaughter. There she is in all her beauty, as you may see. Let him think it over."

The enchanter was almost struck dumb when he caught sight of Truitonne, so hideous did she appear to him. Nevertheless, he could not leave without coming to some sort of agreement with Soussio. "The king has run a thousand risks since he has begun dwelling in a cage." Once, the nail on which the cage had been hanging had broken, and the cage had fallen to the ground with a severe shock to his feathered majesty. Minet, the cat, who happened to be in the room when this accident occurred, gave the poor king a scratch on the eye that nearly blinded him. On another occasion they neglected to give him any fresh water, and he barely escaped having the pip. A little rogue of a monkey got loose, caught hold of some of his feathers through the bars of the cage, and toyed with him as if he were a jay or a blackbird. But worst of all, he was on the verge of losing his kingdom. His heirs were trumping up new stories every day to prove he was dead.

Finally the enchanter came to an understanding with his compeer Soussio: she would bring Truitonne to King Charmant's palace, where she would reside for some months. During that time the king would be allowed to make up his mind to marry her. Soussio would permit him to resume his original form with the proviso that he would become a bird again if he eventually refused to marry her goddaughter.

The fairy presented Truitonne with magnificent dresses made of gold and silver, seated her on a pillion behind herself on a dragon, and proceeded directly to Charmant's kingdom, where they found him with his faithful friend the enchanter. With three taps of Soussio's wand King Charmant was again the handsome, charming, intelligent, and magnificent sovereign he had been before. However, his reprieve was dearly bought. The mere thought of marrying Truitonne made him shudder. The enchanter reasoned with him as well as he could, but made little impression on him. The king was less occupied with the government of his dominions than with devising means to prolong the period Soussio had allowed before he must marry Truitonne.

In the meantime Queen Florine had disguised herself as a peasant. Her hair was disheveled and hanging about her ears to conceal her features, and she wore a straw hat on her head and a sack upon her shoulder. Onward she proceeded, by turns walking and riding. She went by sea and land as fast as she could. However, not being certain of the route, she feared that every turn she took might lead her away from her charming monarch instead of toward him.

One day she stopped to rest beside a fountain whose silvery water flowed over little pebbles. Taking the opportunity of washing her feet, she sat on the grassy bank, tied up her fair locks with a ribbon, and put her feet into the little stream. She looked like Diana bathing on her return from the chase. A little old woman, bent over and leaning on a stout stick, happened to be passing that way and stopped. "What are you doing there so all alone, my pretty girl?"

"My good mother," the queen answered, "I have plenty of company, for I'm beset by sorrows, anxieties, and misfortunes." And upon uttering these words, her eyes filled with tears.

"What? So young and you're crying?" asked the good woman. "Ah, my child, don't give in to sorrow. Tell me truly what's wrong, and hopefully I may be able to comfort you."

The queen willingly told her about all her misfortunes, about the conduct of the fairy Soussio, and how she was presently searching for the blue bird.

The little old woman suddenly drew herself up as straight as possible, changing her whole appearance. She was lovely, young, and superbly attired. She smiled graciously at the queen as she said, "Incomparable Florine, the king you seek is no longer a bird. My sister Soussio has restored him to his former shape. He's in his kingdom. Don't torture yourself, for you will reach it and obtain your goal. Here are four eggs. Break one of them whenever you need help the most, and you'll find something in each that will be useful." In that instant she disappeared.

Florine felt much consoled by what she had heard. Putting the eggs into her sack, she resumed her journey toward Charmant's kingdom. After walking eight days and nights without stopping, she arrived at the foot of an enormously high mountain that was made entirely of ivory and so steep that one could not keep one's footing on it. She made a thousand vain attempts, but slipped back every time, until she became exhausted. In despair at encountering such an insurmountable obstacle, she laid down at the bottom of the mountain and decided to die right there.

Then she remembered the eggs the fairy had given her and took one out of her sack. "Let's see if the lady was merely making fun of me when she promised that the eggs would help me in my need." Breaking the egg, she found some small golden clamps, which she fastened on her hands and feet. With their help she climbed the ivory mountain without the least trouble, for the points of the clamps penetrated the ivory and prevented her from slipping. When she had reached the top, she found herself in just as much trouble with regard to the descent. The entire valley was a sheet of mirrored glass in which upward of sixty thousand women were admiring themselves, for this looking glass was two whole miles in width and six in height. Everyone appeared in it exactly as she wished to be. The carroty-haired women seemed to have locks of gold; a coarse brunette appeared to be a glossy raven black. The old looked young—the young never looked older. In sum, no fault could be seen in this wonderful mirror, and consequently the fair sex from all parts of the world resorted to using it. It was enough to make you die laughing to see the airs and graces that most of these coquettes gave themselves. Nor were men less eager to consult this magical mirror, which pleased them just as well. To some it seemed to give fine, curly hair, to others taller stature or better shape, a more martial mien or a nobler deportment. The ladies they laughed and laughed at them just as much in return.

The mountain was called by a thousand different names as a result. No one had ever been able to get to the top of it. Therefore, when Florine appeared on the summit, the ladies uttered shrieks of despair. "Where is that mad creature going?" they cried. "No doubt she must know how to walk on glass, or the first step she takes, she'll break our mirror to pieces!"

Thereupon a terrific hubbub arose. The queen did not know what to do, for she saw the imminent danger of descending by that road. So she broke another egg, and two pigeons popped out, attached to a tiny chariot that grew sufficiently large for her to sit in comfortably. The pigeons then gently descended with the queen and landed at the bottom without the least accident.

"My little friends," she said to them, "if you'll carry me to the spot where King Charmant holds his court, you won't find me ungrateful."

The civil, obedient pigeons kept going night and day until they reached the gates of the city. Florine got out and gave each of them a sweet kiss worth more than a royal diadem.

Oh, how her heart beat as she entered the city! Staining her face so that she would not be recognized, she asked a group of people she passed where she might see the king. Some of them began to laugh at her. "See the king?" they said. "Ho, what do you want with him, my young slut? Go, go and clean yourself! You are not worthy enough to look at such a monarch."

The queen made no reply, but quietly moved on and asked the next group she met where the best place would be to see the king.

"He'll soon be going to the temple with Princess Truitonne, for he has finally consented to marry her" was the answer.

"Heavens, what tidings! Truitonne, the worthless Truitonne, on the verge of marrying the king?" Stricken, Florine felt like dying, and collapsed dumbfounded on a heap of rubble under a gateway, her face covered by her disheveled hair and her large straw hat. "How unfortunate I am!" she cried. "I've come here only to add to the triumph of my rival and witness her contentment. It was for her, then, that the blue bird deserted me! It was for this little monster that he was guilty of the most cruel inconstancy. While I grieved over him and trembled for his life, the traitor had already turned away and thought no more of me than if he had never seen me. Indeed, he left me to lament his absence without a sigh."

Miserable souls rarely have much appetite, so when the poor queen sought out a lodging for the night, she went to bed without any supper.

Rising with the sun, she hurried to the temple. After repeated rebuffs from soldiers and attendants, she succeeded in obtaining admission. There she saw the king's throne and that of Truitonne, whom the people already looked upon as their queen. How painful it was for such a sensitive lover as Florine! She approached the throne of her rival and paused, leaning against a marble pillar. The king arrived first, looking more handsome and fascinating than ever. Truitonne followed him, richly attired and ugly enough to frighten everybody. She frowned as soon as she noticed Florine. "Who do you think you are to dare approach our august person and our golden throne in this way?"

"I'm called Mie Souillon," replied Florine. "I've come from a distant country to sell you some rare objects." Thereupon, she took out of her sack the emerald bracelets that King Charmant had given to her.

"Aha," said Truitonne, "these are pretty glass ornaments. Will you take five coins for them?"

"Show them to a connoisseur, madam," said the queen, "and then we'll make our deal."

Truitonne, who loved the king as much as such a creature could, was delighted in having a reason to speak to him. Approaching his throne, she showed him the bracelets and requested his opinion with regard to their value. As soon as he saw them, he immediately recalled those he had given to Florine. Sighing, he turned pale and could not speak for some time. At last, fearing that people might notice how upset his conflicting emotions were making him, he made an effort to compose himself and answered, "I believe these bracelets are worth almost as much as my kingdom. I had thought there was only one pair like this in the world, but these are certainly just like the pair I knew."

Truitonne returned to her throne, and once she was seated, she looked less noble than an oyster in its shell. Then she asked Florine what was the lowest price she would ask for the bracelets.

"You would find it difficult to pay, madam," she answered. "I had better propose another kind of bargain to you. If you'll obtain permission for me to sleep one night in the cabinet of echoes, I'll give you the emeralds."

"Gladly, Mie Souillon," said Truitonne, laughing like an idiot and showing teeth longer than the tusks of a wild boar.

The king did not ask where the bracelets came from, not because he did not care about the person who possessed them—in any case, her appearance was not such as to inspire much curiosity—but because he was so overwhelmingly repulsed by Truitonne. Now, it is important to know that when Charmant had been a blue bird, he had told Florine that beneath his apartments was a small room called the cabinet of echoes, so ingeniously constructed that the slightest whispers uttered there could be heard by the king while reposing in his bedroom. And since Florine's intention was to reproach him for his inconstancy, she could not have imagined a better method. After she was conducted to the cabinet that evening on Truitonne's orders, she immediately began her complaints and lamentations.

"The catastrophe that I never dreamed would occur has come about, cruel blue bird," she cried. "You've forgotten me! You love my unworthy rival. The bracelets I received from your disloyal hand could not make you remember me, so entirely have you banished me from your recollection." Here her sobs choked off her speech, and when she was able to speak again, she resumed her lamentations and continued them until daybreak.

The king's servants, who had heard her moan and sigh all night long, asked Truitonne why Florine had made such a disturbance. The queen answered that when she slept soundly, she was in the habit of dreaming and often talked aloud in her sleep. As for the king, a fatal aberration had prevented him from hearing her. Ever since he had fallen so deeply in love with Florine, he could not sleep soundly. So whenever he went to bed, he took a dose of opium in order to gain some rest.

Florine spent part of the next day in a strange, anxious mood. "If he heard me," she thought, "he's certainly showing his cruel indifference. If he didn't hear me, how shall I get him to do so?" Although she did not possess any more of those rare objects, she did have plenty of beautiful jewels. However, she needed something that would particularly catch Truitonne's fancy. So Florine resorted to using her eggs. She broke one, and out sprang a coach of polished steel inlaid with gold. It was drawn by six green mice and driven by a rose-colored rat, and the postilion, also of the rat species, was a grayish-violet color. In the coach sat four puppets who were more sprightly than any ever seen at the fairs of St. Germain or St. Laurent. They could do all sorts of wonderful things, particularly two little gypsies, who could dance a saraband or a jig and hold their own with the famous Leance.

Florine was enraptured at the sight of this new masterpiece of necromancy. Remaining perfectly mum until evening, the time Truitonne usually took a walk, she took up a place on one of the paths and set the mice galloping with the coach, rats, and puppets. This novelty so astonished Truitonne that she called out two or three times, "Mie Souillon, Mie Souillon! Will you take five coins for your coach and set of mice?"

"Ask the men of letters and learned scholars of this kingdom," said Florine, "what such a wonder is worth, and I'll abide by the estimation of the best judge."

Truitonne, who did everything arbitrarily, replied, "Without offending me any longer by your filthy presence, tell me the price."

"All I ask," said Florine, "is to sleep again in the cabinet of echoes."

"Go, poor idiot," answered Truitonne, "you shall have your wish."

Turning to her ladies-in-waiting, she said, "What a stupid creature to reap no greater advantage from such rare objects."

Night came. Florine uttered all the most touching reproaches she could think of, but again it was in vain, for the king never forgot to take his opium. His servants said to one another, "That country wench must surely be mad. What is she muttering about all night?"

"Whatever the case may be," some remarked, "there is both reason and feeling in what she says."

She waited impatiently for morning to ascertain what effect her words had produced. "What?" she cried. "Has this barbarous man become deaf to my voice? Will he no longer listen to his dear Florine? Oh, how weak I am to love him still! How well do I deserve the scorn with which he treats me!" But all her reproaches were for naught, for she had no power over her feelings for him.

There was only one more egg left in her sack that could help her. She broke it, and out came a pie composed of six birds, which were larded, dressed, and quite ready for eating. Yet they sang admirably, told fortunes, and knew more about medicine than Sculapius himself. Florine was enchanted at the sight of such a wonderful thing and carried her talking-pie into Truitonne's antechamber. While waiting for her to come, one of the king's servants came up to Florine and said, "My friend, Mie Souillon, are you aware that if the king did not take opium to make him sleep, you would be disturbing him immensely, for you chatter all night long in the most extraordinary manner."

Now Florine was no longer surprised that the king had not heard her. She took a handful of jewels out of her sack and said, "I'm not afraid of interrupting the king's sleep. So if you'll prevent him from taking opium tonight, assuming I'll be sleeping in the cabinet of echoes, all these pearls and diamonds shall be yours."

The servant agreed to do it and gave her his word. A few minutes afterward Truitonne arrived. She noticed Florine with her pie, which she pretended to be eating. "What are you doing there, Mie Souillon?"

"Madam," replied Florine, "I am eating astrologers, musicians, and physicians."

At that moment all the birds began to sing more melodiously than sirens and then to cry, "Give us a piece of silver, and we'll tell you your fortune." A duck that was particularly prominent called out in a voice louder than any of the others, "Quack! quack! quack! quack! I'm a physician; I cure all disorders and every sort of madness, except that of love."

Truitonne was most surprised by so many wonders. Indeed, she had never seen so many in her entire life. Thinking it an excellent pie, she coveted it. "Come, come, Mie Souillon, what shall I give you for it?"

"The usual price," answered Florine, "permission to sleep in the cabinet of echoes—nothing more."

"Why," said Truitonne generously (for she was in a good mood due to her acquisition of such a pie), "you shall have a gold coin as part of the bargain."

Florine was now happier than she had been for some time because she hoped the king would hear her. So she took her leave of Truitonne with many thanks. As soon as night came, she requested to be led to the cabinet, ardently hoping that the servant would keep his word, and that instead of giving the king his opium, he would substitute something that would keep his majesty awake. When she thought everybody else was asleep, she began her usual lamentations. "How many dangers did I confront searching for you," she said, "while you fled from me and sought to marry Truitonne? What did I do to you, you cruel person, to make you forget your vows? Remember your transformation, my favors, and our tender conversations." She repeated nearly all of them, her memory sufficiently proving that nothing was dearer to her than such recollections.

The king was not asleep and heard Florine so distinctly that he could not imagine where they came from. But his heart, pierced by tenderness, brought back the image of his incomparable princess so vividly that he felt his separation from her just as keenly as he had at the moment the knives had wounded him in the cypress tree. He began to speak aloud on his part, as the queen had done on hers. "Ah, princess," he said, "too cruel to a lover who adored you. Is it possible that you would have sacrificed me to our mutual enemies?"

Florine heard what he said and replied that if he would grant Mie Souillon an audience, he would learn about all the mysteries he had been unable to grasp until now. At these words the impatient king called one of his servants and asked him if he could find a Mie Souillon and bring her to him. The servant answered that nothing could be easier: she was sleeping in the cabinet of echoes.

The king did not know what to think. How could so great a queen as Florine be disguised as a scullion? And yet, how could Mie Souillon have the queen's voice and know such particular secrets unless she were not Florine herself? In his uncertainty he arose and dressed himself in the greatest haste. He descended by a back staircase to the door of the cabinet of echoes. Florine had taken the key out of the lock, but the king had a master key that unlocked every door in the palace.

A lamp at some distance cast a faint light on the scene. Lying on a couch, she was dressed in a light robe of white taffeta, which she wore beneath her coarse disguise, and her beautiful hair bathed her shoulders.

The king entered in a rush, his love getting the better of his anger. The moment he saw for certain it was she, he flung himself at her feet, bathed her hands with his tears, and felt he would die of joy, grief, and

a thousand different emotions that swirled inside of him.

The queen was no less moved. Her heart seemed to stop beating; she could scarcely breathe. She looked earnestly at the king without saying a word, and when she found the strength to speak to him, she had no power to reproach him, for the joy of beholding him again made her forget all of her groundless complaints. At length they explained to each other what had happened and justified what they had done. Their tender feelings were revived more strongly than ever, and the only obstacle that remained was the fairy Soussio.

But at this moment the enchanter who was so fond of the king arrived with a famous fairy, who was none other than the one who had given the four eggs to Florine. After initial compliments were exchanged, the enchanter and the fairy declared that their power had united in favor of the king and queen and that Soussio could do nothing against them. Consequently their marriage could take place without delay.

We may readily imagine the delight of these two young lovers. As soon as it was daytime, the news spread throughout the palace, and everybody was enchanted at the sight of Florine. When the tidings reached Truitonne, she ran to the king's apartments. To her surprise she found her beautiful rival there, and the moment she attempted to open her mouth to abuse her, the enchanter and the fairy appeared and changed her into a sow. Since Truie in French means sow, she still retained part of her name, plus her natural disposition to grumble. She ran out of the room grunting and then into the kitchen courtyard, where long peals of laughter greeted her and completed her despair.

Now that King Charmant and Queen Florine had been rescued from such a hideous person, they thought of their wedding and how elegant and magnificent it would be. Indeed, it is easy to judge how great their happiness was after so many prolonged misfortunes.

When Truitonne tried to force that charming king
To tie a knot which death alone could sunder,
Regardless of the consequences it would bring,
She certainly committed a great blunder.
Of course, it's possible she did not know, a marriage
Unblessed by mutual love is wretched slavery.
But Charmant's bold, uncompromising carriage,
Showed as much prudence, I maintain, as bravery.
Better to be a bird of any hue—
A raven, crow, an owl—I do protest,
Than stick for life to a partner like glue
Who scorns you, or whom you detest.
Too many matches of this sort I've seen,
And wish that now there were some king magician
To stop these ill-matched souls at once and lean
On them with force to keep his prohibition.
He must be vigilant and forbid the banns,
Whenever true affection might be slighted.
And Hymen must be prevented from joining hands,
Whenever hearts have not first been united.

THE GOOD
LITTLE MOUSE

ONCE upon a time there was a king and a queen who loved each other
so much that they needed only each other to be happy. Their hearts and
inclinations were always in unison. Every day they went hunting for hares
and stags or fishing for sole and carp. Sometimes they went to a ball to
dance the bourrée and the pavane. They attended plays, the opera, and
great banquets to eat roast beef and sugar almonds. They laughed, they
sang, they played a thousand pranks to amuse themselves. In short, nothing
exceeded their happiness. Their subjects followed the example set by the
king and queen and emulated them in their pastimes. For all these reasons
this kingdom was called the Land of Joy.

The monarch who was King Joyeux's neighbor, however, happened to
live much differently. A declared enemy of pleasure, he thought of naught
but warfare and causing mischief. He had a grim countenance, a full
beard, and hollow eyes; all skin and bones, he was always dressed in black,
with greasy, dirty hair that stood on end. To please him his men assaulted
and killed all who traveled through his country. He hanged all criminals
himself and delighted in torturing them. When a mother doted on her
little girl or boy, he would send for her and break the child's arms or
wring its neck before her eyes. Thus, his kingdom was called the Land
of Tears.

The wicked king had heard about King Joyeux's happiness, and since he
was very envious, he decided to raise a large army and kill, maim, or
capture him and all his people. He recruited men and arms from everywhere and ordered cannons to be cast. Everyone trembled with fear and
said, "What land is the evil king going to attack? He'll give no quarter."

When everything was ready, he marched toward the country of King
Joyeux, who learned of this bad news and quickly took measures for his
defence. The queen was frightened to death and wept. "Sire, we must
flee," she said. "Let's collect as much money as we can and go to the other
end of the world."

The king replied, "Never, madam, I have too much courage for that. It's better to die than to be branded a coward."

He assembled all his men-at-arms, bid an affectionate farewell to his wife, mounted his beautiful horse, and departed. When he was lost from sight, she began to weep and clasped her hands. "Alas," she cried, "if I should have an infant and the king be killed in battle, I'll be a widow and a prisoner, and the wicked king will torture me in a thousand cruel ways!"

This thought prevented her from eating and sleeping. She wrote to him every day, but one morning, as she looked from the battlements, she saw a courier galloping at breakneck speed. She called to him, "Ho, courier, ho! What news?"

"The king is dead. The battle is lost. The wicked king will soon be here."

The poor queen fainted and was carried to her bed. All her ladies gathered around her, and they wept—some for their fathers, some for their sons—and tore their hair. It was the most distressing sight in the world.

All of a sudden they heard cries of "Murder! Thieves!" The wicked king had arrived with all his wretched followers, killing everyone they encountered. Entering the royal palace in full battle armor, he ascended to the queen's chamber. When she saw him enter, she was so frightened that she hid herself in the bed and pulled the covers over her head. He called her two or three times, but she refused to answer. He grew angry and said fiercely, "I believe you mean to make fun of me. Don't you know that I could strangle you this instant?" He stripped the covers away and tore off her cap. Her beautiful hair fell onto her shoulders, and he twisted it three times around his hand and threw her over his shoulder like a sack of corn. Then he carried her down the stairs and mounted his large black horse. She pleaded with him to have mercy, but he only mocked her, saying, "Cry and lament! You only make me laugh!"

He carried her into his own country, vowing all the way that he would hang her, but was told it would be too cruel, since she was about to become a mother. When he discovered it was true, it occurred to him that if she had a daughter, he would marry her to his son. So he sent for a fairy who lived near his realm to find out which it would be. When she arrived, he entertained her more handsomely than was his custom. Afterward he took her up to a tower, where the poor queen occupied a tiny, ill-furnished garret at the top. They found her lying on the floor on a mattress not worth a sou, and she had been crying day and night. When the fairy saw her, she could not help pitying her. After curtsying to her, she embraced her and murmured, "Take courage, madam, your misfortunes will not last forever. I hope to end them soon."

Consoled somewhat by these words, the queen returned the fairy's embraces and begged her to have pity on a poor queen who had enjoyed the greatest happiness and was now equally as miserable. They were in close conversation when the wicked king exclaimed, "Come, no more compliments. I brought you here to tell me if this slave will have a boy or a girl."

The fairy said, "She'll have a girl, who will be the most beautiful and intelligent princess the world has ever seen." Thereupon, she endowed the unborn princess with innumerable gifts and virtues.

"If she's not beautiful and intelligent," the wicked king said, "I'll hang her to her mother's neck and her mother on a tree, and nothing will prevent me." Upon saying this, he left the room with the fairy, not deigning to glance at the good queen as she wept bitterly.

"Alas, what shall I do?" she said to herself. "If I should have a beautiful little girl, he'll give her to his monkey of a son. And if she's ugly, he'll hang us together. I'm at my wit's end! Perhaps I could hide my infant somewhere so he'd never see it."

As the time drew near for the child to be born, the queen's anxieties increased. No one listened to her laments or tried to console her. Every morning the jailer in charge of her gave her just three boiled peas with a little piece of black bread. She became as thin as a herring, nothing but skin and bones.

One evening as she was spinning (for the greedy king made her work night and day), she saw a pretty little mouse come in through a hole. "Alas, my little darling," she said to it, "what are you looking for here? I have only three peas for myself, and they must last the entire day. If you don't wish to fast, then you'd better depart."

The little mouse raced here and there and danced and capered like a little monkey. It so amused the queen that she gave it the only pea she had left for her supper. "Here, little darling," she said, "eat this. I have nothing more, but you may gladly have it."

As soon as she did, she saw an excellent partridge, wonderfully well roasted, and two jars of preserves appear on the table. "Truly," she said, "a good deed never goes unrewarded." She ate but little, for she had lost her appetite through fasting. She threw some bonbons to the mouse, who was still nosing about for food, and then it began to skip about more than it had before supper.

Early the next morning the jailer brought the queen the three peas, which he placed into a large dish to mock her. The little mouse entered softly and ate all three and the bread as well. When the queen looked for her dinner and could not find a thing, she was very angry with the mouse. "What a wicked little animal!" she said. "If it continues to do this, I'll starve." As she was about to put the cover on the empty dish, she discovered it filled with all sorts of good things to eat. Of course, she was delighted and began to eat them, but while dining, she thought of the prospect of the wicked king ordering her baby to be killed in a few short

days, and she left the table in tears. She raised her eyes to Heaven and exclaimed, "Ah, is there no way to save my child?"

As she did so, she saw the little mouse playing with some long pieces of straw. She picked them up and set to work on them. "If there's enough straw," she said, "I'll make a covered basket in which to put my babe. Then I'll let her down through the window and give her to the first charitable person who consents to care for her." She then continued working with renewed energy. There was plenty of straw, since the mouse kept dragging some into the room as it continued to skip about. At mealtime the queen gave it her three peas, and in exchange she always found a hundred sorts of delicacies. Very surprised by all this, she continually wondered who could be sending her such excellent viands.

One day the queen was gazing out of the window to determine how long the cord should be for letting the basket down. Below her she noticed a shrunken old woman leaning on a stick. "I know your trouble, madam," the woman said. "If you like, I'd gladly be of service."

"Alas, my dear friend," the queen said, "I'd be very much obliged to you. Come every evening to the foot of this tower. As soon as my child is born, I'll let it down to you. You'll nurse it, and if I ever become rich, I'll reward you handsomely."

"I'm not greedy," answered the old woman, "but I am choosy in my eating habits. There's nothing I like better than a plump little mouse. If you find any in your garret, kill them and throw them to me. I'd be very grateful for this, and your baby would be well looked after."

When the queen heard this, she began to weep and could not reply. After waiting some time, the old woman asked her why she was crying.

"There's a mouse that comes into my chamber," she said, "and it's such a pretty little creature that I could never kill it."

"What?" the old woman replied angrily. "You prefer a knavish mouse that gnaws everything to the child you're about to bear? Very well, madam, then you're not to be pitied. You may keep your good company. I'll have plenty of mice without yours. See if I care!" And off she went, grumbling and muttering.

Although the queen had a good meal set before her and the mouse came to dance as usual, she kept staring at the ground with tears streaming down her cheeks.

That same night she gave birth to a wonderfully beautiful princess. Instead of bawling, as other infants do, she laughed at her dear mama and held out her little hands toward her as though she were quite cognizant of what she did. The queen fondled and kissed her most tenderly, all the while thinking sadly to herself, "Poor little darling! Dear child! If you fall into the wicked king's clutches, your life will be over before it starts." She covered her up in the basket with a note tied to her dress that said: "The name of this unfortunate child is Joliette." After leaving her alone a few moments without looking at her, she again opened the basket and found her even more becoming. She kissed her and wept bitterly, not knowing what to do. But just then the little mouse came and got into the basket. "You little creature," the queen said, "you don't know how much your life has cost me. Because of you I may lose my dear Joliette. Anyone else would have killed you and given you to the choosy old woman, but I couldn't agree to do that."

"Don't repent of your deed, madam," the mouse said. "I'm not so unworthy of your friendship as you think."

The queen was frightened to death when she heard the mouse speaking, and her fear increased even more when she saw its little muzzle begin to swell, taking the form of a human face. Its paws became hands and feet, and it suddenly mushroomed in size. When the queen finally summoned enough courage to look at her, she realized that it was the same kind fairy who had come to see her with the wicked king.

"I wanted to test your heart," the fairy said, "and I've discovered it to be good and worthy of friendship. We fairies, who possess immense wealth and treasures, seek only friendship as the sweetness of life, and rarely do we find it."

"Is it really true, beautiful lady," the queen said, embracing her, "that you really have trouble finding friends, being so rich and powerful?"

"Yes," she replied, "for most people only love us out of self-interest, and that does not move us at all. But when you loved me as a little mouse, it was not from self-interest. Even so, I had to test you even more. So I took the form of an old woman. It was I who spoke to you at the foot of the tower, and you were still faithful to me." After saying all this, she embraced the queen. Then she kissed the little princess's red lips and said to her, "I endow you, my child, to be your mother's consolation and to be richer than your father. Always beautiful, you will live a hundred years without sickness or wrinkles or ever becoming old."

Delighted, the queen thanked her and begged that she take Joliette away and look after her, adding that she wanted Joliette to be her own daughter. The fairy accepted and thanked her. She placed the baby in the basket and lowered it to the ground. But she stopped for a moment to reassume the form of the little mouse, and when she descended, the child was nowhere to be found. So she climbed back in fear. "All is lost!" she said to the queen. "My enemy, Cancaline, has carried off the princess. She's a cruel fairy who hates me. And unfortunately, being my senior, she's more powerful than I am. I don't know if I shall be able to recover Joliette from her horrid clutches."

When the queen heard such woeful news, she thought she would die of grief. She cried copious tears and begged her kind friend to try to find the child again no matter what it might cost.

In the meantime, the jailer had come into the queen's apartment and found that she had given birth. He rushed to tell the king, who in turn ran to the queen to ask for the child. She said, however, that a fairy whose name she did not know had appeared and taken it away by force. The wicked king stamped his foot and bit his nails to the quick. "I promised to hang you," he said. "Now I shall keep my word."

He dragged the poor queen into a wood, climbed a tree, and was about to hang her when the fairy, who had made herself invisible, gave him a violent push. From the top of the tree, he fell and knocked out four of his teeth. While his people tried to stick them in again, the fairy carried the queen away in her flying chariot and conducted her to a beautiful castle. She took marvelous care of her, and if the queen had had the Princess Joliette, she would have been perfectly happy. They could not, however, find out where Cancaline had taken her, although the little mouse tried all she possibly could.

As the years flew past, the queen's deep sorrow abated to a small degree. After fifteen years had elapsed, news arrived that the wicked king's son was going to marry his turkey keeper, even though the young girl objected to the match. What's this? A turkey keeper refusing to become a queen? All the same, the nuptial dresses were made, and it was to be such a splendid wedding that people came from a hundred miles around to attend. The little mouse herself went there because she wanted to see this turkey keeper at her ease. Going into the poultry yard, she found the barefoot girl clad in coarse linen and a greasy napkin around her head. Dresses made of gold and silver and diamonds, pearls, ribbons, and lace, lay all about her on the ground; the turkeys were trampling on them, dirtying and spoiling them. While the girl sat on a large stone, the wicked king's son, who was crooked, lame, and blind in one eye, was saying to her roughly, "If you refuse to give me your heart, I'll kill you."

She answered him proudly, "I won't marry you. You're too ugly, and you take after your cruel father. Leave me in peace with my turkeys—I like them better than all your fine clothes."

The little mouse looked at her admiringly, for she was as beautiful as the sun. As soon as the wicked king's son had gone, the fairy assumed the figure of an old shepherdess and said, "Good morning, my darling, your turkeys appear to be quite fine."

The young turkey keeper looked at the old woman sweetly and replied, "They want me to give them up for a paltry crown. What would you advise me to do?"

"My girl," said the fairy, "a crown is very beautiful. You cannot know its value or its weight."

"But I do know," the turkey keeper replied promptly, "and therefore I refuse to accept it. At the same time, I don't know who I am or where my father and mother are. I have neither friends nor relatives."

"You're beautiful and virtuous, my child," the wise fairy said, "and that's worth ten kingdoms. Tell me, I beg of you, who brought you here, since you have neither father nor mother, friends nor relatives?"

"I'm here because of a fairy named Cancaline, who beat me and knocked me around without cause or even pretext. One day I ran away and, not knowing where to go, sat down in a wood. The son of the wicked king happened to be passing by, and he asked me if I'd like to tend his poultry yard. I was very willing to do so and was given the care of the turkeys. He frequently came to see them and me as well. Alas, without any desire on my part, he began courting me more and more, and made me worry a great deal."

After hearing this story, the fairy began to suspect that the turkey keeper might be Princess Joliette. "My child, tell me your name?" she asked.

"I'm Joliette, at your service."

Upon hearing this name, the fairy no longer had any doubts, and she threw her arms around her neck and almost devoured her with kisses. "Joliette, I knew you many years ago, and I'm delighted to find you so discreet and intelligent. I could wish you were cleaner, though, for you look like a little scullion. Gather up these beautiful clothes here and dress yourself in them."

The obedient maiden immediately whipped the greasy handkerchief off her head, and as she shook her head slightly, she was draped entirely by her hair. As bright as the sunlight and as fine as golden thread, it cascaded in ringlets to the ground. With her delicate hands she took some water from a fountain in the yard and splashed her face, which became as clear as oriental pearl. Roses seemed to bloom on her cheeks and lips; her breath smelled of wild thyme; her figure was as straight as a rush. In wintertime they might have taken her skin for the snow, and in summer for the lily.

When she was at last decked in diamonds and fine clothes, the fairy gazed at her miraculous tranformation. "Who do you think you are, my dear Joliette," she asked, "now that you're dressed in such a lively manner?"

"To tell the truth, it seems to me that I'm the daughter of a great king," she replied.

"Would you be happy if this were true?"

"Yes, my good mother," Joliette replied, curtesying to her, "I'd be very glad."

"Well, then," said the fairy, "be content, and I'll tell you more tomorrow."

She quickly returned to her splendid castle, where the queen was busy spinning silk, and as the little mouse she cried out to her, "Will your majesty bet your distaff and spindle to see if I can't bring you the best news you've ever had?"

"Alas," replied the queen, "ever since the death of King Joyeux and the loss of my Joliette, I wouldn't give a pin for all the news in the world."

"There, there. Don't fret anymore," said the fairy. "The princess is wonderfully well. I've just seen her, and she's so very beautiful that it all depends on her if she wants to be a queen." The fairy told her everything from beginning to end, and the queen cried both with joy upon learning that her daughter was so beautiful and with grief that she was a turkey keeper.

"When we were great sovereigns in our own kingdom and lived in such splendor," she said, "my poor dear departed and I never dreamed our child would become a turkey keeper!"

"It's all because of cruel Cancaline," the fairy said, "who knew how much I love you, and to spite me she has placed her in this predicament. She won't be in it any longer, though, or I'll burn my books."

"I won't consent to her marrying the son of the wicked king," said the queen. "Let us go tomorrow to claim her and bring her here."

In the meantime, the wicked king's son had become furious with Joliette. He sat under a tree, where he vented his grief so vigorously that he began to howl. Hearing him, his father went to the window and called, "What are you crying about? Why are you making such a fool of yourself?"

"Our turkey keeper won't love me," he answered.

"What?" the wicked king exclaimed. "She won't love you? I'll make her love you or she will die." Calling his guards, he said to them, "Go and fetch her, for I'll make her suffer so much that she'll repent for being so obstinate."

They went to the poultry yard and found Joliette in a white satin dress embroidered all over with gold, pink diamonds, and more than a thousand yards of ribbon. Never had they seen such a fine lady in all her grandeur. They did not dare address her because they thought she was a princess.

"Please tell me whom you are seeking here?" she said civilly.

"Madam," they said, "we're looking for a miserable wretch they call Joliette."

"Alas, it is I. What do you want with me?"

They instantly seized her and tied her feet and hands with thick cords for fear she would run away. They led her trussed like this to the wicked king and his son. When he saw how beautiful she was, he could not help being a little moved, and no doubt would have taken pity on her had he not been one of the most wicked and cruel men in the world. "Ha, ha! Little rogue, little toad!" he cried. "I hear you won't love my son. He's a hundred times handsomer than you. One of his looks is worth more than your whole person. Come, you'd better love him now, or I'll have you flayed."

Trembling like a pigeon, the princess knelt before him. "Sire, I beg you not to flay me. That would be too cruel. Let me have two or three days to think everything over, and then you may do as you will."

His son was enraged and demanded she be flayed. They agreed at last to lock her up in the tower, where she could see nothing but the sky.

It was then that the good fairy arrived in her flying chariot with the queen. Hearing all that had transpired, the queen began to cry bitterly, saying how unfortunate she always was and that she would rather her child were dead than be married to the wicked king's son.

"Take courage," the fairy said, "I'm going to give them so much trouble that you will be avenged."

When the wicked king retired to bed, the fairy changed herself into a little mouse and hid herself beneath the headrest of the bed. As soon as he lay down to sleep, she bit his ear, and he became enraged. He turned on his other side, but she bit the other ear, and he cried out, "Murder!" He bellowed for someone to come and then they did, they found his two bitten ears bleeding so much that they could not stanch the flow.

While they were searching everywhere for the mouse, she went to the wicked king's son and treated him in a like manner. Calling for his servants, he showed them his flayed ears, and they hastened to bandage them.

The little mouse now returned to the room of the wicked king, who had since become a little drowsy. So she took a bite out of his nose and continued to nibble on it. When he put his hands up to protect himself, she bit and scratched them.

"Mercy, I'm lost!" he cried out. She got into his mouth and nibbled his tongue, his cheeks, his lips, his eyes. When his servants arrived, they discovered him so overwrought that he could scarcely speak. His tongue was so wounded that he had to make signs that it was the mouse. They looked for it in the mattress, in the headrest, and in every corner, but she had already gone to the son, whom she treated even worse by eating his good eye (for he was already blind in one). He arose like a madman, sword in hand. Quite blind, he ran into his father's room, where he met his father, who had also taken his sword and was storming about, swearing that he would kill everyone around if they did not catch the mouse. When he saw his son in such a fury, he scolded him, and the latter was so enraged that in heat of passion he attacked him, for he had not recognized his father's voice. The wicked king was so furious that he wounded his son with his sword. In return, he received a wound, and both of them fell to the ground, bathed in blood.

All their subjects, who hated them mortally, had only obeyed them out of terror, and since they no longer had to fear them, they tied rope around their feet and dragged them into the river, quite delighted to be rid of them. This was how the wicked king and his son met their end.

The good fairy, who knew what occurred, sought out the queen, and they rushed to the black tower, where Joliette was incarcerated behind more than forty locked doors. The fairy struck the great door three times with a wand of hazel wood, and it flew open, as did all the others. They found the poor princess disconsolate and speechless. The queen embraced her and said, "My dear child, I'm your mother, the Queen Joyeuse." She then related to her the story of her life. When Joliette heard all this good news, she almost died with joy. Falling at the queen's feet, she embraced her knees, moistened her hands with tears, and kissed them a thousand times. She hugged the fairy, who had brought her baskets filled with valuable jewels, gold, diamonds, bracelets, pearls, and the portrait of King Joyeux framed by precious stones. All of these she placed before her.

"Let's not lose a moment," said the fairy. "We must bring about a coup d'état. Let's go into the great hall of the castle and address the people." She walked in front with a grave expression, wearing a dress with a train more than ten yards long, and the queen in one of blue velvet embroidered in gold with a much longer train. (They had brought their robes of state with them.) They also wore crowns on their heads as radiant as suns. The Princess Joliette followed, distinguished by her marvelous beauty and modesty. They curtsied to all the people they encountered, commoners and highborn alike, and were soon followed by crowds anxious to learn who these fine ladies might be. When the hall was quite full, the good fairy told the wicked king's subjects that she would give them King Joyeux's daughter, now standing before them, for their queen. She told them they would live very happily under her rule and that, if they accepted her, she would find herself a husband as perfect as she was, who would always be cheerful and banish melancholy from every heart.

At these words everyone exclaimed, "Yea, she shall be our queen! We've been sad and miserable much too long." At that moment a hundred different instruments began to play, and everyone joined hands and danced a round, singing to the queen, her daughter, and the good fairy: "Yea, she shall be our queen!"

Such was their reception, and never has so much happiness reigned. They set the tables, they ate and drank, and then went to bed and slept soundly. When the princess arose next morning, the fairy presented her with the handsomest prince that has ever been seen. She had gone to the very end of the world to fetch him in her flying chariot, and he was as charming as Joliette. The moment she saw him, she loved him. He in turn was captivated by her, and the queen was overjoyed. They prepared a splendid banquet and had wonderfully fine dresses made for the occasion.

Soon thereafter the marrige ceremony was performed amid the greatest rejoicings.

The unfortunate queen,
Whose distress you have seen,
In prison, abandoned, forlorn,
By perils beset,
About her poor Joliette.
She might have wept from the hour she was born,
Had not a kind fay,
Who had many a day,
As a mouse shared her food so short,
With gratitude warm,
Bravely weathered the storm,
And brought their bark safe into port!
Though but a fable,
I'm still quite able
A moral perchance to impart:
To all things be kind,
And let gratitude find
A place forever in your heart.

THE GOLDEN BRANCH

ONCE upon a time there was a king whose austere and melancholy disposition inspired terror in his subjects rather than love. He rarely allowed himself to be seen and put people to death on the slightest suspicion of wrongdoing. Since he always frowned, everyone called him King Grim.

Now, King Grim had a son who was not like him in the least. Nothing could equal his son's intelligence, gentleness, generosity, and overall talents. Unfortunately, though, he also had crooked legs, a hunch on his back that was higher than his head, squinting eyes, and a wry mouth. In short, he was a dwarfish monster, and it was the strangest thing in the world that such a beautiful soul inhabited such a deformed body. Yet it was his singular fate to be doted on by everyone he wished to please. So superior in mind was he to everyone around him that no one could listen to him with indifference. The queen, his mother, decided that he should be called Torticoli, either because she liked that name or because she considered it most appropriate for him, given his twisted body.

King Grim, who thought more about the greatness of his son than his happiness, cast his eyes on the daughter of his near neighbor, a powerful monarch whose dominions, when joined to his own, would make him the most redoubtable ruler on the face of the globe. He thought this princess an eminently suitable wife for Prince Torticoli, especially since she could not have any grounds to criticize his ugly deformities, for she was just as ugly and deformed herself. Called Trognon, she always rode about in a bowl because her legs were out of joint. On the other hand, she was the most pleasant creature in the world; it appeared that Heaven had been anxious to compensate for the injuries of nature by making her so pleasant.

Once King Grim obtained the portrait he had requested of the Princess Trognon, he had it placed under a canopy in a great hall and sent for Prince Torticoli. Commanding him to gaze at the picture with affection, he told him it was the likeness of his intended bride. But when Torticoli took a look, he immediately turned away with an air of disdain that offended his father.

"Aren't you pleased?" he asked sharply.

"No, my lord," replied the prince. "How can I be pleased about marrying a cripple?"

"You're one to talk," said the king. "How can you find fault with this princess when you yourself are a little monster who frightens everyone who looks at you?"

"That's precisely why I object to forming an alliance with another monster," the prince maintained. "I can hardly bear the sight of myself. You can imagine how much worse it would be with such a companion."

"You're afraid you'll perpetuate a race of baboons," the king said insultingly, "but your fears are superficial. You shall marry her. My command should be enough for you to obey."

Torticoli made no reply, but merely bowed respectfully and withdrew.

King Grim was not accustomed to encounter the least opposition, and his son's refusal put him in an awful mood. So he locked him up in a tower built expressly as a prison for rebellious princes. However, there had been nothing like a rebellious prince for two hundred years, and the tower was in great disrepair, and the apartments and furniture were surpassingly antiquated.

None of his guards dared to speak to him. They had been ordered to give him bad food and to wear him down in all sorts of ways. King Grim knew how to make himself obeyed: if he did not get his guards to act out of love, then it was out of fear. Nevertheless, the affection they had for the prince made them want to relieve his sufferings as much as they could.

Since the prince loved to read, he asked for books and was told he might select any he wanted in the tower library. He thought at first that this permission would suffice him, but when he attempted to read several of the books, he found the language so obsolete that he could not understand a word. He put the books down, only to pick them up again to try to decipher something of their contents. At the very least, he hoped to distract himself.

Convinced that Torticoli would soon tire of his imprisonment, King Grim acted as if the prince had already consented to marry Trognon. He sent ambassadors to the neighboring king to request the hand of his daughter, to whom he promised perfect happiness. Trognon's father was delighted to have such a lucky opportunity to marry off his daughter, for few people are willing to burden themselves with a cripple. He accepted King Grim's proposal, and though, to tell the truth, he had not been greatly impressed by the portrait of Prince Torticoli sent to him, he had it placed in a magnificent gallery. Trognon was brought there to look at it, and as soon as she saw it, she lowered her eyes and began to weep. Incensed by the repugnance she showed, he took a mirror and placed it before her. "You weep, my daughter," he said, "but look at yourself and admit that you have no right to complain."

"If I were in a hurry to be married, my lord," she said, "it would, perhaps, be wrong of me to be so fastidious, but I can bear my shame alone. I don't want anyone sharing the misery of having to look at me. Let me remain the unfortunate Princess Trognon all my life, and I'll be content. At least I won't complain."

Despite her excellent reasons, the king did not listen to them and forced her to depart with the ambassadors sent to convey King Grim's proposal. Now, while they are placing her onto a straw litter like a stump of wood to begin her journey, we must return to the tower to see how the prince fares.

One day as the prince was walking in a long gallery, musing sadly about the fate that had caused him to be born so repulsive and to become engaged to a princess even more ill-favored, he happened to look up at the windows. He observed that they were stained with bright colors and had extremely fine designs. Since he had a taste for beautiful works of art, he stopped to examine them, but he could not grasp their meaning because they represented scenes in stories long since forgotten. One thing, however, did capture his attention: there was a man in the series of pictures who appeared to be his spitting image. Depicted at first in the dungeon of the tower, this man could be seen examining a wall. Then he found a golden ramrod and opened a cabinet. There were many other things that drew his attention, but in the greater number of the windows he was attracted mainly by the images of himself. "What could have happened to make me one of the characters here?" he asked. "I wasn't even born then. What fateful idea compelled the painter to amuse himself by creating a man like me?" On the same glass he noticed the figure of a lovely girl whose features were so regular and expression so intelligent that he could not take his eyes off her. In short, he saw a thousand different things, and all the feelings were portrayed so well that he thought he was experiencing in real life events that were actually just a play of colors.

He did not leave the gallery until it was too dark to distinguish anything in the glass. Returning to his room, he picked up the first aged tome that came to hand. The leaves were of vellum with decorated borders, and the binding was made of gold and enameled with blue ciphers. Within, he was quite surprised to find the same subjects in the illustrations as those depicted on the windows in the gallery. In trying to read the manuscript without success, he suddenly noticed that on one of the pages, with an illustration with musicians, the figures began to sing; on another page, where players appeared at Basset and Trictrac, their cards and dice were in motion. Turning the page over, he saw people dancing at a ball; all the ladies were in full dress and marvelously beautiful. He turned the page again and smelled the savory aroma of a splendid dinner; the little figures were all eating, and the largest was no more than a quarter of an inch high. One of them turned toward the prince and said, "To your good health, Torticoli! Try to bring back our queen to us. If you do, it will be to your advantage. If you don't, it will be to your detriment."

At these words the prince had such a violent fit (for he had been trembling for some time) that he let the book drop to one side and fell down as though dead. Hearing him collapse, his keepers ran in. They were deeply attached to him and tried everything they could to help him. As soon as he was able to speak, they asked what the matter was. He replied that he was so weak for want of proper food that his mind had wandered. He felt his imagination had been worked on. "I have seen and heard so many astonishing things in that book that I was struck with fright." His guardians were deeply troubled by all this and gave him something good to eat despite the king's orders. After he had eaten, he picked up the book again and no longer found any of the things he had seen before. This convinced him that he had been under a delusion.

The next day he returned to the gallery, where he again saw the figures in the windows. All were moving about, promenading in avenues, hunting stags and hares, fishing, and building tiny houses. In every one of these miniature scenes his figure could be seen. Wearing garments exactly like his own, it ascended to the dungeon of the tower, where it discovered the golden ramrod. Since the prince had eaten a good breakfast, he was positive that he was no longer imagining things. "This is too mysterious," he said. "Somehow I have to find the means of knowing more. Maybe I can learn more in the dungeon."

Once he had mounted the stairs to it, he struck the wall he had seen, and part of it seemed hollow. Taking a hammer, he knocked down a portion of the wall and uncovered a finely wrought golden ramrod. He was wondering how he might make use of it when he noticed a worm-eaten wooden press in a corner of the room. He tried to open it, but he could not find a lock. In vain he turned it around and looked on each side. At last he spotted a small hole, and thinking that the ramrod might be used there, he inserted it and pulled with all his might until he opened the press. In contrast to the age and ugliness of its outside, the inside was beautiful and contained marvelous treasures. All the drawers were made of engraved rock crystal, amber, or precious stones. When they were taken out, there were smaller drawers on the sides, above, below, and at the back, separated by partitions of mother of pearl. When these partitions were taken out and the drawers opened, each appeared full of the most splendid weapons, rich crowns, and remarkable portraits. Enchanted, Prince Torticoli kept opening drawers until he found a tiny key made of a single emerald, with which he opened a golden compartment at the back of the press. He was dazzled by a glittering carbuncle that formed a large box. He quickly pulled the box out of the compartment, but was shocked when he found it filled with blood. It contained a man's hand cut off at the wrist, but still grasping a miniature case!

Torticoli shuddered at this sight, and his hair stood on end. Trembling so much he could barely stand, he slumped to the floor still holding the box. The sight was so shocking that he had to avert his gaze and sought more than anything to return the box whence he had found it. But thinking that some great mystery was lying behind all of this, he remembered what the little figure in the book had said to him: depending on what he did, his actions would be to his advantage or detriment. He had as much to fear from the future as from the present. Therefore, he reprimanded himself for being so frightened and told himself his fear was unworthy of a brave soul. He summoned the effort to gaze at the hand and exclaimed, "Oh, unfortunate hand! Can't you give me some signs that will help me understand your sad story? If it's within my power to serve you, I assure you I have a generous heart."

His words appeared to excite the hand, for it began moving its fingers and making signs that he comprehended as perfectly as if their meaning had been conveyed in words by the most eloquent lips.

"I want you to know," said the hand, "that you can do a great deal for that person who lost me because of the barbarous act of a jealous fiend. You will see the portrait of an adorable beauty in the miniature case. She's the cause of my misfortune. Go straight to the gallery and focus your attention on the spot where the sun's rays most brightly fall. Search and you'll discover my treasure."

After the hand stopped moving, the prince asked it several questions, but it did not respond. "What shall I do with you?" he remarked. The hand made fresh signs indicating that the prince was to put it back into the press. He did this and then locked everything up again. He hid the ramrod in the wall where he had found it. Now that he was a little accustomed to marvelous events, he descended to the gallery.

Upon entering it, the windows began to clatter and shake in an extraordinary fashion. Looking for the spot where the rays of the sun fell the brightest, he noticed they were falling on the portrait of a youth who was so handsome and had such a majestic air that he felt captivated. On lifting the picture, he found wainscoting made of ebony with moldings of gold, as was the case throughout the rest of the gallery. He did not know how to remove it or even whether he ought to do so. Consulting the windows, he saw that the wainscot was lifted up. He immediately raised it and found himself in a porphyry vestibule ornamented with statues. He climbed a large staircase of agate that had a balustrade engraved with gold. He entered a salon of lapis lazuli, and after passing through numerous apartments whose excellent paintings and rich furniture enchanted him, he eventually reached a small room filled with ornaments made of turquoise. There he saw on a bed of blue and gold gauze a lady who appeared to be asleep. She was an incomparable beauty; her hair was blacker than ebony and highlighted the whiteness of her skin. She seemed to be sleeping uneasily, for her features had the melancholy air of an invalid.

Afraid of waking her, the prince approached quietly. He heard her speaking, and as he listened with great care to her words, he caught these few statements, interrupted by sighs: "Do you think, you perfidious fiend, that I can love you when you have taken me away from my beloved Trasimene? How could you have dared to sever such a dear hand right in front of my eyes from an arm that will always be your dread? Is this the way you intend to demonstrate your respect and love for me? Ah, Trasimene, my dear lover, will I never see you again?"

The prince noticed that her tears found a passage through her closed lids, and as they trickled down her cheeks they resembled those shed by Aurora. He remained transfixed at the foot of the bed, not knowing whether he should wake her or let her remain in her sad slumber. It was already clear to him that Trasimene was her lover and that he had found his hand in the dungeon. A thousand confused thoughts were passing through his mind when he heard some charming music of a group of nightingales and canaries. They sang with such perfect harmony that they surpassed the most pleasant vocalists. At the same moment an enormous eagle entered the apartment. Flying gracefully, he held in his talons a golden branch covered with rubies in bunches like cherries. He fixed his eyes on the lovely sleeper, gazing at her as though she were the sun. Then he spread his great wings and hovered above her, rising and falling almost to her feet.

After some moments he turned toward the prince, approached him, and placed the golden branch with its ruby cherries in his hand. The singing birds raised their voices until their notes pierced the palace roof. The prince began piecing together all the events that had happened and concluded not only that the lady was enchanted, but that he was to have the glorious honor of undertaking an adventure in her behalf. So he advanced toward her and bent one knee to the ground. Touching her with the branch, he said, "Beautiful and charming creature sleeping under an influence unknown to me, I implore you, in the name of Trasimene, to revive all those faculties that you appear to have lost."

The lady opened her eyes, caught sight of the eagle, and exclaimed, "Stay, dear lover, stay!"

But the royal bird uttered a piercing, sorrowful cry and flew away with his little feathered musicians. As this occurred, the lady turned toward Torticoli and said to him, "I followed my heart instead of propriety. I know that I owe everything to you. You have restored the light of Heaven denied me for two hundred years. The enchanter who loved me and has made me suffer so much trouble had reserved this great adventure for you. I have the power to serve you and wish to do so with all my heart. Let me know your wishes. I shall use all the fairy power at my command to make you happy."

"Madam," replied the prince, "if your science enables you to penetrate the secrets of the heart, you certainly must know that despite the calamities that have overwhelmed me, I am less to be pitied than many others."

"That is due to your good sense," replied the fairy. "But please do not shame me. Let me express my gratitude: what do you desire? My power is unlimited. You just need to ask."

"I'd like to restore the handsome Trasimene to you, for his loss has made you so desolate."

"You're much too generous. Don't sacrifice your interests to my own. That great deed must be achieved by another—I'm afraid I can't say anything more on the matter. Just know that this person will be kindly disposed to you. But come, don't deny me the pleasure of obliging you any longer. What do you desire?"

"Madam," said the prince, flinging himself at her feet, "you see my frightful figure. They call me Torticoli in derision. Make me less ridiculous!"

"Go, Prince," said the fairy, touching him three times with the golden branch. "Go. You will be so accomplished and so perfect that no man before or after shall ever be your equal. From now on you will be called Sans-pair, and you'll be justly entitled to that name."

The grateful prince clasped her knees in a silent embrace that testified to his joy. She had him stand up, and he gazed at himself in the mirrors with which the chamber was adorned: Sans-pair could not recognize Torticoli. He was three feet taller, and his hair fell in large curls down to his shoulders. His mien was full of grace and dignity. His features were regular, his eyes sparkled with intelligence. In short, his transformation was worthy of a beneficent and grateful fairy.

"Oh, how I'd like to reveal your destiny to you," she said. "How I'd like to warn you about the shoals that fortune will put in your path and teach you how to avoid them. It would give me great pleasure to add that favor to the one I've just conferred on you. But this would offend the superior genius that guides you. Away, Prince, flee this tower, and remember that the fairy Benigne will always be your friend."

At these words the fairy, the palace, and all the wonders the prince had seen in it disappeared. He found himself in a dense forest more than a hundred miles from the tower in which his father had confined him.

Let us now leave him so that he can recover from his astonishment, and see, first, what happened to the guards that his father had ordered to look after him, and second, to the Princess Trognon.

The unfortunate warders were surprised when their prince did not call for his supper, and thus they entered his chamber. Since they did not find him, they began searching for him everywhere, fearing greatly that he had escaped. Upon realizing that their search was in vain, they were desperate, for they were sure that the king, who was such a terrible tyrant, would put them to death. After thinking over all the different means they could use to appease him, they decided that one of them would lie down on the bed and completely cover himself. Then they would say that the prince was very sick. Shortly afterward, they would pretend that he was dead and bury a wood log. That would get them out of their scrape. This solution seemed perfect, and they immediately began to put their plan into execution. The smallest of the guards was dressed up with a great hump and put in the prince's bed. Then the king was informed that his son was very ill. Since the king thought that he was told this only to make him compassionate, though, he was determined not to relax his severity. This was exactly what the trembling warders had desired, and the more they said about the prince's illness, the more the king expressed his indifference.

As for Princess Trognon, she arrived in a contraption only a foot high and was carried in a litter of straw. King Grim went to meet her, and when he saw her so deformed, seated in a bowl, her skin covered with scales like that of a codfish, her eyebrows joined together, her nose large and flat, and her mouth reaching to her ears, he could not restrain himself from saying, "You may be permitted, Princess Trognon, to despise my Torticoli, and certainly he's very ugly, but to tell the truth, you have him beat when it comes to ugliness."

"My lord," said the princess, "I'm not vain enough to be offended by your rude remarks. Perhaps this may even be your way of persuading me to love your charming Torticoli. But I want you to know that despite my miserable bowl and all my defects, I won't marry him. I prefer the title of Princess Trognon to that of Queen Torticoli."

The king was infuriated by this answer. "Let me assure you," he said, "I won't be contradicted. Your father was your master, and now I've become it since he's placed you in my hands."

"There are matters," the princess responded, "in which we have the power to choose. I warn you that I've been brought here against my will, and I'll regard you as my mortal enemy if you try to force me into this marriage."

The king was even more upset by this response and stomped out. He assigned her to an apartment in his palace and commanded her attendants to persuade her that the best thing she could do was to marry the prince. In the meantime the guards, who feared that the king might learn his son had escaped, made haste to tell him that he was dead. When he heard these tidings, they could not believe how distraught he became. In the midst of a screaming, howling rage, he accused Trognon of being the cause of his loss. So he sent her to the tower to take the place of his dearly departed son.

The poor princess was equally distressed and astonished at finding herself a prisoner. A courageous soul, she felt justified in commenting on such a harsh measure, imagining that the servants would repeat her complaints to the king. Quite the contrary. Nobody dared to mention the subject to him. In addition, she believed that she would be allowed to write to her father in regard to the mistreatment she was suffering and that he would come and rescue her. Her plans on that score were fruitless as well; her letters were intercepted and given to King Grim.

Since she lived with the hope of being rescued, she did not feel that tormented, and every day she went into the gallery to look at the stained windows. As extraordinary as the variety of illustrations may have been, nothing was more so than the pictures of herself in her bowl among them. "Since my arrival in this country," she said, "the artists have derived a strange pleasure out of painting me. Aren't there enough figures to ridicule without mine? Or is it simply that they want to highlight the beauty of that charming young shepherdess by contrasting her with my disfigurement?"

She then gazed at the portrait of a shepherd, whom she could not stop praising. "Aren't I to be pitied," she said, "for being degraded by nature to such an extent as I am? How happy are those who are handsome!" In saying this, tears came to her eyes. Catching a glimpse of herself in a looking glass, she suddenly turned away.

Imagine her astonishment when she discovered a little old woman in a hood behind her, who was half again as ugly as herself. What's more, the bowl in which she pushed herself along had more than twenty holes in it because it had been used so much.

"Princess," this old crone said to her, "I've been listening to your touching complaints and have come to offer you a choice between virtue and beauty. If you choose to be beautiful, you'll be a coquette, vain and utterly gay. If you choose to remain as you are, you'll be virtuous, respected, and utterly humble."

Trognon looked at the person who spoke to her and asked her if beauty was incompatible with virtue.

"No," replied the good woman, "but in your case, it's decreed that you possess only one of the two."

"Well, then," exclaimed Trognon firmly, "I prefer my ugliness to beauty."

"What! You'd prefer to frighten all those who look at you?"

"Yes, madam," the princess said, "I'd rather suffer all the misfortunes in the world than lack virtue."

"I brought with me my white-and-yellow muff expressly for this purpose," the fairy said. "By blowing on the yellow side, you'll become like that remarkable shepherdess who appeared so charming to you, and you'll be loved by that shepherd whose portrait has more than once attracted your attention. By blowing on the white side, you can guarantee that you'll continue along the path of virtue that you've so courageously taken."

"Ah, madam," replied the princess, "please grant me this favor. It will console me for all the contempt that people have shown me."

Thereupon the little old woman handed her the muff of beauty and virtue. Not wanting to make a mistake, Trognon blew on the white side and thanked the fairy, who immediately disappeared. The princess was delighted at the wise choice she had made, and however much she envied the incomparable beauty of the shepherdess in the window, she consoled herself with the thought that beauty passes like a dream; virtue is an eternal treasure, an unalterable quality that endures longer than life.

Still hoping that her father would lead a great army and rescue her from the tower, she awaited the moment with impatience and was dying to ascend to the dungeon of the tower to see the arrival of the help she expected. But how could she manage to climb to such a height? She moved around the floor of her apartment slower than a tortoise, and her women would have to carry her if she wanted to climb up stairs.

Nevertheless, she hit upon a rather clever plan. She knew that the clock was in the dungeon, so she took off the weights and put herself in their place. When they wound up the clock, she was hoisted to the top. Then she looked out of the window opening over the countryside with great anticipation, but she saw nothing approaching. Withdrawing to rest a little, she leaned against the wall that Torticoli—or, as we should now say, Prince Sans-pair—had pulled down and rebuilt but badly. Out tumbled the mortar and with it the golden ramrod, which made a tinkling sound as it fell near Trognon. Noticing it, she picked it up and examined it to determine its use. Since she was more perspicacious than most people, she quickly concluded that it was made to open the press, which had no lock to it. So she proceeded to open the press and was just as enraptured as the prince had been at the sight of all the rare and elegant things she found, for it contained four thousand drawers filled with jewels ancient and modern. At length she found the golden door, the box of carbuncle, and the hand swimming in blood. Shuddering, she would have thrown it away, but found herself checked from letting it go by some secret power. "Alas! What shall I do?" she cried sorrowfully. "I'd rather die than stay here any longer with this amputated hand!"

At that moment she heard a soft, sweet voice that said, "Take courage, Princess. Your happiness depends on this adventure."

"Oh? What can I do?" she replied, trembling.

"You must take this hand to your room," said the voice, "and hide it underneath the pillow of your bed. When you see an eagle, give it to him instantly."

Although the princess was terrified, the voice was so commanding that she did not hesitate to obey. She replaced the drawers and rare objects as she had found them without taking a single thing. Her guards were already in a state of fright, thinking that she had also escaped when they did not find her in her room. As they began looking for her, they were confounded at discovering her in a place they felt she could not possibly have reached except by enchantment.

The next three days she spent without seeing anything in particular. She did not dare to open the beautiful carbuncle box, for the sight of the amputated hand had given her a terrible fright. That night, however, she heard a noise at her window. She got up as best she could, dragged herself across the room, and opened the window. The eagle flew in and made a great noise with its wings to manifest its joy. She quickly gave it the hand, which it took in its talons, and in the next moment it had vanished. In its place stood the handsomest, most strapping young man she had ever seen. His forehead was encircled by a diadem, and his garments were sprinkled with jewels. In his hand he held a miniature. "Princess," he said to Trognon, "for two hundred years a perfidious enchanter has detained me here. Both of us loved the wonderful fairy, Benigne. When I was given preference, he became jealous. Since his art surpassed mine, he determined to use it to bring about my ruin. He commanded me in no uncertain terms never to see her anymore. Such a command went against my love and my rank. I threatened him, and my beloved was so offended at the enchanter's behavior that she in her turn forbade him from ever coming near her. Consequently, the cruel monster decided to punish us both.

"One day when I was by her side, gazing with delight at a portrait she had given me (yet finding it a thousand times less beautiful than its original), the enchanter appeared, and with one blow of his saber he chopped my hand off at the wrist. The fairy Benigne (as my queen is called) felt the anguish of this wound more keenly than I did. She fell onto her couch in a swoon, and immediately I found myself covered with feathers and transformed into an eagle. I was permitted to come and see the queen every day, and despite the fact that I could not approach or wake her, I still had the consolation of hearing her constantly breathe tender sighs and talk in her sleep about her dear Trasimene. I also knew that a prince would restore Benigne to the light of day at the end of two hundred years, and that a princess would give me back my original form by returning my lost hand to me. A famous fairy interested in your glory ordained that it should be so. She was the one who locked up my hand in the press of the dungeon so carefully and has given me the power to show you my gratitude today. Wish for anything, Princess, that can give you the greatest pleasure, and it shall be yours instantly."

"Great king," replied Trognon after a moment of silence, "if I have not answered you right away, it's not because I hesitate to do so, but because I'm not used to such surprising adventures like the present one. It seems more a dream than reality."

"No, madam," replied Trasimene, "it's not an illusion. You'll experience the effects as soon as you tell me what you desire."

"If I were to ask for everything I need to make me perfect," she said, "it would be difficult for you to satisfy me, no matter how much power you may have. So I'll confine myself to the most essential. Make my mind as beautiful as my body is ugly and deformed."

"Ah, Princess!" King Trasimene exclaimed. "You delight me by such a wise and noble choice. But whoever is able to make such a choice like that is already accomplished. Therefore, your body shall become as beautiful as your mind and soul."

So saying, he touched the princess with the miniature of the fairy. She heard all her bones go crick-crack, then stretch, and align into joint. When she stood up, she was tall, beautiful, and straight. Her skin was whiter than milk. All her features were regular. Her air was majestic yet modest, her countenance intelligent and pleasant.

"What a miracle!" she exclaimed. "Can this be me? Is it possible?"

"Yes, madam," Trasimene replied, "it is you. The wise choice you made to be virtuous has brought about the happy change you enjoy. What pleasure it is to me, after all I owe you, to think that I was destined to contribute to it. Never again will you be called Trognon. You are now Brilliante, for your intellect and your charms entitle you to this name."

Suddenly he disappeared, and without knowing how she had arrived there, the princess found herself on the bank of a little river beneath some shady trees. It was the most pleasant spot on earth. She had not yet seen her face, but the water was so clear that she discovered, to her astonishment, that she was the very shepherdess whose portrait she had admired so much in the windows of the gallery. Like her, she had on a white dress trimmed with fine lace, neater than any shepherdess had ever worn. Her waist was wrapped by a band of miniature roses and jasmine, and her hair was adorned with flowers. Nearby she found a gilt crook, and a flock of sheep feeding by the riverbanks knew her voice. Even their sheepdog appeared to be fond of her.

She could not help but be amazed by all these wonders. She had been born the ugliest of human beings and had lived like that up to that moment as a princess. Now she was fairer than the day, even though she was only a shepherdess. Of course, she felt a trifle sorry about the loss of her rank, and these various thoughts troubled her until she fell asleep. She had been awake all night, as I have already told you, and without being aware of it, the journey had covered a hundred miles so that she felt very tired. Her sheep and her dog gathered around and watched over her the way she should have watched over them. Though the noon sun was in full blaze, it did not disturb her because the leaves of the trees screened her from its scorching rays, and the fresh and delicate grass on which she had deposited herself seemed proud of such a beautiful burden. It was there that

> The gentle violets were seen
> Emulating other flowers,
> Peering above the grass so green,
> Scattering incense 'round in showers.

The birds sang sweet concerts, and the zephyrs held their breath so they would not disturb her.

From a distance a shepherd, exhausted by the heat of the sun, spotted this shady spot and hastened toward it. At the sight of the young shepherdess Brilliante, he was so struck with astonishment that he would have keeled over if he had not grabbed a nearby tree for support. She was the same creature whose beauty he had admired in the windows of the gallery and in the vellum pages of the illustrated manuscript. (No doubt the reader realizes this shepherd was no other than Prince Sans-pair.) An unknown power had kept him in this country, and everyone he encountered admired him, for his facility in all manner of skills, his good looks, and his intelligence distinguished him just as much among the other shepherds as his rank would have elsewhere.

He fixed his gaze on Brilliante with a feeling of curiosity and pleasure that he had never felt before. Kneeling beside her, he regarded the assemblage of charms that formed her perfection, and his heart was the first to pay tribute to her beauty that none could ever refuse. While he was steeped in thought, Brilliante awoke, and seeing Sans-pair near her in an elegant shepherd's dress, she instantly remembered him, for she had seen his portrait in the tower.

"Lovely shepherdess," he said, "what happy fate has led you here? You come, no doubt, to receive our worship and our allegiance. Ah, I feel already that I shall be eager above all others to offer to you my homage."

"No, shepherd," she said, "I don't presume to command honors that are not my due. I'd rather remain a simple shepherdess. I love my flock and my dog. Solitude has charms for me, and I desire none other."

"What's this? Young shepherdess, have you come here with the intention of concealing yourself from the mortals who inhabit these lands? Can it be that you'd hurt us so much? At least you could make me an exception, since I'm the first who has offered his service to you."

"No," replied Brilliante, "I won't see you any more than the rest, although I already feel some special esteem for you. But tell me, where I can find some respectable shepherdess with whom I may dwell? Since I'm a stranger here and of an age that does not permit me to live alone, I'd like to place myself under her protection."

Sans-pair was delighted at being entrusted with this task. He conducted her to a tidy cottage that had a thousand charms in its simplicity. It was inhabited by a shrunken old woman who rarely crossed the threshold because she could hardly walk.

"My good mother," said Sans-pair, presenting Brilliante, "here's an incomparable maiden whose appearance alone will make you young again."

The old woman embraced her and told her in a friendly way that she was welcome. Then she apologized that she did not have a better lodging to offer, but that at least she would find the proper affection and care.

"I didn't think I'd find such a favorable and polite reception here. I assure you, my good mother, that I'm delighted to be with you." Then she turned to the shepherd and said, "Please don't neglect to tell me your name so that I'll know to whom I'm indebted for this service."

"They call me Sans-pair," replied the prince, "but now I desire only to be known as your slave."

"And I'd like to know," said the little old woman, "the name of the shepherdess to whom I am offering this hospitality."

The princess told her she was called Brilliante. The old woman seemed charmed by such a lovely name, and Sans-pair said a hundred pretty things about it. Concerned that Brilliante might be hungry, the old shepherdess gave her a clean bowl of fresh milk with brown bread, freshly laid eggs, fresh butter, and a cream cheese. Sans-pair ran to his cottage and brought back strawberries, nuts, cherries, and other fruits. In order to prolong his stay with Brilliante, he asked permission to eat dinner with her. Alas, how difficult it would have been for her to have refused him! She took great pleasure in looking at him, and whatever coolness she affected, she felt stirred in his presence.

After he left her, she thought about him for a long time, and he about her. He saw her every day. He led his flock to the spot where she fed her own. He sang the most passionate songs in her company. He played the flute and bagpipe while she danced, and she displayed such grace and kept such perfect time that he could not show her enough admiration. They each reflected privately on the surprising chain of adventures that they had experienced, and each was filled with suspense. Sans-pair made sure to follow her wherever she went.

> In short, whenever he found the maid alone,
> He painted all the rapture possibly known
> That led fond hearts by Cupid to be united,
> And she discovered shortly that the flame,
> To which she scarcely dared to give a name,
> By Love himself had certainly been lighted.
> And seeing all the danger that she ran,
> An innocent and unprotected creature,
> She carefully avoided the dear man,
> Although it sadly went against her nature.
> In secret, too, her heart would oft implore,
> And ask to let him just adore her.
> Sans-pair, who could not for his life make out
> What caused the change he'd not been told about
> Sought her in vain, to satisfy his doubt:
> Brilliante was never to be seen or heard about.

She avoided him carefully and kept reproaching herself for feeling the way she did for him. "What now?" she exclaimed. "A miserable shepherd! Is this to be my fate? I preferred virtue to beauty. It appears that Heaven rewarded me for that choice by making me beautiful, but this has turned out to be a misfortune. Without these frivolous good looks the shepherd I'm avoiding would not try to please me, and I would escape the shame of blushing at the feelings I have for him." These sad reflections always ended in tears, and her pain was increased by the way she treated her charming shepherd.

Sans-pair was overcome by sadness as well, and he was tempted to reveal the greatness of his birth in the hope that vanity alone might induce her to listen to him more favorably. But he persuaded himself that she would not believe him, and what if she demanded proof? He was not in a position to give her any. "How cruel my fate!" he exclaimed. "Hideous as I was, I would have nevertheless succeeded my father to the throne. A great kingdom makes up for many defects. It would be useless for me now to present myself to him or to his subjects because there's no one among them who could recognize me. And for all the good fairy Benigne has done me in taking my name and ugliness from me, I'm now only a shepherd and the slave of an inexorable shepherdess who cannot stand me. Cruel Fortune!" he said, sighing, "either become more propitious or restore my deformity together with my previous indifference!"

Such were the sad lamentations that the lover and his mistress kept unknown from each other. But despite the fact that Brilliante persisted in avoiding Sans-pair, he was determined to speak to her and sought an excuse that would not offend her. So one day he took a little lamb, adorned it with ribbons and flowers, and put around its neck a collar of painted straw so neatly made that it was a small masterpiece. He attired himself in a robe of rose-colored taffeta covered with English point and carried a crook adorned with ribbons and a small basket. Dressed as he was, not a swain in the world would have dared compete with him. He found Brilliante seated on the bank of a rivulet flowing gently through the thickest part of the wood. Her sheep were scattered about, browsing, for the shepherdess's deep melancholy prevented her from looking after them. Approaching her timidly, Sans-pair gave her the little lamb and gazed at her tenderly. "What have I done, beautiful shepherdess," he said, "to deserve such terrible signs of your aversion? You reproach your eyes when they pay me the least bit of attention. Do my feelings offend you so much that you must flee me? Can you desire anyone more pure or more faithful? Haven't my words and deeds always been marked by respect as well as ardor? But no doubt you love someone else. Your heart is destined for another."

She replied to him immediately:

"Shepherd, if I shun your view,
Should that give alarm to you?
By my flight you can sure tell
I but fear to love too well.
Were my absence caused by hate,
Would my anguish be as great?
Reason would take hold of me,
Love from reason would divorce me.
Even now my fluttering heart
Fails me when I should depart.
Oh, when love becomes extreme,
Stern indeed does duty seem.
And how slowly do we move,
When we flee from those we love!

> Adieu, fair shepherd, I must away.
> I must leave this fatal spot,
> And die without you, though I may,
> If you love me, follow not!"

Upon saying this, Brilliante fled from him. The enamored, desperate prince would have followed her, but his grief so overpowered him that he fainted at the foot of a tree.

Ah, severe and too cruel virtue! Why should you fear a man who cherishes you so much? It is not in his makeup to slight you, and his feelings are perfectly innocent. But the princess doubted herself as much as she doubted him. She could not help seeing the charming shepherd's merits, and yet she was well aware that one must avoid that which appears too pleasant.

Never had anyone in the world undertaken such a task as she undertook at that moment. She tore herself away from the most tender, beloved object she had ever seen in her life! Unable to resist looking back to see if he followed, she saw him fall half dead. Though she loved him, she denied herself the consolation of rescuing him. When she reached the open plain, she lifted up her eyes pitifully, unfolded her arms, and exclaimed, "O virtue! O glory! O grandeur! I sacrifice my happiness to you. O destiny! O Trasimene! I renounce my fatal beauty! Give me back my ugliness, or restore me the lover I am abandoning without causing me to blush!"

After saying this, she stopped, uncertain whether or not she should retrace her steps. Her heart prompted her to reenter the wood, but her virtue triumphed over her emotions. She made the noble resolution never to see him again.

Ever since she had been brought to this spot, she had heard talk of a famous enchanter who lived in a castle that he and his sister had built on the shore of an island. Everyone talked about their great knowledge, which produced some new marvel every day. Brilliante thought that nothing less than magic would efface the image of the charming shepherd from her heart, and so, without saying anything to her charitable hostess, who had treated her like a daughter, she set out on her way. So absorbed was she by her sorrow that she never considered the danger she ran, a beautiful young girl traveling all alone. She rested neither day nor night, nor did she eat or drink, for she was most anxious to reach the castle and be cured of her love. But in passing through a wood, she heard someone singing. Since she thought she heard her own name—moreover, she recognized the voice of one of her companions—she stopped to listen:

> "Sans-pair, of all the village swains
> The handsomest in form and feature,
> Soon came to wear a shepherdess's chains,

Brilliante in name as well as nature.
By every gentle art he sought
To move his enslaver so he could adore her,
But the innocent lass knew nought
Of love, despite the hints he gave her.
Yet in his absence she would sigh,
As though she'd lost her peace forever.
It wasn't often, by the by,
Because he scarcely ever left her.
Stretched on the green turf at her feet,
He sang and piped in rustic fashion:
The maiden confessed his music was sweet,
And caught the tune if not the passion."

"Ah, this is too much!" Brilliante exclaimed, bursting into tears. "Imprudent shepherd, you've boasted of the innocent favors I've shown you.
You've dared to suppose that my weak heart was influenced more by your
feelings than by my own sense of duty. You've made others the confidants
of your mistaken hopes and have made me the theme of idle songs
throughout the woods and meadows." So disturbed was she by this incident
that she believed she could regard Sans-pair with indifference and perhaps
with aversion. "It's unnecessary," she continued, "for me to search any
farther for remedies for my pain. I have nothing to fear from a shepherd in
whom I see so little merit. I'll return to the village accompanied by the
shepherdess whose song I've been listening to." She called to her as loudly
as she could, but nobody answered her. Then again, she kept hearing the
voice every now and then singing very near her, and she became uneasy
and alarmed. The fact is, the forest belonged to the enchanter, and nobody
could pass through it without meeting with some adventure.

More bewildered than ever, Brilliante hastened to make her way out of
the wood. "Has the shepherd I feared become so less threatening to me that
I can now venture to see him again? Or is my heart in league with him and
trying to deceive me? Oh, let me flee, let me flee him! This is the best
thing to do for a princess as unfortunate as I!"

Resuming her journey to the enchanter's castle, she arrived at it and
entered without any obstacle. She crossed several large courts so overgrown
by long grass and brambles that it seemed as if no one had walked on them
for a hundred years. She pushed her way through them with her hands,
scratching them in several places, then entered a hall that admitted light
only through a small hole. The walls were draped with the wings of bats; in
lieu of chandeliers, a dozen live cats were dangling from the ceiling,
screeching enough to drive one crazy; on a long table perched twelve large
mice. Their tails were tied to the table, and each one had a piece of bacon
before it that it could not reach. Thus the cats saw the mice without being

able to eat them, and the mice trembled at the cats while the bacon made them desperate with hunger.

The princess was looking at these tormented animals when she saw the enchanter enter in a long black robe. His head was adorned by a crocodile as a type of a cap, and never in the world has there been such a horrible headdress as this. The old man wore spectacles and carried a whip made of twenty long, live serpents. Oh, how frightened the princess was! How she missed her shepherd, her sheep, and her dog at that moment! She thought only of fleeing, and without saying a word to this terrible man, she ran to the door, but it was immediately covered with spider webs. As soon as she lifted one, she found another, and on lifting that, a third appeared. Then she lifted that and saw a new one, under which was another. In short, there were countless numbers of these villainous doorkeepers made of spider webs.

The poor princess was worn out with fatigue, for her arms were not strong enough to hold up the webs. She would have sat on the floor to rest, but was quickly compelled to rise again by long, sharp thorns growing from it. Again she tried to escape, but could not untangle the webs. The wicked old man observed her and laughed until he almost choked. At length he called to her, "You could spend the rest of your life without succeeding in your goal. You seem to me younger and more beautiful than the fairest lady I've ever seen. If you'll marry me, I'll give you these twelve cats that you see hung up on the ceiling, and you can do what you want with them. These twelve mice on the table here shall be yours as well. The cats were once princes and the mice princesses. At one time or another the little rogues had the honor of pleasing me (for I've always been charming and gallant), but none would love me. These princes were rivals of mine more favored than I was. Jealousy took possession of me. I found means to entice them here, and as fast as I caught them, I transformed them into cats and mice. The most amusing part of the business is that they hate each other as much as they previously loved each other, so that I can scarcely imagine a more complete vengeance."

"Oh, my lord," Brilliante exclaimed, "change me into a mouse. I deserve it just as much as these poor princesses."

"What's this, my little shepherdess?" said the magician. "You won't love me?"

"I've decided never to love."

"Oh, how silly you are," the magician responded. "I'll look after you marvelously. I'll tell you stories. I'll give you the most beautiful dresses in the world. You'll never go anywhere except in a coach or on cushions. You'll be called 'madam.' "

"I've decided never to love," the princess repeated.

"You'd better watch what you're saying!" cried the enchanter angrily. "You'll repent it for many a long day!"

"No matter what," Brilliante replied, "I've decided never to love."

"Aha, you cold creature," he said, touching her. "Since you don't want to love, I'm going to make you into a unique species. In the future you'll be neither flesh nor fish; you'll have neither blood nor bones. You shall be green because you are still in your greenest youth; you shall be agile and sprightly; you shall live in the fields, as you have done; and they shall call you grasshopper."

All of a sudden Princess Brilliante became the most beautiful grasshopper in the world and took advantage of her liberty by skipping quickly into the garden. As soon as she was able to ponder her situation, she exclaimed mournfully, "Oh, my bowl, my dear bowl! What has become of you? Take a look at the result of your promises, Trasimene. Is this, then, the fate that has been in store for me these two hundred years? A beauty as fleeting as that of spring flowers and in the end, a dress of green crape, a singular form neither flesh nor fish, and without blood or bones. I'm very unfortunate! Alas, a crown would have covered all my defects. I would have found a husband worthy of me, and if I had remained a shepherdess, the charming Sans-pair would have kept wishing to win my heart. Now he's fully revenged for my unjust disdain. Here I am, a grasshopper! Doomed to chirrup day and night, while my heart, full of bitterness, invites me to weep."

So did the grasshopper lament as she lay hidden among the tender grass that bordered the banks of a rivulet. But what had Prince Sans-pair been doing after he had been left behind by his adorable shepherdess? The cruel way in which she had parted wounded him so deeply that he did not have the power to follow her and fainted. For a long time he remained unconscious at the foot of the tree where Brilliante had seen him fall. At length the coolness of the ground, or some unknown power, brought him to himself. He did not dare to seek her at her home that day, and his mind kept repeating the words she had said to him,

> "Were my absence caused by hate,
> Would my anguish be as great?"

These flattering words gave him hope, and he believed that time and attention might help make her more grateful. The next day, however, after he went to the old shepherdess with whom Brilliante was staying and heard that she had not been seen since the previous evening, he thought he would die of anxiety. When he went outside, he was overcome by a thousand conflicting thoughts and sat sadly by the side of the river. A hundred times he was tempted to throw himself into the water and put an end to his misery. Finally he took a knife and scratched the following verses on the bark of a nettle tree:

Lovely fountain, river clear,
Smiling valley, fertile plain,
Scenes that once to me were dear,
Alas, you but increase my pain!
The beautiful maid for whom I burn,
To whom your every charm you owe,
Has left you, never to return,
And me to weep forevermore!
When morning in the east appears,
She brings my spirit no relief.
No sun can dry my flood of tears,
No night in slumber lull my grief.
Forgive me, oh, you gentle tree,
That on your breast her name I mark.
How slight the wound to that which she,
Engraved upon my heart so stark.
My steel has left your life untouched.
Her cipher makes you seem more fair.
Yet I have not been left with much,
And sigh for death right now and here. . . .

He stopped writing as a little old woman approached him. She wore a farthingale and had a ruff around her neck, and a roll under her white hair,

and a velvet cap. Her aged countenance had a venerable air. "My son," she said to him, "you've been uttering such bitter cries of grief. Tell me, please, what's caused your sorrow?"

"Alas, good mother," Sans-pair answered, "I'm bemoaning the absence of a lovely shepherdess who's fled from me. I've decided to search all over the world until I find her."

"Go in that direction, my son," the old woman said, pointing toward the castle where poor Brilliante had become a grasshopper. "I suspect you won't have to look for her very long."

Sans-pair thanked her and implored Cupid to stand by his side. The prince met with no adventure on the road of any consequence, but once he had reached the wood of the magician and his sister, he thought he spied his shepherdess. Quickly he began racing after her, only to find the distance separating them growing ever larger. "Brilliante!" he cried. "Adorable Brilliante! Stop for one moment! Please listen to me!" The phantom flitted even faster, and he spent the remainder of the day pursuing it.

When night fell, he saw numerous lights in the castle and, hoping he might find his shepherdess there, ran toward it and entered without any difficulty. After he climbed a staircase, he saw in a magnificent salon a tall old fairy with horrid skin. Her eyes resembled two guttered lamps, and he could see through her jaws. Her arms were like laths, her fingers like knitting needles, and a skin of black shagreen covered her skeleton. Yet despite all this, she wore rouge and patches, pink and green ribbons, a mantle of silver brocade, a crown of diamonds on her head, and a great many jewels all over.

"At last, Prince," she said, "you've arrived where I have long wished to see you. Think no more of your little shepherdess. A passion for one so much your inferior should make you blush. I'm the queen of meteors. I'm your friend and can be of infinite service to you if you love me."

"Love you!" exclaimed the prince, looking at her contemptuously. "Love you, madam? Am I master of my heart? No, I'll never be unfaithful and even if I could change, you'd never be the object of my affections. Choose among your meteors some force that suits you. Love the air, love the winds, but leave mortals in peace."

The fairy was fiercely angry. With two blows of her wand she filled the gallery with frightful monsters, and the prince was obliged to use all his skill and courage to combat them. Some had several heads and arms; others took the forms of centaurs and sirens. There were lions with human faces, sphinxes, and flying dragons. Sans-pair had as weapons only his crook and a small boar spear that he had taken when he had set out on his journey. The tall fairy interrupted the combat every now and then to ask him if he would love her. He always answered that he had sworn to be faithful and could not change.

Provoked by his steadfast position, she conjured up the form of Brilliante. "Look now!" she cried. "You see your mistress at the end of this gallery. Think about what you're about to do. If you refuse to marry me, she'll be torn to pieces by tigers before your eyes."

"Ah, madam," the prince cried, flinging himself at her feet, "I'd die with pleasure to save my beloved mistress. Spare her life and take mine."

"I don't want your life, traitor," said the fairy. "It's your heart and your hand I demand."

While they were talking, the prince heard the voice of his shepherdess complaining. "Are you going to let me be devoured?" she asked him. "If you love me, make sure you do what the queen commands."

The poor prince hesitated and then exclaimed, "Have you abandoned me, Benigne, after all your promises? Come, oh, come to our aid!" No sooner had he spoken than he heard a voice in the air uttering these words most distinctly:

"Leave all to fate, but be constant and seek the golden branch."

The tall fairy, who believed the assistance of so many illusions would assure her of victory, thought she would go mad at finding such a formidable obstacle as the protection of Benigne. "Get out of my sight, wretched and obstinate prince!" she cried. "Since your heart is so enflamed, become a cricket fond of heat and fire!"

Instantly, the marvelously handsome Prince Sans-pair became a dingy cricket who would have burned himself alive in the nearest oven had he not remembered the friendly voice that had encouraged him. "I must seek the golden branch," he said. "Perhaps that will un-cricket me. Ah, if I find my shepherdess there, my happiness will be complete!"

The cricket quickly left the fatal palace, and without knowing which way to go, he commended himself to the protection of the fairy Benigne and set off without ceremony or weapons, for a cricket fears neither robbers nor accidents. At his first resting place, a hole in the trunk of a tree, he found a grasshopper that was so melancholy she could not sing. It never occurred to the cricket that she was a reasoning, intelligent creature and said to her, "Where are you going, friend grasshopper?"

"And you, friend cricket, where are you heading?" she asked in turn.

This reply astonished the enamored cricket very much. "What!" he said. "Can you speak?"

"Why, you speak well enough yourself," she cried. "Do you think a grasshopper has less right to talk than a cricket?"

"I can talk," said the cricket, "because I'm a man."

"And by the same rule," said the grasshopper, "I ought to talk more than you because I'm a woman."

"Have you experienced the same fate as mine?"

"No doubt."

"But, once more, where are you going?" the cricket responded. "I'd be delighted to know that we were destined to stay together a long time."

"I heard an unknown voice in the air," she replied. "It said, 'Leave all to fate and seek the golden branch.' I thought this could only be addressed to me, and without pausing, I set out on my journey, though I have no idea where to go."

Their conversation was interrupted by two mice that came running as fast as they could. They made for the hole at the foot of the tree and flung themselves in headfirst, nearly smothering friend cricket and friend grasshopper, who got out of their way as best they could by squeezing into a corner.

"Ah, madam," exclaimed the biggest mouse, "I've got a pain in my side from running so fast. How is your highness?"

"I've pulled my tail off," replied the younger mouse, "otherwise I would have had to remain on the old sorcerer's table. But did you notice how he pursued us? How happy we are to have escaped from his infernal palace!"

"I'm rather afraid of the cats and the mousetraps, my princess," continued the large mouse, "and I fervently pray that we'll soon be able to reach the golden branch."

"Then you know the road to it?" her mousefied highness asked.

"Know it, madam? As well as I know the road to my own house," replied the other. "It's a wonderful branch. Just one of its leaves would make you rich forever. It provides you with money, it breaks magic spells, it gives beauty and preserves youth. We must set out tomorrow before daybreak."

"We shall have the honor of accompanying you, ladies," said the grasshopper, "if you have no objection. I and the honest cricket whom you see here. Like you, we are pilgrims on our way to the golden branch."

A great many compliments were exchanged between them, for the mice were princesses whom the wicked enchanter had tied to his table, and the high breeding of the cricket and the grasshopper was quite apparent immediately. They all awoke early and set out in solemn silence, for they were afraid some hunters might hear them talking and catch them and put them in a cage. In due time they arrived at a wonderful garden, and planted in the middle of it was the golden branch. The walks contained not sand, but were strewn with small oriental pearls rounder than peas. The roses were crimson diamonds and the leaves were emeralds; pomegranate blossoms were garnets and marigolds topazes, the jonquils yellow brilliants, the violets sapphires, the bluebells turquoises, and the tulips, amethysts, opals, and diamonds. In short, the number and variety of these beautiful flowers were more dazzling than the sun.

The golden branch was the same one Prince Sans-pair had received from the eagle and used to touch the fairy Benigne when she had been enchanted. It had grown as high as the highest trees around it and bore rubies in the form of cherries. As soon as the cricket, grasshopper, and two mice approached it, they recovered their natural forms. What joy filled the breast of the enamored prince at the sight of his beautiful shepherdess! He flung himself at her feet and was about to express all he felt at such a pleasant and unexpected surprise when Queen Benigne and King Trasimene appeared in supreme splendor, for everything matched the magnificence of the garden. Four cupids armed cap-a-pie, with bows at their sides and quivers on their shoulders, supported with their arrows a canopy of gold and blue brocade, under which one could see two splendid crowns.

"Come here, charming lovers," said the queen, extending her arms toward them. "Come and receive from our hands the crowns that your virtue, birth, and constancy deserve. Your toils are about to change into pleasures. Princess Brilliante," she continued, "the shepherd so alarming to your heart is the very prince who was chosen for you by your father and his father as well. He did not die in the tower. Greet him as your husband, and let me look after your happiness and tranquillity."

Delighted, the princess flung herself into Benigne's arms. The tears that flowed down her cheeks showed her extreme joy and rendered her speechless. Sans-pair knelt before the generous fairy, respectfully kissed her hands, and uttered a thousand unconnected sentences. Trasimene embraced him heartily, and Benigne informed them in a few words that she had hardly ever left their sides—it had been she who had suggested to Brilliante that she blow into the white and yellow muff, she who had assumed the form of an old shepherdess in order to take in the princess as a lodger, and she also who had directed the prince which way to go in search of his shepherdess.

"It's true," she continued, "that you have undergone sufferings that I might have spared you had it been in my power, but the pleasures of love must be bought at some cost."

Just then sweet music floated all around them. The cupids hastened to crown the young lovers; the marriage rites were performed; and during the ceremony the two princesses, who had recovered their forms, implored the fairy to use her power to rescue the other unfortunate mice and cats who languished in despair in the enchanter's castle.

"I can refuse you nothing on such a day as this," answered the fairy. So saying, she struck the golden branch three times, and all who had been confined in the castle appeared in their natural forms—each lover finding his mistress. The generous fairy, desirous that nothing should be lacking for the fete, allowed the entire contents of the press in the dungeon to be divided among the company. The value of this present was more than that of ten kingdoms in those days, and you can easily imagine their satisfaction and gratitude. Benigne and Trasimene then crowned this great work by an act of generosity that surpassed all that had come before. They declared that in the future the palace and garden of the golden branch was to be the property of King Sans-pair and Queen Brilliante. A hundred other sovereigns were made their tributaries, and a hundred kingdoms their dependencies.

> When Brilliante had long since suffered,
> A fairy came to see her then,
> And beauty was what she offered,
> A sure temptation to nine maids out of ten:
> Witness the airs, the trouble, and the cost
> To gain or keep it the fair sex has created.
> The temptation, however, on Brilliante was lost.
> She preferred virtue and was well rewarded.
> The rose and lily on the cheek will die
> As quickly as the flowers with which they vie,
> But beauties of celestial virtue born,
> Are immortal as the soul they adorn.

THE RAM

IN those happy times when fairies still existed, there reigned a king who had three daughters. Young and beautiful, all three possessed considerable qualities, but the youngest was the most charming and the favorite by far. Indeed, they called her Merveilleuse. Her father gave her more gowns and ribbons in a month than he gave the others in a year, and she was so good-natured that she shared everything with them so that there might be no misunderstandings.

Now, the king had some evil neighbors who grew tired of keeping peace with him. Therefore, they formed a powerful alliance and compelled him to arm his country in self-defence. Once he had raised a large army, he assumed command and rode off to battle. The three princesses remained with their tutors in a castle, and every day they received good news about the king's exploits. One time he took a city, another he won a battle. Finally he succeeded in routing his enemies and driving them out of his dominions. Then he returned to the castle as fast as he could to see his little Merveilleuse, whom he adored so much.

The three princesses had ordered three satin gowns to be made for themselves—one green, one blue, one white. Jewels were selected to match their dresses—the green enriched with emeralds, the blue with turquoises, and the white with diamonds. Thus attired, they went to meet the king, singing the following verses, which they had written to celebrate his victories:

> "With conquest crowned on many a glorious plain,
> What joy to greet our king and sire again!
> Welcome him back, victorious, to these halls,
> With new delights and countless festivals.
> Let shouts of joy and songs of triumph prove
> His people's loyalty, his daughters' love!"

When the king saw his lovely daughters in such splendid attire, he embraced them all tenderly, but caressed Merveilleuse more than the others. A magnificent banquet was set up, and the king and his three daughters sat down to eat. Since it was his habit to draw inferences from everything, he said to the eldest, "Tell me, please, why have you put on a green gown?"

"Sire," she answered, "having heard of your achievements, I imagined that green would express the joy and hope with which your return inspired me."

"That is very prettily said," the king exclaimed. "And you, my child," he continued, "why are you wearing a blue gown?"

"My liege," the princess said, "I want to indicate that we should constantly implore the gods to protect you. Moreover, your sight is to me like that of Heaven and all the Heavenly Host."

"You speak like an oracle," the king said. "And you, Merveilleuse, why have you dressed yourself in white?"

"Because, sire," she answered, "it becomes me better than any other color."

"What?" the king cried, very much offended. "Was that your only motive, you little coquette?"

"My motive was to please you," said the princess. "It seems to me that I ought to have no other."

The king, who loved her dearly, was so perfectly satisfied with this explanation that he declared himself quite pleased by the little turn she had given to her meaning and the art with which she had at first concealed the compliment.

"Now, then," he said, "I've had an excellent supper, but I won't yet go to bed. Tell me what you all dreamed of the night before my return."

The eldest said she had dreamed that he had brought her a gown with gold and jewels that glistened brighter than the sun. The second said she had dreamed he had brought her a golden distaff to spin herself some shifts. The youngest said she had dreamed that he had married off her second sister and on the wedding day he had offered her a golden vase and said, "Merveilleuse, come here. Come here so you can wash."

Infuriated by this dream, the king knit his brow and made such an exceedingly wry face that everybody saw he was enraged. He retired to his room and flung himself onto the bed, but he could not forget his daughter's dream. "This insolent creature," he said, "she wants to turn me into her servant. I wouldn't be at all surprised if she put on that white satin dress without thinking of me at all. She doesn't take me seriously. But I'll frustrate her wicked designs while there's still time." He rose in a fury, and though it was still dark outside, he sent for the captain of his guards and said, "You heard Merveilleuse's dream. It forecasts strange things against me. I command you to seize her immediately, take her into the forest, and kill her. Afterward, you're to bring me her heart and tongue so I'll be sure you haven't deceived me. If you fail, I'll have you put to death in the most cruel manner imaginable."

The captain of the guards was astounded by this barbarous order. He did not dare argue with the king, however, for fear of increasing his rage and causing him to give the horrifying order to another. He assured him he would take the princess and kill her and bring him her heart and tongue.

The captain strode directly to the princess's apartment, where he had some difficulty in obtaining permission to enter, for it was still quite early. He informed Merveilleuse that the king desired to see her. She arose immediately, and a tiny Moorish girl named Patypata carried her train. A young ape and a little dog who always accompanied her also ran after her. The ape was called Grabugeon and the little dog, Tintin. The captain of the guards made Merveilleuse descend into the garden, where he told her the king was taking in the fresh morning air. She entered it, and the captain pretended to look for the king. When he did not find him, he said, "No doubt his majesty has walked farther on into the wood." He opened a small gate and led the princess into the forest. It was just getting light, and the princess saw that her escort had tears in his eyes and was so dejected that he could not speak.

"What's the matter?" she inquired kindly. "You seem very much distressed."

"Ah, madam," he exclaimed, "how could I be otherwise, for I've been given the most dreadful order that has even been given! The king has commanded me to kill you in this forest and to take your heart and tongue to him. If I fail to do so, he will put me to death."

Turning pale with terror, the poor princess began to weep softly, like a lamb about to be sacrificed. Then she turned her beautiful eyes to the captain of the guards and looked at him without anger. "Do you really have the heart to kill me?" she asked. "I've never done you any harm, and I've always spoken well of you to the king. If I really deserved my father's hate, I'd suffer the consequences without a murmur. But alas, I've always shown him so much respect and affection that he has no just reason to complain."

"Fear not, beautiful princess," said the captain, "I'm incapable of such a barbarous deed. I'd rather have him carry out his threat and kill me. But if I were to kill myself, you would be no better off. We must find some way that will enable me to return to the king and convince him you're dead."

"What way is there?" asked Merveilleuse. "He's ordered you to bring him my heart and tongue, and if you don't, he won't believe you."

Patypata had witnessed everything, though neither the captain nor the princess was aware of her presence because they were so overcome by sadness. Advancing courageously, she threw herself at Merveilleuse's feet. "Madam," she said, "I want to offer you my life. You must kill me. I'd be most happy to die for such a good mistress."

"Oh, I could never permit it, my dear Patypata!" the princess said, kissing her. "After such an affectionate proof of your friendship, your life is as dear to me as my own."

Then Grabugeon stepped forward and said, "You have good reason, Princess, to love such a faithful slave as Patypata. She can be of much more use to you than I. Now it's my turn to offer you my heart and tongue with joy, for I wish to immortalize myself in the annals of the empire of monkeys."

"Ah, my darling Grabugeon," Merveilleuse replied, "I can't bear the idea of taking your life."

"I'd find it intolerable," exclaimed Tintin, "good little dog as I am, if anyone but myself were to sacrifice his life for my mistress. Either I die or nobody dies."

Upon saying this, a geat dispute arose between Patypata, Grabugeon, and Tintin, and they exchanged a great many harsh words. At last Grabugeon, who was quicker than the others, scampered up to the top of a tree and flung herself down headfirst, killing herself on the spot. As much as the princess grieved over her loss, she agreed to let the captain of the guards cut out her tongue since the poor thing was dead. To their dismay, however, it was so small (for the creature was not much bigger than one's fist) that they felt certain the king would not be deceived by it.

"Alas, my dear little ape," cried the princess, "there you lie, and your sacrifice hasn't saved my life!"

"That honor has been reserved for me," interrupted the Moor, and as she spoke, she snatched the knife that had been used on Grabugeon and plunged it into her bosom. The captain of the guards would have taken her tongue, but it was so black that he knew he would not be able to deceive the king with it.

"Look at my misfortune!" the princess said tearfully. "I lose all those I love, and yet my fate remains unchanged."

"Had you accepted my offer," Tintin said, "you would have only had to mourn my loss, and I would have had the satisfaction of being the only one mourned."

Merveilleuse kissed her little dog and wept such bitter tears over him that she became quite exhausted. She turned hastily away, and when she ventured to look around again, her escort was gone, and she found herself alone with the dead bodies of her Moor, her ape, and her little dog. She could not leave the spot until she had buried them in a hole that she found by chance at the foot of a tree. Afterward she scratched these words into the tree:

> Three faithful friends lie buried in this grave.
> They saved my life with deeds most brave.

Then she began to think about her own safety. It was certainly dangerous for her to remain in that forest, especially since it was so close to her father's castle. The first person who saw her would recognize her. Then again, she might be attacked and devoured like a chicken by the lions and wolves that infested it. So she set off walking as fast as she could.

The forest was so enormous, however, and the sun so strong that she was soon nearly ready to collapse from heat, fear, and exhaustion. She looked around in every direction, but was unable to see an end to the woods. Every movement frightened her. She continually imagined that the king was in hot pursuit, seeking to kill her. Indeed, she uttered so many cries of woe that it is impossible to repeat them all here.

As she walked on, not following any particular path, the thickets tore her beautiful dress and scratched her ivory skin. At last she heard some sheep bleating. "It is probably some shepherds with their flocks," she said. "Perhaps they'll be able to direct me to a village where I can disguise myself in peasant garb. Alas, kings and queens are not always the happiest people in the world! Who in all this kingdom would have ever believed that I'd become a fugitive, that my father would want to take my life without reason, and that I'd have to disguise myself to save my neck?"

Even as she made these remarks, she was approaching the spot where she had heard the bleating. Upon reaching an open glade encircled by trees, she was astonished to see a large ram with gilded horns and fleece whiter than snow. He had a garland of flowers around his neck, his legs were entwined with ropes of enormous pearls, and chains of diamonds hung all about him. As he lay on a couch of orange blossoms, a pavilion of gold cloth suspended in the air sheltered him from the rays of the sun. There were a hundred brightly decked sheep all around him, and instead of browsing on grass, some were having coffee, sherbet, ices, and lemonade; others, strawberries and cream, and preserves. Some were playing at *basset*, others at *lansquenet*. Several wore collars of gold ornamented with numerous fine emblems, earrings, ribbons, and flowers. Merveilleuse was so astounded that she remained stock still. Her eyes were roving in search of the shepherd in charge of this extraordinary flock when the beautiful ram ran over to her in a sprightly manner. "Approach, divine princess," he said. "You have nothing to fear from such gentle and peaceful animals of our kind."

"What a miracle! A talking ram!" the princess exclaimed.

"What's that, madam?" the ram replied. "Your ape and your little dog spoke very prettily. Why weren't you surprised by that?"

"A fairy endowed them with the gift of speech, which made everything less miraculous," Merveilleuse stated.

"Perhaps we had a similar experience," the ram answered, smiling sheepishly. "But what caused you to come our way, my princess?"

"A thousand misfortunes, my lord ram," she said to him. "I'm the most unhappy person in the world. I'm seeking a place of refuge from my father's fury."

"Come, madam," the ram replied, "come with me. I can offer you one that will be known only by you, and you will be completely in charge of everything there."

"I can't follow you," Merveilleuse said. "I'm about to die from exhaustion."

The ram with golden horns called for his chariot, and immediately six goats were led forward, harnessed to a pumpkin of such tremendous size that two persons could sit in it with the greatest ease. The hollowed-out pumpkin was dry inside and fitted with splendid down cushions and lined all over with velvet. Getting into the pumpkin, the princess was astounded by such a unique equipage. The master ram seated himself in the pumpkin beside her, and the goats took them at full gallop to a cave. The entrance was blocked by a large stone, but the golden-horned ram touched the stone with his foot and it fell away at once. He told the princess, "Enter without fear."

She imagined that the cave would be a horrible place, and if she had not been so afraid of being captured, nothing would have induced her to go into it, but her fear was so great that she would have thrown herself into even a well to avoid capture. So she followed the ram without hesitation. He walked in front of her to show her the way down, which ran so very deep that she thought she was going at least to the other end of the earth. At moments she feared he was conducting her to the region of the dead.

Suddenly she came upon a vast meadow bursting with a thousand different flowers, whose sweet aroma surpassed that of any she had ever smelled. A broad river of orange-flower water flowed around it; fountains of Spanish wine, rossolis, hippocras, and a thousand other liqueurs formed charming cascades and rivulets. The meadow was home to entire avenues of unusual trees, and partridges greased and dressed better than those eaten at the restaurant La Guerbois hung from the branches. In other avenues the branches were festooned with quails, young rabbits, turkeys, chickens, pheasants, and ortolans. In certain parts, where from afar the atmosphere appeared hazy, it rained bisques d'écrevisse and other soups, foies gras, ragouts of sweetbreads, white puddings, sausages, tarts, patties, jam, and marmalade. There were also louis d'ors, crowns, pearls, and diamonds. Showers so rare—and so useful—would no doubt have attracted excellent company if the great ram had been more inclined to mix in general society, but all the chronicles in which he is mentioned concur in assuring us that he was as reserved as a Roman senator.

Merveilleuse had arrived in this beautiful region during the finest time of the year. Thus, she was fortunate to see that there was also a palace, surrounded by long rows of orange trees, jasmines, honeysuckles, and tiny musk roses, whose interlaced branches formed cabinets, halls, and chambers, all hung with gold and silver gauze and furnished with large mirrors, chandeliers, and remarkable paintings. The master ram told the princess to consider herself the sovereign of this realm. "I have been suffering from grief for many years, and it is now up to you to make me forget all my misfortunes."

"Your behavior is so generous, charming ram," she said, "and everything I see appears so extraordinary that I don't know what to make of it."

No sooner had she uttered these words than a group of the most remarkable and beautiful nymphs appeared before her. They gave her fruit in baskets of amber, but when she stepped toward them, they shrank back slightly. When she extended her hands to touch them, she felt nothing—they were only phantoms. "What does this mean?" she exclaimed. "Who are these things around me?" She began to weep, and King Ram (for so they called him), who had left her momentarily, returned and found her in tears, causing him such despair that he felt he would die at her feet.

"What's the matter, lovely princess?" he inquired. "Has anyone here been disrespectful to you?"

"No," she answered, "I can't complain. It's only that I'm not accustomed to living among the dead and with sheep that talk. Everything here frightens me, and though I'm greatly obliged to you for bringing me here, I'd be even more obliged if you'd bring me back into the world."

"Don't be alarmed," the ram replied. "Please deign to listen to me calmly, and you shall hear my sad story:

I was born to inherit a throne. A long line of kings, my ancestors, had ensured that the kingdom I'd be taking over was the finest in the universe. My subjects loved me. Feared and envied by my neighbors, I was thus justly respected. It was said that no king had ever been more worthy of such homage, and my physical appearance was not without its attractions as well.

I was extremely fond of hunting, and once, when I was zealously pursuing a stag, I became separated from my attendants. Suddenly seeing the stag plunge into a pond, I spurred my horse in after him. This was as unwise as it was bold. But instead of the coldness of water, I felt an extraordinary heat. The pond dried up, and through an opening gushing with terrible flames I fell to the bottom of a precipice, where nothing was to be seen but fire.

I thought I was lost when I suddenly heard a voice saying, "No less fire could warm your heart, ungrateful one!"

"Hah! Who is it that complains of my coldness?" I said.

"An unfortunate who adores you without hope," the voice replied.

Just then the flames were extinguished, and I perceived a fairy whose age and ugliness had horrified me ever since I had known her in my early childhood. She was leaning on a young slave of incomparable beauty, and the golden chains she wore sufficiently indicated who she was. "What miracle is this, Ragotte?" I asked her (since that was the fairy's name). "Have you really ordered this?"

"Who else should have ordered it?" the fairy replied. "Has it taken you this long to learn the way I feel? Must I undergo the shame of explaining myself? Have my eyes, once so certain of their power, lost all their influence? Just look how low I'm stooping! I'm the one who's confessing my weakness to you, who, great king though you may be, are less than an ant compared to a fairy like me."

"I am whatever you please," I said impatiently, "but what is it you demand of me? Is it my crown, my cities, my treasures?"

"Ah, wretch," she replied disdainfully, "if I so desired it, my scullions would be more powerful than you. No, I demand your heart! My eyes have asked you for it thousands and thousands of times. You haven't understood them, or rather, you don't want to understand them. If you had been desperately in love with someone else," she continued, "I wouldn't have interrupted the progress of your ardor, but I had too great an interest in you not to discover the indifference that reigned in your heart. Well, then, love me!" she added, rolling her eyes and pursing her mouth to make it look more pleasant. "I'll be your little Ragotte, and I'll add twenty kingdoms to what you possess already, a hundred towers filled with gold, five hundred filled with silver—in a word, all you can wish for."

"Madame Ragotte," I said to her, "I would never think of declaring myself to a person of your merit at the bottom of a pit in which I expect to be roasted. I implore you, by all the charms that you possess, to set me free, and then we'll consider together what we can do to satisfy you."

"Ha, traitor!" she exclaimed, "if you loved me, you wouldn't seek the road back to your kingdom. You'd be happy in a grotto, in a foxhole, in the woods or the desert. Don't think that I'm such an ingenue. You hope to escape, but I warn you that you'll remain here. Your first task will be to tend my sheep. They are intelligent animals and speak just as well as you do."

Upon saying this, she took me to the plain where we now stand and showed me her flock. I paid scant attention to them, for I was struck by the marvelous beauty of the slave beside her. My eyes betrayed me. The cruel Ragotte noticed my admiration and attacked her. She plunged a bodkin into one of her eyes with such violence that the adorable girl fell dead on the spot. At this horrible sight I threw myself on Ragotte, and with my sword in hand, I would have made her into a sacrificial victim for the spirits of the underworld if she hadn't used her power to freeze me as I stood. All my efforts were in vain. I fell to the ground and sought some way to kill myself and end my agony. But the fairy said to me with an ironical smile, "I want you to become acquainted with my power. You're a lion right now, but soon you'll become a sheep."

As she pronounced this sentence, she touched me with her wand, and I found myself transformed as you now behold me. I haven't lost the faculty of speech, nor the sense of torment caused by my condition. "You are to be a sheep for five years," she said, "and absolute master of this beautiful realm. Meanwhile I'll move far from here so I won't have to see your handsome face. But I'll brood over the hate I owe you."

Then she disappeared and, in truth, if anything could have relieved my misfortune, it would have been her absence. The talking sheep you see here acknowledged me as their king, and they informed me that they were unfortunate mortals who had in various ways offended the vindictive fairy. They had been changed into a flock, and some had to serve longer penances than others. In fact, every now and then they become what they were before and leave the flock. As for the shadows you've seen, they are Ragotte's rivals and enemies whom she has deprived of life for a century or so and who will return to the world later on. The young slave I mentioned is among them. I've seen her several times with great pleasure, although she didn't speak to me. When first I approached her, I was disturbed to discover it was nothing but her shadow. However, I noticed that one of my sheep was giving this phantom a lot of attention and learned that he was her lover. Ragotte had separated them out of jealousy, and this is the reason why I've avoided the shadow of the slave since then. During the past three years I've longed only for my freedom.

"In the hope of regaining it, I frequently wander into the forest," he continued. "It was there that I saw you, beautiful princess. Sometimes you were in a chariot that you drove yourself with more skill than Apollo does his own. Sometimes you followed the chase on a steed that seemed would obey no other rider, or you were in a race with the ladies of your court, flying lightly over the plain, and you won the prize like another Atalanta. Ah, Princess, if I had dared to speak to you during this time in which my heart paid you secret homage, what wouldn't I have said? But how would you have received the declaration of an unhappy sheep like me?"

Merveilleuse was so stirred by all she had heard that she scarcely knew how to answer him. She said something civil, however, which gave him some hope, and also told him that she was less alarmed by the ghosts now that she knew their owners would revive again. "Alas," she continued, "if my poor Patypata, my dear Grabugeon, and the pretty Tintin, who died to save me, could have met with a similar fate, I wouldn't be so melancholy here."

Despite the disgrace of the royal ram, he still possessed some remarkable prerogatives. "Go," he said to his grand equerry (a splendid-looking sheep), "go fetch the Moor, the ape, and the little dog. Their shadows will amuse our princess."

A moment later they appeared, and although they did not approach near enough for Merveilleuse to touch them, their presence was a great consolation to her.

The royal ram possessed all the intelligence and refinement required for pleasant conversation, and he adored Merveilleuse so much that she began to have some regard for him and soon after came to love him. A pretty sheep, so gentle and affectionate, is not a displeasing companion, particularly when one knows that he is a king and that his transformation will eventually end. Thus the princess spent her days peacefully, awaiting a happier future. The gallant ram devoted himself entirely to her. He gave fetes, concerts, and hunts in which his flock aided him and even the shadows played their part.

One day when his couriers arrived—for he regularly sent out couriers for news and always obtained the best—he learned that the eldest sister of Princess Merveilleuse was about to marry a great prince, and the most magnificent preparations were being made for the wedding.

"Ah," the young princess said, "how unfortunate I am to be deprived of witnessing so many fine things! Here I am underground, among ghosts and sheep, while my sister is about to be made a queen. Everybody will pay their respects to her, and I'm the only one who won't be able to share in her joy."

"What reason do you have to complain, madam?" asked the king of the sheep. "Have I refused you permission to attend the wedding? Depart as soon as you please. Only give me your word that you'll return. If you don't agree to that, I'll perish at your feet, for my love for you is too passionate and I'd never be able to live if I lost you."

Touched, Merveilleuse promised the ram that nothing in the world could prevent her return. So he provided her with an equipage befitting her birth. She was superbly attired, and nothing was omitted to embellish her beauty. She got into a chariot of mother-of-pearl drawn by six Isabella-colored hypogriffins that had just arrived from the other end of the earth. She was accompanied by a great number of exceedingly handsome, richly attired officers. These the royal ram had ordered to come from a distant land to form the princess's train.

She arrived at her father's court at the moment the marriage was being celebrated. As soon as she appeared, she dazzled everyone by her glittering beauty and the jewels that adorned her. She heard nothing but acclamation and praise. The king gazed at her with such zeal and pleasure that she was afraid he would recognize her, but he was so convinced that his daughter was dead that he did not have the least inkling who she was.

Nevertheless, she was so afraid that she might be detained that she did not stay to the end of the ceremony. She departed abruptly, leaving a small coral box garnished with emeralds, on which was written in diamonds: "JEWELS FOR THE BRIDE." They opened it immediately, and what extraordinary things they found! The king, who was burning to know who she was,

was despondent about her departure. He gave strict orders that if she ever returned, they were to shut the gates and detain her.

Brief though the absence of Merceilleuse had been, it had seemed like ages to the ram. Waiting for her by the side of a fountain in the thickest part of the forest, he had immense treasures displayed there with the intention of giving them to her in gratitude for her return. As soon as he saw her, he ran toward her, romping and frisking like a real sheep. He lay down at her feet, kissed her hands, and told her all about his anxiety and impatience. His love for her so inspired him that he managed to speak with an eloquence that completely captivated the princess.

A short time afterward, the king was to marry off his second daughter, and Merveilleuse heard about it. Once again she asked the ram for permission to attend a fete in which she took the closest interest. Of course, he felt a pang he could not suppress when he heard her request, for a secret presentiment warned him of a catastrophe. But since we cannot always avoid evil, and since his consideration for the princess overruled any other feeling, he did not have the heart to refuse her. "You desire to leave me, madam," he said, "and I must blame my sad fate for this unfortunate situation more than you. In consenting to your wish, I'll never make you a greater sacrifice."

She assured him that she would return as quickly as she had the first time. "I would be deeply grieved if anything were to keep me from you. I beg you, don't worry about me."

She went in the same pomp as before and arrived just as they were beginning the marriage ceremony. Although everyone was following the nuptials, her presence caused exclamations of joy and admiration that drew the eyes of all the princes to her. They could not stop gazing at her: her beauty, they felt, was so extraordinary that they could easily have been convinced that she was more than mortal.

The king was charmed to see her once more, and he never took his eyes off her, except to order all the doors to be closed to prevent her departure. When the ceremony was nearly concluded, the princess rose hastily in order to disappear in the throng, but was shocked and distressed to find that all the gates locked against her.

The king approached with a respectful, submissive air that reassured her. He begged her not to deprive them so soon of the pleasure of admiring her and requested that she remain and grace the banquet he was about to give the princes and princesses who had honored him with their presence on this occasion. He led her into a magnificent salon, in which the entire court was assembled, and offered her a golden basin and a vase filled with water so that she might wash her beautiful hands. No longer could she restrain her feelings. She flung herself at his feet, embraced his knees, and exclaimed, "Look, my dream has come true! You've offered me water to wash with on my sister's wedding day without anything evil happening to you."

The king had no difficulty recognizing her, for he had been struck by her strong resemblance to Merveilleuse more than once. "Ah, my dear daughter!" he cried, embracing her with tears in his eyes. "Can you ever forgive my cruelty? I wanted to take your life because I thought your dream predicted I would lose my crown. Indeed, it did just that, for now that your two sisters are married, each has a crown of her own. Therefore, mine shall be yours." Upon saying this, he rose and placed his crown on the princess's head, crying, "Long live Queen Merveilleuse!"

The entire court took up the shout. The two sisters threw their arms around her neck and kissed her a thousand times. Merveilleuse was so happy she could not express her joy. She cried and laughed at the same time. She embraced one, talked to another, thanked the king, and in the midst of all this, she recalled the captain of the guard, to whom she was so much indebted. When she asked eagerly to see him, though, they informed her he was dead, and she felt a pang of sorrow.

After they sat down to dinner, the king asked her to relate all that had happened to her ever since the day he had given his fatal orders. She immediately began telling the story with the most remarkable grace, and everybody listened to her attentively.

While she was engrossed in telling her story to the king and her sisters, though, the enamored ram watched for the princess as the hour set for her return passed. Indeed, his anxiety became so extreme that he could not control it. "She'll never come back!" he cried. "My miserable sheep's face disgusts her. Oh, unfortunate lover that I am, what will become of me if I have lost Merveilleuse? Ragotte! Cruel fairy! How you have avenged yourself for my indifference to you!" He indulged in such lamentations for hours, and then, as night approached without any signs of the princess, he ran to the city. When he reached the king's palace, he asked to see Merveilleuse, but since everybody was now aware of her adventures and did not want her to return to the ram's realm, they harshly refused to let him see her. He uttered cries and lamentations capable of moving anyone except the Swiss guard who stood sentry at the palace gates. At length, broken-hearted, he flung himself to the ground and breathed his last sigh.

The king and Merveilleuse were completely unaware of the sad tragedy that had taken place. The king suggested to his daughter that she ride in a triumphal coach and show herself to everyone in the city by the lights of thousands and thousands of torches illuminating the windows and all the great squares. But what a horrible spectacle she encountered as she left the palace gates—her dear ram stretched out breathless on the pavement! Jumping out of the coach and running to him, she wept and sobbed, for she knew that her delay in returning had caused the royal ram's death. In her despair she felt she would die herself.

Now we know that people of the highest rank are subject, like all others, to the blows of fortune, and that they frequently experience the greatest misery at the very moment they believe themselves to have attained their heart's goal.

> The choicest blessings sent by Heaven
> Often tend to cause our ruin.
> The charms, the talents, that we're given,
> May often end on a sad tune.
> The royal ram would have surely seen
> Happier days without the charms that led
> The cruel Ragotte to love, then hurl her mean
> But fatal vengeance on his head.
> In truth he should have had a better fate,
> For spurning a sordid Hymen's chains;
> Honest his love—unmasked his hate—
> How different from our modern swains!
> Even his death may well surprise
> The lovers of the present day:
> Only a silly sheep now dies,
> Because his ewe has gone astray.

FINETTE CENDRON

ONCE upon a time there was a king and a queen who managed the affairs of their realm very badly. As a consequence, they were driven out of their kingdom and had to sell their crowns to support themselves. After that they had to part with their wardrobes, their linen, lace, and all their furniture, piece by piece. Soon the brokers tired of purchasing their goods, for every day something else was sent for sale. When they had disposed of nearly everything, the king said to the queen, "We're exiled from our own country and no longer have any possessions. We must do something to earn a living for ourselves and our poor children. Give some thought as to what we can do. Up to now the only trade I've known is the very pleasant one of a king's."

The queen, who was endowed with a wealth of good sense, asked for a week to think the matter over. At the end of that time she announced, "Sire, there's no need for us to be unhappy. You need only to make nets, with which you can catch both fowl and fish. As the lines wear out, I'll spin new ones. With regard to our three daughters, they're downright idle girls who still think of themselves as fine ladies and would like to continue living in that style without sullying their hands. We must take them so far away that they'll never be able to find their way back again, since we cannot possibly support them as well as they would like."

The king began to weep when he found he had to separate himself from his children, for he was a kind father. The queen was mistress, however, and he agreed to whatever she proposed. "Get up early tomorrow morning," he said to her, "and take your three daughters wherever you think fit."

While they were thus plotting together, the Princess Finette, who was the youngest daughter, listened at the keyhole, and when she discovered her father and mother's plans, she set off as fast as she could in the direction of a large grotto a considerable distance away, which was the abode of her godmother, the fairy Merluche.

400

Finette took two pounds of fresh butter, some eggs, milk, and flour to make a nice cake for her godmother and ensure she would be given a warm reception. She began her journey in good spirits, but the farther she went, the more weary she became. The soles of her shoes were worn completely through, and her pretty little feet became so sore that they were a sad sight to see. Indeed, she became so exhausted that she sat on the grass and cried. Just then a beautiful Spanish horse came by, already saddled and bridled. He had more than enough diamonds on his saddle cloth to purchase three cities. When he saw the princess, he stopped and began to graze quietly beside her. Bending his knees, he appeared to pay homage to her. There-upon, she took him by the bri-

dle and said, "Gentle hobby, would you kindly carry me to my fairy godmother's? You'd do me great service, for I'm so weary that I am ready to expire. If you help me on this occasion, I'll give you good oats and hay and a litter of fresh straw to lie upon."

The horse bent himself almost to the ground, and when young Finette jumped upon him, he galloped off with her as lightly as a bird until he came to a halt at the entrance of the grotto, as if he had known where to go to. In fact, he knew well enough, for Merluche herself had foreseen her goddaughter's visit and had sent the fine horse for her.

As soon as Finette entered the grotto, she made three respectful curtsies to her godmother. Then she took the hem of her gown, kissed it, and said to her, "Good day, godmother, how are you doing? I've brought you some butter, milk, flour, and eggs to make you a cake according to the custom of our country."

"You're welcome, Finette," the fairy said. "Come hither so I may embrace you." She kissed her twice and this delighted Finette a great deal, for Madame Merluche was not one of those fairies one finds by the dozen. "Come, goddaughter," she said, "you'll be my lady's maid. Take down my hair and comb it." The princess took her hair down and adroitly combed it. "I know full well why you've come. You overheard the king and queen discussing how they might lose you, and you want to avoid such a calamity," Merluche said. "Here, you have only to take this skein of unbreakable thread. Fasten one end to the door of your house and keep the other in your hand. When the queen abandons you, you'll easily find your way back by following the thread."

The princess thanked her godmother, who gave her a bag filled with fine dresses made of gold and silver. She embraced her, placed her again on the pretty horse, and in two or three minutes he had carried Finette to the door of her parents' cottage.

"My friend," Finette said to the horse, "you're very handsome and clever, and your speed is as great as the sun's. I thank you for your service. You may now return whence you came."

She entered the house quietly and hid her bag under her pillow. Then she went to bed appearing to know nothing that had taken place. At daybreak, the king woke his wife. "Come, come, madam," he said. "Get ready for your journey."

She got up immediately, took some sturdy shoes, a short petticoat, a white jacket, and a stick. Then she summoned her eldest daughter, who was named Fleur d'Amour; her second, who was named Belle-de-Nuit; and her third, named Fine-Oreille, whom they familiarly called Finette. "I've been thinking all last night that we ought to go and see my sister," the queen said. "She'll entertain us in splendid fashion. We can feast and laugh as much as we like there."

Fleur d'Amour, who despaired of living in such a desert, said to her mother, "Let us go, madam, wherever you please. Just as long as I can stroll somewhere, anywhere." The two others agreed and took their leave of the king. They set off all four together and walked so very far that Fine-Oreille was terrified her thread would not be long enough, for they walked nearly a thousand miles. She always kept behind the others, drawing the thread skillfully through the thickets.

When the queen thought her daughters would be unable to find their way back, she entered a dense forest and told them, "Sleep, my little lambs. I'll be like the shepherdess who watches over her flock for fear the wolf will devour them." Once they had lain down on the grass and fallen asleep, the queen left them there, believing she would never see them again.

Finette had shut her eyes but not gone to sleep. "If I were an evil-natured girl," she said to herself, "I'd go straight home and leave my sisters to die here." (The fact is, they beat her and scratched her until they drew blood.) Yet despite their malice she did not abandon them. She roused her sisters and told them the whole story. They began to cry and begged her to take them with her, promising that they would give her beautiful dolls, a child's set of silver plates, and all their other toys and candy. "I'm quite sure you'll do nothing of the kind," Finette said. "Nevertheless, I'll behave as a good sister should." So saying, she rose and followed the thread with the two princesses, and thus they reached home almost as soon as the queen.

While they were at the door, they heard the king say, "It troubles my heart to see you come back alone."

"Pshaw," said the queen. "Our daughters were much too great a burden for us."

"If you had brought back my Finette," the king said, "I might have felt consoled about the loss of the others, for they loved nothing and nobody."

At that moment they knocked at the door—rap, rap. "Who's there?" asked the king.

"Your three daughters," they replied, "Fleur d'Amour, Belle-de-Nuit, and Fine-Oreille."

The queen began to tremble. "Don't open the door!" she exclaimed. "It must be their ghosts, for they could not have possibly found their way back alive."

The king, who was as great a coward as his wife, called out, "You're lying! You're not my daughters!"

But shrewd Fine-Oreille said, "Papa, I'll stoop down so that you can look at me through the hole made for the cat to come through. If I'm not Finette, I agree to be whipped."

The king did as he was told, and as soon as he recognized her, he flung open the door. Pretending to be delighted to see them again, the queen said that she had forgotten something and had come home to fetch it, but that she would surely have returned to them. They pretended to believe her and went upstairs to a snug hayloft in which they always slept.

"Now, sisters," Finette said, "you promised me the doll. Give it to me."

"Don't hold your breath, you little scamp," they said. "You're the reason why they care so little for us."

Thereupon, they grabbed their distaffs and beat her terribly. After they had abused her as much as they desired, they let her go to bed. However, since she was covered with wounds and bruises, she could not sleep. Because of this, she heard the queen say to the king, "I'll take them much farther in another direction, until I'm positive they'll never return."

When Finette heard this plan, she rose silently to see her godmother again. She went into the chicken yard, where she wrung the necks of two hens, a cock, and two little rabbits that the queen was fattening on cabbages for the next festive occasion. She put them all into a basket and set off, but she had not gone a mile, groping her way and quaking with fear, when the Spanish horse approached at a gallop, snorting and neighing. Thinking that some soldiers were about to seize her, she cried, "Alas, it's all over for me." When she saw the beautiful horse all alone, though, she jumped upon his back, delighted to travel so comfortably, especially since she arrived almost immediately at her godmother's.

After the usual greetings she presented her with the hens, cock, and rabbits, and asked for her sage advice, since the queen had sworn she would lead them to the end of the world. Merluche told her goddaughter not to trouble herself and gave her a sackful of ashes. "Carry this sack in front of you and shake it as you go along. You'll walk on the ashes, and when you wish to return, you'll only have to follow your footsteps," she said. "Don't bring your sisters back with you, though, for they're too malicious. If you do bring them back, I'll never see you again."

Finette bid farewell to her and was given thirty or forty millions of diamonds in a little box, which she put in her pocket to take with her. The horse was ready and waiting and carried her home as before.

At daybreak the queen called the princesses and said, "The king isn't well, and I dreamed last night that I must go and gather some flowers and herbs that'll help him recuperate. There's a particular country where they grow to perfection, so let us be off right away."

Fleur d'Amour and Belle-de-Nuit, who never imagined that their mother intended to lose them again, were quite grieved at hearing that they had to make another long trip. Yet they had to go, and they went farther than any journey had ever been made. Finette, who never said a word, kept behind them and shook her sack of ashes with such wonderful skill that neither wind nor rain spoiled them.

The queen was perfectly convinced that they would not find their way back again, and one evening, when she observed her three daughters fast asleep, she used the opportunity to leave them and returned home. As soon as it was light and Finette found her mother gone, she woke her sisters. "We're alone," she said. "The queen has left us."

Fleur d'Amour and Belle-de-Nuit began to weep. They tore their hair and beat their own faces with their fists. "Alas, what will become of us?" they exclaimed.

Finette was the best-hearted girl in the world, and therefore she took pity on her sisters once again. "See how vulnerable I'm leaving myself," she told them. "When my godmother furnished me with the means to return, she forbade me to show you the way and told me that if I disobeyed her, she'd never see me again."

Fleur d'Amour and Belle-de-Nuit threw themselves on Finette's neck, kissing her so affectionately that it required nothing more to bring all three back together to the king and the queen. Their majesties were greatly surprised at the return of the princesses, and they conversed long into the night. Meanwhile, their youngest daughter, who was not called Fine-Oreille for nothing, heard them concoct a new plan that involved the queen taking them on another journey the next morning. Again Fine-Oreille ran to wake her sisters.

"Alas," she said to them, "we're lost! The queen is determined to lead us into some wilderness and leave us there. I offended my godmother for your sakes, so I don't dare to go to her for advice as I did before."

Faced with such a terrible prospect, they asked each other, "What shall we do, sister? What shall we do?"

At last Belle-de-Nuit said to the two others, "Why should we worry ourselves? Old Merluche doesn't possess all the wit in the world. There are other folks who possess just as much. We need only take plenty of peas and drop them all along the road as we go. Then we'll be sure to trace our way back."

Fleur d'Amour thought this was a remarkable idea, and they loaded all their pockets with peas. But instead of peas, Fine-Oreille packed her bag filled with fine clothes and the little box of diamonds, sensing that they might be gone a long time.

As soon as the queen called them, they were ready to go. "I dreamed last night," she said, "that in a country, which is unnecessary to name, there are three handsome princes who are waiting to marry you. I'm going to take you there to see if my dream was true."

The queen went first and her daughters followed her, confidently dropping their peas, for they were sure of finding their way home. This time the queen went farther than she had ever gone before, and during one dark night she left the princesses. She reached home very weary, but delighted for having gotten rid of the great burden of her three daughters.

After sleeping until eleven, the three princesses awoke, and Finette was the first to discover The queen's absence. Although she was perfectly prepared for it, she could not help crying, especially because she trusted the power of her fairy godmother much more than the cleverness of her sisters. Frightened, she went to them and said, "The queen's gone. We must follow her as soon as possible."

"Hold your tongue, you little hussy," replied Fleur d'Amour. "We can find our way well enough when we choose. There's no need in making such a fuss."

Finette did not dare to answer. However, when they did try to retrace their steps, there were no signs or paths to be found. Since immense flocks of pigeons inhabited that country, they had eaten up all the peas. The princesses began to scream with grief and terror. After spending two days without eating, Fleur d'Amour said to Belle-de-Nuit, "Sister, don't you have anything to eat?"

"Nothing."

She put the same question to Finette.

"Nor do I," she answered, "but I've just found an acorn."

"Ah! Give it to me," one sister said.

"Give it to me," said the other.

Each insisted on having it.

"An acorn will not go far among the three of us," Finette said. "Let us plant it, and maybe a tree will spring from that which will be useful to us."

Although there was scant chance of a tree growing in a country where none were to be seen, they agreed. The only things they could find to eat were cabbages and lettuces, and this was what the princesses lived on. If their constitutions had been delicate, they would have starved a hundred times. They slept almost always in the open air, and every morning and evening they took turns watering the acorn and saying, "Grow, grow, beautiful acorn!"

Indeed, it began to grow so fast that they could watch it grow. When it had reached a certain height, Fleur d'Amour tried to climb it, but it was not strong enough to bear her. Feeling it bend under her weight, she came back down again. Belle-de-Nuit was no more successful. Since Finette was lighter, she managed to climb up and remain there a long time.

Her sisters called to her, "Can you see anything, sister?"

She answered, "No, I can't see a thing."

"Ah, then, the oak is not tall enough," said Fleur d'Amour.

So they continued to water it and say, "Grow, grow, beautiful acorn!" Finette kept climbing it twice a day, and one morning, when she was up in the tree, Belle-de-Nuit said to Fleur d'Amour, "I've found a bag that our sister has hidden from us. What can be in it?"

Fleur d'Amour replied, "She told me it contained some old lace she had brought along to mend."

"I believe it's full of candy," Belle-de-Nuit said. Since she had a sweet tooth, she decided to look. When she opened the bag, she did find a good deal of old lace belonging to the king and queen, but hidden beneath it were the fine clothes and the box of diamonds the fairy had given to Finette.

"Well, now! Was there ever such a sly little scamp?" exclaimed Belle-de-Nuit. "We'll take out all the things and put some stones in their place."

This they did hastily, and when Finette rejoined them, she did not notice what they had done, for she never dreamed of decking herself out in a desert. She thought only about the oak, which quickly became the finest that the world has ever seen. One day when she had climbed it and her sisters as usual had asked if she could see anything, she exclaimed, "I can see a large mansion so very beautiful that I can't find the words to describe it. The walls are composed of emeralds and rubies, the roof of diamonds. It's covered all over with golden bells and weathercocks that whirl about as the wind blows."

"You're lying," they said. "It can't be as beautiful as you say."

"Believe me," Finette replied, "I'm not a liar. Come and see for yourselves. My eyes are quite dazzled by it."

Fleur d'Amour climbed up the tree. When she saw the château, she could talk about nothing else. Greatly curious, Belle-de-Nuit climbed in her turn and was just as enchanted as her sisters at the sight.

"We must certainly go to this palace," they said. "Perhaps we'll find those handsome princes who'll be happy to marry us."

They spent all evening long discussing the subject before they lay down to sleep on the grass. But when Finette seemed to be fast asleep, Fleur d'Amour said to Belle-de-Nuit, "I'll tell you what we should do, sister. Let's get up and dress ourselves in the fine clothes Finette has brought."

"That's a splendid idea," Belle-de-Nuit responded.

Rising, they curled their hair, powdered it, put patches on their cheeks, and dressed themselves in the beautiful gold and silver gowns arrayed with diamonds. What a magnificent sight they made!

The next morning, unaware of her wicked sisters' theft, Finette took her bag with the intention of dressing herself, and was greatly distressed to find nothing in it but flint stones. At that moment she turned and saw her sisters shining like suns. She wept and complained about their treachery, but they only laughed and joked about it.

"I can't believe," Finette said, "that you have the effrontery to take me to the château without dressing and making me as beautiful as you are."

"We have barely enough for ourselves," Fleur d'Amour replied, "and you'll get nothing but blows if you pester us."

"But the clothes you have on are mine. My godmother gave them to me. They don't belong to you."

"If you say one more word about it," they responded, "we'll knock you on the head and bury you without anyone being the wiser!"

Poor Finette did not dare provoke them, but followed them slowly, walking a short distance behind them, as if she were merely their servant.

The nearer they approached the mansion, the more wonderful it appeared. "Oh," Fleur d'Amour and Belle-de-Nuit said, "what fun we'll have! What splendid dinners we'll have! We'll dine at the king's table. But Finette will have to wash the dishes in the kitchen, for she looks like a scullion. If anybody asks who she is, we must take care not to call her 'sister.' We must say she's the little cowherd from the village."

Of course, the lovely, sensible Finette was distressed at being treated so badly.

When they reached the castle gate, they knocked at it, and it was opened immediately by a terrifying old hag. She had just one eye, located in the middle of her forehead, but it was bigger than five or six ordinary ones. Her nose was flat, her complexion swarthy, and her mouth so horrible that it was frightening to behold. She was fifteen feet high and had a waist thirty feet wide. "Unfortunate wretches," she said to them, "what's brought you here? Don't you know that this is the ogre's castle, and that all three of you would scarcely make do for his breakfast? But I'm more good-natured than my husband. Come in. I won't eat you all at once. You'll have the consolation of living two or three days longer."

Upon hearing the words of the ogress, they began to flee, but one of her strides was equal to fifty of theirs. Thus she pursued and caught them, one by the hair and the others by the nape of the neck. Then she tucked them under her arm, took them into the castle, and threw all three into the cellar, which was filled with toads and adders and strewn with the bones of those the ogres had eaten. Desiring to eat Finette right away, the ogress went to fetch some vinegar, oil, and salt to make her into a salad. At that moment, however, she heard the ogre approaching and thought, "The princesses are so white and delicate that I want to eat them all myself." So she popped them quickly under a large tub, from which they could only look through a hole.

The ogre was six times as tall as his wife. When he spoke, the building shook, and when he coughed, they resembled peals of thunder. He had just one huge, filthy eye, and his hair stood all on end. Using a log of wood for a cane, he entered with a covered basket in his hand, from which he pulled fifteen children he had stolen on the road and swallowed them like fifteen freshly laid eggs. When the princesses saw him, they trembled under the tub. They were afraid to cry, lest they be heard, but they whispered to each other, "He'll eat us alive. How can we possibly save ourselves?"

The ogre said to his wife, "You know, I smell fresh meat. Give it to me."

"That's a good one," the ogress said. "You always think you smell fresh meat. It's your sheep that have just passed by."

"You can't fool me. I smell fresh meat for certain, and I'll search everywhere for it."

"Search," she said. "You won't find anything."

"If I do find something, and you've hidden it from me, I'll cut your head off and make a ball out of it."

She was frightened by this threat and said, "Don't be angry, my dear ogre. I'll tell you the truth. Three young girls came here today, and I hid them away. It would be a pity to eat them, though, for they know how to do everything. I'm old and need some rest. You can see that our fine house is very dirty, our bread is badly made, and your soup rarely pleases you. Moreover, I myself no longer appear so beautiful in your eyes ever since I began working so hard. These girls will be my servants. I beg you not to eat them just now. If you should desire one of them some other day, they'll always be within your reach."

The ogre was loath to promise that he would not eat them immediately. "Let me do as I please," he said. "I'll only eat two of them."

"No, you won't eat them."

"Well, then, I'll only eat the smallest."

"No, you won't touch a single one of them."

After a great deal of bickering, he at last promised he would not eat them, but she thought to herself, "When he goes hunting, I'll eat them and tell him they managed to escape."

The orge emerged from the cellar and told his wife to bring the girls to him. The poor princesses were nearly paralyzed with fright, and the ogress had to coax them to come forward. When they were brought before the ogre, he asked them what they could do. They answered, "We can sweep, sew, and spin exceedingly well."

"We can make ragouts so delicious that people are tempted to eat even the plates."

"As for bread, cakes, and patties, people have been known to order them from a thousand miles around."

Since the orgre was fond of good cooking, he said, "Aha! Set these good housewives to work immediately. I say," he asked, testing them, "after you light the fire, how do you know when the oven is hot enough?"

"I throw some butter into it, my lord," Finette replied, "and then I taste it with my tongue."

"Very well," he said, "light the over fire, then."

The oven was as big as a stable because the ogre and ogress ate more bread than two armies could eat. The princess built a terrific fire, until the oven was as hot as a furnace. In the meantime the ogre became impatient waiting for his new bread. So he ate a hundred lambs and a hundred suckling pigs, while Fleur d'Amour and Belle-de-Nuit made the dough. "Well," the mammoth ogre asked, "is the oven hot?"

"You shall see, my lord," said Finette. She threw in a thousand pounds of butter and then said, "It should be tasted with the tongue, but I'm too short to reach it."

"I'm tall enough," the ogre said as he stooped. He thrust his body so far into the oven, though, that he could not keep his balance, and all the flesh was burned off his bones. When the ogress approached the oven, she was astounded to find her husband a mountain of cinders!

Fleur d'Amour and Belle-de-Nuit, who saw how distressed she was, consoled her as well as they were able, but they feared her grief would subside all too soon, and once her appetite returned, she would make a salad out of them, as she had been about to do before. "Don't be discouraged, madam," they said to her, "you'll find some king or some marquis who'll be deligthed to marry you."

She smiled slightly, showing teeth that were longer than most people's fingers. When they saw her in such a good mood, Finette said, "If you would only take off these horrible bearskins that you wrap yourself in and follow the fashion, we'll dress your hair to perfection. Then you'll resemble a star."

"Come," the ogress said, "let's see what you can do. But rest assured that if I find any ladies more lovely than me, I'll make mincemeat out of you."

Thereupon, the three princesses took off her cap and began combing and curling her hair. While they entertained her with their chatter, Finette took a hatchet and struck her from behind with such a blow that her head was sliced clean off her shoulders.

Never was there such rejoicing! Climbing to the roof of the mansion, the three princesses amused themselves by ringing the golden bells. Then they ran through all the apartments, which were made of pearls and diamonds and filled with costly furniture. They nearly fainted with pleasure. They laughed, they sang, they had all they wanted: corn, marmalade, fruit, and dolls in abundance. Going to sleep in beds of brocade and velvet, Fleur d'Amour and Belle-de-Nuit said to each other, "Look at us, we're richer than our father was when he still had his kingdom."

"On the other hand, though, we want to be married, and nobody will dare to come here. People assume this mansion remains a cutthroat den because they don't know that the ogre and the ogress are dead. We must go to the nearest city and show ourselves in our fine dresses. Then we're bound to find some honest bankers who'll be quite glad to marry princesses."

As soon as they were dressed, they told Finette they were going to take a stroll. "But you must stay home and cook and wash and clean the house. We'd better find everything as it should be on our return. If not, you'll be beaten within an inch of your life!"

Poor Finette, whose heart was full of grief, remained alone in the house, sweeping, cleaning, washing, and crying without cease. "How unfortunate," she lamented "that I disobeyed my godmother! All sorts of awful things have happened to me. My sisters have stolen my precious dresses and adorned themselves with my ornaments. If it weren't for me, the ogre and his wife would be alive and well at this moment. What have I gained from killing them?"

Saying this, she broke into sobs until she almost choked. Shortly afterward her sisters returned loaded with Portugal oranges, preserves, and sugar. "Ah," they announced, "what a splendid ball we attended! How crowded it was! The king's son was among the dancers, and we received a thousand compliments. Come take off our shoes and clean them. It's one of your tasks."

Finette obeyed them, and if by accident she let drop a single word of complaint, they jumped on her and beat her savagely. The next day and the next they went out and returned with accounts of new wonders.

One evening Finette was sitting in the chimney corner on a heap of cinders, idly examining the cracks in the chimney, when she discovered a little key lodged in one of them. It was so old and so dirty that she had the greatest trouble cleaning it, but after she had done so, she found it was made of gold. Assuming that a golden key ought to open some beautiful little casket, she ran all over the mansion, trying it in all the locks. Eventually she found it fit the lock of a casket that was a masterpiece of art. When she opened it, she found it filled with clothes, diamonds, lace, linen, and ribbons worth immense sums. She said not a word to her sisters about her good fortune, but waited impatiently for their departure the next day. As soon as they were out of sight, she adorned herself until she looked more beautiful than the sun and the moon combined.

In this altered condition she went to the ball where her sisters were dancing, and though she was not wearing a mask, she had changed so much for the better that they did not recognize her. As soon as she appeared, a murmur arose throughout the gathering. Some were filled with admiration, others with jealousy. Asked to dance, she soon showed that she surpassed all the other ladies in grace as well as beauty. The mistress of the mansion came to her, and after making a respectful curtsy, she asked her name so that she would always have the pleasure of remembering such a marvelous person. Finette replied civilly that her name was Cendron. Now, there was not a lover who did not leave his mistress for Cendron, not a poet who did not write verses about Cendron. Never did such a shabby name cause so much commotion in so short a time. Every echo repeated the praises of Cendron. People did not have eyes enough to gaze at her, nor tongues enough to extol her.

Fleur d'Amour and Belle-de-Nuit, who had previously created a sensation wherever they appeared, were ready to burst with spite as they observed the reception accorded to this newcomer. But Finette extricated herself from all such rivalry with the best grace in the world. Her manners seemed to be those of one born to command. Fleur d'Amour and Belle-de-Nuit, who never saw their sister except with her face covered with chimney soot and looking as dirty as a dog, had completely forgotten how beautiful she was. Consequently, they did not have the slightest inkling who she was. Like all the rest, they paid their respects to Cendron.

As soon as she saw the ball was nearly over, she hurried home, undressed herself quickly, and put on her old rags. When her sisters arrived, they said to her, "Ah, Finette, we've just seen a perfectly charming young princess! She's not a baboon like you. She's as white as snow with a richer complexion than the roses. Her teeth are pearls and her lips are coral. She was wearing a gown so decked with gold and diamonds it must have weighed more than a thousand pounds. How beautiful, how charming she was!" Finette murmured, "So was I, so was I."

"What are you muttering there?" her sisters asked.

She repeated even more softly, "So was I, so was I."

This little game was played for some time. Hardly a day passed that Finette did not appear in a new dress, for the casket was a fairy one. The more she took out, the more it was filled, and every item was so fashionable that all the ladies dressed themselves in imitation of Finette.

One evening when Finette had danced more than usual and had delayed her departure to a later hour, she was so anxious to get home before her sisters that she walked too hurriedly and lost one of her slippers, made of red velvet and embroidered with pearls. She tried to find it on the road, but the night was so dark, that she searched in vain. Thus she entered the house with one foot shod and one foot not.

The next day, Prince Chéri, the king's eldest son, went out hunting and found Finette's slipper. He picked it up and examined it, admiring its diminutive size and elegance. After turning it over and over, he kissed it and carried it home with him.

From that day on, he refused to eat, and his looks underwent a great change: he became as yellow as a quince, thin, melancholy, and depressed. The king and queen, who were devoted to him, had the choicest game and best confiture brought in from everywhere, but they meant nothing to him. He gazed blankly at everything and did not respond when his mother spoke to him. They summoned the best physicians from all around even as far as Paris and Montpellier. After observing him continually for three days and three nights, they concluded that he was in love and that he would die if they did not find the sole remedy for him.

The queen, who doted on her son, burst into tears because she did not know the object of his love and could not help him marry her. She had the most beautiful ladies she could find brought into his chamber, but he did not deign to glance at them. At last she said, "My dear son, you're going to be the cause of our death, for you're in love and you're hiding it from us. Tell us whom you love and we'll give her to you, even if she's just a simple shepherdess."

Taking courage from the queen's promise, the prince drew the slipper from under his pillow. Showing it to her, he said, "Look, madam, this is the cause of my malady. I found this petite, delicate slipper when I went out hunting, and I refuse to marry anyone but the woman who can wear it."

"Very well, my son," said the queen, "there's no need to trouble yourself. We'll organize a search for her."

She rushed to the king with this news. He was very surprised and immediately ordered a proclamation to be made with drum and trumpet: all single women were to come and try on the slipper, and she whose foot fit the slipper would marry the prince.

Upon hearing this, every woman washed her feet with the sorts of waters, pastes, and pomades. Some ladies actually had them peeled, while others starved themselves in order to make their feet smaller and prettier. They converged in hordes to try on the slipper, but no one could fit into it, and the more they came and failed, they more the prince's suffering increased.

One day Fleur d'Amour and Belle-de-Nuit dressed themselves so superbly that they looked astonishingly beautiful.

"Where are you bound?" asked Finette.

"We're going to the capital city where the king and queen reside," they replied. "We're going to try on the slipper the king's son has found. If it fits one of us, the prince will marry her, and then one of us will become queen."

"And why can't I go?" Finette responded.

"Really! You're awfully stupid!" they said. "Go and water our cabbages. That's all you're fit for."

Without a second's thought Finette decided she should put on her finest clothes and take her chance with the rest, for she had a vague suspicion that she would be successful. She was troubled because she did not know her way, for the ball she had attended had not been held in the capital, but she dressed herself magnificently nevertheless. Her gown was made of blue satin and covered with diamond stars. She had a corona of them in her hair and a full moon on her back, and all these jewels glistened so brightly that no one could look at her without blinking. Upon opening the door to go out, she was quite surprised to find the pretty Spanish horse that had carried her to her godmother's. He was covered all over with golden bells and ribbons, and his saddle cloth and bridle were beyond compare. She patted him and said, "You're a most welcome sight, my little hobby. I'm much obliged to my godmother, Merluche." When he knelt down and she bounded atop him like a nymph, she was thirty times more beautiful than fair Helen of Troy.

The Spanish horse galloped off sprightly, his bells ringing ting, ting, ting. When Fleur d'Amour and Belle-de-Nuit heard these sounds, they turned around and saw her coming. They were completely taken by surprise, for they now recognized her both as Finette and Cendron. "Sister!" Fleur d'Amour cried to Belle-de-Nuit, "Look, that's Finette Cendron!"

As the other echoed the cry, Finette passed so close to them that her horse splashed them all over and left their fine dresses dripping with mud. Finette laughed at them and called, "Your highnesses, Cendrillon despises you as you deserve."

Then she passed them like a shot and disappeared. Belle-de-Nuit and
Fleur d'Amour looked at each other. "Are we dreaming?" they asked.
"Who could have supplied Finette with clothes and a horse? It's a miracle!
She's got luck on her side.
Her foot will fit the slipper,
and we'll have made a long
journey in vain."

While they were bemoan-
ing their situation, Finette
arrived at the palace. The
moment she appeared, everybody thought she was a
queen. Guards presented
arms, drums rolled, and
trumpets sounded a flour-
ish. All the gates were flung
open, and those people who
had seen her at the ball preceded her and cried, "Make
room! Make room for the
beautiful Cendron, the wonder of the world!"

Such was the state that she entered the room of the dying prince. Casting
his eyes on her, he was enraptured by the sight of her and prayed fervently
that her foot would be small enough to fit into the slipper. Instantly she
slipped it on and produced its fellow, which she had brought with her for
this purpose. Immediately the cry could be heard: "Long live the Princess
Chérie! Long live the princess who will be our queen!"

The prince rose from his couch and advanced to kiss her hand, and she
was struck by how handsome and intelligent he was. While he paid her a
thousand courteous attentions, the king and queen were informed of the
event. Consequently, they came in all haste. The queen took Finette in her
arms, called her her daughter, her darling, her little queen! She gave her
several magnificent presents, and the generous king added many more.
They ordered the guns be fired, and violins, bagpipes, and every sort of
musical instrument began to play. No one talked of anything but dancing
and rejoicing. The king, queen, and prince begged Cendron to consent to
let the marriage take place immediately.

"No," she said, "I must first tell you my story," which she did in a few
words. When they found that she was born a princess, they again were so
filled with joy that they thought they would burst. And when she told them
the names of her father and mother, they recognized them as sovereigns of
dominions they had conquered. When they informed Finette of this fact,
she immediately vowed that she would not consent to marry the prince

until they had restored the estates of her father. Of course, they promised to do so, for they had upward of a hundred kingdoms, and one more or less was not worth haggling over.

In the meantime Belle-de-Nuit and Fleur d'Amour had arrived at the palace, and the first news that greeted them was that Cendron had put on the slipper. They did not know what to do or say. They decided to return again without seeing her, but when Finette heard they had arrived, she insisted that they come in. Instead of berating and punishing them as they deserved, she advanced to embrace them tenderly and then presented them to the queen. "Madam, these are my sisters. They are very charming, and I ask you to love them."

So confused were they by Finette's kindness that they were rendered speechless. She promised them they could return to their own kingdom, which the king was restoring to their family. At these words they threw themselves on their knees before her and wept for joy.

The wedding was the most splendid that has ever been seen. Finette wrote to her godmother and put the letter along with valuable presents on the back of the pretty Spanish horse. The letter requested that she visit the king and queen, tell them of their good fortune, and inform them they could now return to their kingdom, an errand the fairy Merluche performed most graciously. Thus did Finette's father and mother regain their estates and her sisters later become queens just like her.

> If it's revenge on the ungrateful you want to see,
> Then follow Finette's wise policy.
> Do favors of the undeserving until they weep.
> Each benefit inflicts a wound most deep,
> Cutting the haughty bosom to the core.
> Finette's proud, selfish sisters suffered more,
> When by her generous kindness overpower'd,
> Than if the ogres had made them into a mess,
> For she overcame them with her kindness.
> From her example, then, this lesson learn,
> And give good for evil in your turn
> No matter what wrong may awake your wrath,
> There is no greater vengeance than this kind path.

THE BEE
AND
THE ORANGE TREE

ONCE upon a time there was a king and a queen who lacked nothing but children to make them happy. Since the queen was already old, she was beginning to despair of ever having any when at last she became pregnant and in due time gave birth to the most beautiful girl the world has ever seen. There was great joy in the palace, and everyone tried to find a name for the princess that would express their feeling toward her. In the end they called her Aimée.

The queen had her name, "Aimée, daughter of the King of the Happy Island," engraved upon a turquoise heart. Then she tied it around the princess's neck, believing that the turquoise would bring her good fortune. In this case, however, its vaunted properties failed to work.

One day, when her nurse was seeking some diversion, she took the princess out to sea in the finest summer weather. All at once a tremendous tempest erupted, and it was impossible to land. Since their little boat was used only for pleasure trips close to shore, it was soon ripped to pieces, and the nurse and all the sailors perished. The little princess, asleep in her cradle, remained floating on the sea and was ultimately tossed by the waves onto the coast of a very pretty country.

This land had become nearly deserted ever since the ogre Ravagio and his wife, Tourmentine, had come to live there, for they ate up everybody they could find. Ogres are terrible creatures: once they have tasted fresh meat (this is how they refer to human flesh), they will hardly ever eat anything else, and Tourmentine always discovered some secret way of attracting a victim, for she was half fairy.

When she caught the scent of the poor little princess from a mile away, she ran to the shore to search for her before Ravagio found her, for they were equally greedy. Never have you seen such hideous figures: each had one squinting eye in the middle of their forehead, a mouth as large as an oven's and a large, flat nose, long asses' ears, hair standing on end, and humps in front and behind. Once Tourmentine saw Aimée in her rich

417

cradle, wrapped in swaddling clothes of gold brocade, batting with her wee hands, her cheeks resembling a white rose mixed with a carnation, and her vermilion cupid mouth half open in what seemed to be a smile at the horrid monster who had come to devour her, the ogress was touched with a feeling of pity she had never felt before. She decided to nurse it, even though there was always the possibility she might succumb to temptation and eat it at some later time. She took the child in her arms, tied the cradle on her back, and returned to her cave.

"Look, Ravagio," she said, "here's some fresh meat, very plump and very tender. But if you know what's good for you, you'd better not sink your teeth into it—it's a beautiful little girl. I'm going to raise her and then we'll marry her to our son. They'll have some extraordinary little ogres, and that will keep us amused in our old age."

"Well said," replied Ravagio, "you're as wise as you are powerful. Let me look at the child. She seems beautiful to look at."

"Don't eat her!" said Tourmentine, putting the child in his giant clutches.

"No, no," he said. "I'd sooner die of hunger."

What a miracle to behold! Imagine the ogres Ravagio, Tourmentine, and their young ones caressing Aimée in such a humane manner. But the poor child, who saw only these deformed creatures around her, began to curl her lip and bawl with all her might for her nurse. Ravagio's cave echoed with these cries, and Tourmentine, fearing the noise would frighten the baby even more, carried her into the wood with her six children following her—each one was uglier than the next. As I mentioned before, she was half fairy, and she summoned her power by taking an ivory wand and wishing for whatever she wanted. So she took the wand and said, "I wish, in the name of the royal fairy Trufio, that the most beautiful, gentle, and tame doe in our forests will leave its fawn and come immediately to nurse this little creature that Fortune has sent me."

Immediately a doe appeared, and since the little ogres gave her a warm welcome, she approached the princess and began suckling her. Then Tourmentine carried her back to her grotto with the doe skipping and gamboling after them. The child kept looking at it and petting it. When she was in her cradle and cried, the doe was always there ready to feed her, and the little ogres rocked her.

This was how the king's daughter was raised.

In the meantime she was mourned night and day for many years. At last the king was convinced she had indeed drowned and thought of choosing an heir. He spoke to the queen about this matter, and she told him to do what he judged proper. Since her dear Aimée was dead, she had no hope of having any more children and told him he had waited long enough. "Fifteen years has elapsed since I had the misfortune of losing my daughter, and it would be folly to expect her return now."

The king decided to ask his brother to choose among his sons the one he thought the most worthy ruler and to send him without delay. He gave his ambassadors this message and all the necessary instructions, and they departed. Since they had to sail a great distance, they embarked on some sturdy vessels. The wind was so favorable that they soon arrived at the palace of the king's brother, who ruled over a large domain. He welcomed them graciously, and when they asked his permission to take back one of his sons to succeed their master, he wept for joy.

Since his brother left the choice to him, he told them he would send the one he would have taken for himself, which was his second son, whose inclinations were so well suited to the greatness of his birth that the king found him perfect in every possible way. They sent for Prince Aimé (for this was his name) and no matter how prejudiced in his favor the ambassadors had been beforehand, they were astonished when they saw this eighteen-year-old youth. Cupid, the young god of love himself, could not have matched his beauty. On the other hand, it was a beauty which did not detract from that noble, martial air that inspires respect and affection. He was told how eager his uncle was to have him near him and how his father wanted him to depart soon. So they prepared his equipage, and he took his leave and put to sea.

Let him sail on. Let fortune guide him! We shall now return to Ravagio and see what has transpired with our young princess.

Her beauty blossomed as she grew older, and one could certainly say that Love, the Graces, and all the goddesses combined never possessed so many charms. Whenever she was in the dark cave with Ravagio, Tourmentine, and the young ogres, it seemed that the sun, stars, and skies descended into it. In addition, the cruelty of these monsters had the effect of making her even gentler. From the moment she became aware of their terrible yen for human flesh, she always tried to save the unfortunates who fell into their hands, so much so that she often exposed herself to their fury. She would have been destroyed by them had not the young ogre guarded her like the apple of his eye. Ah, what love will not do! This monster's nature had softened by watching and adoring this beautiful princess. But, alas, how she suffered when she thought she would have to marry this detestable lover! Although she knew nothing about her origin, she had guessed rightly from her rich clothes, the gold chain, and the turquoise that she was highborn, and from the feelings of her heart she believed this even more so. Unable to read, write, or speak any language but the jargon of the ogres, she lived in perfect ignorance of all worldly matters, yet she possessed such fine principles of virtue and such sweet, unaffected manners, it was as though she had been brought up in the most refined court in the universe.

She always wore a tiger-skin dress that she had made for herself. Her arms were half naked, and she carried a quiver and arrows over her shoulder and a bow at her side. Her blond hair, fastened only by a plaited

band of sea rushes, floated in the breeze over her neck and shoulders. She also wore buckskins made of the same rush. In this attire she roved the woods like a second Diana, and she would never have known she was beautiful if the crystal-clear springs had not offered themselves to her as innocent mirrors. (Still, whenever she gazed into them, she did not become vain.) The sun had a similar effect on her complexion as on wax by making it whiter, and the sea air could not tan it. Since she never ate anything but what she caught in hunting or fishing, she often used this pretext to stay away from the cave and avoid looking at those most deformed objects in nature. "Heavens," she cried, shedding tears, "what have I done to make you sentence me to become the bride of this cruel young ogre? Why didn't you let me perish in the sea? Why did you save a life that must be spent in this most deplorable manner? Don't you have any compassion for my grief?" In this way did she address the gods and ask for their aid.

When the weather was rough and she thought the sea had cast unfortunates on shore, she cautiously went to assist them and prevent them from approaching the ogres' cave. Thus, when one night brought a fearful storm, she rose the next day as soon as it was light and ran toward the sea. There she saw a man who had his arms locked around a plank and was trying to reach the shore, despite the violence of the waves continually turning him back. Most anxious to help him, the princess made signs pointing to the easiest landing places, but he did not see or hear her. Sometimes he came so close that it appeared he had but one last step to make when a wave would engulf him and he would disappear.

At last he was thrown onto the sand and lay prone without any signs of life. Aimée approached him, and in spite of his deathlike appearance, she gave him all the assistance she could. She always carried certain herbs with her, and their odor was so powerful that they could revive anyone from the longest fainting fit. Pressing them between her hands, she rubbed some of them on his lips and temples. When he at last opened his eyes, he was so astonished by her beauty and dress that he could hardly tell whether he were in a dream. He spoke first and she responded, but they could not understand each other. Instead they attentively stared at each other with a mixture of astonishment and pleasure.

Until now the princess had only seen poor fishermen whom the ogres might have snared and whom she saved, as I have already noted. What could she have possibly thought when she saw the most handsome man in the world in most magnificent attire? Indeed, it was none other than the Prince Aimé, her first cousin, whose fleet had been driven by a tempest and smashed to pieces on the shoals. Left to the mercy of the winds and waves, their crews had either perished or been cast on unknown shores.

For his part, the young prince was confounded by seeing such a beautiful creature in such savage attire in such a deserted country. When he thought about the princes and ladies he had so recently seen on his departure, he was only more convinced that the being he now beheld surpassed them all by far.

In their mutual astonishment they continued to talk without being able to understand each other; their looks and actions were the sole interpreters of their thoughts. Yet after a few moments the princess suddenly remembered the danger confronting the stranger, and her face showed great distress and melancholy. Fearing she was falling sick, the prince showed deep concern. He tried to take her hand, but she pushed him away and endeavored as best she could to impress upon him that he must fly. She began to run away from him, then returned and made signs for him to do the same. He accordingly ran away from her and returned. When he did, she was angry with him. So she took her arrows and pointed them at her heart to indicate that he would be killed. He thought she wished to kill him and thus knelt on one knee awaiting the blow. When she saw that, she did not know what to do or how to express herself. Looking at him tenderly, she said, "Are you to become a victim of my frightful hosts? Must these very eyes that now gaze on you with so much pleasure see you torn to pieces and devoured without mercy?"

At this she wept, and the prince was at a loss to comprehend the meaning of her actions. She did succeed, however, in making him understand that she did not wish him to follow her. Taking him by the hand, she led him to a very deep cave in a cliff that opened toward the sea. She often went there to bemoan her misfortunes, and sometimes she slept there when the sun became too bright even for her and prevented her from returning to the ogres' cave. Clever and skillful, she had furnished it by hanging butterfly wings of various colors on the walls. In addition, she had spread a carpet of sea rushes on intertwined canes that formed a sort of couch. Clusters of flowers were placed in large, deep shells, answering the purpose of vases, which she filled with water to preserve her bouquets. She had manufactured a thousand pretty things, some with fish bones and shells, and others with sea rushes and canes. Despite their simplicity these articles were so exquisitely made that it was easy to judge that the princess had good taste and ingenuity. The prince was completely surprised by it all, mistakenly thinking that she lived there. Just being there with her delighted him, and although he was not at ease to express the admiration he felt for her, it already seemed he preferred this simple girl's company to all the crowns ordained by his birth and the will of his relations.

Making him sit down, she indicated that she wished him to remain there until she could procure something for him to eat. Then she unfastened the band from her hair, wrapped it around the prince's arm, tied him to the couch, and left. He was dying to follow, but was afraid of displeasing her and so abandoned himself to thoughts that he could not entertain in her presence. "Where am I?" he asked. "What country has Fortune led me to? My vessels are lost, my people are drowned, and I have nothing left. Instead of the crown that was offered me, I find a gloomy rock for a refuge. What will become of me here? What sort of people shall I find? If I'm to judge from the person who's helped me, they're all divinities. But judging by the fear she had that I might follow her—what a rude and barbarous language! It sounds so terrible coming from her exquisite lips—induces me to think something even more unfortunate will befall me than has already occurred."

By turns he found his thoughts entirely focused on reviewing all the incomparable charms of the young savage. His heart was on fire, and he became impatient waiting for her return, for her absence seemed the greatest of all evils.

In fact, she returned as quickly as she could. She had thought of nothing but the prince, and such tender feelings were so new to her that she was not on her guard against them. She thanked Heaven for having saved him from the dangers of the sea, and she prayed that he be preserved from the danger he ran by being so near to the ogres. Brimming with excitement, she walked so rapidly that when she arrived, she felt rather oppressed by the heavy tiger's skin that served as her mantle. When she slumped onto the couch, the prince placed himself at her feet, agitated by her suffering although he was certainly worse off than she. As soon as she recovered from her faintness, she displayed all the delicacies she had brought him: four parrots and six squirrels cooked by the sun, and strawberries, cherries, raspberries, and other fruits. The plates were made of cedar and eagle wood, the knife of stone, the table napkins of large, soft, and pliable leaves.

A shell was used as a cup, and another filled with spring-pure water. The prince expressed his gratitude by all sorts of gestures with his head and hands, and he understood by her sweet smile that all his gesturing pleased her.

Once the hour of separation arrived, however, she made it perfectly clear to him that they must part, and both began sighing and hiding sudden tears. She stood up and would have gone, but the prince uttered a loud cry and threw himself at her feet, begging her to remain. She saw clearly what he meant, but she rebuffed him with some severity, and he knew he had better learn to obey her straightaway.

If truth be told, he spent a miserable night, and the princess fared no better. When she returned to the cave and found herself surrounded by the ogres and their children, especially the frightful young monster that was to become her husband, and thought of the charming stranger she had just left, she felt inclined to throw herself into the sea. Moreover, she was afraid that Ravagio or Tourmentine would smell fresh meat and go straight to the rock and devour Prince Aimé.

These sundry fears kept her awake all night. At daybreak she arose and nearly flew to the seashore, loaded with the best of everything: parrots, monkeys, bustards, fruits, and milk. The prince had not undressed. He had suffered so much from fatigue at sea and had slept so little that he had fallen into a doze toward morning. "What?" she said as she woke him. "I've been thinking of you ever since I left you. I didn't even close my eyes, and you're able to sleep!"

The prince looked at her and listened without understanding her. In turn he declared, "What joy, my darling," he said, kissing her hands, "what joy it is to see you again! It seems ages ago since you left this rock."

He talked for some time to her before he remembered that she could not understand him. When he did, he sighed heavily and fell silent. She then picked up the conversation and told him she was dreadfully afraid that Ravagio and Tourmentine would discover him; she did not believe he would be safe in the rock for any length of time; if he went away she would die, but she would sooner consent to that than expose him to be devoured. Finally she implored him to flee. At this point, tears filled her eyes, and she clasped her hands in a most supplicating manner. Since he could not understand in the least what she meant, he became desperate and threw himself at her feet. She kept pointing to the way out so that at last he understood part of her meaning, and he in turn signaled to her that he would rather die than leave her. So touched was she by this proof of the prince's affection that she took the gold chain with the turquoise heart from her arm, the one her mother had hung around her neck, and tied it around his arm in a most tender manner. Despite the fact that this gesture left him feeling exhilarated, he did not fail to notice the letters engraved on the turquoise. Examining them carefully, he read, "Aimée, daughter of the King of the Happy Island."

Never was anyone so astonished, for he knew that the baby princess who had perished was called Aimée. He was convinced that this heart belonged to her, but he was not sure whether this beautiful savage was the princess, or whether the sea had thrown this trinket onto the beach. He gazed at Aimée with the most extraordinary attention, and the more he looked, the more he discovered a certain family resemblance in her features. In particular, the tender feelings of his heart led him to believe that the savage maiden must be his cousin.

She was astonished as he lifted his eyes to Heaven in thanks, then looked at her and wept, taking her hands and kissing them vehemently. He thanked her for her generosity, and as he refastened the trinket on her arm, he indicated to her that he would prefer to have a lock of her hair, but she hesitated in granting him this favor.

Four days passed in this way. Every morning the princess brought him the food he needed. She remained with him as long as she could, and the hours sped quickly by even though they could not converse. One evening, when she returned rather late and expected to be scolded by the terrible Tourmentine, she was very much surprised at the warm welcome she received. Upon finding a table covered with fruit, she asked if she could have some. Ravagio told her that they were intended for her; the young ogre had been gathering them, and it was now time to make him happy, for he wished to marry her in three days. What tidings! Could there be anything in the world more dreadful for this charming princess? She thought she would die of fright and grief, but she concealed her affliction and replied she would obey them without reluctance, provided they would give her a little more time.

Becoming angry, Ravagio said, "What's to prevent me from devouring you?"

The poor princess fainted with fear in the claws of Tourmentine, and the young ogre, who loved her dearly, so entreated Ravagio on her behalf that he eventually appeased him.

Aimée did not sleep a moment, waiting impatiently for daylight. As soon as it appeared, she flew to the rock, and when she saw the prince, she moaned and wept profusely. He felt as though his heart had stopped. In four days his love for the beautiful Aimée had grown the way a more common ardor develops in four years, and he was frantic to learn what had happened. She knew he could not understand her and could think of no mode of explanation. At last she untied her long hair, put a wreath of flowers on her head and, taking Aimé's hand, made signs to show that they intended her to do what she was doing with another. He understood the impending catastrophe: they were going to wed her to someone else.

He felt that he was bound to die since he did not know of a way to escape. She, too, felt helpless, and so they shed tears together and gazed at each other, indicating that it would be better to die together than be separated.

She stayed with him until evening, but night came all too quickly. Lost in thought as she made her way back to the ogres, she did not pay attention to the paths she was taking and strayed into a part of the wood she seldom frequented. There a long thorn pierced her foot deeply, and luckily for her she was not far from the cave. As it was, she had a great deal of trouble in reaching it, since her foot was covered with blood. Ravagio, Tourmentine, and the young ogres came to her assistance. She suffered a bout of agony as they pulled out the thorn, and even though they gathered herbs and applied them to her foot, she retired very anxious about her dear prince, as may be imagined. "Alas!" she said, "I won't be able to walk tomorrow. What will he think if he doesn't see me? Thanks to my efforts, he now knows they intend to have me wed, and he'll think I haven't been able to prevent it. Who'll feed him? No matter what he does, it will be his death. If he comes looking for me, he's lost. If I send one of the young ogres to him, Ravagio will learn about it," she sighed and then burst into tears. When she arose early in the morning, her wound was too painful for her to walk, and when Tourmentine saw her crawling out, she stopped her and said, "If you take another step, I'll eat you."

In the meantime, the prince realized that the usual hour for their meeting had passed, and he became increasingly distressed and frightened. All the torments in the world seemed less terrible to him than the anxieties that his love caused him. He forced himself to be patient, but the longer he waited, the less hope he had. At length he rushed outside determined to seek his charming princess, no matter what the risk was. Not knowing where he was going, he followed a beaten path that he saw at the entrance of the wood. After walking for an hour, he heard a noise and saw a cave with thick smoke coming from the entrance. Thinking he might obtain some information there, he entered it. Scarcely had he taken a step when he saw Ravagio, who instantly seized him with immense strength and would have devoured him if the cries he uttered in self-defense had not reached the ears of his dear love. At the sound of that voice she felt nothing could stop her. She rushed out of the recess where she slept and into that part of the cave where Ravagio was holding the poor prince. Blanching, trembling as though she herself were to be eaten, she threw herself on her knees before Ravagio and begged him to keep this fresh meat for the day of her marriage with the young ogre. "Then I myself will eat him."

At these words Ravagio was so content in thinking the princess would follow their customs that he let go of the prince and locked him up in the recess where the young ogres slept. Aimée requested that she be allowed to feed him so that he would not grow thin and do honor to the nuptial repast. The ogre consented, and she took the best of everything to the prince.

When he saw her enter, his joy made him forget his wretched condition, but his grief returned when she showed him her wounded foot. For some time they wept together. The prince had no stomach for eating, but his dear mistress cut such delicate pieces with her own hands and gave them to him with so much kindness that he could not possibly refuse them. She made the young ogres bring fresh moss, which she covered with bird feathers, and led the prince to understand it was to be his bed. When Tourmentine called her, she could bid adieu only by stretching out her hand. He kissed it with an ardor that cannot be described, and in her eyes he clearly read the nature of her reply.

As it happens, Ravagio, Tourmentine, and the princess slept in one of the recesses of the cave, and the young ogres slept in the other, where the prince was. It is the custom among ogres that they always sleep with their fine gold crowns on their heads. This is the only luxury in which they indulge themselves, and they would rather be hanged or strangled than forgo it. When they were all asleep, the princess, in thinking of her lover, remembered that although Ravagio and Tourmentine had given their word of honor they would not eat the prince, it would all be over for him if they felt hungry in the night (which was almost always the case when fresh meat was near). The anxiety provoked by this horrid thought troubled her so much that she was about to die from fright. After contemplating the situation for some time, she got up, quickly threw on her tiger skin, and silently groped her way out into the open. Entering the cave where the younger ogres slept, she took the crown from the head of the first one she came to and put it on the prince, who was wide awake but dared not show it, for he was not sure who was performing this ceremony. Afterward, the princess returned to her own humble bed.

No sooner had she crept into it than Ravagio, who had been dreaming of the good meal he might have made of the prince, felt his appetite increasing the more he dwelled on it. He arose in his turn and went into the recess where the little ogres were sleeping. Unable to see clearly and afraid of making a mistake, he felt about with his hand and threw himself on the one who was not wearing a crown. Then he crunched him as he would a chicken. The poor princess, who heard the cracking bones of the unfortunate creature he was eating, swooned in fright at the thought that it might be her lover. For his part, the prince, who was much nearer, was prey to all the terrors born of such a plight.

Morning relieved the princess of her terrible anxiety. Quickly seeking the prince, she made him understand through sign language both her fears and her eagerness to keep him safe from the murderous jaws of these monsters.

She spoke kindly to him, and he would have uttered a thousand kinder words to her but for the arrival of the ogress, who came looking for her children. When she saw the cave filled with blood and her youngest ogre missing, she uttered horrible shrieks. Ravagio soon found out what he had done, but the evil could not be remedied. He whispered to her that he had been hungry and had chosen the wrong one, for he thought he had eaten the fresh meat. Tourmentine pretended to be pacified, for Ravagio was cruel and if she had not taken his apology in stride, he very likely would have devoured her.

Meanwhile, the beautiful princess continued to be tormented by her anxiety, and she was constantly thinking about how to save the prince. For his part, he could think only about the frightful place where this charming girl abided. He knew he would never leave as long as she remained. He would have preferred death to their separation. He indicated this to her by repeated signs as she implored him to flee and save himself. They shed tears, pressed each other's hands, and vowed in their respective languages that they would be faithful to each other until eternity.

She could not resist showing him the clothes she had worn when Tourmentine found her and also the cradle in which she had arrived. Recognizing the arms and emblem of the King of the Happy Island, the prince was overjoyed when he saw this proof of her heritage. The princess, noticing how joyful he became, realized that he had learned something of significance and yearned to know what the emblems meant. But how could he make her aware of whose daughter she was and how closely they were related? All she could make out was that she had great reason to rejoice.

At last the hour for slumber arrived. When they retired to their beds as they had on the previous night, the princess was prey to the same misgivings. So she got up quietly, went into the other cave recess, gently took the crown from one of the little ogres, and put it on her lover's head, who dared not detain her because of the respect and affection he felt for her. The princess was wise to put the crown on Aimé's head, for without this precaution he would have been lost. Startled out of her sleep, the barbarous Tourmentine began mulling over the prince, whom she considered more handsome than the day and tempting food indeed. She was so afraid that Ravagio would eat him alone that she thought she would beat him to it. Without uttering a word, she glided into the young ogres' cave, where she gently touched those heads that had crowns (the prince among them), and one of the little ogres was gone in three mouthfuls. Aimé and his ladylove heard everything and trembled with fear, but Tourmentine, after having accomplished her purpose, now only wanted to go to sleep. So they were safe for the rest of the night.

"Heaven help us!" the princess cried. "Send me some idea of how we can escape our terrible predicament!"

The prince prayed as fervently. At times he felt the urge to attack the two monsters and fight them. But what hope did he have of winning against them? They were as tall as giants, and their skin protected them from pistol shots. He came to the more prudent conclusion that cunning alone could extricate them.

As soon as day arrived and Tourmentine found the bones of her little ogre, she filled the air with dreadful howls. Ravagio appeared to be in as much despair. A hundred times they were on the verge of throwing themselves on the prince and princess and devouring them without mercy. Though the two had huddled in a dark corner, the cannibals knew full well where they could be found. Of all the perils the lovers had encountered, this seemed to be the most pressing. Aimée racked her brains and all at once remembered that the ivory wand which Tourmentine possessed performed wonders. Why this was so, the ogress herself had never been able to tell.

"If these surprising things could occur despite her ignorance," the princess said, "why shouldn't my words have just as much effect?"

Inspired by this idea, she ran to the cave in which Tourmentine slept and looked for the wand, which was hidden in a hole. As soon as she held it in her hand, she said, "I wish, in the name of the royal fairy Trufio, to speak the language of the man I love." She would have made many other wishes, but Ravagio entered, and the princess fell silent. Putting the wand back, she returned noiselessly to the prince. "Dear stranger," she said, "your troubles affect me much more than do my own."

When the prince heard these words, he was struck with astonishment. "I understand you, adorable princess," he said. "You're speaking my language! I hope that you in turn understand that I'm more worried about you than about myself. You're dearer to me than my life, than the light of day, than all that is most beautiful in nature!"

"My terms are much more simple," the princess replied, "but they aren't any less sincere. The way I feel, I'd give everything in the rocky cave on the seashore, all my sheep and lambs—in short, all I possess for the pleasure of beholding you."

The prince thanked her a thousand times for her kindness and begged her to tell him who had taught her so well and in so short a time to speak an unknown tongue. She told him of the power of the enchanted wand, and he informed her about her birth and their relation to each other. The princess was ecstatic, and since nature had endowed her with such marvelous intelligence, she expressed it in such choice and well-turned phrases that the prince fell more in love with her than ever. They pledged their troth to each other forever and promised to live in harmony from the moment they could be wed.

They had little time to make their plans, for they had to flee from these enraged monsters and seek an asylum for themselves as quickly as they could. The princess told her lover that as soon as she saw Ravagio and Tourmentine were asleep, she would fetch their great camel. Then they would mount it and let Heaven conduct them wherever it would. The prince was so delighted he had difficulty containing his joy. Many things that still alarmed him were offset by the charming prospect of the future.

Finally the nightfall they had desired so long arrived. The princess took some meal and kneaded it with her white hands into a cake. In it she put a bean. Then she picked up the ivory wand and said, "Oh, bean, little bean! I wish, in the name of the royal fairy Trufio that you may speak in my voice until you're baked." She put this cake into the hot cinders and then went to the prince, who was waiting most impatiently in the miserable recess of the young ogres. "Let's go," she said, "the camel is tethered in the wood."

"May love and fortune guide us," the prince murmured. "Come, come, my Aimée, let's seek a happy and peaceful abode." By the light of the moon she slipped the ivory wand into a safe place, and when they found the camel, they set out not knowing whither they were bound.

In the meantime Tourmentine, filled with grief, kept turning over, unable to sleep. Putting out her arm to feel if the princess was in bed yet and not finding her, she cried out in a thunderous voice, "Where are you, girl?"

"I'm near the fire," answered the bean.

"When are you coming to bed?"

"Soon," the bean replied. "Go to sleep, go to sleep."

Afraid of waking Ravagio, Tourmentine fell silent. But two hours later she again felt Aimée's little bed and cried out, "What, you little rascal, you won't come to bed?"

"I'm warming myself as much as I can," the bean answered.

"I wish you were in the middle of the fire for all the trouble you're causing," the ogress added.

"I'm there indeed," the bean said. "No one has ever warmed himself nearer."

They continued talking for a while, and the bean kept up the conversation, like a very clever bean. Toward morning Tourmentine again called the princess, but the bean was baked and did not answer. Made uneasy by this silence, she got up angrily, looked about her, called, alarmed everybody, and began searching everywhere. No princess! No prince! No wand! She shrieked so loudly that the rocks and valleys echoed again and again. "Wake up, my poppet! Awake, dear Ravagio! Your Tourmentine has been betrayed. Our fresh meat has run away."

Ravagio opened his eye and sprang into the center of the cavern like a lion. He roared, he bellowed, he howled, he foamed. "Quick, quick! Give me my seven-league boots so I can pursue our fugitives. I'll catch them and eat them before long." Then he donned his boots, which carried him seven leagues at a stride.

Alas, how could our lovers possibly run fast enough to escape such a runner? You may be surprised that with the ivory wand they did not go faster than he did, but the beautiful princess was a novice in fairy art.

They were so delighted now to be together and understand each other that they were overconfident that they would not be pursued. However, as they advanced, the princess caught sight of the terrible Ravagio and cried, "Prince, we're lost! Look, there's that frightful monster coming toward us like a thunderbolt!"

"What shall we do?" the prince exclaimed. "What will become of us? Ah, if I were alone, I wouldn't care about my life, but yours, my dear mistress, is threatened as well."

"Unless the wand helps us, there's no hope," Aimée remarked tearily. "I wish," she continued, "in the name of the royal fairy Trufio that our camel become a pond, that the prince become a boat, and myself an old woman who rows the boat."

The pond, boat, and old woman appeared immediately, and when Ravagio arrived at the water's edge, he cried, "Hola, ho! Old mother, have you seen a camel and young man and woman pass by here?"

The old woman, who kept her boat in the middle of the pond, put her spectacles on her nose. Gazing at Ravagio, she made signs to him that she had seen them passing through the meadow. The ogre believed her and went off to the left. Then the princess wished for her natural form again, and she touched herself with the wand three times and struck the boat and the pond. She and the prince became young and beautiful again. They quickly mounted the camel and turned to the right so that they would not encounter their foe.

While proceeding rapidly, hoping to find someone who could tell them the road to the Happy Island, they lived off the wild fruit of the country, drank water from springs, and slept beneath the trees. Though they feared that wild beasts would come and devour them, the princess had her bow and arrows with which to defend herself. The danger was not so terrible that they were prevented from enjoying the exhilaration of having escaped the cave and finding themselves together. Ever since they had begun understanding each other, they had exchanged the prettiest sentiments in the world. Love generally quickens the wit, but in their case they needed no such assistance because they each had a thousand natural charms and unique ideas constantly at hand.

The prince told the princess that he was extremely eager to reach either his or her royal father's court as soon as possible. "Especially since you have promised to become my wife, provided that our parents consent."

Though difficult perhaps to believe while waiting for this happy day and being alone with her in the forest, where he was at complete liberty to make her any proposals he desired, he conducted himself in such a respectful and prudent manner that the world has never witnessed so much love and virtue together in one person.

After Ravagio had scoured the mountains, forests, and plains, he returned to his cave, where Tourmentine and the young ogres impatiently awaited him. He was carrying five or six people who had unfortunately fallen into his clutches.

"Well," said Tourmentine, "have you found and eaten those runaways, those thieves, that fresh meat? Didn't you at least save me one of their hands or feet?"

"I believe they must have flown off into the sky," replied Ravagio. "I ran like a wolf everywhere without encountering them. I only saw an old woman in a boat on a pond, who gave me some tidings about them."

"What did she tell you, then?" Tourmentine asked impatiently.

"That they had gone to the left," Ravagio replied.

"My word, you've been deceived!" she said. "I suspect you actually spoke to them. Go back, and if you find them, don't give them a moment's grace!"

Ravagio greased his seven-league boots and rushed off again like a madman. Our young lovers were just emerging from a wood in which they had passed the night when they saw the ogre and became greatly alarmed. "My Aimée," said the prince, "our enemy is here. I feel I have enough courage to fight him. Do you think you have enough courage to flee by yourself?"

"No," she cried, "I'll never forsake you. How can you be so unkind as to doubt my love for you? But let's not lose any time. Perhaps the wand may help us. I wish," she cried, "in the name of the royal fairy Trufio, that the prince be changed into a picture, the camel into a pillar, and myself into a dwarf."

Once the transformation was made, the dwarf began to blow a horn. Ravagio approached with rapid strides and said, "Tell me, you little abortion of nature, have you seen a fine young man, a young girl, and a camel pass by here?"

"Ah, I'll tell you," replied the dwarf. "I know that you're searching for a fine chevalier, a marvelously fair dame, and the beast they rode on. I saw them yesterday at this very spot happily enjoying themselves. The fine chevalier received the praise and guerdon of the jousts and tournaments held in honor of Merlusine, who is depicted on this portrait. Many highborn gentlemen and good knights broke their lances here on hauberks, helmets, and shields. The contest was rough, and the guerdon was a most beautiful clasp of gold richly beset with pearls and diamonds. On their departure the unknown dame said to me, 'Dwarf, my friend, without further parley, I'd like you to do me a favor in the name of your fairest ladylove.' 'It won't be denied,' I said to her, 'and I grant it to you, on the sole condition that it's within my power.' 'In case, then,' she said, 'that you should meet an extraordinary giant whose eye is in the middle of his forehead, ask him most courteously to go his way in peace and leave us alone.' With that she whipped her palfrey and they departed."

"Which way?" Ravagio asked.

"By that verdant meadow on the edge of the wood."

"If you're lying, you filthy little reptile," the ogre replied, "you can be sure that I'll eat you, your pillar, and your portrait of Merlusine."

"There's no villainy or falsehood in me," said the dwarf. "My tongue doesn't lie. Not a soul can convict me of fraud. But go quickly if you want to kill them before the sun sets."

The ogre strode away. The dwarf resumed her own figure and touched the portrait and pillar, which also became themselves again. What joy for the lover and his mistress!

"Never have I felt such terrible anxiety, my dear Aimée," the prince said. As my love for you increases every moment, so do my fears when you are in danger."

"As for me," she said, "it seems to me that I wasn't afraid, for Ravagio never eats pictures, and I alone was exposed to his fury, and my figure was not appetizing. No matter what, I would have given my life to protect yours."

In the meantime, Ravagio hunted in vain and could not find the lover or his mistress. Tired as a dog, he retraced his steps to the cave.

"What? You've returned without our prisoners?" Tourmentine exclaimed, tearing her bristling hair. "Don't come near me or I'll strangle you!"

"I saw nothing," he said, "but a dwarf, a pillar, and a picture."

"My word," she continued, "it was them! How foolish I was to leave my vengeance in your hands, as though I were too little to undertake it myself. Now I'll go! I'll put on the boots this time, and I'll go just as fast as you." So saying, she put on the seven-league boots and started off.

What chance did the prince and princess have of traveling quickly enough to escape these monsters with their cursed seven-league boots? They saw Tourmentine coming, dressed in a serpent's skin with startling motley colors. On her shoulder she carried a terribly heavy mace of iron, and as she peered around carefully, she would have seen the prince and princess had they not been at that moment in the thickest part of a wood.

"The matter's hopeless," said Aimée, weeping. "Here comes the cruel Tourmentine, whose sight chills my blood. She's more cunning than Ravagio. If either of us were to speak to her, she'd know us and eat us up without much ado. Our trial will be over as soon as you can imagine."

"Love, Love, do not abandon us!" the prince exclaimed. "Can you find more tender or more pure hearts than ours in your realm? Ah, my dear Aimée," he continued, taking her hands and kissing them fervently, "can it be that you're destined to perish in such a barbarous manner?"

"No," she said, "I have a certain feeling of courage and firmness that reassures me. Come, little wand, do your duty. I wish, in the name of the royal fairy Trufio that the camel become a tub, that my dear prince become a beautiful orange tree, and that I become a bee that hovers around him."

As usual, she struck three blows for each, and the change occurred so suddenly that Tourmentine, who had arrived on the spot, did not notice it. Out of breath, the horrible fury sat down under the orange tree. The princess bee took delight in stinging her in a thousand places, and although her skin was very hard, one sting pierced it and made her cry out. To see her roll and flail about on the grass, one would have thought her a bull or a young lion tormented by a swarm of insects, for this one was worth a hundred. The prince orange tree was dying with fear the princess would be caught and killed. At last Tourmentine, covered with blood, went away, and the princess was about to resume her own form when, unluckily, some travelers passed through the wood and spied the ivory wand. It was such a pretty thing that they picked it up and carried it away.

Nothing could be any more unfortunate than this. The prince and princess had not lost their speech, but it was of little use to them in their present condition. Overwhelmed with grief, the prince uttered lamentations that greatly added to his dear Aimée's distress. At times he would express himself like this:

"The moment was near, when my princess
Was to grant my wishes its crown.
A hope so enchanting—such joyful excess
Left misfortune with nothing but a frown.
O Love, who such wonders can work at your will,
Who rules and sways our world with your dart,
Keep my bee away from all danger, and instill
Her with love that will protect her heart."

"How wretched I am," he continued, "to be locked up within the bark of a tree. Here I am, an orange tree without any power to move. What will become of me if you abandon me, my dear little bee? On the other hand, why must you fly so far from me? You'll find a most pleasant dew on my flowers, and drops sweeter than honey. You'll be able to live on this. My leaves will invite you to couch in them, and you'll have nothing to fear from the malice of spiders."

As soon as the orange tree stopped uttering complaints, the bee replied to him as follows:

"Fear not, Prince, that I should range.
There's nothing my faithful heart can change.
Let your only thought be in time
That you have conquered this heart of mine."

She added to that, "Have no fear that I'll ever leave you. Neither the lilies, nor the jasmines, nor the roses, nor all the flowers of the most beautiful gardens, could induce me to be unfaithful to you. You'll see me continually hovering around you, and you'll know that the orange tree is just as dear to the bee as Prince Aimé was to Princess Aimée."

In short order she shut herself up in one of the largest flowers as though in a palace, and true love, which is never without its consolations, found some even in this union.

The wood in which the orange tree was situated was the favorite promenade of a princess named Linda who lived nearby in a magnificent palace. Young, beautiful, and witty, she would not marry because she was afraid she would not always be loved by the person she might choose for a husband. And since she was very wealthy, she built a sumptuous castle where she admitted only ladies and old men (more philosophers than gallants) and refused to have young cavaliers come near.

One day, when the heat detained her in her apartments somewhat longer than she had wished, she went out in the evening with all her ladies and took a walk in the wood. The perfume from the orange tree surprised her. She had never seen one, and she was delighted to have found it. She could not understand how she had happened to come upon it in such a place. Soon the entire company surrounded it, and Linda forbade anyone to pick a single flower. They carried the tree into her garden, and the faithful bee followed it. Linda was enchanted by its delicious scent and seated herself beneath it. Before returning to the palace, she was about to gather a few of the blossoms when the vigilant bee sallied out humming under the leaves, where she remained as sentinel, and stung the princess so severely that she nearly fainted. That put an end to depriving the orange tree of its blossoms, and Linda returned to her palace quite ill.

When the prince was at liberty to speak to Aimée, he asked, "What made you so angry with young Linda, my dear bee? You've stung her cruelly."

"How can you ask such a question?" she replied. "Don't you have enough sensitivity to understand that you shouldn't offer any sweets except to me? All that's yours belongs to me, and I defend my property when I defend your blossoms."

"But," he said, "you see them fall without being distressed. Wouldn't it be just the same to you if the princess adorned herself with them, if she placed them in her hair or put them in her bosom?"

"No," the bee said, "it's not at all the same thing to me. I know, ungrateful one, that you feel more for her than you do for me. There's also a great difference between a refined person, richly dressed and of considerable rank in these parts, and an unfortunate princess whom you found covered with a tiger's skin, surrounded by monsters who could only give her crude and barbarous ideas, and whose beauty is not great enough to enslave you."

And then she cried, as much as any bee is capable of crying. Some of the flowers of the enamored orange tree were wetted by her tears, and his distress at having disturbed his princess was so great that all his leaves turned yellow, several branches withered, and he thought he would die.

"What have I done, my beautiful bee? What have I done to make you so angry? Ah, doubtless, you'll abandon me. You're already weary of being linked to one so unfortunate as I."

They spent the night exchanging reproaches, but at the break of day a kind zephyr who had been listening to them brought about a reconciliation. He could not have done them a greater service.

In the meantime, Linda, who was dying to have a bouquet of orange flowers, arose early in the morning, descended to her flower garden, and went to gather one. But when she extended her hand, she was so violently stung by the jealous bee that she lost heart. Returning to her room in an awful temper, she said, "I can't make out what kind of a tree we've found. Whenever I try to take the smallest bud, some insects that guard it pierce me with their stings."

One of her maids, a witty, lively chit, said laughingly, "I would advise you, madam, to arm yourself as an Amazon and follow Jason's example when he went to win the golden fleece, and courageously take the most beautiful flowers from this pretty tree."

Linda thought this idea amusing and immediately ordered them to make her a helmet covered with feathers, a light cuirass, and gauntlets, and to the sound of trumpets, kettle drums, fifes, and oboes, she entered the garden, followed by all her ladies, who were armed like she was and who called this fete the "Battle of the Bees and Amazons." Drawing her sword gracefully, she struck the most beautiful branch of the orange tree and said, "Appear, terrible bees, appear! I come to defy you! Are you valiant enough to defend that which you love?"

But Linda, and all who accompanied her, were taken aback when they heard a pitiful "Alas!" issue from the stem of the orange tree and saw blood flowing from the severed branch!

"Heavens!" she cried, "what have I done? What marvel is this?" She took the bleeding branch and vainly attempted to join the pieces together, seized by a terrible fright and anxiety.

The poor bee was desperate when this sad accident befell her dear orange tree. She was about to sally forth and meet her death at sword point in her attempt to avenge her prince, but decided it was better to stay alive for him and remembered a remedy that he would need. She begged him to let her fly to Arabia so she could bring back some balm for him. After he consented and they said tender, affectionate farewells, she started for that part of the world with instinct alone for her guide. To speak more correctly, Love carried her there, and since he flies faster than the swiftest winged creature, she completed this long journey swiftly. She brought back the wonderful balm on her wings and little feet, and soon she cured her prince. It is said that he was cured not so much by the excellence of the balm as by the pleasure it afforded him in seeing the princess bee take so much care of his wound. She applied the balm every day, and he needed a great deal, for the severed branch was one of his fingers. Indeed, if Linda had continued her assault, he would soon have had neither legs nor arms. Oh, how acutely did the bee feel responsible for the sufferings of the orange tree, reproaching herself because of the impetuous manner in which she had defended its flowers.

On the other hand, Linda was so distressed by what she had done that she could neither sleep nor eat. At last she decided to send for some fairies in the hope they would enlighten her about this extraordinary matter, and she dispatched ambassadors loaded with splendid presents to invite them to her court.

Queen Trufio was one of the first who arrived at Linda's palace. No one was as skilled as she in fairy art. She examined the branch and the orange tree; she smelled its flowers and distinguished a surprisingly human scent. Not a spell did she leave untried and at last tapped one so powerful that suddenly the orange tree disappeared, and they saw the most handsome strapping prince in the world. At this sight Linda was petrified. She felt herself struck with admiration and was so drawn to him that she soon lost her former indifference.

The young prince, though, could think of nothing but his charming bee and threw himself at Trufio's feet. "Great queen," he said, "I'm infinitely indebted to you, for you have given me new life by restoring me to my original form. But if you want me to be indebted to you for my peace and happiness—a blessing even greater than the life you've returned to me—restore my princess to me!" Upon uttering these words, he took hold of the little bee, at whom he had never stopped gazing.

"You shall be satisfied," the generous Trufio answered. After she had performed her spells again, the Princess Aimée appeared with so many charms that not a single lady there could avoid feeling envious. Linda herself was uncertain as to whether she ought to be pleased or angry by such an extraordinary incident, particularly by the transformation of the bee.

Finally her reason got the better of her feelings, which were nipped in the bud. She embraced Aimée a thousand times, and Trufio asked her to tell about her adventures. She was under too much obligation to her to refuse this request. The graceful and easy manner with which she spoke interested the whole assembly, and when she told Trufio she had performed so many wonders by virtue of her name and her wand, there was an exclamation of joy throughout the hall, and everyone begged the fairy to complete this great work. Trufio, on her side, felt extremely glad at hearing all she heard and enfolded the princess in her arms.

"Since I was so useful to you without knowing you," she said to her, "you may judge, charming Aimée, now that I know you, how much I'm inclined to serve you. I'm a friend of your father and mother. Let's depart post haste in my flying chariot to the Happy Island, where both of you will be welcomed as you deserve."

Linda begged them to remain one day with her, during which time she gave them costly presents and the Princess Aimée exchanged her tiger's skin for dresses of incomparable beauty. Let all now imagine the joy of our happy lovers. Yes, let them imagine it if they can, but to do that they must have experienced the same misfortunes, have been among ogres, and undergone as many transformations.

At last they departed. Trufio conducted them through the air to the Happy Island, where they were received by the king and queen. They were the last persons in the world they had ever expected to see again, but they beheld them with the greatest pleasure. Aimée's beauty and prudence, added to her intelligence, made her the wonder of the age. Her dear mother loved her passionately. The fine qualities of Prince Aimé's mind were no less appreciated than his handsome person. The wedding was celebrated, and never in the world was anything so magnificent. The Graces attended in their festive attire. The Loves were there without even being invited, and by their express order the eldest son of the prince and princess was named "Faithful Love." Since then they have given him many other titles, and under all these various names it is very difficult to find the Faithful Love such as that which sprang from this charming marriage. Happy are those who encounter him without any misunderstandings.

> Aimée with her lover alone in a wood
> Conducted herself with great discretion.
> To reason she listened—temptation withstood,
> And lost not a jot of her prince's affection.
> Believe not, fair ones, who would captivate hearts,
> That Cupid needs pleasure alone to retain him.
> Love oft from the lap of indulgence departs,
> But prudence and virtue will always enchain him.

BABIOLE

ONCE upon a time there was a queen whose sole desire was to have children. She talked about nothing else and kept lamenting that when the fairy Fanferluche had attended her birth, she had become so infuriated with her mother that she wished the infant's life would be filled with misfortune.

One day when she was sadly sitting alone by the fireside, she saw a tiny woman come down the chimney. Riding on three bits of rushes, she was no bigger than the height of your hand. Her hair was adorned with a sprig of hawthorn, her dress was made of flies' wings, and two nutshells served as her boots. Sailing through the air, she took three turns in the room before she stopped in front of the queen.

"You've been complaining about me for a long time, blaming me for all your misfortunes," she said. "You think, madam, that I'm the one who's prevented you from having children. On the contrary, I've come to announce to you that you'll have an infanta. I fear, however, that she'll cost you many tears."

"Ah, noble Fanferluche," said the queen, "don't deny me your pity and your aid. I'll provide you with all the services in my power, provided the princess you promise me shall be my comfort and not my sorrow."

"Destiny is more powerful than I," the fairy replied. "The only way I can show my affection for you is to give you this white hawthorn. Fasten it to your child's head the moment she's born, and it will protect her from many dangers."

She gave her the sprig and then vanished like lightning, leaving the queen sad and thoughtful. "Why should I yearn for a daughter who will cost me many tears?" she asked. "Wouldn't I be happier without any children?" Only the presence of the king, whom she loved dearly, helped alleviate her grief. Soon she did become pregnant, and during her pregnancy she took great care to inform her intimate friends that the moment the princess was born, they were to place the hawthorn flower on her head.

This she kept in a gold box covered with diamonds, considering it the most valuable thing she possessed.

At last the queen gave birth to the most beautiful creature ever seen. Immediately after the birth her friends attached the sprig of hawthorn to the baby's head. But then all of a sudden, a marvel occurred! She became a monkey, jumping, running, and skipping about the room. Upon seeing this transformation, all the ladies uttered the most horrified cries, and the queen, who was more frightened than anyone, thought she would expire from grief. She cried to them, "Remove the sprig of hawthorn you placed behind her ear!" But they had the greatest trouble in catching the little ape and found that removing the fatal flowers did no good at all. She was still an honest-to-goodness monkey that refused to be nursed like a child and would eat nothing but nuts and chestnuts.

"Barbarous Fanferluche," the queen mourned, "what did I ever do to you for you to treat me so cruelly? What will become of me? What a disgrace! All my subjects will think I've given birth to a monster. The king will be horrified by such a child!" Breaking down in tears, she asked the ladies to advise her what to do.

"Madam," the eldest of her attendants said, "you must tell the king that the princess was stillborn. Then put this ape in a box and let it sink to the bottom of the sea. It would be terrible for you to keep such a little brute alive much longer."

The queen found it difficult to make a decision, but when they told her the king was coming to her room, she was so confused and upset that without further deliberation she told her maid of honor to do what she pleased with the monkey.

They took the monkey into another room, put it in a box, and asked one of the valets to throw it into the sea. He instantly departed on his errand. Now the princess was in grave danger! However, the man got to thinking the box was so beautiful that he did not feel like losing it. Sitting down on the seashore, he took out the monkey with the intention of killing it (for he did not know it was his sovereign). Yet just as he held it in his hands, a terrific noise startled him. He turned his head in time to see an open chariot drawn by six unicorns, resplendent with gold and precious stones. Preceded by a military band, it bore a queen wearing a crown and a royal mantle on cushions of cloth of gold. In her arms she held her son, a child of four years old.

The valet recognized this queen as the sister of his mistress. She had come to see the babe and rejoice with her, but when she had learned that the infant princess was stillborn, she had departed in sadness to return to her kingdom. She was lost in thought when her son cried, "I want that monkey! I want it!" When the queen looked up, she saw the prettiest monkey she had ever seen. The valet tried to escape, but he was stopped.

The queen ordered a large sum of money to be given him for the monkey, and finding it gentle and playful, she named it Babiole. Thus, despite her hard fate the princess fell into the hands of her own aunt.

Once the queen had arrived back in her own realm, the little prince begged her to give him Babiole for a playmate. Since he wanted her to be dressed like a princess, they made her a new dress every day, and they taught her to walk only on her feet. Never was there a prettier or more charming baby monkey: her little face was as black as a jackdaw's with a white ruff around her neck and tufts of flesh color at her ears. Her paws were no bigger than butterflies' wings, and her sparkling eyes indicated so much intelligence that nobody was astonished by anything she did. The prince doted on her and petted her unceasingly. Not only did she never bite him, but when he wept, she wept as well.

She had been with the queen for four years when one day she began to yammer like a child trying to talk. Everybody was amazed by this, and they were to be even more astonished when she began to speak in a voice so clear and distinct that every word was intelligible. "Marvelous!" "Babiole can talk!" "Babiole a creature with reason!" The queen demanded to have her again as part of her own entourage. Therefore, they brought her to her majesty's apartments to the great dismay of the prince. He began to weep, and to console him they gave him cats and dogs, birds and squirrels, and even a pony called Criquetin, which danced a saraband, but all this was not worth even one word from Babiole's lips.

As for Babiole, she was under greater constraints with the queen than with the prince. They required her to act like a sybil and answer a hundred ingenious, learned questions for which she often had no answer. When an ambassador or stranger arrived, they made her appear in a robe of velvet or brocade with a bodice and collar. If the court was in mourning, she had to drag a long mantle of crape after her, and this exhausted her a great deal. They did not allow her to eat what she liked, for the physician always ordered her dinner, which did not please her at all, since she was as self-willed as any ape born a princess might be expected to be. The queen gave her tutors who tested the powers of her intellect most thoroughly. She excelled in playing on a wonderful harpsichord that they crafted for her from an oyster shell. Painters came from all quarters of the world, especially from Italy, to portray her likeness. Her renown spread from pole to pole, for no one had ever heard of a monkey endowed with the gift of speech.

The graceful and witty prince, who was as handsome as a painting of the god of love, was as much a prodigy in his own right. He came to see Babiole and amused himself with talking to her. Their conversations, often changed from gay to grave, for Babiole had a heart, and that heart had not been transformed like the rest of her little body. Therefore, she became deeply attached to the prince, and he in return became only too fond of her.

The unfortunate Babiole did not know what to do. She spent her nights on the top of a window shutter, or on a corner of the chimney piece, unwilling to use the basket prepared for her, which was soft and well lined with wadding and feathers. Her governess (for she had one) often heard her sighing and sometimes complaining. Her melancholy became ever deeper as her reason increased, and she never regarded herself in a looking glass without irritably trying to break it, prompting people to remark constantly, "Once a monkey always a monkey. Babiole will never lose the mischievous nature endemic to her species."

As the prince grew older, he became fond of hunting, dancing, plays, feats of arms, and books, and no longer even mentioned the poor monkey. Affairs were very different on her side: she loved him better at twelve than she had at six, and when she sometimes reproached him for his neglect, he thought he could make up for everything by giving her a choice apple or some sugared chestnuts.

At last Babiole's reputation reached even the kingdom of the monkeys, and King Magot developed a great desire to marry her. With this intention in mind, he sent his most notable councilor to request her hand in marriage from the queen. His prime minister had no difficulty in understanding his wishes, but he would have had great trouble in expressing them if not for the assistance of several parrots and magpies, vulgarly called "mags," who chattered a great deal, while the jackdaws appointed to follow in the train would not stand being outdone in making noise.

This chief of the delegation, a huge monkey named Mirlifiche, had a carriage made for him of cardboard, and on it were painted scenes of the love affair of King Magot and the monkey Monette, well-known in the empire of the monkeys. Monette, the poor creature, had met with a tragic end in the claws of a wildcat that had not liked her frolicsome nature. The happiness of Magot and Monette during their marriage was painted on the carriage along with the natural grief he had shown at her death. Six white rabbits from a capital warren drew the carriage, which was given added distinction by being called a coach of state. After this came a chariot made of straw and painted in different colors. It contained the monkeys destined to attend Babiole, and it was worth more than anything in the world to see how they were adorned. In fact, they looked as if they were going to a wedding. The rest of the cortege was composed of spaniels, greyhounds, Spanish cats, Muscovy rats, hedgehogs, cunning weasels, and shrewd foxes; some of them drew the carriages, others carried the baggage. At the head of it all was Mirlifiche, graver than a Roman dictator and wiser than Cato himself. He rode a young hare that ambled along more easily than any English gelding.

The queen knew nothing of this magnificent delegation until it arrived at her palace, but hearing the shouts of laughter from the guards and common folk, she stuck her head out of a window and gazed at the most extraordinary sight she had ever seen. Mirlifiche, followed by a considerable number of monkeys, advanced toward the chariot of the apes and, giving his paw to the largest, called Gigona, helped her descend. Then he let loose the parrot who was to serve as interpreter and waited until this beautiful bird had presented itself to the queen and requested an audience for him.

Perroquet flew gently into the air, arrived at the queen's window, and said in the prettiest voice in the world, "Madam, his excellency the Count de Mirlifiche, ambassador of the celebrated Magot, king of the monkeys, demands an audience of your majesty to discuss a most important affair."

"Beautiful parrot," the queen responded, caressing him, "first have something to eat and drink, and then I shall allow you to go and tell Count Mirlifiche I bid him and all who accompany him most welcome to my kingdom. If his journey from Magotia has not overly taxed him, he may enter my audience chamber, where I shall await him on my throne with my entire court."

At these words Perroquet kissed his claw twice, flapped his pinions, and sang a short ditty indicating his delight. Off he flew and, perching on the shoulder of Mirlifiche, whispered the favorable reply he had received. Gladdened by the queen's kindness, Mirlifiche immediately requested one of the queen's officers—through the magpie Margot, who had installed herself as second interpreter—to show him to a room where he might rest for a few moments. Immediately they conducted him to a salon paved with marble and painted and gilded all over, one of the best chambers in the palace, and he entered it with his suite.

Monkeys are always great ferreters by profession, and they soon found a corner cupboard where many jars of preserves had been stored. The gluttons got at them instantly. One lifted a crystal cup full of apricots, another a bottle of syrup, one a patty, another some almond cakes. The winged gentry who made up the cortege were very annoyed to be spectators at a feast that lacked hemp seed and millet seed, and a jackdaw, who was a great chatterer, flew to the audience chamber and respectfully approached the queen. "Madam," it said, "I am too devoted a servant of your majesty's to be a willing accomplice in the mess that is being made out of your fine preserves. Count de Mirlifiche himself has already eaten three boxes full. He was crunching the fourth without any respect to your royal majesty when, touched to the heart, I had to come to tell your majesty about it."

"I thank you, my little friend jackdaw," the queen said, smiling, "but there's no need to get upset about my preserves. I'm offering them as a favor from Babiole, whom I love with all my heart."

The jackdaw, ashamed at having made such a great to-do for nothing, withdrew without saying another word. Shortly thereafter the ambassador entered with his suite. He was not dressed precisely in the height of fashion, for since the return of the famous Fagotin, who had cut a remarkable figure in the world, they had not seen a good model. He wore a peaked hat with a plume of green feathers in it, a shoulder belt of blue paper covered with gold spangles, large *canions*, and a walking stick. Perroquet, who passed for a tolerably good poet, had composed a stirring speech and, advancing to the foot of the throne, addressed Babiole:

"Madam, the wondrous power of your eyes
In great Magot's fond passion recognize!
These apes, these cats, this equipage so rare—
These birds—all, all, his ardent flame declare!
When beneath a mountain cat's fierce talons fell
Monette, the beauteous ape he loved so well
And who alone could be compared to you;
When to her spouse she bade a last adieu,
The king a hundred times swore by her shade,
That love should never more his heart invade.
Madam, your charms have indeed effaced
The tender image from his heart that first love traced.
Of you alone he thinks. If you but knew
The state of frenzy he is driven to,
You'd surely be moved to pity. Your gentle breast
Would share his pain, and so restore his rest.
He whom we saw of late so fat, so gay,
Now worn to skin and bone, a constant prey
To heartfelt care that nothing can remove.
Madam, he knows too well what it is to love!
Olives and nuts, his favorite food of yore,
Now seem insipid, and he relishes them no more.
He's dying, and your help alone we come to crave.
It's you alone can snatch him from the grave.
I scorn to tempt you by the grosser bait
Of the choice fare within our happy state,
Where grapes and figs can always be found,
And all the finest fruit the whole year 'round."

Perroquet had scarcely finished his oration when the queen turned her gaze to Babiole, who felt more abashed than anybody had ever been before, for the queen wanted to know her sentiments before she made a reply. She told the parrot to make his excellency, the ambassador, understand that she favored the king's intentions insofar as she had anything to say in the matter.

Signaling that the audience was over, the queen withdrew and Babiole followed her into her room. "My little monkey," the queen said, "I confess that I'll miss you, but there's no way of refusing Magot's marriage proposal, for I still haven't forgotten that his father brought two hundred thousand monkeys into the field against me, and they ate so many of my subjects that we were forced to accept a shameful peace treaty."

"That means, then, madam," Babiole replied impatiently, "that you are set on sacrificing me to this horrid monster to avoid provoking his anger. But I beg your majesty to grant me a few days at least to make up my mind."

"That's only fair. Nevertheless, if you want my advice, decide promptly. Consider the honors in store for you, the magnificence of the delegation, and what maids of honor he's sent you. I'm sure that Magot never did for Monette what he's done for you."

"I don't know what he did for Monette," Babiole said indignantly, "but I know full well that I'm not at all moved by the sentiments with which he honors me." She rose abruptly and curtseying gracefully, went in search of the prince to tell him her troubles.

As soon as he saw her, he exclaimed, "Ah, Babiole, when are we to dance at your wedding?"

"I don't know, sir," she said sadly, "but given my deplorable state of mind, I can no longer guard my secrets. You may think this indecent of me, but I must confess to you that you're the only person I could accept for a husband."

"Me?" the prince said, bursting into laughter. "For a husband? My little monkey, I'm charmed by what you tell me, but I hope you'll excuse me if I don't accept your proposal, for it's clear that our figures, tastes, and manners are not quite suitable."

"I agree with you," she said, "and our hearts are also unlike! You're an ingrate. For a long time I've suspected it, and I feel like a fool for loving a prince who doesn't deserve to be loved."

"But, Babiole, think of how much I'd suffer to see you perched on the top of a sycamore, holding onto a branch by your tail. Believe me, it would be best for your honor and mine if we could just have a good laugh over this matter. Marry King Magot, and for old friendship's sake, send me your first baby monkey."

"You're lucky, my lord, that I'm not at all like a monkey in temperament. A monkey would have already scratched out your eyes, bitten off your nose, and torn off your ears. I, on the contrary, shall simply leave you to muse about the regrets you'll have one day about your unworthy conduct."

She said no more, for her governess came in to fetch her because the ambassador, Mirlifiche, had sent some magnificent presents to her apartments. There was a dressing table made of a spider's web embroidered with

glowworms. An eggshell held the combs, a white-heart cherry served for a pincushion, and all the linen was trimmed with lace paper. Along with these were several shells neatly arranged in a basket: some were to serve for earrings, others for bodkins, and all of them shone as diamonds. Even more splendid were a dozen boxes filled with confiture and a little glass box containing a nut and an olive, even though the key was lost. Babiole, however, cared not a jot for these things. The ambassador informed her in the grumbling language used in Magotia that his king was more moved by her charms than by those of any monkey he had ever seen. He had ordered a palace built for her on the top of a fir tree. He had sent her these presents and also the excellent confiture as a sign of his affection. Indeed, his master could not demonstrate his regard for her in any better way. "But," he continued, "the strongest proof of his tender feelings, and the one of which you ought to consider with utmost sensitivity, madam, is the care he has taken to have his portrait painted as a foretaste of the pleasure you'll have in seeing him."

Thereupon he displayed the portrait of the king of the monkeys, seated on an immense log eating an apple. Babiole turned her eyes away so that they would not be offended by such an unpleasant figure. Grumbling three or four times, she made Mirlifiche understand that she was obliged to his master for his esteem, but that she had not decided yet if she would marry.

Meanwhile the queen, determined not to incite the anger of the monkeys, thought it unnecessary to stand on much ceremony after she had made it clear she would send Babiole where she wanted her to go, and she prepared everything for her departure. At this news poor Babiole was overcome by despair. On the one hand she faced the contempt of the prince; on the other, the indifference of the queen. But more than all this, it was the thought of her intended that made her decide to flee.

This was easily accomplished, for in entering and leaving her room, she used the window as often as the door. Therefore, she scampered away, jumping from tree to tree, from branch to branch, until she came to the banks of a river. Since she was so despondent, she did not even think about the risk she would run by attempting to swim across. Without pausing to look at the river, she flung herself in. Immediately she sank to the bottom, but rather than losing consciousness, she discovered a magnificent grotto ornamented with shells and quickly entered it. There she was received by a very old man whose long white beard descended to his waist. His head was crowned with poppies and wild lilies, and he was reclining on a couch of reeds and leaning against a rock, from which flowed several springs that fed the river.

"Ah, what brings you here, little Babiole?" he asked, extending his hand to her.

"My lord," she replied, "I'm an unlucky monkey! I'm fleeing from a horrible monkey whom they want me to marry."

"I know more of your history than you think," the wise old man stated. "It's true, you do hate Magot, but it's no less true that you love a young prince who treats you with indifference."

"Ah, sir," Babiole cried, sighing, "don't mention it. Just the thought of him makes me even more miserable than I am."

"He won't always rebel against love," continued the host of the fishes. "I know he's destined to marry the most beautiful princess in the world."

"How unfortunate I am!" Babiole continued. "Then he can never be mine."

The good man smiled and said, "Don't upset yourself, my good Babiole. Time is a great master. Just take care not to lose the little glass box that Magot sent you—which by chance you have in your pocket. I can't tell you any more than this. Here's a tortoise who's quite swift. Pray, be seated on him, and he'll conduct you wherever you want to go."

"Now that I'm so indebted to you," Babiole said, "I can't leave you without asking your name."

"They call me Biroquoi," he said, "father of Biroquie—a river, as you see, quite large and quite famous."

Babiole confidently mounted the tortoise and they traveled for some time on the water. At last, after what seemed to be a circuitous route the tortoise reached the bank. It would be difficult to find anything more noble-looking than the tortoise's English saddle and the rest of his harness, complete even to the little pistols contained in the saddle bow in pockets made of two crab bodies.

On Babiole traveled, trusting completely in Biroquoi's promises when all of a sudden she heard a rather loud commotion. Alas, it was the ambassador Mirlifiche with all his followers returning to Magotia, saddened and upset by the flight of Babiole. One of the monkeys in the troop had climbed a walnut tree at dinnertime to knock down the nuts and feed the Magotins, but no sooner had he reached the top of the tree than he looked around and saw poor Babiole on the tortoise, trudging slowly across the open country. Once he spotted her, he began to scream so loudly that all the monkeys around him grumbled, "Whatever is the matter?" As soon as he told them, they immediately sent out the parrots, magpies, and jays, who flew to the spot and identified her. When they reported that it really was Babiole, the ambassador, monkeys, and the rest of the party ran after her and intercepted her.

What bad luck for Babiole! What could be worse than this? They made her get into the state coach, which was immediately surrounded by the most vigilant monkeys, several foxes, and a cock. The latter perched on top of the coach and stood sentinel day and night. A monkey led the tortoise as a rare beast, and thus the cavalcade continued its journey to the great distress of Babiole, who had no other companion than Madam Gigona, a sour-tempered, ill-natured ape.

At the end of three days, during which nothing in particular occurred, the guides lost their way, and the cavalcade arrived at a large, beautiful city unknown to them. Upon viewing a beautiful garden with an open gate, they entered and ravaged it as if it were a conquered territory. One monkey cracked nuts, another swallowed cherries, a third stripped a plum tree. In short, every monkey in the entourage down to the smallest began plundering and stealing.

Now, this city was the capital of the kingdom in which Babiole had been born. Ever since her mother had had the misfortune of seeing her daughter transformed into an ape by the sprig of hawthorn, she had never allowed any ape, monkey, baboon, or anything else that might recall the fatal event to exist in her realm. A monkey was looked upon there as a disturber of the public peace. Imagine, then, the astonishment of her people at the arrival of a cardboard coach, a chariot of painted straw, and the rest of the most extraordinary equipage that has ever been seen since stories were stories and fairies, fairies.

The news spread like lightning to the palace. Appalled, the queen imagined that the monkey folk had designs against her throne, and she immediately summoned her councilors, who pronounced all the intruders guilty of subversion. Determined to make an example of them as a warning to all others in the future, she ordered her guards into the garden to seize all the monkeys. They threw large nets over the trees, and the hunt was soon over. Despite the respect due to the rank of an ambassador, they cruelly threw Mirlifiche into the depths of a dungeon. There he was joined by the rest of his comrades, together with the lady apes and miss monkeys who accompanied Babiole. Babiole herself felt a secret pleasure in this new catastrophe. When unhappiness reaches a certain point, nothing more alarms us, and even death, perhaps, is awaited as a boon. Such was her situation—her heart was tortured by the recollection of the prince who had spurned her, and her mind by the frightful image of King Magot, whose wife she was to become.

We must not forget to mention that her dress was so pretty and her manners so superior that her captors could not help considering her a marvelous creature, and when she spoke, their surprise was even greater. They had often heard mention of the remarkable Babiole. The queen who had found her, unaware of her niece's transformation, had frequently written to her sister that she had a marvelous monkey and begged her to come and see it. But the troubled mother had always skipped such passages in her letters. At length the guards captivated by Babiole carried her into a large gallery, where they erected a miniature throne, on which she seated herself with more the air of a sovereign than of a captive ape. Just then the queen happened to be passing through the gallery and was so struck with surprise at her pretty mien and the graceful salutation she gave her that nature spoke in favor of the infanta despite herself.

The queen took Babiole in her arms. The little creature, herself moved by feelings unknown to her until that moment, threw herself on the queen's neck and said such tender, winning things that all those who heard her were filled with admiration.

"No, madam," she said, "it's not the fear of imminent death (with which you threaten the unfortunate race of monkeys, so I've learned) that induces me to seek means to please and pacify you. The termination of my life is no great calamity to me, for my feelings are so far above the beast I appear to be that I'd be sorry if the least step were taken to save my life. It's for you yourself that I love you, madam. Your crown moves me much less than your merits."

What reply could anybody have made to such a polite and respectful Babiole? The queen, as mute as a fish, opened her eyes wide and imagined she was dreaming. Her heart was palpitating so much that she had to carry Babiole into her room. When they were alone, she said, "I want you to tell me all about your adventures immediately, for I feel that of all the animals that I keep in my menageries and in my palace, I shall love you the best. I'll even promise you that, for your sake, I'll pardon the monkeys that have accompanied you."

"Ah, madam," Babiole said, "I don't want to intercede on their behalf. It's been my misfortune to be born an ape, and the same cruel fate has given me the power of understanding that will be my torment as long as I live. What am I to feel when I see myself in a looking glass, a little, ugly black creature with paws covered with hair, a tail, and teeth always ready to bite, and at the same time knowing that I have a mind, that I possess some taste, refinement, and feeling!"

"Are you capable of love?" the queen asked.

Babiole sighed without replying.

"Oh!" the queen continued. "I beg you, tell me if you love a monkey, a rabbit or a squirrel, for if you aren't engaged, I have a dwarf who would make a superb husband for you."

At this proposition Babiole became indignant, and the queen burst out laughing. "Don't be angry," she said. "Come, now. Tell me how you happened to gain the power of speech."

"All that I know about my past," Babiole said, "is that your sister had hardly left you after the birth and death of your daughter than she saw one of your valets, who was about to drown me on the seashore. I was snatched from his grasp by her orders, and by a miracle that astonished everybody I found that I had the power of speech and reason. I was given tutors to teach me several languages and to play various instruments. Gradually I became aware of my misfortune, madam, and—but what's the matter, madam?" she cried, observing the queen's face had turned completely ashen and was covered with cold sweat. "There's an extraordinary change in your countenance."

"I'm dying," the queen said in a feeble voice that was barely audible. "I'm dying, my dear, unhappy child! Ah, today I've found you again." As she uttered these words, she fainted. Alarmed, Babiole ran for help. The ladies-in-waiting rushed in to give her water, unlace her, and put her to bed. Babiole smuggled herself into bed with her. No one noticed it, she was so little.

When the queen recovered from the lengthy swoon caused by the princess's account of her past, she requested to be left alone with the ladies who knew the secret of her daughter's fatal birth. She told them what had just occurred. In turn they were so amazed that they did not know what advice to give her. She commanded them, however, to tell her what they thought would be best to do in such a sad situation. Some suggested that the monkey should be smothered, others were for shutting it up in a hole, and a third party proposed sending it again to be drowned in the sea. The queen wept and sobbed. "She has so much good sense," she said. "What a pity to see her reduced by a magic bouquet to this miserable condition! But after all, she is my child. It's I who called down the wrath of the wicked Fanferluche on her. Do you find it just that she must suffer for this fairy's hatred for me?"

"Nevertheless, madam," said her eldest lady, "you must protect your honor. What would the world think if you declared yourself the mother of a monkey infanta? It's unnatural for someone so beautiful to have such a child."

The queen lost all patience with such reasoning, whereas the old lady and all the others insisted with equal passion that the little monster ought to be exterminated. Finally the queen decided to have Babiole locked up in a château where she would be well fed and well treated for the rest of her days.

When the princess heard the queen announce her decision to imprison her, she slipped quietly from the bed, leaped from a window onto a tree in the garden, and escaped into the great forest beyond, leaving everybody to wonder what had become of her. She spent the night in the hollow of an oak, where she had time to contemplate the cruelty of her destiny, but what gave her the most pain was the necessity of leaving the queen. All the same, she preferred a voluntary exile that would allow her to enjoy her liberty than to remain a prisoner forever.

As soon as it was light, she continued her journey, not knowing where she was bound. A thousand times she reflected about the bizarre nature of her extraordinary birth. "What a difference," she exclaimed, "between what I am and what I ought to have been!" Ever more swiftly did the tears flow from Babiole's little eyes.

Every morning at daybreak she resumed her flight. Fearing that the queen would have her pursued, or that some of the monkeys had escaped from the dungeon and would carry her against her will to King Magot, she fled without following road or track. She traveled so far that she eventually came to a vast desert where there were no houses, trees, fruits, herbs, or springs. She entered the desert without giving it much thought, and when she became hungry, she discovered too late how unwise she was to travel through such a barren country. Two nights and two days elapsed without her being able to catch even a worm or a gnat. The fear of death came over her. She was so weak that she felt she was about to faint, and she stretched herself along the ground. That's when she recalled the olive and nut in the little glass box, and thought to make a slender meal out of them. Encouraged by this ray of hope, she took a stone, broke the box to pieces, and began to eat the olive.

No sooner had she bitten into it, though, than a torrent of fragrant oil poured forth. As it dripped onto her paws, they became the most beautiful hands in the world. Extremely surprised, she cupped some of the oil in her hands and rubbed herself all over with it. What a miracle! She made herself so beautiful that no one in the universe could match her looks. Feeling herself, she found that she had large eyes, a small mouth, and a handsome nose. She was dying to see herself in a mirror, and it occurred to her to make one out of the largest piece of her broken box. Oh, how delighted she was when she saw herself! Her head was well formed, her hair was in a thousand curls, and her complexion bloomed like the flowers of spring. Moreover, her clothes had grown as large as she was.

When the first moments of her surprise had passed, her hunger pangs became more urgent, and her distress on that score increased twofold. "Ah," she said, "why must a young and beautiful princess born as I am perish in this sad spot? Oh, cruel fortune that has brought me here, what do you have in store? Is it to heap more affliction on me that you have brought about this charming, unexpected change in my person? And you too, venerable river Biroquoi, who so generously saved my life, will you let me perish in this frightful desert?"

The infanta cried in vain for help, for all was deaf to her pleas. Her torments of hunger increased to such a degree that she took the nut and cracked it. As she flung away the shell, she was astonished as she watched architects, painters, masons, upholsterers, sculptors, and a thousand other kinds of craftsmen emerging from it. Some drew plans for a palace, others built it, still others furnished it. Some painted apartments glistening with blue and gold, and others laid out gardens. A magnificent meal was set forth, and sixty princesses dressed finer than queens, led by squires and followed by the pages, paid her the highest compliments and invited her to the banquet awaiting her. Without waiting to be urged, Babiole immediately entered the salon and ate as a starving person might be expected to eat, while endeavoring to maintain the air of a queen.

She had scarcely risen from the table when her treasurers placed before her fifteen thousand chests as large as hogsheads, filled with gold and diamonds, and inquired if she would like them to pay the workmen who had built her palace. She answered that this was the fair thing to do provided that they also built a city and married and remained in her service. They all consented, and the city was built in three quarters of an hour, although it was five times larger than Rome. What a number of miracles to come from a nut!

The princess decided to send an illustrious envoy to her mother and convey some reproaches to the young prince, her cousin. After she dispatched her ambassadors with her instructions, she amused herself by watching such games as the run at the ring, for which she always distributed the prizes. She also entertained herself with cards, plays, hunting, and fishing, for the architects had plotted a river that ran through the palace gardens.

The report of Babiole's beauty spread throughout the universe, and kings came to her court from the four corners of the earth—giants taller than mountains and pygmies smaller than rats. One day several knights broke their lances during a grand tournament, and a quarrel erupted between them. Soon they began fighting in earnest and wounded each other. Greatly offended by this conduct in her presence, the princess descended from her balcony to determine who the guilty parties were. When they were unhelmed, she was most surprised to find her cousin among them! Though not dead, he was so nearly gone that she almost died of grief and alarm at the sight.

She had him carried into the most elegant room in the palace, where everything possible to speed his recovery was made available—physicians from Chodrai, surgeons, ointments, broths, syrups. The infanta herself made the bandages and prepared the liniment. They were watered with her tears, and those tears alone would have been a balsam to the wounded prince. Indeed, wholly besides his half-dozen sword cuts and as many lance thrusts that had pierced him through and through, he had been so deeply wounded by Babiole's bright eyes (for he had been at the court incognito for some time), that he was incurable for life. It is easy, therefore, to imagine what he felt when he read in the countenance of that beautiful princess how grieved she was at seeing him so badly hurt.

I shall not pause to repeat all that his heart prompted him to say to thank her for her kindness. Those who heard him were astonished that a man so ill could express himself with so much warmth and gratitude. The infanta, who blushed more than once at his words, begged him to be silent, but the ardor of his speech so carried him away that he suddenly suffered into a spasm of agony. Up to this moment she had shown great fortitude, but now it completely gave way. She tore her hair, uttered wild shrieks, and gave everyone reason to believe that her heart was easily conquered. Otherwise, how could she fall so desperately in love with an utter stranger in such a short time? Of course, those in Babiola (this was the name she had given to her kingdom), did not know that the prince was her cousin and that she had loved him since childhood.

He had been traveling when he had chanced to arrive at this court, and since he had known no one to present him to the infanta, he had thought to perform five or six heroic deeds before her, that is, to cut off the arms or legs of several knights in the lists, but he had found none polite enough to permit him to do so. Consequently, he had joined in a furious general combat. The strongest had overthrown the weakest, and the weakest, as I have told you before, was the prince.

Babiole was in such a state of distraction that she ran out on the high road without coach or guards. Plunging into a forest, she soon fainted at the foot of a tree. The fairy Fanferluche, who never slept so that she could be always on the watch for opportunities to do mischief, came and carried her off in a cloud that was blacker than ink and flew faster than the wind. For some time the princess remained unconscious, and when she eventually came to herself, she was bewildered at finding herself quite near the Arctic pole. The floor of a cloud is not solid, and as she dashed back and forth, she felt as though she were treading on feathers and would easily fall through if the cloud were to open but a hair. She found no one to confront, for the wicked Fanferluche had made herself invisible. Left alone, with time to muse about her dear prince and the condition in which she had left him, she immersed herself in the most painful feelings that a human being has ever experienced. "What now?" she exclaimed. "Once again I've been able to keep going without the man I love. When will my heart ever shudder at imminent death? Oh, if the sun would only roast me, he'd do me a favor. Or if I could drown myself in the rainbow, how happy I'd be! But, alas, the entire zodiac is deaf to my plea: the centaur has no darts, the bull no horns, the lion no teeth. Perhaps the earth will be more obliging and offer me the sharp point of a rock on which I may impale myself. Oh Prince, my dear cousin, why aren't you here to watch me take the most tragic leap that a despairing lover could devise?"

So saying, she rushed to the end of the cloud and sprang from it with the force of an arrow from a bow. All who saw her thought it was the moon falling, and since it was then on the wane, its many admirers stayed on for some time. Not seeing it again, they went into deep mourning, convinced that the sun had played this wicked trick out of envy. Much as the infanta desired to kill herself, she did not succeed, but fell into the glass bottle in which the fairies usually keep their ratafia in the sun. But what a bottle! Not a tower in the world is so large. Fortunately it was empty or she would have drowned in it like a fly. The six giants guarding the bottle recognized the infanta immediately, for they were the same giant suitors who had been residing at her court. The malignant Fanferluche, who did nothing without calculation, had transported them there, each on a flying dragon, and these dragons guarded the bottle when the giants slept. Many a time during the days Babiole was in this bottle, living like the chameleons on air and dew, did she long for her old monkey's skin.

Since no one knew of her imprisonment, the prince was unaware of it as well. Having escaped death, he continually asked for Babiole from his sick bed. From the melancholy of all his attendants he saw clearly enough that a general pall of sorrow pervaded the court concerning some matter that his innate discretion prevented him from attempting to discover. But as soon as he regained his health, he begged them so earnestly for tidings of the princess that they had not the heart to conceal her loss from him. Some who had seen her enter the forest maintained that she had been devoured by lions, while others believed she had destroyed herself in a fit of despair. Still others imagined she had taken leave of her wits and was wandering about the world.

Since the last of these notions was the least dreadful and gave the prince a flicker of hope, he adopted it and departed on Criquetin, the horse I mentioned before. (I neglected to say, however, that he was the eldest son of Bucephalus, and one of the finest horses of the time.) The prince let the bridle fall slack on his neck and gave him his head. He kept shouting "Infanta! Infanta!" but only his own echoes replied. Eventually he came to the banks of a large river. Thirsty, Criquetin bent his head to drink while the prince kept on shouting, "Babiole, lovely Babiole! Where are you?"

Then he heard a voice whose sweetness seemed to charm the waters say to him, "Advance, and you shall learn where she is."

Upon hearing this, the prince, whose courage was equal to his love, clapped both his spurs into Criquetin's flanks. Into the river he plunged and swam until he came to a whirlpool, which rapidly sucked in the water. Down into it they went, horse and man, and the prince was certain they would drown. Fortunately, however, he arrived at the abode of the worthy Biroquoi, who was celebrating the marriage of his daughter with one of the richest and deepest rivers in the country. All the aquatic deities were assembled in the grotto. Tritons and sirens performed the most delightful music, and the River Biroquie, lightly attired, danced the Hay with the Seine, Thames, Euphrates, and Ganges, who had certainly come a long way to make merry together.

Criquetin, who had impeccable manners, halted respectfully at the entrance of the grotto, and the prince, who had even better manners than his horse, made a respectful bow and inquired if a mortal like himself might be permitted to attend such a splendid party. Biroquoi replied affably that he did them both an honor and a pleasure. "I've expected you for some days, my lord," he continued. "I'm interested in your fate and that of the infanta who is so dear to me. You must gain her release from that fatal bottle in which the vindictive Fanferluche has imprisoned her."

"Ah, what's this I hear?" the prince cried. "The infanta's in a bottle?"

"Yes," said the sage. "She's suffering a great deal, but I warn you, my lord, that conquering the giants and the dragons that guard it will not be feasible unless you follow my advice. You must leave your good steed here and mount a winged dolphin that I've been breaking in for you for some time."

He had the saddled and bridled dolphin brought out, and it leaped and pranced so skillfully that Criquetin was jealous of him. Biroquoi and his friends quickly armed the prince. They gave him a glittering cuirass made from the scales of golden carp and placed on his head the shell of a huge snail that was overshadowed by the tail of a large cod, raised in the form of an aigrette. A naiad tied a belt of eel around his waist, and another hung a tremendous sword made from a gigantic fish bone. Lastly, they gave him the shell of a great tortoise for a shield. Thus armed, even the smallest gudgeon would have taken him for the god of sole, for to tell the truth, this young prince had a certain air rarely encountered in mortals.

The hope of soon recovering the charming princess he adored infused him with a joy he had not experienced since her loss, and the faithful chronicle of these events maintains that he ate with an excellent appetite while staying with Biroquoi, and that he thanked him and the entire company with extraordinary eloquence. He then bade farewell to Criquetin and mounted the flying dolphin, who immediately set off. Toward evening the prince found himself at such tremendous heights that he entered the kingdom of the moon to take a short rest. The marvelous things he saw there would have detained him for some time had he been less anxious to gain his beloved infanta's release.

Morning had just dawned when he discovered her surrounded by giants and dragons, which the fairy, by the power of her wand, had kept beside her. Never imagining that anyone would have the power to rescue the princess, she felt perfectly satisfied with the vigilance of her terrible guards.

As she had for the past few months, the beautiful princess raised her mournful eyes to Heaven. She was addressing her sad complaints to it when she saw the flying dolphin and knight come to rescue her. She never thought such an event possible, even though her own experience had taught her that certain people learn to do the most extraordinary things. "Is it because of some fairy's malice that this knight is being transported through the air?" she asked. "Alas! How I pity him if he is doomed to be imprisoned in a flagon like me."

While she was pondering this situation, the giants caught a glimpse of the prince hovering above their heads. Thinking he was a boy's kite, they cried to one another, "Catch hold, catch hold of the line! It will amuse us."

As they stooped to search for the line, however, the prince attacked them with sword in hand, slashed them to pieces as you would cut a pack of cards, and scattered them to the winds.

Hearing the tumult of this furious combat, the infanta turned around and recognized her young prince. What joy to know he was alive! But what terror to see the danger he courted among those horrible giants and dragons rushing at him! She uttered fearful shrieks and almost died at seeing him in such danger. But the enchanted bone with which Biroquoi had armed the prince never struck in vain, and the light dolphin dipping up and down at exactly the right moment was also such a wonderful help that the ground was covered with the bodies of these monsters in no time.

The impatient prince saw his infanta through the glass, and would have smashed the bottle to pieces had he not been afraid of wounding her. He decided, therefore, to descend through its neck. When he touched bottom, he flung himself at Babiole's feet and respectfully kissed her hand.

"My lord," she said, "I find it necessary, in order to retain your good opinion, to give you my reasons for the tender interest I took in your recovery. I want you to know that we are close relations: I am the daughter of your aunt, that very Babiole whom you found in the form of an ape on the seashore and who afterward had the weakness to show an affection for you that you spurned."

"Ah, madam," the prince said, "do you really think I can believe such a miracle? To say that you were an ape and loved me. To think that I was aware of it and rejected the greatest of all blessings!"

"At this point I'd hold a rather bad opinion of your taste if I knew you felt any affection for me then. But let us fly from here, my lord. I'm weary of being held prisoner, and I'm afraid of my enemy. Let us seek out my mother and tell her all of these extraordinary events. They will be of great interest to her."

"Come, madam, let us go," said the enamored prince, taking Babiole in his arms and mounting the winged dolphin. "Let us bring her back the most lovely princess the world has ever boasted."

The dolphin rose gently into the air and steered his flight toward the capital, where the queen was leading a life of sheer melancholy. The disappearance of Babiole had deprived her of sleep, for she could not stop thinking about her and the pretty speeches she had made. Despite the fact that she was just a monkey, the queen would have given half her kingdom to see her once more.

As soon as the prince arrived, he assumed the disguise of an old man and requested a private audience with her majesty. "Madam," he said to her, "I've studied the art of necromancy ever since I was a boy. You may judge this from the fact that I know how much Fanferluche hates you and how terrible the consequences have been for you. But dry your tears, madam. That Babiole who was once so ugly is now the most beautiful princess in the world. She will shortly be at your side if you will forgive your sister for the cruel war she has brought upon you, and cement the peace by allowing the marriage of your infanta with your nephew."

"I can't imagine that such things are possible," the queen replied, weeping. "You wish to allay my sorrow, wise old man, but I've lost my dear child. I no longer have a husband. My sister claims my kingdom, her son is equally unjust toward me, and I'll never seek their alliance."

"Destiny has ordained otherwise," the prince said. "I'm commissioned to inform you so."

"Alas," the queen responded, "what advantage would there be to my consenting to their marriage? The wicked Fanferluche has too much power and malice. She'd always oppose it."

"Don't you worry about that, madam," the old man replied. "Just promise me that you won't object to the desired match."

"I'll promise anything," the queen said, "on the condition that I can see my dear daughter once again."

Withdrawing, the prince ran to the spot where the infanta was awaiting him. She was surprised to see him in disguise, and he therefore explained that for some time past a conflict had existed between the two queens and caused considerable bitterness. "I have, however, finally persuaded my aunt to accede to our wishes." The princess was delighted and went with him to the palace. All who saw her pass by were so struck by the perfect resemblance to her mother that they dropped everything and followed her to discover who she could be.

As soon as the queen saw her, her heart began to beat so strongly that she needed no other proof to verify the old man's story. The princess flung herself at the queen's feet, and the queen raised her into her arms. After remaining silent for some time, they kissed away each other's tears and expressed every conceivable feeling that can be imagined on such an occasion. Then the queen glanced at her nephew, welcomed him graciously, and repeated the promise she had made to the necromancer. She would have said more, but the commotion she heard in the palace courtyard drew her to the window, and she had the pleasant surprise of viewing the arrival of her sister. The prince and infanta, who were also looking out the window, perceived the venerable Biroquoi in the royal suite, and even good Criquetin was one of the party. Upon seeing one another, they uttered shouts of joy and ran to meet one another. The magnificent wedding of the prince and infanta was celebrated on the spot in spite of the fairy Fanferluche, whose power and evil were at last thwarted.

The friendship of the wicked we should fear,
Their fairest offers are wisely to be declined.
Even while protesting that they hold us dear,
In secret our peace has often been undermined.

The princess, whose adventures I've related,
Might have considered her happiness achieved,
If, from the fairy who her mother hated,
The fatal hawthorn had not been received.

Her transformation to an ugly ape
Could not exempt her from the tender passion.
Regardless of her features and her shape,
She dared to love a prince—"the glass of fashion."

I know some well in this, our present day,
Ugly as any monkeys in creation,
Who, nevertheless, venture a siege to lay
To the most noble hearts in all the nation.

But I suspect, before they win a lover,
They must to some enchanter pay their duty,
Who can inform them where they may discover
The oil which gave Babiole her beauty.

THE YELLOW DWARF

ONCE upon a time there was a queen who had only one daughter, but that one was worth a thousand. Since the queen was a widow, nothing in the world was as dear to her as the young princess, and she was so afraid of losing her affection that she never corrected any of her faults. Is it any wonder that this marvelous being began to view her beauty as more divine than mortal? She appeared nearly always dressed as Pallas or Diana, followed by the principal ladies of the court attired as nymphs. And since she knew she was destined to wear a crown, she became so vain of her inherent charms that she snubbed everyone around her. If all this weren't enough, the queen capped her daughter's vanity by naming her Toutebelle.

When the princess reached the age of fifteen, the queen had her portrait painted by the best artists and sent it to several kings with whom she was on friendly terms. As soon as they saw this portrait, everyone without exception yielded to the inevitable power of her charms. Some fell ill, others lost their wits, and those fortunate enough to maintain their health and senses rushed to her court. No sooner did they lay eyes on the fair original than the poor princes became her devoted slaves.

Never in the world was a court more gallant and polite. Twenty kings vied with one another in endeavoring to please the princess. After spending three or four hundred million francs on a single entertainment, they felt more than repaid by her curt response: "It was pretty." The queen was delighted by all the worship that her daughter was receiving. Not a day passed that the princess did not find seven or eight thousand sonnets and as many odes, madrigals, and songs, sent to her by all the poets in the universe. Toutebelle was the sole theme of all the prose and verse written by the authors of the time. All the bonfires were made with these compositions, which burned and sparkled better than any other sort of fuel.

No one ventured to claim the honor of proposing to become her husband, though everybody wanted to. Yet how could anyone touch a heart like hers? A man might have hanged himself five or six times a day to

459

please her, and she would have thought it but a trifle. Her lovers complained bitterly about her cruelty, and her mother, now that she wanted her to marry, saw no means of inducing her to decide in favor of one of them. "Won't you soften that intolerable pride of yours and stop criticizing all the kings who visit our court?" she asked. "I want to give you one for a husband. Don't you want to please me?"

"But I'm so happy," Toutebelle replied. "Please permit me, madam, to enjoy my serene indifference. If I were to change, you might be very sorry."

"Yes," said the queen, "I'd be angry if you were to love anyone beneath you. But look at those who want you, and you will see that none are more worthy than the suitors you have."

This was quite true, but the princess had such a high opinion of her own perfection that she considered herself worth someone even better. After some time had passed, her obstinate determination to remain single upset her mother so much that she now regretted her extreme indulgence, even though it was too late. Not knowing what to do, she journeyed all alone to consult a famous fairy called the fairy of the desert. Gaining access to her, however, was no easy task, for she was guarded by a pride of lions. The queen's plight would have been hopeless if she had not known that she had to feed these beasts a cake made of millet seed, sugar candy, and crocodiles' eggs. She made one of these cakes herself and put it into a hand basket.

Since she was not accustomed to walking so far, she lay down at the foot of a tree to take a short rest. Gradually she fell asleep, and on reawaking she found her basket empty. The cake was gone, and to complete the calamity, she heard the tremendous roars of the great lions coming ever nearer, for they had detected her scent.

"Alas, what will become of me?" she exclaimed piteously. "They're going to devour me!" Weeping, not having strength to flee, she clung to the tree under which she had slept. Just then she heard, "Psst! Psst! Ahem! Ahem!" She looked all around her and, raising her eyes, saw a little man up in the tree. He was no more than a foot tall, and he was eating oranges. "I know you quite well, Queen," he said, "and I know you're afraid the lions will devour you. To be sure, you have good reason to be afraid, for they've devoured many before you, and to make matters worse, you have no cake."

"I must prepare myself to die!" the queen said, sighing. "Alas, I'd die much happier if my dear daughter were but married!"

"What? You have a daughter?" the yellow dwarf exclaimed. (He was given this name because of the color of his skin and because he dwelled in an orange tree.) "Truly, I'm delighted to hear it, for I've sought a wife by land and sea. Look, if you promise her to me, I'll save you from lions, tigers, or bears."

Looking at him, the queen was scarcely less frightened by his horrible little figure than by the lions. She pondered for some time without replying.

"What, you hesitate, madam?" he cried. "You can't be very fond of life."

At that very moment the queen perceived the lions on the top of a hill charging toward her. Each had two heads, eight feet, four rows of teeth, and their skin was as hard as rock and as red as morocco. At this sight the poor queen trembled more than a dove that spots a falcon, and she cried out with all her might, "My lord dwarf! Toutebelle is yours."

"Oh," he said disdainfully, "Toutebelle is too much of a belle. I don't want anything to do with her. You may keep her."

"Ah, my lord," the troubled queen continued, "don't reject her. She's the most charming princess in the world."

"Very well," he said, "I'll accept her out of charity, but remember the gift you've given me!"

Suddenly the trunk of the orange tree opened and the queen rushed headlong into it just as it closed, thwarting the lions of their prey. The queen was so upset that she did not see that a door had been constructed inside the tree as well. Eventually she noticed it and, opening it, saw a field of nettles and thistles surrounded by a muddy ditch. Not far from the door stood a low-roofed cottage thatched with straw, and from it emerged the yellow dwarf, grinning mirthfully. Wearing wooden shoes and a jacket of coarse yellow cloth, he had large ears and no hair and looked just like a little villain. "I'd be delighted, my lady mother-in-law," he said, "to show you the little château in which your Toutebelle will reside with me. She may keep an ass in this field of nettles and thistles to ride about on. This rustic roof will shelter her from inclement weather. She'll drink this water and eat some of the frogs that live off it freely. And she'll have me day and night beside her—handsome, gay, and gallant, as you see me—for I'd be very angry if her shadow were to follow her better than I could."

The unfortunate queen was suddenly struck by the wretched life the dwarf planned for her daughter, and since she could not stand such a terrible prospect, she fainted dead away without uttering a word in reply. In this state was she transported to the palace and placed neatly in her own bed with the finest nightcap and most beautiful ribbons that she had ever worn. When the queen awoke and recalled what had happened to her, she could not believe it was true, for when she found herself in her palace with her ladies and her daughter by her side, there was little to show that she had been in the desert, that she had encountered such great dangers, and that the dwarf had saved her from them by making such a hard condition as the gift of Toutebelle. Nevertheless, the rare lace of the cap and the beauty of the ribbon astonished her just as much as the dream she assumed she must have had.

Due to her extreme anxiety, she fell into a melancholy so extraordinary that she could scarcely speak, eat, or sleep. The princess, who loved her mother with all her heart, was very concerned about her. She asked her frequently to tell her what the matter was, but the queen kept giving excuses. Sometimes she answered that she was not feeling well, other times that one of the neighboring states threatened to declare war against her.

Toutebelle saw clearly enough that these were plausible reasons, but also that there was something else at the bottom of the matter that the queen carefully concealed from her. Unable to suppress her disquiet, she decided to seek out the famous fairy of the desert, whose wisdom was widely celebrated in the region. She also desired her advice about marrying or remaining single, for everybody kept urging her to choose a husband. With her own hands she carefully kneaded the cake that had the power to appease the fury of the lions. That evening she pretended to go to bed early, but instead went out by a back staircase, her face covered by a large white veil that came down to her feet. All alone she took the road toward the clever fairy's grotto.

When she arrived at the fatal orange tree of which I have already spoken, however, she found it so laden with fruit and blossoms that she was overcome by an irresistible desire to pick some. Setting her basket on the

ground, she plucked some oranges and ate them. When she turned to look for her basket and the cake again, they had disappeared. Already quite distressed, she was jolted when suddenly, right beside her, appeared the frightful dwarf whom I described before.

"What's troubling you, fair maid? Why are you weeping?" he asked.

"Alas, who wouldn't weep?" she replied. "I've lost my basket and my cake, which I need to insure my safe arrival at the abode of the desert fairy."

"Ah, and what do you want with her, fair maid?" the little monkey asked again. "I'm her kinsman, her friend, and just as clever as she is."

"My mother has lately been so despondent that I tremble for her life," the princess replied. "I think that I may be the cause of it all. You see, she wants me to marry, and I must confess that I haven't met anyone yet whom I deem worthy of me. This is why I want to consult the fairy."

"Don't trouble yourself, Princess," the dwarf said. "I'm better suited to enlighten you about such subjects than she. Your mother regrets that she has promised your hand in marriage—"

"The queen's promised me to someone?" the princess cried, interrupting him. "Oh, you must be mistaken. She would have told me, for I'm far too interested in this affair for her to arrange my engagement without seeking my consent beforehand."

"Beautiful princess," said the dwarf, suddenly flinging himself at her feet, "I hope that her choice will not displease you when I tell you that it is I who is destined to enjoy such happiness."

"My mother wants you for her son-in-law?" Toutebelle exclaimed, retreating a few steps. "You must be insane!"

"I don't really care about this honor," the dwarf said angrily. "Here come the lions! In three bites they'll avenge me for your unjust disdain."

All at once the poor princess heard the loud roars of the approaching monsters. "What will become of me?" she cried. "Is this how my young days are to end?"

The wicked dwarf looked at her and laughed contemptuously. "At least you'll have the glory of dying a maiden," he said, "and not disgracing yourself by having a person of your dazzling worth united with a miserable dwarf like me."

"For mercy's sake, don't be angry," the princess begged, clasping her beautiful hands. "I'd rather marry all the dwarfs in the universe than perish so frightfully."

"Regard me well, Princess, before you give me your word," he replied, "for I don't want to take advantage of you."

"I've looked at you more than enough," she said. "The lions terrify me more than your looks. Save me! Save me or I'll die of fright!"

Scarcely had she uttered these words than she fainted. When she at last recovered from her swoon, she found herself, without knowing how she got there, in her own bed lined with the finest linen in the world, the most beautiful ribbons on her dress, and a ring made of a single red hair, which fitted her finger so tightly that the skin would have come off sooner than the ring.

When the princess saw all these things and remembered what had taken place that night, she fell into a melancholy that shocked and upset the entire court. More alarmed than anyone, her mother asked her hundreds of times what the matter was, but the princess persisted in concealing this incident from her. At length the great estates of the kingdom became impatient to see the princess married, and they assembled in council. Afterward they obtained an audience with the queen, whom they petitioned with the request that she choose a husband for her daughter as soon as possible. She answered that she desired nothing better, but that her daughter demonstrated so much repugnance to marriage that she advised them to talk to the princess herself about the subject, whereupon they left immediately.

Toutebelle had lost a good deal of her haughtiness since her encounter with the yellow dwarf. She saw no other way of escaping her dilemma than by marrying a great king with whom the little monkey would not dare to dispute such a glorious prize. To the members of the council she gave a more favorable answer than they had expected: "Although I would consider myself content to remain single all my life, I agree to marry the king of the gold mines." This was a powerful, handsome prince who had loved her passionately for several years and who until that moment had never dared to hope that she would in the least return his affection.

You can well imagine how ecstatic he was when he received such glorious news, and you can also imagine the rage of all his rivals when they learned about the extinction of the fond hopes they had nourished. But Toutebelle could not marry twenty kings. She had already had a great deal of difficulty in choosing one, for her vanity was as great as ever, and she was still fully convinced that nobody in the world was suitable enough for her.

Everything necessary for the finest celebration that the universe has ever seen was prepared. The king of the gold mines sent home for such prodigious sums that the sea was swamped with the ships that returned with them. Agents were dispatched to all the most refined and gallant courts, particularly that of France, to purchase the rarest materials for the wardrobe of the princess. Of course, she had less need than anybody for ornamentation to highlight her beauty, which was so perfect that it was impossible to embellish. As the blissful day approached, the king of the gold mines never left the side of his charming princess.

The evident importance of becoming acquainted with the character of her future husband induced the princess to observe him carefully. As a result she discovered in him so much merit, so much sense, such deep and delicate feeling—in short, such a fine mind in such a perfect body—that she began to return his affection to some degree. They spent happy moments wandering in the most beautiful gardens in the world, where they found themselves at liberty to express their mutual sentiments, a pleasure often heightened by the charms of music. The king, always gallant and amorous, sang verses of his own composition to the princess. The following is one she especially liked:

> "The groves for you have donned a richer green.
> The fields reveal the brightest flowers seen.
> Your footsteps fall, fresh blossoms spring;
> Within your bowers, the sweet birds sing.
> All nature smiles, around, below, above,
> All hail the daughter of the god of love!"

Everyone in the palace was filled with joy but the king's rivals. Enraged by his success, they left the court and returned to their own dominions, too overwhelmed by grief to be able to bear the pain of witnessing Toutebelle's marriage. In fact, they took their leave of her in such a touching manner that she could not help pitying them.

"Ah, madam," the king of the gold mines asked her on that occasion, "why are you being so unfair to me today? These lovers were more than repaid for their sufferings by one glance from your eyes, and yet you've blessed them with your pity."

"I'd be angry," Toutebelle said, "if you were indifferent to the compassion I've shown those princes who have lost me forever. It's proof of your sensitivity, and I'm indebted to you for it. But, my lord, their position is so different from yours. You have good reason to be satisfied with my conduct toward you, and they have little cause to congratulate themselves. So don't let your jealousy get the better of you."

Disarmed by how kindly the princess received a reproach that might have annoyed her, the king of the gold mines threw himself at her feet, kissed her hand, and asked her pardon a thousand times.

At last the day they had awaited so fervently arrived. Everything was ready for the marriage: trumpets and musical instruments announced the commencement of this grand fete all over the city; the streets were carpeted and strewn with flowers; the people flocked in crowds to the great square in front of the palace. In a state of rapture, the queen had scarcely gone to bed before she got up again long before daybreak to give the necessary orders and to select the jewels the princess was to wear. She was diamonds down to her very shoes, which were also fashioned of them. Bought at an enormous price, her gown of silver brocade was striped with a dozen rays of the sun, and their radiance was matched only by the beauty of the princess. A magnificent crown adorned her head. Her hair fell to her feet in wavy curls. Her majestic form glittered brilliantly among the crowd of ladies who accompanied her.

The king of the gold mines was no less magnificent in his appearance, and his happiness was apparent in his every look and gesture. No one approached him who did not return loaded with his generous gifts, for he had ordered a thousand barrels to be filled with gold and large sacks of pearl-embroidered velvet to be crammed with coins. Placed around the banquet hall, each held a hundred thousand and were given indiscriminately to all who held out their hands. The result was that this pleasant ceremony drew many people who had scant regard for the other entertaining events during the wedding festivities.

The queen and princess advanced to meet the king and proceeded with him to the altar. As they passed through the long nave, they saw two large turkey cocks drawing a very clumsily made box. Behind them came a tall old crone, whose great age and decrepitude were as striking as her ugliness. She walked with a crutch and wore a black taffeta ruff, a red velvet hood, and a farthingale all in tatters. She took three turns around the gallery with her turkey cocks before she said anything. Then, stopping in the center and brandishing her crutch in a threatening manner, she cried, "Ho, ho, queen! Ho, ho, princess! Do you think you can break your promises to my friend the yellow dwarf with impunity? I'm the fairy of the desert! Don't you realize that if it weren't for him and his orange tree that my great lions would have devoured you? We don't put up with such insults in fairyland. Ponder quickly the consequences of what you're about to do, for I swear by my cap that you shall marry the dwarf, or I'll burn my crutch."

"Ah, Princess!" the queen exclaimed, bursting into tears. "What do I hear? What was the promise you made?"

"Ah, Mother!" Toutebelle cried sorrowfully. "What was the promise you yourself made?"

The king of the gold mines was enraged by this interruption and by the wicked old woman's opposition to his marriage. He advanced toward her, sword in hand, and placing the point to her throat, he cried, "Leave this palace forever, or you'll pay for your maliciousness with your life."

No sooner had he said these words than the lid of the box popped open with a terrific noise and shot to the ceiling. Out came the yellow dwarf, mounted on a large Spanish cat. In a wink he had assumed a position between the fairy of the desert and the king of the gold mines.

"Not so quick, young man," he said. "Don't think you can assault this illustrious fairy. You're going to have to deal with me alone! I'm your foe, nay, I'm your rival. The faithless princess who means to wed you promised to be mine, and I promised to be hers. Look and see if she doesn't have a ring of my hair on her finger. Try to remove it and you'll learn how inferior your power is to mine."

"Miserable monster," the king replied, "you have the audacity to declare yourself the lover of this divine princess? You're nothing but a monkey, whose hideous figure is painful to behold. I would have long since eliminated you if you had really been worthy of dying by my hand."

Stung to the quick, the yellow dwarf stuck his spurs into the sides of his cat, who began squalling horribly. As the cat flew here and there, it terrified everyone except the brave king, who pressed the dwarf so closely that he drew a large cutlass from his side and challenged the king to single combat.

The dwarf descended into the palace courtyard amid an extraordinary uproar, and the enraged king followed him with rapid strides. No sooner had they confronted each other, as the entire court watched from the balconies, than the sun suddenly became as red as blood, and it grew so dark that they could scarcely see each other. Such thunder and lightning exploded that the world seemed to be coming to its end. The two turkey cocks appeared at the yellow dwarf's side: they were twin giants larger than mountains, spewing so many flames from their mouths and eyes that each one looked like a fiery furnace. Still, none of these horrors frightened the dauntless young king. Through his intrepid glare and swirling sword he reassured all who were interested in his welfare and brought embarrassment to the yellow dwarf.

Alas, the king's mettle failed him when he saw the fairy of the desert— her head covered with long serpents like Tisiphone, mounted upon a winged griffin and armed with a lance—rush at his dear princess and strike her with such a fierce blow that she fell into the queen's arms bathed in her own blood. That tender mother was more deeply wounded by the blow than even her daughter, and she uttered shrieks and groans that are impossible to describe. As soon as he saw this, the king's reason abandoned him, and he ceased fighting. Immediately he dashed to rescue the princess or to die with her, but the yellow dwarf anticipated his movements. Leaping with his Spanish cat onto the balcony, he snatched the princess from the arms of the queen and the ladies who surrounded her. Then he jumped onto the roof of the palace and disappeared with his prize.

Paralyzed with astonishment, the king witnessed this extraordinary incident in utter despair. Not only did he have no power to prevent it, but to complete his disgrace, he felt his eyesight fail him as an irresistible power carried him off through a vast expanse of some vacuum. What misfortunes! Love, cruel Love! Is this how you treat those who acknowledge you as their lord?

The wicked fairy of the desert had no sooner laid eyes on the king of the gold mines than her barbarous heart was touched by his charms. Marking him as her prey, she carried him off to the depths of a frightful cave, where she bound him with chains anchored to a rock in the hope that the fear of impending death would make him forget Toutebelle and do whatever she desired. As soon as they had arrived, she restored his sight. Through the power of fairy art, she acquired the graces and charms denied her by nature, and appeared before him as a lovely nymph who just happened to show up at that spot by chance.

"What do I see?" she cried. "Can it be you, charming prince? What's happened to you? What misfortune has brought you to languish in this miserable abode?"

Deceived by her appearance, the king replied, "Alas, fair nymph, I don't know why the infernal fairy has brought me here. Although she prevented me from seeing when she carried me off and hasn't shown herself since, I do know from her voice that it was the fairy of the desert."

"Ah, my lord," the false nymph exclaimed, "if you are in the power of that woman, you won't escape without marrying her. She has snared more than one hero, and of all beings in the world, she is the most obstinate when she sets her mind on something."

While she thus pretended to take a great interest in the king's distress, he caught sight of the nymph's feet, which resembled those of a griffin. The fairy of the desert could always be recognized by her feet, which remained unaltered no matter how she changed herself. Pretending not to notice, the king continued conversing as though he fully trusted her. "I don't feel any aversion toward the fairy of the desert," he said, "but I can't stand her protecting the yellow dwarf and keeping me in chains like a criminal. What have I done to offend her? I loved a charming princess, but if the fairy restores my liberty to me, I feel that gratitude will induce me to love no one but her."

"Are you sincere about this?" the nymph asked, faltering.

"There's no need to doubt me," the king replied. "I'm not experienced in the art of deception, and I must confess that my vanity would be more flattered by the attention shown by a fairy than by a mere princess. But even if I desperately loved her, I'd show her nothing but hatred until I had regained my liberty."

Deceived by these words, the fairy of the desert decided to transport the king to a spot as beautiful as the cave he now inhabited was horrible. Compelling him to get into her chariot, to which she now harnessed swans instead of the bats that usually drew it, she flew with the king of the gold mines from one pole to the other. What a shock the king received, though, enroute! While coursing through the boundless ethereal regions, he caught a glimpse of his dear princess in a castle made entirely of steel. Its walls reflected the rays of the sun and became burning glass sheets that scorched to death all who approached them. The princess was reclining in a bower beside a streamlet, and one of her hands was beneath her head, while the other appeared to be wiping away tears. As she lifted her eyes to Heaven, imploring its aid, she saw the king pass by with the fairy of the desert. Just as she had used her skillful magic power to appear beautiful in the eyes of the young monarch, so she also seemed to be the most marvelous creature in the world to the princess.

"What now?" she exclaimed. "Aren't I sufficiently wretched in this inaccessible castle where the dreadful yellow dwarf has transported me? Must the demon of jealousy torture me to complete my misery? Must I learn through this extraordinary incident that the king of the gold mines is unfaithful to me? Now that I'm out of sight, he obviously believes that he's absolved from all his vows. But who is this formidable rival whose fatal beauty surpasses mine?"

While the princess mused, the enamored king was in mortal agony at being whisked away from the dear object of his affections. If he had not been so fully cognizant of the fairy's power, he would have risked escape either by killing her or by using some other means that his love or courage might have proposed. But what could be done against so powerful a being? "Be patient," he told himself. "You must wait for the right opportunity to free yourself of her clutches."

Having seen Toutebelle as well, the fairy sought to discover in the king's eyes what effect the sight of his darling had induced in his heart. "No one but myself," the king said, interpreting her glances, "can tell you what you want to know. This unexpected meeting with an unhappy princess with whom I had an attachment has aroused some feelings in me. But you are so far superior to her in my mind that I'd rather die than be unfaithful to you."

"Ah, Prince!" the fairy said. "Dare I hope that I've inspired you with sentiments so favorable?"

"Time will convince you, madam," he replied. "But if you want to convince me that I'm in your good graces, you'll not refuse me when I ask you to protect Toutebelle."

"Reflect on what you ask of me," said the fairy, frowning and looking askance at him. "Do you want me to use my skills against the yellow dwarf, my best friend, in order to release a proud princess from his power—a princess whom I must still regard as my rival?"

The king sighed without replying. What answer could he make to such an calculating fiend?

They arrived at a vast prairie sprinkled with a thousand different flowers. A deep river surrounded it, and streams from many fountains flowed gently beneath tufted trees offering refreshing shade. In the distance could be seen a superb palace whose walls were made of transparent emeralds. As soon as the swans drawing the fairy's chariot had descended beneath a portico roofed with rubies and paved with diamonds, thousands of lovely nymphs appeared from every quarter and advanced to receive them with loud shouts of joy and the following song:

"When victory is what Love seeks to gain,
Defiance is idle—we struggle in vain.
Resistance gives force to the weapons he wields.
The greater the hero, the sooner he yields."

The fairy of the desert was delighted at hearing this allusion to her conquest. Leading the king into the most superb apartment known in the memory of fairies, she left him alone for a few minutes so that he would not think that he was utterly her prisoner. For his part, he felt certain that she was not far off and that no matter where she was keeping herself, she had an eye on all his actions. Therefore, he advanced to a large looking glass and addressed it by saying, "Loyal counselor, let me see what I can do to make myself more pleasant to the charming fairy of the desert, for I'm terribly eager to please her." Thereupon, he combed and powdered his hair, put a patch on his cheek, and upon noticing a suit of clothes on a table more magnificent than his own, he changed into them as quickly as possible. When the fairy reentered, she was so ecstatic that she could not control her joy.

"I appreciate the pains you've taken to please me," she said. "You've found the secret of pleasing me without searching for it. You must judge, sir, whether it will be difficult to continue to do so."

The king, who had his reasons for saying sweet things to the old fairy, kept flattering her, and by degrees he obtained permission to take a daily walk by the seaside. She had used her art to make that coast so dangerous and terrifying that not a captain was courageous enough to navigate in the vicinity. Thus she had nothing to fear by granting this favor to her captive. It was, however, some comfort to him to be able to indulge in solitary musings uninterrupted by the presence of his wicked jailer.

After having strolled for some time on the sands, he stooped and inscribed the following lines in them with a cane that he carried at his side:

At last I am at liberty to weep:
My tears in torrents now unchecked may pour,
And ease my laboring bosom's anguish that's so deep.
Alas! I shan't behold my love anymore.
Oh you, that make this rock-girted shore
To mortals inaccessible! Dread sea,
Whose mountain billows as the wild winds roar,
Now high as Heaven, now low as Hell, can flee.
Your state, compared to mine, is calm tranquillity.

Toutebelle! Oh cruel destiny! Forever,
Forever lost! The idol of my heart!
You gods, when dooming me from her to sever,
Why didn't you ask my life as well to part?

Spirit of Ocean, whoever you are.
If it be true that even beneath the wave
Love has the power to reach you with his dart,
Rise from your pearly grotto, your coral cave,
And from despair a fond and faithful lover save.

As he finished, he heard a voice that irresistibly attracted his attention. Noticing the tide rising in an extraordinary manner, he quickly turned around and saw a female of extraordinary beauty. Her torso was adorned only by her waist-long hair, and the breeze brushed it gently so that her hair floated on the water. She held a looking glass in one hand and a comb in the other, and her lower extremities took the form of a long fish's tail furnished with fins. Needless to say, the king was astounded by such an extraordinary sight.

As soon as she was near enough to speak, she said, "I know of your sad predicament with your lost princess as well as the bizarre attachment that the fairy of the desert has for you. If you're willing, I'll take you away from this fatal spot. Otherwise you may languish here another thirty years."

The king knew not how to reply to this proposal. Though he needed no inducement to escape from captivity, he feared the fairy of the desert had taken this form to deceive him. As he hesitated, the siren, who could read his thoughts, said, "Don't think I'm laying a trap for you. I'm too honest to want to serve your enemies. The conduct of the fairy of the desert and the yellow dwarf has incensed me. I see your unhappy princess daily, and her beauty and merit have aroused my compassion. So, let me repeat, if you'll trust me, I'll rescue you."

"I trust you completely," the king said, "and I'll do whatever you command. But since you've seen my princess, please tell me some news of her."

"We'd lose too much time by talking here," said the siren. "Come, I'll take you to the steel castle and leave a figure here on the shore that will resemble you so closely that it will deceive the fairy."

She immediately cut some sea rushes and made a large bundle of them. Blowing on it three times, she said, "Sea rushes, my friends, I order you to lie motionless on the sand until the fairy of the desert comes to take you away." The rushes became covered with skin and so resembled the king of the gold mines that he was astonished by the transformation. The figure wore clothes exactly like his, and its countenance was pale and wasted, as if he had drowned. The friendly siren then made the king sit on her large fish's tail, and in this manner, agreeable to both, they plied the sea together.

"Now," the siren said, "I'll gladly tell you what transpired after the fairy of the desert had wounded Toutebelle and the wicked dwarf carried her off on the back of his horrible Spanish cat. The princess lost so much blood and was so terrified by all that had occurred that her strength failed her, and she was unconscious the entire journey. Despite her condition, the yellow dwarf did not stop to help her in the least until he had safely arrived in his terrible steel palace, where he was welcomed by the most beautiful nymphs in the world, whom he had already transported there. They vied with one another in their eagerness to serve the princess. She was put into a bed with sheets made of gold and covered with pearls as large as walnuts."

"Ha!" exclaimed the king of the gold mines, interrupting the siren. "So he's married her. I feel faint! I'm going to die!"

"No," she said, "compose yourself, my lord. Toutebelle's vigor has protected her from the violence of that hideous dwarf."

"Proceed, then," the king said.

"What more can I tell you?" the siren continued. "She was in the grove when you flew over it. She saw you with the fairy of the desert, who was so well disguised that she appeared to be more beautiful than the princess herself. You cannot imagine how desperate she is. She believes you love the fairy."

"Good heavens!" the king cried. "She believed that I love the fairy? What a mistake she's made! What must I do to put these matters right?"

"Consult your own heart," the siren replied with a gracious smile. "When we are deeply in love, we need no advice about such things."

Even as she spoke, they arrived at the steel castle. The side facing the sea was the only border that the yellow dwarf had not fortified with those formidable walls that burned everyone who approached them. "I know for certain," the siren said, "that Toutebelle sits beside the same fountain that you saw when you passed over the castle gardens. But you'll have some foes to contend with before you can approach her. Here is a sword: armed with it you may dare to brave the greatest dangers. But beware that you never let it drop. Adieu, I'm going to rest beneath the rock you see over yonder. If you need my help to convey you and your dear princess any farther, I won't fail you, for her mother is my best friend and it was for her sake that I went to find you."

So saying, she gave the king a sword fashioned from a single diamond, which glistened more brightly than the rays of the sun. The king understood its incalculable value, and since he could find no words to express his gratitude, he begged her to make amends for his deficiency by imagining all that an honest heart could feel under such great obligations.

We must now say a word about the fairy of the desert. When she found that her charming lover had not returned, she went in search of him. Down to the seashore she walked with a hundred maidens in her train, all bearing magnificent presents for the king. Some carried large baskets filled with diamonds, others golden vases marvelously wrought; many were carrying ambergris, coral, and pearls; others had bales of amazingly rich materials on their heads while still others bore fruit, flowers, and even birds. Thus you can imagine the feelings of the fairy who followed this bounteous troop when she saw the sea rushes that exactly resembled the king of the gold mines. The sight of him dead caused her such pain that she uttered a dreadful shriek that pierced the skies, shook the hills, and echoed even in the infernal regions. The Furies, Megara, Alecto, and Tisiphone, could not have assumed a more terrible aspect than did the fairy of the desert at that moment. Throwing herself on the apparent corpse of the king, she wept, she howled, she tore apart fifty of the most beautiful maidens accompanying her, immolating them to the manes of her dearly departed. After this she invoked eleven of her sister fairies to appear and help her construct a stately mausoleum in which she might deposit the remains of the young hero. Like the desert fairy every one of the eleven was deceived by the appearance of the sea rushes. This circumstance is rather surprising, for fairies generally know everything, but the clever siren proved in this case that she knew more than they.

Even as they were collecting porphyry, jasper, agate, marble, statues, emblems, gold, and bronze to immortalize the king they believed dead, he was thanking the charming siren and implored her to continue protecting him. She kindly promised she would and vanished from sight. Nothing was left but for him to advance on the steel castle.

Guided by his love, he strode forth to inspect every part of the castle and discover his adorable princess. But he encountered trouble all too quickly. Four terrible sphinxes surrounded him, and when they lashed out with their sharp talons, they would have quickly torn him to pieces if the diamond sword had not proved as useful as the siren had predicted. No sooner had he flashed it before the eyes of these monsters than they fell powerless at his feet, and he dealt each of them its death blow. When he advanced again, he encountered six dragons covered with scales harder to pierce than iron. Alarmed though he was, his courage remained unshaken, and he made such good use of his redoubtable sword that he cut each one in half with one blow. He was hoping he had surmounted the greatest obstacles when a most embarrassing one presented itself. Twenty-four beautiful, graceful nymphs advanced toward him with long garlands of flowers, which they stretched across his path to impede his progress.

"Where do you wish to go, sire?" they asked. "We've been entrusted to protect these regions. If we permit you to pass, we shall all experience a wealth of misfortunes. For mercy's sake, don't continue. Do you want to stain your victorious hand with the blood of twenty-four innocent maidens who have never done anything to displease you?"

Irresolute, the king stood transfixed before them. He who professed such respect for the fair sex and eagerly championed them to the death on every occasion was presently to destroy a group of the fairest! But while he was hesitating, he heard a voice say: "Strike! Strike! or your princess is lost forever!"

Swayed by these words, he did not utter a word in reply to the nymphs, but instead he rushed upon them, broke through their garlands, attacked them without mercy, and scattered them about.

This proved his last obstacle before he found himself entering the grove in which he had previously seen Toutebelle, who was seated beside the fountain, pale and suffering. Trembling as he approached her, he would have thrown himself at her feet, but she fled from him as hastily and indignantly as if he had been the yellow dwarf. "Don't condemn me without hearing me out," he said. "I'm neither unfaithful nor guilty of any intentional wrong toward you. I'm an unhappy lover who was compelled despite himself to offend you."

"Ah, cruel prince," she exclaimed, "I saw you sail through the air with a lady of extraordinary beauty. Was it despite yourself you made that voyage?"

"Yes, Princess," he replied, "it was. The wicked fairy of the desert was not satisfied with chaining me to a rock. So she dragged me in her chariot to one of the ends of the world, where I would still be languishing in captivity if it were not for the unexpected assistance of a beneficent siren who brought me here. I've come, my princess, to release you from the power of the villain who holds you prisoner. Don't reject the aid of the most faithful of lovers!"

He flung himself at her feet and caught the hem of her gown to detain her, but in so doing, he unfortunately let the formidable sword drop to the ground. The yellow dwarf, who lay hidden beneath the leaves of a lettuce, no sooner saw it fall from the king's grasp than he sprang forward and seized it, for he was aware of its power.

The princess uttered a terrified shriek at the sight of the dwarf, but her anguish only exasperated the little monster. With two cabalistic words he conjured up two giants, who bound the king with chains and fetters.

"Now," the dwarf said, "I'm master of my rival's fate, but I'll spare his life and give him liberty to leave this place, provided you consent to marry me immediately."

"Oh, I'd rather die a thousand deaths!" the enamored king exclaimed.

"You die? Alas, my lord," said the princess, "what could be more terrible for me than such a calamity?"

"Your becoming the victim of this monster. Can any horror exceed that?"

"Let's die together, then."

"No, Princess," the king answered. "Grant me the consolation of dying for you."

"Before I allow that," the princess said, turning to the dwarf, "I will consent to your wishes."

"In front of my eyes?" the king exclaimed. "In front of my eyes you intend to make him your husband? Cruel princess, life will be hateful to me!"

"No," the yellow dwarf said, "you will see no such thing. A beloved rival is too dangerous to be endured."

With these words, despite the tears and shrieks of Toutebelle, he stabbed the king in the heart and laid him dead at his feet. Unable to bear life without her lover, the princess fell on his body, and her spirit quickly fled to join his. Thus this illustrious but unfortunate pair perished without the siren being able to help, for the power of the spell had been centered in the diamond sword.

The wicked dwarf preferred having the princess dead than seeing her in the arms of another, and once the fairy of the desert was informed of what had occurred, she destroyed the mausoleum she had erected and developed as much hatred for the king as she had formerly felt love.

The friendly siren was overwhelmed with grief by such a great misfortune, but she could obtain no other favor from Fate than the permission to change the two lovers into palm trees. Their two bodies, which had been so perfect during life, became two graceful trees, and since they still cherished a faithful love for each other, they joined their branches in fond embraces and immortalized their ardor by that tender union.

Those who in danger on the stormy main
Vow hecatombs to all the gods they know,
When safe on shore they find themselves again,
Not even near their altars do they care to go.
In peril anyone will swear anything for his sake,
But let the tragic tale of poor Toutebelle
Warn you no promise in your fear to make
You would not gladly keep when all is well.

THE GREEN SERPENT

ONCE upon a time there was a great queen who, having given birth to twin daughters, invited twelve fairies who lived nearby to come and bestow gifts upon them, as was the custom in those days. Indeed, it was a very useful custom, for the power of the fairies generally compensated for the deficiencies of nature. Sometimes, however, they also spoiled what nature had done its best to make perfect, as we shall soon see.

When the fairies had all gathered in the banquet hall, they were about to sit at the table and enjoy a magnificent meal. Suddenly the fairy Magotine entered. She was the sister of Carabossa and no less malicious. Shuddering when she saw her, the queen feared some disaster since she had not invited her to the celebration. However, she carefully concealed her anxiety, personally went looking for an armchair for the fairy, and found one covered with green velvet and embroidered with sapphires. Since Magotine was the eldest of the fairies, all the rest made way for her to pass and whispered to one another, "Let us quickly endow the infant princesses, sister, so that we may get the start on Magotine."

When the armchair was set up for her, she rudely declined it, saying that she was big enough to eat standing. She was mistaken in this, though, because the table was rather high and she was not tall enough to see over it. This annoyance increased her foul mood even more.

"Madam," the queen said, "I beg you to take your seat at the table."

"If you had wished me to do so," the fairy replied, "you would have sent an invitation to me as you did to the others, but you only want beauties with fine figures and fine dresses like my sisters here. As for me, I'm too ugly and old. Yet despite it all, I have just as much power as they. In fact, without boasting about it, I may even have more."

All the fairies urged her strongly to sit at the table, and at length she consented. A golden basket was placed before them, containing twelve bouquets composed of jewels. The fairies who had arrived first each took a bouquet, leaving none for Magotine. As she began to mutter between her teeth, the queen ran to her room and brought her a casket of perfumed Spanish morocco covered with rubies and filled with diamonds, and asked her to accept it. But Magotine shook her head and said, "Keep your jewels, madam. I have more than enough to spare. I came only to see if you had thought of me, and it's clear you've neglected me shamefully."

Thereupon she struck the table with her wand, and all the delicacies heaped on it were turned into fricasseed serpents. This sight horrified the fairies so much that they flung down their napkins and fled the table. While they talked with one another about the nasty trick Magotine had played on them, that cruel fairy approached the cradle in which the princesses, the loveliest children in the world, were lying wrapped in golden swaddling. "I endow you with perfect ugliness," she quickly said to one of them, and she was about to utter a malediction on the other when the fairies, greatly disturbed, ran and stopped her. Then the mischievous Magotine broke one of the window panes, dashed through it like a flash of lightning, and vanished from sight.

All the good gifts that the benevolent fairies proceeded to bestow on the princess did not alleviate the misery of the queen, who found herself the mother of the ugliest being in the universe. Taking the infant in her arms, she had the misfortune of watching it grow more hideous by the moment. She struggled in vain to suppress her tears in the presence of their fairy ladyships, whose compassion is impossible to imagine. "What shall we do, sisters?" they said to one another. "How can we ever console the queen?" They held a grand council about the matter, and at the end they told the queen not to give into her grief since a time would come when her daughter would be very happy.

"But," the queen interrupted, "will she become beautiful again?"

"We can't give you any further information," the fairies replied. "Be satisfied, madam, with the assurance that your daughter will be happy."

She thanked them very much and did not forget to give them many presents. Although the fairies were very rich, they always liked people to give them something. Throughout the world this custom has been passed down from that day to our own, and time has not altered it in the least.

The queen named her elder daughter Laidronette and the younger Bellotte. These names suited them perfectly, for Laidronette, despite her boundless intelligence, became too frightful to behold, whereas her sister's beauty increased hourly until she looked thoroughly charming.

After Laidronette had turned twelve, she went to the king and queen, and threw herself at their feet. "Please, I implore you, allow me to shut myself up in a lonely castle so that I will no longer torment you with my ugliness." Despite her hideous appearance, they could not help being fond of her, and not without some pain did they consent to let her depart. However, since Bellotte remained with them, they had ample consolation.

Laidronette begged the queen not to send anyone except her nurse and a few officers to wait on her. "You needn't worry, madam, about my being abducted. I can assure you that, looking as I do, I shall avoid even the light of day."

After the king and queen had granted her wishes, she was conducted to the castle she had chosen. It had been built many centuries before, and the sea crashed beneath its windows and served it as a moat. In the vicinity was a large forest in which one could stroll, and in several fields leading to the forest, the princess played various instruments and sang divinely.

Two years she spent in this pleasant solitude, even writing several volumes recording her thoughts, but the desire to see her father and mother again induced her to take a coach and revisit the court. She arrived just as they were to celebrate the marriage of Bellotte. Everyone had been rejoicing, but the moment they saw Laidronette, their joy turned to distress. She was neither embraced nor hugged by any of her relatives. Indeed, the only thing they said to her was that she had grown a good deal uglier, and they advised her not to appear at the ball. "However, if you wish to see it, we shall find some hole for you to peep through."

She replied that she had come there neither to dance nor to hear the music, that she had been in the desolate castle so long that she had felt a longing to pay her respects to the king and the queen. Painfully aware that they could not endure the sight of her, she told them that she would therefore return to her wilderness, where the trees, flowers, and springs she wandered among did not reproach her for her ugliness. When the king and queen saw how hurt she was, they told her reluctantly that she could stay with them two or three days. Good-natured as always, though, she replied, "It would be harder for me to leave you if I were to spend so much time in your good company." Since they were all too eager for her to depart, they did not press her to stay, but coldly remarked that she was quite right.

For coming to her wedding the Princess Bellotte gave her a gift of an old ribbon that she had worn all winter in a bow on her muff, and Bellotte's fiancé gave her some zinzolin taffeta to make a petticoat. If she had expressed what she thought, she would have surely thrown the ribbon and rag of zinzolin in her generous donors' faces, but she had such good sense, prudence, and judgment that she revealed none of her bitterness. With her faithful nurse she left the court to return to her castle, her heart so filled with grief that she did not say a word during the entire journey.

One day as she was walking on one of the gloomiest paths in the forest, she saw a large green serpent at the foot of a tree. As it reared its head, it said to her, "Laidronette, you aren't the only unhappy creature. Look at my horrible form. And yet at birth I was even handsomer than you."

Terrified, the princess heard not one half of this. She fled from the spot, and for many days thereafter did not dare to leave the castle, so afraid was she of another such encounter.

Eventually she tired of sitting alone in her room, however, and one evening she went for a walk along the beach. She was strolling slowly, pondering her sad fate, when she noticed a small gilt barque painted with a thousand different emblems gliding toward her. With a sail made of gold brocade, a mast of cedar, and oars of eagle wood, it appeared to be drifting at random. When it landed on the shore, the curious princess stepped on board to inspect all of its beautiful decorations. She found its deck laid with crimson velvet and gold trimmings, and all the nails were diamonds.

Suddenly the barque drifted out to sea again, and the princess, alarmed at her impending danger, grabbed the oars and endeavored in vain to row back to the beach. The wind rose and the waves became high. She lost sight of land and, seeing nothing around her but sea and sky, resigned herself to her fate, fully convinced not only that it was unlikely to be a happy one, but also that this was another one of the fairy Magotine's mean tricks. "If I must die, why do I have such a secret dread of death?" she asked. "Alas, have I ever enjoyed any of life's pleasures so much that I should now feel regret at dying? My ugliness disgusts even my family. My sister is a great queen, and I'm consigned to exile in the depths of a wilderness where the only companion I've found is a talking serpent. Wouldn't it be better for me to perish than to drag out such a miserable existence?" Having thus reflected, she dried her tears and courageously peered out to discover whence death would come, inviting its speedy approach. Just then she saw a serpent riding the billows toward the vessel, and as it approached her, it said: "If you're willing to be helped by a poor green serpent like me, I have the power to save your life."

"Death is less frightful to me than you are," the princess exclaimed, "and if you want to do me a kind favor, never let me set eyes on you again."

The green serpent gave a long hiss (the manner in which serpents sigh), and without saying a word it immediately dove under the waves.

"What a horrible monster!" the princess said to herself. "He has green wings, a body of a thousand colors, ivory claws, fiery eyes, and a bristling mane of long hair on his head. Oh, I'd much rather die than owe my life to him! But what motive does he have in following me? How did he obtain the power of speech that enables him to talk like a rational creature?"

As she was entertaining these thoughts, a voice answered her: "You had better learn, Laidronette, that the green serpent is not to be despised. I don't mean to be harsh, but I assure you that he's less hideous in the eyes of his species than you are in the eyes of yours. However, I do not desire to anger you but to lighten your sorrows, provided you consent."

The princess was dumbfounded by this voice, and the words it uttered seemed so unjust to her that she could not suppress her tears. Suddenly, though, a thought occurred to her. "What am I doing? I don't want to cry about my death just because I'm reproached for my ugliness!" she exclaimed. "Alas, shouldn't I perish as though I were the grandest beauty in the world? My demise would be more of a consolation to me."

Completely at the mercy of the winds, the vessel drifted on until it struck a rock and immediately shattered into pieces. The poor princess realized that mere philosophizing would not save her in such a catastrophe, and grabbed onto some pieces of the wreck, so she thought, for she felt herself buoyed in the water and fortunately reached the shore, coming to rest at the foot of a towering boulder. Alas, she was horrified to discover that her arms were wrapped tightly around the neck of the green serpent! When he realized how appalled she was, he retreated from her and said, "You'd fear me less if you knew me better, but it is my hard fate to terrify all those who see me."

With that he plunged into the surf, and Laidronette was left alone by the enormous rock. No matter where she glanced, she could see nothing that might alleviate her despair. Night was approaching. She was without food and knew not where to go. "I thought I was destined to perish in the ocean," she said sadly, "but now I'm sure that I'm to end my days here. Some sea monster will come and devour me, or I'll die of hunger." Rising, she climbed to the top of the crag and sat down. As long as it was light, she gazed at the ocean, and when it became dark, she took off her taffeta petticoat, covered her head with it, and waited anxiously for whatever was to happen next. Eventually she was overcome by sleep, and she seemed to hear the music of some instruments. She was convinced that she was dreaming, but a moment later she heard someone sing the following verse, which seemed to have been composed expressly for her:

> "Let Cupid make you now his own.
> Here he rules with gentle tone.
> Love with pleasure will be sown.
> On this isle no grief is known."

The attention she paid to these words caused her to wake up. "What good or bad luck shall I have now?" she exclaimed. "Might happiness still be in store for someone so wretched?" She opened her eyes timidly, fearing that she would be surrounded by monsters, but she was astonished to find that in place of the rugged, looming rock was a room with walls and ceiling made entirely of gold. She was lying in a magnificent bed that matched perfectly the rest of this palace, which was the most splendid in the universe. She began asking herself a hundred questions about all of this, unable to believe she was wide awake. Finally she got up and ran to open a glass door that led onto a spacious balcony, from which she could see all the beautiful things that nature, with some help from art, had managed to create on earth: gardens filled with flowers, fountains, statues, and the rarest trees; distant woods, palaces with walls ornamented with jewels, and roofs composed of pearls so wonderfully constructed that each was an architectural masterpiece. A calm, smiling sea strewn with thousands of vessels, whose sails, pendants, and streamers fluttered in the breeze, completed the charming view.

"Gods! You just gods!" the princess exclaimed. "What am I seeing? Where am I? What an astounding change! What has become of the terrible rock that seemed to threaten the skies with its lofty pinnacles? Am I the same person who was shipwrecked last night and saved by a serpent?" Bewildered, she continued talking to herself, first pacing, then stopping. Finally she heard a noise in her room. Reentering it, she saw a hundred pagods advancing toward her. They were dressed and made up in a hundred different ways. The tallest were a foot high, and the shortest no more than four inches—some were beautiful, graceful, pleasant, others hideous, dreadfully ugly. Their bodies were made of diamonds, emeralds, rubies, pearls, crystal, amber, coral, porcelain, gold, silver, brass, bronze, iron, wood, and clay. Some were without arms, others without feet, others had mouths extending to their ears, eyes askew, noses broken. In short, nowhere in the world could a greater variety of people be found than among these pagods.

Those pagods who presented themselves to the princess were the deputies of the kingdom. After a speech containing some very judicious ideas, they informed her that they had traveled about the world for some time past, but in order to obtain their sovereign's permission to do so, they had to take an oath not to speak during their absence. Indeed, some were so scrupulous that they would not even shake their heads or move their hands or feet, but the majority of them could not help it. This was how they had traveled about the universe, and when they returned, they amused the king by telling him everything that had occurred, even the most secret transactions and adventures in all the courts they had visited. "This is a pleasure, madam," one of the deputies added, "which we shall have the honor of occasionally affording you, for we have been commanded to do all we can to entertain you. Instead of bringing you presents, we now come to amuse you with our songs and dances."

They began immediately to sing the following verses while simultaneously dancing to the music of tambourines and castanets:

> "Sweet are pleasures after pains,
> Lovers, do not break your chains;
> Trials though you may endure,
> Happiness they will insure.
> Sweet are pleasures after pains,
> Joy from sorrow luster gains."

When they stopped dancing and singing, their spokesman said to the princess, "Here, madam, are a hundred pagodines, who have the honor of being selected to wait on you. Any wish you may have in the world will be fulfilled, provided you consent to remain among us."

The pagodines appeared in their turn. They carried baskets cut to their own size and filled with a hundred different articles so pretty, so useful, so well made, and so costly that Laidronette never tired of admiring and praising them, uttering exclamations of wonder and delight at all the marvels they showed her. The most prominent pagodine, a tiny figure made of diamonds, advised her to enter the grotto of the baths, since the heat of the day was increasing. The princess proceeded in the direction indicated between two ranks of bodyguards, whose appearance was enough to make one die with laughter.

She found two baths of crystal in the grotto ornamented with gold and filled with scented water so delicious and uncommon that she marveled at it. Shading the baths was a pavilion of green and gold brocade. When the princess inquired why there were two, they answered that one was for her, and the other for the king of the pagods.

"But where is he, then?" the princess asked.

"Madam," they replied, "he is presently with the army waging war against his enemies. You'll see him as soon as he returns."

The princess then inquired if he were married. They answered no. "Why, he is so charming that no one has yet been found who would be worthy of him." She indulged her curiosity no further, but disrobed and entered the bath. All the pagods and pagodines began to sing and play on various instruments. Some had *theorbos* made out of nut shells; others, bass viols made out of almond shells, for it was, of course, necessary that the instruments fit the size of the performers. But all the parts were arranged in such perfect accord that nothing could surpass the delight their concert gave her.

When the princess emerged from her bath, they gave her a magnificent dressing gown. A pair of pagods playing a flute and oboe marched before her, and a train of pagodines singing songs in her praise trailed behind. In this state she entered a room where her toilet was laid out. Immediately the pagodines in waiting, and those of the bedchamber, bustled about, dressed her hair, put on her robes, and praised her. There was no longer talk of her ugliness, of zinzolin petticoats, or greasy ribbons.

The princess was truly taken aback. "To whom am I indebted for such extraordinary happiness?" she asked herself. "I was on the brink of destruction. I was waiting for death to come and had lost hope, and yet I suddenly find myself in the most magnificent place in the world, where I've been welcomed with the greatest joy!"

Since the princess was endowed with a great deal of good sense and breeding, she conducted herself so well that all the wee creatures who approached her were enchanted by her behavior. Every morning when she arose, she was given new dresses, new lace, new jewels. Though it was a great pity she was so ugly, she who could not abide her looks began to think they were more appealing because of the great pains they took in dressing her. She rarely spent an hour without some pagods coming to visit and recounting to her the most curious and private events of the world: peace treaties, offensive and defensive alliances, lovers' quarrels and betrayals, unfaithful mistresses, distractions, reconciliations, disappointed heirs, matches broken off, old widows remarrying foolishly, treasures discovered, bankruptcies declared, fortunes made in a minute, favorites disgraced, office seekers, jealous husbands, coquettish wives, naughty children, ruined cities. In short, they told the princess everything under the sun to entertain her. She occasionally saw some pagods who were so corpulent and had such puffed-out cheeks that they were wonderful to behold. When she asked them why they were so fat, they answered, "Since we're not permitted to laugh or speak during our travels and are constantly witnessing all sorts of absurdities and the most intolerable follies, our inclination to laugh is so great that we swell up when we suppress it and cause what may properly be called risible dropsy. Then we cure ourselves as soon as we get home." The princess admired the good sense of the pagodine people, for we too might burst with laughter if we laughed at all the silly things we see every day.

Scarcely an evening passed without a performance of one of the best plays by Corneille or Molière. Balls were held frequently, and the smallest pagods danced on a tightrope in order to be better seen. What's more, the banquets in honor of the princess might have served for feasts on the most solemn occasions. They also brought her books of every description—serious, amusing, historical. In short, the days passed like minutes, although, to tell the truth, all these sprightly pagods seemed insufferably little to the princess. For instance, whenever she went out walking, she had to put some thirty or so into her pockets in order for them to keep up. It was the most amusing thing in the world to hear the chattering of their little voices, shriller than those of puppets in a show at the fair.

One night when the princess was unable to fall asleep, she said to herself, "What's to become of me? Am I to remain here forever? My days are more pleasant than I could have dared to hope, yet my heart tells me something's missing. I don't know what it is, but I'm beginning to feel that this unvarying routine of amusements is rather insipid."

"Ah, Princess," a voice said, as if answering her thoughts, "isn't it your own fault? If you'd consent to love, you'd soon discover that you can abide with a lover for an eternity without wishing to leave. I speak not only of a palace, but even the most desolate spot."

"What pagodine addresses me?" the princess inquired. "What pernicious advice are you giving me? Why are you trying to disturb my peace of mind?"

"It is no a pagodine who forewarns you of what will sooner or later come to pass," the voice replied. "It's the unhappy ruler of this realm, who adores you, madam, and who can't tell you this without trembling."

"A king who adores me?" the princess replied. "Does this king have eyes or is he blind? Doesn't he know that I'm the ugliest person in the world?"

"I've seen you, madam," the invisible being answered, "and have found you're not what you represent yourself to be. Whether it's for your person, merit, or misfortunes, I repeat: I adore you. But my feeling of respect and timidity oblige me to conceal myself."

"I'm indebted to you for that," the princess responded. "Alas, what would befall me if I were to love anyone?"

"You'd make a man who can't live without you into the happiest of beings," the voice said. "But he won't venture to appear before you without your permission."

"No, no," the princess said. "I wish to avoid seeing anything that might arouse my interest too strongly."

The voice fell silent, and the princess continued to ponder this incident for the rest of the night. No matter how strongly she vowed not to say the least word to anyone about it, she could not resist asking the pagods if their king had returned. They answered in the negative. Since this reply did not correspond in the least with what she had heard, she was quite disturbed. She continued making inquiries: was their king young and handsome? They told her he was young, handsome, and very charming. She asked if they frequently received news about him.

They replied, "Every day."

"But," she added, "does he know that I reside in his palace?"

"Yes, madam," her attendants answered, "he knows everything that occurs here concerning you. He takes great interest in it, and every hour a courier is sent off to him with an account about you."

Lapsing into silence, she became far more thoughtful than she had ever been before.

Whenever she was alone, the voice spoke to her. Sometimes she was alarmed by it, but at others she was pleased, for nothing could be more polite than its manner of address. "Although I've decided never to love," the princess said, "and have every reason to protect my heart against an attachment that could only be fatal to it, I nevertheless confess to you that I yearn to see a king who has such strange tastes. If it's true that you love me, you're perhaps the only being in the world guilty of such weakness for a person so ugly."

"Think whatever you please, adorable princess," the voice replied. "I find that you have sufficient qualities to merit my affection. Nor do I conceal myself because I have strange tastes. Indeed, I have such sad reasons that if you knew them, you wouldn't be able to refrain from pitying me."

The princess urged him to explain himself, but the voice stopped speaking, and she heard only long, heavy sighs.

All these conversations made her very uneasy. Although her lover was unknown and invisible to her, he paid her a thousand attentions. Moreover, the beautiful place she inhabited led her to desire companions more suitable than the pagods. That had been the reason why she had begun feeling bored, and only the voice of her invisible admirer had the power to please her.

One very dark night she awoke to find somebody seated beside her. She thought it was the pagodine of pearls, who had more wit than the others and sometimes came to keep her company. The princess extended her arm to her, but the person seized her hand and pressed it to a pair of lips. Shedding a few tears on it, the unseen person was evidently too moved to speak. She was convinced it was the invisible monarch.

"What do you want of me?" she sighed. "How can I love you without knowing or seeing you?"

"Ah, madam," he replied, "why do you make conditions that thwart my desire to please you? I simply cannot reveal myself. The same wicked Magotine who's treated you so badly has condemned me to suffer for seven years. Five have already elapsed. There are two remaining, and you could relieve the bitterness of my punishment by allowing me to become your husband. You may think that I'm a rash fool, that I'm asking an absolute impossibility. But if you knew, madam, the depth of my feelings and the extent of my misfortunes, you wouldn't refuse this favor I ask of you."

As I have already mentioned, Laidronette had begun feeling bored, and she found that the invisible king certainly had all the intelligence she could wish for. So she was swayed by love, which she disguised to herself as pity, and replied that she needed a few days to consider his proposal.

The celebrations and concerts recommenced with increased splendor, and not a song was heard but those about marriage. Presents were continually brought to her that surpassed all that had ever been seen. The enamored voice assiduously wooed her as soon as it turned dark, and the princess retired at an earlier hour in order to have more time to listen to it. Finally she consented to marry the invisible king and promised him that she would not attempt to look upon him until the full term of his penance had expired. "It's extremely important," the king said, "both for you and me. Should you be imprudent and succumb to your curiosity, I'll have to begin serving my sentence all over again, and you'll have to share in my suffering. But if you can resist the evil advice that you will soon receive, you'll have the satisfaction of finding in me all that your heart desires. At the same time you'll regain the marvelous beauty that the malicious Magotine took from you."

Delighted by this new prospect, the princess vowed a thousand times that she would never indulge her curiosity without his permission. So the wedding took place without any pomp and fanfare, but the modesty of the ceremony affected their hearts not a whit.

Since all the pagods were eager to entertain their new queen, one of them brought her the history of Psyche, written in a charming style by one of the most popular authors of the day. She found many passages in it that paralleled her own adventures, and they aroused in her a strong desire to see her father, mother, sister, and brother-in-law. Nothing the king could say to her sufficed to quell this whim.

"The book you're reading reveals the terrible ordeals Psyche experienced. For mercy's sake, try to learn from her experiences and avoid them."

After she promised to be more than cautious, a ship manned by pagods and loaded with presents was sent with letters from Queen Laidronette to her mother, imploring her to come and pay a visit to her daughter in her own realm. (The pagods assigned this mission were permitted, on this one occasion, to speak in a foreign land.)

And in fact, the princess's disappearance had affected her relatives. They believed she had perished, and consequently her letters filled them with gladness. The queen, who was dying to see Laidronette again, did not lose a moment in departing with her other daughter and son-in-law. The pagods, the only ones who knew the way to their kingdom, safely conducted the entire royal family, and when Laidronette saw them, she thought she would die from joy. Over and over she read the story of Psyche to be completely on her guard regarding any questions that they might put to her and to make sure she would have the right answers. But the pains she took were all in vain—she made a hundred mistakes. Sometimes the king was with the army; sometimes he was ill and in no mood to see anyone; sometimes he was on a pilgrimage and at others hunting or fishing. In the end it seemed that the barbarous Magotine had unsettled her wits and doomed her to say nothing but nonsense.

Discussing the matter together, her mother and sister concluded that she was deceiving them and perhaps herself as well. With misguided zeal they told her what they thought and in the process skillfully plagued her mind with a thousand doubts and fears. After refusing for a long time to acknowledge the justice of their suspicions, she confessed at last that she had never seen her husband, but his conversation was so charming that just listening to him was enough to make her happy. "What's more," she told them, "he has only two more years to spend in this state of penance, and at the end of that time, I shall not only be able to see him, but I myself shall become as beautiful as the orb of day."

"Oh, unfortunate creature!" the queen exclaimed. "What a devious trap they've set for you! How could you have been so naive to listen to such tales? Your husband is a monster, and that's all there is to it, for all the pagods he rules are downright monkeys."

"I believe differently," Laidronette replied. "I think he's the god of love himself."

"What a delusion!" Queen Bellotte cried. "They told Psyche that she had married a monster, and she discovered that it was Cupid. You're positive that Cupid is your husband, and yet it's certain he's a monster. At the very least, put your mind to rest. Clear up the matter. It's easy enough to do."

This was what the queen had to say, and her husband was even more emphatic. The poor princess was so confused and disturbed that, after having sent her family home loaded with presents that sufficiently repaid the zinzolin taffeta and muff ribbon, she decided to catch a glimpse of her husband, come what may. Oh, fatal curiosity, which never improves in us despite a thousand dreadful examples, how dearly you are about to make this unfortunate princess pay! Thinking it a great pity not to imitate her predecessor, Psyche, she shone a lamp on their bed and gazed upon the invisible king so dear to her heart. When she saw, however, the horrid green serpent with his long, bristling mane instead of a tender Cupid young, white, and fair, she let out the most frightful shrieks. He awoke in a fit of rage and despair.

"Cruel woman," he cried, "is this the reward for all the love I've given you?"

The princess did not hear a word. She had fainted from fright. Within seconds the serpent was faraway. Upon hearing the uproar caused by this tragic scene, some pagods ran to their post, carried the princess to her couch, and did all they could to revive her. No one can possibly fathom Laidronette's depths of despair upon regaining consciousness. How she reproached herself for the misfortune she had brought upon her husband! She loved him tenderly, but she abhorred his form and would have given half her life if she could have taken back what she had done.

These sad reflections were interrupted by several pagods who entered her room with fear written on their faces. They came to warn her that several ships of puppets with Magotine at their head had entered the harbor without encountering any resistance. Puppets and pagods had been enemies for ages and had competed with each other in a thousand ways, for the puppets had always enjoyed the privilege of talking wherever they went—a privilege denied the pagods. Magotine was the queen of the puppets, and her hatred for the poor green serpent and the unfortunate Laidronette had prompted her to assemble her forces in order to torment them just when their suffering was most acute.

This goal she easily accomplished because the queen was in such despair that although the pagods urged her to give the necessary orders, she refused, insisting that she knew nothing of the art of war. Nevertheless, she ordered them to convene all those pagods who had been in besieged cities or on the councils of the greatest commanders and told them to take the proper steps. Then she shut herself up in her room and regarded everything happening around her with utter indifference.

Magotine's general was that celebrated puppet Punch, and he knew his business well. He had a large body of wasps, mayflies, and butterflies in reserve, and they performed wonders against some lightly-armed frogs and lizards. The latter had been in the pay of the pagods for many years and were, if truth be told, much more frightening in name than in action.

Magotine amused herself for some time by watching the combat. The pagods and pagodines outdid themselves in their efforts, but the fairy dissolved all their superb edifices with a stroke of her wand. The charming gardens, woods, meadows, fountains, were soon in ruins, and Queen Laidronette could not escape the sad fate of becoming the slave of the most malignant fairy that ever was or will be. Four or five hundred puppets forced her to go before Magotine.

"Madam," Punch said to the fairy, "here is the queen of the pagods, whom I have taken the liberty of bringing to you."

"I've known her a long time," Magotine said. "She was the cause of my being insulted on the day she was born, and I'll never forget it."

"Alas, madam," the queen said, "I believed you were sufficiently avenged. The gift of ugliness that you bestowed on me to such a supreme degree would have satisfied anyone less vindictive than you."

"Look how she argues," the fairy said. "Here is a learned doctor of a new sort. Your first job will be teaching philosophy to my ants. I want you to get ready to give them a lesson every day."

"How can I do it, madam?" the distressed queen replied. "I know nothing about philosophy, and even if I were well versed in it, your ants are probably not capable of understanding it."

"Well now, listen to this logician," exclaimed Magotine. "Very well, Queen. You won't teach them philosophy, but despite yourself you'll set an example of patience for the entire world that will be difficult to imitate."

Immediately thereafter, Laidronette was given a pair of iron shoes so small that she could fit only half her foot into each one. Compelled nevertheless to put them on, the poor queen could only weep in agony.

"Here's a spindle of spider webs," Magotine said. "I expect you to spin it as fine as your hair, and you have but two hours to do it."

"I've never spun, madam," the queen said. "But I'll try to obey you even though what you desire strikes me to be impossible."

She was immediately led deep into a dark grotto, and after they gave her some brown bread and a pitcher of water, they closed the entrance with a large rock. In trying to spin the filthy spider webs, she dropped her spindle a hundred times because it was much too heavy. Even though she patiently picked it up each time and began her work over again, it was always in vain. "Now I know exactly how bad my predicament is. I'm wholly at the mercy of the implacable Magotine, who's not just satisfied with having deprived me of all my beauty, but wants some pretext for killing me." She began to weep as she recalled the happiness she had enjoyed in the kingdom of Pagodia. Then she threw down her spindle and exclaimed, "Let Magotine come when she will! I can't do the impossible."

"Ah, Queen," a voice answered her. "Your indiscreet curiosity has caused you these tears, but it's difficult to watch those we love suffer. I have a friend whom I've never mentioned to you before. She's called the Fairy Protectrice, and I trust she'll be of great service to you."

All at once she heard three taps, and without seeing anyone, she found her web spun and wound into a skein. At the end of the two hours Magotine, who wanted to taunt her, had the rock rolled from the grotto mouth and entered it, followed by a large escort of puppets.

"Come, come, let us see the work of this idle hussy who doesn't know how to sew or spin."

"Madam," the queen said, "it's quite true I didn't know how, but I was obliged to learn."

When Magotine saw the extraordinary result, she took the skein of spider web and said: "Truly, you're too skillful. It would be a great pity not to keep you employed. Here, Queen, make me some nets with this thread strong enough to catch salmon."

"For mercy's sake!" the queen replied. "You see that it's barely strong enough to hold flies."

"You're a great casuist, my pretty friend," Magotine said, "but it won't help you a bit." She left the grotto, had the stone replaced at the entrance, and assured Laidronette that if the nets were not finished in two hours, she was a lost creature.

"Oh, Fairy Protectrice!" the queen exclaimed, "if it's true that my sorrows can move you to pity, please don't deny me your assistance."

No sooner had she spoken than, to Laidronette's astonishment, the nets were made. With all her heart she thanked the friendly fairy who had granted her this favor, and it gave her pleasure to think that it must have been her husband who had provided her with such a friend. "Alas, green serpent," she said, "you're much too generous to continue loving me after the harm I've done you."

No reply was forthcoming, for at that moment, Magotine entered. She was nonplussed to find the nets finished. Indeed, they were so well made that the work could not have been done by common hands. "What?" she cried. "Do you have the audacity to maintain that it was you who wove these nets?"

"I have no friend in your court, madam," the queen said. "And even if I did, I'm so carefully guarded that it would be difficult for anyone to speak to me without your permission."

"Since you're so clever and skillful, you'll be of great use to me in my kingdom."

She immediately ordered her fleet to make ready the sails and all the puppets to prepare themselves to board. The queen she had heavily chained down, fearing that in some fit of despair she might fling herself overboard.

One night when the unhappy princess was deploring her sad fate, she perceived by the light of the stars that the green serpent was silently approaching the ship.

"I'm always afraid of alarming you," he said, "and despite the reasons I have for not sparing you, you're extremely dear to me."

"Can you pardon my indiscreet curiosity?" she replied. "Would you be offended if I said:

"Is it you? Is it you? Are you again near?
My own royal serpent, so faithful and dear!
May I hope to see my fond husband again?
Oh, how I've suffered since we were parted then!"

The serpent replied as follows:

"To hearts that love truly, to part causes pain,
With hope even to whisper of meeting again.
In Pluto's dark regions what torture above
Our absence forever from those whom we love?"

Magotine was not one of those fairies who fall asleep, for the desire to do mischief kept her continually awake. Thus, she did not fail to overhear the conversation between the serpent king and his wife. Flying like a Fury to interrupt it, she said, "Aha, you amuse yourselves with rhymes, do you? And you complain about your fate in bombastic tones? Truly, I'm delighted to hear it. Proserpine, who is my best friend, has promised to pay me if I lend her a poet. Not that there is a dearth of poets below, but she simply wants more. Green serpent, I command you to go finish your penance in the dark manor of the underworld. Give my regards to the gentle Proserpine!"

Uttering long hisses, the unfortunate serpent departed, leaving the queen in the depths of sorrow. "What crime have we committed against you, Magotine?" she exclaimed heatedly. "No sooner was I born than your infernal curse robbed me of my beauty and made me horrible. How can you accuse me of any crime when I wasn't even capable of using my mind at that time? I'm convinced that the unhappy king whom you've just sent to the infernal regions is as innocent as I was. But finish your work. Let me die this instant. It's the only favor I ask of you."

"You'd be too happy if I granted your request." Magotine said. "You must first draw water for me from the bottomless spring."

As soon as the ships had reached the kingdom of puppets, the cruel Magotine took a millstone and tied it around the queen's neck, ordering her to climb to the top of a mountain that soared high above the clouds. Upon arriving there, she was to gather enough four-leaf clovers to fill a basket, descend into the depths of the next valley to draw the water of discretion in a pitcher with a hole in the bottom, and bring her enough to fill her large glass. The queen responded that it was impossible to obey her: the millstone was more than ten times her weight and the pitcher with a hole in it could never hold the water she wished to drink. "Nay, I cannot be induced to attempt anything so impossible."

"If you don't," Magotine said, "rest assured that your green serpent will suffer for it."

This threat so frightened the queen that she tried to walk despite her handicap. But, alas, the effort would have been for naught if the Fairy Protectrice, whom she invoked, had not come to her aid.

"Now you can see the just punishment for your fatal curiosity," the fairy said. "Blame no one but yourself for the condition to which Magotine has reduced you."

After saying this, she transported the queen to the top of the mountain. Terrible monsters that guarded the spot made supernatural efforts to defend it, but one tap of the Fairy Protectrice's wand made them gentler than lambs. Then she proceeded to fill the basket for her with four-leaf clovers.

Protectrice did not wait for the grateful queen to thank her, for to complete the mission, everything depended on her. She gave the queen a chariot drawn by two white canaries who spoke and whistled in a marvelous way. She told her to descend the mountain and fling her iron shoes at two giants armed with clubs who guarded the fountain. Once they were knocked unconscious, she had only to give her pitcher to the canaries, who would easily find the means to fill it with the water of discretion. "As soon as you have the water, wash your face with it, and you will become the most beautiful person in the world." She also advised her not to remain at the fountain, or to climb back up the hill, but to stop at a pleasant small grove she would find on her way. She could remain there for three years, since Magotine would merely suppose that she was either still trying to fill her pitcher with water or had fallen victim to one of the dangers during her journey.

Embracing the knees of the Fairy Protectrice, the queen thanked her a hundred times for the special favors she had granted her. "But, madam," the queen added, "neither the success I may achieve nor the beauty you promise me will give me the least pleasure until my serpent is transformed."

"That won't occur until you've spent three years in the mountain grove," the fairy said, "and until you've returned to Magotine with the four-leaf clovers and the water in the leaky pitcher."

The queen promised the Fairy Protectrice that she would scrupulously follow her instructions. "But, madam," she added, "must I spend three years without hearing any news of the serpent king?"

"You deserve never to hear any more about him for as long as you live," the fairy responded. "Indeed, can anything be more terrible than having made him begin his penance all over again?"

The queen made no reply, but her silence and the tears flowing down her cheeks amply showed how much she was suffering. She got into her little chariot, and the canaries did as commanded. They conducted her to the bottom of the valley, where the giants guarded the fountain of discretion. She quickly took off her iron shoes and threw them at their heads. The moment the shoes hit them, they fell down lifelessly like colossal statues. The canaries took the leaky pitcher and mended it with such marvelous skill that there was no sign of its having ever been broken.

The name given to the water made her eager to drink some. "It will make me more prudent than I've been," she said. "Alas, if I had possessed those qualities, I'd still be in the kingdom of Pagodia." After she had drunk a long draught of the water, she washed her face with some of it and became so very beautiful that she might have been mistaken for a goddess rather than a mortal.

The Fairy Protectrice immediately appeared and said, "You've just done something that pleases me very much. You knew that this water could embellish your mind as well as your person. I wanted to see to which of the two you would prefer the most, and it was your mind. I praise you for it, and this act will shorten the term of your punishment by four years."

"Please don't reduce my sufferings," the queen replied. "I deserve them all. But comfort the green serpent, who doesn't deserve to suffer at all."

"I'll do everything in my power," the fairy said, embracing her. "But since you're now so beautiful, I want you to drop the name of Laidronette, which no longer suits you. You must be called Queen Discrète."

As she vanished, the queen found she had left a pair of dainty shoes that were so pretty and finely embroidered that she thought it almost a pity to wear them. Soon thereafter she got back into her little chariot with her pitcherful of water, and the canaries flew directly to the grove of the mountain.

Never was a spot as pleasant as this. Myrtle and orange trees intertwined their branches to form long arbors and bowers that the sun could not penetrate. A thousand brooks running from gently flowing springs brought a refreshing coolness to this beautiful abode. But most curious of all were the animals there, which gave the canaries the warmest welcome in the world.

"We thought you had deserted us," they said.

"The term of our penance is not over yet," the canaries replied. "But here is a queen whom the Fairy Protectrice has ordered us to bring you. Try to do all you can to amuse her."

She was immediately surrounded by all sorts of animals, who paid her their best compliments. "You shall be our queen," they said to her. "You shall have all our attention and respect."

"Where am I?" she exclaimed. "What supernatural power has enabled you to speak to me?"

One of the canaries whispered in her ear, "You should know, madam, that several fairies were distressed to see various persons fall into bad habits on their travels. At first they imagined that they needed merely to advise them to correct themselves, but their warnings were paid no heed. Eventually the fairies became quite upset and imposed punishments on them. Those who talked too much were changed into parrots, magpies, and hens. Lovers and their mistresses were transformed into pigeons, canaries, and lapdogs. Those who ridiculed their friends became monkeys. Gourmands were made into pigs and hotheads into lions. In short, the number of persons they punished was so great that this grove has become filled with them. Thus, you'll find people with all sorts of qualities and dispositions here."

"From what you've just told me, my dear canary," the queen said, "I've reason to believe that you're here only because you loved too well."

"It's quite true, madam," the canary replied. "I'm the son of a Spanish grandee. Love in our country has such absolute power over our hearts that one cannot resist it without being charged with the crime of rebellion. An English ambassador arrived at the court. He had a daughter who was extremely beautiful, but insufferably haughty and sardonic. In spite of all this, I was attracted to her. My love, though, was greeted with so much disdain that I lost all patience. One day when she had exasperated me, a venerable old woman approached and reproached me for my weakness. Yet everything she said only made me more obstinate. When she perceived this, she became angry. 'I condemn you,' she said, 'to be a canary for three years, and your mistress to be a wasp.' Instantly I felt an indescribable change come over me. Despite my affliction I could not restrain myself from flying into the ambassador's garden to determine the fate of his daughter. No sooner had I arrived than I saw her approach in the form of a large wasp buzzing four times louder than all the others. I hovered around her with the devotion of a lover that nothing can destroy, but she tried several times to sting me. 'If you want to kill me, beautiful wasp,' I said, 'it's unnecessary to use your sting. You only have to command me to die, and I'll obey you.' The wasp did not reply, but landed on some flowers that had to endure her bad temper.

"Overwhelmed by her contempt and the condition to which I was reduced, I flew away without caring where my wings would take me. I eventually arrived at one of the most beautiful cities in the universe, which they call Paris. Wearily, I flung myself on a tuft of large trees enclosed within some garden walls, and before I knew who had caught me, I found myself behind the door of a cage painted green and ornamented with gold. The apartment and its furniture were so magnificent that I was astounded. Soon a young lady arrived. She caressed me and spoke to me so sweetly that I was charmed by her. I did not live there long before learning whom her sweetheart was. I witnessed this braggart's visits to her, and he was always in a rage because nothing could satisfy him. He was always accusing her unjustly, and one time he beat her until he left her for dead in the arms of her women. I was quite upset at seeing her suffer this unworthy treatment, and what distressed me even more was that the blows he dealt the lovely lady served only to increase her affection.

"Night and day I wished that the fairies who had transformed me into a canary would come and set to rights such ill-suited lovers. My wish was eventually fulfilled. The fairies suddenly appeared in the apartment just as the furious gentleman was beginning to make his usual commotion. They reprimanded him severely and condemned him to become a wolf. The patient lady who had allowed him to beat her, they turned into a sheep and sent her to the grove of the mountain. As for myself, I easily found a way to escape. Since I wanted to see the various courts of Europe, I flew to Italy and fell into the hands of a man who had frequent business in the city. Since he was very jealous of his wife and did not want her to see anyone during his absence, he took care to lock her up from morning until night, and I was given the honor of amusing this lovely captive. However, she had other things to do than to attend to me. A certain neighbor who had loved her for a long time came to the top of the chimney in the evening and slid down it into the room, looking blacker than a devil. The keys that the jealous husband kept with him served only to keep his mind at ease. I constantly feared that some terrible catastrophe would happen when one day the fairies entered through the keyhole and surprised the two lovers. 'Go and do penance!' the fairies said, touching them with their wands. 'Let the chimney sweeper become a squirrel and the lady an ape, for she is a cunning one. And your husband, who is so fond of keeping the keys of his house, shall become a mastiff for ten years.'

"It would take me too long to tell you all the various adventures I had," the canary said. "Occasionally I was obliged to visit the grove of the mountain, and I rarely returned there without finding new animals, for the fairies were always traveling and were continually upset by the countless faults of the people they encountered. But during your residence here you'll have plenty of time to entertain yourself by listening to the accounts of all the inhabitants' adventures."

Several of them immediately offered to relate their stories whenever she desired. She thanked them politely, but since she felt more inclined to meditate than to talk, she looked for a spot where she could be alone. As soon as she found one, a little palace arose on it, and the most sumptuous banquet in the world was prepared for her. It consisted only of fruits, but they were of the rarest kind. They were brought to her by birds, and during her stay in the grove there was nothing she lacked.

Occasionally she was pleased by the most unique entertainments: lions danced with lambs; bears whispered tender things to doves; serpents relaxed with linnets; a butterfly courted a panther. In short, no amour was categorized according to species, for it did not matter that one was a tiger or another a sheep, but simply that they were people whom the fairies had chosen to punish for their faults.

They all loved Queen Discrète to the point of adoration, and everyone asked her to arbitrate their disputes. Her power was absolute in this tiny republic, and if she had not continually reproached herself for causing the green serpent's misfortunes, she might have accepted her own misfortune with some degree of patience. However, when she thought of the condition to which he was reduced, she could not forgive herself for her indiscreet curiosity.

Finally the time came for her to leave the grove of the mountain, and she notified her escorts, the faithful canaries, who wished her a happy return. She left secretly during the night to avoid the farewells and lamentations, which would have cost her some tears, for she was touched by the friendship and respect that all these rational animals had shown her.

She did not forget the pitcher of discretion, the basket of four-leaf clovers, or the iron shoes. Just when Magotine believed her to be dead, she suddenly appeared before her, the millstone around her neck, the iron shoes on her feet, and the pitcher in her hand. Upon seeing her, the fairy uttered a loud cry. "Where have you come from?"

"Madam," the queen said, "I've spent three years drawing water into the broken pitcher, and I finally found the way to make it hold water."

Magotine burst into laughter, thinking of the exhaustion the poor queen must have experienced. But when she examined her more closely, she exclaimed, "What's this I see? Laidronette has become quite lovely! How did you get so beautiful?"

The queen informed her that she had washed herself with the water of discretion and that this miracle had been the result. At this news Magotine dashed the pitcher to the ground. "Oh, you powers that defy me," she exclaimed, "I'll be revenged. Get your iron shoes ready," she said to the queen. "You must go to the underworld for me and demand the essence of long life from Proserpine. I'm always afraid of falling ill and perhaps dying. Once I have that antidote in my possession, I won't have any more cause for alarm. Take care, therefore, that you don't uncork the bottle or taste the liquor she gives you, or you'll reduce my portion."

The poor queen had never been so taken aback as she was by this order. "Which way is it to the underworld?" she asked. "Can those who go there return? Alas, madam, won't you ever tire of persecuting me? Under what unfortunate star was I born? My sister is so much happier than I. Ah, the stars above are certainly unfair."

As she began to weep, Magotine exulted at her tears. She laughed loudly and cried, "Go! Go! Don't put off your departure a moment, for your journey promises to benefit me a great deal." Magotine gave her some old nuts and black bread in a bag, and with this handsome provision the poor queen started on her journey. She was determined, however, to dash her brains out against the first rock she saw to put an end to her sorrows.

She wandered at random for some time, turning this way and that, thinking it most extraordinary to be sent like this to the underworld. When she became tired, she lay down at the foot of a tree and began to think of the poor serpent, forgetting all about her journey. Just then appeared the Fairy Protectrice, who said to her, "Don't you know, beautiful queen, that if you want to rescue your husband from the dark domain where he is being kept under Magotine's orders, you must seek the home of Proserpine?"

"I'd go much farther, if it were possible, madam," she replied, "but I don't know how to descend into that dark abode."

"Wait," said the Fairy Protectrice. "Here's a green branch. Strike the earth with it and repeat these lines clearly." The queen embraced the knees of her generous friend and then said after her:

> "You who can wrest from mighty Jove the thunder!
> Love, listen to my prayer!
> Come, save me from despair,
> And calm the pangs that rend my heart asunder!
> As I enter the realm of Tartarus, be my guide.
> Even in those dreary regions you hold sway.
> It was for Proserpine, your subject, that Pluto sighed;
> So open the path to their throne and point the way.
> A faithful husband from my arms they tear!
> My fate is harder than my heart can bear;
> More than mortal is its pain;
> Yet for death it sighs in vain!"

No sooner had she finished this prayer than a young child more beautiful than anything we shall ever see appeared in the midst of a gold and azure cloud. He flew down to her feet with a crown of flowers encircling his brow. The queen knew by his bow and arrows that it was Love. He addressed her in the following way:

> "I have heard your tender sighs,
> And for you have left the skies.
> Love will chase your tears away,
> And try his best in every way.
> Shortly shall your eyes be blest
> With his sight you love the best.
> Then the penance will be done,
> And your foe will be overcome."

The queen was dazzled by the splendor that surrounded Love and delighted by his promises. Therefore, she exclaimed:

> "Earth, my voice obey!
> Cupid's power is like my own.
> Open for him and point the way
> To Pluto's dark and gloomy throne!"

The earth obeyed and opened her bosom. The queen went through a dark passage, in which she needed a guide as radiant as her protector, and finally reached the underworld. She dreaded meeting her husband there in the form of a serpent, but Love, who sometimes employs himself by doing good deeds for the unfortunate, had foreseen all that was to be foreseen: he had already arranged that the green serpent become what he was before his punishment. Powerful as Magotine was, there was nothing she could do against Love.

The first object the queen's eyes encountered was her charming husband. She had never seen him in such a handsome form, and he had never seen her as beautiful as she had become. Nevertheless, a presentiment, and perhaps Love, who made up the third in the party, caused each of them to guess who the other was. With extreme tenderness the queen said to him:

> "I come to share your prison and your pain.
> Though doomed no more the light of heaven to see,
> Here let but love unite our hearts again,
> No terrors these sad shades will have for me!"

Carried away by his passion, the king replied to his wife in a way that demonstrated his ardor and pleasure. But Love, who is not fond of losing time, urged them to approach Proserpine. The queen offered Magotine's regards and asked her for the essence of long life. Proserpine immediately gave the queen a phial very badly corked in order to induce her to open it. Love, who is no novice, warned the queen against indulging a curiosity that would again be fatal to her. Quickly the king and queen left those dreary regions and returned to the light of day with Love accompanying them. He led them back to Magotine and hid himself in their hearts so that she would not see him. His presence, however, inspired the fairy with such humane sentiments that she received these illustrious unfortunates graciously, although she knew not why. With a supernatural effort of generosity she restored the kingdom of Pagodia to them, and they returned there immediately and spent the rest of their days in as much happiness as they had previously endured trouble and sorrow.

> Too oft is curiosity
> The cause of fatal woe.
> A secret that may harmful be,
> Why should we seek to know?

> It is a weakness of womankind,
> For witness the first created,
> From whom Pandora was designed,
> And Psyche imitated.

> Each one, despite a warning, on the same
> Forbidden quest intent,
> Did bring about her misery and become
> Its fatal instrument.

> Psyche's example failed to save
> Poor Laidronette from erring.
> Like warning she was led to brave.
> Like punishment incurring.

> Alas, for human common sense,
> No tale, no caution, schools!
> The proverb says, Experience
> Can make men wise, and change dumb fools.

> But when we're told, yet fail to listen
> To the lessons of the past,
> I fear the proverb lies quite often,
> Despite the shadows forward cast.

PRINCESS ROSETTE

ONCE upon a time there was a king and a queen who had two handsome boys who grew as splendidly as the day. Whenever the queen gave birth to a child, she sent for the fairies and asked them to tell her what would happen to the infant. From her next pregnancy she had a baby girl who was so pretty that once you laid eyes on her, you had to adore her. The queen gave a grand celebration, and all the fairies came to see the baby. When they were about to depart, she said, "Don't forget about your good custom. Please tell me what will happen to Rosette"—for that was the name they had given to the princess.

The fairies replied that they had left their magic books at home. "We'll come and tell you another time."

"Ah," the queen said, "that bodes me no good. You don't want to upset me by predicting some misfortune. But I beg of you, tell me everything. Don't hide a single thing."

They made every sort of excuse, but these only increased the queen's desire to know. At last the chief fairy said to her, "We fear, madam, that some amour of Rosette's will be the cause of some great catastrophe involving her brothers, an affair that will cost them their lives. That's all that we can foresee regarding this beautiful little girl, and we're very sorry we can't tell you anything more pleasant."

Once they had departed, the queen remained so melancholy that the king could not avoid noticing. He asked her what the matter was. She answered that she had been sitting too near the fire and had burned all the wool off her spindle.

"Is that all?" the king asked. He went up into the loft and brought her more wool than she could spin in a hundred years.

When the queen continued in low spirits, the king again asked her what the matter was. She told him she had lost one of her green satin slippers while walking by the riverside.

"Is that all?" the king asked. He sent an order to all the shoemakers in the kingdom, and they furnished her majesty with ten thousand green satin slippers.

Even so, she continued to be sad. The king again asked her what ailed her. She told him that she had been eating too hastily and had swallowed her wedding ring, which had slipped off her finger. Now, the king knew she had told him a lie, for he had the ring safe in his possession. "My dear wife," he said to her, "you're not telling the truth. Here's your ring, which I had put away for safekeeping."

Caught in her lie, the queen was mortified, for lying is the most disgraceful thing in the world. Seeing that the king was angry, she told him what the fairies had predicted about little Rosette and asked him if he knew how to remedy the situation. The king became despondent and eventually told the queen, "I don't see any other way to save our two sons than by killing the little girl while she is in her swaddling clothes."

But the queen exclaimed that she would sooner die than let such a cruel thing occur. She told the king that he must think of something else. Thus the king and queen became totally absorbed by this matter.

One day the queen learned of an old hermit who lived in a hollow tree in a great forest near the city. People traveled from all parts of the world to seek his advice. "I must see him as well," the queen said. "The fairies have told me of the danger, but they've forgotten the remedy."

She rose early the next morning and mounted a beautiful white mule shod with gold. Two of her maids of honor accompanied her, each on a stately horse. When they neared the forest, the queen and her ladies dismounted, out of respect for the hermit, and went on foot to the tree he inhabited. He objected to the sight of women, but when he saw it was the queen, he said to her, "Welcome. What can I do for you?"

She told him what the fairies had said about Rosette and requested his advice. He told her she should put the princess into a tower, which she should never be permitted to leave. The queen thanked him, gave him a handsome present, and returned with her information to the king.

When the king heard this report, he ordered a great tower to be built as quickly as possible. Rosette was put into it, and to keep her from being bored, the king, queen, and her two brothers went to see her every day. The elder was called the great prince and the younger the little prince. They were deeply devoted to their sister, for she was the most beautiful and charming creature in the world. Just one look from her was worth more than a hundred gold coins. When she was fifteen, the great prince said to the king, "Papa, my sister is old enough to be married. Won't we soon be going to her wedding?" The little prince said the same thing to the queen, and their majesties answered them evasively without mentioning a word about marriage.

Some time later the king and queen fell gravely ill and died on almost the same day. Extremely sad, everyone dressed in black, and the bells tolled throughout the city. Rosette was inconsolable about the loss of her good mama. After the king and queen were buried, the dukes and marquises of the kingdom placed the great prince on a throne of gold and diamonds with a magnificent crown on his head and robes of violet velvet embroidered all over with suns and moons. The whole court then shouted three times, "Long live the king!" and there was nothing but rejoicing.

Almost immediately the king and his brother had a talk and said to each other, "Now that we are in power, we'll take our sister out of the prison in which she has spent so many years."

They only had to walk across the garden to reach the tower, which had been built as high as possible because the late king and queen had intended to keep the princess in it all her life. Rosette was embroidering a beautiful robe on a frame set before her, but when she saw her brothers, she rose and took the king's hand. "Good morning, sire," she said, "you are now king, and I'm your humble servant. I beg of you, let me leave this tower, where I've been very, very bored."

With that she began to weep. The king embraced her and told her not to cry, for he had come to take her out of the tower and conduct her to a fine château. The prince had his pockets full of sugar almonds, and he gave some to Rosette while saying, "Come, let's leave this vile dungeon. The king will soon find you a husband. You won't need to worry any longer."

When Rosette saw the beautiful garden, filled with flowers, fruits, and fountains, she was so astonished that she could not utter a word. Indeed, she had never seen anything like it before. Looking all around as she walked, she sometimes stopped and gathered fruit from the trees or flowers from the beds. Her little dog, named Fretillon, who was as green as a parrot, had but one ear, and danced delightfully, ran ahead of her, bow-wow-wowing with a thousand jumps and capers.

Fretillon was amusing the company when all of a sudden he ran into a small copse. Following him, the princess was astonished to find a great peacock with his tail spread. It was so very, very beautiful that she could not take her eyes off it. The king and the prince rejoined her and asked her what was delighting her so much. She pointed to the peacock and asked them what it was. They told her it was a type of a bird that people sometimes eat.

"What?" she exclaimed. "How can they dare kill such a beautiful bird and eat it? I want you to know that I'll never marry anyone but the king of peacocks, and when I'm queen, I'll make sure that peacocks will never be eaten."

Nothing can describe the astonishment of the king. "But, sister," he said, "where are we to find the king of the peacocks?"

"Wherever you like, sire, but I'll marry nobody else but him."

After she had made up her mind, the two brothers conducted her to their château, where they were obliged to bring the peacock as well and place it in her room, for she was extremely fond of it. All the ladies, who had never seen Rosette before, rushed forward to pay tribute to her. Some brought her preserves, others sugar, others dresses made of gilt materials, beautiful ribbons, dolls, embroidered shoes, pearls, and diamonds. Everywhere she was entertained, and so well-bred and polite was she, that she knew just how to kiss hands and curtsy when any pretty thing was given to her, and neither gentleman nor lady left dissatisfied with their reception.

While she was chatting with the fine company, the king and the prince deliberated on how they might find the king of the peacocks, if such a thing existed. They decided to have a portrait of the princess made, and it was so finely painted that it did all but speak. Then they said to her, "Since you won't marry anyone but the king of the peacocks, we're going to travel together all over the world in search of him. If we find him, we'll be very happy. Take care of the kingdom until we return."

Rosette thanked them for the trouble they were taking and said she would carefully govern the kingdom. Moreover, she told them that she would amuse herself during their absence by looking at the beautiful peacock and making Fretillon dance. None could refrain from shedding tears as they said their farewells.

Thus, the two princes proceeded on their journey and asked everybody they met, "Do you know the king of the peacocks?" And since everybody answered, "No, no," they kept traveling farther and farther. At last they went so very far that they reached a place nobody had ever seen. It was the kingdom of mayflies, and never had they seen so many in their life. The flies made such a buzzing that the king was afraid he would never be able to hear clearly again. He asked one who seemed the most sensible among them, if he knew the whereabouts of the king of the peacocks.

"Sire," the mayfly said to him, "his kingdom is thirty thousand miles from this place. You've taken the longest road to it."

"And how do you know that?" the king asked.

"Because," the mayfly replied, "we know you very well. We spend two or three months every year in your gardens."

Upon hearing this, the king and his brother embraced the mayfly. Indeed, they became great friends and dined together. They saw all the sights of the kingdom and marveled at all the rare things there. Just one leaf in this country was worth a gold coin. After viewing every last thing, they set out again to finish their journey, and since they had been told the way, it did not take them long to reach their goal. Soon they saw trees decked with peacocks; every part of the kingdom was so full of them that you could hear them scream and chatter two miles away.

The king said to his brother, "If the king of the peacocks is a peacock himself, how does our sister intend to marry him? We'd be mad to consent. That would make for a pretty alliance! Some little peachicks for nephews!"

The prince was also troubled by this. "It's a most unfortunate whim she's got into her head," he said. "What could have induced her to imagine there was a king of the peacocks somewhere in the world?"

When they arrived at the principal city, they found it filled with men and women, who not only dressed in clothes made of peacock feathers but also wore a great deal of them all over as ornaments. They met the king, who was driving out in a fine petite coach of gold and diamonds, drawn by twelve peacocks in full regalia. The king of the peacocks was so very handsome that the king and the prince were charmed by him. He had long, curly blond hair, an exceedingly fair complexion, and wore a crown of feathers from a peacock's tail. When he saw the two brothers, he surmised that they must be foreigners, since their garments were so different from those worn by his people. Just to be sure, he ordered the coach to stop and had them called over to him. The king and prince approached him, and after paying their respects, they said to him, "Sire, we have come a great distance to show you a beautiful portrait."

So saying, they took the large portrait of Rosette out of a valise. After the king of the peacocks had examined it carefully, he said, "I can't believe that such a beautiful maiden like her exists in the world."

"She's a hundred times more beautiful," said the king, her brother.

"Oh, you must be jesting," the king of the peacocks replied.

"Sire," the prince said, "my brother is a king just like you. He's called the king, and I'm the prince. This portrait is of our sister, the princess Rosette. We've come here to ask you if you'll marry her. She's beautiful and virtuous, and we will give her a bushel of golden crowns."

"Yes, certainly, I'll marry her with all my heart," said the king, "She'll have everything she wants at my court. I'll shower her with love, but let me tell you that I expect her to be as beautiful as her portrait. If it flatters her in the slightest degree, I'll put you both to death."

"Of course, we consent," the brothers said.

"You consent!" the king responded. "Then off to prison with you. You'll remain there until the princess arrives."

The brothers did not resist in the least because they were perfectly certain that Rosette was more beautiful than her picture. Once they were put in prison, the king of the peacocks had them looked after in admirable fashion, and he frequently went to see them. The portrait of Rosette was kept in his castle, and he was so crazy about it that he could not catch a wink of sleep. Since the other king and his brother were in prison, they wrote a letter to the princess, requesting her to pack her clothes immediately and to come as soon as possible because the king of the peacocks was waiting for her. They did not, however, tell her they were prisoners, for fear of alarming her.

When she received their letter, she was so overcome with joy that she thought she would die. She told everybody that the king of the peacocks had been found, and he wanted to marry her. They kindled bonfires, fired guns, and had feasts of sugar almonds all over the kingdom. For three days she gave everyone who came to see her a slice of bread with butter and jam, some wafers, and a glass of Hypocras wine. After displaying such generosity, she left her beautiful dolls to her best friends, and her brother's kingdom in the hands of the wisest old men in the city. She recommended strongly that they were to take great care of everything, to spend very little, and to increase the monies by the time the king returned. She also asked them to keep her peacock safe and took only her nurse, her foster sister, and her little dog Fretillon to accompany her.

They put to sea in a boat and carried with them the bushel of gold crowns and clothes enough to change their dresses twice a day for ten years. They did nothing but laugh and sing all the time. The nurse asked the boatman, "Are we approaching, are we approaching the kingdom of peacocks?"

He answered, "No, no."

Another time she asked him, "Are we approaching? Are we approaching?"

He answered "Yes, yes."

As soon as he said this, she went to the stern of the boat, sat down beside him, and said, "If you want, you can make yourself a rich man for the rest of your life."

"I should like it very much."

"If you want," she continued, "you can earn some fine gold coins."

"I desire nothing better."

"Well, then," said the nurse, "you must help me tonight. When the princess is asleep, we'll throw her into the sea. As soon as she is drowned, I'll dress my daughter in the princess's fine clothes, and we'll conduct her to the king of the peacocks, who'll be happy to marry her. And for your reward we'll fill your purse with diamonds."

The boatman was astounded by the nurse's proposition. He said it was a pity to drown such a beautiful princess, and that he felt pity for her. But the nurse took out a bottle of wine and made him drink so much that he could no longer refuse her anything.

The princess lay down as soon as it was dark, as was her custom. Little Fretillon snuggled at the bottom of the bed and did not move a paw. Rosette was sleeping soundly when the wicked nurse fetched the boatman and led him into the princess's cabin. Without disturbing her, they lifted her up along with her feather bed, sheets, and counterpane. The foster sister helped them with all her might, and they flung the whole lot into the sea. The princess was so sound asleep that she never woke. By a stroke of good luck, however, the feather bed was stuffed with phoenix feathers, which are very rare and never sink in water; she floated on her bed just as if it were a boat. Still, the water gradually soaked through the mattress. Disturbed by this, Rosette tossed from side to side and roused Fretillon. He had an excellent nose and, smelling sole and codfish so close to him, he began to bark. He barked so much that he woke all the rest of the fish, and they began to swim about. The large fish bumped their heads against the princess's bed, which spun around and around like a whirligig because there was nothing to steady it. She was quite taken aback and wondered, "Is our boat dancing on the water? I've never been so uncomfortable as tonight."

Fretillon kept making a frightful commotion. The wicked nurse and the boatman heard him a long way off and said, "There's that little rogue of a dog drinking with his mistress to our good health. Let's quickly make for shore."

They were just in sight of the city of the king of the peacocks. His majesty sent a hundred coaches drawn by all sorts of rare animals, and by the time the boat approached, they were waiting on the beach. There were lions, bears, stags, wolves, horses, oxen, asses, eagles, and peacocks. The coach intended to convey Princess Rosette was drawn by six blue monkeys who could jump, dance the tightrope, and do all sorts of amusing stunts. Each one had a beautiful harness made of crimson velvet and plated with gold. There were also sixty young ladies whom the king had selected to entertain the princess. They were dressed in all sorts of colors, among which gold and silver would seem quite ordinary by comparison.

The nurse had taken great pains to deck out her daughter. From head to foot she had covered her with Rosette's diamonds and robes. Still, despite this finery, she looked uglier than an ape. She had greasy black hair, squinting eyes, crooked legs, and a great hump in the middle of her back. Moreover, she was an ill-tempered slut who was constantly grumbling. When the servants of the king of the peacocks saw her step out of the boat, they were so very surprised that they could not speak.

"What does this mean?" she said. "Are you asleep? Come, come, bring me something to eat. You're a nice set of rascals. I'll have you all hanged!"

On hearing this threat, they said to one another, "What a vile creature. She's as wicked as she is ugly. What a fine wife for our king! It certainly wasn't worth having her come from the other end of the world."

Meanwhile, she kept pretending to be the mistress. For next to nothing she doled out slaps and blows with her fist to everybody around her. Since her entourage was huge, she proceeded slowly and sat in her coach like a queen. All the peacocks perched in the trees to salute her as she passed had been prepared to cry, "Long live beautiful Queen Rosette," but when they saw she was such a horrible fright, they cried, "Fie! fie! How ugly she is!"

Extremely furious and mortified, she said to her guards, "Kill those rogues of peacocks who are insulting me!"

The peacocks flew away quickly and made fun of her.

The scoundrel of a boatman, who witnessed all this, said in a whisper to the nurse, "Friend, all is not well with us. Your daughter should have been more beautiful."

"Hold your tongue, fool," she replied. "You'll bring us bad luck."

A messenger was sent to inform the king that the princess was approaching.

"Well," he asked, "have her brothers told me the truth? Is she more beautiful than her picture?"

"Sire," he replied, "it's enough if she's just as beautiful, isn't it?"

"Yes, surely," said the king, "I'll be perfectly satisfied with that. Let us go and see her," for he knew by the great commotion they were making in the court that she had arrived, and he could not distinguish anything they were saying except, "Fie! fie! How ugly she is!" He thought they were speaking about some dwarf or animal she might have brought with her, for it never occurred to him that they were referring to her.

Completely unveiled, the portrait of the princess was carried on the end of a long staff, and the king walked in solemn procession behind it. He was followed by all his barons, his peacocks, and the ambassadors from the neighboring kingdoms. The king of the peacocks was extremely impatient to see his dear Rosette. However, when he finally saw her, he nearly died on the spot. He flew into the greatest rage in the world. He tore his clothes and would not go near her, for she was frightening. "How dare they!" he exclaimed. "Those two scoundrels I've got in prison have some nerve to mock me and to think I would marry a baboon like that. They'll die for this. Go this instant and lock up that impertinent girl, her nurse, and the fellow who brought them here. Fling them into the lowest dungeon of my great tower."

Meanwhile, the imprisoned king and his brother, who knew the day on which their sister was to arrive, had put on their best clothes to welcome her. Yet, instead of opening their prison and setting them at liberty as they had hoped, the jailer came with some soldiers and made them descend into an utterly dark cell filled with horrid reptiles, where they were up to their necks in water. Nobody was ever more astonished or more miserable. "Alas," they cried to each other, "this is a sad wedding for us! What can have brought such great misfortune upon us?" They did not know what in the world to think, except that they were doomed to die, and they were completely overcome with sorrow. Three days passed without their hearing a word. At the end of the three days the king of the peacocks came and insulted them through a hole in the wall.

"You assumed the titles of king and prince just to trap me into marrying your sister," he cried. "Now I know you're nothing but vagabonds who aren't worth the water you drink. I'm going to give you judges who will make quick process of you. The rope that will hang you both is all ready."

"King of the peacocks," the king angrily, "don't be so rash, for you may have cause to repent. I'm truly a king like you. I have a fine kingdom, robes, crowns, and good money. Ha, ha! you must be joking if you're talking about hanging us. Tell me, what have we stolen from you?"

When the king heard him speak so boldly, he did not know what to think, and he was somewhat tempted to let them and their sister go free and not put them to death. However, his trusted servant—verily a flatterer, this one—encouraged him to stick to his convictions. He told him that if the king did not take vengeance on them, everybody would laugh at him and think him a petty monarch not worth a penny. So the king swore that he would not forgive them and ordered their trial to take place. It did not last long, for all that was needed was the portrait of the real Princess Rosette side by side with the person who had assumed Rosette's name. Consequently, the brothers were condemned to lose their heads as false traitors who had promised to give the king a beautiful princess in marriage and had only offered an ugly country wench. The court went in full state to the prison to read the sentence to the prisoners, who declared that they were not guilty of lying. They maintained that their sister was a princess fairer than the day, that there was some mystery which they could not understand, and they demanded the postponement of their execution for seven days. The king of the peacocks, who was greatly incensed, was reluctant to grant them this reprieve, but he eventually consented.

While all this was happening at court, we must return to poor Princess Rosette. When day broke, she was greatly astonished, and Fretillon also, to find themselves in the middle of the sea without the boat or

any help. She began to weep so bitterly that all the fish pitied her. She did not know what to do or what would become of her. "There's no doubt but the king of the peacocks gave orders to have me thrown into the sea," she said. "He's gone back on his promise to marry me and ordered me to be drowned to get rid of me. What a strange man. I would have showed him so much love. We would have lived so happily together."

After saying all this she wept more bitterly, for she could not help loving him. During the next two days she continued to float on the ocean, first on one side and then the other, soaked to her bones. The cold water was enough to kill her, and she was all but benumbed. If it had not been for little Fretillon, who warmed her heart, she would have died a hundred deaths. Of course, she was also tremendously hungry, and when she saw oysters in their shells, she took as many as she chose and ate them. Fretillon had little liking for them, but he was obliged to eat something. When it grew dark, Rosette became terrified and said to her dog, "Fretillon, keep on barking, for I'm afraid the sole might eat us."

He barked all night, while the princess's bed floated ever closer to the shore. On the coast there was a good old man who lived all alone in a little hut, which nobody ever visited. He was very poor and cared nothing for worldly goods. When he heard Fretillon bark, he was quite surprised, for dogs seldom came by. He thought some travelers had lost their way and came out of his hut to help them. All of a sudden he saw the princess and Fretillon floating on the water, and when the princess caught sight of him, she stretched out her arms and cried to him, "Good old man, save me, for I'm dying out here. I've been like this for two days!"

When he heard her speak so despondently, he had great compassion for her and went back into his dwelling to get a long boat hook. He waded into the water up to his neck, and two or three times the thought he would drown. Finally he managed to pull the bed to the shore. Rosette and Fretillon were greatly relieved to be on dry land. The princess thanked the good man warmly and, wrapping herself up in the bed covers, she walked barefoot into the hut, where he made a small fire for her with dry leaves and took his dead wife's best gown with stockings and shoes out of a chest, and the princess put them on. Dressed like a peasant, she looked as lovely as the day, and Fretillon danced around her to her delight.

The old man saw plainly that Rosette was a lady of breeding, for the coverlet of her bed was made of gold and silver, and her mattress made of satin. He requested her to tell him her story and assured her that he would keep it a secret if she wished. She recounted everything and wept a great deal, for she was still under the belief that it was the king of the peacocks who had ordered her to be drowned.

"What shall we do, my daughter?" the old man asked her. "You're a great princess accustomed to delicacies, and I have nothing to give you but black bread and radishes. You'll fare badly with me. If you'll take my advice, you'll let me go and tell the king of the peacocks that you're here. I'm sure that if he had seen you, he would have married you."

"Ah," exclaimed Rosette, "he's a wicked creature and wants to kill me. But if you have a little basket, let us tie it around my dog's neck, and he'll bring back something to eat."

The old man gave the princess a basket. Then she tied it around Fretillon's neck and said to him, "Go to the best saucepan in the city and bring me whatever you may find in it."

Fretillon ran to the city, and since there were no saucepans better than the king's, he entered the royal kitchen, took the lid off the largest, skillfully removed its contents, and returned to the hut.

Then Rosette said to him, "Go back to the pantry and bring me the best of everything."

Fretillon returned to the pantry and filled his basket with white bread, muscatel, and all sorts of fruits and preserves. He was so loaded down that he could hardly wag his tail.

When the king of the peacocks called for his dinner, there was nothing in the saucepan or the pantry. The servants could do nothing but stare at one another, while the king was in a frightful rage. "Very well," he said, "there's no dinner for me. But take care that the spit is set up this evening, and that you roast something excellent for me."

When evening arrived, the princess said to Fretillon, "Go to the city, enter the best kitchen, and bring me some nice roast meat."

Fretillon did as his mistress ordered him and, knowing no better kitchen than the king's, he stole into it quietly while the cooks' backs were turned and took all the roast meat off the spit. It was so nicely prepared that the mere sight of it whetted one's appetite. Fretillon returned home to the princess with his basket quite full. She sent him back immediately to the pantry, and he returned with all the royal preserves and sugar almonds.

The king, who had not dined at noon, was famished and desired to sup early, but there was nothing to set before him. He worked himself up into an awful rage and went to bed supperless.

The next day at lunch and supper time it was exactly the same, and the king had to go without eating or drinking. Each time he was ready to sit down at the table, his servants discovered that everything had been carried off.

His trusted servant was greatly disturbed and, fearing the king would die, he

concealed himself in a corner of the kitchen and kept his eye constantly on the boiling pot. He was quite surprised to see a little green dog with one ear enter quietly, take off the cover, and put all the meat into his basket. He followed it to see where it was going, and when he saw it leave the city, he followed it to the good old man's hut. Then he returned right away to tell the king that all his boiled and roast meat was being taken day and night to the hovel of a poor peasant. The king was most astonished and ordered the man to be brought before him. Desiring to keep the king's favor, the servant decided to go himself. He took the archers of the guard with him, and they found the old man dining with the princess and eating the king's boiled meat. They tied them up with rope and seized Fretillon as well. As soon as they arrived at the palace, they notified the king, who replied, "Tomorrow will be the seventh and last day I granted to those impudent impostors. They shall die with these thieves who have stolen my dinner."

After saying this, he entered the hall of justice. The old man fell on his knees and said he would confess everything. While he was speaking, the king gazed at the beautiful princess and felt sorry that she was weeping. And when the good man declared that she was Princess Rosette and had been thrown into the sea, the king jumped three times for joy, even though he was faint from not having eaten for some time. He embraced Rosette even as he untied the rope that bound her, and assured her that he loved her with all his heart.

Directly afterward, the king sent for the princes. Believing that the time had come for their execution, they approached sadly with their heads hung down. The nurse and her daughter were also brought out. When they looked at one another, a general recognition took place. Rosette hugged her brothers, and the nurse, her daughter, and the boatman flung themselves on their knees and begged for mercy. The joy was great that the king and the princess forgave them. The good old man was richly rewarded and lived for the rest of his days in the palace. The king of the peacocks made all sorts of amends to the king and his brother, and apologized for the way he had treated them. The nurse restored the rich clothes and bushel of gold crowns to Rosette, and the wedding festivities lasted fifteen days. Everybody was satisfied all the way down to Fretillon, who from that day on never ate anything but the wings of partridges.

> Heaven watches over us, and when Innocence
> Stands in danger, it rushes to her defence,
> Rescues, and avenges her. Now the sight
> Of poor Rosette on the ocean in such a plight,
> Just like fabled Halcyon in her nest,
> Drifting at the pleasure of the reckless gale,
> Awakens pity in each gentle breast.
> One fears a tragic end to such a tale:
> Perish she must, the reader can't help thinking,
> Either amid the stormy billows sinking,
> Or swallowed up by some rapacious whale.
> Fretillon was the humble instrument
> Of Providence and saved his mistress
> From the hungry fish and then was sent
> To find her food and brought back quite a dish.
> How many are there nowadays who need
> The help of dogs that come from such a steadfast breed!
> Rosette was saved and took pity on her foes.

Oh, you who on those perpetrators of your woes
Would like to have vengeance, no matter what the cost,
Let her example not be lost;
But treasure this lesson while you live—
The noblest vengeance still is to forgive.

THE WHITE CAT

ONCE upon a time there was a king who had three brave, handsome sons, and he was afraid lest they become eager to reign during his lifetime. He had even heard rumors that they were seeking to win over adherents to help them take over the kingdom. The king knew he was growing old, but his mind was still alert, and he had no desire to yield a position he still filled worthily. Therefore, he thought that the best way to keep them from growing restive was to tantalize them with promises that he would always avoid fulfilling.

One day he called them into his room, and speaking to them kindly, he remarked, "You'll agree with me, my dear sons, that my great age prevents me from managing the affairs of state as assiduously as before. I fear my subjects may suffer from this circumstance, and I want to transfer my crown to one of you. To deserve such a gift, however, it is only just that you in turn try to please me. Now, since I contemplate retiring to the country, I believe that a pretty, faithful, and intelligent little dog would make an excellent companion. So, instead of showing preference to my eldest, I declare that

whichever one of you brings me the handsomest little dog will immediately become my heir."

The princes were exceedingly surprised by the king's inclination for a

515

little dog, but the two younger realized they could profit from this proposition and gladly accepted the task, while the eldest was too timid or too respectful to stand up for his rights. So they took leave of the king, who distributed money and jewels among them and added, "Return without fail next year on the same day and hour, and bring me your little dogs."

Before setting out, they withdrew to a castle a mile from the city and gathered their most intimate friends for several splendid banquets. There the three brothers pledged eternal friendship to one another. They would act without jealousy or regrets in this particular affair, they declared, and the successful candidate would be willing to share his fortune with the others. At last they departed, agreeing to meet at the same castle on their return before proceeding together to the king. So that they might not be known, they refused to take any assistants and even changed their names.

Each took a different road. The two elder met with many adventures, but let me recount only those of the youngest. He was well mannered and possessed a gay, cheerful temperament, even though his courage was most intrepid. He had a noble figure, a striking face, regular features, and fine teeth. He was very talented in all those skills that a prince was expected to perform: he could paint, he sang with a pleasant voice, and played the lute and *theorbo* with a sensitivity that charmed everyone. In short, he was a highly accomplished young fellow.

Scarcely a day passed that he did not purchase dogs. They were big and little: greyhounds, mastiffs, bloodhounds, pointers, spaniels, water dogs, lapdogs. The instant he found one handsomer than the next, he let the previous one go, since he could not have possibly led around thirty or forty thousand dogs by himself, and he remained firm in his determination not to have gentlemen, servants, or pages in his company.

Continuing on without any fixed destination, he was surprised one night by a thunderous rainstorm in a forest, and he lost the path he was following. So he took the first he could find, and after having walked a long way, he saw a glimmer of light that indicated there was some habitation nearby in which he might find shelter until morning. Guided by the light, he came to the gate of the most magnificent castle you could ever imagine. This gate was made of gold and covered with carbuncles, and their pure, vivid light illuminated everything in the vicinity. It was this light that the prince had perceived at a distance. The walls were transparent porcelain of various colors, and the histories of all the fairies from the beginning of time were painted there. The famous adventures of Donkey-Skin, Finette, the Orange Tree, Gracieuse, Sleeping Beauty, the Green Serpent, and a hundred others, were not omitted. He was delighted to see Prince Sprite among them, for he was his uncle, according to the legends of Brittany. The rainstorm prevented him from lingering before this mural because he was being drenched to the skin. Besides, he could hardly see anything beyond the rays cast by the gate's carbuncles. Thereupon he returned to the golden gate, where he saw a kid's foot dangling from a chain of diamonds. He admired all the magnificence and apparent security in which the owners of the castle seemed to live. "Indeed," he said to himself, "what's to prevent thieves from cutting off this chain and pulling the carbuncles off the gate? They could make themselves rich for the rest of their lives."

Pulling the kid's foot, he immediately heard a bell ring, which by its sound seemed to be made of gold or silver. A moment later the gate was opened without his seeing anything but a dozen hands, each holding torches, suspended in midair. He was so astonished that he hesitated to move forward. However, he felt other hands that gently pushed him forward. Therefore, he advanced with some distrust, and to be on the safe side, he kept his hand on the hilt of his sword. On entering a vestibule entirely decorated with porphyry and lapis lazuli, he heard two enchanting voices raised in song:

> "Be not startled by the hands you see.
> Have no fear in this delightful place.
> There's nothing here except a lovely face,
> Nothing at all but love to flee."

Unable to believe that he was being invited so graciously for the purpose of eventually being harmed, he let himself be pushed toward a large coral gate that opened before his eyes. Into a salon of mother-of-pearl he entered and then passed through several apartments variously ornamented with such an abundance of paintings and jewels that he was captivated by the sight of them. Thousands and thousands of lights, from the vaulted roof of the salon down to the floor, illuminated parts of the other apartments, which were also filled with chandeliers, girandoles, and stages lined with wax candles. Such magnificence was so resplendent that he had difficulty imagining how all this had been made possible.

After passing through sixty rooms, he was stopped by the hands that had been guiding him and watched as a large easy chair moved by itself toward the fireplace. At the same instant a fire was lighted, and the hands, which appeared to him handsome, white, small, plump, and well shaped, began to undress him, for he was soaked, as I have already told you, and they were afraid he would catch cold. Although they did not reveal themselves, they gave him a splendid shirt suitable for a wedding day and a morning gown made of rich golden material embroidered with emerald ciphers. The bodiless hands carried over a dressing table that had everything he needed. Nothing could be more magnificent. They combed him with a lightness and pleasing skill. Finally, they dressed him again, not in his own clothes, but with others much richer. He observed all that took place with silent wonder and a certain alarm that he could not altogether conquer.

After they had powdered, curled, perfumed, attired, and adorned him to look handsomer than Adonis, the hands led him into a hall that was superbly gilt and furnished. All around were paintings of the stories about all the most famous cats: Rodilardus hung by the heels in the Council of Rats, Puss in Boots, Marquis of Carabas, The Writing Cat, The Cat That Became a Woman, Witches in the Shape of Cats, and their Sabbath and all its ceremonies. In a word, these paintings were highly unusual.

A table was set with two places, each with a golden *cadenas*. The buffet astonished him, for it held innumerable cups of rock crystal studded with a thousand rare stones. The prince was trying to figure out why there were two place settings when he saw several cats take their places in a small orchestra that had been designed expressly for them. One held a music book with the most extraordinary notes, another held a roll of paper to beat time with, and the rest had miniature guitars.

Suddenly each cat began to mew in a different tone and strummed the strings of their guitars with their claws, producing the strangest music that he had ever heard. The prince would have thought he was in the lower regions if he had not found the palace so marvelously beautiful; this fact alone prevented him from making such an error. He was, however, obliged to stop up his ears, and he laughed heartily at the sight of the various postures and grimaces of these novel musicians.

As he pondered the odd things that had already happened to him in the château, he saw a figure scarcely a foot tall enter the hall. This puppet was draped with a long black crape veil, and the two cats preceding it, wearing cloaks and swords, were also dressed in deep mourning. A large retinue of cats followed, some carrying rat traps filled with rats and others mice in cages. The prince could not get over his astonishment. He did not know what to think. The little black figure approached, and as it lifted its veil, he perceived the most beautiful white cat that ever has been or ever will be seen. In a very youthful, melancholy air she began mewing so softly and sweetly that it went straight to his heart. "Prince," she said, "you are welcome. My mewing majesty regards you with pleasure."

"Madam cat," the prince said, "it's very generous of you to receive me with so much ceremony, but you don't appear to me to be any ordinary little animal. Your gift of speech and the superb castle you inhabit are sufficient evidence to the contrary."

"Prince," the white cat replied, "please forgo paying me these compliments. I'm plain in my speech and my manners, though I have a generous heart. Come, let them serve supper. And put an end to the concert, for the prince doesn't understand what they are singing."

"Are they actually singing words, madam?" he inquired.

"Yes, indeed," she answered. "We have poets here of considerable talent, and if you remain among us for long, you'll become convinced of this fact."

"You need only say so, and I'll believe it," the prince responded politely. "All the same, madam, I regard you as a most unusual cat."

The supper was placed on the table by the hands of invisible bodies. First, there were two soups, one of pigeons and the other of very plump mice. The sight of the latter prevented the prince from touching the former, believing that the same cook had concocted both, but the cat, who guessed from his face what was going on in his mind, assured him that their meals had been cooked separately and that he could eat it with the perfect assurance that it contained neither rats nor mice. The prince did not wait to be told twice, for he felt that the pretty cat had no wish to deceive him.

At that moment he noticed to his surprise that she had a miniature set in a bracelet on her paw. He begged her to show it to him, supposing it to be that of some Master Minagrobis. He was astonished to find the portrait of an extraordinarily handsome young man who resembled himself so nearly that he could not have asked for a better likeness. Sighing, the white cat became even more melancholy, lapsing into a profound silence. The prince saw clearly that there was some unusual story connected with the portrait, but did not venture to ask any questions for fear of displeasing her. Instead, he entertained her by telling all the news he had and in the process found her well acquainted with the various concerns of princes and other events occurring in the world.

After supper the white cat invited her guest to enter a salon, in which was constructed a theater where twelve cats and twelve monkeys danced a ballet. One party was dressed as Moors, the other as Chinese. You can easily imagine the leaps and capers they performed, and every now and then they gave each other a scratch or two. So did the evening end, and the white cat bade "Good night" to her guest.

The hands who had been his conductors so far took hold of him again and led him into an apartment quite different from any he had seen, for it was not so much magnificent as it was elegant. All the decorations were made of butterflies' wings whose various colors formed a thousand different flowers. There were also the feathers of exceedingly rare birds that perhaps have never been seen anywhere else. The furnishings of the bed were made of and tied with a thousand bows of ribbon. Large mirrors hung from the ceiling to floor in frames of chased gold representing a thousand tiny cupids.

The prince went to bed without saying a word, for there were no means of talking with the hands that waited upon him. He slept but little and was wakened early by a muffled noise. The hands immediately lifted him out of bed and dressed him in hunting attire. Looking into the castle courtyard, he saw more than five hundred cats, some of whom led greyhounds in the slips, while others blew horns. It was a grand holiday. The white cat was going to hunt and wanted the prince to accompany her. The officious hands gave him a wooden horse, and though he made some objection to mounting it, saying that he could never become a knight-errant like Don Quixote, his resistance was useless. It had a bridle and saddle embroidered with gold and diamonds, and in fact it went at full gallop and kept pace wonderfully. The white cat rode a monkey, the handsomest and proudest ever seen. She had thrown off her long veil in favor of a dragoon's cap, which made her look so bold that she frightened all the mice in the vicinity. Never was there a more charming hunting party. The cats outran the rabbits and hares, and as fast as they caught them, the white cat had a *curée* made in her presence, and a thousand skillful feats were performed to the great delight of the whole company. The birds, in turn, were by no means safe, for the kittens climbed the trees, and a great monkey carried the white cat up even to the nests of the eagles so that their eaglets were at her mercy.

Once the hunt was over, the white cat took a horn, and though it was about the length of one's finger, it emitted a call so clear and loud that it was easily heard ten miles away. As soon as she had sounded two or three flourishes, she was surrounded by all the cats in the country. Some rode chariots through the air, and others came in boats by water. Never before had so many cats been gathered, nearly all dressed in different fashions. Attended by this splendid entourage, the white cat returned to the castle, requesting the prince to accompany her. He was perfectly willing to do so, even though all this caterwauling smacked of a witch's festival.

As soon as they reached home, she put on her long black veil and dined with the prince, who was hungry and did justice to the good cheer. They brought him some liqueurs, which he sipped with great satisfaction, and they soon made him forget all about the little dog he was to find for the king. He no longer thought of anything but mewing with the white cat, that is to say, remaining her kind and faithful companion. He spent his days by amusing himself in pleasant ways, followed by ballets, carousals, and a thousand other events that provided him with a good deal of entertainment. Even the beautiful cat herself frequently composed verses and sonnets so full of passionate tenderness that made him suspect she had a susceptible heart, for no one could speak as she did without being in love. Unfortunately, her secretary, who was an old cat, wrote in such a vile scrawl that it is impossible to read them today, even though her works have been preserved.

The prince had forgotten all about the land of his birth. The hands of which I have spoken continued to wait upon him, and he regretted sometimes that he was not a cat so he could spend his whole life long in such excellent company. "Alas," he said to the white cat, "how wretched I'll be when I must leave you! I love you so dearly! Either become a woman or make me a cat."

Amused by his wish, she gave him some mysterious answers that he did not understand in the least.

A year flies by quickly when one has neither care nor pain, when one is merry and in good health. The white cat knew when the prince was supposed to return, and since he had forgotten it, she reminded him. "Don't you know," she asked, "that you have only three days left to look for the little dog that your father desires? Your brothers have already found several that are very beautiful."

The prince's memory of his task returned to him, and he was astonished by his negligence. "What secret spell could have made me forget the most important thing in the world to me?" he exclaimed. "My honor and fortune are staked on this. Where shall I find a dog that can win the kingdom for me, or a horse swift enough to complete the journey, in such a short time?"

Seeing him become so anxious and sad, the white cat said to him sweetly, "Prince, do not be distressed. I'm your friend, and you may stay here one more day. Although it's five hundred miles from here to your country, the good wooden horse will carry you there tomorrow in less then twelve hours."

"I thank you, beautiful cat," the prince said, "but I cannot simply return to my father without bringing him a little dog."

"Wait," said the white cat, "here's an acorn that contains one more beautiful than the Dog Star."

"Oh, madam cat," the prince cried, "your majesty is jesting with me."

"Put the acorn to your ear," she replied, "and you'll hear it bark."

He obeyed her, and immediately the little dog went "bow-wow." The prince was extremely delighted, for any dog that could be kept in an acorn was bound to be diminutive indeed.

He was going to open the acorn, so eager was he to see the dog, but the white cat told him that the dog might catch cold on the journey, and it would be better for him to wait until he was in his royal father's presence.

He thanked her a thousand times and bade her a most tender farewell. "I assure you," he said, "that the days I have spent with you have flown by so quickly that I deeply regret leaving you behind. Although you're the sovereign here and all the cats that compose your court possess much more wit and gallantry than ours, I'd be honored if you came with me."

The cat replied to this invitation only with a deep sigh: "Prince, depart."

The prince was the first to reach the castle where he had agreed to meet his brothers. Arriving shortly thereafter, they were surprised to see in the courtyard a wooden horse that curveted with more grace than the horses in the riding schools. When the prince came forward to receive them, they embraced several times and recounted their travels to one another, though our prince kept the bulk of his adventures a secret from his brothers. Showing them an ugly turnspit, he remarked, "I think it's so beautiful that I've selected it for the king." Despite the close friendship of the brothers, the two elder felt a secret joy at their young brother's awful taste. Since they were sitting at a table, they nudged each other's feet by way of signifying that they did not have much to fear from him.

The next morning they set out together in the same coach. The king's two elder sons carried a few little dogs in baskets so beautiful and delicate that everyone was afraid to touch them. The youngest son carried the poor turnspit, which was so filthy that nobody could bear the sight of it. As soon as they set foot in the palace, everybody surrounded them

and welcomed them back to court. Once they had entered the king's apartment, he was at a loss to make a decision, for the little dogs given to him by his two elder sons were nearly equal in beauty. In fact, the two brothers had already begun to dispute the right of succession when their younger brother reconciled them by taking out of his pocket the acorn that the white cat had given him. He opened it immediately, and everybody saw a tiny dog lying on cotton. He got up and jumped through a ring without touching any part of it.

The prince placed it on the floor, and instantly it began dancing a saraband with castanets that was as sprightly as the most celebrated Spanish dancer. It was a thousand different colors, and its hair and ears swept the ground.

The king was dumbfounded, for how could he possibly criticize the beauty of Toutou?

Nevertheless, he was by no means inclined to give over his crown, for the smallest fleur-de-lis in its circlet was dearer to him than all the dogs in the universe. Therefore, he told his sons that he was gratified by the trouble they had taken. Indeed, they had succeeded so well in fulfilling his first request that he wanted to test their ability again before he fulfilled his promise. "You have a year to travel over land and sea in quest of a piece of cloth so fine that it will pass through the eye of a needle used to make Venetian point lace."

All three were extremely disappointed to learn that they were obliged to undertake a new voyage of discovery, but the two elder princes, whose dogs were less beautiful than that of the youngest, readily consented. Both went their own ways without declaring their friendship to him as they had done before, for the trick of the turnspit had rather cooled their ardor.

Our prince remounted his wooden horse, and since he did not wish for any assistance other than that obtained from the friendship of the white cat, he set off at a gallop toward the castle where she had so kindly received him. He found all the doors open, and the windows, roofs, towers, and walls were all illuminated by a hundred thousand lamps, which produced a brilliant effect. The hands that had attended him so well advanced to meet him and took the bridle of the excellent wooden horse, which they led to the stable while the prince entered the white cat's apartments.

Wearing her morning cap, she was lying in a little basket on a fine mattress of white satin. She seemed in low spirits until she saw the prince. Then she cut a thousand capers and played as many gambols to show him her delight. "Whatever hope I had that you'd return," she said, "I confess, Prince, that I didn't want to deceive myself by indulging in it. I'm generally so unfortunate in matters that concern me that this is a pleasant surprise."

The grateful prince caressed her a thousand times and told her about the success of his journey, which she knew perhaps better than he did. "Only now the king wants a piece of cloth that can pass through the eye of a needle." In truth, he believed it was impossible to find such a thing, but he did not hesitate to ask her to make the attempt, relying implicitly upon her friendship and assistance. Becoming more serious, the white cat told him it was a matter that demanded consideration. Fortunately, there were some cats in her castle who spun extremely well. She intended to put a claw to it herself and speed up the work as much as possible. "Rest assured that you have no need of searching any farther for what you will more readily find in my castle than in any other place in the world."

The hands appeared bearing torches, and the white cat and prince followed them. They entered a magnificent arbor running along the side of a large river, over which was to be shot an astonishing display of fireworks.

Four cats were simultaneously to be burnt there, for they had been tried and sentenced in due form for having eaten the roast meat, cheese, and milk, provided for the white cat's supper, and even of having conspired against her life with Martafax and L'Hermite, two famous rats of that country, and regarded as such by La Fontaine, a very dutiful historian. It was well-known there had been a great deal of intrigue in the matter, and that the majority of the witnesses had been bribed. Despite all this, the prince managed to obtain their pardon. The fireworks did not harm anyone, and never had such splendid skyrockets been seen before.

Afterward, a splendid supper was served. This gratified the prince more than the fireworks because he was famished: the wooden horse had carried him at such a rapid pace that he had never ridden so hard before in his life. The following days were spent like those of the previous year and the ingenious white cat set forth a thousand diverse entertainments to regale her guest. Our prince was probably the first mortal who ever found so much amusement among cats without human company.

The truth is, the white cat possessed charming, sweet, and well-rounded qualities. She was wiser than a cat is allowed to be, and the prince was sometimes astonished by her knowledge. "No," he said, "it's not natural for you to possess all these wonderful qualities I've discovered in you. If you love me, charming pussy, explain to me what miracle has enabled you to think and speak so perfectly that you might be elected a member of the most famous Academy of Arts and Sciences?"

"Stop questioning me, Prince," she said. "I'm not allowed to answer, and you may conjecture as much as you like without the least contradiction from me. Let it suffice that I'll always have a velvet paw for you, that I take a tender interest in all that concerns you."

The second year slipped away like the first—without their being aware of it at all. The prince could scarcely think of anything he desired without the diligent hands instantly providing him with it, whether it be a book, jewel, picture, or antique medal. He had but to say, "I want a certain gem in the cabinet of the Great Mogul or of the King of Persia, or such a statue in Corinth or any part of Greece," and it was instantaneously before him, without his knowing how it came or who brought it. This pastime was not without its charms, for it is sometimes very pleasant to possess the finest treasures in the world.

The White Cat, who constantly attended to the prince's welfare, warned him that the hour of departure was approaching. There was no need to worry, however, about the piece of cloth he needed. She had made a most wonderful one for him, and she added that she intended this time to furnish him with an equipage worthy of his birth. Without waiting for his reply, she told him to look into the great courtyard of the castle. He saw an open calèche made of gold and enameled in scarlet with a thousand gallant

emblems that stimulated the mind as much as the eye. It was drawn by twelve horses as white as snow, four-and-four abreast, bearing harnesses of scarlet velvet embroidered with diamonds and plated with gold. The calèche was lined to match, and a hundred coaches followed in its train. Each was led by eight horses and filled with superbly attired noblemen of high bearing. There was as well an escort of a thousand bodyguards, whose uniforms were covered so much with embroidery that you could not see the stuff they were made of. Most striking about this cavalcade was the portrait of the white cat, which could be seen on the emblems on the calèche or the uniforms of the bodyguards or attached by a ribbon to the doublets of those who formed the train, as if it were a new order with which she had decorated them.

"Go," she said to the prince. "Appear at the court of your father in such a sumptuous state that your magnificence may make an impression on him and prevent him from refusing again to bestow you with the crown you deserve. Here's a walnut. Crack it only in his presence, and you'll find in it the piece of cloth you asked of me."

"Charming white cat," he said, "I must confess that your kindness has so infused me that, if you consent, I'd prefer spending my life here with you than enjoying all the grandeur that I have reason to expect elsewhere."

"Prince," she replied, "I'm convinced that you have a good heart, a rare quality among princes. Usually they want to be loved by everyone. Rarely do they want to love anyone themselves. You're proof that the rule has its exception. I give you credit for the affection you've demonstrated for a white cat that, after all, is good for nothing but catching mice."

The prince kissed her paw and departed. We would have some difficulty in believing the speed with which he traveled if we were not already aware of the pace at which the wooden horse had previously covered the five-hundred-mile distance from the castle. Impelled by a like power, these swift steeds traveled for twenty-four hours straight and stopped only when they reached the king's palace.

The two elder brothers had already arrived, and when they did not see the youngest prince, they congratulated themselves on his negligence. "Here's a piece of good luck!" one whispered to the other. "He's either dead or very ill. He won't be our rival in the important business about to be decided." They immediately displayed their cloths, which were so fine that they could pass through the eye of a large needle, though not that of a small one. Elated by this, the king used it as a pretext to deny their claims. He ordered the magistrates to bring the needle that he had selected out of the City Treasury, where it had been carefully kept during the princes' absence. There was a good deal of murmuring when he did this. The friends of the princes, particularly those of the eldest, whose cloth was made of the finer material, protested, "It's downright chicanery." "The king is too cunning and deceptive." The king's followers contended that he was merely bound by the conditions he had proposed. The matter seemed settled when suddenly they heard a fine flourish of trumpets, kettle drums, and oboes, announcing the arrival of our prince in all his pomp and accoutrements. The king and his two other sons were all equally thunderstruck by such splendor.

After the prince had respectfully greeted his father and embraced his brothers, he revealed a box dotted with rubies. In it was the walnut. He cracked it expecting to find the boasted piece of cloth, but instead found a hazel nut, which he also cracked. Lo, he was surprised to find a cherrystone! Everybody looked at one another, and the king laughed up his sleeve at his son, who had been naive enough to believe he could bring a whole piece of cloth in a walnut. Yet, why shouldn't the prince have believed it when he had already given the king a dog that had emerged from an acorn? Therefore, he cracked the cherrystone and found a kernel. A great murmur arose in the room. Everyone was convinced that the young prince had been duped in this adventure, but he did not respond to the courtiers' raillery. Opening the kernel, he found in it a grain of wheat and in the grain of wheat a millet seed. In truth, he began to have doubts himself and muttered between his teeth, "White cat, white cat, you've fooled me!" Instantly he felt a cat's claw on his hand give him such a scratch that blood began to flow. He knew not whether this scratch was given to encourage or to dishearten him, but he nevertheless opened the millet seed, and the entire company was astonished when he drew out a piece of cloth four hundred yards long, so wonderfully wrought that all the birds, beasts, and fish were depicted in their natural colors along with the trees, fruits, and plants of the earth; rocks, rare gems, and shells of the ocean; the sun, the moon, the great and lesser heavenly bodies. There were also portraits of all the kings and lesser sovereigns reigning in the world at that time, with those of their wives, mistresses, children, and all their subjects, not omitting the smallest urchin—everyone in his particular walk of life accurately represented and dressed in the garb of his country.

When the king saw this piece of cloth, he became as pale as the prince had become red with bewilderment when he had not at first found it. The needle was produced, and the prince passed and repassed the cloth through the eye of it six times. The king and the two elder princes looked on in sullen silence, except at those moments when the beauty and uniqueness of the cloth forced them to acknowledge that nothing in the universe could compare to it.

The king heaved a deep sigh and, turning toward his sons, said, "Nothing gives me as much consolation in my old age as observing the deference paid by you to my wishes. Consequently, I want to put your obedience to a new test. Go and travel for another year, and he who at the end of it brings back the most beautiful maiden shall marry her and be crowned king on his wedding day. It's necessary anyway that my successor should marry, and I pledge my troth that I'll no longer defer bestowing the reward I have promised."

This unjust decision went especially against our prince, for the little dog and piece of cloth were worth more than ten kingdoms. He was so well bred, though, that he would not contest his father's will, and he promptly reentered his calèche. His whole entourage followed him, and he took the road back to his dear white cat. She knew the day, the very moment he would arrive. The entire way was strewn with flowers; thousands of vases exuded perfume everywhere and particularly within the castle. The white cat was seated on a Persian carpet under a pavilion of cloth of gold in a gallery, and from there she saw him approach, received by the hands that had always attended him. All the cats climbed up into the gutters to welcome him with a desperate squalling.

"So, Prince," the white cat said, "you've returned once more without a crown."

"Madam," he replied, "your generosity has placed me in a position to obtain it, but I'm convinced that it would have given the king more pain to part with it than the pleasure I would have gained from acquiring it."

"It matters not at all," she said. "Nothing shall be overlooked if you want to win it, for I'll help you in this affair. Since you're obliged to return with a beautiful maiden to your father's court, I'll find one who'll help you obtain the prize. In the meantime, let us be merry. I've ordered a naval combat between my cats and the terrible rats of this country. My cats will perhaps be embarrassed a little, for they're afraid of water. On the other hand, they would have too much of an advantage, and one ought to equalize matters as much as possible."

Admiring the prudence of madam puss, the prince heaped praises on her and accompanied her to a terrace that overlooked the sea.

The ships in which the cats embarked were large pieces of cork, on which they managed to sail conveniently enough, and the rats had bound several eggshells together for their navy. The battle was long and cruel. The rats flung themselves into the water and swam much better than the cats so that they triumphed and were defeated alternately twenty times. However,

Minagrobis, admiral of the feline fleet, reduced the rattish race to utmost despair when he devoured the general of their forces, an old rat of great experience, who had been around the world three times in splendid ships where he had been neither captain nor common sailor but simply a lickspittle. The white cat would not permit the utter destruction of all these poor unfortunate creatures. A smart politician, she calculated that if there were no more rats or mice left in the country, her subjects would live in a state of idleness that might work to her disadvantage.

The prince spent this year as he had the two previous ones, hunting, fishing, or playing chess, which the white cat did extremely well. He could not help occasionally questioning her as to the miraculous power that enabled her to speak. He asked her whether she was a fairy, or been transformed into a cat, but since she never said anything but what she chose, she never gave answers that did not wholly suit her. Consequently, her replies consisted of a number of fragments that signified nothing in particular, and he clearly perceived she was not inclined to share her secret with him.

Nothing flies faster than time spent without trouble or sorrow, and if the cat had not been careful to remember the day when the prince had to return to court, he certainly would have forgotten it. On the eve of his departure she told him that everything depended on him taking home one of the most beautiful princesses in the world. "The hour to destroy that fatal work of the fairies has finally arrived. You must cut off my head and tail and fling them quickly into the fire."

"Me?" the prince exclaimed. "Blanchette, my love! I can't be so barbarous as to kill you! Ah, you undoubtedly mean to test my heart. But rest assured that it is incapable of forgetting the love and gratitude it owes you."

"No, Prince," she replied, "I don't suspect you of ingratitude. Well I know your worth. Neither you nor I control our destiny in this matter. Do as I bid you, and then we'll both begin to be happy. On my word of honor as a noble cat, you'll discover that I'm truly your friend."

The eyes of the young prince welled up with tears at the mere thought of being obliged to cut off the head of his little kitten, so pretty and so charming. He said all the most tender things he could think of in order to induce her to spare him such a trial. However, she persisted in replying that she wanted to die by his hand, and that only this way would he prevent his brothers from obtaining the crown. In a word, she urged him so earnestly that he drew his sword tremblingly, and with a faltering hand he sliced off the head and tail of his dearly beloved cat.

The very next moment he beheld the most charming transformation imaginable. The body of the white cat swelled in size and changed suddenly into that of an indescribably perfect young maiden. Her eyes enthralled everyone's heart, and her sweetness held them captive. Her form was majestic, her demeanor noble and modest, her spirit, gentle, her manners, engaging. She was, in sum, the most charming being in the world.

The prince was so struck with amazement at the pleasant sight of her that he thought he was enchanted. He could not speak or open his eyes wide enough to take her in enough. His astonishment became even greater when he saw an extraordinary number of lords and ladies enter the room. Each had his or her cat's skin flung over a shoulder as they advanced and threw themselves at the feet of their queen. "How great is our pleasure at seeing you restored to your natural form!" She received them with signs of affection that clearly indicated the goodness of her heart, and after spending a short time in their company, she requested that they leave her alone with the prince, to whom she told the following tale:

I don't want you to think, my lord, that I've always been a cat, or that my birth was an obscure one in the eyes of men. My father was king of six realms. He loved my mother tenderly and gave her complete liberty to do whatever she liked. Her great love was traveling, and shortly before I was born, she took a journey to a certain mountain about which she had heard the most extraordinary tales. While traveling there, she was told that she was then passing near an ancient fairy castle, the most beautiful in the world. At least this is what people believed according to legend. Since nobody ventured there, they could not know for certain, but they did know that the fairies had in their garden the finest, most delicious, and most delicate fruit that one could ever eat.

My mother immediately had such an overwhelming desire to taste some that she turned her steps toward the castle. She arrived at the gate of that superb edifice, which blazed with gold and azure on all sides, but when she knocked, nobody appeared to answer. It seemed as if everyone in the castle were dead. Her desire grew in proportion to the obstacle. She sent for ladders so that her attendants might climb over the garden walls, and they would have succeeded had not the said walls visibly increased in height, even though no one was seen to cause this. They lengthened the ladders by tying two or three together, but they broke under the weight of those who mounted them, and the attendants were either crippled or killed.

The queen was in despair. She saw the large trees laden with what looked like delicious fruit, and was determined to eat some or die. Ordering several splendid tents to be pitched before the castle, she remained there six weeks with her entire entourage. She neither slept nor ate, but sighed unceasingly and talked of nothing but the fruit in the inaccessible garden. In the end she fell dangerously ill without anyone being able to find a cure for her illness, for the inexorable fairies had never appeared so much as once since she had set up the tents. All her officers were deeply troubled. Nothing was to be heard but sobs and sighs, and the dying queen kept asking for fruit from her attendants and cared only for that which was denied her.

"One night, awakening from a doze, she opened her eyes and saw an ugly, decrepit old woman seated in an armchair at the head of her bed. Even as she stared, shocked that her women had allowed a stranger to come so near her, the old woman said, "We think your majesty is very obstinate in persisting in your desire to eat our fruit, but since your life is precariously hanging on this, my sisters and I consent to give you as much as you can eat on the spot as well as whatever you can carry away with you. However, you must give us something in exchange."

"Ah, heavens! I can't purchase such fruit at too high a price."

"We wish to have the daughter whom you are about to bring into the world," she said. "As soon as she is born, we'll come and fetch her, and she'll be brought up among us. There are no virtues, charms, or accomplishments with which we shall not endow her. In a word, she'll be our child, and we'll make her happy. But be advised that your majesty will not be allowed to see her anymore until she is married. If this proposal is agreeable to you, I'll cure you instantly and lead you into our orchard. Even though it's night, you'll be able to see well enough to pick whatever fruit you desire. If what I have said does not please you, then good night, Queen, I'm going to bed."

"Hard as the condition may be that you impose upon me," the queen replied, "I'll accept it sooner than die, for I know I cannot live another day, and my infant would therefore perish with me. Cure me, wise fairy," she continued, "and don't postpone for one moment the opportunity of enjoying the privilege you've promised."

The fairy touched her with a golden wand, saying, "Let your majesty be free from all the ills that confine you to this bed!"

It seemed to the queen that someone had instantaneously stripped off a heavy, stiff robe that had oppressed her, though some portions of it still clung to her, apparently in the places most affected by her disorder. Sending for all her ladies, she told them with a smiling countenance that she was quite well and was going to get up. "Soon those gates of the fairy palace, so well bolted and barred, will be opened for me to enter, and I'll be able to eat the fine fruit and take away as much as I like."

All of her ladies thought the queen was seeing things in her delirium because she wanted the fruit so much. Instead of replying, they began to weep, and some went to waken all the physicians to come and see the state their majesty was in.

This delay exasperated the queen, but when she ordered them to bring her clothes to her instantly, they refused. She flew into a passion, turning red with rage. This they attributed to fever, but once the physicians arrived, felt her pulse, and went through the usual ceremonies, they could not deny that she was in perfect health. Her women, who realized the mistake that their zeal had caused them to make, tried to atone for it by asking her majesty's pardon and dressing her as quickly as possible. Peace was restored, and the queen quickly followed the old fairy, who was still waiting for her.

She entered the palace, which required nothing to make it the most beautiful place in the world. Two other fairies, somewhat younger than the one who conducted my mother, received her at the gate and welcomed her graciously. She asked them to lead her straight into the garden and to those espaliers where she would find the best fruit.

"Everything is equally good," they said to her, "and if it weren't for the fact that you desire the pleasure of picking it yourself, we need only call the fruit we wish for, and it will come to us here."

"I implore you, ladies," the queen said, "to show me such an extraordinary sight."

The eldest fairy put her finger into her mouth and whistled three times. Then she cried, "Apricots, peaches, nectarines, *brunions*, sherries, plums, pears, *bigaroons*, melons, muscatel grapes, apples, oranges, lemons, gooseberries, strawberries, raspberries, come at my call!"

"But," the queen said, "all the fruit that you've summoned cannot be found at the same season."

"In our orchard," they replied, "we have all the fruits of the earth. They're always ripe, always excellent, and they never spoil."

Meanwhile, the fruit rolled in over the floor pell-mell, but without being bruised or dirtied. So, the queen, eager to satisfy her longing, threw herself on them and took the first that came to hand, devouring rather than eating it.

After having partly satisfied her appetite, she begged the fairies to let her proceed to the espaliers so that she might have the pleasure of choosing the fruit on the tree and then gathering it. "We freely give you permission," they said, "but remember the promise you've made us. You won't be allowed to rescind it!"

"I'm convinced," she said, "that you live so well here, and this palace appears to me so beautiful that if I did not love my husband dearly, I'd propose remaining here with you along with my daughter. Therefore, you need have no fear about by retracting my word."

Completely satisfied, the fairies opened all their gardens and enclosures to her. She remained there three days and three nights without wishing to go out again because she found everything so delicious. She gathered the fruit to take home with her, and since it did not spoil, she had four thousand mules loaded with the fruit. In addition, the fairies gave her the most exquisite golden baskets in which to carry it and many other precious items. They promised her that I would be educated like a princess and that they would make me a model of perfection and choose a husband for me. "You will receive notice of the wedding, and we hope you will attend."

The king was delighted by the queen's return, and the entire court rejoiced as well. There were nothing but balls, masquerades, runnings at the ring, and banquets, at which the queen's fruit was served as a delicious treat. The king preferred to eat the fruit over anything else offered him, but he knew not of the bargain the queen had made with the fairies.

He often asked her where she had traveled to find such good things. One time she told him that she had found them on an almost inaccessible mountain. Another time she said they grew in some valleys. Other times she named a garden or great forest. Surprised by so many contradictions, the king questioned those who had accompanied her, but she had so strictly forbidden them to tell anyone of her adventure that they dared not talk about it. Eventually the queen became uneasy about the promise she had made the fairies, and as the time for her to give birth approached, she fell into an alarming state of melancholy. She kept sighing constantly and looked worse and worse every day. After a great deal of probing, she informed him of everything that had occurred with her and the fairies, and how she had promised to give them the daughter she was about to bring into the world.

"What?" said the king. "We have no other children. You know how much I want some, and for the sake of eating two or three apples you gave away our daughter? You have no feelings for me!" He overwhelmed her with a thousand reproaches, which were almost the death of my poor mother, but that did not satisfy him. He had her locked up in a tower and surrounded it with soldiers to prevent her from having communication with anyone except the officers of her household. These, too, he changed so they were not the same as those who had been with her at the fairy castle.

The misunderstanding between the king and the queen threw the whole court into consternation, and everybody changed into clothes more suitable to the general sorrow. The king, for his part, appeared inexorable. He never saw his wife, and as soon as I was born, he had me brought into the palace to be nursed, while she remained a most unhappy prisoner.

The fairies, knowing all that took place, became annoyed. They regarded me as their property and my detention as a theft. Before seeking vengeance appropriate to their anger, they sent a grand embassy to the king to warn him that he had better set the queen free, restore her to his favor, and surrender me to their ambassadors so that I could be nursed and brought up by the fairies. The ambassadors were so little and deformed (for they were hideous dwarfs) that they did not have the power to persuade the king to comply with their request. He refused bluntly, and if they had not taken their departure instantly, something worse might have befallen them. When the fairies heard of my father's conduct, they were highly indignant, and after demolishing his six kingdoms by inflicting every ill they could devise on them, they let loose a terrible dragon that poisoned the air wherever he breathed, wilting all the trees and plants, and devoured man and child.

In the throes of despair, the king consulted all the wise men in his dominions as to what he should do to protect his subjects from the misfortunes that were overwhelming them. They advised him on the one hand to seek out the best physicians and the most excellent remedies throughout the world, and on the other, to offer a free pardon to all criminals under the death penalty who would agree to fight the dragon. The king approved of this advice and acted on it immediately, but without success, for the pestilence continued and the dragon devoured all those who attacked him. Finally the king turned to a fairy who had been his friend from childhood. She was very old and rarely left her bed. Going to see her, he reproached her a thousand times for permitting fate to persecute him without coming to his rescue. "What would you have me do?" she said. "You've irritated my sisters. They're as powerful as I am, and we rarely act against one another. Try to appease them by giving them your daughter. The little princess rightfully belongs to them. You've put the queen in prison. What has that charming woman done for you to treat her so severely? It would be best if you decided to keep your wife's pledge to the fairies. I assure you, you'll be rewarded greatly if you do."

My father loved me dearly, but seeing no other way of saving his kingdoms from the lethal dragon, he told his friend he would take her advice. He was willing to surrender me to the fairies since she had assured him that I'd be cherished and treated as a princess of my rank ought to be. He also agreed to allow the queen to come back to the court. Finally he told the fairy that she should name the person who should carry me to the fairy castle, and it would be done. "You may even remain in its vicinity if you desire, to witness the celebration that will take place there."

The king told her that he would go there with the queen within a week's time and asked her to notify her sister fairies of his intention so that they might make the necessary arrangements.

As soon as he returned to the palace, he sent for the queen and received her with as much affection and regard as he had exhibited rashness and anger when he imprisoned her. She was so changed and melancholy that he would hardly have recognized her if his heart had not assured him she was the same person he had formerly loved so tenderly. With tears in his eyes he implored her to forget the misery he had caused her and assured her she would never again experience anything like that on his account. She replied, "I brought it upon myself by my imprudence in promising our daughter to the fairies. If anything could excuse my actions, it was the condition to which I had been reduced at the time."

The king then informed her that he had decided to place me in the hands of the fairies. The queen, in her turn, opposed this intention. It seemed as if some fatality was hanging over this affair, and that I was forever doomed to be a subject of dissension between my father and mother. After she groaned and wept for a considerable time without obtaining her goal (for the king saw too clearly the fatal consequences of hesitating, and our subjects continued to perish as if they were answerable for the faults of our family), she consented to all he desired, and everything was prepared for the leave taking.

I was placed in a mother-of-pearl cradle ornamented with the most elegant things that art could ever conceive. Hanging from every side were garlands and festoons of flowers made of jewels, whose different colors reflected the rays of the sun with such dazzling splendor that you could scarcely look upon them. The magnificence of my swaddling surpassed that of the cradle, if that be possible, for all the bands of my clothes were formed of large pearls. Twenty-four princesses of royal blood carried me on a delicate litter. Though their dresses were all different, they were not allowed to wear any color but white in token of my innocence. The entire court accompanied me according to rank.

While we were climbing the mountain, we heard a melodious symphony more and more distinctly. At length thirty-six fairies appeared, for the trio of before had invited their friends to accompany them. Each was seated in a pearl shell larger than that in which Venus arose from the ocean. Seahorses, which seemed rather awkward in getting overland, drew these pearl cars, and though the occupants wore more sumptuous finery than the greatest queens in the universe, they were at the same time old and ugly hags.

The dragon who had been their instrument of vengeance followed them in chains of diamonds. They carried olive branches to signify to the king that his submission had found favor with them, and when I was presented, their caresses were so extraordinary that they seemed to have no other goal in life except to make me happy. They took me in their arms, kissed me a thousand times, endowed me with various gifts, and then began to dance the fairy brawl. It is a very lively dance, and it's hard to imagine how well these old ladies jumped and capered. Afterward, the dragon that had devoured so many people crawled forward, and the three fairies to whom my mother had promised me seated themselves upon it. Then they placed my cradle between them and struck the dragon with a wand. It immediately spread its great, scaly wings, which were finer than gauze and glittered with all sorts of extraordinary colors, and in this way did they return to their castle. On seeing me aloft on this terrible dragon, my mother could not help shrieking over and over again. The king consoled her, saying "My friend the old fairy has assured me that no misfortune will befall her. She'll be as well taken care of as if she had remained in our own palace." The queen was calmed by this assurance, though she continued to be distraught at the idea of being separated from me for such a long time. She felt she was to blame for everything, for if she had not insisted on eating the fruit of that garden, I would have been brought up in my father's realm and would never have suffered the misfortunes that I still must relate to you.

Know, then, Prince, that my guardians had built a tower expressly for my abode, and it had a thousand beautiful apartments suitable for each season of the year, magnificent furniture, and amusing books. But it was without doors so that one could only enter it by the windows, which were set very high. Atop this tower was a beautiful garden ornamented with flowers, fountains, and green arbors, where you could remain cool on the hottest of dog days. Here was the place where I was brought up by the fairies, and the care they took of me even exceeded what they had promised the queen. She would have thought every day was my wedding day. I was taught everything befitting my age and rank. I didn't give them much trouble because I learned almost everything with the greatest ease. My docility pleased them, and since I never saw another soul, I might have lived there in perfect tranquillity for the rest of my life.

When the fairies came to see me, they were always mounted on the terrible dragon I have already mentioned. Since they never mentioned the king or queen and called me their daughter, I believed myself to be so. Nobody lived with me in the tower except a parrot and a small dog that they had given me to amuse myself, for the creatures were endowed with reason and conversed remarkably well.

On one side of the tower was a path lined with deep ruts and trees that so choked the road that I had never seen anyone pass by since I had been shut up there. But one day when I was at the window talking with my parrot and my dog, I heard a noise. Looking all around, I noticed a young cavalier who had stopped to listen to our conversation. I had never seen a young man before but in a painting, and I was glad that chance provided me with this opportunity. Not dreaming of the danger that accompanies the pleasure of contemplating such a charming object, I leaned forward to gaze at him, and the more I looked, the more was I delighted. He made a profound bow, stared at me, and seemed frustrated that he could not find a way to converse with me, for my window was very high and he feared being overheard, since he knew well enough that I was in the castle of the fairies.

The night came suddenly upon us, or, to be more precise, it came without our noticing it. He blew his horn two or three times, entertaining me with a few flourishes. Then he took his leave, and I was unable to ascertain which way he had gone because the night was so dark. I remained meditative, no longer feeling the same pleasure in talking to my parrot and dog that I had felt before. They said the prettiest things in the world to me, for fairy creatures are very witty, but my mind was preoccupied and I was too naive to conceal it. Perroquet noticed it, and since he was a shrewd bird, he revealed no sign of what was going on in his mind.

As soon as it was light, I got up and ran to my window. Of course, I was most pleasantly surprised to see the young knight at the foot of the tower. He was so magnificently dressed that I imagined that it must be partly on my account, and I wasn't mistaken. He addressed me through a sort of speaking horn, informing me that until then he had been indifferent to the charms of all the beautiful women he had seen, but now he was so overwhelmed by my beauty that he could not imagine how he could live without seeing me every day. Greatly pleased by this compliment, I was at the same time very disturbed that I dared not reply, for I would have been compelled to cry out with all my might and run the risk of being better heard by the fairies than by him. I threw him some flowers I had in my hand that he received as a favorable sign. Kissing them several times and thanking me, he asked me if I would approve of his standing under my window every day at the same hour, and if so, to throw him something else. A turquoise ring I had on my finger I instantly pulled off and flung to him. Then I gave him a signal to depart as quickly as possible because I heard the fairy Violente mounting her dragon on the other side of the tower to bring me my breakfast.

The first words she uttered on entering my room were "I smell the voice of a man here. Search, dragon!"

Oh, how upset I was! My heart was sinking, for I was afraid the monster would fly out through the opposite window and follow the cavalier. "Indeed, my good mama," I said (for the old fairy liked me to call her so), "you're jesting, surely, when you say you smell the voice of a man. Is it possible to smell a voice? And if so, what mortal would be rash enough to venture climbing this tower?"

"What you say is true, daughter," she replied. "I'm delighted to hear you reason so nicely, and I suppose the hatred I bear all men sometimes makes me imagine they're near." Giving me my breakfast and my spindle, she said, "After you've had your breakfast, don't forget to spin, for you did nothing yesterday, and my sisters will be angry with you." In fact, I had been so preoccupied by the stranger that I had found it quite impossible to spin.

As soon as the fairy was gone, I rebelliously tossed my spindle aside and ascended to the terrace to look out as far as I could see. I had an excellent telescope, and there was nothing to interrupt the view. In every direction I looked until I discovered my cavalier on the summit of a mountain. He was resting beneath a rich pavilion of gold cloth and surrounded by a large entourage. I was convinced that he was the son of some king who reigned in the vicinity. Since I feared that if he returned to the tower, he would be discovered by the terrible dragon, I fetched my parrot and told him to fly to the mountain. "There you will find the person who had spoken to me. Beg him in my name never to come again, for I fear my vigilant guardians will surely do him harm."

Perroquet carried out his task like a clever parrot. The courtiers were all surprised to see him flying at full speed, and watched him perch on their master's shoulder and whisper in his ear. The king (for that's what he proved to be) was both delighted and troubled by this message. My anxiety on his account he found encouraging, but the many obstacles barring him from speaking to me distressed him. Still, he was bent on wooing me and asked Perroquet a hundred questions. Perroquet asked him as many in return, for he was naturally inquisitive. The king gave him a ring to bring to me in return for my turquoise. It was a turquoise as well, but much finer than mine, for it was shaped like a heart and encircled by diamonds. "It's fitting," he told the parrot, "that I treat you as an ambassador. Therefore, let me give you my portrait. Show it to no one but your charming mistress." He tied the miniature under the bird's wing, and the ring he brought me in his beak.

I awaited the return of my little green courier with an impatience I had never known before. He told me that the person to whom I had sent him was a great king. "I was most kindly received by him, and you may rest assured he only lives for your sake. Despite the grave danger in coming to the foot of the tower, he is determined to brave everything rather than renounce the pleasure of seeing you."

These tidings greatly perplexed me, and I began to weep. Perroquet and my little dog Toutou did their best to console me because they loved me with a great deal of tenderness. Then Perroquet gave me the king's ring and showed me his portrait. I confess I had never been so delighted as by being able to regard the king's image closely, since I had only seen him at a distance. He appeared to me much more charming than I had supposed. A hundred notions rushed into my mind, some pleasant, some distressing, and my conflict made me appear extraordinarily anxious.

The fairies who came to see me noticed it. They remarked to one another that I undoubtedly tired of my dull life. "It's time we find her a husband of the fairy race." Several were proposed and eventually they settled on little King Migonnet. His kingdom was some five hundred miles away, but that was, of course, a trifle for them.

Overhearing their discussion, Perroquet darted away to give me an account. "Ah," he said, "how I'd pity you, my dear mistress, if you were to become the queen of Migonnet. He's a frightful monkey. I'm sorry to relate this, but to tell you the truth, the king who loves you wouldn't condescend to have him for his footman."

"Have you seen him, Perroquet?"

"Indeed, I have," the bird continued. "I was brought up on the same branch with him."

"What? On a branch?" I exclaimed.

"Yes," he said, "he has talons like an eagle."

I was extremely disturbed by this account. I gazed at the charming portrait of the young king, certain he had given it to Perroquet so I could have the opportunity of beholding him. When I compared it to the description of Migonnet, I felt I had nothing more to hope for in life, and I was determined to die rather than marry this creature.

I did not sleep a wink that night, talking matters over with Perroquet and Toutou. I dozed a little toward daybreak, and since my dog had a good nose, he smelled the king at the foot of the tower and woke Perroquet. "I'll wager" he said, "the king's below."

Perroquet replied, "Hold your tongue, babbler. Just because your eyes and ears are almost always open, you envy others their peace."

"Wager something, then," insisted good Toutou. "I'm sure he's there."

"And I'm sure he's not," replied Perroquet. "Didn't I forbid him to come here in my mistress's name?"

"Oh, you amuse me with your forbiddances," my dog exclaimed. "A man in love consults only his heart." All at once he began roughly tugging Perroquet by the wings, making him quite vexed. The clamor they made woke me, and they told me what had started their quarrel. I ran, or rather flew, to my window, and I saw the king, who extended his arms toward me and said through his horn that he could no longer live without me. "I implore you, find some way to escape from your tower, or find some way I can enter." He called upon all the gods and all the elements to witness that he would marry me immediately and make me one of the mightiest queens in the world.

I ordered Perroquet to tell him that what he desired was quite impossible. Nevertheless, relying on his pledge and the oath he had taken, I was willing to attempt to carry out his wishes. But I implored him not to come every day since he might eventually be observed, and the fairies would show him no mercy.

He withdrew filled with joy at the hope I had given him, and I found myself in a great quandary when I began to consider the promise I had made him. How was I to escape from a tower that had no doors? I had no one to help me but Perroquet and Toutou! I? So young and inexperienced and timid? After considering this, I decided against an attempt that would never succeed, and I sent word to that effect by Perroquet to the king. At first he was going to kill himself before the bird's eyes, but then he charged him to persuade me either to witness his death or to bring him some comfort. "Sire," exclaimed my feathered ambassador, "my mistress is more than willing. She just lacks the means."

When the bird repeated to me all that had transpired, I felt more wretched than ever. The fairy Violente came to see me and noticed my eyes red and swollen. She observed that I had been crying and said, "Unless you tell me the cause, I shall burn you alive."

Her threats were always terrible, and I replied, trembling, that I was tired of spinning and wanted instead to make some nets to snare the young birds that pecked the fruit in my garden. "Cry no longer, my daughter," she said. "I'll bring you as much twine as you need." Indeed, I received it that very evening, but she advised me to concern myself less about working than about my personal appearance since King Migonnet was expected to arrive shortly. I shuddered when I heard these fateful tidings and gave no reply.

As soon as she had left, I began to make two or three pieces of net with the object of constructing a rope ladder, which I succeeded in doing very well, though I had never seen one. As it happens, the fairy never furnished me with as much twine as I needed and continually said to me, "Why, daughter, your work is like that of Penelope. You never make any progress, and yet you keep asking for more material."

"Oh, my good mama," I replied, "it's easy for you to talk. Don't you see I'm very awkward at my work and burn a good deal of it? Are you afraid I'll cause your ruin because of the thread?" My naive air amused her, though she was a very ill-tempered and cruel creature.

I sent Perroquet to tell the king to be under the window of the tower on a certain evening, and he would find the ladder and learn the rest when he arrived. I fastened it as securely as possible since I was determined to make my escape with him. However, when he saw it, he did not wait for me to descend, but mounted it eagerly and jumped into my room just as I was preparing everything for my flight.

The sight of him so delighted me that I forgot all about the danger. He renewed all his vows and implored me not to postpone becoming his wife. We took Perroquet and Toutou as witnesses of our marriage. Never was a wedding between two persons of such exalted rank celebrated with less fanfare or commotion, and never were two hearts so perfectly happy as ours.

Day had not dawned when the king left me. I had told him of the fairies' dreadful intention to marry me to little Migonnet, and my description of this creature horrified him as much as it had me. The hours seemed long years to me after the king's departure. Running to the window to follow him with my eyes despite the darkness, I saw to my astonishment a fiery chariot in the air being drawn by winged salamanders. It flew so fast that I could scarcely follow it, and it was escorted by several soldiers mounted on ostriches. I didn't have time to distinguish who the ugly creature was speeding through the sky, but I easily surmised that it must be either a fairy or an enchanter.

Shortly afterward, the fairy Violente entered my room. "I bring you good news," she said. "Your lover has just arrived. Be prepared to receive him. Here are some dresses and jewels for you."

"And who has told you," I exclaimed, "that I desire to be married? It's not at all my desire. Send King Migonnet away again. I won't add a pin to my dress. I don't care whether he thinks I'm beautiful or ugly. I'm not going to be his."

"What's this I hear?" the fairy responded. "We have a young rebel here? We've a head without any brains in it! I won't be trifled with, I warn you—"

"What will you do to me?" I cried, reddening at the names she had called me. "Can you make life more miserable for me than it is already? I live in this tower with only a dog and a parrot, and I see only the horrible form of a dreadful dragon several times a day."

"Ha, you ungrateful little wretch," the fairy said, "you haven't deserved in the least all the care and consideration we've shown you. I've often told my sisters we'd reap nothing from all our labors!" She departed to find them, and when she told them about our quarrel, they were just as taken aback as she was.

Perroquet and Toutou scolded me, vowing that if I continued to be so insolent, I'd suffer the terrible consequences. I felt so proud of possessing the heart of a great king that I despised the fairies and the advice of my poor little companions. I didn't dress myself, and I took pleasure in mussing my hair so that Migonnet might think me ugly.

Our meeting took place on the terrace. Arriving in his fiery chariot, he was tinier than the smallest dwarf I'd ever seen. Supporting himself on a pair of diamond crutches, he walked on his eagle's talons and on his knees at the same time because he had no bones in his legs. His royal mantle was only a half yard long, and yet more than a third of it dragged on the ground. His head was as large as a peck measure, and his nose was so big that a dozen birds sat on it, warbling to entertain him. He had such a bushy beard that canaries made their nests in it. His ears rose more than a foot above his head, but they were not so noticeable because of the high-pointed crown that he wore to make him appear taller. The flames of his chariot roasted the fruit, scorched the flowers, and dried up the fountains, and his chief equerry was obliged to lift him. But as soon as he was brought near me, I fled into my room and locked the door and all the windows.

Extremely angry with me, Migonnet returned to the fairies and they begged his pardon a thousand times for my rudeness. To appease him, for they feared him a great deal, they decided to bring him into my room while I slept to tie me hand and foot, place me in his fiery chariot, and take me away with him. After conceiving this plan, they scarcely said a cross word to me about my rude behavior to him. Instead they merely advised me to think about making amends.

Perroquet and Toutou were astonished by such kindness on their part. "Do you know, mistress," my dog said, "I have some sneaking suspicions. My lady fairies are acting strangely, particularly Violente."

I laughed at these fears, while I awaited my dear husband's arrival with great anxiety. He was too impatient to keep me waiting long. I threw him the rope ladder, fully determined to flee with him. He mounted it sprightly and said such tender things that even now I don't dare recall them to mind.

While we were conversing together, as calmly as if we had been in his own palace, the windows of my room suddenly burst open. The fairies entered on their terrible dragon. Migonnet followed them in his fiery chariot flanked by all his guards on their ostriches. Fearlessly drawing his sword, the king thought only of rescuing me from the most dreadful fate that ever awaited a mortal. In brief—I don't know whether I should tell you this, my lord—those barbarous creatures set their dragon on him, and the beast devoured him before my eyes.

Driven to despair by his fate and my own, I flung myself at the jaws of the horrible monster, hoping he would swallow me along with all that I loved in the world. He was quite willing to comply, but the fairies were even crueler than the dragon and would not permit it. "We must save her so that her agony will be prolonged," they cried. "A speedy death is too mild a punishment for this unworthy creature!"

They touched me, and I found myself immediately transformed into a white cat. Then they conducted me to this superb palace, which used to belong to my father. They transformed all the lords and ladies of the kingdom into cats, left only the hands visible of the rest of his court, and reduced me to the deplorable condition in which you found me. Finally, they informed me about my birth and the death of my father and mother, and told me, "You will be released from your catlike form only by a prince who exactly resembles the husband we have just eliminated."

"It is you, my lord, who bear that resemblance," she concluded. "You have the same features, the same air, the same voice. I was struck by it the moment I saw you. I knew about everything that happened, and I'm equally aware of all that will happen. My troubles are about to end."

"And mine, lovely queen," said the prince, flinging himself at her feet. "How long will they last?"

"I already love you more than my life, my lord," the queen said. "You must return to your father, and we'll be able to ascertain there how he feels about me, and if he'll consent to what you desire."

Leaving the castle, the prince gave her his hand as she stepped into a chariot much more magnificent than those she had previously provided for him. The rest of the equipage matched the brilliance of the chariot, and even the hooves of the horses were shod with emeralds and nailed with diamonds. Such a thing has perhaps never been seen except on that occasion. I shall not repeat the pleasant conversation that took place between the queen and the prince on their journey. If her beauty was incomparable, her mind was no less superb, and the equally perfect young prince exchanged all sorts of charming thoughts with her.

As they neared the castle in which the prince was to meet his two elder brothers, the queen entered a little rock of crystal, the points of which were ornamented with gold and rubies. Completely surrounded by curtains so that no one could see in, it was carried by some handsome young men superbly attired. Remaining in the chariot, the prince saw his brothers walking with two extremely beautiful princesses. As soon as they sighted him, they came forth to greet him and inquired, "Have you brought a lady with you?" He replied that he had experienced bad luck on his journey and had encountered only surpassingly ugly hags. "The only rare item I've brought back is a little white cat."

They began to laugh at his naiveté. "A cat?" they exclaimed. "Are you afraid the mice will eat up our palace?"

The prince admitted that he had been rather unwise in selecting such a present for his father.

Thereupon, they continued on their way to the city. The elder princes rode with their princesses in open carriages made of gold and azure, and their horses' heads were adorned with plumes of feathers and aigrettes. Nothing was more radiant than this cavalcade. Our young prince followed them, and behind him came the crystal rock, which everybody gazed at with wonder. Meanwhile the courtiers hastened to inform the king that the three princes were coming.

"Are they bringing beautiful ladies with them?" the king asked.

"It would be impossible to find any that could surpass them" was the answer, which appeared to displease him.

The two princes eagerly ascended the palace stairs with their wonderful princesses. The king received them graciously and could not decide which deserved the prize. He looked at his youngest son and said, "Have you returned alone this time?"

"Your majesty will see a little white cat in this rock," the prince replied. "It meows so sweetly and has such velvet paws that you'll be delighted with it." The king smiled and went to open the rock himself, but as soon as he approached it, the queen made it fly into pieces by means of a spring, and she suddenly appeared like the sun after it has been hidden in the clouds. Her hair fell in loose ringlets over her shoulders down to her very feet. She was crowned with flowers, and her gown was made of thin white gauze lined with rose-colored taffeta. As she made a most dignified curtsy to the king, he was so overcome by this wondrous appearance that he could not resist exclaiming, "Behold the incomparable beauty who deserves the crown!"

"My liege," she announced, "I come not to deprive you of a throne you fill so worthily, for I was born the heiress to six kingdoms. Permit me to offer one to you and one to each of your elder sons. I ask of you no other recompense than your friendship and this young prince for my husband. Three kingdoms will be quite enough for us."

The king and the entire court joined in shouts of joy and astonishment. The marriage was celebrated immediately, as well as those of the other two princes, and the court subsequently spent several months enjoying entertainment and pleasures of every kind imaginable. Finally each couple departed to reign over their own dominions. The beautiful white cat came to be immortalized in her realm due to her goodness and generosity as well as her rare talent and beauty.

> The handsome young prince was fortunate to find
> An illustrious princess beneath a cat's skin,
> Worthy to be adored and much inclined
> To share the throne her affection won for him.

> The willing heart is easily subdued
> By enchanting eyes set for conquest.
> When love's soft flame is fanned by gratitude,
> The charm will have more power and be full of zest.

> I cannot overlook that mother
> Who paid so dearly for her whim.
> Like Eve before she did not care about the other,
> And was well prepared to sacrifice her kin.

> Mothers beware and learn from this greedy queen!
> Don't tamper with a daughter's lot
> Or gratify the appetite and act so mean.
> Condemn her conduct and remember what she got.

THE BENEFICENT
FROG

ONCE upon a time there was a king who had waged war against his neighbors for many years. After an adverse campaign in which several battles had gone against him, they began to besiege his capital city. Since he was concerned about his queen, who was pregnant, he begged her to withdraw to a remote fortified castle. The queen begged him to allow her to remain near him, for she wanted to share his fate, and uttered piercing cries when he placed her in a coach and ordered her to depart. He promised her that he would disguise himself and steal away secretly to visit her, but he did so only to keep up her hopes, for the castle was faraway and surrounded by a thick forest. In fact, if one did not know the roads well, it was difficult to find. (He himself had visited it only once in his life.)

The queen set out, distressed at leaving her husband to confront the dangers of war. The guards that he had commanded to accompany her traveled by short stages, fearing she would be exhausted by such a long journey. At last she arrived at the castle very disquieted and melancholy. After she had sufficient rest, she wanted to make excursions in the vicinity, but she found nothing there to amuse her. Everywhere she looked, she saw immense forests that increased rather than diminished her sorrow. As she gazed at them sadly, she sometimes said, "What a difference between this abode and the one in which I've resided all my life! If I stay here much longer, I'll die. Who can I talk to in these solitary confines? To whom can I unburden my heart? What have I done to the king for him to banish me? It seems as though he wants to make me feel all the bitterness of his absence by sending me away to this horrid castle."

Such were her lamentations, and although the king wrote to her every day with hopeful tidings of the siege, she became all the more miserable and determined to return to him. She knew the officers he had placed around her had been ordered to prevent her from traveling to him unless he sent a courier expressly for that purpose, and she gave them no hint of her intention. On the pretense that she occasionally wanted to go hunting, she had a chariot made just big enough for herself. In it she followed the dogs so closely that the huntsmen could not keep up. As soon as she had learned how to control her chariot perfectly, she was in a position to go wherever she liked. Only one obstacle remained—she was unfamiliar with the roads in the forest—but she deluded herself into believing the gods would protect her on her journey.

After offering them sacrifices, she announced her intention to go on a grand hunt, at which she requested everyone to be present. She intended to go in her chariot, and each person was to take a divergent route so that the wild beasts would not be able to escape. They separated accordingly, and the young queen, thinking she would soon see her husband again, had dressed herself to great advantage. What with her hat covered with feathers of different colors and her vest ornamented with jewels, her uncommon beauty gave her the appearance of a second Diana. While her entourage was occupied by the pleasures of the chase, she gave her horses their head and urged them to go faster by her shouts and a few flicks of her whip. From a fast trot they broke into a gallop and finally took the bits between their teeth. Soon the chariot seemed to be propelled onward by the winds, and the poor queen repented her temerity. "What have I undertaken?" she cried. "I certainly won't be able to control the horses. They're too spirited and unmanageable. Alas, what will become of me? Ah, how would the king feel if he knew I was in danger? I know he loves me dearly and sent

me from the capital only to provide me with greater safety. How have I repaid his tender care of me! What's worse, my dear unborn may also be the victim of my imprudence."

The air resounded with her lamentations. She invoked the gods and the fairies for help, but they had abandoned her. Suddenly the chariot overturned. She lacked the agility to jump quickly enough, and her foot became caught between the wheel and the axle. It was nothing less than a miracle that she escaped from such a terrible accident with her life.

She was sprawled on the ground at the foot of a tree, unconscious and speechless, her face covered with blood. In this condition she remained for a long time. When she at last opened her eyes, she saw a gigantic woman clothed only in a lion's hide standing beside her. Her arms and legs were bare, and her hair was tied up with the dried skin of a serpent, whose head was hanging on her shoulders. She had a stone club in her hand for a staff and a quiver full of arrows at her side. Such an extraordinary figure convinced the queen that she was dead. Indeed, after such a serious spill she could not imagine how she could still be alive. In a low tone she murmured, "I'm not at all surprised that mortals are so unwilling to die. What one sees in the other world is frightful."

The giantess could not help laughing at the queen's presumption that she was dead. "Come to your senses," she said. "You see, you're still alive, but your fate will scarcely be less sad. I'm the fairy lioness, and I live nearby. You must come and spend your life with me now."

The queen looked sorrowfully at her and said, "If you'd take me back to my castle, madam lioness, and let the king know what price he must pay for my ransom, he'll give you half his kingdom, for he loves me dearly."

"No," the fairy replied, "I'm sufficiently rich. For some time now I've been bored living alone. You have some wit, and perhaps you'll amuse me." Upon saying this, she transformed herself into a lioness, placed the queen on her back, and carried her down to the bottom of her terrible grotto. As soon as she arrived, she cured the queen of the wounds she had received by rubbing her with a magic balm.

How astonished and distressed the poor queen was to find herself in this frightful abode! One had to descend ten thousand steps to reach this spot, which was at the very center of the earth. The only light, except that from several large lamps, came from the reflection of a lake of quicksilver. This lake was filled with monsters, whose various forms might have terrified a more courageous queen. Great screech owls and ravens and other birds of sinister omen could be heard there. In the distance rose a mountain from which streams trickled into a pool that was all but stagnant. These were all the tears that had ever been shed by unfortunate lovers and collected in reservoirs by compassionate cupids. The trees had neither leaves nor fruit, and the ground was covered with briars and nettles. The food was suitable to the climate of such an odious land. Dried roots, horse chestnuts, and wild berries were all that could be found to relieve the hunger of the unfortunate creatures who fell into the hands of the fairy lioness.

As soon as the queen was able to move about, the fairy told her to build herself a hut, since she would be remaining with her for the rest of her life. Hearing this, the queen could not refrain from weeping. "Ah, what have I done to you to make you want to keep me here?" she exclaimed. "If my death, which I feel approaching, will provide you with any pleasure, kill me at once, for this is all I venture to get from your pity. But don't condemn me to a long and wretched existence separated from my husband."

The lioness ridiculed her distress and advised her that she had better dry up her tears and try to please her, otherwise she would be the most miserable person in the world.

"What must I do, then, to soften your heart?" the queen asked.

"I'm very fond of fly pies," the fairy said. "Catch enough flies to make a large and excellent pie."

"But," the queen said, "I don't see any here, and even if there were, it's not light enough to catch them. And if I were to catch them, I've never made pastry. You're giving me an order that I can't carry out."

"No matter," the merciless lioness said. "Do as I say."

The queen did not respond. She thought that, in spite of the cruel fairy, she had but one life to lose, and in her wretched predicament what did she have to fear? Instead of looking for flies, she sat under a yew tree and began uttering sorrowful lamentations: "How distressed you'll be, my dear husband," she said, "when you begin looking for me and can't find me! You'll imagine I'm dead or unfaithful, and I'd prefer your mourning the loss of my life than that of my affection. Perhaps they'll find the fragments of my chariot in the forest and all the ornaments that I wore in the hope of pleasing you. If you find all this, you'll be convinced that I'm dead. How can I be certain that you won't give your heart to someone else? But at any event, I won't know it, for I'll never be allowed to return to the world."

She would have continued lamenting in this manner for much longer

had she not heard the mournful croaking of a raven over her head. She raised her eyes, and thanks to the scant light glimmering on the bank, she saw a large raven preparing to eat a frog in its talons. "Although there's no hope for me," she said, "I won't neglect saving a poor frog who's in as much trouble in its way as I am in mine."

Grabbing the first stick she could find, she made the raven abandon its prey. The frog fell to the ground and remained stupefied for some time. When it had regained its senses, it said, "Beautiful queen, you're the only kindhearted person I've met in these regions."

"What miracle enables you to speak, little frog?" the queen asked. "And who are the people you've seen here? I myself have yet to see any."

"All the monsters in this lake," the little frog replied, "lived in the world at one time. Some of them were kings, and others had the trust of their sovereigns. There are even some here who were mistresses of kings and cost the state a good deal of precious blood—they are those whom you see transformed into leeches. Fate sends them here for a specified time, but none of them return any better or improve their faults."

"I can easily understand," the queen said, "that herding so many wicked people together does not tend to aid their reformation. But with regard to yourself, good friend frog, what are you doing here?"

"Curiosity led me here," she replied. "I'm half fairy. My power is limited in certain things and extensive in others. If the fairy lioness recognized me in her domain, she'd slay me."

"How is it possible that a raven was about to eat you when you're half fairy?" the queen asked.

"A few words will make you understand," the frog replied. "When I have my little hood of roses on my head, I assume great power and fear nothing. But unfortunately, I had left it in the marsh when this wicked raven pounced upon me. I confess, madam, that if it hadn't been for you, I'd be no more, and since I owe you my life, your wish is my command if I can do anything to comfort yours."

"Alas, my dear frog," the queen said, "the wicked fairy who holds me captive wants me to make her a fly pastry. There are no flies here, and even if there were some, I can't see well enough to catch them. Please, I run a great risk of being beaten to death."

"Leave it to me," the frog said. "I'll provide you with plenty before long."

She immediately rubbed herself with sugar, and more than six thousand frogs, friends of hers, did the same. She then went to a storehouse filled with flies, for the wicked fairy lioness kept them expressly for tormenting certain unfortunate souls. As soon as the flies smelled the sugar, they settled onto it, and the friendly frogs returned at full gallop to the queen. Never has there been such a catch of flies, nor a better pastry than the one she made for the fairy lioness. When she presented it to her, the fairy was at a loss to understand how she had caught them.

Exposed to all the influences of the poisonous air, the queen cut down some cypress trees to use in building her hut, and the frog came to offer her generous services. She placed herself at the head of all those who had gone fly-catching, and they helped the queen in constructing a petite edifice that was the prettiest in the world. No sooner had she gone to bed, however, than the lake monsters, envious of her repose, came to torment her by making the most horrible clamor ever heard. Terrified, she got up and fled from the hut, which was just what the monsters wanted. Taking immediate possession was a dragon who had formerly been the tyrant of one of the finest kingdoms in the world.

The tormented queen complained of this outrage, but she was met only with ridicule. The monsters hooted at her, and the fairy lioness told her that if she kept annoying her with her complaints, she would break every bone in her body. So the queen was obliged to hold her tongue, sharing her woes only with the frog, who was certainly the best creature in the world. They wept together, for as soon as the frog had obtained her hood of roses, she was able to laugh and cry like anyone else.

"I have so much affection for you," she said, "that I'll rebuild your habitation, even though all the monsters of the lake will be furious."

She began cutting the wood on the spot, and the queen's petite rustic palace was built so quickly that the queen slept in it the same night. The frog took care of everything needed, including a bed of creeping thyme and wild thyme. When the wicked fairy found that the queen no longer slept on bare earth, she sent for her.

"Who are the men or gods that protect you?" she asked. "This land, which never gets rain other than showers of sulphur and fire, has never produced as much as a leaf of sage. Nevertheless, I've learned that scented herbs are growing along your path."

"I don't know why, madam," the queen said. "If I may attribute it to anything, it is to my infant yet unborn, who will perhaps be less unfortunate than myself."

"Be that as it may, I have a yearning for a bouquet of the rarest flowers. See if your little brat's good fortune will supply them for you. If it fails to do so, I shall not fail to apply stripes to your hide, for I administer them often and wonderfully well."

The queen broke down in tears. Such threats were anything but pleasant for her, and the impossibility of finding any flowers plunged her into despair. She returned to her small dwelling, and her friend the frog came to her.

"How melancholy you seem," she said to the queen.

"Alas, my dear friend, how could I be otherwise? The fairy demands a bouquet of the finest flowers. Where shall I find them? You see those that grow here. And yet I must pay with my life if I don't satisfy her."

"Charming princess," said the frog graciously, "I must try to get you out of this predicament. I've had dealings with a certain bat here. She's a good creature and can travel faster than I. I'll give her my hood of roses, and with this aid she'll find you some flowers."

The queen made her a low curtsy, for there is no way of embracing a frog, and she immediately went to speak to the bat. In a few hours the bat returned, hiding some beautiful flowers under her wings. The queen quickly carried them to the wicked fairy, who was more surprised than she had ever been in her life, since she could not fathom what miraculous forces were helping the queen.

Since the queen was constantly looking for ways to escape, she told the good frog of her wish. "Madam," the frog replied, "permit me first of all to consult my hood, and we'll act according to its advice." Placing it on a rush, she burned some slips of juniper wood, some capers, two green peas. Over this fire she croaked five times. After this incantation she donned the hood of roses and began to speak like an oracle. "Destiny, ruler of all, forbids you to leave these regions," she declared. "You'll give birth here to a princess more beautiful than the mother of the loves. As for what may follow, you must not worry. Only time will be able to relieve you."

The queen lowered her eyes and tears fell from them, but she was determined to trust her friend. "Whatever may come," she said, "don't desert me. Please stand by me at the birth since you've decreed that it must take place here."

The good frog promised her to be her Lucina and consoled her as much as she could.

Now it is time to return to the king. While his enemies were besieging him in his capital city, he could not regularly send couriers to the queen. After making several sallies, however, he compelled his enemies to abandon the siege. He was elated by this success, not so much for himself as for his dear queen. Now he would be able to fetch her home without fear. He was as yet unaware of her disaster, for none of his officers had dared inform him of it. They had found the remains of the chariot in the forest along with the runaway horses and all the amazonian ornaments she had worn with the idea of rejoining him. Since they had no doubts she had perished and believed her body had been devoured by wild beasts, they agreed among themselves to convince the king that she had died suddenly. At this sad news he thought he would die of grief himself. Hair torn, tears shed, mournful exclamations, sobs, sighs, and other duties of bereavement—none were lacking on this occasion.

After spending several days wishing to see no one, he returned to his capital city dressed in deep mourning, which he felt more in his heart than his attire could ever proclaim. Ambassadors of the neighboring kings came to offer their condolences, and afterward he dedicated himself to providing peace for his subjects, exempting them from war and procuring extensive commercial ventures for them.

The queen knew nothing of these matters. The time for her to give birth arrived, and all turned out well. Heaven blessed her with a baby princess, who was as beautiful as the frog had predicted. They named her Moufette, and the queen, despite some difficulty, for the barbarous lioness had a great desire to eat the infant, obtained permission from the fairy to nurse it.

By the time Moufette had turned six months old, she was already the wonder of her age. The queen continually gazed at her with affection mixed with pity and said, "Ah, if your father could see you, my poor child, how delighted he'd be! How dear you'd be to him! But perhaps at this very moment he's beginning to forget me. He thinks we're buried forever in the shades of death. Perhaps at this very moment another woman occupies that place in his heart he once accorded to me."

These sad reflections cost her many tears. When the frog, who truly loved her, saw her weep one day, she said, "If you wish, madam, I'll go and find your husband. The journey is long and I travel slowly, but sooner or later I think I can accomplish it."

No proposal could have been more warmly received. The queen clasped her hands, even made Moufette join hers, to show madam frog how obliged she would be if she would undertake the journey. She assured her that the king would not be ungrateful to her. "But," she continued, "what use will it be if he learns I'm in this miserable abode? He cannot possibly rescue me."

"Madam," the frog replied, "we must leave that worry to the gods, and take care of that which depends on us."

They took their leave of each other immediately. The queen wrote to the king with her own blood on a small piece of linen, for she had neither ink nor paper. She begged him to trust the worthy frog in all respects, and she would give him all the news concerning her.

The frog took a year and four days to ascend the ten thousand steps from the black plain into the world, and she took another year preparing her equipage, for she was too proud to appear in a great court like a paltry little frog from the marshes. She ordered a litter to be made large enough to hold two eggs conveniently; it was entirely covered with tortoise shell outside and lined with the skin of young lizards. She had fifty maids of honor—some were those little green queens who hop about the meadows—and each was mounted on a snail with an English saddle, her leg placed on the bow with a dainty air. Preceding the snails were several water rats dressed as pages, charged with looking after her. In short, nothing was ever so pretty as this. Above all, her hood of marvelous roses, always fresh and blooming, suited her better than anything. She was rather a coquette in her way, which induced her to use rouge and patches. (They even said she used makeup, as most of the ladies did in that country, but once the matter was investigated, it became clear that her enemies had spread scandalous rumors.)

Seven years she spent on her journey. During this time the poor queen suffered indescribable pain and hardships, and without the beautiful Moufette to console her, she would have died a hundred times over. This wonderful child never opened her mouth without charming her mother, and she even tamed the heart of the fairy lioness. In fact, after the queen had spent six years in this horrible abode, the fairy allowed her to go hunting, on the condition that all she killed would be for her.

How delighted the poor queen was to see the sun once more. She had become so unaccustomed to it that at first she feared she would go blind. As for Moufette, she was so skillful, even at the age of five, that she always hit her target when she shot. As a result, mother and daughter managed to temper the ferocity of the fairy lioness quite a good deal.

The frog traveled day and night over hill and dale, and at last neared the king's capital city. She was surprised when she encountered dancing and feasting everywhere she went. People laughed, people sang, and the closer she approached the city, the greater the joy and merrymaking appeared to be. Her marshy equipage surprised everyone she passed. Indeed, they all followed after her, and the crowd became so thick when she entered the city that she had a good deal of difficulty in reaching the palace, where everything was in a state of great magnificence. The king, who had been a widower for eight years, had at last yielded to the pleading of his subjects, and he was on the point of marrying a princess who was certainly far less beautiful than his wife, but who was nevertheless very charming.

Emerging from her coach, the good frog entered the king's palace, followed by her retinue. She did not need to request an audience, for the monarch, his fiancée, and all the princes were all too eager to learn why she had come.

"Sire," she said, "I don't know whether my news will cause you pain or pleasure. The wedding soon to take place convinces me of your infidelity to the queen."

"Her memory has remained dear to me," the king said, shedding tears he could not hold back. "But you must know, pretty frog, that kings can't always do as they wish. For eight years my subjects have been urging me to remarry. They want me to give them an heir to the throne. Therefore, I've chosen this young princess, who appears to me most charming."

"I advise you not to marry her," said the frog, "for polygamy is a hanging matter. The queen's not dead. Here's a letter written in her own blood that she entrusted to me. You have a little princess called Moufette, who is more beautiful than all the goddesses combined."

The king took the scrap of linen on which the queen had scribbled a few words, kissed it, and bathed it with his tears. He showed it to everyone around him and remarked, "I recall her handwriting perfectly." He asked the frog a thousand questions, and she promptly gave sensible answers to all of them. His fiancée and the ambassadors appointed to witness the celebration of her marriage made very wry faces. "Sire," asked the most eminent among them, "how can you trust the assertion of a toad like this and break such a solemn vow? This scum of the marsh has the impertinence to come and tell lies at your court and enjoy the pleasure of an audience!"

"Mr. ambassador," the frog said, "I want you to know that I'm not the scum of the marsh. And since you force me to show my powers: come fairies and vassals! I command you to appear!"

All the frogs, rats, snails, and lizards revealed themselves accordingly, but they no longer had the forms of these nasty wee creatures. Their figures were lofty and majestic, and their countenances pleasing, their eyes brighter than the stars. All wore crowns of jewels on their heads, and on their shoulders were royal mantles of velvet lined with ermine with a long train carried by a male or female dwarf. At the same moment trumpets, kettle-drums, oboes, and drums pierced the air with lively, martial airs. All the fairies and vassals began to dance a ballet so sprightly that their final jump carried them up to the ceiling. The attentive king and the intended queen were even more thunderstruck when all these honorable dancers suddenly transformed into flowers—jasmine, jonquils, violets, pinks, and tuberoses. They formed an exquisite parterre, and the swaying of the flowers stimulated everyone as much by their scent as by their grace.

A moment later the flowers vanished and several fountains appeared in their place. They rose rapidly and fell into the large moat that flowed at the foot of the castle. It was populated with little painted and gilded galleys so pretty and gay that the princess invited her ambassadors to descend with her and sail about. They did so willingly since they thought it an entertainment that would be followed by a happy wedding.

As soon as they were embarked, the galley, stream, and all the fountains disappeared, and the frogs became frogs again. The king asked what had happened to his princess. The frog replied, "Sire, you have no right to anyone but your wife. If I were not such a great friend of hers, I wouldn't care in the least about the wedding you were preparing to celebrate, but your wife is so good and your daughter Moufette so lovely that you shouldn't lose a moment in trying to set them free."

"I confess to you, madam frog," the king said, "that if I could believe my wife is alive, there's nothing in the world I wouldn't do to regain her."

"After all the wonders I've performed in your presence," she replied, "it seems to me that you ought to be convinced of what I say. Leave your kingdom in good hands, and don't delay your departure. Here's a ring that will enable you both to see the queen and speak to the fairy lioness, although she's the most terrible creature in the world."

The king no longer cared a whit for the princess, who had been chosen for him, and as his affection for her abated, his former love for the queen grew more fervent than ever. Consequently, he prepared to depart all alone and gave some valuable presents to the frog.

"Don't be discouraged," she said. "You'll have tremendous difficulties to overcome, but I trust you'll succeed in accomplishing your goal."

Comforted by these promises, the king left in search of his dear queen with no other guide but his ring.

As Moufette grew older, her beauty increased so greatly that all the monsters of the quicksilver lake fell in love with her. The most hideous dragons came crawling to her feet. Although she had seen them since early childhood, her beautiful eyes could not get accustomed to them. She would flee and hide in her mother's arms.

"Shall we be staying here much longer?" she asked. "Will our troubles never end?"

The queen would give her hope in order to console her, but deep down she had none herself. The frog's absence, her profound silence, the long years without receiving any news of the king—all this, I say, tormented her a great deal.

Little by little the fairy lioness became accustomed to taking the queen and princess with her when she went hunting. She was fond of good eating and liked the game they caught for her. For their part, though all she gave them in reward for their trouble was the feet or head of their catch, they were greatly thankful just to be permitted again to see the light of day.

When hunting, the fairy took the form of a lioness, and the queen and her daughter rode on her through the forest. The king, conducted to this same forest by his ring, had stopped to rest when he saw them shoot past like an arrow from a bow. They did not see him, and as soon as he endeavored to follow them, he lost sight of them completely.

Despite the queen's continual troubles, her beauty had not diminished in the least. She appeared to him more lovely than ever, and all his affection for her was rekindled. Moreover, he was certain the young princess with her was his dear Moufette, and he was determined to die a thousand deaths rather than to abandon his attempt to recover them. Soon the kind ring conducted him to the dark abode in which the queen had resided for so many years, and as he descended to the center of the earth, he was quite astonished by what he saw there.

The fairy lioness, who knew everything, was aware of the day and hour he would arrive, though she would have given anything if fate had joined her and arranged things otherwise. In any event, she decided to resist the power of the king with all her might. Therefore, in the middle of the quicksilver lake she built a crystal palace that floated on the waves, and she locked the poor queen and her daughter in it. Then she told all the monsters in love with Moufette, "You'll lose this beautiful princess if you don't help me defeat a knight who's coming to carry her off."

The monsters promised to leave nothing in their power undone. Surrounding the crystal palace, the lightest among them took positions on the roof and parapets. Others stationed themselves at the doors and the rest in the lake.

Guided by his faithful ring, the king went first to the mouth of the fairy's cave, where she lay in wait in her guise as lioness. The moment he appeared, she attacked. He drew his sword with a courage she had not anticipated, and as she swung her paw to drag him to the ground, he lopped it off at the elbow. A horrible cry she roared as she fell. Approaching her, he put his foot on her throat and swore by his faith he would kill her. Despite her unconquerable fury she could not help trembling before him.

"What do you want?" she asked. "What do you intend to do with me?"

"I want to punish you for abducting my wife," he replied fiercely, "and I want you to give her back to me, or I'll strangle you this instant."

"Look at that lake," she said, "and you'll see she's in my power."

Looking in the direction she pointed, the king saw the queen and her daughter in the crystal castle, which glided like a galley over the quicksilver lake even though it had neither oars nor rudder. He thought he would die of both joy and grief, and called to them as loudly as he could. They heard him, but how could he reach them? As he began seeking a way, the fairy lioness disappeared.

He ran along the edge of the lake, but when he had nearly reached the transparent palace on one side, it receded from him with astonishing speed to the other, and thus was he continually thwarted. Afraid that he would gradually tire of this effort, the queen cried out to him not to lose courage. The fairy's object was to exhaust him, she indicated, but true love was not to be turned back by any obstacles. With that she and Moufette extended their hands to him and implored him with their gestures to continue. Upon seeing this, the king was moved more than ever to help them. In a thunderous voice he swore, "By the rivers Styx and Acheron, I shall remain in these miserable regions for the rest of my life rather than return without you."

He must have been endowed with wonderful perseverance, for he underwent a terrible ordeal, worse than any king in the world. The ground, covered with brambles and thorns, was his bed; he ate nothing but wild fruit more bitter than gall; and he continually had to defend himself against assaults from the lake monsters. A husband who could endure all this to regain his wife must certainly have lived in the time of fairies, and his trials indicate the epoch in which my story occurred.

Three years passed without the king seeing any hope of success. Nearly going mad, he was on the verge of throwing himself into the lake a hundred times, and he would have done so if he had thought this fatal step would release the queen and princess from their sorrows. One day he was running as usual, first on one side of the lake and then on the other, when a horrible dragon called to him and said, "If you'll swear to me by your crown, by your scepter, by your royal mantle, by your wife and your daughter, to give me a certain tidbit I'm fond of, and which I'll request when I so desire it, I'll take you on my wings. And despite all the monsters who guard this crystal castle, I promise you that we'll carry away the queen and Princess Moufette."

"Ah, dragon dear to my soul!" the king exclaimed, "I swear to you and to all your kind that I'll feed you to your heart's content and be your humble servant besides."

"Don't pledge your word," the dragon replied, "if you don't intend to keep it, for you'll be plagued by terrible evils that will torment you for the rest of your days."

The king reaffirmed his pledge, for he was dying with impatience to rescue his dear queen, and he mounted the dragon's back as he would have the finest horse in the world. At that same moment the monsters advanced to intercept him. As they began fighting, nothing could be heard but the sharp hissing of serpents, and nothing could be seen but fire. Sulfur and saltpeter rained down pell-mell! When at last the king reached the castle, the monsters redoubled their efforts—bats, owls, ravens, all attempted to prevent his entrance—but the dragon with his claws, teeth, and tail, tore the boldest of them to pieces. In turn, the queen, who was witnessing this furious combat, kicked down her prison walls and armed herself with the pieces to help her dear husband. At last they were victorious. As the king and queen embraced each other, the enchantment was broken: a thunderbolt pierced the lake, causing the water to evaporate.

Everything vanished, the kind dragon with all the rest, and before the king could guess how he had been transported to his capital city, he found himself seated with the queen and Moufette in a magnificent hall with a banquet table before them spread with delicious dishes. Never was anyone so astonished or joyful as they. All their subjects ran to gaze upon their queen and the young princess, who via the same series of miracles were so superbly dressed that the crowd was dazzled by their jeweled radiance.

You can easily imagine that this fine court was soon consumed by all kinds of entertainment. They had masquerades, runnings at the ring, and tournaments that attracted the greatest princes in the world. Though Moufette's lovely eyes riveted them all to the spot, among the handsomest and most skillful was Prince Moufy, who took the honors in most of the events. Everyone sung his praises. For her part, the young Moufette, who had formerly spent all her days among serpents and dragons, did not hesitate to recognize Moufy's merit. Not a day passed that he did not conceive of some new gallantry to please her, for he loved her passionately. He entered the lists to establish his intentions to marry her, and he revealed to the king and queen that his realm was so beautiful and extensive that it deserved their particular attention.

The king told him that Moufette was at liberty to choose her own husband, and that he would not oppose her inclination in anything. In a like manner, he advised the prince to do his utmost to please her, for this was his only way to happiness. The prince was delighted with this answer, since he had gathered from several conversations with her that she was not indifferent to him. After proclaiming his intentions to her, she told him, "And I want none other but yourself for my husband." Moufy was ecstatic with joy. He threw himself at her feet and beseeched her in the most affectionate terms never to forget the promise she had just made.

He ran straight to the king and queen's apartment and informed them of the progress he had made in his suit and begged them not to defer his happiness a moment longer. They consented with pleasure. Indeed, Prince Moufy was endowed with so many excellent qualities that he seemed the only one worthy of the marvelous Moufette. The king wanted to arrange their engagement before the prince returned to his kingdom, where he was obliged to go to give orders for his marriage. Moufy would have preferred to have remained rather than depart without full assurance of happiness on his return. The Princess Moufette bade farewell, shedding many tears. Although I am not certain why, it appears she was tormented by a presentiment that a dark cloud hung over them. The queen, who saw the prince overwhelmed with grief, gave him her daughter's portrait and implored him, for the love of them both, to forego some of the pomp of his return home rather than allow it to prevent his speedy return.

"Madam," he said, "I shall never have as much pleasure in obeying you as on this occasion. My heart is much too vested in this for me to neglect anything so essential to my happiness."

After he departed, the Princess Moufette spent her time awaiting his return by singing and playing various instruments she had been learning for the past several months and which she now played remarkably well. One day when she was in the queen's chamber, the king entered with his cheeks bathed in tears. After embracing his daughter, he exclaimed, "Oh, my child! Oh, unfortunate father! Oh, unhappy king!"

He could say no more, for sighs choked his tongue. Terrified, the queen and princess asked what was wrong. Finally he told them that an enormous giant, an ambassador from the dragon of the lake, had just arrived. This ambassador was charged with demanding that the king live up to the promise that he had given as the condition on which the dragon had helped conquer the monsters. The dragon now demanded to have Princess Moufette so he could eat her in a pie. The king was bound by the most sacred oaths to give the dragon whatever he desired, and in those days kings did not break their word.

Upon hearing these sad tidings, the queen locked the princess in her arms. "They'll have to take my life before I'll give up my daughter to this monster!" she shrieked. "Let him take our kingdom and all we possess! Unnatural father, could you be a party to such a barbarous act? Never! Put my child into a pie? Ah, I can't bear the thought of it! Send this cruel ambassador to me, and perhaps my torment may move him to pity."

The king did not reply, but went to the giant and brought him straight to the queen. She threw herself at his feet, and with her daughter she beseeched him to have pity on them, to persuade the dragon to take all that they had and spare Moufette's life. However, the giant told them it did not depend on him at all. "The dragon is too obstinate and too fond of good living, and when he gets a notion in his head like eating some tidbit, all the gods combined cannot change his whim." He advised them as a friend to submit with good grace, or even worse things might befall them. Upon hearing these words the queen fainted, and the princess would have as well if she had not been obliged to help her mother.

No sooner did this sad news spread throughout the palace than the entire city echoed with sighs and lamentations, for Moufette was idolized. The king delayed for several days, unable to make up his mind to give her up, and the giant began to grow impatient and threatened him in a terrible manner. In private, the king and queen said, "Could anything worse have happened to us? If the dragon of the lake came to devour us all, we'd be much less distressed. If he only eats our Moufette in a pie, we'll be devastated."

The giant informed them he had received fresh news from his master: if the princess would marry a nephew of his, he would consent to let her live. "This nephew is a handsome and strapping prince, and she could live very happily with him."

This proposal softened their majesties' grief a little, but when the queen spoke to the princess, she found her more averse to this proposal than to her death. "I won't be guilty, madam, of preserving my life by an act of infidelity," she said. "You promised me to Prince Moufy, and I'll never belong to anyone else. Let me perish. My sacrificed life will guarantee you a peaceful existence."

The king seconded the queen, speaking to his daughter about this matter with the greatest affection imaginable. However, she remained firm in her decision, and finally he agreed to take her to a mountain top where the dragon of the lake was to come for her.

Every preparation imaginable was made for this sad sacrifice. Not even those sacrifices of Iphigenia and Psyche were so mournful. Nothing was seen but funeral dress, pale faces, and consternation. Four hundred young girls of the first rank accompanied her, wearing long white robes and cypress wreaths on their heads. She herself was borne on a black velvet litter left uncovered so that everyone could see this masterpiece of the gods. Her disheveled locks lay strewn on her shoulders, tied here and there with crape, and the wreath she wore was of jasmine mixed with marigolds. She seemed to be moved only by the grief of the king and queen, who followed behind, overwhelmed by their affliction. The giant, armed from top to toe, walked alongside the litter containing the princess, eyeing her longingly, for he was getting his share of her to eat. The air was filled with sighs and sobs, and the road was inundated by the tears that were shed.

"Ah, frog! Frog!" the queen cried. "You've forsaken me. Alas, why

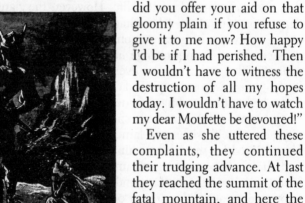

did you offer your aid on that gloomy plain if you refuse to give it to me now? How happy I'd be if I had perished. Then I wouldn't have to witness the destruction of all my hopes today. I wouldn't have to watch my dear Moufette be devoured!"

Even as she uttered these complaints, they continued their trudging advance. At last they reached the summit of the fatal mountain, and here the shrieks and lamentations swelled to such a pitch that nothing so distressing had ever been heard. The giant told them, "All of you, take your leave and retire."

The king and queen withdrew and then climbed another mountain with their entire court, for there they could see what was about to happen to the princess. They had been there only a short time when they observed a dragon with a tail nearly half a mile in length aloft in the sky. Though he had six wings, he could scarcely fly because his body was so heavy. He was entirely covered by large blue scales and long, fiery darts. His tail was in fifty curls and a half. Each of his claws was as large as a windmill, and his wide-open mouth displayed three rows of teeth as long as an elephant's tusks.

. As he slowly approached, the dear, loyal frog mounted a sparrow hawk and flew rapidly to Prince Moufy. Although he was locked in his room, she wore her hood of roses and entered without a key.

"What are you doing here, unfortunate lover?" she said to him. "You're dreaming about Moufette's charms, and yet at this very moment she's threatened by a frightful calamity. Here's a rose leaf. By blowing on it I can transform it into a beautiful horse, as you will see."

No sooner had she spoken than a green horse with twelve hooves and three heads appeared. The mouth of one head spouted fire, another bombshells, and the third cannonballs. She gave him a sword eighteen yards long and lighter than a feather. Then she armed him in a single diamond that he donned like a coat, and although it was as hard as crystal, it was so flexible that it did not inconvenience him in the least.

"Away!" she cried. "Fly to defend the princess you adore. The green horse will carry you to her. After you've rescued her, let her know what role I've played in her rescue."

"Generous fairy," the prince cried "I cannot tarry to express my gratitude at present, but I declare myself your most faithful servant forever."

He mounted his three-headed horse, which immediately set off at a full gallop. With its twelve hooves it raced faster than three of the finest mounts combined, so fast, in fact, that in no time he arrived at the top of the mountain. There he spied his dear princess all alone and the frightful dragon slowly approaching her. The green horse belched fire, bombs, and cannonballs, which greatly amazed the monster. He received twenty cannonballs at his throat, which damaged his scales but slightly, and the bombs knocked out one eye. Enraged, he would have engulfed the prince, but Moufy's eighteen-yard sword was of such fine-tempered steel that he wielded it as he pleased, by thrusting it in up to the hilt or lashing the dragon with it as with a whip. All the same, the prince would not have avoided the fury of this monster's claws if not for the impenetrable diamond armor.

Moufette recognized him from afar, for the diamond that encased him was crystal-clear, and she was seized with the most mortal fright that a woman in love could ever feel. Meanwhile, the king and queen began to feel a ray of hope in their hearts at the extraordinary appearance of a horse with twelve hooves and three heads spouting missiles and flames and a prince encased in diamonds and armed with such a formidable sword. Not only had he arrived at the critical moment, but he fought with the utmost valor. The king placed his hat upon his cane, and the queen tied her handkerchief to the end of a stick, to make signs of encouragement to the prince. Their retinue did the same, but he did not need their encouragement, for his heart alone, fired by the danger in which he saw his mistress, was all he needed to spur him on.

He stopped at nothing! The earth was covered with darts, claws, horns, wings, and scales of the dragon. The monster's blood flowed in a thousand places. (Its blood was blue, while that of the horse was green, which mixed strikingly on the ground.) The prince fell five times, but always managed to recover. He remounted his horse each time and sallied anew into the shower of cannonballs and floods of Greek fire of which the world has never seen the like. At last the dragon's strength failed him. As he fell, the prince gave him a thrust in the belly that opened a frightful gash. And what is even more incredible, yet as true as the rest of the story, is that the handsomest and most charming prince ever seen emerged from this gaping wound. His dress was of blue cut velvet with a gold ground embroidered with pearls, and he had a small Greek *morion* covered with white feathers on his head. With open arms, he ran to embrace Prince Moufy.

"How much I'm indebted to you, my generous benefactor!" he said. "You've just rescued me from the most frightful prison to which a sovereign could ever be confined. I was condemned to it by the fairy lioness, and for sixteen years I've been pining within. Her power was such that she would have compelled me to devour this beautiful princess against my will. Lead me to her feet so that I may explain my misfortunes to her."

Surprised and delighted by such an astonishing incident, Prince Moufy treated the prince with the greatest civility, and they rushed to join the lovely Moufette. She in turn gave the gods a thousand thanks for such unexpected happiness. The king, queen, and the entire court had already hastened to her side. Everyone spoke at once and no one was heard. They cried nearly as much out of joy as out of sorrow.

To ensure that nothing was missing at the fete, the good frog appeared overhead, mounted on a sparrow hawk that had golden bells on its talons. When they heard the tinkling, they all looked up and saw a hood of roses shining like the sun and a frog as beautiful as Aurora. The queen advanced toward her and took one of her little feet. All of a sudden the wise frog transformed herself into a noble queen with the most charming countenance in the world.

"I've come to crown Princess Moufette's constancy," she said. "She preferred sacrificing her life to being unfaithful. This is a rare example in the age in which we live, but it will be much more so in future times."

She then took two myrtle wreaths and placed them on the heads of the happy lovers. After striking her wand three times, she made the dragon's bones rise and form a triumphal arch in commemoration of the great battles.

Finally, all the handsome members of this large company advanced toward the city, singing nuptial hymns as loudly as they had chanted dirges before. The marriage took place the very next day, and you can easily imagine all the joy that accompanied it.

The queen, whose portrait I have painted here,
Amid the horrors of that gloomy lake,
Had for her life but little cause to fear:
Friendship with love united for her sake.

The grateful frog felt, like the monarch, bound
To make the greatest effort in her cause.
Opposed to the lioness and her cruel ways, they found
The means to save the queen from her most fatal claws.

Husbands so constant, friends brave and true,
Assisted our sires long ago to much of all their glory;
And by that fact, kind reader, I'm sure you
Are bound to guess the period of my story.

BELLE-BELLE
OR
THE CHEVALIER FORTUNÉ

ONCE upon a time there was a very good, mild king. He was a powerful monarch, but his neighbor, the Emperor Matapa, was more powerful still. In the last of the great wars they had waged against each other, the emperor had won a tremendous battle. After killing or taking prisoner the greater portion of the king's officers and soldiers, Matapa besieged and conquered the king's capital city, and took possession of all its treasures. The king had just enough time to save himself and the queen, his sister, who had become a widow at a very early age. Though intelligent and beautiful, she was, to tell the truth, also proud, violent, and difficult to approach.

The emperor sent all the king's jewels and furniture to his own palace, and he carried away an extraordinary number of soldiers, women, horses, and anything else that he found useful or pleasant. After he had ravaged the greater part of the kingdom, he returned triumphant to his own, where he was joyously received by the empress and his daughter.

In the meantime, the defeated king was not inclined to accept his misfortune lightly. Rallying the remnants of his troops around him, he gradually formed the nucleus of an army. To increase their numbers as quickly as possible, he issued a proclamation requiring all the noblemen of his kingdom to come and serve him in person, or to send a well-mounted and armed son disposed to support all his ventures.

Now, there was an old nobleman, eighty years of age, who lived on the frontier of the kingdom. He was a wise and prudent man, but fortune had not been kind to him, and he found himself reduced almost to poverty after having been quite wealthy at one time. He would have endured such straits if his three beautiful daughters had not been compelled to share his fate. They were so understanding that they never grumbled at their misfortunes, and if by chance they discussed them at all with their father, they did so more to console him than to add to his disquiet. Without the least desire to seek a better life, they lived with him in their rustic setting.

When the king's proclamation reached the ears of the old man, he called his daughters to him, looked at them sorrowfully, and said, "What can we do? The king has ordered all the noblemen of his kingdom to join him in order to fight against the emperor, and if they refuse, he intends to levy a heavy tax. I'm not in a position to pay the tax, and therefore I'm in a terrible dilemma. This will either be my ruin or my death."

His three daughters were just as distressed as he himself, but they implored him to have courage, for they were convinced that they would find some way out of this predicament. The next morning the eldest daughter went looking for her father, who was walking sadly in an orchard that he tended by himself.

"Sire," she said, "I've come to ask your permission to join the army. I'm tall and strong enough. Let me dress myself in male attire and pass for your son. Even if I don't perform a single heroic deed, I'll at least save you the journey or the tax, and that is a great deal in our situation."

Embracing her affectionately, the count at first objected to such an extraordinary proposition, but she argued so convincingly that he finally had no choice but to consent. All he had to do now was to provide her with the clothes suitable to the person she was to represent. So he furnished her with arms and gave her the best of his four plough horses. Then they bade their tender farewells to each other.

After traveling for several days, she passed through a meadow bordered by a quickset hedge. There she saw a shepherdess who was trying with the greatest difficulty to drag one of her sheep out of a ditch into which it had fallen.

"What's the matter, good shepherdess?" she asked.

"Alas," replied the shepherdess, "I'm trying to save my sheep. It's drowning, and I don't have the strength to drag it out."

"I'm sorry about your plight," she said, riding off without offering her any help.

The shepherdess immediately cried out, "Good-bye, disguised beauty!"

Our lovely damsel was bewildered when she heard that. "How is it possible," she remarked, "that I could be so easily detected? That old shepherdess only saw me for a moment, and yet she knew that I was disguised! What am I to do now? Everyone will know who I am, and if the king finds out, my shame will be great, and so will his anger. He'll think my father's a coward, who shrinks from danger."

After much reflection she decided to return home. The count and his daughters had been talking about her, counting the days she had been gone, when they saw her enter. She told them about the incident with the shepherdess, and the good man responded that he had warned her about this. "If you had listened to me, you would never have set out. Why, it's impossible not to detect a maiden in a man's attire."

Once again, this little family was in a predicament and did not know what to do. Then the second daughter went to the count in her turn and said, "My sister had never been on horseback, so it's not surprising that she was discovered. If you'll allow me to go in her place, I promise that you'll be satisfied with me."

Nothing the old man said in opposing her intention had the slightest effect on her. So he was forced to consent, and she put on different clothes, took some other arms, and another horse. After she had equipped herself, she embraced her father and sisters a thousand times, determined to serve the king bravely. But in passing through the same meadow where her sister had seen the shepherdess and her sheep, she saw her again trying to drag a sheep out of the bottom of the ditch.

"Unfortunate creature that I am!" cried the old woman, "half my flock have perished this way. If someone would help me, I could save this animal, but nobody wants to stop and assist me."

"If you took better care of your sheep, shepherdess, they wouldn't fall into the water," the fair cavalier responded. Without giving her any other consolation, she spurred her horse and rode on.

The old woman bellowed after her, "Good-bye, disguised beauty!"

These words upset our amazon a great deal. "What bad luck! She's recognized me too! Now I've experienced the same fate as my sister. I'm not any luckier than she was, and it would be ridiculous for someone with my effeminate appearance to join the army. Everybody would see right through my disguise!"

She returned at once to her father's house, quite disturbed that she had failed to complete her mission. Though her father received her affectionately and praised her for having had the good sense to return, he fell into a depression. What's worse, he had been put to the expense of purchasing two useless suits of clothes and the other accoutrements. The good old man, however, kept his sorrow to himself, not wishing to add to that of his daughters.

At length the youngest girl came to him and begged him most urgently to grant her the same permission he had granted her sisters. "Perhaps," she said, "it's presumptuous of me to hope I'll succeed where they haven't. Nevertheless, I'd like to try. I'm taller than they are, and as you know, I go hunting every day. This exercise has prepared me in some degree for war, and my great desire to relieve you in your distress has inspired me with extraordinary courage."

The count loved her more than either of her sisters, for she cared for him so tenderly that he regarded her as his chief consolation. She read interesting stories to amuse him, nursed him in his illness, and gave him all the game she killed. Consequently, he argued against her plan much more than he had with her sisters, doing all he could to change her mind. "Do you want to leave me, my dear child?" he asked. "Your absence will be the death of me. If fortune should really smile on you and you should return covered with laurels, I won't have the pleasure of witnessing them. My old age and your absence will bring about my demise."

"No, my dear father," said Belle-belle (for this was her name). "Don't think for a minute that I'll be away that long. The war will soon be over, and if I find any other way of fulfilling the king's orders, I won't hesitate to take advantage of them. I assure you, though my absence will be upsetting to you, it will be even more distressing to me."

At last he granted her request, and she made a plain suit of clothes for herself because her sisters' clothes had cost so much that the poor old count's finances would not allow more expense. She was also compelled to take a very bad horse since her two sisters had nearly crippled the other two. All this, however, did not discourage her. She embraced her father, received his blessing with respect, and as her tears flowed with his and those of her sisters, she departed.

In passing through the meadow I have already mentioned, she found the old shepherdess, who was trying to pull yet another sheep out of the deep ditch.

"What are you doing there, shepherdess?" Belle-belle stopped and asked.

"I can't do anything more, my lord," the shepherdess replied. "Ever since daylight I've been trying to save this sheep in vain. I'm so weary, I can scarcely breathe. There's hardly a day that passes when some new misfortune doesn't befall me, and I have nobody to help me."

"I'm truly sorry for you," Belle-belle said, "and to prove it, I'll help you."

She instantly dismounted from her horse, which was so calm that she did not bother tying it to prevent its running away. Even though she suffered a few scratches as she jumped over the hedge, she plunged into the ditch and labored so diligently that she succeeded in dragging out the dear sheep. "Don't cry anymore, my good mother," she said. "Here's your sheep. Despite the fact that it's been in the water a long time, it seems quite lively."

"You won't find me ungrateful," the shepherdess said. "I know you, charming Belle-belle. I know where you're going and what your intentions are. When your sisters passed through this meadow, I recognized them as well and knew their every thought. But they were so heartless and ungracious toward me that I managed to prevent their journey. Things will be different in your case. Let me prove it to you, Belle-belle, for I'm a fairy and take pleasure in rewarding those who deserve it. Just watch. You have a miserably poor horse, and now I'll give you a real one." As she spoke she struck the ground with her crook, and instantly Belle-belle heard a neighing behind a bush. Whirling about, she saw the most dashing horse in the world prancing in the meadow.

Belle-belle, who was fond of horses, was delighted to see one so perfect. The fairy called this fine stallion to her and, touching it with her crook, she said, "Faithful Comrade, I wish you better harnessed than the Emperor Matapa's best horse." Within seconds Comrade bore a green velvet saddle-cloth embroidered with pearls and rubies, a saddle to match, and a bridle of pearls with a gold bit and gold studs. In short, not a horse in the world was as magnificent as this one. "You've seen only the least remarkable thing about this horse," the fairy remarked. "Pray, let me enumerate his many other qualities. In the first place, he eats only once a week, and it's not necessary to look after him, for he knows the present, past, and future. I've had him a long time, and I've trained him as I'd train my own horse. Whatever you wish to know, or whenever you need advice, you need only consult him. He'll give you such good counsel that most sovereigns would be blessed to have ministers like him. Consider him more as your friend than your horse. Lastly, your attire is not to my liking. Let me give you something more becoming."

She struck the ground with her crook, and a large trunk sheathed with Turkey leather appeared. It was studded with gold nails and bore Belle-belle's initials. Plucking from the grass a gold key made in England, the fairy opened the trunk, revealing an interior lined with Spanish leather and profusely embroidered. Everything within came in dozens: twelve suits, twelve cravats, twelve swords, twelve feathers, and so forth. The coats were woven with so much embroidery and so many diamonds that Belle-belle could barely lift them. "Choose the suit that pleases you most," the fairy said, "and the others will follow you everywhere. You need only to stamp your foot and say, 'Turkey-leather trunk, come to me brimming with linen and lace,' " or " 'Turkey-leather trunk, come to me brimming with jewels and coins,' and it will instantly appear before you, whether you are outdoors or in. You must also assume an alias, for Belle-belle will not suit the profession you're about to enter. It occurs to me that you might call yourself the Chevalier Fortuné. Of course, you ought to know who I am. Therefore, let me appear in my natural form." All of a sudden the old woman's skin was shed, and the fairy became so astonishingly beautiful that Belle-belle was dazzled. Her dress was made of blue velvet trimmed with ermine, and her hair was entwined with pearls and adorned by a superb crown.

Transported by her admiration, Belle-belle threw herself at the fairy's feet as a show of her respect and inexpressible gratitude. The fairy raised her and embraced her affectionately. She told her to don a suit of green and gold brocade, and Belle-belle swiftly obeyed. Afterward she mounted her horse and continued her journey so overwhelmed by all the extraordinary things that had just taken place that she could think about nothing else.

Eventually she began to ponder the unexpected good fortune that had helped her attract the kindness of such a powerful fairy, "Because in truth," she said, "she didn't need me to save the sheep. A simple stroke of her wand would have brought an entire flock back from the antipodes if it had wandered off there. I was lucky indeed to have been in a position to oblige her. The trifling service I performed on her behalf is the cause of all she's done for me. She knew my heart and approved of my sentiments. Ah, if my father could see me now, so magnificent and so rich, how delighted he would be! But in any case, I'll have the pleasure of sharing with my family the wealth she has bestowed upon me."

As she finished making these different observations, she arrived in a beautiful, populous city. She attracted a great deal of attention, and the people followed and gathered around her. "Have you ever seen a cavalier more handsome or strapping, or more handsomely dressed?" they cried. "Look how gracefully he manages that superb horse!" They saluted him most respectfully, and he returned their greetings with a kindly, courteous air. As soon as he had stopped at an inn, the governor, who had been out walking and had admired him in passing, sent a gentlemen to say that he hoped he would come and make his lodgings in his castle. The Chevalier Fortuné (we will now use this name when discussing Belle-belle) replied that since he had not yet had the honor of making his acquaintance, he would not take that liberty. However, he would come to pay his respects. In addition, Fortuné requested of the governor a man whom he could trust with something of consequence that he wanted to send to his father. The governor responded immediately and sent him a very trustworthy messenger.

Asking him to wait since his letters were not ready yet, Fortuné shut himself in his room and, stamping his foot, he said, 'Turkey-leather trunk, come to me brimming with diamonds and coins!" Within seconds it appeared but without its key. Where was he to find it? What a pity to break a golden lock enameled with so many different colors! Then again, he dared not trust a locksmith, for no sooner had he mentioned the cavalier's treasures than thieves would descend to rob or even kill him.

He looked for the key everywhere, but the more he looked, the more hopeless his search appeared. "How disturbing!" he cried. "I cannot avail myself of the fairy's generosity, nor send my father any of the treasures she's given." In the midst of his musing, it occurred to him that his best course of action would be to consult his horse. So he went to the stable and whispered, "I beg of you, Comrade, tell me where I can find the key of the Turkey-leather trunk."

"In my ear," the horse replied.

Fortuné peered into the horse's ear and spied a green ribbon. Drawing it out, he found the key he needed. He opened the Turkey-leather trunk, which contained more than a bushel of diamonds and coins. The chevalier filled three caskets, one for his father and two others for his sisters. Then he gave them to the governor's man and told him not to stop night or day until he arrived at the house of the count.

This messenger made a swift journey, and when he told the old man that he had brought him an onerous casket from his son, the cavalier, the count wondered what could be in it. "Belle-belle started with so little money that she had no means to buy a thing or even to pay the journey of the man in charge of this present." But after reading the letter that his dear daughter had written, he thought he would die from joy. What's more, the sight of the jewels and gold confirmed the truth of her story. The most extraordinary thing was that when Belle-belle's two sisters opened their caskets, they found not only bits of glass instead of diamonds but also false coins, for the fairy did not want them to benefit from her kindness. Thinking their sister was laughing at them, they were extremely angry at her, and when the count noticed this, he gave them the greater part of the jewels he had just received. As soon as they touched them, though, they changed like the others. Therefore, they concluded that an unknown power was working against them and begged their father to keep the rest for himself.

The handsome Fortuné did not wait for the messenger to return before he left the city. His business was too urgent; he was bound to obey the king's orders. Paying his visit to the governor's house, he discovered that many people had assembled to see him. His personality and manners revealed such an air of goodness that they could not help but admire and even adore him. He said nothing except what was pleasant to hear, and when so many people crowded around him, he did not know how to account for such an unusual circumstance, especially because he had spent his entire life in the country.

He continued his journey on his excellent horse, which amused him by telling him a thousand stories of the most remarkable events in ancient and recent history. "My dear master," he said, "I'm delighted to have you as my owner. I know you possess a wealth of frankness and honor. Certain people with whom I lived a long time made me weary of life because their circle of friends were so unbearable. Among them was a man who pretended to be my friend. When he spoke in my presence, he placed me above Pegasus and Bucephalus. But as soon as I was out of sight, he called me a jaded and sorry nag. He pretended to admire my faults in order to induce me to commit greater ones. One day, when I tired of his caresses, which properly speaking were treacherous, I gave him such a severe kick that I had the pleasure of knocking out nearly all his teeth. Whenever I've seen him since then, I've told him with the utmost sincerity that it's not right for his mouth to be as handsome as others because he opens it too often to abuse those who do him no harm."

"Ho, ho," the chevalier cried, "you're full of spirit. Aren't you afraid that someday in the heat of passion this man will pass his sword through you?"

"It wouldn't matter, my lord," Comrade replied. "In any case, I'd be aware of his intention before he knew it himself."

As they continued this conversation, they approached a vast forest, and Comrade said to the chevalier, "Master, a woodcutter who lives here may possibly be of great service to us. He is one who has been endowed with gifts."

"What do you mean by that term?" Fortuné interrupted.

"I mean that he's received one or more gifts from fairies," the horse replied. "You must hire him on to accompany us."

Just then they reached the spot where the woodcutter was working, and the young chevalier approached him with a gentle, winning air. He asked him several questions about these woods, if there were many wild beasts there and if he was allowed to hunt them. The woodcutter responded to all of this like an intelligent man. Fortuné then inquired what had happened to the men who had been helping him chop down so many trees. The woodcutter replied that he had felled them all by himself. "It took only a few hours, and I have many others yet to cut to make a load for myself."

"What? Do you mean to say you'll carry off all this wood today?" the chevalier asked.

"Ah, my lord," replied Strongback (for this is what people called him), "my strength is quite out of the ordinary."

"So you make a great deal of money, I suppose?" Fortuné said.

"Very little," the woodcutter replied. "The people hereabouts are poor. Everyone works for himself without asking for his neighbor's help."

"Since you live in such a poor region," the chevalier remarked, "you have only to decide to leave it and travel to another. Come with me and you'll have everything you desire. Whenever you believe it's time to return, I'll give you money for your return journey."

Thinking he would never get a better offer than this, the woodcutter laid his ax aside and followed his new master.

As they passed through the forest, they came upon a man in a glade who was roping his legs so tightly together that it seemed he could do naught but hobble. Stopping, Comrade said to his master, "My lord, here's another gifted man you'll need. You must take him with you."

Fortuné approached this man and with his usual grace asked him, "Why are you tying your legs like that?"

"I'm going hunting," he said.

"What?" the chevalier asked, smiling. "Do you mean to say you can run better when your legs are bound like that?"

"No, my lord," he replied. "I'm aware that I won't be too fast, but that's my goal. There's not a stag, roebuck, or hare I can't outrun when my legs are free. As a result, I always run right by them, they escape, and I rarely have the pleasure of catching them!"

"You seem to be an extraordinary fellow," Fortuné said. "What's your name?"

"They've given me the name of Swift," the hunter replied, "for I'm well-known in this region."

"If you'd like to see another," the chevalier responded, "I'd be happy to take you with me. You won't have difficult tasks, and I'll treat you well."

Swift was not particularly well off, and he gladly accepted the offer.

Continuing his journey, followed by his new servants, Fortuné spied a man binding his eyes on the border of a marsh the next morning. The horse said to his master, "My lord, I advise you to hire this man as well."

Fortuné immediately asked him why he was binding his eyes.

"I see too clearly," he said. "I can spot game more than four miles away, and I always kill more than I wish when I shoot. Therefore, I'm obliged to bind my eyes, for I wouldn't have any game left once I caught sight of all the animals around me."

"You're a very talented fellow," replied Fortuné.

"They call me the Sharpshooter," the man said, "and I wouldn't abandon this occupation for anything in the world."

"Well, despite what you've just said, I'd like to invite you to travel with me," the chevalier said. "You won't be prevented from exercising your talent."

The Sharpshooter made some objections, and Fortuné had more difficulty in persuading him than the others, since sportsmen as a lot are fond of their freedom. However, he eventually succeeded and left the marsh with his new servant.

A few days later he passed by a meadow in which he saw a man lying on his side, and Comrade said, "Master, this man is most gifted. I can see that you'll need him very much."

So Fortuné entered the meadow and asked the man what he was doing.

"I want some herbs," he replied, "and I'm listening to the grass as it grows to find out which ones I'll need."

"What?" the chevalier remarked. "Are your ears so sharp that you can hear the grass grow and know what's about to sprout?"

"That's why they call me Hear-all," said the man.

"Very well, Hear-all," Fortuné continued, "would you like to join me? I'll give you such high wages that you won't have any regrets."

The man was delighted by such a handsome proposition and joined the others without hesitation.

Continuing his journey, the chevalier saw by the side of a highway a man whose cheeks were so inflated that he looked rather droll. He was facing toward a lofty mountain two miles away where fifty or sixty windmills were standing. The horse said to his master, "Here's another of our gifted ones. Do all you can to make him come with you."

Fortuné, who had the power of fascinating everyone he saw or spoke to, approached this man and asked him what he was doing.

"I'm blowing a little, my lord," he said. "I want to get all those mills turning."

"It appears to me that you're rather far off," the chevalier replied.

"On the contrary," the blower remarked, "I'm afraid I'm too near. If I weren't retaining half of my breath, I'd upset the mills and perhaps the mountains they stand on. I do a great deal of harm this way without intending to, and I can tell you, my lord, that once, when my mistress had treated me badly, I went into the woods to indulge my sorrow, and my sighs tore the trees up by their roots and created a great deal of confusion. So in these parts they now call me Boisterous."

"If they're tired of you," Fortuné said, "and you'd like to come with me, I have some men who'd keep you company. They too possess unusual talents."

"I have a natural curiosity for anything out of the ordinary," Boisterous replied, "and so I accept."

Immensely pleased, Fortuné proceeded on his way. After passing through a densely wooded country, he came to a large lake that was fed by several springs. On its shore was a man who was staring at it attentively. "My lord," Comrade said to his master, "this man will nearly complete your entourage. You'd do well to induce him to join you."

The chevalier promptly approached him and asked, "Tell me, what are you doing?"

"My lord," the man replied, "you'll see as soon as this lake is full. I intend to drink it in one swig, for I'm still thirsty, although I've already emptied it twice."

Accordingly, he stooped down to drink, and in a few minutes left hardly enough water for the smallest minnow to swim in. Just as surprised as his followers, Fortuné asked, "My, are you always so thirsty?"

"No," the man said. "I only drink like this for a wager or when I've eaten something too salty. I'm known in these parts as Tippler."

"Come with me, Tippler," said the knight. "I'll give you wine to tipple, which you'll find much better than spring water."

This promise pleased the man very much, and he decided on the spot to join the others.

When the chevalier was within sight of the general meeting place set for the king's forces, he noticed a man eating so greedily that although he had more than sixty thousand loaves of Gonesse bread before him, he seemed determined to eat every last crumb. Comrade said to his master, "My lord, this is the final man you need. Please make him come with you."

The chevalier approached him, smiling. "Do you really mean to eat all this bread for your breakfast?"

"Yes," he replied. "My only regret is that there's so little, but the bakers are lazy fellows and refuse to extend themselves whether you're hungry or not."

"If you require so much every day," Fortuné remarked, "there is hardly a country you wouldn't bring to the brink of starvation."

"Oh, my lord," replied Gorger (as people called him), "I'd feel badly if I always had such a huge appetite. Neither my property nor that of my neighbors would be enough to satisfy it. To tell the truth, I only feast in this fashion every now and then."

"My friend Eater," Fortuné said, "join me and I'll show you good cheer. You won't regret choosing me for a master."

Comrade, who had a good deal of sense and forethought, then warned the chevalier to forbid his men from boasting about the extraordinary gifts they possessed. So Fortuné lost no time in gathering them around him and said, "Listen to me, Strongback, Swift, Sharpshooter, Hear-all, Boisterous, Tippler, and Gorger. If you want to please me, you'll keep your talents an inviolable secret. In return, I guarantee that I'll try my utmost to keep you satisfied."

Each one of them took an oath to obey Fortuné's orders, and soon after, the chevalier, who stood out more because of his good looks and graceful demeanor than his magnificent attire, entered the ravaged capital city on his excellent horse, followed by the finest attendants in the world. He lost no time in procuring for them horses and uniforms laced with silver and gold. After taking lodgings in the best inn, he awaited the day set for the review. In no time he became the talk of the city, and the king, made aware of his reputation, was eager to meet him.

All the troops assembled on a vast plain, and there the king arrived with his sister and the entire court. Because the queen had not forsworn pomp despite the misfortunes of the kingdom, Fortuné was dazzled by so much splendor. But if the king and his sister attracted his attention, they were just as much struck by his incomparable beauty. Everyone asked who that handsome, graceful young gentleman was, and the king passed close by him and gave him a signal to approach. Dismounting immediately to make a low bow, Fortuné was unable to help blushing when the king gazed at him so earnestly, and this additional color heightened the radiance of his complexion.

"I'd like to hear from your own lips," the king said, "who you are and what your name is."

"Sire," he replied, "I'm called Fortuné, without having any reason for bearing this name up to now, for my father, who's a count on the frontier, has been living in great poverty, although he was born of a rich and noble family."

"Fortuné, whoever has served as your godmother has done well to bring you here," the king replied. "I feel a particular affection for you, for I remember your father. He once rendered me a great service. Let me reward him by favoring his son."

"That's quite just of you, brother," said the queen, who had not spoken yet. "And since I'm older than you and am more familiar with the service this count rendered the state, I request you to let me take charge of rewarding this young chevalier."

Enchanted by his reception, Fortuné could not sufficiently thank the king and queen. He did not, however, venture to extol his feeling of gratitude because he believed silence more respectful than talking too much. The little he did say was so correct and to the point that everyone applauded him. Afterward he remounted his horse and mixed among the noblemen who accompanied the king, even though the queen called him away every minute to ask him a thousand questions. Turning toward Floride, her favorite confidante, she asked softly, "What do you think of this chevalier? Have you ever seen anyone with a nobler demeanor or more regular features? I confess to you, I've never laid eyes on anyone more charming."

Floride agreed with the queen wholeheartedly and lavished praise on the chevalier, for he seemed just as charming to her as to her mistress. For his part, Fortuné could not help regarding the king from time to time. He was the handsomest prince in the world, and his manners were most engaging. Belle-belle, who had not renounced her sex with her dress, felt fervently drawn to him.

After the review, the king told Fortuné, "I fear this war will be a bloody one, and I've decided to keep you near me." The queen, who was present, exclaimed that she had also been thinking the same thing. He ought not to be exposed to a long campaign, and since the place of premier *maître d'hôtel* was vacant in her household, she would give it to him.

"No," the king said. "I intend to make him my squire."

Thereupon, they argued with each other as to who would have the pleasure of promoting Fortuné. Since the queen feared revealing the secret emotions already exciting her heart, she at last yielded to the king's wish.

Hardly a day passed that Fortuné did not call for his Turkey-leather trunk and take out a new garment. He was certainly the most magnificent prince at the court. Sometimes the queen asked him how his father could afford to give him such clothes. Other times she would jest with him, "Tell the truth," she said, "you have a mistress, and she's the one who sends you all these beautiful things."

Though Fortuné blushed, he replied respectfully to the various questions the queen put to him. He also performed his duties remarkably well. He had come to appreciate the king's merits and became more attached to him than he had wanted. "What will be my fate?" he said. "I love a great king without any hope of his loving me. Nor will he ever know what I'm suffering."

In turn, the king overwhelmed him with favors, and he found nothing to his liking unless it was done by the handsome chevalier. Meanwhile the queen, deceived by his dress, seriously contemplated arranging a secret marriage with him, and the inequality of their birth was the only issue that troubled her. She was not the only one who entertained such feelings for Fortuné, however, for the most beautiful women at the court were taken with him. He was swamped with tender letters, assignations, presents, and a thousand gallantries, but he replied to all of them with so much indifference that they were certain he had a mistress in his province. No matter how much he tried to be modest at the great entertainments of the court, he always distinguished himself. He won the prize at all the tournaments. He killed the most game when he went hunting. He danced at all the balls with more grace and skill than any other courtier. In short, it was delightful to watch him and hear him speak.

Anxious to be spared the shame of declaring her feelings for him, the queen asked Floride to make him understand that a young and beautiful queen's many signs of kindness ought not to be a matter of indifference to him. Floride was taken aback by this request, for she herself had been unable to avoid the fate of all those who had seen the chevalier, and she thought it would be too nice on her part to give her mistress's interests precedence over her own. So whenever the queen gave her an opportunity of talking to him, she told him only about the queen's bad temperament and what injustices her attendants suffered from her instead of speaking about her beauty and noble qualities. Floride also told him how badly she abused the power she had usurped in the kingdom. Finally she drew a comparison between their feelings and said, "I wasn't born a queen, but really I ought to have been one. I have so much generosity in my nature that I'm eager to do good for everybody. Ah, if I were in that high station," she continued, "how happy I'd make the handsome Fortuné. He'd love me out of gratitude even if he could not love me from inclination."

Quite dismayed by this conversation, the young cavalier did not know what to say. Therefore, he vowed to avoid any future tête-a-têtes with her.

When Floride returned, the impatient queen constantly inquired,"What impression did you make for me on Fortuné?"

"He esteems himself so little," she said, "and he's so bashful that he won't believe anything I tell him about you. Or he pretends not to believe it because he's absorbed by some other matter."

"I think so too," said the distressed queen. "But I can't imagine that he'd curb his ambition to advance himself."

"And I can't imagine," Floride replied, "that you'd use your crown to capture his heart. You're so young and beautiful and possess thousands of charms. Is it necessary for you to take recourse in the splendor of a diadem?"

"One may have to take recourse in anything possible," the queen replied, "if it becomes necessary to subdue a rebellious heart."

Floride saw clearly that she could not possibly put an end to her mistress's infatuation. Every day the queen expected some positive result from the confidante's work, but she made such little headway with Fortuné that the queen was eventually compelled to seek some means of speaking to him herself. She knew that he was accustomed to take a walk early every morning in a copse in front of the windows of her apartment. So she arose at daybreak, and as she watched his habitual path, she saw him approaching with a melancholy and distracted air. She called Floride immediately. "You've spoken the truth," she said. "Fortuné is without a doubt in love with some lady at this court or in his province. See how sad he looks."

"I've noticed this sadness in all his conversations," Floride replied. "You'd do well to forget all about him."

"It's too late," the queen exclaimed, sighing deeply. "Since he's already entered that green arbor, let's go there. I want you alone to come with me."

The girl did not dare to stop the queen no matter how much she wanted to, for she feared the queen would induce Fortuné to fall in love with her, and a rival of such exalted rank is always dangerous. As soon as the queen had taken a few steps into the wood, she heard the chevalier singing. His voice was very sweet, and he sang these words to a melody then current:

> "How rare a thing it is for love and peace
> To dwell together in the same heart!
> When my joys begin to surge, my fears increase,
> That they, like a morning dream, will soon depart!
> Dread of the future robs my soul of rest,
> Most unhappy I am when most blessed!"

Fortuné had composed these verses, stirred by his feelings for the king, the favor the king had shown him, and his fear of being found out and forced to leave a court that he preferred above any other in the world.

Stopping to listen, the queen was distraught. "What shall I do?" she whispered softly to Floride. "This ungrateful young man doesn't want to honor or please me. He believes himself content with this conquest of his. He sacrifices me to another."

"He's at that age," Floride replied, "when reason has yet to establish its rights. If I may venture to give some advice to your majesty, forget such a giddy fellow so incapable of appreciating his good fortune."

The queen would have preferred a different answer from her confidante. Casting an angry look at her, she hastened onward and entered the arbor where the knight was. She pretended to be surprised to find him there and to be upset at his seeing her in such disarray, although she had taken great pains to make herself magnificently attractive. As soon as she appeared, he made to withdraw out of respect for her, but she asked him to remain so that he might aid her in walking.

"I was wakened this morning most pleasantly by the singing of the birds. The fine weather and pure air induced me to come outside and listen more closely to their warbling. How happy they are! Alas, all they know is pleasure. Grief does not trouble them!"

"It appears to me, madam," Fortuné replied, "that they're not entirely exempt from pain and sorrow. They're always in danger of a murderous shot or deceitful snares of sportsmen. Moreover, birds of prey make war against these little innocents. When a hard winter freezes the ground and covers it with snow, they die for want of hemp or millet seed, and every year they have difficulty finding a new mistress."

"So you think, then, chevalier," the queen said, smiling, "that this is a difficulty? Some men have a fresh one every month—but you appear surprised by this, as if your heart were not of the same stamp. Can you not change your heart like this?"

"I'm unable to predict how I'd act," the chevalier said, "for I've never been in love. I do believe, however, that if I formed an attachment, it would end only when I breathed my last."

"You've never been in love?" cried the queen, looking so earnestly at him that the poor chevalier changed color several times. "Fortuné, how can you possibly declare this to a queen who reads in your face and your eyes the passion that occupies your heart? Just now I heard the words you sang to that new melody that's just become so popular."

"It's true, madam," the chevalier replied, "that those lines are my own. My friends ask me every day to write drinking songs for them, although I never drink anything but water. There are others who prefer love songs. So I sing about love and Bacchus without being a lover or a drinker."

As the queen listened to him, she trembled so with emotion that she could scarcely keep standing. All that he told her had rekindled the hope in her bosom that Floride had sought to extinguish. "I'd think you were sincere," she said, "but I'd indeed be surprised if you hadn't found one lady at this court sufficiently lovely to attract your attention."

"Madam," Fortuné replied, "I try so hard to carry out the duties of my office that I have no time for sighing."

"You love nothing, then?" she responded vehemently.

"No, madam," he said, "my heart is not so gallant. I'm a kind of misanthrope who loves his liberty and doesn't want to lose it for anything in the world."

Sitting down, the queen gave him the kindest of looks. "There are some chains so beautiful and glorious," she replied, "that anyone might feel happy to wear them. If fortune has made this your destiny, I'd advise you to renounce your liberty."

As she spoke, her eyes revealed her meaning too clearly for the chevalier to mistake what she meant. He already had strong suspicions and was now convinced they were correct. Fearing the conversation might lead even further, he looked at his watch and held up his hand. "I must beg your majesty to permit me to go to the palace," he said. "It's time for the king to get up, and he asked me to be at his side."

"Go, callous youth," she said, sighing profoundly. "You're doing the right thing by paying court to my brother, but remember, it's not wrong to pay some attention to me."

The queen followed him with her eyes, then let them fall. After reflecting on what had just transpired, she blushed with shame and rage. Her grief was further augmented by the fact that Floride had witnessed everything, and she noticed a smirk of satisfaction on her face that implied: "You would have done better had you taken my advice instead of speaking to Fortuné." She pondered all this for some time. Then she took her tablets and wrote these lines, which she later had set to music by a celebrated court composer:

> "Behold! Behold! The torment I endure!
> My victor knows, but covers the clue.
> My heart shows, but it can't have a cure,
> Still stung by the shaft he's shot so true.
>
> "He's not concealed his coldness or disdain,
> He hates me, and his hate I should return;
> But ah, my foolish heart tries in vain,
> For it only has love for him to burn!"

Floride played her part cleverly: she consoled her as much as she could and gave her some hope to keep her going. "Fortuné thinks himself so beneath you, madam," she said, "that perhaps he failed to understand what you meant. It seems to me that he's already said a good deal by assuring you that he doesn't love anyone."

It is so natural for us to expect our hopes will be fulfilled that the queen was eventually encouraged to believe she had a chance with Fortuné. She was unaware that the malicious Floride, who knew all too well the chevalier's indifference toward her, wanted to induce him to speak even more forthrightly and offend the queen by his coolness.

As for Fortuné, he was most confused, for he was caught in a cruel dilemma. He would not have hesitated to leave the court if his love for the king had not detained him despite himself. Never did he go near the queen except when she held her court, and then always in the king's entourage. She noticed this change in his conduct instantly and responded by giving him the opportunity of paying her attention several times. He steadfastly refused to do so. But one day as she descended into her gardens, she saw him cross one of the grand avenues and suddenly enter the copse. When she called to him, he was afraid of displeasing her by pretending not to hear and approached her respectfully.

"Do you remember, chevalier," she said, "the conversation we had together some time ago in the green arbor?"

"I'd never forget that honor," he answered.

"No doubt the questions I put to you then were distressing," she said. "Ever since that day you've so avoided me that I haven't been able to quiz you further."

"Since it was happenstance alone that gave me that opportunity," he said, "I thought it would be presumptuous of me to seek another one."

"Why don't you say instead that you've been avoiding my presence, you ungrateful man?" she demanded, blushing. "You know quite well how I feel about you." Fortuné cast down his eyes in an embarrassed and modest manner, and since he hesitated to reply, she continued, "You seem dismayed. Go! Don't try to answer me. Your silence speaks louder than words."

She would have perhaps upbraided him more, but she spotted the king coming their way. She advanced toward him, and upon noticing how melancholy he was, she asked him to tell her the reason.

"You know," the king said, "that about a month ago I received news that an enormous dragon was ravaging the country. I thought my soldiers could kill him and issued the necessary orders for that purpose. But they've tried everything in vain. He devours my subjects, their flocks, and anything he encounters. He poisons all the rivers and springs wherever he quenches his thirst, and ruins the grass and the herbs wherever he lies."

While the king was talking to her, it occurred to the irritated queen that this would be an opportune way to take her resentment out on the chevalier. "I'm aware of the bad news you received. As you saw, Fortuné was just with me and told me all about it. But, brother, you'll be surprised at what I have to tell you. He's implored me most insistently to ask you for permission to go and fight this terrible dragon. Indeed, he's so skilled in the use of arms that I'm not surprised he's willing to be so daring. Besides, he's told me he has some secret power that he can use to put the most lively dragon to sleep, but that must never be mentioned because it doesn't show much courage on his part."

"No matter how he does it," the king replied, "it will bring him great glory and be of great service to us if he succeeds. But I fear he's overzealous, and it may well cost him his life."

"No, brother," the queen added, "there's no need to fear. You know that he's naturally sincere and thus has no intention in dying so rashly. In short,

I've promised to obtain what he wants, and if you refuse him, it will kill him."

"I'll grant your wish," the king said, "but I confess, I do so with a great deal of reluctance. Come, let us call him." He then made a signal for Fortuné to approach and said kindly, "I've just learned from the queen that you want to fight the dragon that is devastating our country. It's such a bold decision that I scarcely believe you've considered the danger involved."

"I've depicted all this to him," the queen said. "But he's so eager to serve you and to distinguish himself that nothing can dissuade him, and I predict he'll succeed."

Fortuné was taken aback by what the king and queen said. Though he quickly grasped the queen's wicked intentions, his natural deference would not permit him to expose them. So he had not responded and simply let her continue. He contented himself by making low bows so that the king thought he was now pleading with him directly to grant him what he desired. "Go, then," the king said, sighing, "go where glory calls you. I know you're skillful in everything you do, especially in the use of weapons. Perhaps this monster won't be able to avoid your blows."

"Sire," the chevalier replied, "no matter what the outcome of this combat, I'll be satisfied. Either I'll rescue you from a terrible scourge, or I'll die for you. But grant me one favor dear to my heart."

"Ask for whatever you wish," said the king.

"May I be bold enough to ask for your portrait?" Fortuné said.

The king was very pleased that he had thought of obtaining his portrait at a time when he should have been occupied with far more weighty matters, and the queen resented once again that he did not make the same request of her. However, he would have had to possess a superabundance of goodness to desire the portrait of such a wicked woman.

Once the king had returned to his palace and the queen to hers, Fortuné mulled over the consequences of the pledge he had made. Going to his horse, he said, "My dear Comrade, I have a good deal of news to tell you."

"I know it already, my lord," he replied.

"What shall we do, then?"

"We must set out posthaste," the horse said. "Go and get the king's order commanding you to fight the dragon, and then we'll do our duty."

These words comforted our young chevalier, and the next morning he awaited the king in a riding dress just as handsome as all the others that he had taken from the Turkey-leather trunk. As soon as the king saw him, he exclaimed, "What? You're ready to go?"

"Your commands cannot be executed too quickly, sire," he replied. "I've come to take my leave of your majesty."

The king could not help feeling pity for Fortuné, seeing that such a young, handsome, and accomplished gentleman was about to expose himself to the greatest danger a man could ever face. He embraced him and gave him a portrait framed by large diamonds. Fortuné accepted it joyfully, for the king's noble qualities had made such an impression on him that he could not imagine anyone in the world more charming. If Fortuné was upset at leaving him, it was much less from the fear of being devoured by the dragon than from being deprived of the presence of one so dear.

The king added a general order to Fortuné's commission, calling upon all his subjects to aid and assist Fortuné whenever he might be in need. Taking leave of the king, Fortuné went to the queen so that nothing might be taken amiss. She was sitting at her dressing table, surrounded by several of her ladies. She changed color when he appeared, and she began reproaching herself for what she had done. He saluted her respectfully and asked her if she would honor him with her commands since he was on the point of departure. These last words completely disconcerted her, and Floride, who did not know that the queen had plotted against the chevalier, was thunderstruck. She would have liked to have had a private chat with him, but he carefully avoided such an embarrassing situation.

"I pray to the gods," the queen said, "that you may conquer the dragon and return triumphant."

"Madam," the chevalier replied, "your majesty does me too much of an honor. You're sufficiently aware of the danger to which I shall be exposed; however, I'm full of confidence. Perhaps, on this occasion, I'm the only one who has hope."

The queen understood very well what he meant. No doubt she would have replied to this reproach if fewer persons had been present. The chevalier returned to his lodgings and ordered his seven excellent servants to get their horses and follow him. "The time has arrived to prove what you can do." Not one failed to rejoice at having a chance to serve him. In less than an hour everything was ready, and they set out with him, assuring him they would do their utmost to carry out his commands. And, as soon as they had reached the open country and had no fear of being seen, each one gave proof of his talent. Tippler drank the water from the lakes and caught the finest fish for his master's dinner. Swift hunted some stags and caught a hare by its ears, despite the doubles it made. The Sharpshooter gave no quarter to partridges and pheasants, and when the game was killed by the one, the venison by another, and the fish plucked from the water, Strongback carried everything cheerfully. Even Hear-all made himself useful: he found truffles, morels, mushrooms, salads, and fine herbs by listening to where they grew in the ground. So Fortuné rarely had to pay anything to cover the expenses of his journey. He would have been greatly amused at the sight of so many extraordinary events if he had not been so troubled by all that he had just left. Even as the king's qualities continued to impress him, the queen's malice seemed so great that he could not help hating her.

As he was riding along lost in thought, he was aroused from his reverie by the shrieks of a host of poor peasants whom the dragon was devouring. Seeing some who had escaped and running away as fast as they could, he called to them, but they would not stop. So he followed and spoke to them, and he learned that the monster was not far distant. When he asked them how they had managed to escape, they told him that since water was scarce in this region, they had only rain water to drink and had made a pond to conserve it. After making his rounds, the dragon went to drink there and uttered such tremendous roars when he arrived there that he could be heard a mile away. So alarmed did everybody become that they hid themselves and locked their doors and windows.

The chevalier entered an inn, not so much to rest as to seek some sage advice from his handsome horse. After everyone had retired, he went into the stable and asked, "Comrade, how are we to conquer this dragon?"

"My lord," he said, "let me dream about it tonight. Then I'll tell you what I think tomorrow morning."

Accordingly, the next morning when the cavalier came again, the horse said, "Let Hear-all listen to discover if the dragon is close by." Hear-all lay on the ground and heard the rumble of the dragon some seven miles away. When the horse was informed of this, he said to Fortuné, "Tell Tippler to drink up all the water in the pond and have Strongback carry enough wine there to fill it. Then you must scatter dried raisins, pepper, and other herbs around the pond that will make the dragon thirsty. Order all the inhabitants to lock themselves up in their houses. And you, my lord, must stay there and lay in wait with your attendants. The dragon won't fail to drink at the pond, he'll relish the wine, and then you'll see how it will all end."

As soon as Comrade had indicated what was to be done, they all set off on their tasks. The chevalier himself went into a house that overlooked the pond, and no sooner had he done so than the frightful dragon arrived at the pond and took several draughts. Next, he partook of the breakfast they had prepared for him, and then he drank more and then more, until he became intoxicated. Unable to move, he lay on his side, his head hung down, his eyes closed. When Fortuné saw him like this, he knew he did not have a moment to lose. Emerging from the house, sword in hand, he courageously attacked the dragon. Wounded on all sides, the dragon tried to stand up so he could fall on the chevalier, but he lacked the strength because he had lost too much blood. The chevalier was overjoyed that he had reduced him to this sorry state, and called his attendants to bind the monster with cords and chains so that the king would have the pleasure and glory of putting an end to his life. Once they had nothing more to fear from the beast, they dragged him to the city, Fortuné at the head. On approaching the palace, he sent Swift to the king with the news of his great success.

Such tidings seemed incredible to everyone until they actually saw the monster tied on a machine constructed for the beheading.

The king descended and embraced Fortuné. "The gods have reserved this victory for you," he said. "I feel more joy at your safe return than at the sight of this horrible dragon reduced to this condition, my dear chevalier."

"Sire," he replied, "it would please me if your majesty would give the monster his death blow. I brought him here expressly to receive it from your hand."

The king drew his sword and terminated the existence of one of his most cruel enemies. Everybody uttered shouts of joy at such unexpected success. Floride, who had been fretting unceasingly, soon heard about the return of her handsome chevalier and ran to tell the queen. She in turn was so astonished and confounded by her love and her hatred that she could not respond to her confidante's news. She had reproached herself hundreds of times for the malicious trick she had played, but she preferred to see him dead than so indifferent to her. She did not know whether she should be pleased or sorry that he had returned to disturb her peace.

Eager to tell his sister of this extraordinary event, the king entered her chamber, leaning on the chevalier's arm. "Here's the dragon slayer," he said. "This faithful subject has performed for me the greatest service that I could have ever demanded. Since you were the one, madam, to whom he first expressed his desire to fight this monster, I hope you appreciate the courage with which he exposed himself to utter peril."

Composing herself, the queen honored Fortuné with a gracious reception and a thousand praises. She thought him handsomer than when he went away, and the way she gazed at him indicated that her heart was not cured of its wound.

She did not, however, want to leave it up to looks alone to explain how she felt. So, as she was hunting with the king, she left off following the hounds, saying she felt suddenly indisposed. Turning to the young chevalier nearby, she said, "Do me the pleasure of remaining with me. I want to get down and rest a little. —Go," she continued, speaking to those who accompanied her, "don't leave my brother!" She dismounted from her horse with Floride and sat by the side of a stream. There she remained for some time in deep silence, trying to think of the best way to start the conversation.

Finally she raised her eyes and fixed them on the chevalier. "Since good intentions are not always obvious," she said, "I fear you haven't grasped the motives that induced me to urge the king to send you to fight the dragon. I have presentiments that never mislead me, and I felt certain that you'd prove yourself brave. Your rivals have not thought highly of your courage because you didn't join the army. That's why I felt you needed to perform some act of valor to stop their tongues from wagging. Perhaps I ought to have told you what they had been saying about you, but I feared any consequences resulting from your resentment. So I thought it better for you to silence such evil-minded people by demonstrating your intrepid conduct in action rather than by exerting influence that would mark you as a favorite, not a soldier. Thus you see, chevalier, that I longed to do something that might contribute to your glory, and you'd be very wrong if you were to judge otherwise."

"The distance is so great between us, madam," he replied modestly, "that I'm not worthy of the explanation you've been so kind to give me, or the care you took to imperil my life for the sake of my honor. The gods protected me with more beneficence than my enemies had hoped, and I'll always esteem myself lucky to serve the king or you and to risk my life, the loss of which is a matter of more indifference to me than one might imagine."

This respectful reproach from Fortuné nettled the queen, for she wholly comprehended his meaning, but he was still too pleasing for her to feel alienated by such a sharp reply. On the contrary, she pretended to sympathize with his sentiments and asked him, "Tell me again how skillfully you conquered the dragon."

Fortuné had carefully avoided telling anyone how his men had helped him defeat the dragon. He boasted of having faced this redoubtable enemy alone, and that his own skill and courage, even to the point of rashness, had enabled him to triumph. The queen, who scarcely paid attention to what he was saying, interrupted to ask whether he was now convinced of her sincere concern in his affairs. She would have pressed the matter further, but he interrupted her by saying, "Madam, I hear the blast of the horn. The king approaches. Does your majesty want your horse to go and meet him?"

"No," she said spitefully. "It's sufficient for you to do so."

"The king would blame me, madam," he added, "if I were to leave you by yourself in such a dangerous place."

"I can dispense with your attention," she replied imperatively. "Be gone! Your presence annoys me!"

At this command, the chevalier made a dignified bow, mounted his horse, and disappeared from her sight. Concerned by how she would react to this fresh offence, he consulted his fine horse. "Let me know, Comrade," he said, "if this queen, who's much too passionate and angry, is going to find another monster for me."

"No, she won't find another one," the handsome horse replied. "But she herself is more of a dragon than the one you've killed, and she'll certainly put your patience and virtue to the test."

"Will she cause me to fall out of favor with the king?" he cried. "That's all I fear."

"I won't reveal the future to you," Comrade said. "Just know that I'm always on the alert." He stopped talking, for the king had appeared at the end of an avenue. Joining him, Fortuné reported that the queen had not felt well and had commanded him to remain at her side.

"It seems to me," the king said, smiling, "you're very much in her good graces, and you speak your mind to her rather than to me. I've not forgotten that you asked her to procure the illustrious opportunity of fighting the dragon."

"I won't dare to contradict you, sire," the chevalier replied, "but I can assure your majesty I make a great distinction between your favors and those of the queen, and if a subject were permitted to make his sovereign a confidant, I'd be most delighted to declare my feelings to you—"

At that point, the king interrupted him abruptly by asking him where he had left the queen, who meanwhile was complaining to Floride of Fortuné's indifference to her. "I'm finding the sight of him more and more hateful," she cried. "Either he leaves the court, or I must withdraw from it. I can no longer tolerate the presence of an ungrateful youth who dares show me so much contempt. Any other mortal would be enraptured to know he pleased a queen who's so powerful in this kingdom! He's the only one in the world who doesn't. Ah, the gods have selected him to disturb my tranquillity!"

Floride was not at all sorry that her mistress was so displeased with Fortuné, and far from endeavoring to oppose her displeasure, she augmented it by recalling a thousand other disturbing signs that the queen had perhaps not wanted to notice. Thus her rage increased, and she began devising some new way to destroy the poor chevalier.

As the king rejoined her and expressed his concern about her health, she said, "I confess I was very ill, but it's difficult to remain so with Fortuné near. He's so cheerful, and his ideas are quite amusing. So I must tell you, he's implored me to obtain another favor from your majesty. He's asked, with the greatest confidence of success, to be allowed to undertake the most rash enterprise in the world."

"What now, sister?" cried the king. "Does he want to fight another dragon?"

"Several all at once," she said, "and he's certain he will triumph. Do you want me to tell you? Very well, he boasts he'll compel the emperor to restore all our treasures, and he doesn't even need an army to achieve this."

"What a pity," the king replied, "that this poor boy has to exaggerate so much."

"His fight with the dragon has made him think of nothing but great adventures," the queen remarked. "But what risk do you run if you permit him thus to serve you?"

"I risk his life, which is dear to me," the king replied. "I'd be extremely sorry to see him throw it away so recklessly."

"No matter what you decide, he's bound to die," she said. "I assure you that his desire to recover your treasures is so strong that he'll pine away if you refuse him permission."

The king felt deeply distressed. "I can't imagine," he said, "how these notions get into his head. I'm extremely disturbed to find him so foolhardy."

"The fact remains," the queen replied, "he's fought the dragon and conquered him. Perhaps he'll succeed equally well in this adventure. I'm seldom deceived by my presentiments, and my heart tells me he'll also accomplish this mission. Please, brother, don't oppose his zeal."

"Let him be called," the king said. "In any case, I must inform him of the risk he runs."

"That's just the way to exasperate him," the queen replied. "He'll think you won't let him go, and I assure you he won't be deterred by any consideration for himself, for I've already said all that can be thought about the subject."

"Very well," the king cried, "let him go. I consent."

Delighted with this permission, the queen sent for Fortuné. "Chevalier," she said, "thanks be to the king. He's granted you the permission you desired so much—to seek out the emperor Matapa and by guile or by force, recover the treasures he's taken from us. Prepare to depart as speedily as when you fought the dragon."

Fortuné was shocked. Was this the extreme to which the queen's malice and fury had driven her? On the other hand, he was pleased by the prospect of laying down his life for a king so dear to him. So without objecting to this monstrous task, he knelt and kissed the king's hand. For his part, he was very much moved, and even the queen felt a degree of shame in witnessing the respect with which he received this order to charge toward certain death.

"Can it be possible," she said, "that he has some affection for me? Rather than disavow what I've supposedly done on his behalf, he prefers to suffer without a complaint. Ah, if this were true, I'd wish a good deal of harm to myself for having caused him so much!"

The king said little to the chevalier before he remounted his horse, and the queen entered her chariot again, feigning a return of her indisposition. Fortuné accompanied the king to the end of the forest and then reentered it to converse with his horse. "My faithful Comrade," he said, "it's all up with me. I must die. The queen has plotted a course I'd never have expected."

"My charming master," the horse replied, "don't alarm yourself. Although I wasn't present when all of this occurred, I've known about it for some time. The mission isn't as terrible as you imagine."

"You don't realize that this emperor is the most wrathful man in the world," the chevalier said. "If I suggest to him that he restore all that he has taken from the king, he'll answer by having me strangled and thrown into a river."

"I've heard of his violent ways," Comrade said, "but don't let that prevent you from taking your attendants with you. If you perish there, we'll all perish together. However, I trust we'll have better luck than that."

Somewhat consoled by this, the chevalier returned home, issued the necessary orders, and then received the king's commands along with his credentials. "You'll tell the emperor for me," he said, "that I demand my subjects he holds in bondage, my soldiers who are prisoners, my horses that he rides, and all my goods and treasures."

"What shall I offer him in exchange for all these things?" Fortuné asked.

"Nothing," replied the king, "but my friendship."

The young ambassador's memory was not overburdened by these instructions. He departed without seeing the queen, and though she was offended, he had no reason to treat her with any respect. Besides, what worse could she do to him in a fit of rage that she had not already done in the throes of love? Passions of this kind seemed to him to be the most dreadful thing in the world. Even her wily confidante was exasperated with her mistress for wanting to sacrifice the flower of chivalry.

Taking all he needed for his journey in the Turkey-leather trunk, Fortuné was not satisfied simply with attiring himself magnificently, but wanted his seven attendants to make just as fine an appearance. They all rode on their excellent horses—indeed, Comrade seemed to fly through the air rather than gallop over ground—and soon arrived at Emperor Matapa's capital city. Larger than Paris, Constantinople, and Rome put together, it had so many people that all the cellars, garrets, and lofts were inhabited.

Fortuné was surprised to see such a tremendous city. He demanded an audience with the emperor, but when he announced the purpose of his mission, even though his ample grace made his speech more effective, the emperor could not help smiling. "If you were at the head of five hundred thousand men," he said, "one might listen to you, but they tell me you have but seven."

"I've not undertaken this task, my lord," Fortuné said, "to make you restore what my master wishes by force but by my very humble remonstrances."

"It doesn't matter which way you choose," the emperor responded. "You'll never succeed—unless you can accomplish a task that's just come to my mind; find a man who has such an appetite that he can eat for his breakfast all the hot bread baked for the inhabitants of this great city."

The chevalier was most pleasantly surprised by this proposal, but since he did not answer right away, the emperor burst into a fit of laughter. "It's perfectly natural to respond to a ridiculous request with a ridiculous answer."

"Sire," Fortuné said, "I accept your offer. Tomorrow I'll bring a man who'll eat all the fresh bread and likewise all the stale bread in this city. Just order it to be brought to the great square, and you'll have the pleasure of seeing him devour it down to the very last crumb."

The emperor agreed, swearing he would put him to death if he did not keep his word, and people talked of nothing but the madness of the new ambassador for the rest of the day.

Fortuné returned to the hotel where he had taken up residence and called for Gorger to come to him. "Now's the time for you to prepare yourself to eat bread," he said. "Everything depends on it." Thereupon he told him what he had promised the emperor.

"Don't worry, master," Gorger said. "I'll eat until they weary of feeding me."

Since Fortuné was afraid of any exertion on Gorger's part, he forbade him to have supper so he would be better able to eat his breakfast, but this precaution was not really necessary. The next morning, the emperor, empress, and princess took seats on a balcony so that they would have a better view. Arriving with his small retinue, Fortuné saw six mountains of bread higher than the Pyranees rising in the great square. This sight made him turn pale, but it had the opposite effect on Gorger. Delighted by the prospect of eating so much good bread, he asked them not to keep the smallest morsel from him and declared, "Nothing will be left even for a mouse." The emperor and the entire court amused themselves at the expense of Fortuné and his attendants, but Gorger, becoming impatient, demanded the signal to begin.

At a flourish of drums and trumpets, he immediately threw himself on one of the mountains of bread and devoured it in less than a quarter hour. All the rest he gulped down at the same rate. Everyone was astonished and, wondering if their eyes had deceived them, they had to satisfy themselves by touching where they had placed the bread. That day everyone, from the emperor to the cat, was compelled to dine without bread.

Delighted by his great success, Fortuné approached the emperor and asked respectfully if he were pleased by the way he had kept his word with him. The emperor, who was rather irritated at being duped this way, said, "Monsieur Ambassador, it won't do to satisfy such hunger without also slaking thirst. Therefore you, or one of your men, must drink all the water in the fountains, aqueducts, and reservoirs in the city, and all the wine in the cellars."

"Sire," Fortuné said, "you're trying to make it impossible for me to obey your orders. However, I don't mind endeavoring to fulfill this task if I can expect that you'll restore what I've requested for my master."

"I'll do so if you succeed in your undertaking," the emperor stated.

When the chevalier inquired if the emperor would like to be present, he replied that he would certainly attend such an extraordinary event. Thereupon, he got into a magnificent chariot and drove to the fountain of lions, where seven marble lions spouted torrents of water that formed such a mighty river that the inhabitants of the city usually crossed it in gondolas.

Tippler approached the great basin, and without taking a breath, he drained it so dry that the bewildered fish cried out for vengeance. Then Tippler turned to all the other fountains, aqueducts, and reservoirs and did the same. In fact, he could have drunk the sea, he was so thirsty. After seeing such an example, the emperor was convinced Tippler could drink the wine as easily as the water, and he watched his disturbed subjects refuse to give up their wine to him. But Tippler complained that they were being unfair, for he needed the wine to settle his stomach. Not only did he expect all the wine, but also the spirits. Fearing to appear miserly, Matapa consented to Tippler's request.

Once this feat was accomplished, Fortuné reminded the emperor of his promise. At these words the emperor looked very stern and told him he would consider it. Thereupon he convoked his council and expressed his extreme annoyance at what he had promised the young ambassador. Indeed, he had thought the conditions he had set for Fortuné were so impossible to fulfill that he would not have to comply with them. After he had spoken, his daughter, one of the loveliest creatures in the world, remarked, "You're aware, sire, that until now I've beaten all those who have dared to race against me. You must tell the ambassador that if he can reach a certain designated spot before me, you'll stop procrastinating and keep your word."

The emperor thought her advice was excellent and embraced his child. The next morning, he received Fortuné graciously and said, "I have one more condition, which is that you or one of your men must run a race with my daughter. I swear by all the elements that if she's beaten, I'll satisfy your master in every respect."

Since Fortuné did not refuse this challenge, Matapa added that the race would take place in two hours, and immediately informed his daughter that she should get ready. She did so with alacrity, for she had raced since childhood, and soon appeared in an avenue of orange trees three miles long and so beautifully graveled that not a stone the size of a pin's head could be seen in it. She wore a light rose-colored taffeta dress embroidered down the seams with gold and silver spangles; her beautiful hair was tied by a ribbon in back and fell carelessly on her shoulders; she wore extremely pretty slippers and a belt of jewels that displayed her figure sufficiently to prove that none had ever been as lithe. Even that of the young Atalanta could never have matched hers.

Fortuné arrived, followed by the faithful Swift and his other attendants. The emperor took his seat with his entire court. The ambassador announced that Swift would have the honor of running against the princess.

The Turkey-leather trunk had furnished him with a holland suit trimmed with English lace, scarlet silk stockings, feathers to match, and exquisite linen. He looked very handsome in this garb, and the princess accepted him as her competitor. But before they started, she had a liqueur brought to her that she used to strengthen her and give her additional speed. Swift said he ought to have some as well, and that the advantages ought to be equal. "Gladly," she said, "I'm too just to refuse you."

She immediately poured some out for him, but since he was not accustomed to such potent liquid, it went quickly to his head. Turning around two or three times, he collapsed at the foot of an orange tree and fell fast asleep. Meanwhile the signal for starting had already been given three times, and the princess had kindly waited for Swift to wake up. Finally, feeling the grave importance of freeing her father from his predicament she set off with wonderful grace and speed. Since Fortuné was at the other end of the avenue with his men, he was unaware of what was happening until he saw the princess a half mile from the finish line running all alone. "Ye gods!" he cried, speaking to his horse. "We're lost. I see nothing of Swift."

"My lord," Comrade said, "Hear-all must listen. Perhaps he'll be able to tell us what's going on."

Hear-all threw himself onto the ground, and although he was two miles from Swift, he could hear him snoring.

"Truly," he said, "he has no intention of coming. He's sleeping as though he were in bed."

"Ah, what shall we do?" Fortuné cried again.

"Master," Comrade said, "Sharpshooter must shoot an arrow at the tip of his ear to wake him."

The Sharpshooter took his bow and aimed so well that he indeed pierced Swift's ear. Woken by the pain, he opened his eyes to see the princess near the finish, and he heard shouts of joy and mounting applause. At first astonished, he soon regained the ground he had lost in slumber. The very winds seemed to bear him, and nobody could follow him with their eyes. In short, he arrived first with the arrow still in his ear, for he had not had the time to extract it.

So astonished was the emperor by the three events that had occurred since the ambassador had arrived that he believed the gods favored him, and that he better not defer keeping his word. "Approach," he said to Fortuné, "I want you to hear from my own lips that I consent to your taking as much of your master's treasures from here as you or one of your men can carry. Indeed, you couldn't have expected that I'd ever do more than that or that I'd let either his soldiers, his subjects, or his horses go."

Making a profound bow, the ambassador said that he was very much obliged to him. "Pray give your orders to execute your will."

Deeply mortified, Matapa spoke to his treasurer and then rode to a palace just outside the city walls. Fortuné and his attendants immediately asked for permission to enter all those rooms where the king's furniture, rareties, money, and jewels were deposited. The emperor's servants hid nothing from him, but reminded him of the condition that only one man carry them. Strongback made his appearance and carted off all the furniture in the emperor's palace, five hundred statues of gold taller than giants, coaches, chariots, and countless other articles. Everything was taken, and Strongback walked so jauntily, it seemed as though his back bore not a pound.

When the emperor's ministers saw the dismantled palace—sans chairs, chests, saucepans, or even a bed to lie on—they rushed to warn him. You can imagine how astonished he was when he learned that one man carried everything. Exclaiming, "I shall not stand for this," he commanded his guards and musketeers to mount and quickly follow the robbers.

Although Fortuné was more than ten miles away, Hear-all told him that he heard a large body of cavalry galloping toward them, and the Sharp-shooter with his excellent vision spotted them at a distance. Having just arrived on the banks of a river with his men, Fortuné said to Tippler, "We don't have any boats. If you could drink some of this water, we might be able to ford the river."

Tippler instantly performed this task. The ambassador was anxious to make the best use of his head start and get away, but his horse counseled, "Don't worry. Let our enemies approach."

They appeared on the opposite bank, and since they knew where the fishermen moored their boats, they speedily embarked in them and rowed with all their might. Then Boisterous inflated his cheeks and began blowing. So tumultuous became the river that the boats were upset, and the emperor's host perished without a single soldier escaping to tell the news.

Fortuné's men rejoiced at this event, and each one's thoughts turned to what reward he might demand as his just deserts. They wanted to make themselves masters of all the treasures they had carried away, and a great dispute arose among them about how to divide everything.

"If I had not won the race," the runner said, "you'd have had nothing."

"And if I hadn't heard you snoring," Hear-all said, "where would we have been then?"

"Who would have wakened you if it weren't for me?" the Sharpshooter responded.

"In truth," Strongback added, "I admire your arguments. But it's clear to me that I should have first choice since I've been carrying it all. Without my help you wouldn't have the opportunity of sharing it."

"You really mean without mine," Tippler responded. "The river that I drank like a glass of lemonade would have defeated you."

"You would have been much more defeated if I hadn't upset the boats," Boisterous said.

"I've been silent up till now," interrupted Gorger, "but I must remark that it was I who started this chain of events. If I had left just a crust of bread, everything would have been lost."

"My friends," Fortuné said commandingly, "you've all done wonders, but we ought to leave it to the king to acknowledge our services. I'd very much regret if we were to be rewarded by some other hand than his. Believe me, let's leave all to his will. He sent us to recover his treasures, not to steal them. Just the thought of it is so shameful that I beg you never to mention it again. I assure you, I shall do everything I can to ensure that you'll have nothing to regret even if the king neglects you."

Deeply moved by their master's remonstrance, the seven gifted men fell at his feet and promised him that his will would be theirs. Onward they went and soon completed their journey. As they approached the city, though, the charming Fortuné was troubled by a thousand different concerns. On the one hand, he was overjoyed at having performed such a great service for the king he loved so tenderly, and the hope of his favorable reception made him eager to return. On the other hand, he feared irritating the queen again and suffering torments anew from her and Floride.

When he finally arrived at the city gates, everyone was overwhelmed by the immense quantity of valuables he had brought back with him, and they followed him with a thousand acclamations. The sounds soon reached the palace, and the king could not believe the extraordinary event taking place. He ran to the queen to tell her about it, and at first she was thunderstruck, but quickly regained her composure. "You see," she said, "the gods protect him, and he's fortunately succeeded. I'm not surprised that he's always ready to undertake what appears impossible to others."

As she uttered these words, she saw Fortuné enter. He informed their majesties of the success of his journey, adding that the treasures were in the park. Since there was so much gold, jewels, and furniture, there was no other place large enough to put them in. You can easily imagine that the king demonstrated a good deal of affection for such a faithful, zealous, and charming subject.

The presence of the chevalier and all the successes he had achieved reopened the wound in the queen's heart, which had never been quite healed. She thought him more charming than ever, and as soon as she was at liberty to speak to Floride, she began complaining again. "You've seen what I've done to destroy him," she said. "I thought it the only way of forgetting him. Yet, some sort of irrefutable fate keeps bringing him back to me again. Whatever reasons I had to despise a man so much my inferior, and who's returned my affections with the meanest ingratitude, I can't help but love him still, and I've determined to marry him privately."

"To marry him?" Floride cried. "I can't believe this! Have I heard you rightly?"

"Yes," the queen replied. "You've heard my intentions, and you must help me. Bring Fortuné to my room this evening. I myself shall declare to him how far I'm willing to go because of my love for him."

In despair at being chosen to assist the queen in her plans to marry Fortuné, she tried every possible argument to dissuade the queen from seeing him. She maintained that the king would be angry if he discovered this intrigue, that perhaps he would order the chevalier to be executed. At the very least he might condemn him to life in imprisonment, and she would never see him again. However, all her eloquence was in vain. Seeing that the queen was beginning to get angry, she decided that there was nothing to be done but obey her.

She found Fortuné in the palace gallery, where he was having the golden statues arranged that he had brought from Matapa, and she told him to come to the queen's room that evening. This order made him tremble, and Floride noticed his distress. "Oh," she said, "how I pity you! What unlucky fate caused the queen to lose her heart to you? Alas. I know one less dangerous than hers, but it's afraid to reveal itself."

The chevalier was not eager for further explanation, for he had endured too much already. Since he cared not a jot for pleasing the queen, he dressed himself so plainly that she could not possibly think him distinguished. Yet even though he dispensed with his diamonds and embroidery, he could not efface the qualities of his person. He was charming and remarkable no matter what he wore. In a word, he was incomparable.

On the contrary, the queen went to great pains to heighten the luster of her appearance by an extraordinary display, and she was quite pleased to see how tongue-tied Fortuné was. "Appearances," she said, "are sometimes so deceptive that I'm delighted to have the chance to defend myself against the charges you no doubt have brought against me in your heart. When I induced the king to send you to the emperor, my object may have seemed to destroy you. Nevertheless, believe me, handsome chevalier, I knew how everything would turn out. I had no other object than to provide immortal glory for you."

"Madam," he said, "you're too far above me to condescend to any explanation. I would never presume to inquire into your motives. The king's commands are sufficient justification for me."

"You're making light of the explanation I want to give you," she remarked. "But the time has come to demonstrate how much I care for you. Approach, Fortuné, approach. Receive my hand as a pledge of my faith."

The poor chevalier was utterly thunderstruck. Twenty times he was on the verge of declaring his sex to the queen, but he did not dare to do so and could only respond to her show of love by an excessive coldness. He tried to explain to her the innumerable reasons why the king would be angry if he were to hear that a subject in his own court had ventured to contract such an important marriage without his sanction. After the queen vainly endeavored to remove the obstacles that alarmed him, she suddenly assumed the voice and countenance of a Fury. Flying into the most violent rage, she threatened him with a thousand punishments, heaped abuse on him, fought and scratched him. Then she turned her rage on herself. She tore her hair, scratched her face and throat until they bled, ripped her veil and lace. Finally she cried out, "Help, guards! Help!" As they rushed into her room, she bellowed at them, "Fling that wretch of a chevalier into a dungeon!"

Running to the king to demand justice for the way that young monster had violated her, she told her brother that Fortuné had had the audacity some time ago to declare his feelings for her. She had hoped that by being severe and sending him away, she could cure him. As the king might have observed, she had used every opportunity to have him removed from the court. However, he was such a villain that nothing could change him. The king could see for himself to what extremes he had gone to possess her. She insisted on his being brought to justice, and that if she were denied such satisfaction, she wanted to know why.

The manner in which she spoke to the king alarmed him, for he knew that she was one of the most violent women in the world. She had a great deal of power and could cause turmoil in the kingdom. Therefore, Fortuné's rash actions demanded an exemplary punishment. Everybody already knew what had happened, and his own feelings should have prompted him to avenge his sister. But, alas, who was to be the target of his vengeance? It was a gentleman who had exposed himself to numerous perils in his service. Indeed, the king was indebted to him for the peace and all his treasures, and he had a particular affection for him. He would have given half his life to have saved his dear favorite. So he explained to the queen how useful he had been to him, the services he had rendered the kingdom, his youth, and everything else that might induce her to pardon him. Yet she would not listen and demanded his execution.

The king, realizing that he could not avoid having him tried, appointed the mildest and most tender-hearted judges in the hope they would weigh the offence as lightly as possible. His assumption, though, was mistaken. The judges wanted to establish their reputation at the expense of this unfortunate prisoner. Since it was an affair of great notoriety, they were extremely severe and condemned Fortuné without deigning to hear his side: he was sentenced to be stabbed three times in the heart with a dagger because it was his heart that was guilty.

The king trembled at this sentence as though it had been passed on himself. He banished all the judges who had pronounced it, but could not save his beloved Fortuné. The queen exulted because of the punishment the chevalier was to suffer, and her eyes thirsted for the blood of her illustrious victim. The king made various attempts to intercede, but they served only to exasperate her.

Finally, the day set for the terrible execution arrived. Off they went to lead the chevalier from his prison. Because he had been placed in isolation, he was unaware of the crime that he had allegedly committed and merely imagined that he was to be persecuted once again because of his indifference to the queen. What distressed him most was his belief that the king shared the queen's rage against him.

Meanwhile, Floride was inconsolable at seeing the predicament in which her lover was placed and made a most drastic decision: she was prepared to poison the queen and herself if Fortuné was doomed to die a cruel death. From the moment she knew the sentence, she was overcome with despair, and she thought about nothing but how to execute her plan. The poison she procured, however, was not as powerful as she desired. After she had given it to the queen, her majesty seemed not to feel the slightest effects. Instead she ordered the charming chevalier to be brought into the palace square so that the execution could take place in her presence. The executioners brought him from his dungeon according to custom and led him like a tender lamb to the slaughter. The first person who caught his eye was the queen in her chariot, who wanted to be as close as possible in the hope that his blood might splatter her. The king meanwhile had locked himself up in his chamber so that he might freely lament the fate of his beloved favorite.

After they tied Fortuné to the stake, they tore off his robe and vest to pierce his heart. Imagine everyone's astonishment when they uncovered the alabaster bosom of Belle-belle! Immediately the populace realized Fortuné was an innocent girl unjustly accused. So upset and confused was the queen by this sight that the poison began to rampage through her veins. After a series of long convulsions, she recovered only to utter agonized lamentations. The people, who loved Fortuné, had already freed her and ran to announce the wonderful news to the king. He, who had succumbed to the deepest grief, now felt joy take the place of sorrow. Racing into the square, he was delighted to see Fortuné's transformation.

The last sighs of the queen subdued his rapture somewhat, but when he thought about her malice he could not feel sorry for her. He decided to marry Belle-belle in order to repay her for the great debt he owed her, and he declared his intentions to her. You can easily imagine that his wish had been the goal of all that she had ever desired, and it was not the crown she had wanted but the worthy monarch for whom she had long cherished the greatest affection.

The day was set for celebrating the king's marriage, and when Belle-belle reassumed her female attire, she appeared a thousand times more charming than in the garb of the chevalier. Consulting her horse with regard to her future adventures, she was assured that she would have nothing but pleas-

ant ones. In gratitude for all the good services he had rendered, she had a
stable built of ebony and ivory, and she installed the best satin mattress on
which he could take his repose. As for her seven followers, they were
rewarded in proportion to their services. Comrade, however, disappeared,
and when they came and told Belle-belle, the queen was distressed, for she
adored him and ordered her attendants to look for her horse everywhere
they could. They did this for three whole days in vain. On the fourth day
she was so worried that she got up before sunrise and descended into the
garden. Then she crossed the wood and entered a large meadow, calling
from time to time, "Comrade, my dear Comrade! Where are you? Have
you deserted me? I still need your wise advice. Come back, come back, and
give it to me!" While calling out like this, she suddenly noticed a second
sun rising in the west. Stopping to gaze at this miracle, she was immensely
astonished as she watched it advance toward her by degrees. Within moments she recognized her horse, whose trappings were set with jewels and
led a chariot of pearls and topazes drawn by twenty-four sheep. Their wool
was of gold thread and purl and extremely radiant. Their traces were made
of crimson satin and covered with emeralds, and their horns and ears were
ornamented with carbuncles. Belle-belle recognized her fairy protectress in
the chariot, and she was accompanied by the count, her father, and her
two sisters, who called out to her. They clapped their hands and made
affectionate signs to her, intimating that they had come to her wedding.
Thinking she would die from joy, she did not know what to do or say to
show her delight. She got into the chariot, and this splendid equipage
entered the palace, where everything had already been prepared to celebrate
the finest wedding ceremony that had ever taken place in the kingdom.
Thus the enamored king bound his destiny to that of his mistress, and the
story about this charming adventure has circulated for centuries and been
passed down to our own.

> The lion roaming Lybia's burning plain,
> Pursued by the hunter, galled by countless darts,
> Is less to be dreaded than that woman vain,
> Whose charms are disdained and foiled in her arts.

> Poison and steel are trifles in her eyes,
> As agents of her vengeance and her hate;
> The dire effects that from such passions rise
> You've now seen in Fortuné's strange fate.

> Belle-belle's change saved her innocent soul,
> And struck her royal persecutor down.
> Heaven protects the innocent and plays its role
> By defeating vice and rewarding virtue with a crown.